The Land of Hugh

W.T. LEWIS

BALBOA
PRESS

A DIVISION OF HAY HOUSE

Balboa Press books may be ordered through booksellers or by contacting:

Balboa Press
A Division of Hay House
1663 Liberty Drive
Bloomington, IN 47403
www.balboapress.com
1 (877) 407-4847

This is a work of fiction. All of the characters, names, incidents, organizations, and dialogue in this novel are either the products of the author's imagination or are used fictitiously.

Scripture quotations marked KJV are from the Holy Bible, King James Version (Authorized Version). First published in 1611. Quoted from the KJV Classic Reference Bible, Copyright © 1983 by The Zondervan Corporation.

Print information available on the last page.

ISBN: 978-1-5043-9902-9 (sc)
ISBN: 978-1-5043-9904-3 (hc)
ISBN: 978-1-5043-9903-6 (e)

Library of Congress Control Number: 2018904639

Balboa Press rev. date: 04/24/2018

Table of Contents

Dedication to those who Inspire

To my Family, Colene, Billy and Melody for inspiring my life in so many ways that they cannot know.

To Nicole, for bringing into this world my Grandsons Mathew, Jacob and Trevor, who reminded me of what it is to be a child again.

And also to Cynthia Humes, for taking a struggling writer and painting his words into a Spiritual work of Art. Her understanding of the story concepts was uncanny. She also inspired me by her expertise in taking my words and almost mystically transforming them into a spiritual articulation, which reflected my entire intent and purpose for the Land of Hugh.

—W.T. Lewis

"For most people, the truth is a lie, and the lie is truth."

In trying to create from love, mankind confuses it with desire, and so fails miserably; "I" then make manifest your desires in the energy of your expectations—but not necessarily always with the desired effect, for that is inflected by man's own lack of faith and wisdom. Man provides the energy, feeling, and form, and I choose the matter in how it is used according to one's limited beliefs.

Mankind gladly gives his wealth, greed, adoration, fear and power to his adversaries and leaders, and then viciously murders his Saints, Saviors, Redeemers, and Divine Teachers. The list is endless.

Never forget, Hugh! This is humankind's legacy, and is mostly due to their ignorance of divine wisdom and weak discipline. By not using these two attributes, man allows me to create endless temptations to surround and infect their lives. Humankind does not yet realize that all creation in this universe is from his or her own power; until they do, this power will flow through the mind and be subject to mankind's conscious will, which is nothing more than desire!

—Abaddon to Hugh

The Land
OF HUGH

Story written by W. T. Lewis

C'mon, boy. Let's go home.

PROLOGUE

Most of us have the ability to trace our lives and see how we have created the personalities we believe are us. This "us-personality" reflects perfectly the sum total of everything we experience. Hugh's journey is based on this truth.

A few may see this journey as fantasy; some may see a simple thoughtful story or perhaps a guide, while to others it may encourage their own quest for truth. However this story reveals itself to each of you, we must be aware that even out of fantasy, truth is discovered.

Hugh's family, his friends, and even his adversaries contribute to a deeper understanding of his incredible journey, a journey that reveals questions and answers concerning the deepest secrets of Soul. The questions asked have preoccupied humankind since man and woman first looked to the stars in search of their Creator. The answers are timeless truths revealed through a boy's journey to save his family.

From this timeless journey of Soul, the eternal quest is revealed to those who are ready to take a step further in their own growth. Time and time again, Hugh awakens to his own personal understanding of life's meaning. As you journey with Hugh, you will participate in a young boy's spiritual awakening as he learns life's universal purpose through the eyes of a child—an open and fresh perspective that most of us lose over time. Throughout his journey, he discovers the divine magic that allows us to experience being something more than we once thought we were, and that open mindedness and compassion when combined with knowingness, truly allows mankind to learn that the only true miracle in life is a changed consciousness. Keep your mind and heart free, and you may be nudged to reconsider traditional values of your own reality.

So as I write, I dream. I dream of helping ignite the eternal spark hidden within each and every one of us, and possibly reintroduce the reader "To Soul."

W. T. Lewis

2 Corinthians 12.2: I knew a man in Christ above fourteen years ago, (whether in the body, I cannot tell; or whether out of the body, I cannot tell: God knoweth;) such an one caught up to the third heaven.

To those of us who seek truth within

Chapter 1 ~ Bristol

Gray clouds drift through morning light while dissipating mists hover above lush meadows. Slowly, the township of Bristol awakens.

The Baptist church in our town square with its white steeple reflects serenely on the surface of Amity Pond, partially shaded by assorted pine, cherry, maple, and dogwoods. Next to the church lies the common ground where a small road weaves like a snake crawl through Bridge Park, then blends onto Main Street where roads and side streets spread like spider webs weaving our lives and homes together in the quaint hamlet town.

Bristol, like a lot of east coast small towns, has that special feature that makes it like a big family—it doesn't take long to find yourself becoming charmed and acquainted with the folk in this New England township. A mile from the town center a small road veers to the right. A marker partially hidden by weeds reads "Dogwood Circle."

Sugar maples on both sides of this quiet country road intricately intertwine with dogwoods, forming a cathedral of limbs, flowers, and leaves. Morning light breaks in golden shafts near a bend on the road; a house sits on a small hill surrounded by azaleas and willows. This is me family's home, and this is where our story begins as it happened to me.

****

Since I was four I've spoken with a stutter.

It started before me family moved from Ireland to America. Me parents—Ann and Clark Bailey—and I were vacationing in Scotland at some underground caves and I wandered off and lost me way. While searching for me parents, I went deeper and deeper in the caves until I was hopelessly lost. I was told later a search party was sent to find me, but for about four hours I was on my own. While wandering in the darkness I remember stumbling upon a colony of bats. Startled by me intruding on 'em, bats started flying in every direction, striking me head and landing on me clothes and even getting caught up in me hair.

I don't remember much after that, but between the bats flying, the rats and spiders crawling all in the darkness, I was pretty scared.

I was finally found huddled against a crevice in the cave too frightened to say anything or move, and for several days, I didn't speak at all.

When finally I did speak, I stuttered.

The stammering combined with me Irish dialect and New England mix makes it difficult enough sometimes for people trying to understand what

I'm saying. I don't care all that much, but for sure I'm shy and a tad introverted, preferring to keep to me self a bit…it's odd though, the only time I don't stammer is when I'm singing, or in me dreams.

Sunlight flickers across me bedroom wall as I'm trying to remember the dream I'm just waking from; I crawl deeper under the covers, protecting me from morning chill and glare of reality. Footsteps clattering on the hardwood floor in the hall makes me emerge from my cocoon, and as I do the bright sun evaporates me memory of the dream…Mum's voice abruptly interrupts and wakens me thoughts. "Hugh…you awake? Wake up, boy—breakfast is cooking!" I'm ignoring her, hoping she'll go away…and then she knocks louder on the door.

"Hugh! Get yourself up before breakfast gets cold!"

I bury meself deeper in me pillow, trying to ignore the intrusion: just five minutes more is all I'm asking. Snuggling further in me bed I'm thinking about last night playing video games and watching old horror shows with me mate Billy. Billy had to be home before midnight, so I ended up watching the last horror movie alone.

Delicious smells of French toast and bacon float in my room beckoning me to crawl out from under warm coverins'. Pulling on me shirt, jeans, and shoes I look in the mirror and catch a glimmer of light reflecting in me green eyes, flexing a muscle on my skinny arm then pulling me cap over light brown shaggy hair I stagger half asleep into the den. Mum and me younger sister Melody have already set up TV trays; before sitting down I mumble to me mum, "B-br-breakfast in fr-front of the tele. H-ho—ow come?"

Wiping her small hands on the apron around her waist, she's staring at me with a glare in her Irish green eyes, her red hair bristles from morning wake up.

"Well, good morning to you, too, and just where's your cheery greeting manners?" Still a little sleepy, I slump into me chair and say a little clearer and louder, "Morning, Mum. B-bu-but why th-the TV trays?"

"'Tis Dagwood and Blondie movies from the 1940s that's a' playing this morning and you know how much Da' likes watching 'em; now grab a tray and take your cap off afore you eat, I'll have your plate in a smidge."

I like the old movies, too; even for a ten-year-old like me they are simple compared to modern tele. Life, laughter, and just plain living seemed to be a lot easier to come by back then.

Smells of breakfast cooking are making me even hungrier, and I complain, "Mum, I'm j-u jus-tt about starving!"

Just then me Da' walks in. Bending his lanky body, he kisses Mom on the cheek while tickling her small waist, "Morning to you, darling, how are you? Yum, something smells good."

Mom's giggling and squirming as he continues tickling. Da' always knows how to make Mom smile even when she's getting a little frustrated. "I'm just fine and dandy, now don't tickle. C'mon, Clark, stop it. If ya' don't, I'll just drop your plate, for sure." Putting the plate on his tray, she puts her arms around Da's shoulders. "We're eating in front of the tele this morning, so would ya' mind to be sitting down?"

Da' takes a glass of orange juice and sits in his favorite chair. "What's the occasion?"

Before anyone can answer, we hear a scratching at the door. Melody jumps up a-shouting, "I'll get it!" As the door opens a flash of pale yellow fur almost matching Melody's blonde hair slides across the wooden floor then rushes straight to the den. I'm suddenly staring into the face of our large Labrador, Cody; tilting his head slightly to the left his face is asking "Where's me breakfast?" He knows what he wants, and in most cases how to get it; he's expecting French toast and bacon like the rest of us.

I pass his bowl around saying, "Okay, o-kaay, let's all g-gi-give Cody a li-t-little." Everyone shares a wee portion, the tele's turned on and we begin breakfast.

I'm almost through eating when there's a knock at the door; me mate Billy comes in. I completely forgot that today we're supposed to find a tree to build our tree house.

Billy sits on the couch and watches the end of the show with us. Then grabbing me cap, we run outside chasing each other up a path leading behind our property. Cody comes a'running from the bushes to join us. Invigorating smells from the countryside ignite our senses, filling us with a fearless innocence and awareness of life. Running deeper into the woods we catch our breath when we stop to wait a bit, watching Cody smell a tree, chase a squirrel, and then begin to leave his mark on a favorite bush. While we were waiting for Cody to finish his business, Billy asks, "Hey, how did the river monster die in that old movie last night?"

Thinking back last night to the old black and white movie, I replied with a sly smile, "Like a-all m-m-monsters b-being...st-stu-pid, doing something dumb... then getting wa-wasted w-without kno-knowing wh-what a dumb thing it did."

Billy picked up a stick and threw it for Cody. "I got home just before my dad got mad, so I did right by leaving before it was over."

I start running again, at the same time shouting, "At-ttt least you were s-s-sm-marter than th-the mo-m-monsteeeeer!"

We hear Cody barking in the distance, so we take off toward the noise. Billy tries to outrun me, but I get to Cody first. Cody's barking like crazy at a patch of meadow grass, and then I hear a movement. A deer springs from the tall grass and runs off, then leaps an ole stack fence by the meadow before he swiftly disappears. Encouraged by me standing behind him, Cody gives chase. Billy runs up alongside me; I notice he's staring at the tree the deer stood under before running off. Taking a few steps toward the tree, I whisper to Billy, "Ch-check out th-the treeeee!"

Like me, he's just staring, and then he says, "Dang...it's old! Look how thick the trunk is and those roots are like the arms of an octopus!"

He's right, the huge sugar maple is old—really, really old. Thick, long lower limbs are reaching about five feet from the ground, higher branches snake to the sky reaching maybe a hundred feet or more then spreading out like a canopy creating shadows on the trees below; it's freaking enormous.

I say as much to meself as to Billy, "H-how co-cou-uld we h-haave m-m-missed seeing this tree before?"

Billy grabs one of the lower limbs, and then pulling himself up, he replies, "I don't know, but this is the tree—so let's climb!" Being heavier than me, Billy struggles to get to the top limbs, which are growing in a pattern that's allowing us an easy and fast climb. I'm like a skinny monkey quickly passing Billy.

I'm halfway up when I come to a crisscross of large limbs that's weaving a wide flat spot across the middle section of the tree. I yell down to Billy, "This is brilliant! W-wait u-u-until Da' sees this!"

Just then, sunlight breaks through the clouds. Tiny arrows of gold light pierce the interior creating scattered shafts of light that are bouncing and twinkling against resting dewdrops; smaller branches dance to gentle breezes while blue skies peek between higher branches. Climbing deeper into the interior of the tree I discover a dense area of limbs providing the perfect perch; a squirrel sitting above me starts a'chattering while his tail's thumping, probably telling me to stop all the noise. Billy hollers out from below, "Hey! Come on down! Let's get some rope and build a swing."

Small limbs, dead twigs, dried cattails, and wet meadow grass slap our faces and arms as we run from the woods and deeper into the meadow—the meadow grass is thick and more dew drops splash against our flushed faces. As we leave the woods behind, I'm talking as we are running. "We'll n-nee-eed s-sm-small boards for a-at-attaching the rope for us to c-c-climb."

Billy speeds up his running and replying at the same time; "Aw, don't worry about boards. Let's get the rope up and make sure it reaches the ground." Within minutes, we are running up to Billy's garage.

Amidst all the hanging tools, ladders, and other junk are two coils of rope hanging in the corner. Climbing up on the counter, Billy grabs one coil and tosses it to me. He next picks out a jar of nails and a hammer, and then jumps down. Satisfied with our goods, we go running back to the tree, all the while trying to talk between heavy breaths. Running and trying to talk at the same time with me stammer is so impossible even I can't understand me own words. Cody gets to the tree first with us right behind; how did he know where we were going? I don't know how, but he did.

In seconds, Billy is already above me in the tree. Holding one end of the rope, he's dropping the other end to me. I pull meself to the lower branches and the rope drops into me hands; I dangle it about three feet from the ground: it's perfect! Climbing down, Billy's red hair blazes from streaks of sunlight striking his head; grabbing the rope, he swings to the ground Tarzan-fashion. "It works perfect! We found our tree!"

After supper, I'm sitting with me Da' on the front porch showing him plans I drew of the tree house. After looking at 'em for a few minutes, he stands up and walks to the porch railing, his thin frame almost disappearing behind post shadows. Looking at the plans again, he sits next to me and says, "Son, these are good, they are, but where you gonna build it, lad?"

"Da', you ca-an't believe b-bu-but we found a huge old tr- treeee past th-the meadow! Ya' go-gotta see it-it for yourself."

Da' hands back me drawings and says, "I'll tell you what, lad, when morning comes, for sure we'll go see this tree." I barely sleep that night as me mind's constantly thinking of the giant maple.

Next morning, Billy, Cody, Da' and me are off to the woods, and soon enough we are approaching the tree. Da' stops for a moment and stares. Taking off his cap, he's scratching his thinning brown hair and then says, "Never have I seen such a tree as this! It's perfect, tis a grand tree for your tree house and if you want, I'll help ya' to build it." That afternoon we drive to the hardware store in Amity to buy materials needed to start.

Days are passing and building the tree house becomes the center of all the free time me, Billy, and Da' can squeeze from our schedules. By the time school's out, we are halfway finished—and by the second week of summer, it's nearly completed—and by the middle of July, it's done! With help from me Da', it's more than any of us hoped or imagined.

Built on four limbs thirty feet from the ground, a rope ladder drops through the center floor. We used what Da' calls pressure treated two by fours for the framing and two by sixes for the rafters and flooring. Plywood covers the sides and floor joists; the hole in the floor allows us to climb directly through the middle.

A large open window with a tarp covering allows a direct view into the heart of the tree. At least five boys can fit comfortable, plus an old couch we hauled up. It's freaking beautiful, and I can't wait for our first sleepover.

****

Flashlights, fishing poles, a gas lantern, drinks, snacks and some comics are stacked in the corner. Me mates Paul and Matt are freaking at the size of the tree and even more amazed by the tree house. One by one each of us climbs through the hole in the floor; it's like entering another world, a world mixing with our imagination and our own reality. The tree has its own smells, its own primitive roughness, and its own views; the large open window is giving way to endless branches cascading out into the approaching darkness. We imagine alien creatures peering at us from the branches—it seems a perfectly mysterious night for a sleepover.

Da' built the windowsill wide and low enough to sit on so we could watch the sky or look into the heart of the tree; for sure, it's the best sitting in the whole tree. So while me mates prepare their bedding, I'm sitting and watching as the sun slowly sinks and the last bit of light fades into darkness. Twilight is filling gaps between leaves, as birds are fluttering to their branches settling in for the night.

After unrolling the sleeping bags and leaning the fishing poles against the opposite wall, the tree house takes on a warm cozy feeling. Grabbing our flashlights we are pushing and shoving each other almost fighting to get to the window first. Directing the flashlights into the tree's interior a different world reveals itself; our intrusive beams light up limbs flickering in the leaves. Birds have stopped their chattering and gone to sleep, while darkness awakens us to its mysteries leaving us wondering. Limbs reach out into blackness, disappearing into empty pockets of space.

Billy comes over to the window and leaning over to me, he whispers, "It's sure quiet at night." One of the flashlights points upward about twenty feet, and two small round discs of lights flash back in the darkness.

I put me light directly into the staring eyes, and softly squeak, "Look a-at th-thaat."

"What?"

"Up th-there where I'm pointing. Yoo-you sees i-it?"

"I don't see nothing."

"There—wh-wh-ere the tw-oo branches sp-split."

A large barn owl twists its head, staring unblinking at us down below. "I see it, it's a big un." The owl slowly lifts its wings and drops, Matt shrieks and ducks back into the tree house; the owl turns and glides right in front of us.

Billy leans out the window and says, "What's the matter, Matt? Afraid the big ole owl is gonna getcha?"

"It's not funny. I thought it was headed through the window."

"Awwww, it p-p-pro-b-bably s-sa-saw...a mouse or s-so-something."

"Well, it was scary stuff; wonder if anything else might be out there?" Matt, the smallest of us, looks out the window again, then ducking his head back, he dives on his sleeping bag. A few minutes later a bat cuts across the top of the tree. We didn't know it then, but we eventually learned that at night the tree comes alive: creatures moving silently through its branches; bugs a'quivering and humming; leaves rustling; and the tree itself creaking against its own weight.

Pulling the lantern from me bag, I begin pumping gas into the wick while Billy's sorting out Twinkies, plastic tubes of chips, and a bag of chocolate cups so we can eat. Munching and drinking sodas and trying to see which one of us can make the most noise while eating, our chewing sounds are almost blocking out the whispering noises from the darkness. I grab comics from the corner and throw 'em in the middle of the floor. After a few arguments it's decided we'll read from me own horror comic, Dark Shadow.

Paul begins reading first.

From boy to boy the story is unfolding; our imaginations come alive, while at the same time we are cringing at every sound out of the darkness. When it's my turn, I look at each boy one by one as I read. *"Silent k-k-killers stalk th-the wo-woods, searching for v-victims foolish e-enough t-to be out a-a-lone, no one w-wa-was safe from the mo-m-monster's b-bl-bloooood lust!"* Me mates listen with eyes wide as the story unfolds in their minds. Each is lost in his imagination; me stammering somehow makes the story even scarier.

Just as I'm getting to the scariest part, a loud crash rattles the tree house.

Matt yells out, "What the hell's that?" Then he's pulling his sleeping bag over his head. Even I feel the hair on me arms rise. Looking around at each other, no one's daring to speak, when suddenly, another even louder crash shakes the tree! Something big is colliding with the rear wall; no one says anything as I quickly drag the lantern closer to us. Crowding together against the far wall, a sudden unearthly scream penetrates the darkness. Something or someone wails, the tree house shakes again, and yet another heavy crash rattles the roof, and then all hell breaks loose! It's as if a bunch of banshees are screaming and yelling while attacking our fort. Matt's screaming again now and yelling, "Stop it! Stop it!" from inside his sleeping bag.

Paul yells at him to shut up, and then all becomes eerily silent except the sound of our breathing. We're searching around us; whatever landed on the roof is now silent. Imagining a werewolf like in the comic, we are certain it's crawling on the roof ready to spring; Matt points out of his sleeping bag with a single shaky finger at the rope ladder in the center of the tree. "It moved!"

I can't believe it! Then it moves again!

The rope is jerking and bouncing back and forth...something's climbing up the ladder! Heavy breathing is heard. No one moves; flesh is crawling on me arms; the breathing is closer seeming to be in the room with us. Billy pulls something from his pack, and then looking at us he puts his finger to his lips and whispers, "Shh!" He leans over the hole in the floor, and drops something over the edge. All is quiet for a few seconds when suddenly a wild scream explodes in the darkness and the rope goes slack. We hear a loud voice cursing, and then quickly it begins fading into the night.

A huge grin is on Billy's face; his red hair and large freckles are highlighted by lantern light, and his eyes were glowing playfully. He lifts a plastic bag for us to see and says, "Don't know who or what's out there, but whatever it is, it didn't like what I dropped on top of it."

"What is it?" Paul whispers. Billy holds the empty bag higher and closer to the light.

He reads aloud: *Shultz Liquid fertilizer.*

"Whatever was coming up the rope got a face full," he said, "it's for my mom's potted plants; I brought it for a prank, just in case we needed it."

Brilliant! I gotta admit I'm impressed, Billy was thinking way ahead of any of us. Slapping him on the shoulder, I say, "Th-that was some ssm-smart t-th-think-i-ing."

We're laughing so hard we forget for a moment something or someone tried coming into the tree house. Matt whispers loudly from still inside his bag. "I wonder who it was that was out there."

Billy nudges the sleeping bag with his foot and says, "Who said it was a...who?"

Paul then steps over to Matt's sleeping bag while looking at us with an evil grin, and then pointing to the bag. "Um...don't worry about it, Matt..." We all exchange looks and then look again down at Matt's sleeping bag. We're all thinking the same thing; at the same time we all jump on Matt's bag with him inside, wrestling and grabbing at him for a few minutes.

After a while we take a rest and then Paul says, "Let's get some sleep—we gotta get up early." Still wondering what or who attacked us, we crawl into our sleeping bags. Lantern light casts a soft orange glow in the tree as we talk for a while before going to sleep.

I lay quietly thinking me thoughts, wondering over the night's events as sounds from the woods fade…soon there was only silence. Listening for any remaining night sounds, I notice a familiar high-pitch ringing in me ears. I listen more closely; me concentrating on the sound makes the ringing even louder as though it's coming from inside of me. I'm feeling the sound as much as I'm hearing it. Listening closer, the ringing grows more intense, and then it shifts abruptly, seeming to be ringing all around—even vibrating inside of me—then it changes again, getting higher.

I've been hearing this sound throughout me whole life—mostly at night when I'm alone in bed just thinking or listening. I always wonder what it is; sometimes I think it sounds like buzzing bees or mosquitoes. Doctors on the tele say if you're hearing sounds, then you must have tinnitus—ringing in the ears—but this isn't the same. These sounds are clear and have a rhythm. I've always liked the rhythm. It's comfortable, almost familiar.

The sound abruptly shifts again, sounding more like a humming sound, like the noise the refrigerator makes, and then the tone gets louder. The vibrating feeling has more power tonight than ever before, and as I'm listening, I fall asleep.

As I sleep, I dream.

I'm watching meself on a path walking through a thicket of trees. The path is leading into a forest and I sense for sure I'm searching for something: what it is, I don't know. The twisting and turning path is leaving me with a feeling that what I'm looking for is just around the next bend, but it never is. At a steep dip in the path, a rustling from the woods gets me attention; the bushes separate and a movement catches me eye. A young man appears from the shadows wearing a dark green cloak with a hood. A glimmering translucent light radiates around him and dark blonde hair peeks out from his hood. The young man approaches within a few feet, then he stops and stares deeply into me eyes. Feeling the intensity of his stare, I feel strange—it's as if he's probing or searching someplace deep inside me. Keeping his eyes locked on mine, he steps even closer and then his hood falls away; his eyes shine like fire! He pulls a sword from behind his back and then holds it in front of him. Instantly, I'm overwhelmed with a powerful fragrance of jasmine and sandalwood. I know these smells well, because me mum always burns incense with these aromas. The warrior pauses, and the familiar smells are releasing sensations within me; great feelings of happiness and a wondrous sense of freedom burst inside of me. The young man says nothing…something queer is happening to me. He continues staring as if he's trying to tell me something; then slowly, in a soft but brilliant light, he begins fading…and then he's gone.

I hear a faint whistling, sorta like flutes; the sounds are following the fading light and the exciting feelings in me blend into warm surges of energy that's rushing through me, leaving the most profound feeling of joy and peace I've ever known.

I'm alone again and still dreaming. I'm sitting on the window ledge in the tree house, a mystical copy of the original. Gazing into the intense starry night, for a moment I'm free, free'er than anything I can ever remember. Turning to look at me mates, I see the four of us in our bags sleeping. I sit staring…at the same time, I'm confused. How can I be sleeping over there when I'm sitting here on the window ledge? Suddenly, I'm back in my sleeping bag.

I open me eyes, and for a moment I don't know where I am or even who I am—it's confusing. I look around; it's almost morning outside. Faint sounds of a high single note flute still rings in me ears.

Powerful feelings of excitement and wonder are flowing through me. Sitting up, I hear the other boys breathing. What could the dream have meant? I feel I should know the young warrior, but that's impossible! How could I know him? I'm sure the dream was trying to tell me or warn me of something. It was like the warrior was trying to steer me from something bad, and at the same time, the vivid dream awakened something deep inside me, something I haven't felt before... something real and powerful and something so wonderful. Seeing me own self sleeping kinda freaked me out, but for now I think I'll keep this—the dream, the message, whatever it was—me own secret.

The other guys are waking up; we grab our fishing gear and set off to Amity Pond. Climbing down the tree, we see large chunks of watermelon strewn about. Paul exclaims, "I bet that's what we heard slamming against the walls last night!"

"Well, duh. I just wonder who it was," Matt replies.

With a shrug, Billy mumbles again, "Maybe not who, but what."

Morning goes quickly. Fishing is good, but we release our catch back into the pond; no one wants to scale or eat them: the fun is in catching and releasing. Toward late morning it's getting time to go home. Matt and Paul live in the opposite direction of me home and as they turn to go, Paul calls out, "Last night was really cool; can we do it again?"

"You be-bet! Ma-maybe ne-next-we-we-eeeeek, I'll check."

Billy and I cut through the woods back to the tree house. After getting me gear and saying goodbye I start back home. Walking into the meadow, I see Cody's running from the other side to greet me, but before he gets to the middle of the meadow, the big buck we had seen before reappears from out of the edge of shadows—it stands like a statue at the edge of the forest, watching us.

At the sight of the deer, Cody freezes and stares back; I also stop and stare. The buck takes a step forward, then leaps and swiftly crosses the meadow—in a flash, he's gone. I continue staring for a moment and then say, "C'mon boy, l-let's go home."

The sound of the screen door slamming is almost drowned out by me yelling, "I'm ho-home—hello? Is a-an-anyone heeeere?"

No answer; we are home alone. Cody curls up on the den floor and falls asleep while I go to me room to change. Falling down on me bed, I can't think of anything but the weird feelings about seeing me body sleeping while I was sitting on the window ledge, still dreaming. And then there's the young warrior with the brilliant eyes...

Chapter 2 ~ Collision

A few days after the sleepover, Mum and Da' decide where we're going for our vacation. After a whole lot of talking, they decide on a Caribbean cruise. None of us have ever been on a ship before and the cruise is for ten days. We leave in two weeks—first, we got to fly to Florida, and from there we board the ship.

During the next two weeks, I spend most of me time at the tree house. I'm treasuring being alone while watching life unfold within me new world.

At times I fall asleep or daydream what it's like being a bird, or being a squirrel leaping from limb to limb. Life is slower here in our tree, and my mind often gets quiet just from the simplicity around me—these quiet times offer moments to wonder at the meaning of life and what I might become when I grow up.

Sometimes I just practice on me guitar or try thinking of words for a song; I love music. No matter what, though, I'm always thinking of the powerful dream I had that first night in the tree house. From this tree I freely create a world from me imagination...a world of magic, discovering, and mystery.

Melody sometimes comes to the tree house with her cat Namo; she also loves the quiet beauty of the giant tree and woods. Da's been here a few times and together we'd be talking and enjoying new discoveries in the tree. He seems to relax when he's here; these are the times that bring us closer than ever. Time spent with me Da' is something I really love. It makes me realize what me family means to me, not only as a whole family, but each as an individual.

The morning before our vacation starts, I wake up excited. Mom's up early gathering, packing, and making sure last-minute details are being taken care of. Melody's friend Judy will be taking care of Namo while Billy's watching Cody. Tomorrow we leave for Florida!

Walking into the kitchen, I see Mom's brewing some coffee. I reach into the cupboard and grab a box of Cap'n Crunch for breakfast. Pouring it in me bowl, I ask, "Mum, can I go t-to-to the t-t-tree-hoo-use after breakfast?" Mom's quiet for a moment. Then turning to me, she says, "You can go only if ya' take me with you." I stop pouring cereal into me bowl and stare at her. She's never asked to see the tree house before. Finishing pouring me cereal I say, "Grr-ea-attt! But you better ch-chaa-ange, as we'll be wa-walking through the m-mea-meadow to-toooo get there." She smiles, gives me a tight hug and says, "Tis be only a few moments to change into some jeans and me tennies."

Practically inhaling me cereal, I finish and put the bowl in the sink just as Mom returns.

Walking down the deck stairs leading from the kitchen, Cody comes running to see what's going on. He's jumping in circles when he sees me and Mom walking toward the meadow. Racing ahead of us, his head is high as he sniffs at the wet morning air; the excitement of having Mom with us makes him act like a puppy.

Entering the meadow, Mom gradually slows her walking and then finally stops. She stares across the tall grass that's sparkling with morning light. Flowers and small trees dot the dew-covered meadow gradually merging with the pine forest. The smells are intoxicating as we walk deeper into the grass. Neither of us says much; our thoughts are absorbed in trying to identify each new scent and reacting to the pitter patter of the chirping birds and buzzing insects. Deep, thick grass folds beneath our feet as we go further into the meadow. Morning sunlight bounces off thousands of dewdrops sparkling like diamonds. Looking up just in time, we see a gray fox spring from behind a large bush and dash through the meadow, running behind her are three kits. Mom's staring at the fox and her kits as they reach the edge of the meadow; the vixen looks back as if inviting us to come closer into her domain, Cody takes off after them and then...they are gone.

As we go deeper into the woods, Mom spins around, she's walking backwards and swinging her arms almost like dancing, and at that moment it seems as if she's a young girl again. She's looking at me and then says, "How striking that fox was—I don't think I've ever seen one as beautiful and majestic."

"I-I th-th-think she lives a-a-around the e-ed-edge of the wo-oo-woods."

Walking toward the end of the meadow where the fox disappeared, we enter a shaded glen. Smells of moss and pine are flooding our senses; a small stream gurgles as water splashes over small rocks to the right of us, adding to the peaceful ambience. Light streams through the tall pines while shimmering over a shadowed carpet of green moss covering rocks and fallen tree limbs. Looking over at me, Mum asks, "How're ya' feeling about entering into junior high in the fall?"

I pick up a rock and throw it at nothing.

"I h -have many f-f-fee-li-lings about it, but mo-more than any-th-thing else, I feel ne-nervous about how di-dif-different I'm told it'll beeeeee..."

"Tis for sure, Hugh, you know life is about change, nothing stays the same, that's how we grow in spirit." Looking up from the path we are walking, I know she's trying to tell me about changes in me own life, such as feelings and me body. Feeling shy I nod, at the same time I'm thinking how life's taking a big step for me, a step that's going to be asking for me to take more responsibility for me thoughts and for the actions created from those thoughts. Mum reaches for me hand and we walk together into the clearing where the huge tree stands in shattered sunlight. Shafts of light pierce through a gray mist surrounding the tree; tips of tall limbs and upper leaves appear almost faded against the foggy sky. Looking up, we both are staring at the flowing limbs interlacing and forming a wide canopy. A ladder Da' built is leaning against the tree, making it easier climbing than the rope. Mom climbs slowly and mindfully, being careful as she takes each step higher into the thick folds of leaves and limbs. When she's entering the tree house, I'm right behind her.

Quickly I run over to the far wall. "M-Mom, lo-l-look at this!" Proudly, I lift the canvas covering the window, which opens the view into the heart of the tree.

Stepping closer to the window, Mum stares into the massive interior of the tree; she takes a deep breath, the tree's inner world opens as in a vision. Vast tangles of limbs and leaves are winding first upward and out, and then crossing each other creating a living cave. Cardinals, jays, and chickadees hop and flutter from limb to limb, each singing—or in the case of the jays, squawking—their own special songs. Squirrels race around larger limbs, chasing each other in their morning play; shafts of light move on every breeze that's wafting through the branches; dew shimmers on wet leaves. Pieces of blue sky peek between limbs that bend in rhythm with the morning breezes. Butterflies, with their myriad colors, flitter gently from one limb to another. The spectacle of abundant life and vibrant color together create a scene like a fairy glen; all the life this tree shelters now accepts the tree house as part of their reality.

Mum continues staring in wonder at the beauty unfolding from the window, without turning, she softly whispers, "I had no idea tis be so lovely."

Kicking off me shoes, I sit on the windowsill. Leaning against the frame I cross me arms over my chest and say, "I'm glad you came today Mom, I-I've re-rea-lly come to-to love this p-place and I'm h-hap-happiest when I-I'm h-heeeere." Mum can't take her eyes from the beauty unfolding in front of her; tears glisten in her eyes as she realizes—like me—what a precious gift this tree is to our family for sharing, enjoying, and loving together.

Ann Bailey doesn't have many happy moments in her life, not because they aren't there, but because she either ignores them or she just can't see how precious ordinary moments are. While growing up, she lived with parents who fought constantly and eventually divorced. Her mother remarried a man who was cruel and abusive to Ann and her siblings. This abuse caused the children to grow up fast while simultaneously losing faith and trust in other people. Ann's a good mother and a loving person, but there are moments when she still feels like a victim, and those are the times when she needs to be alone. Ann tries, but she can't forgive and forget; she therefore struggles constantly to create her future from her past, but the results leave her present partially shaded in sadness. This lack of trust in others makes life miserable at times, and combined with the culture shock of leaving Ireland, a deep and dark expanse has created emotional dark areas within her. For the most part she tries to hide from the darkness, but attachments to her past are so deeply rooted that even her supportive family can't help her to let them go. Doctors prescribed drugs for depression, discussed a bi-polar disorder, and treated her for other forms of possible mental problems, but nothing seems to work for long, so the family learns to live with it the best they can. The upcoming cruise is hopefully going to allow her to pay attention to something other than herself, perhaps providing a temporary escape.

Noticing his Mom's pleasure as she stares into the tree, Hugh's thinking about this almost magical moment he is having with his mom when he says, "I'll n-nev-never…forget this m-mo-mor-morning, Mom. I didn't kn-know until n-noow how happy this place ma-kkes pe-people feel."

For this moment it is as if they are both children and best friends at the same time, laughing and talking about things never discussed before. The midmorning sun creeps overhead; by and by, it's time to head home.

Walking back toward the house, Hugh thinks how his mom's looking through different eyes at him. She seems to have grown today, and so has he; she understands him in new ways, just like Hugh sees his mother in different ways, too.

Arriving at the house, Mum asks if I have me things packed and ready for the vacation. I go check one more time to make sure I haven't forgotten anything. I'm going through me suitcase when she walks in and asks if I need any help. "I think I-I have e-ev-everything—all the clothes I-I'll need, a few books, my bi-bin-binocu-lars and spare shoes. What else do I ne-neeeed?"

"We're going to stop in Cozumel—have ya' packed your mask and flippers? There's great diving and snorkeling there."

I hadn't thought about the swimming, so I go to the closet to find me diving equipment. The flippers are tucked away in the corner where I left them. I feel for the diving mask and it's also exactly where I left it. I'm about to pack the mask when I see a crack in the faceplate; it's small, but for sure it will allow water to leak in.

"Darn, Mom, it-it's cracked! Wh-what am I g-gonna d-d-do now?"

Calmly she walks over, takes the mask, and examines it. "Well, tis for sure ya' can't be using this, so we'll have to run down to the mall and get a new one. Let's go right now and get back before Da' comes home."

Climbing into the minivan, I buckle up and ask Mom, "The old maa-ssk is just a-a toy, can I g-get a p-p-profess-sio-nal mask like in the ma-ma-magazines?"

"I don't see why not; let's see what we can find." She pulls out of the driveway and heads down Dogwood Circle toward town.

Driving down the quiet country road, I'm thinking about the kind of mask to get when Mom pulls out on Main Street past the town square. She's likely still thinking about the tree house and all the beauty she had seen this morning; tis for sure they were wonderful feelings of peace we felt. Approaching the main thruway into Bristol, I'm thinking how Mom's so happy and content—maybe she's thinking the world might be a nice place to live in after all.

Ann Bailey's thoughts are on her family.

She's realizing how much she has to be thankful for, especially with the vacation just a day away. Such thoughts of gratitude run through her mind as she pulls out on to the highway. The vehicle behind her doesn't slow down as it changes lanes; neither Hugh nor his mom sees the truck as it comes hurtling down upon them.

There's a loud horrific crash, and Hugh hears his mother's scream, sees a brilliant flash of light, and then his consciousness withdraws into darkness.

CHAPTER 3 ~ A FAMILY LOST

When the call came informing him of the accident, Clark's world plunged into hell; it's two in the morning now, and he's been home for just an hour; he and Melody had been at the hospital the entire day.

Staring into the dimly lit fire, Clark's thoughts race through his mind while flames flicker within dying embers...firelight casts shadows against bare walls. A thin, dark-haired man in his late thirties sits alone with his head in his hands. Aloud, he asks some age old questions. "Why, God? Why us? How could this happen? Why would you allow such a terrible thing to come into our lives? I can't see any reason for this. What kind of God does this?"

Doctors worked feverishly for hours on both Ann and Hugh; their injuries are extensive and both are in a deep coma. The surgeon explained to Clark that due to the seriousness of the injuries, their brains have shut down certain areas to block the pain and trauma. So far, both have survived the injuries, but now their bodies are barely even responding to touch. Ann suffers severe head wounds and internal injuries, as well as a broken pelvis, leg and shoulder.

Hugh also suffered head injuries, though not as extensive as his mother's; his arm is broken along with minor internal injuries. Given the type of injuries Hugh sustained, the doctors are puzzled why he has not regained consciousness. Clark spent the day and most of the night waiting to hear whether the operations would save their lives. Finally, the nurse told him there was nothing he could do and he might as well go home and get some rest.

Staring into the fire, Clark has never felt as helpless as he does now. Melody fell asleep while they drove home and is now in bed. Clark's exhausted, but still can't sleep; today they were supposed to fly to Florida to meet the ship for their long-planned vacation. A stream of thoughts keeps him from sleep.

Why? I just don't understand God. Me family is everything and now they're gone. For years, Annie and I have struggled to build a life for our family, both carrying the load together. Now to suddenly have it all vanish within a few moments makes no sense. How could life do this to us?

They aren't bad people! He believes in God! He tries to do right with his business and his family: how can he go on without Annie and Hugh? How will he take care of Melody and explain this to her?

He suddenly feels so incomplete.

Cody lies in front of the low fire, his gentle eyes locked on his master. He senses something is different. He feels his master's sadness, but all he can do is stay at his side and give him unconditional love, as is his nature. Throwing a few logs on the fire, Clark sits back, reaches for a faded photograph of his family from the end table, and slowly begins to nod, eventually letting the peaceful arms of sleep take him into its unknown world, thereby escaping for a short time the torment life has plunged him into.

The faded photograph rests on his chest.

A soft touch to his shoulder wakens him. It is already late morning as Melody kneels by her father's side, looking for answers only he can provide, answers that to a child's collapsing world are difficult to come by. Reaching out, Clark pulls her close. Somehow he needs to go deep within and find the strength to hold her world together.

"Da', are Mommy and Hugh going to be okay?"

Clark thinks for a minute before answering, and then he says, "Ah, lass, the doctors for sure have done a wonderful job with the both of them, tis now in God's hands; we have to have faith, so try to keep good thoughts darling think of us all being together again. Tis the best medicine we have to give them and ourselves." Leaning her head against her daddy's chest she silently thinks about what life has done to her world. She can't really understand life without Mom and Hugh—it's something that simply doesn't register in her eight-year-old mind. She knows her mom and Hugh are in great danger. She feels they need Dad and her now more than anything else in the world.

Within the protective shield of her youth, the understanding of the sadness and pain she feels associates itself with not having her mother and brother at home, but for now, she rests her body and mind in the arms of her dad.

Walking the sanitized halls of the hospital, echoes of their steps ring in his ears; suffering and fear hang like a dark shadow as Clark and daughter get closer to his wife and son's room. Glancing at strangers without names lying ill behind glass panes Clark tries to ignore the images, but can't help wonder Why? Why all this sorrow, this suffering, this pain? This living in fear is it so necessary or are we just going through life in vain? Not knowing what to expect the prospect of death settles like a graveyard mist over their minds and hearts causing both to see the world as surreal or a terrible dream.

Having received special permission for Ann and Hugh to share a room rather than sending Hugh to the juvenile wing made walking into their room like a nightmare times two.

Wrapped in bandages almost head to foot, Ann lay as in death, yet she's alive. Bandaged but not as extensively, Hugh lies motionless in a bed separated by white curtains. The darkest part of what's happening is seeing all the tubes and lifelines penetrating their bodies as they lie in deathly silence. Sitting next to Ann, Clark gently takes her hand; she's so strong in her love, and now so must he be, not only for his daughter but also for his wife and son. His love has always been strong but now comes the intense test of his deepest strength. Melody takes Hugh's hand as her father has with her mom and holds it gently but firmly.

The door swings open and a doctor enters. The doctor walks over to Ann's bed to examine some equipment, and after writing some notes on the chart at the end of the bed, he looks tenderly at Clark holding Ann's hand, and after glancing over at the young girl holding the boy's hand, he feels compelled to interrupt and say something. "Mr. Bailey? I'm Dr. Orvitz. I'm your wife and son's treating physician."

Still staring at his wife, Clark asks, "What's to become of me family? Are they ever going to be with us again?"

The doctor's silent for a moment, then moving closer to Ann's bed he bends forward, looking directly at Clark over the rim of his glasses he gently asks, "Do you mind if I sit here with you for a while?" Setting the clipboard down, Dr. Orvitz pulls a chair up and sits across from Clark. He touches Ann's wrist, pauses, then slowly shakes his head, and says, "We don't really understand or appreciate all the workings of the mind, Mr. Bailey. Even with all our high tech equipment and knowledge, we still can't explain the miracle of the human spirit."

The doctor smiles hopefully. "I've seen cases that defy all known medicine and logic, which we as doctors are supposed to know; yes, your wife has suffered a traumatic shock along with serious injuries. But the fact that she's even alive is a compliment to her spirit. I suppose the final outcome is in the hands of the Creator—or maybe in the hands of her own spirit. The body for the most part repairs itself, but I can't tell you much about the mind—it remains mostly an enigma. As for the boy—I'm puzzled. He suffered injuries, but none of which should have sent him into a coma like this. Besides his broken arm and a mild concussion, he suffered some internal injuries that we have already repaired. He should have regained consciousness by now."

Dr. Orvitz tweaks some switches on the machine attached to Ann again, and continues, "I'm sure that both Hugh and Ann in some way feel your presence, but on what level I don't know; I do know that it will take patience, love, and strength of spirit to journey back to this world, and that's where you and your daughter come in; your love and attention is the best medicine they can receive right now."

Clark looks at Annie and then over to Hugh, somewhere deep in his heart he senses a battle is growing. He doesn't know about the medical part of his wife's and son's injuries; he only knows it just can't end like this. His world has gone to hell and it seems no matter what, he is following close behind. Slowly dropping his face into his hands, his head, and fingers begin to tremble as the enormity of what is happening spreads deeper into his mind. He whispers out loud, "Oh, God! I miss 'em."

The fear of losing his wife and son builds a deep darkness within, leaving Clark gasping for breath. As the darkness grows and creeps over his mind, he struggles to suppress the horror; he can't allow himself to surrender to the hopelessness—if not for himself, then for Melody. Despair, fear, and darkness continuously take turns seeking to overtake his mind. His shaky hands still covering his face, he tries to stay calm, but he feels himself sinking—succumbing to his mind's overwhelming fear. He cries out in his thoughts. Oh, God, help me, help me, please! Nothing but the hissing and beeping of the life support machines is heard.

And then something happens.

His mind quiets for a second, and then he hears it!

At first it's faint, hardly perceptible—just a strange rumbling, like distant summer thunder. The sound soon expands, rolling through his entire being, becoming more intense with each second; the strange sound expands within him. He listens more closely; the sound changes to a deep humming then it slowly forms a slow pounding rhythm similar to his heartbeat. Faint forgotten feelings begin growing from within, feelings he has not felt since he was a small child; slowly but steadily a gentle warmth spreads throughout his mind and into his heart. The darkness fades a little. Waves of steady energy from within his mind move into his feelings gently giving him an awareness of assurance; the warmth spreads.

Clark slowly begins to realize that he isn't alone anymore in this nightmare, for the first time since the accident he feels hope, and for a brief moment he understands, sees, and feels this situation as the challenge that it is, not only for his wife and son, but for him and Melody as well. The life of his family is at stake with their very souls being attacked. Now is the time to grow, and to somehow bring from the deepest part of him, the courage to challenge darkness and fear. The strange vibrating sound fills him momentarily with a calm confidence and a rising hope, but there's also something else...what, he doesn't know; but as a husband, a father, and a man, he will find the strength to fight back. The villain has arrived— and it has invaded his family's soul.

A father takes his daughter's hand and walks out of the hospital; he leaves with something more than when he had entered—possibly a flicker of hope, and perhaps a growing faith.

CHAPTER 4 ~ THE JOURNEY BEGINS

Drifting in nothing…nothing but a deep and murky darkness that I feel more than I see…The shadowing darkness hovers like suspended nothingness… beyond this emptiness is something else, something tremendously huge…shadows perhaps? I can't know for certain, shapes are constantly fading and disappearing. Shapeless shadow forms move within darker ones, ominous shadows fade, replacing the emptiness with a thick grayish fog that's throbbing like a living breathing thing. Vaporous shadows move to rhythms of slow beating drums—each beat forms darker shadows that dissipate within the fog. Swirling mists waver like flickers of silvery dust: sparkling for a brief second, and then repeating itself. I struggle for consciousness, trying to pull me thoughts together; the last thing I remember was me mum's screaming, and then…darkness.

Where am I? Where's me mum?

From the deepest part of the shadows a round, coppery transparent sphere slowly melts into the center of swirling grayish mists; it isn't moving—just a' floating in front of me, floating within desolate sounds of distant drums. Staring intently at the sphere, I feel myself gently being pulled forward. The cloud thins. I struggle to see more clearly, but the fog smothers me even further, the shining sphere keeps moving and receding further and further into the mist. Me vision tries to follow, and then for a moment the image clears; bits of color sparkle like flakes of glitter, and the darkness of me mind fades. I try to hold a thought, but me thoughts only slip away more. Thoughts disappear into the fading darkness, drawing me deeper into the mist—slowly at first, but definitely pulling me…almost like being pulled within me own thoughts. What's happening to me? Is this even real?

Feelings expand within me. Shadowing images form and then separate; a part of me feels like it's being left behind somewhere, as in a dream. Floating further into the misty light, I'm moving forward and deeper, always following the sphere. The fog slowly and gently dissipates…everything very softly and so gently changes…a glittering golden light flutters against a background of faded pastels like distant rainbows moving to slow distant drums.

I move through the now starry but still misty light, following the shining globe; something is compelling me to keep going. A spiraling light appears within the evaporating fog and it swirls around me; the golden sphere fades into the light, while a haunting melody pulses through me like an invisible wave, and then ever so slowly, it fades. A powerful feeling of confidence and a great love bubbles from within me. I no longer have a beating heart separate from me mind—instead I am just one of many rhythmic pulse's flowing out of me own heart, and with each pulse love continues to move me forward. Me mind stretches again, expanding further. I try anchoring onto anything, but again I'm vanishing in the light slowly fading within the love…Something odd is happening—maybe it's something divine, or something I can only describe as holy, as I'm moving within the light I'm becoming more than what I'd been. I'm becoming different—something is changing. I swirl faster and faster, deeper into the light, I feel a tremendous push and then I hear a loud popping like a cork being pulled from a bottle. Me last thoughts are of me mum, and then darkness overtakes me again.

Slowly and very gently, I begin to emerge out of a deep darkness. Opening me eyes, I stare above into a cloudless sky; sittin' up, I look around; I'm stunned with the vision forming before me.

Something has changed also within me: my head is crystal clear, and my thoughts are sharp, articulate, focused, and more commanding. It's as if my mind has developed years in the span of a nap! A comforting feeling embraces me and I feel no stress, urgency, or fear: only curiosity and wonder. My eyes seem to see everything in brighter hues and longer distances. Deep endless valleys lay around me, all surrounded by rolling hills and sparkling waterfalls tumbling down huge mountains. Meadows with endless flowers are enshrined within deep glens and woods, all spreading before me as if in a divine vision. Streams flow into pools of crystal clear waters that empty into vast rivers, and then they gently disappear into the distant horizon. Mountains stand like guardians on each side of the valleys, extending high above as if reaching for heaven. The intensity and clarity of the crystal blue sky is intoxicating, and the setting appears timeless: feelings of morning, noon or late afternoons are all gone. This is like another reality—beautiful, but totally different than me own world. The light in the sky is rich, dark, and bright at the same time.

Clear, soft, brilliant hues of colors fade in and out of the scene in front of me. The tree I lie under stands crookedly like a twisted work of modern art: all gnarled and thick. Even as it's growing upward, it grinds against itself, spreading its limbs outward in a circular motion amid mysterious fading ribbons of pink, white, and silver light that merges and then disappears to only reappear again. Around me trees form small shaded glens with brooks and streams bubbling along twisted pathways. Even though the mountains are great distances away, I see them almost telescopically—they are giant monoliths of granite shaped into huge cones with waterfalls cascading between crevices, while throwing out soft mists that are reflectin' rainbows against sheer cliffs. It's hard to look away from the almost magical beauty and light. The clarity and brightness of colors beg for description, but how can words of man describe a garden that a God must have tended, and therefore touches me Soul itself? As I become more aware of the surrounding environment, the impact of what's happening begins to sink in. Again, I ask meself: Where am I? What has happened? Where's me mum? What is this place? Have I died?

Slowly, I stand up, look around, and then I look down at me own body. Nothing could have prepared me for what's now happening! No longer am I in me small boy's skinny body! I've changed from a young boy into a young teen, with longer, stronger legs and arms and hands. Reaching up to me face and head, I feel hair that's longer and thicker than my old hair. I'm also wearing different clothes; my pants are dark beige and seem to be made from soft linen, but thicker; they're not tight, but then again they're not loose either; the pants pool into moccasin-like boots made from some unknown material; a white long-sleeved shirt with brown laces coming down from the neck a few inches is tucked into me pants, which is held up by a belt winding through a thick ring of silver rather than a buckle. I look again over the unfolding landscape, trying to make sense of what's happening. I know one thing for sure—I'm not in the world I was born in. I feel so odd, so strange; me mind, me vision, and me body are all different.

I sit up on the small hill gazing over the valley trying to adjust to these strange new sensations and thoughts. After a while, I stand up again; I gotta figure out what to do.

Looking around, it occurs to me that maybe I can find someone or something that can give me a clue about where I am. Rising up unsteadily on me legs like a newborn colt, I stumble a short distance from the tree, slowly trying to get used to this new body and strange landscape.

Down from the hill I see a path leading into the distance, and I set off toward it. Stepping onto the little path I again see a breathtaking vivid glen lying before me, walking just a bit further down the hill, I enter the shaded glen.

Still marveling at the brightness and clarity of the scenery and colors, I hear a faint noise. Stopping for a moment to listen more closely, I hear it again; the sound is coming from the bottom of the hill. Maybe it's someone who can help me or at least answer some questions, I consider. Carefully I walk further down the pathway. Just left of the hill, the path twists around large exotic plants and then opens up to an even larger pathway. As I'm nearing the sound, I try to move more smoothly and quietly in hopes of not startling who—or whatever—is making the noise. Crunchin' down behind some bushes alongside the path, I peer over the top in the direction to where the noise is coming from; a wide flowing stream just beyond some boulders; a stream with water sparklin' a misty golden light. Water forms small pockets along the edges of the stream near the boulders. Beautiful trees and a few flat rocks line the edges of the shore. Small flowers and leaves of various colors float on the water's surface as the stream winds its way deeper into the valley. A large flat rock sits at the junction where the stream pours into a small jetty, and on that stone I see the most peculiar-looking creature I've ever seen or imagined. I keep hidden in the bushes, but carefully inch forward as much as I can to better view this odd sight.

The creature moves and acts human, but from the rear it appears more like a small, slim teddy bear. Its feet are lightly covered with a soft fur, but there are toes. The body's about four feet tall and is covered with short fine hair except the chest area, which is bare skin. The arms are human-shaped and also covered with hair, and the hands are small like a child's. Its head is round with long, slightly pointed ears on the sides, so long that they extend almost to the top of the head. The face seems quite close to a human, and it has a small button nose.

Large, expressive, blue eyes—almost like a baby's—peek out from its charming face; it isn't a disagreeable face at all, just different. The little person wears a brown vest and dark green pants. The strange creature dips its arms into the water and splashes vigorously. I watch hardly breathing trying not to scare the little person away, but suddenly it turns its head and looks directly where I'm hiding. I remain quiet and don't dare stir. Abruptly the creature stands up and walks directly to where I'm scrunching behind the bushes, when it's about five feet from where I'm hiding; it looks into me face and smiles. The eyes twinkle and the little round nose wiggles back and forth as a small grin emerges. I can't help but stare and smile back. It takes a few steps closer and reaches out to touch me cheek, and at that point, I step out from the bushes. The little person's eyes widen when it sees how tall I really am, I step a few feet closer. I'm about to speak to the creature when I feel a powerful push inside me head; then a musical androgynous voice springs into me mind or maybe in me thoughts—I'm not sure.

"*I am Kaylu of the Wuskies, greetings.*"

I step back!

I hear the words clearly and feel the feelings of the greeting, but there's no sound from the little person.

"I…I…I'm Hugh."

Kaylu looks up at me with a questioning look on his face then sends another thought. "*You talk with sounds from your mouth; can you not think words and pictures?*"

Squatting down I look directly at the little person and say, "I a-am a stranger to this p-place, I think in w-wo-words and p-pi-pic-tures, but al-always use sounds to e-ex-express the thoughts and images in me mind."

The little person looks intently at me, and then replies by simply projecting words again into me mind. "*It must be difficult to understand everyone you meet when they're all making different sounds.*"

I think about this for a moment before I finally say, "We ma-manage to get ac-ac-across what we wa-want." He continues staring at me like a cat might focus curiously at a bug crawling across the floor; then quickly he turns back to the stream.

Reaching the water's edge, he stoops and picks up the handle to what looks like some sort of tool, then dipping it into the stream, rubs it clean. I watch silently, thinking maybe I'd be interrupting something. Picking up what looks like an axe, he dips it into the water to wash it, and once finished, he carefully wraps the tools in a white cloth and ties them with two pieces of thin rope.

I inch forward and ask, "Excuse m-meeeee, but I-I was wo-wo-wondering if you can tell me wh-where I am?"

Kaylu looks up at me and grins again, and a thought comes into me mind. "*I do not understand? You are here with me next to the stream.*"

I'm quiet for a moment thinking about his words, and then I ask, "I mean, wh-what l-land am I in? I-I am not from this p-place, and am lost."

Kaylu's silent for a moment and then replies. His voice in me mind is almost musical and has a whimsical flavor to it. "*You must be from a world of Light* and Darkness; sometimes new travelers appear in this land, not knowing how they got here."

"Yes! Tis what hap-ha-happened t-to meeee! I was wi-with me mum, th-there was a crash and then I-I'm here; the last thing I-I re-rem-remember is dar-darkness." The little creature is silent; he picks up his package of tools and walks by me without stopping. I get a feeling in me mind of compassion and understanding, but I hear no words.

"W-wait! I need he-help! P-please tell me where I-I am. Wh-whaat place is this?"

He stops, turns and walks back to where I'm standing, and words again enter me mind. "I normally avoid getting involved with newcomers; it is always so confusing. The questions never stop, and your language is odd—even for one who speaks only with sounds."

I'm silent; I really don't know what to say. I'm thinking about how to respond, trying to form the right words, when again I feel a push in me mind and me thoughts are gone; the little creature's musical words rings within me mind. "If you listen without asking too many questions, I will give you as much information as I can."

I breathe a sigh of relief and follow Kaylu back to the rocks by the stream. We find a comfortable place to rest and I reach down to scoop up some water for a drink. Just as me hand is about to touch the clear pool, I stop: staring back at me from the slow, rippling water is a reflection, but it isn't mine—the face staring back isn't really a stranger's face—it's me own—only older. I stare into the pool's reflection and examine the face staring back. The hair is wavy, a might long, and hanging over me face a little; the chin is square and strong; the eyes are mine, but they shine more clearly and seem set deeper. The reflected image is an older version of what I will look like in the future! I'm thinking I look at least thirteen. Kaylu sits down next to me, and staring into the stream alongside me, he says, "You seem surprised at your reflection."

I stand up, a bit shaken, and then I kneel down and settle myself again. "I look d-dif-different from the way I look back in me ow-own' world; how did I g-g-get older? And w-what is this p-place?"

Kaylu reaches over to get his knapsack again, and words manifest effortlessly within me thoughts. *"You are in the land of Quatron, which is part of the world of Tirkuti; my people are called Wuskies. Wuskies live north of the great mountains and I'm returning to my land after a long journey."*

Kaylu continues to project words and images to me; it seems that once the words enter me mind, they stay there as part of me own knowledge. My comprehension and retention of this type of communication is astonishing; not only can I understand what he sends, but I can also feel the feelings that Kaylu feels. The feelings seem to be injected somehow within his words, as are his images. In this multidimensional way, he communicates the words, the feelings, and the sights of the history of this strange and beautiful land; it is as if I actually live his story in my mind.

According to Kaylu, Quatron has four central capitals, each located in the center of its own province. Kaylu comes from the north; there are three more provinces where various types of beings live. A fifth capital is located in Offland, but little is known of this strange place; some say it's used as a portal to other worlds. Kaylu and his people are gatherers and builders: they build homes, towns, dams and other assorted things inhabitants might need. They don't limit themselves to only their own lands, and travel to the other provinces as well. I have arrived in the Providence of Tusha, which is primarily inhabited by Tuzas.

The Tuza people are dreamers, artists, writers, and anything else that has to do with arts, learning and even what some call magic. Their primary goals are creating beautiful works of art, poetry, landscaping, and keeping history in written form: they always walk in truth. The Tuzas had asked Kaylu to design a new temple in their capital city of Ahirit. It is known that occasionally newcomers appear from what is called the lower worlds, and when this happens, usually they are met and escorted to a community where they can learn and adjust to their new world. Some of those called the Old Ones are aware of how and why this happens. In certain situations, newcomers are escorted to one of these wise ones for instructions as to their mission in this new world. Kaylu doesn't know why I was sent to this land, but he did suggest that maybe I needed to find the Old Ones or a learned Traveler to discuss this matter.

After a while, I'm finding it easier to receive me new friend's thoughts and then respond with me talking words. Kaylu tells me that in time I, too, will communicate with thoughts instead of the primitive way of sounds from the mouth. Kaylu can't tell me why I'm here, or the whereabouts of others like me, but my mind and body being older isn't a surprise to him. It seems that when newcomers arrive in this world, their bodies are created in a fashion that exemplifies their finest strengths, intelligence, and beauty. Whether the person is old, young, female, or male doesn't matter; each newcomer starts his or her new life in the best body and mental condition that the mind can create.

I'm absorbing all the information he's giving me, and this increase in awareness allows me to digest the knowledge and adjust me thinking accordingly.

As I'm listening, I interrupt to ask a question. "Kaylu, if a person is gi-gi-given a perfect body, why do-dooo…I still have this sp-speech imp-p-edim-m-ment when I speak?"

"The speaking part isn't a physical handicap, but some kind of fear you need to overcome. However, there is one thing that does puzzle me. Normally, previous newcomers arriving in this land don't remember their old lives, whereas you seem to remember everything about your past life."

He was right. In fact, my entire other life still exists within me—me Da', Melody, Mom, Cody, and me best friend Billy—they are all still a part of who I was and still am. It's as if the "I" of me old life appeared in this new world with a new body, new awareness, and new intelligence, but still possesses all the attachments and memories of my life with me family and friends, plus the same goals and all that I love. I remember the tree house and me family getting ready to leave on a vacation. I remember Mum and me leaving to go to the store, and then I remember the accident, and after that, I recall nothing except waking up in this strange world. Kaylu listens to me talk about my old life and everything that's happened, and I somehow know he is beginning to think I may be different from any newcomers he has met or heard of. For some reason, he feels he was placed in the location where we met in order for him to help me through this time of change.

By the time Kaylu finishes his first lesson, both of us are famished. He opens his bundle and places some packets of food on the rock we're resting on, then motions for me to eat. I pick up what looks like a roll and taste it. "Oh…my…God! It's delicious!" It was like cinnamon and honey, but with some other exotic flavor I can't identify. "Wh-what kind…of b-br-bread is this?"

"It is called comb bread; it's made from the honeycomb of the bees in my land—the honeycomb is made from various flowers and extracted from the bee hives."

"It's d-d-delicious!" I reach for another roll as Kaylu then pours a drink from a canister into two cups. I take a sip. "This is really go-good, too. What's it m-ma-made from?"

Kaylu looks at me in surprise and points to the stream. *"It's merely water from the stream."*

I can't believe it! The water tastes like nothing I ever tasted before: it's fresh, sweet, and has a deep, rich flavor that's unbelievably satisfying to the thirst. I dip me cup into the stream and again taste the water; it's the same sweet, rich refreshing flavor. "Wow! If o-o-only the wa-wa-water tasted this g-g-good back home!"

After the meal Kaylu suggests we head north. *"Maybe we can find someone who can help; it may be important that you discover why you were sent to this land with all your memories and feelings still intact. Maybe we should talk to one of the Old Ones."* I agree. I'm just so grateful I found someone who would take the time to help me. Preparing to leave, I mention I have a feeling there's something I need to find, and whatever it is, I'm sure it's going to be necessary if I'm ever to get back to me family.

CHAPTER 5 ~ THE DREAM

Driving home from the hospital with Melody, Clark's mind can't stop going over the events of the past two days. Between the shock and pain, he's slowly realizing that throughout this whole experience only his faith, love, patience, and inner strength will sustain him, not only him but his daughter's as well. Faith may very well determine whether this nightmare ends well or badly. The doctors just updated their findings about Annie and Hugh's condition this morning.

Annie's still in a deep coma, her injuries are life-threatening. Hugh's injuries, although much less serious than his mother's, are baffling the doctors. No medical reason exists as to why Hugh is still in a coma; his brain isn't injured, his body's injuries are healing, and they never were life-threatening in the first place, so what's keeping him in his deep sleep? The doctors can only speculate, and none gives an answer that makes any sense.

What's he to do? Where can he go for help?

Pulling into the driveway and parking, Clark opens the front door. Immediately he senses the empty loneliness, it's the same feeling he fought at the hospital. The first thing he must do is try to bring some normalcy for Melody and himself.

Watching her play with her cat, he asks Melody to feed Cody and Namo while he looks to see what they have for dinner. Entering into the kitchen, Clark feels a kind of emptiness; he imagines Annie standing by the stove, preparing dinner as she has so many times. Shaking his head, he opens the refrigerator to see what's available. Cody comes into the kitchen, wagging his tail. Reaching down and patting him, Clark thinks how grateful he is to have such a warm, wonderful friend as Cody; here's this big ole dog, giving his love without ever expecting anything in return. If only I could love as unconditionally. I love me family and enjoy them to the fullest, yet in reality I see now that I always expected something in return from them...obedience, comfort, respect or even demanding their love in me own way. Tis a selfish man I've been; now I'm giving me love and all I get back is loneliness, misery, sadness, and haunting memories.

Why can't I just love without expecting something in return? Even now, when all seems lost, I still look for something for my misery. Tis as if the meaning of love really has no meaning when selfishly demanding something back. Maybe there's something more to what we call love; if so, how do I experience it?

After dinner, Melody turns on the tele hoping it will take their minds off the sad events swallowing their lives. TV is different tonight for Clark. He does not feel himself letting go and entering the story; he clearly sees the actors acting, but he is disgusted and a bit surprised by the obvious foolishness of the plot and silly things that people get so upset about—they are only illusions. Most of the shows are written bundled up within a web of assumptions, with the characters pained by the desire of wanting something and their not getting it.

Clark found himself trying to count how many times each actor said the word "I". As he watches, he thinks about this one small word and how much control it generates in our lives. Could I or anyone else go through one day without using the word "I"? If we could, how much might it change our point of view and attitude?

He continues to think about the word "I."

Isn't the world, day in, and day out, mainly caught up in satisfying the little me, or "I"? Our lives are always so desperate; our thoughts are constantly revolving around this one little word that invades our lives, even to the smallest details. Everything always seems to come back to "I."

Clark sees his life as not much different from the TV shows. Even though on the surface it seems he's doing everything for his family, he suspects deeper down that it's all about him, about the "I." He realizes with some shock and embarrassment that the "I" always strives for its own needs to be satisfied.

"I" want the perfect family.

"I" want the perfect house.

"I" want the perfect dog.

"I" want the perfect job.

Why? Because that's what "I" want...and now it's all gone, and "I" am miserable.

Tis for sure the foolishness, the selfishness, and most of all, the illusions that one gets trapped by constantly, this desire for all such things I think "I" want, but I know it is not what I really need.

Why is he even thinking about this? Why does it even seem important now? His mind seems to be on automatic pilot as he continues puzzling this realization through.

Through the "I," I've manipulated me loved ones mostly to conform to what I want, to the choices I've made. The wins, the losses, the joys, and sadness were all my own choices, and all of them have created the situation where I am now.

As he's thinking these thoughts and watching the tele, he fitfully drifts off to sleep.

As he sleeps, he dreams.

Sitting on a park bench surrounded by heavy fog, Clark tries to see through the thickening mist. Peering deeper, he hears a very faint sound. The sound moves closer, and then suddenly it's all around him; it sounds like the hum a refrigerator sometimes makes. The sound grows steadily louder as the fog further thickens. Soon it becomes impossible to see anything, and to make matters worse, it's getting darker. Suddenly, from out of the fog he feels a cool breeze blowing and stroking his face. He feels a sensation erupting from within his mind, like a sucking vacuum, or maybe more like a push in the air itself; then, right next to him sits Hugh.

The boy looks at his dad without saying a word. Clark reaches out to touch him, but he can't move; his arms feel as if they are made of stone, and the more he tries, the harder it feels to move forward.

Hugh seems to be trying to speak, but he can't; Clark tries to move, but to no avail. Staring into his son's eyes, he feels like Hugh's trying to tell him something, but Hugh begins slowly fading into the gray mist, and as he does so, the humming intensifies. Clark feels another push within his mind, and then his son's voice echoes within him: *"Da'! I'm all right! I've gotta find Mom. Don't give up on us. Please, Da'! Don't give up!"*

Clark's head jerks up and he's instantly awake! His skin is wet and clammy, and his shirt is damp with sweat. His head rings with his son's words, and even more than this, he somehow feels his son's feelings as if they are his own. The dream leaves Clark's mind like a feather blown uncontrollably aloft at the caprice of the wind; his mind feels as if it is slipping silently away, and in its place is a feeling of confusion. The confusion seems laden with a sense of urgency and desperation, as if time is running out.

Clark sits up from the chair, puzzled and confused. What was Hugh trying to say?

Are his son and wife struggling to get back to him?

The more he thinks, the faster these feelings seem to leave him; somehow, his son managed to communicate with him, which in itself is the miracle he was hoping for.

The next morning, Clark begins making phone calls and sending emails. He needs to open up his schedule beyond the brief vacation he had planned. He needs to arrange for enough time away from his work and clients to learn how he can help Hugh and Annie. After a day of calling, shuffling, and rearranging his workload for the next three months, he is free to do whatever he can to get his family back. After last night's dream, he's convinced his son is looking for his mom: this has to be the reason for his coma, but why? And even more, how can that work? This he doesn't know, but he knows he has to find a way to help.

Not understanding about religion, dreams, God, death or all that other stuff, or even how and why this is happening, Clark senses that somehow, someway, he and his son will try to find Annie together.

The look on Hugh's face while they were sitting on the bench haunts Clark's thoughts; neither could touch one another, but then almost magically his son's thoughts were transmitted into his mind. Why had he felt so immobile, as if he were embedded in cement? The more he tried reaching out, the heavier and stiffer he became. Even though it was a dream, he can't ever remember having such a lucid and vivid experience, nor of having the same awareness he normally has when awake. Why did Hugh vanish when he got excited by seeing him? Maybe if he searched he might find either a book or some information online that could help explain his dreams. What if he could learn to communicate with him again? Clark remembers a friend who talked a lot about dreams; he hasn't seen him in years, but still has his phone number—possibly his friend could direct him to something that might help?

At this point, Clark is willing to try anything.

Chapter 6 ~ The First Realm

Kaylu and I walk a path leading toward a great range of mountains. Up to this point, our communicating is through my spoken words and his thoughts. Slowly, though, I'm learning about Kaylu's more efficient way of communicating. I gradually understand that communicating by words via me mouth actually distorts and limits the true meaning of what I want to say.

Kaylu explains it to me like this.

Speaking with words filters out the purity of what you actually mean. This is partly due to me words first starting out of a feeling and an impulse; a thought rises in the mind, and then this communication begins running through me brain, and along the way, it attaches to me ego, emotions, fears, analysis, and me own biased judgments. All these factors exist within the perimeters of me own limited perspective of reality. This brain filtering happens almost instantaneously in me brain, and causes an effect that I react to by speaking words saturated with these mind attachments. So by the time the message is relayed, it's no longer a message with pure feelings or clear images; my true meaning gets lost in the translation. When we are little children, we have minds that are still free and unfiltered; children may not know grammar all that well, but they communicate more purely. As we grow, we develop opinions and experiences. Our ego grows, too, so it blends with feelings, emotion, judgments, fears, and desires. By allowing fear and attachments to infect our thoughts, we lose the ability to communicate in a pure state. When Kaylu communicates with me, I not only get his message's basic meaning, but I get multiple things at once—I experience his thoughts, feelings, intentions, and clear images, not just the words of his thinking. This higher form of communication is so pure, so complete that it's impossible for the sender to exaggerate, lie, or manipulate, and it's impossible for the receiver to misinterpret or misunderstand. Truth is just sent and truth is simply received.

But if I'm to learn this higher way of communicating, I'll have to change the way I think, my attitude, and the way I perceive things. So as we journey deeper into this remarkable land, Kaylu begins to instruct me in some basic mental contemplations and breathing exercises. Kaylu explains that the exercises will over time create the changes in me necessary for me to send and receive this higher form of communication.

"To communicate in universal concepts, you must feel that you're part of everything around you. This feeling is necessary and required to project feelings and thoughts to another. You cannot identify with the world around you in clarity

if you remain the objective viewer; instead, you must reach a proper balance. Your judgment of things around you must be tempered so that you feel as if you're thinking from the whole—from a knowing feeling that each external object is just an extension of yourself. Once you start to master this stance, objectivity begins to establish itself within you. It does so by your not judging circumstances purely from the mind or purely from emotions. You must learn to think in universal concepts, but still retain your individuality. By learning these basic techniques, you become not only the observer, but the observed as well, with a sense of detachment and compassion. I am going to suggest something more, but before you choose to accept or reject what I am going to ask, I want you to think about it first."

"And…wh-what's that?"

"Do not speak the word 'I' for a while."

"I'm s-s-s-sorry, wh-what did you say?"

"Don't use the word 'I' for a while."

"Why n-n-not?"

"Every time you speak using the word 'I,' you automatically separate yourself from the object you are encountering and give control of your thoughts to your mental and emotional self or the ego. Using the word 'I' instantly makes what you say something more personal, and it also allows judgments from the ego, emotions, and mind to manifest themselves. These judgments from the ego and other passions of the mind cause you to muddle your thought process, which causes you to react from emotions or feelings. It is a subtle distinction, but over time, 'I' has become so much a part of the mind that you do not recognize the subtle takeover. This takeover eventually comes to form most of your personality, which is what causes the separation between Soul and the mind.

"'I' is the most powerful survival tool of the brain, mind, and its passions. 'I' actually created the boy you know as Hugh, and eventually the adult you will become. This adult personality will continue to build barriers between Soul and the mind. It does this through desire, which also creates fear of loss of that which is desired. In trying to escape fear, the mind or ego forms even stronger attachments to the external world through the growing personality. The mind wraps around the external world self-created dramas, passions, and clinging to material possessions. It wraps these with emotion, whose power is like a strong glue, creating a very tight bond. These barriers ultimately prohibit Soul from being in control; this is sometimes called, 'A loss of Grace.'"

I feel overwhelmed; sensing this, Kaylu pauses. Nodding toward a log on the side of the road, I silently beckon my companion to take a seat beside me. Kaylu joins me, and I sit up straight-backed and bent toward him with my eyes locked on his so that I can give his words my undivided attention.

"The 'I' blends itself so well with the other senses—especially your feelings— it is barely detectable until it is too late. Once the 'I' is in control, it then attaches to each passion such as desire, lust, anger, fear, joy, pleasure, vanity, and other feelings, even attaching to your thoughts and concepts of reality. These attachments create an attitude, which affects how you respond to the outside world. So mind creates myriad states of desires that exist only to satisfy the pleasure centers and the ego. The mind seeks the accumulation of material objects, power, or wealth, and especially, mind seeks attention.

"When the 'I' is fully in control, the mind, emotion, and the personality run our lives, eventually serving only the ego; this causes even more drama and chaos. Soul—the real self—is blocked from participating in the earthly existence, except in its most base state: as only the life force. This takeover by the mind is at the heart of most problems facing humankind.

"The mind and the ego are not completely bad; indeed, the use of the 'I' is a natural function, and in many ways it helps to form the experiences needed for the growth of Soul. For those of us who have evolved to higher states and gained access to the higher forms of communication you are seeking to learn, one must constantly retain awareness of <u>how</u> the 'I' might seek to take control. When beings understand <u>how</u> this happens, then this advanced understanding eventually allows Soul to take back control of the mind, instead of the mind controlling Soul. The discipline of not using the word 'I' will help you become aware of the difference between the mind and Soul."

After listening to Kaylu, I'm still confused, but I understand well enough to start Kaylu's assignment. I'm thinking this first exercise is just changing out a single word, so it is going to be easy. But after just a couple seconds, I find meself slipping and constantly using the word "I." Me mind is getting all confused; it's like me mind is infected with a computer virus that makes only gibberish come out as I stumble over me words, sentences, and even me thoughts. This is too difficult; is there any word I could substitute for "I" that somehow makes sense but doesn't ruin the exercise? Even in me own thoughts, I use "I" on a continuous basis; what word could possibly be used that would somehow identify "me," but not the "separate" me that is apart from everything else? Using me name for a while seemed to help, but it felt awkward; "Hugh" sounds too much like "you," and is also too closely related to the ego-inflicted "I."

Then Kaylu suggests using the word "Soul," which he says will help connect me to my real self.

At first, using "Soul" instead of "I" is not only difficult, but confusing. I feel like there is another person inside of me watching every word and even me thoughts flowing. After a while, using "Soul" and deleting the "I" word gradually leads to feelings of oneness. This experience actually begins to make me feel somehow larger, as if I am a part of everything around me. New feelings—along with deeper thoughts and broadened concepts—creep into me mind; some don't feel foreign so much as akin to memories long forgotten. I also discover that "I" want, react, and desire a lot of things that "Soul" doesn't really want or need.

Kaylu persistently tries to clarify and explain this process in his projected mental statements.

"The mind is naturally curious, and by its nature, it asks questions on almost anything that pops into its realm. Most of the times, these questions are unnecessary; they cause distractions to the Soul and create illusions in our lives. When this happens, a person ponders not only unimportant items but also imagined illusions. He is constantly creating drama through his mental imagination, and from this drama, humankind lives in fear of what might happen or might not happen. Through these feelings of fear, the 'I'-imagined events eventually manifest as a reality in life."

"So, it's tr-true that wh-what we fear most e-even-eventually comes upon us?"

"Absolutely, you always are the creator of your own reality. You create life's events by what you think, feel, and imagine, and by practicing this no 'I' exercise, you will find yourself becoming quieter, more watchful, and far more aware—not only of things outside of yourself, but also of your own mind. When you do say something, it will have far more substance and meaning than all the mundane menial thoughts and desires that the 'I' normally creates in your mind."

Kaylu reaches down and picks up a twig, making lines in the dirt as he talks.

"If you do this mental exercise diligently, it will increase your awareness and allow you to expand and accept a feeling of unity—first from within, and then finally in the outer world as well. This expansion of consciousness also assists in bringing these inner and outer realities together as one, and at the same time, it allows you to become objective to what the mind is thinking and feeling. You become the observer of your thoughts and emotions before they even have time to manifest.

"The greatest benefit and gift from this exercise is that mind begins to form a conscious awareness of your true self or what we can call the Soul. This new awareness then begins to fade the concept of duality or opposites from your consciousness. Over time, you will understand that Soul lives only in the 'now' and knows no opposites—only oneness."

I agree to stick with the exercise, and I persist in controlling the "I" by replacing it with the word "Soul"—even in me thoughts.

"I" ask one final question.

"This is all fi-fine, but due to m-m-me lack of kn-knoww-ledge or re-re-relationship with what you call 'Soul,' I still fi-fi-find m-me-me-self-limited about f-f-feeling this one-oneness y-you describe."

Kaylu smiles and replies in a musically toned thought stream. *"Keep practicing. It will all unfold within you at your own natural pace. See our journey as if you were thinking and telling a story as a third person; this will balance your mind and prepare you for the mental expansion that is required when using your mind instead of your mouth to speak."*

So from this point on, "Soul" tries.

****

The first part of our journey seems to last forever.

"We've been wa-walking a long ti-time; when does i-it get dark?"

Kaylu looks at me in a strange way, almost as if he doesn't understand the question. It was then that the realization hit me that there is no sun shining in the sky!

"Kaylu? Wh-wh-where's th-the sun?"

Kaylu looks at me with that questioning expression again on his face; *"What is the sun?"*

We both stop walking. Soul looks up at the sky and then at Kaylu. "W-what is th-the sun? You m-mean you don't know wh-what the sun is?"

Kaylu again looks at the sky, searching for the image that me mind is projecting, but he has never seen anything like that.

"Where's the l-light c-co-coming fr-rom? What m-makes it-it day-t-time?"

Kaylu stretches out both of his arms and turns around. *"There is always light; what else could there be?"* That's when Soul realizes that neither of us has a shadow—at least not a shadow in the traditional sense. In fact, nothing in this world has a shadow! Kaylu tries, but he just can't relate to me mental images of nighttime and daytime, nor can he relate to the concept of a big ball of fire up in the sky giving off heat and light for a world to survive. As sure as the idea of a sun was foreign to him, the feeling was mutual as Soul tried to understand a world bathed in perpetual light without a sun. Kaylu couldn't explain the source of light for his world—and he really didn't seem concerned.

Due to this sunless condition, me whole concept of time is becoming distorted and Soul feels it will eventually collapse. Although there are no shadows in this land, there are darker colors in different areas that block light to some extent, so darkness isn't unknown to Kaylu. A box with a lid on it has no light when it's closed; in a home, there's less light but not darkness, and the same holds with a cave. Having no days or shadows to measure time forces me mind to forget about urgency. Soul soon stops worrying when we will arrive somewhere, or when we will finish what we are doing by a certain time. Released from my earthly concept of time, combined with the vibrant colors and piercing beauty of the landscape, is changing me whole concept of reality. Kaylu said this process Soul was undergoing is the way a person moves their awareness into closer alignment into the "Here and Now."

The landscape constantly changes as we walk further from the stream. Distant mountains keep drawing closer, and soon the road becomes a steep pathway through hills and forests. Trees grow to great heights, some bearing fruit, and others, nuts and berries. Though there is less light in these woods, it never becomes dark.

Pure, clear crystal rocks gleam and sparkle as they thrust out of the ground, reminding me of the white quartz rocks in the deserts and caves back home. Blue crystals and red sapphires are scattered throughout the terrain, sparkling in the light. A constant twinkling of colored lights dances around us. This mysterious and surreal land with its brilliant cobalt blue sky is amazing. Jagged peaks rise around us, making me feel as if we are at the top of the world. Colorful, exotic flowers and their rich fragrances saturate the senses with memories of things that occurred long ago.

Entering a large meadow covered with these exotic blooms, Kaylu explains. *"These are the flowers of memories. When you smell them, you can focus on the images of what this world was like in the past or on your own past memories; sometimes people become spellbound and go deep into the memories of this area and never come out. They live only in their past, forgetting the present and unable to create a future; they live in the illusions of dead images, however, there is no need to fear this happening to us: the time is not right for the flowers to release their most intoxicating aromas."*

Nevertheless, even out of season, the floral scent fills me mind mostly with images of me mum: the shape of her eyes, the way she walks, her own special smell, and laugh. These memories are making me feel like Mom is attached to this entire experience in some way. Soul gathers a handful of these herbs and tucks them away in me tunic, inspired by an unspoken understanding that they might come in handy later. As we descend into a huge valley, the feeling of someone or something watching us creeps into me mind; who or what is it? Soul has no clue, but the feelings persist.

Wildlife such as birds and a few unfamiliar ground animals abound; a squirrel, then some bunnies and deer flash by. Coming down the high trail leading out of the hills, we enter another valley that is not only vast, but contains a tremendous lake in its center. Kaylu carefully steps over the little ridges at the bottom of the hill, and as he heads directly toward the lake, his thoughts enter me mind.

"This is Anami, which means Timeless Lake. It has been here longer than anyone can remember. Even in the old legends that are older than the mountains, this lake has been sung about. All rivers and streams from the south country empty into this lake, and then new rivers and streams pour into the North Country; all are born from Anami."

We stare across the great waters. After a while, Kaylu looks up and speaks within me mind. *"Everything will change once we are on the other side."*

It's difficult to pull me eyes from the serene beauty unfolding all around us; the lake is magnificent in every respect. Hundreds of rivers and streams flow into Anami from the south side, while great waterfalls slide gracefully into light turquoise blue waters. Waterways of every size flow along peacefully, slowly merging with the lake that's melting into a vast blue oneness. Many of the waterfalls from surrounding mountains cascade hundreds—perhaps even thousands—of feet, spraying fine, white, silvery tentacles across the lake. The mist refracts light, creating rainbows that dance across the water in patterns that fade and reappear as vibrant clouds. The shifting lights make me think of the aurora borealis in the Northern Hemisphere of Earth, except this has far more mystical colors, and instead of being in the night sky, these skim across the surface of the great lake.

Standing alone on these mesmerizing, mystical shores, a feeling of the oneness of life creeps into me mind; colors are getting brighter and clearer, and Soul sees and experiences a deeper insight into everything. The air itself is refreshing, highly intoxicating, and seemingly alive; it whispers memories of long ago. The sky radiates dark blue, with shades growing lighter as it descends to the horizon, similar to the light that might come from a perpetual sunset. Small distant stars and faded moons seem ethereal. At this high level of sense intensity, Soul experiences the entire vision as a vibration within me. Without this higher awareness, Soul couldn't possibly appreciate its full impact. Comprehending, absorbing, and feeling everything with this new heightened state of awareness defies description. These evolved senses allow me to experience this beautiful lake and this entire world at a level far beyond me former, normal human senses. The closest Soul can come to describing this world and this new power of awareness is what Soul imagines can only be "Heaven."

Shifting patterns of soft pink light melt against the impossibly blue sky, while ribbons of light undulated in and out in a way that's as effortlessly natural as any of the wonders of this amazing new world. Some of these ribbons of light are in colors whose names Soul doesn't know, but here they feel as familiar to me as me own thoughts and memories. Large, exquisite birds with exotic colors and beautiful plumage drift in and out of the dazzling mist. In the center of the lake stands an island. Two mountains arise from the center of the island, pressing upward to heights so high that all perspective is lost, making it impossible to judge how tall they really are. Soft rings of clouds with pastel colors circle their tops. Looking down at the shore we are standing on, sparkles burst all around me. The sand is not sand as Soul previously understood; this sand is made from fine gold flakes and white sparkling grains. Soul reaches down; the tiny particles are just as soft as they look, and the shores sparkle in the light as if trillions of tiny diamonds are sprinkled throughout the gold crystals.

Kaylu's wonderful, musical voice floats into me mind. "*This lake is considered holy in our world; it is the source of all life. Those who the lake accepts can experience a new birth; for others, they experience a feeling of bliss and contentment that lasts for a while and then fades. For the most fortunate, to immerse in its accepting waters is the sacrament of a new birth in which all ills and troubles disappear, and only happiness, wisdom, and love remain.*"

Standing at the shoreline Soul wonders; how are we ever to get to the northern side? It's so immense, and we have no boat to carry us over the waters. Reading me mind, Kaylu quickly explains, "*We must build a raft to cross the waters. There's enough wood along the shoreline to easily build what we need, and my tools and ropes will help us bind the wood into a large enough raft for both of us. If we hurry, we can reach the island before we must sleep.*"

Kaylu begins picking out bits of driftwood for the raft, instructing me to gather some of the diverse fruits from the trees and luscious berries from all of the vines growing in abundance around us. He then uses his skills and tools to build a raft not only large enough for the two of us, but also for a small lean-to for storing his bag and the fruit. The rope he has seems thin, and far too weak to support the weight and pressure of the large logs; however, it proves to be far stronger than it looks. Because the rope is so thin, it can be coiled in great lengths, which allows more than enough rope to bind the raft securely. When we complete the raft, he begins carving a simple oar from a flat piece of wood he found; when the first is finished, he begins on the second, and soon we have two paddles, perfect in size and shape. Fashioning a long, thick pole, he then centers it directly in the middle of the raft. Wedging it securely, he walks over to a large growth of plants with huge leaves attached to them. The leaves look more like giant elephant ears than common foliage. Using his rope, Kaylu weaves some of the large leaves together to form a perfect sail that can be controlled by pulling on the rope tied to the bottom limb.

With everything in place, Kaylu motions for me to help push the raft into the warm waters. The raft is durable, and floats high in the water. All this is done in an amazingly short time from only wood and plants growing along the lake's shore.

Handing me a paddle, he instructs me to man the left side of the raft while he does the right. Soul feels like Tom Sawyer and Huckleberry Finn rafting down the Mississippi River.

There's no ripple on the surface, and the water's like glass—so clear that we can see the bottom, where a rich display of incredible water plants and shellfish thrive. Moving swiftly we draw closer to the island. Each stroke of our paddles sends us gliding faster; it seems almost effortless to move across the warm waters.

We glide into colored clouds wafting just above the surface of the water. Entering the soft mist, we hear an ethereal sound all around us, like clear instrumental strings similar to the strumming of several guitars, but somehow deeper, richer, and more melodious then than anything Soul has ever heard before. A background of musical chords much like a piano then mingles within the vibration of the strings. It dawns on me that every time we stroke the water, the small rippling waves are the source of the music; the rhythms are light and in perfect harmony as they dance and merge within me thoughts. The music of the moving water floats outward, and my newly enhanced senses and acute hearing easily pick up their vibrations, and the movement of even the smallest waves of music reverberate in me body.

Soon we approach the island's shores and arrive in a small cove sheltered by tall trees and high rocks forming a natural wall. Quietly, we float into a peaceful stream. Trees looking like giant palms bend down to form a canopy near the shoreline of the cove, and a mixture of willows and huge trees with bright red and orange leaves nestle beside plants with huge beautiful flowers melting into the palms and ferns. Chirping birds flutter from tree to tree, trilling amazing melodies. The stream empties into what looks to be a wide river flowing into the interior of the island, Kaylu motions to help him turn the raft in the direction of the river.

Gliding along with the current, we continue deeper into the interior of this inviting island. Strange and wonderful flowers growing to gigantic sizes— perhaps five feet across and easily thirty feet high—waft a sweet, fresh fragrance. Their floral breeze constantly wavers over us as we travel deeper inland, and the aroma is enticing, impelling us to keep going. Each bend reveals a different type of landscape, a series of waterfalls gush from high natural rock formations on both sides of us. Kaylu nods for me to look to our right in the direction he's pointing.

Soul sees an amazing sight.

Situated along the small hills close to the riverbed are small trees with pinkish-white flowers. There must be thousands of them, but what's astonishing is that each flower is twinkling from its own center, like sunlight hitting a diamond. Kaylu looks over at me and says, *"This is the gemstone forest; each flower grows a small cluster of clear crystals that absorbs light and then reflects it back, causing them to sparkle. Eventually the crystals fall from the flower, and the process begins over and over again."*

The river widens and the current becomes stronger, taking us deep into the heart of the island. Kaylu uses the leaf sails to guide the raft; the gemstone flowers and trees along the river fade. In their place, high canyon walls border both riverbanks. The walls are tremendously high. To see the top, Soul has to bend his neck backward, and in some areas the canyon walls presses close, creating narrow alleys where the current speeds us along at an even faster pace. These huge canyons are colored with dozens of shades of brown that then turn to a light metallic yellow streaked with reds; the colors merge again into darker browns, finally fading to a pyrite yellow—it's entrancing. Huge waterfalls flow from side canyons, forming small rivers that are joining ours. As we float onward, the canyons gradually begin to recede. In their place are rolling hills covered with tall, green grass and expansive fields of flowers. Small streams burble from the hills off the banks and into the river. Kaylu points just ahead to a large meadow covered with flowers and green grass; however, what Kaylu is pointing to isn't the sloping meadow, but rather a structure above it.

Never has Soul seen or heard the likes of what this structure is; even in me wildest imagination Soul could never create what we are seeing. On the hill sits a gothic palace with a single high square turret, winding stairways and balconies encircling the structure, but what's even more amazing is that it appears to be made entirely from pure crystal! Crystal towers reflect colors of the rainbow, and more striking, the metallic blue sky casts small areas in light cyan, while mirror-like walls reflect the translucent teal hill it is built on. The meadow leads up to the very structure's gates; as balmy breezes blow across the meadow grasses, the warm winds caress the palace, and it seems to come alive and pulse into vibrant transparency. Ribbons of light fade in and out from the celestial sphere, which enhances the illusion of a living, breathing, ethereal structure even more. The Palace is blanketed in a white and blue translucent mantle; light sparkles like dancing diamonds—first silvery, and then picking up various colors—throwing out a steady glow of ever-changing brilliance that holds me spellbound. The structure is huge. To enter, we must pass through a tremendous gate covered with emeralds, diamonds, rubies, and other precious gems all embedded in a crystal setting and framed with pure white gold. If Soul thought he had seen beauty before, all becomes pale and fades from me mind as we gaze on this palace of light. Kaylu directs the raft toward the meadow, and as we come closer to the shore he projects his thoughts to me. "*This is the heart of the island; the inhabitants live here alongside their teacher, who is known as Jotan. Jotan is also known as one of the Ancient Ones.*"

Soul gazes at the low waterfalls flowing from the hilltops on both sides of the crystal structure; the luminous turrets and walls capture and reflect the water's movement, somehow adding more spirituality to the already serene stillness flowing into the world around it. Kaylu says, "*We must stop here and ask permission to proceed.*"

He maneuvers the raft to the shore where the meadow begins; stepping onto the shore we hear or feel a sound in the distance. The sound slowly starts vibrating through us; the tone is similar to high ringing bells—not loud, and similar to the gentle tinkling of sleigh bells. Tying the raft to a wooden dock, we walk up a garden path leading through the meadow. Walking on the meadow cover is like walking on a soft, thick carpet. As we approach the fabulous palace, the tinkling bells become clearer.

Arriving at the entrance to what now seems to be a city instead of just a single structure, Soul is stunned at the beauty of the huge jeweled gates. As we step closer, a strange voice mingles with me own thoughts. Soft as a whisper, words begin to echo and merge through me mind: *"Who is it that comes to us?"*

Kaylu returns the impression with his own: *"Kaylu of the Wuskies asks permission to enter with this newcomer."*

Silence…then a clear, rich soft voice again enters me mind. *"What are you called, newcomer?*

Thinking better of saying anything with me mouth, my mind tries to send me answer through projection. *"My name is Hugh."*

A solitary clap of a large bell reverberates throughout the fabulous city, and the tone echoes the sound of me name: *Huuuu…* Long and melodious spirals of wind blow through trees; their whispering vibrates throughout every fiber of me body, and the doors slowly swing open. Kaylu nods for me to follow.

Stepping through the gates, Soul sees a vision only hinted at in fables.

Streets paved with gold and silver cobblestones accent dwellings of great beauty. The homes appear to be fashioned from the same type of translucent material as the palace; each reflects colors that brighten, fade, and then repeatedly emerge again. Within these undulating rainbow colors is a constant twinkling and sparkling throughout the city. Lush flowers grow over balconies on vines that twist and turn along doorways and windows. The light is brilliant to me eyes, but even in the great light my sense of sight has improved to such a degree that distance and intensity don't matter; whatever Soul looks at is magnified into crystal clarity, allowing me to see and feel, even from a distance, as if we are right next to it. Walking down the narrow lane, we don't see anyone else; Soul wonders where the citizens might be. Birds glide down and alight atop welcoming fountains that spill over into elaborate canals that enter the dwellings. Other than these, we see no other life.

We enter a small park in the center of the city. Small pathways lead out in every direction, each joining paths that apparently extend out to other areas of the city. Kaylu chooses a path pointing to a great structure towering over the entire city. Walking through this transcendent city Soul begins to sense having been here before; even though all this beauty seems overwhelming, it's nevertheless like déjà vu. Surely, this is a place Soul has visited in the past…or is it?

Before long, we are standing in front of the great tower that we had espied from the river; the doors swing open, and as we step in—cautiously—the huge doors shut behind us. Me heart skips and me stomach feels light; we move forward, searching for anything close to our expected sense of reality, when all a sudden again my name floats in me mind like a soft breeze: *Huuuu…*

CHAPTER 7 ~ THE COUNCIL

Kaylu's small hand takes mine as we enter a large circular room. The light grows more intense; we can barely make out the high, yawning ceilings through the glare. Upon approaching the center of the room, a semicircle of what appear to be thrones on a horseshoe-shaped disc slowly pulse in and out of the light. As the light fades more, me sight adjusts, and Soul watches as brilliant, pulsing figures crystalize into images of motionless men and women seated on the thrones.

A rich, smooth female voice—comforting, but direct—enters me mind. *"Hugh, we have been expecting you."*

All is silent for a moment, then using me mind, Soul answers, *"Who are you? Can you help me?"*

Silence hovers in me thoughts and then a voice nudges me; this time, it's a distinctly powerful male voice. *"You have many questions, Hugh—some that we can answer, and others we cannot. We are the Council of Jotan; some know us as the Old Ones. We govern, and we help and assist Jotan. By probing your mind, we have learned what has happened to you since you entered this world. We can teach you if you trust and allow us. Jotan is waiting for you, but before you are presented, we must prepare you."*

Again, with a slight mental projection, Soul addresses the council. *"Soul has many questions, but what Soul most wants to know is this: what is me purpose here?"*

The female voice again enters me mind.

"Patience, Hugh. You have only just begun your journey. There are many adventures awaiting you, but none can take place unless you are willing to learn. In our world, knowledge is a great power; especially if the knowledge is given at the right time. If you are to succeed in your quest, then know there are dangerous obstacles you will find in your path. Without the patience and willingness to learn and grow, you will not be prepared to overcome them. We have not created this journey; we are only a small part of what will come."

Me mind races and panic rises; only just begun me journey? Obstacles? To find the reason for being here, Soul must rely on any assistance available; right now, the Council seems ready to help.

The male voice again comes into me mind.

"You are new to this world. There are many strange and wonderful things for you to learn, but just as there are wonderful things for you to experience and learn from, there are also many things you must learn to forget. Dangerous opponents will seek you out and try to stop you from accomplishing your goal."

"Why would anyone want to stop me?"

The same voice replies, *"Your journey is much greater than you can imagine. The journey you are about to take is one of discovery—one that each Soul must eventually experience. When even one Soul succeeds in what you are attempting, what is gained makes that one Soul a threat to systems that control endless universes. Because of this, most who attempt it do not succeed. Your journey is yours and yours alone. It is not the places or the events of the journey that are as important as the journeying itself. The way is not impossible; each Soul is given opportunities to free itself, but doing so is difficult. In taking this journey, you must forget much of what you've already learned and what you think you are."*

Soul scans the face of each member of the council, and then says, *"Whatever is necessary for me to learn to go forward will be learned with gratitude and acceptance, but Soul has one more question."*

The council remains silent, waiting for me to continue.

"Will me family ever be together again?"

And again, only silence; then another voice rolls through me mind, and this time it's a young male voice—strong and precise, but also compassionate and direct.

"If you succeed in this journey, Hugh, you will have the power to make your life any way you wish, but know this! Every Soul takes the journey to power and truth. Each takes a different path, but all travel the same road. All learn eventually the ultimate answer that allows them to control their destiny: you are no exception.

"Upon success, your desires, priorities, and needs will be far different from what you have currently; it will then be up to you to choose. Only you can decide the right course to finish your existence in the lower worlds. If this is clear...then choose."

For a few seconds, me mind processes all this. Soul replies, *"Soul wants to learn."* Silence again. No bells, no sounds, no voices—only silence.

The light fades, and the Old Ones manifest themselves before us even more clearly and distinctly: they are majestic and beautiful. Their long, luxurious ivory robes are fringed by soft beige trim along their hooded necklines, sleeves and entire plackets gracing the front of each gown. The sandals each Old One wears match the same deep shade of chestnut as the burnished carvings of intricate symbols and animals on their thrones. As the light fades even more, the immensity of the room inspires awe: enormous murals stretch across the walls, depicting scenes from what seem ages long gone, and elaborate panel carvings display mysterious patterns and symbols. The polished crystal floor reflects the paintings and carvings like a mirror, giving the room an appearance of a surreal house of mirrors, yet its intensity was probably the most real thing either one of us has ever experienced.

A strong male voice echoes within me mind. *"Before you learn the knowledge for your journey, you must first rest and refresh yourself. Feel free to explore the city and its wonders, but never go alone, for even in the beauty and peace of our city, danger hides and waits for the innocent. We will provide you with a guide; use him if you decide to wander outside the doors of our tower."*

Kaylu thanks them, and then a boy appears from a doorway to our left and gestures for us to accompany him.

A revelation comes upon me.

"Kaylu! Me communicating: it's with me mind! Even better, there's no more stuttering!"

Kaylu's musical voice enters me mind as he replies, *"This is only one of the benefits of communicating without sounds; congratulations."* The boy leads us to another part of the tower to a modest room just large enough for both of us to feel comfortable. Two daybeds covered by tan cotton blankets sit on each side of the room. A water fountain stretches along one wall, with water spilling over into a transparent fountain bowl mounted on a thin counter where cups, towels, and a large bowl of fruit and bread sit. We've traveled far since Soul entered this world; Soul has no idea how long we've been traveling, or what time it is—all Soul knows is that we're tired. This no morning, noon or evening business is beginning to affect me mind, which hasn't yet completely accepted the idea of no night nor any way of telling time; all we really want to do is sleep.

Sitting on the small bed, the light somehow fades and a welcoming darkness envelops the entire room. Me eyes are soon heavy, and it isn't long before we both are in a deep, dreamless sleep.

Upon awakening, Soul is totally refreshed and hungry. Sitting up, the room begins to lighten until something like morning light streams through the window. Kaylu is still sleeping on the other side of the room, but hunger stirs me; the fruit, bread, and a dish containing what looks like butter are irresistible. A knife next to the dish helps me to slice the fruit and spread the butter on the bread, and soon the pangs of hunger are but a fleeting memory.

After eating, it's time to look around. A door in the corner of the room catches me attention; taking the handle and easing it open, there is another room much smaller than our sleeping quarters. Its walls are lined with light gray mosaic tiles, and there doesn't appear to be a roof. Light beams down and reflects off the floor, which is made from the same crystal as the throne room. A statue of an angel holding a tipped vase in its hands emerges high above atop the far wall. As the door closes behind me, water gushes from the vase and a sheet of warm water like a miniature waterfall cascades to the crystal floor and drains into small holes in the floor.

A shower!

Having slept in the same dusty clothes from traveling and building the raft, nothing could be better right now than a refreshing shower. Slipping out of me clothes, Soul crosses the room and steps under the angel. Hot, powerful streams splash over me; rivulets ran down over me body, and me mind relaxes. The warm water pelts my skin and hair, seeming to clean the dirt and grime off without any need of scrubbing. The longer Soul stays under the water, the cleaner me body feels; it's like being renewed—no shower has ever felt so invigorating!

As water continues to pour over me, everything becomes more clear and me confidence soars. This shower is helping to make me feel comfortable: not only with this new body, but about my entire situation. Somehow, a sense that what's happening to me is something that's meant to be enters me mind. After some time, Soul reluctantly steps away to retrieve me clothes, and then is delighted again in the miracle of simple pleasures to find a large, soft towel next to me clothes, which are now somehow sparkling clean, pressed, and even scented! Quickly dressing, and using a hair brush that—like the towel—simply appeared next to the clothes, Soul steps into the other room feeling like a new person. Kaylu's awake and Soul tells him of the next room and shower. Kaylu excuses himself and enters the shower room. Walking onto the terrace to gaze over the city, Soul remembers the Council's invitation to explore. Walking back into the room, it isn't long before Kaylu emerges looking refreshed and also eager to explore.

"*Did you notice anything different about the shower?*" Kaylu asks.

"*You mean that it was probably the best shower Soul ever had?*"

"*Yes; that's because the water is from Anami.*"

Leaving the little room, we are greeted by Tomas, a boy about my age and size, who tells us he is to be our guide whenever we are outside the towers. His clothes are simple but clean, and they fit him perfectly. It's obvious he is glad to be our escort; he's friendly and answers all of our questions about the city. As he takes us through the doors of the great tower, the sight that meets us is unexpected. Instead of the city being deserted, there seem to be people everywhere. Some are standing in groups, talking and laughing, while others are sitting quietly by fountains with friends or by themselves. The homes are alive with people passing in and out, and there doesn't appear to be any type of shop or store as far as we can see.

"*Tomas, where did all these people come from? When we entered the gates earlier, the city was deserted.*"

Tomas waves his arm around indicating the city around him. "*When you entered the gates, most of the population was in the streets doing the things they always do; however, since you are newcomers, they didn't wish you to see them until you met with the council. It was quite easy to put a block in your mind, so that you could only see deserted streets. The people were all here when you walked the streets and entered the towers.*" Looking around at all the faces, Soul wonders how it was possible that they could all have been there without his even sensing their presence. Tomas explains this is a natural ability of the citizens, and Kaylu isn't surprised in the least, or if he is, he isn't showing it.

Only happiness resides here—no bickering, no police, no pollution—everything seems to run by itself. Entering a great park, Soul is struck by the nobility of the citizens; each has a look of wisdom, confidence, and peace. Children are playing everywhere within the park, laughing, running or swimming in the many ponds fed by reservoirs overflowing into one another. Adults gather in groups, laughing and talking, while some sing with musicians playing exotic instruments. Artists paint on large canvasses, and still others are lecturing to groups; everyone is busy doing whatever he or she desires. Beautiful young women and men are dancing, playing and running through meadows of flowers. Trees spread out for miles, while beautiful waterfalls cascade from cliffs surrounding the park. Me body begins to relax; the stress of the journey and thoughts of my quest drift away as we walk along and behold new wonders at every turn. After a short time in the park, Soul is at a loss as to what he's feeling—slowly, realization dawns that this feeling is a new energy. It's joy and freedom! And what a freedom it is! This inspiring feeling comes from deep inside and ignites me senses, making me to want to run and dance, and to shout with joy at the beauty and freedom around me and inside.

Tomas smiles and says, "*Hugh, you can do exactly what you feel. This is the purpose of life; we as citizens of this city try to express the deepest feelings that come from within us. No one works for a living in the sense that you know, simply because there is no need to. This new feeling is because of the waters of Anami that you showered in; you have been accepted."*

Tomas waves his arms in a circle at the people.

"All of this and more exists because the people have become creative in every aspect of their lives. They, too, have been accepted. What you are seeing and what you are feeling is the result of the joy and peace that comes from being here. There are no leaders, no police, no priests, and no religions. With the love that comes from within, everyone lives harmoniously in joy and peace. Those that dwell here are blessed; they have earned the right to stay, and while they are here, it is understood that they develop their positive virtues and talents, and share them with others. No one judges or criticizes your actions, so feel free to do whatever it is that you feel within. You would not be here unless your dominating desire is love."

By this time, Soul is bursting with a flood of energy and joy. Soul takes off running; feeling the intoxicating, fresh air caressing me face and hair, my feet seem to have wings. Soul could run for hours, with every step lighter than the last—jumping over bushes, leaping streams with the grace of a gazelle—even gravity can't hold me down. Soul leaps and spins in the air effortlessly, each time coming back to earth in what seems to be a controlled floating. Watching me, Kaylu laughs at my antics, and soon he's climbing trees and jumping alongside me as if we were both small children. Soul is totally enjoying this experience. It's like a dream, only this is for real; in fact, it's so real that the world Soul left behind seems to be only an illusion—a poor facsimile of this enchanted land of joy, peace, and love. After a while, with feelings of exhilaration still pulsing throughout me body, we return to Tomas. Soul has the heart of a child in this older body, and even if my intellect has grown, me heart still feels a child's excitement. The freedom to run, jump, and play allows me to feel calmer and in more control of me emotions and mind. This physical exertion is just what I need to begin sorting out the balance of these new powers within me.

Tomas asks, *"Would you like to listen to one of the talks being given by the teachers?"*

Soul isn't too excited about listening to someone lecture, but then Kaylu's melodious voice rings in my mind. *"Remember, Hugh, do not judge or analyze what you see or hear. Keep yourself open and see what there is to learn."* Looking over at me new friend, for a moment a sense of kinship flows between us that is deep and sincere; looking back at Tomas, Soul nods in assent.

Tomas takes me arm and walks over to a small meadow; the grass is deep and has a rich chartreuse green color. A huge tree with limbs and leaves spread out like a large canopy stands at the center of the meadow. Nearly a dozen children sit underneath its limbs on the thick grass, listening to an older man who is sitting on a stone bench, gesturing with his hands.

Tomas brings me into the circle and holds me arm up. *"This is Hugh. He has come to listen. Is he welcome?"*

The elderly man looks at us and smiles. *"You are most welcome, young sir. Sit...listen carefully and learn."*

CHAPTER 8 ~ A TIME TO GROW

Clark scans page after page of the books recommended by his friend Darwin. A student and teacher of mystic religions, Darwin teaches spiritual science and metaphysical spiritual paths that orthodox teachers normally shun. But as Clark had been told, most experts agree that all religious thought is built from a foundation of mystical teachings.

Clark doesn't understand all of what the books are saying, and most did not seem to pertain to what he was seeking anyway. If he could just find something to point the way, he knows he would recognize it. Darwin had written down some titles about spiritual matters such as dreams, out-of-body experiences, and visions. Normally, such teachings would never interest him, but since Annie's and Hugh's accident, plus with the dream he had about Hugh, Clark has developed feelings and thoughts that convince him there has to be more. Books he has perused so far were complicated, to say the least: mostly abstract metaphysical concepts that aren't easily understood. Surely, with the thousands of religious teachings available through the Internet and the books at the library, he should find the answers he's looking for; he just needs to be persistent. One thing is certain; the dream with Hugh has caused changes in Clark in ways he isn't able to understand. From just this one dream, he's developed a craving to understand the mysteries of the Soul. The morning after that dream, he felt he had been left stranded in unknown territory. Something is now pushing him forward to pursue answers to big questions—questions about life's purpose, immortality, and God. When moments of doubt cloud his mind, he always returns to the mental picture of Hugh sitting by his side in the dense fog. Has his own lack of knowledge and experience prevented him from communicating with Hugh? Does it matter that he can't understand the meanings of his dreams? Or are the strange new sensations and feelings he wakes with after each night's sleep what truly matters?

Since the dream with Hugh, Clark falls asleep each night and his dreams are strange; it's like going to school, only what he's learning isn't clear to him. Each morning he has different feelings that create the need to continue to seek answers. These feelings push him forward, causing him to explore any and all venues that might assist him in reaching his son to help him find Annie; life has taken strange roads for him and his family. His daughter also seems to be in a world of her own.

Before the accident, Melody was a warm, friendly child, always laughing. Now she's distant, distracted, and she looks like she has seen more than she should have, especially at her tender age. No longer does she play with her friends, preferring instead to stay close to home. She cleans and takes care of chores that she would have shunned before the accident. Once there had been a normal, happy eight-year-old girl; now, to others, she seems well beyond her years—more quiet and reserved. But even with this more distant attitude, she's still lovingly attentive to her mother and brother, and like her mother, Melody has patience and great compassion. At times, she stays for hours, just holding their hands, telling them she's there for them and not to ever give up. When Clark asks about her feelings, she simply says she's sad.

Melody is indeed having experiences beyond anything Clark could understand. She doesn't fully grasp the significance of those times when a deep understanding surfaces in her mind. She knows that when these moments come, she always feels a deep love for her mother and brother, and that this love leaves her with a sense of hyper-clarity. Her brother and mom need her and Dad's help, and it's the kind of help she doesn't fully comprehend yet. She feels herself growing closer to grasping something within her, something deep and vast; when needed most, this something is a power that will guide her and give her strength.

Melody goes to the tree house almost daily. She feels closer to her mother and brother while there than anywhere else, even sometimes when at the hospital. At the tree house, she feels a silent happiness; quiet moments reveal small discoveries within her. Today, she is again at the giant tree. Resting her arms on the large windowsill, she thinks about her mother and Hugh, and the sounds of the whispering wind, falling leaves, and tweeting birds merge together forming one melodious symphony conducted only for her. For Melody, listening to the sounds of nature is music itself.

Staring out into the tree, she daydreams about walking with Hugh through a beautiful land filled with light; her mother is just ahead of them as they all move deeper into an enchanted land of Light and Sound.

She keeps the tree house clean and always brings some bread crusts or tidbits for the animals living in the tree. To her delight, soon the animals become so used to her calm and gentle presence that they accept food directly from her hand; squirrels come up to the windowsill, waiting impatiently until she hands them a few nuts or pieces of cookies. Birds are more cautious, but eventually they, too, succumb to her charms and wait patiently on branches next to the window. These visitations are her secret; she decides to keep them to herself to set them apart from the ordinary, and in some way they seem to her to be her very own exclusive way to communicate with her brother and mother. She doesn't think her father would understand anyway, so for the time being, it remains her private experience to use as an escape from the sadness that hangs like a cloud in their lives. At home, everything—from the pictures on the wall to her brother's room, to her mom's clothes, to evening dinners without them—all remind her of the loss she is suffering. She doesn't know it but the times she spends at the tree house are healing her, and at the same time she's being taught. The lessons aren't particularly clear, but slowly, Melody is changing; this solitary preparation is most important and necessary for what lies ahead.

Walking home one day from her visit to the tree house with Cody, she's enjoying the sunset and the warm breezes; everything smells of approaching summer. Entering the meadow, she hears the snap of a small branch, and turning in its direction, Melody sees a large deer emerging slowly from under a flowering magnolia. His antlers disappear in the tree's low branches, but his tan fur flashes like copper from the red rays of the setting sun; as the buck looks directly at her, Cody freezes. Staring back, the deer takes a small step forward. He bends his head without taking his eyes from her, and so she, too, nods. The buck then steps back under the tree and disappears into the woods. Melody stands motionless for a moment, and then reaching down, she pats Cody and says, "C'mon, boy. Let's go home."

CHAPTER 9 ~ SERMON UNDER THE TREE

The teacher sits on a bench shaded by the canopy of an enormous tree. A natural spring bubbles from the center of a garden nearby; a few animals such as deer and birds wander in and out, not bothered in the least by our presence. As the bubbles murmur in melodic rhythms, the spring is surrounded by exotic sparkling crystal plants, flower blooms, and trees. The scene gives a peaceful, serene feeling. The speaker wears a red, long-sleeved robe; his head is wrapped in a matching turban. His countenance reflects wise and gentle eyes, and a snow white beard blends perfectly with his face; his skin isn't withered as in old age but remains supple and luminous as in youth. The teacher waits for a moment while we find a place to sit, and then, without taking his eyes from me, and in a voice echoing within me mind, he begins.

"Soul cannot be found until it becomes lost."

There is silence for a moment, and then he continues. *"All Souls are moving back to the source from which they are created; much like the salmon that crosses great distances and hurdles to get back to where it was born, so it is with Soul. The difference is that Soul's journey is eternal. It is a quest that never ends, constantly driven by a compelling force that eventually moves Soul into the understanding of what it really is. Even with the discovery of the self, Soul continues to grow—for growth is Soul's forever journey. As Soul grows, its ability for giving grows. From the gift of giving, the mind finally understands that every Soul that has ever been, still, and always will exist each an essential part of the Creator's essence, each moving through their destiny throughout the rooms of heaven. This journey of Soul comes in many forms; the form depends on Soul's level of unfoldment and evolution."*

For a moment the speaker is silent as he looks at each person in the group. Then he says, *"To be that which you are now in body, mind, and spirit has taken eons of spiritual evolution. This evolution encompasses the physical, mental, and psychic components of man. Unfoldment occurs as Soul moves through all the diversified forms existing in creation and life, including matter itself."*

People are still gathering around the elderly gentleman. Then someone asks, *"How can we at some time be matter itself? Are we not conscious living beings when we are created?"*

The elderly teacher gently smiles and then continues. *"When Soul begins its journey of discovery, it is like a clean slate. In order to adjust and exist in the worlds of matter, energy, space, and time it must become a part of that reality, it must absorb aspects of the lower kingdoms so it can grow. Soul's journey continues so it becomes that which it must learn from. The consciousness of Soul is almost non-existent when it first embarks on the journey of life, it is just a tiny spark born from the Creator. Within the framework of this tiny spark is complete perfection, much like the tiny seed of the acorn that eventually produces a magnificent tree. As Soul experiences the fundamental forces of creation, this spark or divine perfection gradually comes into awareness of itself; it learns over and over again, thereby gathering experiences that it requires for maturing and expanding its awareness, Soul always seeks truth…some find truth before others, and when Soul finds truth it finds itself. From this experience of truth, Soul is often compelled to share its wisdom with those who are also ready to receive; truth once absorbed as part of Soul becomes what man knows as wisdom. This tiny spark of consciousness created from the Creator is fanned by the properties of whatever experience it is going through. This spark is known as Soul.*

"This process continues as Soul journeys through all the lower kingdoms known as lower states of consciousness. We each as Soul are like parts of a shattered mirror, reflecting our experiences throughout the ages; we reflect these experiences by being the person who we are right now.

"The final act of Man is to discover his true self. Upon this discovery, he then reflects the glory of the Creator, and the Creator then reflects the glory of Soul. The man Jesus said it very well long ago. 'Now is the Son of man glorified, and God is glorified in him. If God be glorified in him, God shall also glorify him in Himself.'"

The Speaker glances at me, smiles slightly, and then continues. *"All Souls are part of a unified whole guided by the higher collective consciousness of Over-Souls that have unfolded or remembered their divine state of being. This collective consciousness—working universally within all life—is the secret behind the building blocks of matter, energy, space, and time. All existence is connected through this divine chemistry, which unites all things as one. Just as humanity is created from the Star Dust of Creation, Soul is a part of the Supreme Creator—a true child of the One Creator."*

The teacher becomes silent for a moment so that his words could take effect with those listening, Kaylu leans forward and asks, *"Do we always have forms or bodies that we inhabit, and if so, why? How do we become free? How do we become what we are originally created to be?"*

The teacher again slowly looks around at the people gathering, and then continues. *"When Soul gains enough experience and is aware enough to form its personal relationship with the Creator, then, and only then, will it divest itself of all form and continue its journey as an individual unit of spiritual awareness, never forgetting its unity with all life. Man's perception then becomes that of Soul discovering its divine state of being, which is the same as the Creator, only in miniature. This is known as 'The Living Truth.'"*

The elderly man stops for a moment. His movements and gestures are slow but precise—as if every movement is precious and has a purpose greater than we can see.

He continues. *"In truth, each atom or Soul has the power of creation embedded within its self but knows it not; this power of creation is the connecting fiber that binds all of life together as one great family. The power I speak of is sometimes called love. Love is the glue that holds creation together; without love, there's nothing! Can you imagine an existence of nothing?"*

Mental murmurs arise from the crowd; a few whispered thoughts gurgle up as each in their way try to understand what he's asking. The elderly gentleman bends over and picks up a fallen twig. After staring at it for a few moments, he continues while still gazing at the twig.

"What humankind calls 'spirit' is actually love or the omnipotent essence which flows from the Creator. Soul has the same essence flowing from it; the amount that flows is measured by our own unfoldment or awareness as Soul. Each of us has the same ability as the Creator, which is to allow love to flow unconditionally. In its purest state, this omnipotent power is a concentration of love that magnifies all reality, including our human love and experiences, which in turn become our stepping stones to freedom. This ultimate love breaks down to form all reality as we know it, unconditional love in turn allows this creative current to fulfill its divine purpose."

Soul asks, *"What divine purpose?"*

"Divine purpose is interpreted differently for each Soul, but for spirit in general, it consists of uplifting, recreating, and providing an existence from which Soul can grow and gather the experience necessary for each to ultimately know its divine self. For Soul, it is difficult sometimes to understand the dances of life and our individual purpose, especially when we exist in forms we believe to be us; however, Soul is much more. Soul is not only the sum total of everything it has experienced, whether it is in the lower forms or the higher, but Soul more importantly is a true child of its Father, the Creator."

A small girl sitting in the front row raises her hand and asks, *"Why isn't everybody aware of this knowledge? If they were, wouldn't life for all be better?"*

The wise teacher smiles at the child then gestures for her to sit beside him. The little girl curls up into his flowing robes, and he hands her the twig, which somehow now has lovely flowers growing from it. *"As I have stated, each of you is the culmination of every experience you have had throughout the ages. At some time, Soul will experience the divine, and when this happens, Soul grows in such a way that the divine sets its eternal path to Soul's true home; it is done firmly and with unfathomable determination. When this happens, the divine becomes a part of who you consciously are.*

"To reach the point where each of you are currently in your growth has taken untold ages of experience, discipline, and growth; you have earned the right to the awareness that you possess, the great value of this awareness allows you to grasp truth. Nevertheless, those who have not the ears to listen, nor the eyes to see, experience the journey of understanding from only the mind. However, no Soul will be kept from its ultimate destiny with the Creator; each of you someday will remember to remember why you are here in the first place."

A little boy from the group walks shyly over as if being pulled by some irresistible force and sits next to the teacher. The teacher puts his arm around the child's shoulder. *"The first phase of your own divine purpose as Soul is to go into the lower worlds and be the Creator...but unfortunately, soon after your arrival, Soul begins to forget who it really is and from whence it came. The mind blocks out the agreement you made with the Creator in the beginning of your journey.*

"*Upon birth in a body of flesh, the Soul essence is squeezed into a very small, dense physical container, then you are labeled according to species, gender, race, name, and so on. You forget who you really are and why you were sent here; you now strive to live up to-the labels that define you in the worlds of matter, energy, space, and time. Even though we take on many forms to gain experience, we are never just the actual form we are encased in, for Soul is made perfect from the Creator's own image; it only lacks the awareness of what perfection actually is. For the Soul that does not know its true form and its truth, it becomes like the master prostrated before his own servants, not understanding that he, himself, is the master of many mansions. Soul must learn to accept the responsibility that goes with the power the Creator allows us to have. If not, we become like the beggar pleading with whatever gods we create for help.*"

The wise old teacher slowly stands up and walks into the small crowd of people who now form a circle around him. Searching out each person's gaze in turn, he says, "*The schoolhouse we call life is not really a school of lessons as much as it is a reminder of what we are not. To those who are not ready for the next step in their spiritual unfoldment, I speak in riddles, but for those who can see the continuity of existence in the face of a newborn babe, or hear it in the whisper of the wind, to those I speak and they will know.*"

More people gather around the wise teacher as he slowly walks deeper into the growing crowd. He stops for a moment not far from where we are sitting and begins speaking again. He has the ability to direct his thoughts to each one of us as if we are his only listener; his thoughts somehow penetrate completely within the circle of Souls, and as his words project in me mind, Soul feels deep care and warmth for this man. Soul hears and feels his voice echoing throughout me mind like a deep disappearing whisper, his wise words are felt as well as heard from within.

"*Everything we are is already encoded within our Spiritual DNA. It is only waiting for each of us to unravel the code through the language of Soul, which is the Sound Current.*"

Soul asks at the same time as many others, "*What is the 'Sound Current'?*"

Singling me out, the wise teacher is silent for a moment as he studies me. Then he says, "*Within the divine journey, each Soul is eternally connected with the Creator through Its voice. This voice is the Audible Life Stream and primal essence flowing from our Creator, and without this connection, we are lost. This connection has many forms, but its purest is called the Bani, also known as the Shabda, Logos, Spirit, or the Music of the Spheres. Some call it the 'Voice of God.' It is the essence that permeates all existence: a flower cannot bloom, and a child's smile cannot manifest without it, Planets cannot complete their spiritual evolutionary cycle without it. It is what makes existence grow, from the tiniest neutron/proton, to the heart of the Creator. Nowhere does it not exist, for it is life itself!"*

The wise man again looks directly at me and says, *"Some know it as the Word, or as it is said in the Holy Bible of the earth world, 'In the beginning was the Word, and the Word was with God, and the Word was God. The same was in the beginning with God. All things were made by him; and without him was not any thing made that was made.' Simply said, the Sound Current is the essence of the Creator flowing outward to all existence. It is 'Its Voice,' calling Soul back to its true home."*

The Wise One's eyes continue to drill into me as his thoughts project. *"It takes courage, patience, and love to proceed on the path of truth. For those who are bold enough to walk the razor's edge, great hardships sometimes come into their lives; these hardships sometimes trigger a remembrance of that ancient agreement with our beloved Creator. When this happens, we begin to recall that our sole purpose is to be the individual living manifestation of the one we are born from...In that moment of awakening, we begin peeling away the mundane human labels and the journey takes on a new significance. Constantly, life is testing us to see whether we are capable of grasping the divine truth lying deep within our hearts. Each of you at some time will be the one who will bring and express heaven in all you think, say, and do."*

Someone asks out loud, "How can we learn these truths? I mean, how on an individual level?"

"As we awaken to Soul's purpose, we inherently know that truth is found in our daily experience. Our reason for existing is right in front of us, every moment of every day—to be the vessel through which the Creator finds fullness of expression in an individualized manner, when this occurs, divine truth is allowed to interact with all creation."

The same person asks aloud again, "How do we find and recognize this deeper meaning in everyday life? Are there others to show us? And if so, how do we find them?"

The wise man looks over the audience again. With a voice that echoes in the breezes, the leaves, and grass we are resting on, he whispers from within our own hearts and minds.

"Those we interact with daily are reflections of abilities, attitudes, and lessons we need to observe in order to help us remember, some Souls indirectly and directly show us the hidden powers or Sound Current lying dormant within us. All life is your teacher—especially those we call friends and family—and yes, even our adversaries. They may not know this consciously, but nevertheless, we would not be with them if an exchange of spiritual values were not transpiring. For those who will one day find the Word within themselves, then from that moment on, they are taught by spirit itself. To the aware Soul, truth is everywhere, and always at once are they being taught: this teaching is in every experience they encounter whether it is what may seem dark or negative does not matter, all is teaching Soul through the Word. The Creator manifests through the Word directly or maybe in a poem, a lover, stories, music, and nature. Sometimes it

may come from a speaker under a tree or even a book. All existence is a vessel for the Word to manifest, this Word has many aspects of power but again the most important aspect is that it is audible. That one can hear it, and participate in its unbridled joy and freedom, is the greatest living promise and gift from the Creator. Soul without the Word in the human form is like a bird without wings who longs to fly. Some even poetically compare the Soul without the Word like a song without music. There are the few who find the Word through the natural course of their lives: they are the fortunate ones. For those Souls, they become what some call a guardian angel—always guiding each man, woman, and child, always pointing the way to truth—but even more than this, Soul finally comes into the understanding that the greatest teacher of all is love. For in truth, love and the Word are one."

The more Soul listens to the wise teacher, the more Soul begins to open up. Powerful and marvelous feelings of understanding are growing from within me; in some mystical way Soul is beginning to understand what the teacher is conveying. With this understanding comes new feelings, new thoughts that are joyful, deep, and profound; the teacher pauses for a few seconds, then he walks closer to me and continues. *"The way of the Light and Sound is within each of us; the way leads to freedom. This is why we cannot judge or impose our will on someone else, for to do so limits our experience and suppresses freedom for others and the freedom we ourselves are striving to gain. Do not hate those who seem to harm or misdirect you, for within their actions lie deep lessons, which in reality are gifts of opportunity. Our families and friends are more than parents, brothers, sisters, or companions. They are Souls we have been interacting with throughout eternity, and they are gaining from you as much as you gain from them. Each of us chooses to be with the ones we love and the ones we disdain. For this reason, and this reason alone, we must learn to control our emotions and direct our energy as a creative power by gently reminding others that we are all from the same source."*

The speaker slowly turns around and looks behind him at the garden for a few seconds, then he looks back at his audience and says, *"Life can be likened to an ocean. Love is the boat that carries each of us through the storms on the journey home. We are each living, walking, breathing eternal examples of the Creator's love. This love expresses itself in limited forms until we remember the unlimited source we come from. The Creator's love allows each of us to become eternal. Once we remember, we then become Travelers of Heaven—our goals are gone, our desires have dried up. No longer do we need forms to express ourselves, because we are now a part of all forms, and most of all, we recognize that our divine hearts are formless, unlimited, abundant, and all powerful, and even more importantly, we are free."*

The teacher again falls quiet, looking at each listener in front of him before continuing to speak; his searching eyes seem to be looking for something within each and every one of us. *"For those who act and voice themselves as Soul instead of the 'I,' they are the ones who spirit forms a conscious connection to, and thereby allows Soul to take control of the mind, emotions, and life itself."*

The teacher slowly turns his gaze again upon me. As Soul looks into the wise man's face, his eyes appear to grow deeper and softer; then very slowly, they start expanding into twin luminous pools of light. Soul can't tear away from the power and love emanating from the two expanding circular waves of power. The Wise Teacher's expression changes, too. With his head tilted slightly, he smiles gently. He continues to pour his love into me, even as this transmission somehow pulls at me, sending surges of energy that change into invisible circular waves of Light and Sound; they then explode within me mind, heart and Soul. My heart becomes saturated with this electric current of love, but there's something else, something even more than this; for a brief second, Soul is a pair of eyes looking at the entire universe, feeling the power of suns, moons, stars, galaxies, and every life form existing...for one brief instant, Soul is pure spirit. Then...Soul is the Creator! Just as briefly, Soul is again in me mind, looking at the wise old man in front of me. Tears moisten me eyes as Soul fathoms the power of the gift just given. For one brief moment, Soul isn't just a part of creation, but is actually creation itself, with the inborn ability to use the atoms/Souls within the Creator's body to aid in me journey home, but even that understanding doesn't matter in comparison to the intense overwhelming feeling of love.

Nothing exists but love.

Love is me resting place, a shelter from the storm. Only love exists, all else is illusion.

My mind again slowly begins to awaken and me senses come to life. The teacher smiles and then transfers his gaze to the other listeners; upon dismissing them, he turns back and holds his hand out to me. *"Come, you have many things to remember, and you had best do it alone."* Soul takes his hand and rises up, and then thanking the wise one, Soul walks alone into the garden behind him.

Tis true, Soul needs to be alone. Soul needs to think about and understand what just happened. In trying to analyze the whole experience Soul slowly realizes mind can never bring the entire experience to a total understanding, only me heart is capable of understanding what just happened. The more Soul tries to think about the experience, like cool mist drying up in the morning light, it moves further from me memory. The mind just can't hold on to what the heart is experiencing. Then, like a volcano exploding inside me, an awareness creeps throughout my consciousness and slowly Soul realizes something more; then Soul knows! It isn't the mind that's accepting the great awareness that Soul is experiencing, but the heart...but why? Why is my heart capable of holding this feeling and not me mind? The answer drifts into me thoughts like water seeking its level.

The mind of itself is not capable of creating love; instead, it creates desire and confuses Soul. Mind is only a vehicle for love to flow through to the world outside; the heart is the actual vessel that holds divine wisdom and all the love existing within me. The rhythm of me heart is the Creator itself speaking to me, keeping me alive and calling me home. The heart unlike the mind isn't limited to the amount of love it can give or receive. The more Soul thinks of what has taken place, the more the experience abandons mind and creeps into me feelings and heart. The heart is me awareness, my true consciousness of Soul. Love again takes over me entire being; this experience was never intended for me mind but solely for me heart alone to experience without limitations.

Soul walks a short distance into the garden feeling different from the lad who walked into the park. Soul is again more than what he'd been before, this is the understanding that love allows me to experience. Tis only the heart that changes, mind will always remain the same with all the attachments, desires, and habits. If the mind is to grow and change it will have to surrender to the heart.

Soul remembers a great secret from the wise teacher's sermon under the tree. Before the lecture, the mind directed me heart and limited me. To experience true freedom, however, the <u>heart must direct the mind,</u> for the heart is really the abode of Soul!

Kaylu is waiting by the entrance to the park.

Soul turns and says to the little Wuskie, *"We are ready to meet with Jotan."*

CHAPTER 10 ~ NEW FRIENDS

We enter the main tower with Tomas. We are expecting to see the Council before meeting Jotan; however, Tomas instead walks briskly down a corridor leading to another part of the tower. Soul is anxious to meet the great Soul governing this great city, and wonders what this powerful being will be like. Will he be as impressive as the council? Jotan must be brilliant in comparison.

We finally come to a wooden door with a silver latch. Tomas stops and turning to face us, says, *"Hugh must go the rest of the way by himself. Jotan sees only one visitor at a time."*

"What? Wait!" I blurt out in talking words. "I'm not ready! What about the Council? Don't we need to meet them first before I meet Jotan?"

Tomas smiles. *"Hugh, the Council already prepared you while you were in the park."*

Soul looks around wide-eyed, "But how?"

"You received the Gaze of the Master—that's all that is necessary."

Trying to stop the panicking feeling growing inside, Soul reverts back to projecting me thoughts. *"I thought I was ready to meet Jotan, but not alone!"* I send out a pleading thought to Tomas. *"'I' need Kaylu to go with me, he has been by me side since arriving in this world. He's my friend and fellow traveler; 'I' need him with me!"* Then in desperation, I exclaim loudly in me voice, "I INSIST that Kaylu be presented to Jotan, too!"

Kaylu quickly turns and looks at me, and then projecting his words in me mind, he says, *"Don't revert back to using 'I', my friend. You are not quite ready; even now your 'I' insists on something Soul does not want or need."*

My mind's confused, but Soul knows it's right. "I" suddenly feel foolish. Soul could never act so desperate due to fear. "I" now see so clearly the difference between Soul and the "I."

Tomas shakes his head. *"'I' am sorry, but Kaylu will have to stay behind with me."*

The "I" is beginning to feel intimidated, and Soul needs to take back control of the mind. The "I" doesn't think it can meet this magnificent being by itself. But Soul can.

Kaylu puts his hand on me shoulder. *"It will be all right. Remember what you experienced in the park; I will be right here, so do not worry about me. Sometimes we have to face things on our own and this seems to be one of those times."*

Tomas steps in front of me and takes the silver handle in his hand. With a twist and a pull, he opens the wooden door and steps aside to let me enter. Soul walks through the door, not knowing what to expect.

Entering a large, sparsely decorated room, Soul notices the floor is no longer made from crystal but from stone. A few comfortable looking chairs sit along a low stone ridge wall to me right, and a stone balcony is to me left. Soul wonders at the stone work; the rest of the city is made from crystal, but here in this one room, all is different. On my right side a long open window runs the length of the room. The green tapestry rug in the center of the room has designs of trees and flowers intricately woven into its border. The high ceilings are made entirely from light beige stones, each perfectly fitted to mesh with each other. For a moment, Soul thinks of the story *The Wizard of Oz,* when Dorothy is about to meet the great and powerful Oz; Soul walks across the room expecting to hear a voice project into me mind any second, but instead there is only silence.

Feeling awkward, Soul is confused and nervous. Moving over to the long window, Soul peers over the ledge and discovers a magnificent garden below. A breeze brushes me face; its floral fragrance caresses me. Fruit trees with pears, apples, apricots, and cherries grow along the edge of a pond with small waterfalls splashing into a sparkling pool, and beside the pond, a beautiful gazebo stands.

Shifting back to the low wall, Soul notices an open entryway across the room.

Soul impulsively hastens to the entry, tramps down a flight of steps leading out to the garden, and upon emerging onto a beautiful path encircling the pond, veers off into the woods.

Passing a secluded meadow shaded with tall pines and ferns, Soul takes another path that branches off uphill, and then gradually begins to level out. Giant ferns and trees covered with a soft moss surround me. Me nose catches a faint whiff of sandalwood, reaching the top of a little hill Soul comes upon a small grove of large trees similar to oaks. Lush moss and clover carpet the rolling ground. The trees somehow cast shadows, making it cooler than the meadow. Soul sees a wooden structure beneath a giant oak tree—a shanty so primitive and spare that it seemed as if a child had constructed it. Soul thinks perhaps this is the wrong place? But the inner impulse pulls Soul toward the lone cabin in the glen.

The structure is put together with small limbs and logs, and the entryway has no door—like a clubhouse that children might make. Yet somehow the structure appears neat and tidy. Feeling this trek must have gone off course, Soul turns back to leave when a warm feeling begins enveloping me, the warmth beckons me forward to the cabin. Wonderful feelings slowly rise inside me upon approaching the hut. A few steps away from the door, the warm energy intensifies and penetrates deeper into me consciousness: all concerns and apprehensions start melting away, a comforting lightness soothes me, Soul bends down and walks through the door.

If Soul thought the council was grand sitting on their thrones radiating light and power, then Soul was sure that Jotan would be even greater. But this was decidedly not so, for sitting on a small rug in the center of the cabin is a small boy who looks to be five or six, younger than me back on earth. Blonde curls flow down to his shoulders and his amazing bright turquoise blue eyes contrast with his lightly tanned skin. He wears no shirt, only light brown shorts and small moccasins. His face and hands are smudged lightly with dirt, and at first, he ignores me and seems to be building something from wooden sticks on the rug. After a few seconds, he slowly turns his face toward me and smiles. With sparkling eyes, the boy sends his thoughts to me mind.

"I am Jotan. Would you like to play?"

Reaching for my hand, he motions for me to sit. At the touch of his fingers, another surge of warm energy begins flowing into me body, wave after wave of peace and joy enters me heart. Soul smiles and sits next to the young boy. A whimsical, relaxed, and curious feeling opens within me all at the same time. Without saying a word, Soul watches the little boy as he rolls sheets of paper together tightly into small sticks. Soul again feels like the small boy living in me heart; all questions and attitudes about Jotan float away like smoke on a breeze. Jotan smiles and looks up at me.

"I know why you are here, Hugh. Maybe I can help you, but right now I'm building something. Perhaps you can help me?" Using a small flat board and rolling paper underneath it, Jotan keeps rolling the paper tighter and tighter. He adds a little sap to the edges of the paper from a dish, then Jotan projects words into me mind as he works. *"The sap is like glue and sticks the ends together so I have what looks like a stick, but is really tightly bound paper—sort of like the paper sticks left over after eating a lollipop, but thicker and longer."*

Placing the newly formed stick next to a pile of previously rolled sticks, he reaches around and picks up another dish containing what looks like muddy water, but is of a thicker consistency. He dips his fingers into the bowl and explains, *"This is crushed brown berries added to a little earth and water—it makes an excellent dye."* He dips his fingers into the dye, and then picking up one of the white paper sticks, he begins rolling the stick gently between his fingertips.

A pattern of color begins to emerge onto the white stick, giving it a light beige color with dark textured streaks from where his fingernails embedded the dye deeper, similar to a barber pole.

Within moments the stick is finished.

Placing it with a pile of other sticks, Jotan smiles and hands me the board and a sheet of paper. Brushing his hands on his shorts, he asks, *"Would you like to try?"*

Soul takes the flat board from Jotan's hand and clumsily tries to roll the paper, Jotan giggles as he observes me struggling to roll the paper together. *"It seems easy when you watch someone else doing it. You need to start the roll with your fingers, and once the paper is started, you can use the block to roll it tighter and tighter."* After a few tries, Soul begins to get the feel for how to get the paper started.

"What do you do with the sticks once you've roll them?" Soul asks.

"I build things; I can build almost anything I want with paper sticks."

"Why do you build things with paper?"

Jotan picks up a few of the sticks and looks at them closely. Contemplating them for a few moments, he replies, *"Well, I mainly build things with these because they are so flexible."* He takes a stick and carefully bends it to form a small arch, demonstrating that the stick doesn't break or even crack, even when he bends the stick straight again. *"I can make them any size I wish, and shape them to form whatever I want to build. With enough of them glued together, I build toy cabins, tables, forts, and towers, but the best thing I like to build is ships."*

Ships! *"How do you do that?"* Jotan giggles and points to some shelves alongside the little cabin's rear wall. Sure enough, there, sitting on the shelves, are three magnificent ships of all different sizes, resembling the old Spanish galleons that sailed the oceans during the times of pirates. One has paper sails colored with light brown dyes; another has open white sails made from flat pieces of paper bent slightly to look as if the wind were blowing them. The third ship is brown with cloth sails rolled up around each mast. Each ship is different, but made from the same materials.

Jotan reaches out his hand, and then gently touching me chin, he turns my face directly into his own and says, *"You are going to have to be flexible for where you have to go, Hugh."*

As Jotan stares into me eyes, Soul somehow falls headlong into the child's deep crystal ice blue eyes; Soul sees in those eyes the age of the universe and the wisdom of all that has been and all that will be. In this child's face, there is a kindness beyond description; compassion and profound understanding radiate from his very being, but most of all, Soul sees and feels power!

The small boy smiles slightly and then says, *"Your mother is being held prisoner by one who has taken her fear and created a prison around her. This prison is like my paper ships...an illusion put together with the fabric of her mind. This illusion is what you must overcome, not only in you, but you also must show others the illusion the mind creates over their lives. Your mother is a long way from here; you will have to travel through different worlds to get to her. I can give you some tools to assist in this quest, but when you meet the challenges that await you, it is your heart that will be your most powerful weapon. There are those who will use your mind, your emotions, your memories, and all that you think you are to stop you from saving her. Your physical body along with your mother's, are both in a deep sleep on your earth world, and they are out of danger for now.*

"Your quest is to free your mother's Soul, and by doing so you both can re-enter the life you left. The little boy sleeping in your world—the one you know as Hugh—lives on within you. Keep his innocence in your thoughts and heart, for it will be your greatest power when you need it most.

"There are many reasons for this happening to you, Hugh, but these you will discover within your journey. While you travel, remember this. Life is simple; the basic things around you can be used to overcome any dangers that await you and others. The imagination is also one of your weapons; it is most powerful when combined with the heart. The things you are going to experience will test Soul more than anything you have ever imagined, but within these tests, you must understand one thing more than anything else!"

Jotan's voice gets deeper and penetrates deep within my mind. *"The mind is a wonderful tool for Soul to use, but it is a terrible master."*

He pauses for a moment giving me time to take in what he's saying. Soul asks, *"Why does everyone keep telling me there are things or others who want to stop me? We haven't done anything wrong or hurt anyone."*

Jotan is quiet for a moment, and then picking up another piece of paper, he begins rolling it under the board; as he does, he speaks. *"There are powers that* exist contradictory to what Soul's true purpose is. These powers exist both inside and outside the mind, and even in the outlying realms of creation. Your journey is at a stage where experiences and circumstances are creating energies that cause ripples or waves. These waves disrupt flows of power that control vast worlds in the universe of matter, energy, space, and time. At some point, you will touch others, who will then also cause disruptions within these negative systems; this threatens those who control the minds of humankind and others. But know this, Hugh: this negative power also exists within you, and it is one of the powers within that you must overcome and take control of more than anything else."

Jotan speaks without looking up while rolling another stick.

"Your mind has automatic functions that sustain life, such as breathing, healing, dreaming, and keeping all within your body in balance. You are free consciously of having to learn any of the mechanics of this sympathetic nervous system. It's this unconscious activity that constantly performs billions of necessary actions that keep the body alive, which in turn allows the conscious mind to be free to perform its one divine purpose—to express yourself as Soul in the lower worlds. To accomplish this, mind must be brought back under the control of Soul."

Jotan picks up another piece of paper and starts rolling it. As he works, he continues speaking to me mind. "The mind craves sensations. Once it experiences a pleasurable feeling, it wants to feel it as often as possible; you know this as habits. It does not matter what kind of sensation—whether it is perverted, passionate, silly or loving—the mind by itself responds with no moral concepts, this is the function of Soul. The mind by itself responds to the sensation only. Mind is similar to a lump of clay; everything it experiences, every sensation it feels, begins to carve grooves into it, and the deeper the groove, the more treacherous the habit. If repeated often enough, it becomes addictive. If this happens, mind will then constantly replay the same thoughts, the same habits, or fears, pleasures, and attachments. It is difficult to overcome a lifetime of habits; the only way to change these addictions is to replace them with something more powerful. You will hear this over and over as your journey progresses."

Soul thinks for a moment and then asks, "What is more powerful than feelings and me own mind?"

Jotan stops rolling the paper. Staring deeply into me eyes, he says with his thoughts, "The only thing more powerful than these mental addictions exists beyond the mind. You must bring yourself continuously to the awareness that the Creator is an infinite being, always acts to your benefit, and exists as a part of you. By doing this, you manifest and express the Creator as an individual entity within you. You then begin to understand that all power flows out from you and through all things; it flows as a benediction and a blessing to all creation. This power is always in a state of giving, and exists beyond the lower powers of the mind. Giving your thoughts to something beyond the mind's comprehension allows Soul to have control over the mind. The discipline of giving yourself to a higher power starts as faith, and as faith grows, something wonderful happens. Soul begins to take control of the mind and begins to create its own reality based on divine principles. Faith then grows into knowingness, and knowingness allows whatever is needed in your life to be made manifest. *This is accomplished by using the imagination of the mind with such clarity that Soul responds with an emotional confirmation. Soul then directs the mind to build the matrix that allows you to receive what you need most.*" Jotan picks up the stick he's rolling and dips it into the brown dye, and then setting it alongside the other sticks, he continues, "*There are basic disciplines that you will need to learn. Kaylu has started you on the path, but soon you will have to advance to techniques that will carry you even beyond mind.*

"*Remember this, Hugh. Your emotions are not generated by the heart, but constructed by the mind through feeling. Emotions become habits and are powerful addictions. They are easily created by the mind and are usually a byproduct of desires—either unfulfilled or fulfilled. Unfulfilled desires are the building blocks for attachments, doubts, anger, and fear, all of which create negative attitudes. These negative attitudes form the matrix for all the unhappy events and chaos found in humankind. However, emotions can be useful if used properly and under the control of Soul, but they can also cause you great danger. What I am telling you is that you— yourself—are your greatest enemy. You can be the final hindrance to freeing yourself and your mother. You must outsmart the mind as the fox outsmarts the hounds. It is for you to learn that man cannot use mind to defeat mind. That is impossible!*

"*From this journey, you will learn the difference between the mind and your true self. When you accomplish this, then you will have found what you are seeking. The exercise Kaylu has you doing, which replaces the word 'I' with the word Soul, allows you to begin the process of re-introducing the mind to who you really are: Soul.*"

Turning away, Jotan continues to bend his paper sticks again, each in the same shape as the other. As he does, he continues speaking in me mind. "*Our thoughts are like these paper sticks. We can bend them into any shape we wish; unfortunately, because of the mind's ability to form habits, people keep creating the same thoughts over and over, just like I bend these sticks in the same shape over and over. It is when you infuse imagination with feeling and combine this with disciplined thought that finally allows you to create what you desire. With your thoughts, you build your own universe—just as I build my ships.*

"*Sometimes something happens, either something wonderful or perhaps something sad or disastrous. This happens for a purpose most of humankind cannot see. These life-changing events are created by Soul to bend your thoughts another way.*"

Jotan holds up a stick before me and bends it in a different direction.

"*The mind resists change but the heart embraces it, these life changing events allows change to your heart which helps you to grow. It may not look like this from the limited perspective of the mind, but in the larger picture many people are affected by one person's change of heart or consciousness. Changing your thoughts about how you perceive reality is probably one of the most difficult challenges a person will attempt. In the history of your world great spiritual giants have changed the thoughts of billions by simply changing their own way of thinking. We are all a part of the Creator and what affects one Soul will in time affect many others. Demonstrating miracles, magic or mystical experiences are not what the Travelers know as true miracles.*"

Jotan leans closer...placing his hand on me shoulder, he projects his words into me mind with tremendous clarity and force. *"A changed consciousness is the one and only true miracle. One person in a million realizes this! Even when Soul finds this greatest of mysteries he learns it is one of the most difficult tasks Soul will encounter. Once accomplished, Soul finds that change is what it was created for; the secret of all secrets becomes an open book to him. He now knows that within him is a kingdom waiting for him to recognize and control. It has always been there...but Soul has forgotten it in favor of the illusionary thoughts and false realities of the mind."*

Jotan pauses for a moment. Again, he looks down at his sticks. Taking one in his hand, he begins to glue it to another using the sap, and then without looking up, he continues to project his voice. *"Before you go, there is one other aspect of the Creator's power that you must understand. The power I speak of is love. Love is a self-giving universal force, and it must find action in humankind's physical lives. Man must take this most wonderful thing into his spiritual, mental, and muscular activities. If not, love remains something just for poets and idle conversation. In other words, love must become action in all your thoughts, words, deeds, and feelings, if not then man will fail in his most sublime purpose. When mankind moves and thinks in love, then all goes well. When he cannot move in love, but rather moves in fear only, he finds that fear and love cannot exist together. Either the power of love will manifest freely, or the complications inherent in fear will temporarily paralyze everything. At certain points, your journey will require you to live, act, and breathe love. If you do not, you will fail."*

Looking up at me, Jotan smiles a gentle smile with both his eyes and lips. *"Go now. What you need for your journey is waiting. Use these resources wisely, for as all things in the lower worlds, they, too, are limited to the laws of this universe."*

Soul wonders at the great wisdom falling from the child's lips. Jotan turns back to his playing and Soul turns to leave the little cabin.

Passing through the marvelous glen, circling the pond, and ascending the stairs back to the stone room, Soul still feels the power of the small child's words—especially those of love. Soul opens the stone room's wooden door with the silver handle and walks over to Tomas and Kaylu. Tomas motions for us to follow; we walk to another section of the tower leading down a hall to a dark chamber. My mind is at ease, and Soul still feels the wonderful energizing boost of Jotan's words. Like an expanding cloud, my awareness continuously grows, expanding upward. It feels like Soul has entered a dream in which everything is more colorful than real life: more vibrant, more clear.

Entering a dimly lit chamber, we discover an ornately carved chest illuminated by a single shaft of sparkling crimson light. We fall silent; what is in this treasure chest set in the center of this otherwise empty room? Tomas carefully opens its lid and directs me to reach inside. Slowly, Soul reaches inside and comes upon something that seems to pulsate, as if it were alive, drawing back me arm, Soul pulls a brilliant blazing sword from the chest. Never could Soul have imagined a sword such as this! Its handle is molded from pure silver and studded with diamonds; the grip is solid and fits my hand so perfectly that it feels as if it were purposely designed for me. Beautiful etchings carved along both edges of the blade shine like a mirror. As long as my arm, the blade is made from some type of metal that Soul can't identify; its color shifts, from steely blue, then to violet, and again on to silver as Soul turns the sword over in the dim light. The cross hilt is fashioned from gold and tipped with blue-green emeralds on both ends. As Soul holds the sword up into the light, a feeling of confidence seems to flow into me from the tip of the sword into my fingers and down through my arm and then throughout my body.

Tomas reaches back into the chest and pulls out a pair of boots. *"Try these on, they should fit you perfectly."*

Soul rests the sword against the side of the chest and sits down. Taking off my old boots, Soul pulls on the new knee-high boots. Dark brown, with designs of gold thread sewn into the top depicting a circle within a circle, the boots insides are of soft white cotton to warm the feet. Although sturdily built, standing up, they felt like walking on a soft pillow. The soles are a rubbery substance: firm, thick, and durable. The artwork and design is intricate and detailed. And they do fit me perfectly.

Glancing again into the chest, Soul notices something else. Reaching down, Soul picks up an object wrapped in silk linen the color of blue sky. Tomas carefully reaches out to take the object from me. Then laying the bundle down on the edge of the chest, he unfolds the delicate cover, exposing a small book no bigger than the <u>Reader's Digest</u> books me Da' receives every month in the mail. However, this book's beautiful, burgundy-brown stained wood cover features swirling patterns carved into them. The designs are encrusted with small symmetrical jewels, gleaming with colors of blue, red, emerald, and gold. White diamonds on the edges enhance small pearls shimmering in various shades of pink, blue, and violet in the pale light.

Tomas picks up the book and hands it to me. *"This is <u>The Way of the Traveler</u>. Within its pages, you will find the wisdom you will need to pass the dangers of not only your own mind, but those of others, also."*

Soul leafs through the pages, whose edges are gilded and words embossed in silver. The pages themselves are made from some type of parchment material— soft but firm, without any type of wear on them. A purple silk cord to be used as a bookmark is secured to the spine of the book, and looking down randomly at one of the pages, Soul reads,

> The way of the traveler is often riddled with tests and obstacles that are constantly put in his way. Some of these obstacles are placed to bar his way from moving forward, and some are there to test his strength, spiritual stamina, and discipline.

"Of all the gifts you have received," Tomas emphasizes, *"this book is the most precious. <u>The Way of the Traveler</u> will teach you to prepare for your journey. This book will teach you how to use the sword and boots, and even more important, it will teach you the ways to travel from one realm to another. The book is created from*

the eternal hand that guides the ages, down from the ancients and even beyond. It will show you the meaning of your dreams, as well as the initial secrets of the Light and Sound. When all else has forsaken you, resort to its pages and without fail, you will soon understand what you must do."

Soul closes the book and slips it into my tunic, making sure it's fastened in well. Lifting the sword, Soul then places it into the scabbard fastened to my back, and another sudden feeling of confidence rushes through me. The boots help support me in a way Soul isn't accustomed: they makes me feel taller, straighter, and more in control of me movements, and it's a pleasure just taking a few steps to test the feel.

Tomas admires me and says, "You cut a rather striking figure. Now it is up to you how you use these gifts; bear in mind that the sword is not only a weapon, but also a multipurpose tool, as are your boots."

Stepping away from the chest, Soul notices Kaylu waiting at the doorway and strides toward him. Kaylu is plainly excited by the gifts. After exiting the chamber, Tomas closes the door behind us and continues to explain our next steps. "We have pouches for you with food, water, and a complete change of clothes. When you are on the road, try to take time to read the holy writings in _The Way of the Traveler_. It is permitted and even advised to share the wisdom with your companion, Kaylu. What is in the book is not a secret; however, it is to be read only by those who are ready to go beyond their everyday reality. For those who are not at the awareness level to understand true freedom, what they read in the book will not appear to be wisdom, but seem instead to be meaningless words that seem to have no value."

Kaylu looks over at Tomas and says, "I have heard of this book; it is a blessing just to gaze on its page! For me, seeing this is worth our entire journey, no matter what else comes to pass."

As we walk through the city toward the main gate, once again Soul is awed by the beauty and power of this place and the nobility of its people, including Kaylu; Soul could be very content to stay here and live in this happy, wonderful land forever. However, deep inside Soul knows he cannot stop; he must complete this journey to bring me family back together.

Soul feels encouraged by the guidance and even simple presence of Tomas. However, sensing my thoughts, when we finally reach the magnificent entry gate, Tomas stops and stretches his hands out to me, slowly shaking his head. "Hugh, I am to go no further. As much as I would like to join you, I cannot leave at this time. This is not due to a prohibition from the council, but is my own choice; I have duties to finish here before you will see me again." Tomas bows deeply and walks slowly away. Half-turning, he raises his hand and mentally projects to the both of us, "May the blessings be."

Sobered by the sense of finality in the abrupt departure of Tomas, we silently walk—deliberately, purposefully, now just the two of us—through the beautiful meadow leading back to the river.

Approaching the shore, we see someone standing on the dock, apparently waiting for us. The figure raises his hand to his mouth and shouts, "Helloooooooo!" Soul can clearly see the man waving at them. Focusing me attention on the figure,

Soul sees him with tremendous clarity; he is at least one hundred yards from us, and he is tall—very, very tall, standing at least seven feet. Even though he isn't well-muscled, he is not gangly either. His clothes are well-worn, but clean. He wears a light blue tunic and a darker gray robe draped over his shoulders. His bald head and sharp features suggest he has seen hard times. They look as if they had been shaped by the wind, not unlike the strong angled sides of a rocky canyon. His eyes are as steely as his face is rugged; his mouth is firm with a slight smile molded on the lower lip. His face expresses calmness and contentment. The man waves to get our attention. Kaylu slows his pace and gestures to me to do the same. *"We must be careful. We cannot trust anyone until we know for sure their intention."*

As we approach, we see what appears to be a large raft or boat of some kind. The original raft we used isn't in sight, but we recognize our meager supplies now piled on the rear of the new craft. We stand at the dock, sizing up this imposing but friendly man, who apparently has found and outfitted a larger vessel for our trek and is now waiting for us. He takes a step forward, and with a beckoning wave of his hand, motions for us to come closer. Soul feels warmth toward this giant, and walks briskly forward to greet him. My eyes catch those of the stranger and the man's face breaks into a wide grin, showing perfect white teeth. Soul feels a friendly attitude emanating from his warm smile and craggy face. Kaylu steps forward, too, and without so much as a word, he nods to the man, who apparently is now projecting a greeting to him.

Soul feels a nudge in me mind, and words manifest in me thoughts.

"My name is Dandi. I have been asked by Jotan to serve you as a boatman and guide. I am to take you down the river to the other side of the island."

Soul struggles for a moment, trying to remember how to project me thoughts; then, with a sudden push from me mind, Soul responds. *"Thanks, we appreciate the help."*

Kaylu smiles, and at the same time he sends a stream of thoughts to me. *"We will remain talking without sounds and without using the word "I," which is necessary to strengthen the recognition of your true self along with your focus and your imagination. These strengths will be necessary as we travel closer to and within the other realms."*

Dandi helps us onto the raft and with a long pole, pushes away from shore. He then says, *"We have a long trip to the opposite side of the island. There is food and water in the storage bag along with your rope and supplies; feel free to eat and drink what you like."*

The boat drifts away from the shore and soon joins a strong current directed toward a passage cut through steep canyons. Soul looks back at the marvelous city of crystal, reminiscing about the beautiful park and the wise teacher's counsel under the tree. Soul smiles; although Jotan appeared to me as a small boy, Tomas told me that Jotan normally manifests himself as pure energy dancing on waves of Light and Sound. Jotan's natural form is all-pervading, which allows him to keep all the workings of the reality that he governs in balance. Soul was most fortunate, Tomas informed me, for Jotan rarely appears in form to anyone. Soul smiles again, remembering the small, wise boy who taught me how to make paper ships. Soul will miss this wonderful place, yet there are no regrets. Soul was accepted with trust and love, and this warm acceptance gives Soul the confidence that whatever awaits, the knowledge and power will be there to protect me. Soul only has to learn how to access and use them.

Drifting along, Soul can't take my eyes off the never-ending spectacle of beauty unfolding completely around us as we slowly float to the steep canyon's entrance. Kaylu taps me on the shoulder and points to my left: the vision is astounding.

The canyon walls are made of pure crystal; waterfalls on one side of the canyon reflect off the other crystal wall, making there appear to be twin falls. All three of us look back one more time to see the Crystal City silhouetted against the sky and the crystal canyon's entrance. The view is more awesome and magnificent than words could describe; the Creator carved a gorge with this river that is a divine and mystical work of natural art. We sit in our humble craft plying the undulating water, entranced by the beautiful waterfalls continuously reflected, like we are in a hall of mirrors. Light sparkles off edges, crevices, and precipices and into the clear turquoise waters reflecting our boat. Like a puzzle, it is difficult to see where one set of images begins and another set starts. Mist billows from the cascading waterfalls, creating shattered rainbows that float along the sides of the canyon accompanying us as we move deeper into this surreal land of wonders. Floating through this unimaginable canyon, Soul falls silent and humbled by the unrestrained beauty that touches all of us. Too soon, we drift out of the cool, glorious canyon and emerge to find warm, tropical jungles and valleys of starkly different—yet still exquisite—majesty. The river expands, growing wider and deeper. Soul, too, feels he is expanding and growing wider and deeper.

As the current picks up speed it moves us closer to another part of this island paradise. Soul asks Dandi where he is from. The giant is silent for a moment, just staring out over the magical river and then without turning, he projects into our minds the ancient story of his people.

"I am from the far side of this world. My people have lived for ages on the other side of the great waters that separate us from the rest of the world. Hundreds of thousands of eons ago, a race of giants spawned us. This ancient race was very powerful, for they had learned the power of the mind; with this power, they learned to travel throughout the known world and even deep into the universe itself, exploring countless worlds.

"As their knowledge, technology, and power grew, so their appetite for domination grew. Eventually, their resources empowered them to discover and subdue all of the races of this world, and their dominion even extended to some outside worlds. However, this was long ago, and today only fragments and oft-vague allegories seem to remain of our history. On some worlds, however, they left reminders of their visits in the form of large statues and temples."

Soul remembers stories of people finding buried skeletons of some ancient race of giants. Could they be connected to what Dandi was describing?

Dandi continues. "As the avarice of my ancestors to control grew, they became consumed with power. Eventually, they lost the truth of what life's purpose is. Although they lost the wisdom of the ancients, they gained the vast knowledge of the mind, through which they created many marvels: great sciences, cults, religions, weapons of wars, and all sorts of devices. These creations were sometimes held to be resources for good, but ultimately, we have realized instead that they were merely used to keep people enslaved to an elite ruling class. This ruling class created a false history, and thus manufactured and perpetuated a fear that was more powerful than any of their technology. Their tools of fear—both technical and mental—infected most facets of the citizens' lives. Combined with their advanced technology, their propaganda brought them almost limitless power. Fear, combined with the passions of the body and emotions, were the fodder that fed the mind power. Yet the mind, even though it seemed all-powerful, became undisciplined, and this lack of discipline was due to the loss of the ancient wisdom of the Creator. This fear spread throughout the lands and worlds they dominated, even creeping into the minds of the citizens. That same fear eventually diminished the citizens' memories of life's divine purpose, along with love, tolerance, justice, and the freedom to make choices.

"Laws became one of the more powerful tools to control every phase of the citizens' lives. This was one of many ways fear was used to control the masses. The leaders created this fear from their own minds, and they knew what they had gained they couldn't keep.

"Fear cannot keep Soul wrapped in its illusion of power forever, nor could fear keep freedom and truth from seeping back into the minds of all the Souls they now held in their power. This predictable loss was the greatest fears of the leaders and elites. To compensate for this, the leaders created religions based on dogma, rules, rituals, and fear of an eternal hell or attachment to a promised heaven. Each religion established itself as the one true faith; they even created wars to justify their beliefs. These wars went on between the most powerful of the teachings—for after all, what better way to show to the followers of each teaching that the leaders were needed to protect them not only spiritually but also physically? The governments deceptively protected their people from their own rulers; by working hand in hand with other cooperative governments, the elite used the same methods in collaboration with their allies: the all-powerful religions. The masses were fed lies on a constant basis by their leaders, who injected their own fears and terror into the societies they held captive. The more they fed the citizens imagination, the more securely they enslaved them."

While listening to Dandi, Soul was struck by how many similarities there were to my own world.

Dandi continues. *"To inject this fear deeper into the minds of their citizens, the leaders conspired to perform attacks on their own cities. They caused massive monetary inflation and placed the countries in debt through abusive taxes, wars, and the misuse of the trust given to them. All their lies were mass-produced and spread through their controlled media channels.*

"Using these psychological and terrorist tactics, the leaders created ever more laws limiting more of the people's freedoms. All this and more was perpetrated in the name of government protection for the citizens. However, in trying to control other worlds and cultures, they eventually lost control of their own root citizens. And so revolutions erupted; chaos became rampant. Finally, the end of their power was upon them.

"A long time ago, in the hazy age of its greatest preeminence, this powerful civilization fell. The citizens, too, deserved blame; by allowing their leaders to amass great wealth and power, the citizens trembled like sheep in a flock guarded by wolves, yielding to all their demands, manipulations, and machinations in the hope of being spared. This subjugation replaced wisdom and even common sense. Our civilization was not defeated by an outside enemy, but by enemies within. Through scientific marvels, they gained power and knowledge, which took them to the mind's greatest heights; their downfall left but little of their former grandeur."

Dandi is silent for several long moments as we drift. Then he continues, *"I am born of the new race. We call ourselves Seres. We have not forgotten that an ancient race of geniuses created a society that held the most powerful energy of the mind and then fell for their lack of spirituality. Because of this corrupted mind power, the people stopped growing closer to the Creator. They worshiped only the mind power and their gods of desire, thinking that was the ultimate way."*

Kaylu shifts closer to Dandi. He, too, is entranced by the giant's story, especially by the strong feelings Dandi projects into his words. For a moment, Dandi sits still and silent, scanning the currents of the widening river. He pauses to push his long pole back deep into the river, propelling us deeper into middle of the channel, and he resumes his story.

"The power of the leaders, their passions and emotions, may have seemed great, but in the end, it, too, was illusory and deception at its worst. So, the great empire crumbled. From its ruins, a gentler and wiser race of people sprung forth. We look no different, but our people thrive instead on feelings of love and charity. Our focus is on individual freedom, and we again have learned the old ways, 'The Ways of the Creator.' Now we have a simple way of life, leaving all the technological miracles behind. With the natural simple ways of Soul, we began to experience a life that mandates truth and freedom for all. This change in our hearts, also changed our culture and our society: we became seekers of truth. That vast empire no longer exists; ancient ruins and relics stand as a reminder of our forefather's folly—ruins and ancient fables, along with myths, whisper their story."

Dandi is quiet for long moments as he reflects. *"Only a few hundred thousand of our kind still exist; but I think we are a credit to this world, for we pass truth freely to all Souls we meet."*

Soul listens intently as Dandi projects the story into me mind, allowing me to feel the great power of their past. Soul could feel something lost, but at the same time, something greater gained. By the time the story ends, Kaylu and Soul understand and appreciate the boatman more deeply and comprehensively than if we had taken years to get to know someone else normally; it is as if we have known Dandi forever. It's astonishing that we can feel as close as we do to someone we just met.

Kaylu projects to me, *"This is one of the more positive aspects of learning to communicate from Soul. It creates a bond that allows you to see and feel what a person is made from and where his heart truly lies."*

Dandi lives a simple life and has no family; Soul now feels bonded to the gentle giant, and understands his need to share his story and connect with others.

As we float into the deeper parts of the island, my eyes begin to tire. Lying down to rest, Soul hears Kaylu questioning Dandi about what is waiting for us on the far side of the island. For the most part, Dandi describes it as yet another beautiful place to experience. However, somehow it is what he doesn't say that seems to concern Kaylu. We will have to be patient and wait to see what the journey will bring, Soul thinks. Kaylu has similar thoughts as he, too, drifts off into a restful sleep, leaving our new friend Dandi in charge, sitting tall in the raft, slowly maneuvering us down the slow, wide channel.

CHAPTER 11 ~ THE PATH OF THE WARRIOR

Time stands still as we drift with the current. The river has expanded into what seems a sea, endless in length and width: no signs of physical progress mark our journey. Neither darkness nor sun traverse the sky, so Soul can't really know how long we have traveled in this void.

Dandi is quiet. Since his deeply personal revelations about his people's past, he neither offers conversation, nor shy away from answering questions. Dandi doesn't sleep as much as Kaylu or me, either. Our silent sentry at the front of our boat is ever guarding, ever guiding, us. And watching—always watching. Dandi is impervious to the anxiety and agitation Soul feels in this seemingly endless interval.

Soul decides to use this time to examine the gifts Jotan had given me. Soul quickly discovers that The Way of the Traveler isn't like any book Soul has read before. Somehow, it actually speaks to me mind; it's a subtle difference at first, but after reading only a few pages, the new concepts and ideas in its pages somehow project directly into me mind. Soul feels and hears the words as if a conversation is in progress, similar to the way Soul converses with Kaylu and Dandi.

The feeling is unsettling.

Placing the book aside, Soul is startled by a deep, humming sound. Soul cannot figure out where the sound is coming from; Soul looks everywhere for the source, but finds nothing beyond the boat and his fellow travelers. Thinking that perhaps a hidden threat is lurking nearby, Soul pulls the sword from its scabbard. Once drawn, Soul discovers the sword itself is vibrating, and it is then Soul realizes the sound comes from the sword as well.

Holding the sword in front of me, the sound becomes deeper and vibrates throughout me whole body. Every cell absorbs the vibration. The sensation isn't unpleasant—in fact, it's quite the opposite. Soul relaxes, sits down, and closes me eyes. Grasping the hilt, Soul knows this implement holds power. Just like The Way of the Traveler, this sword projects an understanding of its powers and capabilities into me mind. The hair on me neck stands up as Soul slowly extends the sword and moves it in gentle circles; as with the book, Soul feels and hears the sword, as if entering into conversation with it. The sword reveals that when used properly, it can teach the possessor the fine art of defense. The sword teaches Soul that like a compass of destiny, it can be used to point out the direction in which the traveler should go.

Soul extends the sword's tip so that it touches the wooden deck of the boat in front of me. With hands resting on the hilt, Soul drops me head, absorbing these new feelings flowing into my body, and my mind relaxes. Effortlessly, Soul stares deep into me mind's eye.

Then something happens.

At first, it's just a fleeting flicker, but soon Soul sees a faint light pulsing deep within me inner vision. Focusing on the light, it grows brighter and moves closer, vibrating to a rhythm both felt and heard from the sword. Gradually, the pulsating light-sound joins the cadence of me own beating heart. With each throb, soft light fills my inner vision, eventually encompassing the entire screen of me mind's eye.

As light within expands, it grows brighter, becoming bright as the sun itself. However, as bright as it is, it doesn't hurt me inner eye. Gradually, a small dark spot the size of a pinhole appears in the center of the light. The spot keeps growing with every beat of me heart. It becomes so large it forms a circle within the light, like a dark donut hole. Me heart pounds faster! A great anticipation is building inside of me even as a part of me remains calm and detached. The round light moves closer in me inner vision, and then moves back out; it approaches closer again, until with one swift rush, the light completely floods me inner vision.

Soul hones into the center of the light. Tiny flashes, like glimmering stars, appear inside the light's dark center, and Soul is being drawn into the star-studded darkness. The flashes grow not only in size, but also in clarity, and me total awareness abruptly locks in on the blackness. Then, Soul sees a great vision: vast universe's bursts into me consciousness of planets, galaxies, stars, and great colored gas clouds, with uncountable suns and moons whirling around inside them. Unexpectedly, Soul senses an almost magnetic pull from these great orbs, drawing me into the swirling energy of this brilliant universe, and Soul accelerates away together with the expanding universe.

Suddenly, me head jerks back with a gasp, and me eyes open wide. Kaylu and Dandi are sitting in front of me, and neither seems to have noticed anything happened. Me vision blurs, and thoughts slow down, as if me mind is asleep, but another part of me is awake.

Slowly, mind and senses merge back together. Soul feels small, sluggish, and heavy as if confined in a thick container.

For a brief moment, when self was being pulled through the light, Soul felt limitless and free: a strange new feeling, but what a brilliant sensation! The feeling is fleeting, but the memory burns in my consciousness. Never will Soul forget what had just been seen and felt for that brief moment, nor will Soul forget the powerful sense of freedom and universal connectedness.

The sword stops vibrating. Soul slips it back into the scabbard and places the book back into me tunic. Soul just experienced entirely new realizations and sensations, leading to exceptional insights, yet somehow this vision seems to be familiar, as if it were all part of a natural function of me own mind and body. My mind may not understand exactly what just happened, but Soul knows that whatever it was, it's designed for me to learn from. It's like discovering a new part of me, as if an extra sense has opened from within.

Soul notices new landscapes on the horizon, and moves up and takes a seat next to Dandi.

"*How much further are we going?*"

Dandi turns, and with a knowing look, smiles and responds, "*Beyond those hills stand the great cliffs. Once we pass those, we will see a village, which is where our journey ends and where yours begins.*" Soul is silent for a few moments; is there something that should be said? Soul remains at a loss as to how to respond. Dandi, slightly smiling, looks up the river and then says, "*You know, Hugh, there are many journeys we travel. Some are great distances. Others can be closer than you might think.*"

Puzzled, Soul stands, stretches his legs, and sits down on the barrel next to Dandi, slowly rubbing his hands on his knees. "*What do you mean?*"

Without turning, Dandi replies, "*My people are familiar with the art of opening up the latent senses that all men have deep within them. When a person learns this lost art, it in itself becomes a journey, for when he awakens to his true self, he remembers the ancient promise and reason for the existence of Soul.*"

Soul is quiet for a moment, remembering me family and friends. Were they all part of a plan Soul didn't recognize? Were these other senses Dandi is mentioning what he just experienced? Soul is thinking of me old life: playing with Cody, running through green meadows and forests, working on the tree house with me Da'. For a moment, Soul is ten years old again and just wants to go home.

Dandi turns again and looks at me. Then in almost a whisper, his voice enters me mind. "*The real journey lies within each person. It always takes great courage and patience to learn truth. Truth is something most will not respect or recognize. So to compensate for this loss of grace, they create the illusion of a love for external objects. Whether their love is for religion, family, the opposite sex, a career, or maybe all of these, people will resist changing their consciousness to discover the truth that has always existed within them. You have been given a great gift, Hugh.*

"*You are experiencing circumstances that are taking you closer to your own truth than ever before. Remember, no matter what happens in your life, you and you alone must choose to pursue the final goal. You now believe freeing your mother is your quest, but soon you will realize that seeking to free her is only one aspect of your great journey. This journey has never been far away, it has always waited within, waiting patiently for you to discover it.*"

Strange stirrings of memories drift into me mind, spurring a cascade of profound feelings, including confusion. One thing is for sure. The gentle giant is telling me something Soul has waited a long time to hear.

Kaylu then joins us at the front of the boat. He places his small hand on my shoulder and says, "*So far, you have received assistance every step of the way, but soon, you will find there are others who will do everything in their power to stop you from finding what you seek. When you confront them, remember: all life is teaching us, preparing us for its challenges. However, even as life's opportunities can assist us, so can life's obstacles try to stop you. Gird your strength, young friend, for there are no guarantees you will succeed: at least, you must try.*"

The boat continues gliding along, silently and swiftly. What's happening to me? Like the boat, Soul flows silently and swiftly along to an unknown and mysterious but incredibly precious destination.

CHAPTER 12 ~ THE DOOR OPENS

Sunday morning light beams through the kitchen window.

Clark pours himself another cup of coffee.

It's been more than six weeks since the accident. Things are the same for Annie and Hugh; both are still trapped in a coma, with no sign of their waking up any time soon. Clark spends a large part of his day at their bedsides talking, holding their hands and gently stroking their foreheads as if they could sense him in some way. The doctors have no answers.

After the first month passed by, with no medical explanations, Clark takes a new path.

He begins surfing the internet and reading books on the subject of comas and the mechanics of the subconscious mind. He learns about ancient spiritual techniques that supposedly allow man to build a bridge from the conscious mind to the subconscious: wishful thinking, perhaps, but why not try? So far, he's made no distinct progress by trying them, but his dreams are more vivid, and he does seem to be having more memorable dreams than usual—but nothing else. The techniques described in the books are basic exercises associated with vibrations and sounds that can be heard only from what they describe as the inner ear. He reads that he must learn to focus the mind's eye while listening for these so-called inner sounds. Both the inner ear and the inner eye are the two spiritual senses of Soul in the human body.

Some of the books he skims mention this inner eye as being the eye of Soul, or the spiritual eye. Others call it the window to the Soul. Imagination is the key to this third eye, which is located just between the brows; even though everyone uses this little known organ, most are not aware of its true function, or even that it exists.

His reading at times prompts memories of himself as a young boy: how he would daydream such wonderful fantasy worlds in his mind! How real they seemed then; sometimes he'd lose himself for hours in his make-believe world, and after returning to his ordinary life, various objects would crack the veil and draw him back under their spell. Slowly, as he reads further, Clark's skepticism softens and his inner eye opens; just for glimpses at first, but with practice, he finds he can sustain a vision for longer and longer stretches. With his fledgling success in accessing his inner eye, he next trains his attention on developing his inner ear. He reads that when used with the imagination, both these organs assist the mind by increasing awareness and perception. This expansion in awareness is said to open a deeper understanding of life and can actually unlock the mind, setting free the Soul of man. These inner senses are set on automatic; all people use them on a constant basis, but most do so at a subconscious level. These inner senses work as naturally as our other senses that react to daily events and activities. Supposedly, this inner ear hears sounds or feels vibrations that normal hearing cannot tune into. When a person exercises these two inner senses of Light and Sound through meditation, prayer or contemplation, over time they can become as artfully deployed as his outer senses. The sources promise that by using the inner eye and the inner ear together, in concert with visualizing a goal or desire, a person can achieve even the most elusive of goals. Clark's intense desire to communicate with his wife and son and to know they live—and someday they'll come back into his life—feeds his persistence.

So although much of this study and reading seems boring at first, and despite his too-rational mind resisting their messages, Clark reads and re-reads the passage until these new concepts gradually begin to sink in, and the reading gets easier and more interesting. Ideas of dreams, spirit, love, sound, light, and the true form of man—the Soul—became all-consuming subjects in his life. Maybe this development is his destiny; or perhaps this is because of his love for his family? Or possibly, it's simply the time in his life when he's ready to learn this type of knowledge. It might be that there is no reason that could ever be known for sure; Clark only knows that the seed has been firmly planted and spawned roots.

Unknown to Clark, tonight's circumstances will help him take a giant leap forward.

It is late evening, and Melody is asleep. The house is still and quiet. Firelight flickers in the den fireplace while burning embers exhale their last breaths. Clark stirs the dying coals, bringing them temporarily back to life. Staring deeply into the fire, Clark thinks about his life's trajectory, and he wonders about Annie and where she might be right now. Leaning back comfortably on a large pillow in front of the hearth, he thinks about the teachings, spiritual exercises, and techniques he is studying. Taking several long deep breaths to relax, he closes his eyes and imagines his son. Slowly he focuses his attention on the inner eye.

Using his son's image as the focal point for his imagination, he gently etches his son's image deeper and more sharply into his inner vision. It's exasperating at first, but he persists. Bit by bit, images become clearer in the inner eye, keeping his attention focused Clark holds the image in place. He sees Hugh as a boy of four. Controlling his imagination further, he ages the image of Hugh, watching him grow up until he has reached his age now. Memories of tender moments with his son evoke the unconditional love Hugh always gave. As his son grows in this meditation stream, Clark remembers the walks they'd take together. The little secrets between a father and son—making wishes beside "fairy" trees; that moment together being surprised by the sudden flight of a pheasant flushed out of the tall grasses as we walk slowly in morning light; Hugh's delighted shrieks of laughter and unyielding questions. These memories allow Clark to hear his son's voice vibrate through him, and even more, to feel what he's imagining. Listening deeply, the sounds of the house settling and the last few crackles of embers in the fire fade; the sounds within begin to resound. He now understands the readings that claim focusing one's attention simultaneously on both Light and Sound is one of the most powerful spiritual exercises a novice can attempt.

The first several times he tries this technique, his mind creates things he fears. His thoughts are scattered, projecting images relating to nothing of importance. He discovers that it doesn't matter what the image is, his mind's main intent seems meant to distract him. Whether it's something he fears or desires, even if it's the shape of a pretty woman, the mind is relentlessly distracting. No matter what he does to try to stop it, often the mind simply tags along with images and feelings: sometimes of sorrow, sometimes of fear. Anger invades his thoughts in myriad ways. Sometimes, he pictures his past with images of better times, or what might have been. Then he itches, and of course, he has to scratch.

The previous meditation failures allow him to begin to understand how the mind, even though it is his greatest tool, is also his greatest adversary. If only he could learn to just be still!

Struggling and listening at the same time, he keeps his focus on the inner eye. Shadowy images appear within his mind, constantly trying to distract him. As battles rage between his thoughts, he remembers a passage in the Bible his mother used to read him. "Be still and know I am God."

But how difficult this is to do?

Eventually the body rests, the mind becomes quiet, a little success shapes a new perception while the warmth of the low burning fire makes him feel warm and content. Again the phrase comes to mind, "Be still and know I am God."

Slowly, he notices a difference in mind's activity. Things are clearing, and the mind isn't as unruly. Taking several deep breaths, he calls Hugh's name in a long chant while focusing on the inner eye and listening. He listens to the sound of his voice as he calls out to his son. By drawing his attention away from unceasingly trying to calm the mind, the mind no longer maintains its control. Slowly, the mind unwinds; Clark opens himself to this effortless method; a faint, high-pitched, continuous ringing in his ears is becoming clearly audible. The sound changes, becoming more like a buzzing mosquito. The pitch goes up and down, similar to the continuously changing melody of buzzing bees. He becomes more entranced; the buzz is all around him. As the sound continues, something else is happening. He notices his focus is more centered. Staring directly into his inner eye, his mind relaxes and allows his whole being to concentrate on the buzzing. Wherever his focused attention is placed, the vision/sound begins to grow into a brighter area. He watches a growing, pulsating light that gets brighter by the second. The light moves with a slow rhythm, fading in and out. The rhythm of the sound blends, moving in a slow, swirling motion. Soft pastel colors fade into the fringes of the swirling light. Colors change to shades of green, blue, and yellow, all merging into one, then disappearing into another and then reappearing, slightly brighter. The light becomes more brilliant, with a clarity that is astounding. The sound changes to a deep humming like lips pressed together. The humming interacts with the swirling light. Light and sound merge. Taking a deep breath, he calls out his son's name again. The sound carries the light with a beauty and synergy like a pair of Olympic ice skaters dancing together as one to music. His attention locks on the great swirling mass of light growing deeper and brighter by the second. Not knowing why, a deep feeling nudges him to call to his son...to call his name again into the swirling light. Breathing in deeply, and then slowly exhaling, he sings Hugh's name each time he breathes out, pouring his heart, his mind, his whole being and his love into the word: *Huuuu...*

He listens closely to the sound, and exults in the deep vibrations drawing out of and across his lips. Sounds from deep within like a bubbling fountain move through his being; his son's name mixes with the light within him. Clark's heart pounds while his voice echoes the sound of Hu. Light shimmers within pastel shades of orange, blue, and yellow, all constantly arching in and out of each other until they form a circular rainbow effect. From the center of those colored lights, a piercing white light emerges.

With every beat of his heart, the light pulsates. With every pulse, a color flows outward to the edge of his vision. There is no house, no den, no chair, no fire, no body; just Light and Sound. Rings of colored light emanate from around the circle of light. Every inward breath causes the light to expand; colors continue to widen. His heart beats faster! Struggling to stay calm, his breathing becomes deeper.

Faster than thought, the light envelops his inner vision that then opens to an immense universe, whose clarity he could find no words to describe; its immensity staggers his imagination. Stars, planets, moons, swirling nebulae, meteors, spiraling giant colored gas nebulae all open up to him.

He feels a pull.

The pull is gentle at first, then more insistent. In an instant, he's moving through vast, unbounded universes. Though he's traveling at astounding speeds, he sees all clearly with full comprehension. Just as he is becoming aware of what's happening, he feels himself slowly being pulled back—like a stretched rubber band, slowly snapping back. Everything begins to fade. Faintly he hears the sound of his son's name echoing throughout the star system. Clark barely moves as his consciousness nudges his mind to resume control. His brain feels like a muscle or a hand that has gone to sleep. It takes a few moments, but then he starts to awaken. Soon he is completely back to his normal self.

And yet not.

Rubbing his face, he looks around, his eyes adjusting gradually to the low firelight. His ears still ring, and he reminds himself to stay calm; if he doesn't, he knows this precious experience will vanish. Squinting at his watch, he notes that it has been fifteen minutes since he first sat down. Standing up, he stretches and walks to the bedroom. Lying down on his bed, his mind reflects on what has just happened. All he can think about is his son's name echoing throughout his mind and body, then disappearing into the universe that exists within. Drifting off to sleep, Clark listens to Hugh's name as it echoes like warm summer thunder, rolling over and over his body, calling out to him, reminding him of things unknown, but with a promise that the door is now open.

CHAPTER 13 ~ THE WISDOM POOL

The river narrows again. Soul sees the shoreline from each side; it would still be a hard swim if it had to be done. Soul cuts some fruit into pieces to share. Dandi points up ahead and says, *"Our journey ends there, where the great lake swallows the river."*

We are looking but we see very little due to the high canyon walls we are drifting through. Just ahead where a bend in the river is blocking our view, we hear enchanting music growing louder. Pipes, flutes, and voices blend with some sort of stringed instruments, all playing as one. The boat draws closer to the magnetic, almost hypnotizing music. Tones and rhythms awaken memories of happy times. Soul feels and sees me fondest experiences through the rhythm of instruments and voices. As intoxicating as the music is, it doesn't entice us into unknown mysteries. On the contrary, the music enhances our senses to a joyful higher perception.

As we round the bend, a village comes into view. Dandi stands and gestures toward the trees, *"This is the village of Rhoads. It is a village designed for commerce and cultural events. It also prides itself on its social unity, but at the same time, unity emerges from blending with each citizen's special individuality."* At first glance the village is almost invisible due its blending aspects with the natural surroundings, but as people move in and out of the forest, we quickly put things in perspective. As our boat-raft enters into a large lagoon, more details of the village are revealed.

The people of Rhoads have high cheekbones and wide eyes; they range in coloring from light-skin blondes to warm bronze skin with dark hair. They are of average height, all in excellent health, vigorous, happy, and seemingly ageless. Children run, skip, and hop from steps leading into the green forest. We step onto dry land. In seconds people are approaching as if melting from the forest. Soul sees that hundreds of people are living within the forest. Dandi raises his hand and utters a sound from his mouth, which is greeted with smiles and then a silent communication begins.

The communication is strange and mysterious; Soul watches the movements and expressions on the villagers' and Dandi's faces. It's weird not being included in their communicating, but thrust into the role of the observer, Soul realizes the varied expressions and gestures are themselves a type of language; it seems that whatever is being said is conveyed not only in projected thoughts and images, but also with gestures and facial expressions. After just a little while, Soul begins to make a little sense out of the Rhoads language. All of a sudden, in me mind there comes the now familiar sensation of a push; words sound within, despite their being far away. Soul keeps watching, feeling, processing the gestures and expressions.

A kind voice speaks up within me.

"Welcome, traveler. We are the people of Rhoads. We welcome you and your friends to our home."

Soul starts to reply and then realizes the words in my mind are from the villager who is gesturing to me. Somehow Soul understands the gestures along with his kindly expression. Soul sends back a greeting not only in projected words, but also through a gesture of me own, one that me Da' taught me. The villager smiles and steps forward to grasp me outstretched hand.

"What a wonderful language the traveler speaks," the villager says.

As Soul shakes his hand firmly as me Da' taught, Soul sends a greeting, *"Thank you, we appreciate your kindness."*

The villager's eyes twinkle even more as he clasps me hand. Soul senses a thought followed by a feeling melting into me mind. *"We know of your journey, traveler. May the blessings be."*

A powerful wave of energy flows into me mind and body. Without thinking, Soul places my other hand on top of the villager's; with a smile and a nod, Soul sends genuine feelings of kindness back to the villager. He says. *"My name is Olgera. I am the speaker for our village; I will also act as your guide."*

Soul nods again while at the same time sending me name to the villager. *"I am Hugh."*

An anxious look appears on Olgera's face; he asks, *"You are the Hu?"*

Soul looks at Dandi for a moment, then turns to Olgera and says, *"I am not 'the Hugh.' My name is Hugh. I'm just Hugh, a traveler looking for me family."* Olgera looks puzzled for a moment, then nods and gestures for us to follow him.

After walking a few steps toward the forest, Olgera points up to the giant trees. *"There's the entrance to our village."* Looking up into the trees, me mouth drops open, and all three of us stare in silence. The giant trees are the actual village!

Roads, buildings, homes, gardens, and tunnels are intricately carved into the trunks and limbs of the massive trees which make up the entire village. The carvings are so much like the trees themselves that if we hadn't been shown they were there, we would never have realized the existence of the remarkable village despite walking and moving throughout the area.

Olgera's thoughts manifest again within me. *"We created the entire village from the grove of the giant trees. We have lived here for eons with not one tree ever dying. The village is built with ancient skills."*

Soul stares in awe. The roots of these giant trees are at least fifteen feet high with a width of more than thirty feet. Olgera continues speaking. *"Look closely, you can see a door carved into one of the roots. The door leads to a tunnel, which then leads into the village. We made the design to look like natural tree bark, but if you look closely you can see the actual designs and patterns that make up the carving."*

As we approach the tunnel entrance the door swings open, and we step through. At once melodious music floats like a whisper to our ears. Soul walks deeper into the tunnel and the music fades until it can barely be heard. My attention diverts to the construction of the tunnel; it is simply a hollow passage bored through the center of the tree's root, yet the tree itself doesn't seem to be affected by its construction.

The smell of the vibrant natural wood and fragrances from luscious plants waft past as we walk deeper into the living tunnel.

Olgera continues to explain the village's construction. *"Energy permeates this passage—you can feel it as you walk deeper into the next tunnel—the energy you feel defines the living force that is the tree."* As the path spirals upward, steps appear leading us to a soft light illuminating the entire passageway. Streams of golden light with fine glittering dust motes are coming from openings or cracks. We ascend to the top of the stairway, a faint smell of pine mixed with jasmine floats through the air. Within seconds we emerge from the living tunnel onto a huge upper branch of the giant tree.

Olgera points to the path in front of us and says. *"This branch is at least 40 feet wide, and as it grows away from the trunk, it widens even more."* Along the edges of the branch-path smaller branches are neatly cut so they resemble a hedge-like fence lining the entire walking distance of the huge branch. The massive branch has been turned into a road with natural gardens and wooded sides to it. The tree road reaches out, eventually touching other branches that overlap each other to form a bridge of paths crisscrossing each other throughout the entire grove of trees. Our guide walks up a few more stairs carved from the lower limb onto another limb and then onto a pathway leading toward the center of what Soul thinks is the single tree they are standing on. The limb slopes downward then up again, twisting and turning in long sweeping curves then disappearing into the interior of the great trees. Growing on the sides of the pathway are flowers of various sizes and colors, some growing above our heads as hanging vines from branches above. Vines intertwine with others that are different types of plants entirely. A spongy green moss grows in patches on the limbs creating a soft pleasant sensation as we walk through this remarkable village in the trees.

Birds of various shapes, colors, and sizes flutter from tree to tree. Some perch in branches along the pathway whistling melodious tunes. The spectacle of color bursting from the assorted flowers along with exotic natural aromas is almost too much for the senses to take in. This entire splendor blends with patches of golden light and cobalt blue skies, peeking through the canopy of leaves. The sights make us momentarily forget why we are here.

As we near the center of the village, we see homes built in niches and corners of the giant trees; some are in the upper branches, while others are below us. The homes are carved so intricately into the natural lines of the tree itself that only a window opening or a door is visible. Some homes have outside platforms where people are gathering for some type of event. Others are next to pools of water collected in the cradle of a limb or in the deep impressions much like knotholes of the tree.

No matter where we are, all the dwellings are surreal and serenely beautiful. For me to explore the sights and wonders of this village in the trees would be a blessing, but our guide doesn't stop to allow us time to enjoy the scenery.

While we are walking Olgera explains about the trees.

"The giant trees have natural irrigation channels growing inside their trunks; these living pumps pull water from the ground and constantly distribute the water through their leaves much like a fine mist. Each tree also sends oxygen into the atmosphere providing life to all within their influence."

Soul thinks of the giant Sequoias and Redwoods in Northern California, and marvels at the similarities—except these trees are ever so much larger. We keep walking closer to the center of the grove. Soon we are approaching what looks like the heart of the giant trees. Sounds of birds and wind fade, overtaken by the sounds of water falling from great heights. We enter a densely shaded area of closely bound limbs. Giant ferns are growing from the trees limbs, and rich, dark green moss carpets the small glen. As we walk, a fine spray of water droplets occasionally sprinkles our faces. Curious children peek out from behind ferns, limbs, and various plants above and below us. The path leads to a center of several giant trees merging in a circle, their limbs forming a large cradle. In the cradle is a shimmering pool of water.

Tumbling waterfalls feed the pool, enhancing the scene to an unimaginable beauty something almost divine. Falls cascade down onto numerous giant limbs from above before splashing into the clear pool, some of the falling water collects in smaller cradles above the pool then when it fills they overflow and form smaller waterfalls that ultimately splash in the larger pool in front of us. Rainbows shimmer through the mist of falling waters. Light peeps between the limbs and breaks through as long shafts of golden light the shafts of light merge to create an unimaginable feeling of tranquility and peace. Exotic flowers of every size and color form a ring around the pool with vines extending out and growing over a stone bridge that crosses it. With an outstretched arm, Olgera projects a thought to us. *"Welcome, travelers, to holy ground. Behold the Wisdom Pool."*

Soul stands momentarily in awe, trying to take in something like a mysterious mystical dream. Scents from the splashing water, exotic plants, and flowers fill me senses. Dandi slowly kneels down while staring at the unfolding beauty in front of us; he too is awestruck at the living waters that seem to communicate with an unknown silence. The pool somehow relays a deep personal feeling for each to understand in his way.

Olgera again sends us more explanation. *"These waters flow from several large streams originating from the great mountains above the grove of giant trees. It is the life force for the trees and our village. The great falls have existed for as long as anyone can remember. Beyond the mountain lays a land that is much different from what you and your friends have experienced so far. However, before you can travel to the other side, you must take in the wisdom of the pool, this takes place inside this grove of living trees."*

As we walk closer to this living pool, Olgera explains, *"Each of you should spend time alone listening to the waters. Take your time, walk alone among the trees. Listen as they call you and then to what they tell you. I will return at the proper time to take you where you can rest before going to the cave that leads to the other side of the mountains."* Olgera instructs us to separate; being alone is of utmost importance to communicate with the Wisdom Pool. He bids farewell and slowly fades into the trees.

Dandi stays where he is; he finds a comfortable spot, sits down, and closes his eyes to listen to whatever wisdom he might gain. Soul sets off alone into the trees nearing the edge of the great pool as Kaylu heads in the opposite direction from me.

Walking along the banks of the beautiful waters Soul marvels at the great beauty of the giant trees and waterfalls. As I stare around me, the awesome images of the giant trees and the mystical waters begin moving me thoughts to wondering about life. Me thoughts wander back to me home in Bristol and my family. Why does the mind keep thinking of them? These thoughts are always causing me to ask questions which cause me then to worry about them. Questions ricochet through me mind as Soul walks along the edge of the clear pool.

My mind is having a hard time comprehending and accepting all that's happening in such a short time. I'm in a new body, feeling like its mine, but knowing it's only an older version of meself or the boy lying in some hospital.

Since entering this strange world, me mind no longer behaves or believes as it did before. Taking the "I" from me speaking is proving to be an incredible tool to remember myself as Soul. The changes being born within me seem to be taking me somewhere….but where? This land has shown me great beauty, a beauty far beyond anything ever imagined, and yet it doesn't seem so strange. Somewhere in me memories these feelings aren't as unfamiliar as they should be. Like a memory that's within me that's grasping and touching a feeling to identify with, this process is making everything seem familiar, but then instantly it's gone—like smoke drifting away on the wind. Is there a connection between this place and the tree house that me and Da' built?

Questions and more questions blow through me mind like leaves churning in brisk autumn winds. As me mind gropes for answers, Soul barely notices the little inlet along the water's edge. Standing under a giant fern looking out over the pool of shimmering water, Soul feels alone, alone like a lost child. A part of me wants to be home with me family; to feel the warm covers of me bed and to smell breakfast being made would be heaven. Simple pleasures which are so ordinary now are so precious. Yet here I am, in this mystical land of unrivaled beauty, and I only want to be with me family, to be home again. Sitting on a flat root protruding over the edge of the glistening waters, me mind's thinking of a sadness and loneliness that is growing inside. The mind and feelings of a ten-year-old boy can't contain meself any longer. Feelings burst within like a shattered dam, tears stream down me face, me mind and feelings are homesick in an awful way. Tears fall, each one reflecting the waterfalls spilling from the trees above, each tear drops into the

Wisdom Pool, becoming one with the mystical waters. My heart is that of a child who misses his family, and because Soul is a child at heart, within me tears is comfort. For a moment, a door opens within me mind, allowing Soul to flee and escape the prison my mind creates; once free, Soul's heart freely feels the love that memories create, this same love soothes the loneliness, filling me with a warm glow.

Sitting on the water's edge, Soul focuses on these new warm feelings, at the same time projecting those same feelings outward to the beauty of the great falls. Love gently fills me with confidence letting me know Soul isn't alone in this journey. After all, are not Kaylu and Dandi with me? Hadn't Jotan given me great gifts to assist in my quest? Me mind slowly is becoming quieter, soon it no longer fires question after question. Contentment spreads throughout me mind and body, relaxing and soothing me even further. Soul is merging with me child's heart forming a presence within me that at first is mysterious. Feelings gently encourage me to go forward and allow the presence to enter me mind.

My thoughts become deeper telling me that what lies ahead is unknown; but whatever it is, there's a force within that always will be there to assist.

Maybe it's God?

Can I ever know for sure?

Will Soul ever be able to go back home again?

Soul doesn't know.

What Soul does know is that he is where he's supposed to be at this very moment. This is no accident or coincidence; this journey has a destiny and a purpose, it's supposed to happen. Soul shouldn't fear it but embrace it for all that it offers in whatever way it chooses. Kneeling down Soul scoops up some water to drink, as Soul marvels at the deep richness of the water, it races through me body. Soul feels a presence again but stronger; a presence not just within me but also beside me. Looking around to see who might be there Soul sees no one. The presence becomes stronger. Soul isn't frightened only curious about what it might be. Very gently, and even more silently, me own feelings merge with the presence which allows it to gently slip into me mind. Strange, wonderful new feelings creep into me consciousness. These feelings expand my heart, it feels like it is stretching outward connecting to the natural beauty surrounding me; soon the presence is even more, much, much more. Small ripples move across the waters, each ripple rides the water until it hits shore, as it does it becomes a part of me own mind. Soul feels the cool waters lapping at the edge of the pool. The waterfalls become me blood, racing through me veins. The trees me bones, the sky my spirit, for the first time in my life Soul consciously feels the extension of all things as a part of meself. The power of the trees is merging in me heart; the coolness of the wind becomes me own breath.

How is this possible?

Soul sits motionless, allowing the presence to merge further; no longer is Soul the boy sitting on the root by the pool. Soul for the moment is an open vessel ever expanding and growing, again Soul is becoming something more than before. Me awareness expands, the more it does the more vast Soul becomes; every creatures pulse is my own. Soul sees through their eyes as well as feeling the warm light gently caressing the leaves. The roots of the giant trees are my roots, the skies my freedom! The past no longer matters, nor does the future, for surely Soul exists only Now!

"Now" is the only moment that is real! Just as "now" is always moving into another "now," and then merging into "here"-ness, perception of life becomes transparent, Soul transforms into the "Traveler of One Moment," becoming the recipient of the Wisdom Pool. Ripples of small waves flow forward brushing me boots at the shore. I close me eyes, spread my arms, and lift me face upward to the waterfalls and giant trees, letting their presence flow freely into me mind and heart. A cool breeze caresses my face, words flow from the wind and waters...they flow into me, and the waters then in some mystical way speak from within. The words are bold and direct, saturated with a power of love beyond description; I listen carefully.

"Uphold, keep, and perpetuate this moment, my child, for you are now thrice blessed. Know that you are not alone, and know that you are eternal." Soul kneels on one leg, bows me head, and listens.

"All life is connected to the rhythm of your heart; this connection has many names and is interpreted in many ways. For you, the connection is love. Love will give you courage, love will give you peace, love will give you power! But more than any of this love will give you freedom. This freedom once understood must be given back to all life if you are to keep it within your heart, for giving is love's very nature." The words bubble from deep within making me own feelings holy.

The Wisdom Pool continues to teach.

"Try to suppress freedom or love, and it will transform into limitations and passions of a lower nature, this lower nature has many faces which are the barriers that all life must overcome in order to find true peace and eternal life. So stop limiting your love, and all life becomes your gift.

"Forgiveness is one of the vehicles love travels on, eventually though, even forgiveness must be left behind for as you begin to experience true freedom you find that in its limitless way it is always expanding, expressions of forgiveness dissipate like drops of water in the hot desert. For how can you forgive when you do not condemn? How can you forgive when you do not judge? How can you forgive when you do not create expectations from the actions, thoughts or feelings from yourself or others?"

As Soul listens, my consciousness opens even deeper within me mind. Soul asks a question with me thoughts. *"How can any man become as you say? Humans all judge—we especially judge those who try to harm us and our loved ones."*

The waters become still, and from the stillness, melodious voices speak as one. *"The question you ask is true, and as all things divine, your question is rooted in simplicity."*

A small series of ripples move toward the shore again voices as one, ring within my mind.

"In man's attempt to grow into the divine, he must release the many chains that keep Soul tied to the mind. Forgiveness is one of the keys to unlock these chains, once used however you must throw the key away. Like its Father, Soul is eternal, the arrows and poisons of man's mundane earthly existence cannot pierce or harm it in any form. To truly understand this nonjudgmental and unconditional state of awareness, each man only needs to know that every thought, every action, and experience affects himself and all life as he knows it. To become what he truly already is, man must provide a foundation for Soul to emerge through his human consciousness and reveal itself as the Creator. Forgiveness of yourself and kindred spirits provides the only way. Once through this state of consciousness Soul continues

to rise even beyond forgiveness. Know that all is exactly as it should be, and that nothing is out of balance, the trembling of a leaf helps shape the movement of waves in the mighty oceans. All is connected in such a way that makes life one, so it is true that a ripple in the waters of a small puddle affect the movement of a solar cycle within the physical universe. The only way to know this one reality is to become it, this is a sacred gift but an offering not given lightly...only earned. The remembrance of the divine self can only be received by those who are ready to let go of all they think they are and all they expected to be. The tears you now shed are only a reflection of your heart letting go of something small in order to gain something more, this is the unending cycle of all life; embrace it and gain all, or deny it and lose yourself."

Soul looks up for a moment at the giant trees and the cascading waters sweeping across the pool and says, "I have been told that I am to confront danger in this journey of mine. Can you tell me what Evil is?"

The waters ripple across the surface, and words again echo deep within my being. "Evil is an expression of fear and lack of experience coupled with a lack of understanding. For in reality, evil is a lesser good absent of love. Do not let the evil of others turn you away from the one reality that is love. Evil is as a small child who does not understand the consequences that go with actions that harm others and himself, actions always return to the sender, some of which cause what you know as evil. But know this Soul! No Soul has ever ceased to exist, life never dies it only transforms. Evil is the illusion created by mind to control Soul, to rise above evil one only need's to become that which he already is...Soul. Only in the mind does evil and death occur. Evil deeds are timed to ultimately bring experiences which become part of life's balanced cycles in the worlds of Matter, Energy, Space, and Time."

The waters become calm; all becomes silent. Soul asks another question. "What is death?"

The waters gently swirl in small whirlpools in front of me, and then wisdom again pours into me mind. "What humans call death is only a threat to the personality that is created from the fabric of the mind, or what your world calls 'ego.' When understanding of the mind is gained, then Soul lets go of even this limited concept called death. Death is an expansion from one level of growth to another; it is a necessary step in Souls journey to the Creator. Death only comes to the mind not the Soul! Death is the loss of a limited perspective of reality in exchange for a larger concept of reality governed by freedom. Mind exists within its limitations and what you call death is one of its tools to keep man from freeing himself. The mind of itself cannot ever experience true freedom or true love, what's even truer is, the mind cannot ever experience the entirety of the Creator but only aspects of the Creator's love, creation, and power. Mind can and will experience the sensation of these aspects in the form of human love, passions, desires, joy, attachments, and emotions, even the wonders of the outlying Universe, but never the first cause or the source of truth. Mind's greatest tool is man's fear of death...but on the other hand, mind's greatest fear is death. Evil is fear's tool to survive in a world of madness and unknowingness. Evil and death only survive among those who have forgotten who they truly are and their divine purpose."

The waters became calm for a moment; soon ripples again gently brush my boots.

"*You have received what you can, Soul. Only bits and pieces of this experience will survive in your conscious mind, but know this: in your heart, in your Soul, all this and much more exists; it exists throughout eternity as the essence of your true self.*"

My mind wants to ask more questions. Once again, the water ripples and then becomes smooth like glass. "*We leave you with the opportunity to ask one more question that you feel is important to you.*"

Soul hesitates for a moment, and then looking directly into the pool asks in me whispering voice, "What is God?"

The waters ripple and then calm, slowly becoming still again.

"*Listen, my child, and listen well, for this answer is being given to your mind so it must be approached with care. Deepest truth knows no opposites such as good or evil, these concepts exist only in the mind. Nevertheless, since you are currently experiencing reality from the mind, we will explain. Any action that carries you closer to the God of your mind is considered a door to freedom and good, any action that carries you away from that conceptual God is considered illusion, however once you have transcended the mind you'll realize, all actions causing change are to be considered a positive movement toward discovering the one truth within yourself. When this truth is known then the God of your mind fades. This God of the mind is composed of choices which are determined by desire, love, joy, fear, anger, pleasure, loss, and attachments; all these are within your mind God and all these will spin you into deluded actions that halt man from knowing his one deepest Truth. Right action is critical to the true self, always be aware of what you say do or think, not knowing that your decisions result in the right or wrong action delays you from perceiving or experiencing the true Creator. The effect of another person's choices and actions that you follow may also delay the ultimate experience, actions that harm others or yourself halt your progress temporarily.*"

The Wisdom Pool's voice within me increases in clarity and tempo. "*What binds you with every action, and every thought throughout all the worlds and heavens, is the one power that is unending and constant; this power is known as love, it is the very essence of the Creator. Love is the cement that holds all life intact and binds the universes together. Without love, there would be no life; indeed, there would be no existence. All would be void. This is universal truth, and you will experience it over and over until it becomes so much a part of you that you become it. So, the true Creator exists outside the mind. This is because mind always resides in duality or what you know as opposites; it cannot do otherwise, for mind is created from the twins pillars of creation: a positive flow and a negative flow. The true one Creator exists only in oneness. This oneness springs forth when one lets go of everything but love. Divine love exists always as oneness. The closest your mind can come to understanding and knowing the Creator is for you to look into my waters.*"

The sound of melodious voices echo within me mind, filling me momentarily with an ecstasy of Soul; in that one moment, Soul understood how one must become the experience in order to know it.

The voices fade and the waters become perfectly still. Soul leans over and stares into the waters; only my image is reflected back. Soul keeps staring expecting to see God at any moment, but still only my face is reflected. Water gently dances from limb to limb lightly splashing in the pool before me. As my reflection stares back, a surge like an ocean wave pulsates within me; overwhelming feelings engulf me, crashing against me mind, and after the feelings recede and disappear, they again begin building upon itself to an even more powerful state. My mind desperately tries to hold to these waves, but like waking from a dream, they slip away—leaving only fragments and shadows of their meaning. However, even with the fleeting memories of what Soul heard and felt, my heart fills with compassion. Soul continues staring at the reflection, hoping for God to show itself. As Soul watches, more realizations bubble up from within me heart into me mind. Love is what propels me to find Mom; love is also the vehicle that carries me to experience what it is that Soul needs in order to be free. For one precious moment, Soul knows that in freeing my mom, Soul is being given the opportunity to also free meself.

Still staring at me reflection, Soul slowly stands to leave, even while lingering to stare into the clear waters, still only seeing meself. Perhaps a little uncertainty is floating in me mind—probably because God is not showing itself. I turn again to leave.

Walking along the water's edge, Soul soon leaves the Wisdom Pool behind and returns to where Dandi is sitting under a great fern growing from the base of a giant tree. The gentle giant is motionless. Soul stands back a short distance, trying not to disturb the little giant's silence. Dandi then calls out in me mind. *"I am not contemplating any longer, my young friend; come closer."*

Soul approaches. *"We have much to talk about when Kaylu arrives."*

Dandi nods, then stretching as he stands he says, *"I have been told the circumstances that have brought you and Kaylu into my life; we are connected in a way I never would have anticipated, and it seems we may be traveling together a bit longer than I thought."*

Soul is growing more and more close to this little giant, even more than he consciously realizes. Warm feelings of friendship and trust flow between them. This trust in Dandi was felt almost from the moment we first met, and now it flows uninhibited. From around a giant root Kaylu ambles into the little glen where we are gathered; a smile spreads across the face of the little Wuskie. As he approaches, he gestures for us to sit; the ground is soft with thick moss. All three of us sit, warmed by shafts of light coming from between the trees.

Dandi speaks first. *"As I sat by the giant fern and listened, my hearing sharpened, and it wasn't too long before a gentle wind slowly whispered for me to feel the trees, and to embrace their age and wisdom. The wind was cool as it whispered its message, and as I listened, I felt myself shifting from my normal awareness to something deeper, something wiser. The next thing I knew, I was part of the giant trees, the waters, and even the wind. The giant trees are timeless, their roots run deep into the ground, deeper than anyone can imagine. From their collective awareness, I was shown the past, the present, and what I perceive as my future. I'm to travel beside you, Hugh; for if I do, I will find the truth about my people, my world, and myself. By helping you in your mission, I will find answers to my own truth. So with your acceptance, I make myself your servant in whatever way is needed."*

Soul looks about and picks up a large tripartite shaped red leaf. Soul offers me hand, clasps Dandi's huge palm, and says, "*A seed drops into the soil; the soil nurtures the seed, and their merger becomes the tree; each is separate, but all are joined; and so this tripartite leaf, divided into three parts and yet one, we three are independent, but a single Brotherhood of the Leaf. Soul accepts you as my companion with honor and trust. From this moment onward, we are brothers to the end.*"

Dandi nods his approval and then looks at Kaylu, who says, "*I, too, have been shown the path I must follow. It is with humility and trust that I, too, join in your quest, Hugh; for now I know you are sent to this world for reasons that affect not only us as your companions, but all life in this world and yours. The adventures we face together will mold us into what the Creator has ultimately already designed us to become.*"

We stand up together. Soul pulls me sword and holding it in the center of our circle, intones. "*We will be as one, in the Brotherhood of the Leaf; let no power break this bond of trust, loyalty, and love. Benefit for one will forever be benefit to all.*" More shafts of light pierce the trees above bathing us in a warm diffused glow, causing the sword to shimmer with a dazzling blue gold glow.

CHAPTER 14 ~ THE POWER

The three of us walk back toward the village. Within a short time, Olgera meets and escorts us the rest of the way. When we arrive at the center of the village, Olgera stops at a huge tree and says, *"You can rest here and refresh yourselves; supplies and directives will be given when you leave. While you are here, enjoy the hospitality of our people."* He opens a doorway set in the side of the giant tree, and we all step through and walk along a limb leading to the entrance of a wondrous tree house.

Upon entering, we find ourselves in a room wholly carved from the inside trunk of the tree itself; its walls are sanded and polished to a smooth, marble-like finish, revealing the wonderfully wide, wavy grains of the tree. Windows on each side of the large room open to vistas of the village sprawling deep into the interior of nearly interlocking trees. Three neatly made beds sit against the far wall; on a counter next to each are large wooden bowls holding fruit and bread. To our left, a candle burns low in a simple candleholder, looking oddly rustic as it sits atop a lustrous wood ledge carved with human figurines standing beside the great falls. Next to the candleholder are three basins filled with water; three towels are draped over ornamented hooks. After washing and eating, we lay down to rest.

Soul awakens alone to birds singing and wind rustling through trees. Me sword lies next to me, my boots at the bottom of the bed; Dandi and Kaylu have already risen and gone, probably exploring. Splashing water on me face from the wooden basin, Soul slides the scabbard over me head. While pulling me boots on, the door swings open.

Olgera walks in and announces, *"It is time for you and your friends to go to the Dark Cave. I have furnished you with packs of food and a water bag for you to refresh yourself along the way."*

Olgera walks over to the bed I'm sitting on. Putting his hand on my shoulder, he stares for a moment into me eyes; patterns of thoughts and images flood into me mind, and Olgera's voice echoes somehow in between the ideas and visions. *"I'm to give you information about the next step in your journey. Listen well, young traveler, for this information will help you pass through the Dark Cave and on into the Land of Light and Darkness."*

Soul finishes pulling on me boots as Olgera sits down beside me to provide more guidance. *"Up to this time, you have seen only our world of light, which is but a small fragment of what awaits you. So far, you have been prepared and given tools to help you survive your journey—especially as you go through the cave—but what you have experienced in this world is nothing compared to the wonders and terrors that await anyone attempting the journey you are now embarking upon. As you* pass through the Dark Cave, many changes will come upon you. It is what you have learned in this land that is your protection; do not be fooled by the illusions that will be thrust upon you."

Soul is confused. "What sort of illusions do you mean?"

Olgera is quiet for a moment then continues, "Listen closely, and I will explain. During part of your passing through this Dark Cave, you will be in a darkness that no man can imagine; learning to trust your intuition is imperative. Your sense of hearing will be increased once inside, but your vision will be less acute. All the passions of your body and its senses will be tempted: trust in your heart, nothing else. Do not believe anything you see, feel or hear. Trust only in the wisdom you have gained, for your mind is going to become your greatest adversary while you pass through the cave. Once you have made it through, your mind will again be the valuable tool it was originally designed to be. This is of utmost importance for anyone in the cave, but especially so for you, Hugh; indeed, if you succeed and make it through the Dark Cave, your mind will become among the highest and most discerning of disciplined machines." Olgera pauses silently for a moment, and then, dramatically moving closer, he whispers, "There are others who are watching you; they do not want you to succeed, and they will do everything within their power to stop you."

Me heart thumps as Olgera continues to project his words into me mind. "Be careful; be watchful, for as you pass through the cave, two things are of utmost importance. The conscious mind—or what you know as Hugh—is not who you really are; passing through the cave, this personality known as Hugh or the 'I' will begin to lose power over the mind. In order for the personality to stop this loss of control, the mind will bring out all the fears and attachments that you have accumulated as a part of your life experiences. You must travel the fine line between reality and illusion: the razor's edge of sanity and insanity. If you succumb to the mind, then all is lost; you will never leave the Dark Cave."

Soul stares at Olgera for a moment and then asks, "Are you saying that the illusions that appear will be of me own making?"

Olgera nods and replies, "Not just of your making, but those of your companions as well. You must understand—the grains of wisdom you have gained and the even greater wisdom you are seeking—is power itself! It can help you overcome any illusion, but only if you trust this wisdom; if you remember what you have gained in our land then in times of danger, it will be the only thing that can release you from the grip of the lower mind, or that which you know as the human person 'Hugh.' There are parts of your personality that are of a positive nature. These positive parts must survive as the thick folds of darkness gather heavily around you. The cave acts as a filter when you pass through it; you will leave behind that which has always held you back from knowing your true self. Deciding which parts are of a positive nature, and which parts are of a negative nature, is the test you are about to encounter. The best way I can make you understand this challenge is to remind you of the very basics that you learned as a child in play."

"What do you mean?" I ask aloud.

Olgera smiles. *"Remember the first time that your father showed you a magnet when you were a small child? Remember how you were amazed at its ability to attract iron objects? It appeared to be magic at the time. Now do you remember what happened when another magnet was applied to the first?"*

Soul thinks for a moment, and then replies, *"Yes, it either pulled the other magnet even more powerfully, or it repelled it."*

"Exactly!" Olgera nodded. *"It attracted it even more powerfully and clamped it securely, but this happened only if the positive pole was facing the negative pole."*

Soul allows the mind to think back to that special day with me Da', and then says, *"Yes; Soul remembers playing with the magnets, thinking how wonderful it was how they reacted to each other."*

Olgera bends forward, and prompts Soul further, *"But what happened when you turned around one of the magnets, and put two positive or two negative poles together?"*

Soul replies, *"The two wouldn't go together; instead, they repelled each other."*

"Yes!" Olgera exclaims. *"Now apply that same principle to the two natures of your mind. Your lower mind—or what is called the conscious mind—has been brought up to understand itself as belonging to a human boy, and from birth, taught to always want or desire something. The conscious mind learns to live within labels and rules of what his society, family, or friends have taught him."*

Soul looks at Olgera and considers how to respond, but the force of Olgera's mind floods into me thoughts. *"Wait! Listen; I will explain. This desire, this wanting, is not only taught since your physical birth, but the impulse has been inbred into your very species for eons. This wanting for more and more could be for anything, say a new toy, some tasty food, or not wanting to get up in the morning because you wanted more time to stay comfortable in warm, protective blankets."*

Soul smiles, thinking of his bed back home, as Olgera continues.

"Realize the depth of this unquenchable grasping; from the moment you were born, your conscious mind was wanting; either it wanted food, wanted your diapers changed, or even wanted your mother's love. This grasping is a negative energy that attracts all sorts of things, and it is a part of all life. Without this energy, life could not exist in the lower worlds of Matter, Energy, Space, and Time. The energy is what it is, and it has a purpose. You see, Hugh, it is not the object that creates desire, but the habit of wanting that creates desire. Man is born into a world that when he sees something he deems desirable, he wants to possess it. This desire for possession breeds attachment, and attachment spins into more wanting and desire. This necessary negative energy is finally perverted into greed. Once you have attained the object of one desire, another desire for yet another object or experience begins to sink its claws into your heart, and this then spirals into more wanting. It is a vicious circle that enforces and builds the negative power within the mind. As you mature, the mind attaches itself to the body and the senses; feeling has now become the next victim of this energy. The more pleasurable stimuli you get, the more you want, and the mind is no longer a tool for your true self to use—instead,

the mind becomes a creature of desire and habit, accumulating illusions. When Soul enters into a physical body, it is in a state of giving: this is felt and seen by anyone who looks into a newborn babe's face. This state of giving is a powerful positive force for the unfoldment of Soul. But because of the law of duality existing in the physical universe, very quickly the consciousness of giving begins to divide. Part of it transforms into a consciousness of wanting. This degree of wanting is different with each individual mind. This transformation is necessary in order for Soul to have experiences that eventually lead it back to its true self. Human experiences should be grounded and based on careful discrimination, common sense, piety, and empathetic understanding—ultimately these create that wisdom which merges mystical truth with human reason. Survival is the sole mission of the lower mind. Over time, desire pushes the higher, giving mind deep down into the subconscious. This happens at a very early age, so instead of becoming a creature of giving, humankind becomes creatures of desire! This loss of Soul's control over the mind allows the undisciplined mind to create a personality formed through reactions to the outer world. Man begins to respond to the world outside of him, forgetting the world within. This is the key to the lower mind's survival and power."

Olgera stands and walks over to a window. Pausing for a second, he turns back to me and Soul senses his discomfort with this subject. *"Once the negative power has gained almost total control of the mind, it takes over the senses. Now the desire is going for more than just external things. Soul's inner kingdom is invaded with the same insidious power of desire that steals its way into the deepest parts of humankind. This invasive force is what man constantly fights within himself. Some call this force karma, sin, or cause and effect; others allude to it in the expression that you Reap what you sow. Whatever the name, eventually it must be eliminated in order for Soul to be free. Once the invasion of man's inner world is complete, man is left with two channels of energy constantly at odds with each other: the positive and the negative. These twin energies wrestle for control, and the outcome of their struggle determines man's journey. Understanding the flows of these two energies is the key to spiritual freedom. The negative energy by itself flows away from the center of the Creator, while the positive energy flows toward it. Man's mind, controlled by the domineering negative energy manifested through the desirous ego, clamps together with man's positive side, effectively locking Soul tightly into a self-created prison: like the two magnets that attract each other through opposite poles. Soul has no control as the real self; instead, it is a slave to the mind with its desires, its senses, its attachments for material possessions and emotional satisfaction, even as it avoids the difficult or fearful in its pursuit of only the pleasure principle. These attachments constantly grow throughout life, causing ever more tension, stress, and fear; this reinforcing energy is how the whole human dilemma begins and ends. The human mind becomes controlled by its wanting instead of giving, eventually becomes a liability instead of an asset."*

Olgera stops for a moment, and in his hesitation, Soul interrupts. *"But most of the things we desire are things that make our lives more comfortable, so what is so wrong with that?"*

"There is nothing necessarily wrong with most objects themselves; the problem arises in the very act of desiring and constant wanting of things, and attachment to those things a person accumulates. You see, you form attachments for these objects, projecting onto them an illusory essence; this is what creates problems within humankind. Desire sends man spinning outward into a reality of chaos, a realm of illusion and fears, so he forgets his reasons for taking on a human body in the first place.

"Originally, the mind was a tool for the real self—the Soul—to learn and express itself as a vehicle for the essence of the Creator. Eventually, the real self is to become a co-worker with the Creator. Instead, by losing itself in the realm of the mind and in its world of desire, Soul has forgotten its one true divine mission. Part of the journey of Soul is to remember the distinction between the mind and Soul. The mind is a highly efficient machine, capable of wonders that most men never even dream about, let alone actually create and experience. Combined with desire, mind forms the core factors of all human problems, whether they are mental, emotional, political, individual, economical, racial, religious, cultural or psychological. Desire even creeps into our most private and personal relationships to cause chaos. Many times during man's existence, he is given the opportunity to overcome this wanting negative energy and again become a spiritual being totally giving of itself. This giving is not what you would normally think of as giving, but this you will learn later—for now, just know that consciously creating your own destiny and current experience modeled after the nature of the Creator is what the Creator intended for each of us. The Creator has formed the perfect plan for each of its children to benefit from.

"To those controlled by the mind, existence seems to be chaotic, evil, dangerous, and at times even pleasurable and most desirable, which to some extent is correct. But those few who are ready to take back their kingdoms are the chosen ones who become spiritual warriors. You as Soul are now at that stage. You may not have known you were ready, but nevertheless you are, or else you would not be here now. If a man can change his consciousness, then he is truly creating a miracle, for in reversing his attitude, which is created by his mental perception of reality, he is turning the lower mind's negative wanting power into a positive giving power. Once this process is reversed, then just like the magnets facing each other from the same pole, the conscious and the subconscious minds repel each other, and this sets free the real individual self, or Soul.

"In truth, it takes both the negative and the positive working together in balance to eventually set Soul free. This setting free is a most wonderful and powerful thing in man's life, for when freed, Soul begins to remember its covenant with the Creator. Soul becomes free to explore all aspects now, of not only its earthly existence, but as a child of the Creator, Soul can explore the universes within as well as the universes without. This reversing of attitude is a natural function. Just as in nature the positive is always changing into the negative, and the negative is always transforming into the positive, as Soul we have the power and ability to create this change too, it just takes discipline. If one settles into a deep contemplation and uses the forces of Light and Sound, one can actually feel this power pressing against his inner eye as it opens up his awareness. Once opened, the reversal of the way he has always thought begins; this is a common experience for those who practice meditation or enter into deep prayer. It simply comes down to detaching yourself from most of what you were taught as a human.

"There is no problem with having the comforts of life so long as you realize they are only borrowed and temporary; to gain true freedom, one must let them go without feelings of loss. In reality, you and all life forms are much more than what the mind and its attachments try to convince you.

"Attachment comes in every conceivable form, and this variety is what traps you. It is the seed of all evil, all fear, and all vanity; the mind creates it and then infects the heart. Once the heart is in its grip, it is difficult to extract by yourself. Take care of your heart. Do not let sick feelings of possession, nor painful aches for either loss or gain enter your heart: if they do, you fall victim to the chronic disease that infects most of humankind.

"So far, you have been taught that man creates emotional attachments to his material possessions. Often far more serious is the emotional attachment that can arise in those who create gods out of their minds. When a person emotionally attaches himself to these creations, he calls it religion. These religions are not for the survival of Soul, but for the survival of the mind. Religions assist the mind power to feel as if it is eternal; belief in religions makes man feel he is connected with whatever gods he worships. Combined with personality, emotion, and religion, the mind has a very potent capacity to not only create the illusion of existence, but also endow it with a false sense of individualism and delusions of immortality. By mind's very nature, mind separates us from our true father until we as Soul eventually wake up.

"Remember this! Soul does not need religions for its survival. This existence is already assured by the Creator. In reality, religions need man for _their_ survival. This is not to say that religions are not needed; they can function like steppingstones in mire, or like rungs on a ladder. We have a saying about your world. It is good to be born in a church, but disastrous to die in one.

"Understand this! Once the individual changes his attitude, transmuting it into a positive and detached state, or what is often known as the detached way of life, he gains everything, for now he is a magnet of love. The more love he gives, the more love he gains. All the heavens sing in his glory, for he is now the true son of the Creator, doing its works.

"Know this! Only one man in a million actually accomplishes this illustrious change. And this is so because change does not come all at once; there are many, many levels to experience while one is unfolding the dark, suffocating cloak that hides the true, perfected state of your self. This quest will feel like you have started at the bottom of a deep trench, and you must strive and trudge your way upward and ever inward to reach the doorway of the divine kingdom.

"Remember: when danger is near you, in the highest sense you are the actual creative power personifying your thoughts and feelings into actual forms. The form you now exist in is your own creation. Try to remember, Hugh: as you journey through the Dark Cave, nothing can harm you except what you, yourself, allow into your own universe."

Chapter 15 ~ A Choice

Since the accident a month ago, Clark has been forced to adjust his work schedule and direct financial opportunities to his associates; he now divides his time between caring for Melody in the hospital, or investigating and studying to find a solution. He pores over stories about paranormal experiences, ancient teachings concerning life after death, interpretation of dreams, meditation techniques, and anything else he thinks might, just might, help him connect with his son. Ann's doctors continue to list her condition as grave; if anything, she is sinking deeper into her coma, falling further into a world no one has been able to reach. Hugh's condition is much less desperate than his mother's. Lately, however, it has become obvious to the doctors and Clark that Hugh will not be coming out of his coma anytime soon.

Sitting by his son's bedside, Clark whispers Hugh's name in the chanting fashion he discovered from yesterday evenings inner experience. That night left him hopeful that he could come closer to making some sort of contact.

After a quick knock on the door, Doctor Orvitz enters the hospital room, followed by a woman. "Mr. Bailey, I'm glad you are here, I have someone for you to meet." Motioning to his colleague, Doctor Orvitz explains, "This is Dr. Stepp, an associate of mine. I have asked her for a consultation, and she has been examining your wife and son for the last week. We'd like to go over her findings with you."

Clark stands and shakes Dr. Stepp's hand. "It's nice to meet you; I wasn't aware you are part of the medical team treating me wife and son."

Dr. Stepp is a small, forty-ish woman, whose ebony hair is slick-backed and tied in a tight ponytail. Her sharp features are somewhat softened by large, dark framed glasses. "Well, actually, I'm the newest member to your medical team. I have some expertise in coma patients, and from what Dr. Orvitz informs me, this is a most unusual case; can we go to my office, Mr. Bailey? We should be more comfortable there."

Clark steps over to his wife's bedside, leans down to kiss her on the forehead and whispers, "Goodbye, Annie. I'll return soon."

They enter the doctor's office and Clark takes a chair. Dr. Orvitz offers him some coffee and then says, "Mr. Bailey, Dr. Stepp has spent a great amount of time examining and running tests on both your wife and son, and she'd like to discuss the results with you in detail, if that's all right with you."

Clark turns to Dr. Stepp and says, "Let's do it."

"Okay, may I call you Clark?"

"Please do."

"In the course of my career, Clark, I've examined hundreds of coma patients. Never have I seen a case like this; your wife's severe head injuries support why she's in such a deep coma. However, given her injuries, it's highly unusual for her to sink so deeply. Usually a patient like this remains unconscious for a while and then begins to improve. However, in your wife's case, our EEG and other tests show her brain function is slowing down. Due to this, she has moved into unknown territory as far as comas are concerned. There are many different theories that have been tested. Usually, the first steps are to have the patient scanned, measured, and probed for several days; I have been doing these, plus I conducted what is known as a PET/CT scan, which reveals how much energy your wife's brain is using, and an MRI that shows which parts of her brain are damaged; our entire team has used numerous tactics to try to bring about a response. While one team peppers her with questions, audiotapes, pictures, and other sensory prods, an FMRI machine tracks her brain activity to look for evidence of awareness and the possibility of establishing communication. We also glue tiny electrodes to her scalp to pick up electrical signals through electroencephalography (EEG); by repeating this process, we detect fluctuations in her awareness. We use these tests to create a diagram of the recovery of her consciousness. A schematic, or what you might call a blueprint, has recently been created that offers tentative explanations for some of the surprises we have seen. This blueprint shows no single consciousness center of her brain; instead, her consciousness appears to be arranged in a type of circuit consisting of a collective of centers situated in different brain regions, and they show a dynamic state that seems to be made possible by this circuit, this active coalition of parts. The circuit diagram focuses on the links between the central thalamus, cortex, and regions such as the globus pallidus and the striatum, which closely regulates the level of stimulation between cortex and thalamus…"

Dr. Orvitz interrupts. "Dr. Stepp, can you explain a bit more about what all this means?"

Dr. Stepp picks up the test results in front of her, stares at them for a moment, and with a sigh drops them back on the desk. "To be honest, due to Mrs. Bailey's state, we haven't a clue."

Shaking his head, Clark abruptly blurts out, "Hold it, please! I have no idea what you guys are talking about! Can't you keep it simple and speak in layman's terms?"

Dr. Stepp takes off her glasses and says, "I apologize—you are right, of course. Clark, the bottom line is this. Most patients either die or begin to improve when they reach your wife's state. Granted, we don't understand the total power of the mind's healing process, but in your wife's situation, she has descended to a level that has never been recorded to my knowledge in an otherwise living patient."

The doctor's report is not only shocking, but more painful than Clark has ever felt; all he can do is sit there in silence, listening to this woman telling him that according to modern science, his wife should be dead.

Dr. Stepp continues. "In your son's case, it's even more confusing. Hugh has suffered only minor head injuries: injuries that should never have put him into a coma. Up to last week, the likelihood of him awakening was very positive. However, within the past twenty-four hours, something is happening that we can't explain. Running tests and recording his brain activity have shown that his subconscious activity is actually stepping up, while the activity in the conscious area of his brain has almost ceased to register. But that's not all. Periodically, Hugh's conscious mind responds with high activity for a few moments, but then it disappears. With each jump in conscious activity, he seems to dive back into the coma at a deeper level. I believe it is possible—but highly unlikely—that Hugh's brain could be mapping a new neural pathway that could be tapping into unknown areas of the mind. This has never been seen or experienced by any patient that I'm aware of. At this juncture in our examination, we decided to test your son's brain activity exactly at the same time as your wife's. This test has indicated another most bizarre medical phenomenon: it seems that just as his mother descends, Hugh follows; however, before he descends, his conscious mind seems to make an effort to pull out of the coma, or maybe he's trying to waken and communicate, but on some level we can't understand. Just this morning, your wife's brain activity slowed; within minutes, your son's brain activity jumped. Then after about thirty minutes, the activity leveled out and began to slow down. The way it's going right now, your son isn't improving, but instead, he seems to follow your wife's pattern. We think your son might be conscious on some level, but he is aware his mother is dying and he does not want to return without her. This brings us to a problem that needs to be addressed. Clark, you're going to have to make some decisions concerning both of them as far as their continued treatment."

Clark is silent. He can't believe what he's hearing; this woman just told him what he suspected all along—Hugh is somehow in sync with his mother and trying to save her! Clark doesn't understand exactly what's happening medically, but he can grasp the significance of the situation, even if the doctors didn't.

Dr. Stepp continues. "Clark, the information Dr. Orvitz and we've gathered shows no significant improvement for either your son or wife for over a month. If this trend continues, they could live for years, and their care would not only cost a great deal of time and money, but the emotional pain that your family would have to endure in itself would be staggering. We see you're suffering, and since both patients are not improving, some tough decisions are going to have to be made."

Clark is quiet, trying to grasp what the doctor just told him. Then he says, "What kind of decisions are you talking about?"

Dr. Stepp leans a little closer over the desk, and without hesitation she says, "If your son is somehow influenced by your wife's condition, we believe the only chance your son has of recovering is to disconnect your wife's life support; otherwise, your son will continue to deteriorate at the same pace as your wife. If your son is to have any chance of coming out of his coma, he must focus all his energy on himself instead of following his mother. If he reaches a level where there's no return, he's lost; in other words, are you ready to risk both their lives, or do you want to give your son the chance he needs in order to wake up?"

Clark sits motionless, remembering his dream and Hugh's plea, *"Da'! I'm all right! I've gotta find Mom. Don't give up on us. Please, Da'! Don't give up!"*

Clark stands up; he knows what the doctor is saying makes sense, but he also knows his son is somehow trying to save his mother. If he chooses to let his wife die, Hugh would possibly come back, but on the other hand, it is entirely possible his son could give up and never return. If he keeps his wife alive, it is possible Hugh might find a way to save her and return to this world again. How can he make such a decision? No one should be put in such a position to choose one over the other, or try to save both at the risk of losing them both. "How long do I have before I need to make a decision?"

Dr. Stepp answers, "We'll need to know within twenty-four hours. If the MRI and EEG show deterioration, it only makes it riskier for your son. We're sorry to put you in this position, but it's critical we do something soon."

Clark offers his hand and shakes Dr. Stepp's. "I appreciate your forthrightness and honesty. I understand, and I'll let you know what my decision is within twenty-four hours." He knew this experience was going to be rough, and he knew that his lack of understanding would be tested at some point, but he never fathomed that he'd be thrust into this dilemma. How could he choose?

Clark walks out of the hospital as if in a dream. What guidelines could he use to make such a choice? He loves his wife and his son; does he have the faith and trust in Hugh to help his mother? As he drives home, his mind is racing. Trust, patience, courage—these are easily talked about, but when confronted with the very core of what they represent, the mind runs in fear. All sorts of images are forming in his mind. What if he makes the wrong choice? What if his lack of trust kills both of them? How could he face himself? What about Melody? Could he ever look her in the face again knowing he didn't made the right choice as a father?

Why? Why, God, are you doing this to me?

Why do I deserve this? I can't make these kinds of choices! Hopeless and lost feelings rush through him. "I should just drive forever and never stop, I never needed to confront this impossible situation. Continuing home, his mind just keeps racing almost as if it had a life of its own. When he finally arrives, Melody's back from school playing with Cody in the yard. He hates coming back with this burden lying on his heart; how can he even begin to explain to Melody what is happening? Nevertheless, he has no choice: she needs to know what he's up against; she needs to realize the seriousness of what he is about to decide.

Melody comes running as he steps out of the car. "Da', I'm glad you're home early! Can we go for a walk with Cody to the tree house?"

Clark tries to smile, looking at his daughter with piercing tenderness. Why not? Perhaps it would be better to talk while they walk through the meadow.

It's an Indian summer day and slightly overcast; not too warm, but with a promise of fall to be here soon. Even at the end of summer the meadow is still a lush green, making both of them feel warm and safe. Father and daughter watch the light on the meadow change as the sun lowers past the horizon; the two amble toward the woods while light shifts to a soft and serene shine gilding the grass and leaves. Both are entranced as the meadow becomes bathed in gold; entering the pathway leading to the woods, the sun on their backs is like a herdsman, lazily driving them home. As the two saunters toward the tree house, Clark wonders. Will the sun ever shine more beautifully than right now? Sunlight penetrates their minds and hearts like a birthday candle awakens a warm and hopeful moment. They pass the little brook, whose rippling waters cast flashes into pockets of shadows, and overhead light stretches long fingers over the meadow eastward in perfect beauty, as if it were the only land existing for the beams of light. Warm moist air wafts the aromas of Mother Nature. Nothing more is needed to make a paradise of the meadow; Clark felt he could either laugh or cry.

Looking at his daughter bathed in the soft light, his throat catches as he ponders how beautiful she is; mustering courage, he takes her delicate hand in his and begins to explain what is on his mind. "I was at the hospital today to see your mom and brother. It seems I have to make a decision and you need to be part of that decision."

"What do we have to decide on, Da'?"

"The doctors say your mother's not doing as good as they'd like. The coma seems to be getting worse, and the doctors haven't seen any improvement. Your brother is also getting worse; each time your mother goes deeper into her coma, within moments Hugh follows the same pattern."

Melody squeezes her father's hand. "Da', that's because Hugh is trying to help Mom!"

Clark stops in his tracks and stares dumbstruck at his daughter. "What did you say?"

"Dad, I know that Hugh is trying to help Mom. I thought you knew it, too."

"Well, I suspected, but how do you know?"

Melody picks up a small branch, and twirling it in her slender fingers she begins to tell him of a dream she had after the accident. "Hugh's in the dream, and he tells me he is going to save Mom and to trust him. He wanted me to tell you when the time was right—I guess this is the right time."

"Why didn't you tell me about this sooner?"

Melody calmly looks up at her father. "Da', Hugh said that if I waited when the right moment came, it would help you make the right choices, so it's important to wait. I wanted to tell you sooner but it didn't feel like the right time—now it does."

Clark squeezes his daughter's hand. "Thanks, honey, it has helped. We must make a very important decision and to be truthful, I didn't know what choice to make until just now." The tree house finally comes into view at the end of the pathway. As Clark looks up into the limbs, he realizes all the boundaries and limitations he constantly builds; lately these seem to be fading from his mind, changing his world in ways he doesn't understand. In this moment, he suddenly sees the real world through the faith and trust of a child. He now knows the world we're living in leaves no trace, it has no time, and will leave no anniversary; the moment is fleeting, but as it fades it leaves an impression in his mind of how often adults fail to appreciate a child's faith.

The next day Clark arrives at the hospital with his daughter. Entering Dr. Ovitz's office, he feels at peace with what he has to do.

Dr. Orvitz is seated at his desk and Dr. Stepp is perched in a side chair, leaning over her notepad writing. As Clark and Melody walk in, Dr. Stepp places the pad down, smiles, and says, "Thank you, Clark, for coming. I know this is a hard decision for you, but I'm sure it will be for the best." Dr. Stepp motions to Clark and Melody to sit at a small table next to Dr. Orvitz, but both instead remain standing.

Dr. Stepp explains, "I have taken the liberty of drawing up the preliminary consent order on your wife." Pushing some papers on the table toward Clark, she continues, "Once you've given consent, we can get the proper documents in place for the courts."

Clark sits down; Melody remains standing at his side. Clark thinks how smug Dr. Stepp looks...as if the choice about his family is hers alone to make. She assumes the choice will be what she presented yesterday; she has no thought of his possibly holding another viewpoint or even the chance of there being another avenue. It is a matter of fact with her—there is no other way. Clark gently pushes the papers back toward the center of the table and says, "Dr. Stepp, I appreciate your input and your expert opinion in trying to help make our decisions easier. Undoubtedly, not everyone is equally fit to determine medically the ramifications or the details you believe exist to decide on this type of situation...however, after much thought and discussion with me daughter, I've decided that the survival of me family now and in the future isn't based on medicine alone. I've analyzed and contemplated the situation and realize I have more confidence in my son and wife than I do with medicine. I believe my wife and son are not insignificant bystanders in this situation but participants as much as—if not more than—you or I. The decision is a family one, it is a decision of trust, faith, and courage. We have as a family decided that the journey Ann and Hugh have started will continue— whatever happens will not be in our hands, but in the hands of something far more knowledgeable than you or I. I want the support system to stay on. I stand by this decision with me wife, daughter, and son."

After a moment of stunned silence, Dr. Stepp abruptly stands up. "Perhaps you don't understand, Mr. Bailey! Your insurance is running out; within a few weeks the insurance company will dispute continuance anyway, thereby forcing the situation into a far more drastic procedure. I am trying to give you the opportunity of making the decision based on medical facts instead of financial distress."

As Clark stands and puts his arm around Melody's shoulders, he replies, "I will confront the insurance when that time arrives, but for today and until all options are played out, the support stays on!"

Dr. Stepp looks at Dr. Orvitz. "Are you going to sit there and allow this? You know what my superiors are going to say!"

Dr. Ovitz clears his throat and says firmly, "Dr. Stepp, Mr. Bailey has made his decision and I stand one hundred percent behind him. I also remind you, Dr. Stepp, you were made a part of our medical team due to the insurance company's insistence; your expertise in this field is unquestionable, but even you know that in cases such as this there is no right or wrong answer. To your employers, the case is based on sterile medical facts, and above all else, dollars; to us as doctors, it's based on clinical analyses, research, and past experience that proves no doctor can tell the future. I have seen many things in the medical field I can't explain. I have seen what some call miracles, and as a professional, I'm not encouraged to discuss that, but remember this: our profession is called a medical practice…it's called practice for a very solid reason. Think about it!"

Dr. Stepp picks up the consent papers and notepads, and without any goodbyes, walks angrily out of the office. Clark moves toward the door and then turning, looks at Dr. Orvitz and says, "I understand you have to follow certain rules and criteria when it comes down to something like this, but I want you to know that what you just said confirms my decision, and I thank you for your candor and support."

Nodding sympathetically, Dr. Ovitz replies, "Mr. Bailey, you're quite welcome. Some of us in the medical field are constantly at odds with big insurance companies that don't see the human side of our situation. This is sad; however, it's what society has created. We place our trust in people of power who then become the architects of our future, and in most cases, the manipulators of our fate; it's a pleasure to meet someone like you. Seldom do I meet a man who not only questions but also rebuffs the schemes for more dollars and more control from the powers that be."

Walking down the sterile hospital hallway, their steps echoing, Clark and Melody somehow feel heavier, laden down with the realization that this journey has become increasingly more difficult. Now they must support each other through not only love, but also patience, courage, and faith; all these qualities are going to be needed as they approach their darkest moments.

Chapter 16 ~ The Cleansing

Soul stands at the entrance of the Dark Cave; Kaylu and Dandi stand behind me waiting for my signal to proceed. Soul knows the dangers that lay ahead but even more, Soul understands exactly what the outcome will be if we fail to keep control of our minds. Olgera's instructions and information was projected directly into me consciousness, and so has become a part of me awareness; neither Kaylu nor Dandi know except what I briefly told them. Carefully we discussed what is to be expected, and that it's not too late to turn back. Both insisted they intend on staying and confronting whatever lay inside the ominous dark opening. Soul looks at me friends, smiles and says, *"Well, guys, are ya' ready?"*

We duck into the massive maw of the mountain.

The cave is large; ceilings disappear into darkness. It isn't wide, but it's still roomy. Light from the entrance illuminates the first dozen or so yards, and then like fading daylight disappears: only darkness looms ahead.

The fresh air is invigorating, smelling of damp earth. Mists from the falls spray lightly against our faces, and as we descend deeper, we round a turn and the cave's entrance completely vanishes into darkness. Soul reaches around for the safety rope we tied around our waists to link us together, tugging the rope to make sure me mates are at me side. Soul slows down and stops to project words to me mates' minds, "Let's light a torch before we go any further." Both companions agree simultaneously. Soul lights me torch first mainly because of me being in the lead. Then Soul realizes somethings different about me communicating. Before, Soul would send thoughts to only one individual at a time. Now it seems as natural as breathing to send me thoughts to both of them at once; the thoughts from me companions return to me simultaneously with clear images and words, not confusing at all. Soul thinks about this briefly but shrugs it off as part of the knowledge gained from Olgera. Lighting the torch makes me more comfortable, at least now we can see the cave walls. Looking about we see various colors merging and blending as we move forward. Light greens on the wall blend into pale tans, yellow, and dark browns. Some parts of the wall are smooth and arched, gracefully ascending to the distant ceiling. The ground is rough, somewhat jagged but passable, as we cautiously move ahead. Occasionally we glimpse the path, which looks like a dried-up streambed. Torchlight bounces against the wall allowing us to see the width of the cave, which is about fifty feet across. The walking becomes easier and we begin to make progress.

Strange feelings flutter inside our guts as we descend farther into blackness, our steps certain as the torch burns brightly: it can burn for hours if needed. As we descend deeper into the bowels of the mountain, Soul feels a startling clarity of mind, this clarity makes me confident and secure. Logically speaking, with the torch lighting our way, me sword in its scabbard, and the three of us tied together, nothing should impede our journey. Soul grows in confidence— in fact, more confident than Soul could ever remember. Me mind is keen and observant, mental communication with Kaylu and Dandi is articulate and clear, their responses are simple to follow even if they respond at the same time. The moist air is drying up; it's now more of a mild dry breeze that carries mysterious scents. Shadows play tricks, growing larger on the high walls as we descend further into the cave, leaping and then disappearing. Up ahead a few feet, the streambed divides, one way to the left and the other curving to the right. Which way do we go? Standing still at the crossroads, none of us knows what to do; holding the torch closer to the entrances only makes us more confused and undecided. Choosing the wrong direction could make us lost forever in the mountain, but then again, perhaps one way was as good as the other? Did both passages lead out?

Soul sends me thoughts to me two friends. "*We have to decide…does anybody have any idea what direction we should go?*"

Kaylu walks ahead a few feet, sniffing the air. "*Close your eyes, let the wind tell you the direction.*"

Soul thinks for a moment and then remembers Olgera's wisdom, "*Your sight will be less important while your other senses will expand.*" Closing me eyes, Soul lets the breeze drift its scents to me.

At first Soul can't identify anything but after concentrating for a moment a slight fragrance fills me nostrils. Apples! actually the smell of apple pie! drifts into me senses. The aroma intensifies, as if the pie was set right in front of me. The smell brings back warm memories, especially those of me mother and family times together. Chilly winter nights when Mom's baking a pie, Da' standing with his hands on her shoulders and whispering in her ear, Cody's lying with me in front of the fireplace watching the tele, while me sister colors with her crayons…so many memories flood me mind…simple innocent memories. The warm aroma of baking pie is coming from the path turning to the right. Soul wants to follow the heady scents with conjured images of home. It has to be the correct way, it's so inviting, so loving, how could it be anything else? The aroma invites me forward in warm delicious bursts of memories and scents.

Veering to the right, Soul feels me sword vibrate. At first, Soul thinks it is just the scabbard shifting, but as Soul continues to the right, the vibration makes itself more obvious. Reaching back and pulling out the sword the vibration increases. Holding the sword in front of me, Soul takes a few steps forward and the vibrations intensify almost to an angry buzzing sound: Soul stops. What's happening? Is the sword telling me to stop or go forward? Shifting the point of the sword to the left the vibration fades; as the sword further veers to the left, the vibration stops entirely but the blade suddenly gives off a slight glow. The sword glows more brightly with each step along the new path.

Soul stops again. What to do? Follow the light, or follow the sound? With me eyes closed and pointing the sword toward the left, me sense of smell guides me. At first, just for an instant, the aroma of cool fresh air and damp earth wafts into me senses. As me senses fill with the aroma, the mind slowly loses all the images and memories created by the baking pie scents. Like a morning fog lifting from a meadow, everything seems clear: opening me eyes, Soul looks at me comrades who are standing and watching me.

Soul says, *"We go to the left."* Olgera's words ring through me; the mind creates illusions to trap us, especially illusions that stimulate the emotions. Remembering Olgera's words, me awareness and confidence is reinforced. Me body and mind are me own worst enemies; intuition points to the left so this is the way we will go. All three of us realize what just happened. We are naturally more prone to follow the body senses or even respond to our mind's fond memories, these senses and images create powerful desires for someone who hasn't learned differently. Soul sees clearly how his human mind creates emotions, memories, and feelings, which in turn sometimes create confusion. Decisions made based on the senses can sometimes lead a person to a world of sensory illusions, diverting him from life's real journey thus carrying him through a life of redundancy and repeated erroneous choices.

Walking along the path leading to the left we see the streambed widen. Cave walls melt away to merge with much larger caverns, shadows reach high into the darkness and the three of us look like insignificant bugs moving among the meandering streambeds, nooks, and crannies.

After a while Kaylu and Dandi move more slowly, more cautiously, every so often they slow to a stop and look about; both appear as if their minds are far away. Soul keeps pressing forward, yet allowing for the constant delays. Something's happening. We're all feeling strange; in some ways it's like being disconnected from who we really are. Strange thoughts and images appear in me mind—seemingly from nowhere—causing unexpected feelings and emotions to erupt inside me. Each of us is traveling through this cave not as a group, but as individuals: seeing, feeling, and experiencing the surroundings in our own way. Can we hold out? Are we strong enough to see through the illusions created from the blackness as it probes, touches, and expands our minds? What may seem like reality is actually a steady mixture of each other's own images emerging from a store within our minds; we need to take control of the false illusions. My advantage over Dandi and Kaylu comes from the teachings that Jotan and Olgera gave me.

Kaylu abruptly stops, and we all stumble as our tethers jerk us back together. Kaylu glances around with glazed eyes and says, *"Wait! Something's wrong! This cannot be the way."*

Dandi asks, *"What's wrong?"*

Kaylu stands still and silent for a moment, a faraway look on his face. He mumbles some words, not projecting them from his mind, but spilling actual words from his mouth.

Soul moves closer. *"Are you ok?"*

Kaylu stares momentarily into the vastness of the cavern and slowly says aloud, "I do not understand what I am feeling or seeing."

Soul places me hand on Kaylu's shoulder. *"It's all right Kaylu. Tell me, what's wrong?"*

Kaylu steps back, shaking off my friendly gesture, and starts talking, again not with his mind but his mouth. "This place must be the ancestors of your gods? People like you are everywhere; metal objects are moving across flat rock trails, and giant metal birds fly across the sky leaving streams of clouds behind them. So many people living in high rock caves; sounds come from everywhere. No silence, no stillness…only the constant movement of chaotic thoughts. The air is hard to breathe. These life forms—these humans? They are so scared and angry, they are confused, sad, happy, lustful, angry, and selfish all at the same time! Everything is about wanting." He looks at me and Dandi with a glazed look in his eyes, and says in a low and tremulous voice, "Greed lives within everything!" He turns his face to me, his eyes opening even wider. "Your world has forgotten its purpose!" He trembles as thoughts, words, and feelings engulf him.

Soul doesn't understand what is happening. *"Kaylu, it's me, Hugh! We're in the cave! You're creating these images yourself."*

Kaylu looks at me; his eyes reflect confusion. *"Me, how? Can I create things I have never imagined? Never seen? Never experienced? Surely, we are lost forever in this dark place!"* Me friend trembles even more; the look on his face is growing dark, fear is taking possession of him.

Kaylu shuts his eyes tightly and clutches his head, assailed by images being pushed into his mind; every image has feelings attached. He gazes up for a moment and then with a gasp, he moans. *"Oh, my! This is what you meant; yes now I understand! How can people live in this world of confusion? Now I see! Now I know what you tried to tell me. I see the fireball in the sky, I see the sun!"* Kaylu staggers to his knees, falling in the streambed moaning, he whispers while shadows and light twist and turn inside his mind. Looking again at me, but now with pity, he repeats softly, *"How can you live in this world?"* Soul stares at Kaylu dumbfounded, trying to understand; he's seeing my world, but how?

Images invade Kaylu's imagination even more, making his pain even more intense. The images have to be coming from me, but how? I'm not thinking about what he is seeing. Dandi kneels next to Kaylu and says to him, *"Listen, my friend, you are seeing dead images stored within Hugh—you are tapping too deeply within his being."*

Kaylu opens his eyes; his voice wavers as he asks, *"Can you see them, too? Why can't you see as I do into this world of darkness and light? All is a part of me and a part of us; can you not see the truth in this?"*

Soul looks at Dandi and asks, *"What's he talking about? He's not making sense!"*

Dandi holds Kaylu's body to his chest and then looks up at me. *"You must remain calm…your thoughts and feelings are killing him!"*

Soul stares at the gentle giant with mouth agape. Is he mad also? How could me thoughts and feelings kill anyone?

Dandi speaks calmly as he holds Kaylu in his massive arms. *"Thoughts and feelings are real things, they can either destroy or create—it depends on whether the mind is in control or whether something higher has control."* Dandi's quiet for a moment, then looking at Kaylu, he explains further, *"Hugh, no matter how close we are to our loved ones or friends, we are each still individuals. In your world, people exist in what appears to be a separate reality, but even though it appears separate, it's really connected to all. Your world's reality is one that neither Kaylu nor I comprehend; apparently it exists as nearly pure desire—unceasing wanting— trapping the citizens in fear and attachments. The cave expanded those images inside you, making them appear within Kaylu's own thought patterns: they are now real to him."*

What's his giant friend saying?

Soul sends a thought, *"Dandi, in my world we are individuals; each of us lives and thinks how we wish. Each of us creates individual goals. We strive to be different; no one wants to feel like sheep being led to the slaughter, yet you say in my world we live by emotion or instincts, like ants or honey bees?"*

Dandi replies, *"Don't you see, Hugh? Your world is mostly comprised of minds that accept the same reality!"*

"What do you mean? None of us are alike. I like certain things, I'm white, I'm male, I love me family, I believe in God. Do you know that there are billions in my world who don't have the same life as me? Some are poor, some are rich, some are crippled or diseased, and others are healthy. Some people are black, some brown, some red or yellow; we have many different religions. Why, we're so different that we have major wars over our differences."

Dandi shakes his head. *"You don't understand, Hugh. Your perception of reality or existence is exactly the same as every higher life form in your world. You as individuals justify war in order to condone your differences and opinions, yet you feel obligated to constantly interfere in one another's lives and force them to change to your ideas. Can't you see? Every part of your reality is based on a wanting mind. Your species have created the chaotic world you live in with all its rules and limitations. In creating the reality that humans accept and live by, they have lost their purpose for existing."*

Soul tries to understand what Dandi is saying; it doesn't make sense! *"Dandi, what's wrong with wanting to make our lives better? Everyone needs something in life or what's the purpose of living?"*

"Hugh," Dandi responds, *"the heart of your world's existence is not about objects, but the desire for objects! Your whole world exists on the same energy of desire! It does not matter what the object of desire is, just the energy alone binds all. Existing by this desire has created a world that demands each life center its existence on the core of mental aberrations that humankind's undisciplined minds create from the time of birth to the time of death. It does not matter if one is richer or poorer; nor does it matter whether you are of a certain color or race. All the mind wants is for you and your world to fulfill its desire, to want and strive for the illusions that you believe you need and think are real. Mind even creates the illusion that some of you are more disciplined than others, either in materialism, or in your religious or moral*

concepts, and even in your feelings of love. Some have better bodies than others, so the mind makes them think they are better, or even a superior being. The human desire to want to help is formed from the foundation of wanting. It does not matter whether it is considered good or bad, it only matters that it is a desire. In becoming slaves to desire, humans forget they are created to give. Instead of helping one another, they strive to accumulate more wealth, more things. Kaylu is now a part of your desire consciousness, desire is invading his being."

Soul can't grasp the total meaning of what Dandi is trying to tell me, but maybe he's right! What else can be happening to Kaylu? Humans hardly ever change their habits. Instead, they only grow more deeply entrenched, sucked into the mind's power; we are taught to surrender, to work as a team with school, friends, family, sports, work, religious beliefs or whatever.

Working together is not deceptive, however. What's false is the feeling of being alone and accepting the principles and rules that govern every aspect of the mind. On one hand, you have the "I" concept, that which makes you feel apart. On the other hand, you have the "team" concept; the team awareness is the universal acceptance of images and applied principles that rule and control us as individuals and as a society. Rightly so, this has become accepted as an essential part of being human. Sometimes it's obvious; we see this in the herd instinct or in some animal species that despite instincts of self-preservation, conduct mass suicides. The illusion of individualism is so well-manipulated that we cannot see the trap that is sprung on us. As humans we too conduct mass suicides each time we send thousands of soldiers to battle thousands of other soldiers, or when we accept someone else's laws and concepts and allow them to rule over us; we then stop living our own dream but attach ourselves to theirs. My world has not realized that when a person is trying to include someone as his contemporary, in most cases, it's because he's troubled and wants the companionship of another to share his mood.

That's it! This cave has enhanced my limited and incorrect concepts, allowing the mind to drag me companions into my troubled universe, forcing its perception of reality into their very being. What a malignant virus we humans really are. Soul remembers a saying in the Bible how the seeker becomes lonelier as he journeys closer to the Creator. It's obvious that someone who doesn't accept the principles or concepts of leaders, family, governments, or even friends would be lonely indeed. Each of us must come to an understanding that the Creator doesn't train its children to become automatons as the materialistic world does. To know your true self, to touch your true power, and to experience total freedom, you must become a complete, individualistic person.

Dandi interrupts my thoughts. *"Hugh, you have been mentally in contact with Kaylu far longer than you have with me. Due to this, he is now linked to your subconscious thoughts. This is why he is seeing your world—he is not only seeing it, but has become a part of it as far as feeling."*

Soul finally realizes what is actually happening.

Those individuals who rebel against society are the type of person usually struggling to get free, so he acts differently; he goes against society's accepted terms and conditions. He stops playing the people-pleaser game. For those who turn to

God at this crucial stage, they find that their detachment grows but so does their compassion. A person's eccentricities are not a sign of true freedom but usually a sign of his struggle to be free. Soul sees how freedom in the human consciousness acts in contradiction with true spiritual freedom. How can someone who wants true freedom live within a society, obey its laws, surrender to its customs and be a slave to the passions of the body and the mind? How does someone who is participating within the limitations of the mind know freedom? Soul looks over at Dandi and asks, *"What needs to be done?"*

Dandi rests Kaylu against a large boulder on the side of the streambed. Straightening up and then taking me shoulders in his massive hands, he looks deep into me eyes. *"Be still."*

Soul finds itself creating streams of thoughts and images that seem endless, how can Soul be still? How can Soul defeat the mind with mind? It's impossible! These images and feelings deceive us into believing we've reached success—it's only later in life or even on our deathbed that we see the subtle trap that again we have lost ourselves in.

"Hugh, try to focus! Concentrate on something that symbolizes all you have learned in our world." While trying to focus on what Dandi is saying, a light gently forms within me mind's eye, and an image appears; it isn't clear at first, but as Soul focuses, it becomes recognizable. The image floats forward from the dark corridors of me mind and crystallizes sharply: within the light is the childlike face of Jotan. His simplicity, his love, patience, and trust all filter into me mind and then me feelings. As it flows throughout me being, Soul feels the very nature or Soul of this world, of its people, and its natural caring for all. It isn't all the inventions, cities or even the images of humans that are attacking Kaylu. It's the confusion, the lies, the hate, the anger, the hunger for power, and the desire for material objects and everything else that man has become. But more than all of this is the look of fear in me friend's face. Never has Soul seen a trace of fear in his face, yet now it's swallowing this gentle, brave, and loving creature.

Dandi bends over Kaylu and says, *"All the mind's negative aspects are the food that has nurtured and fed your own fear Hugh; these have now infected Kaylu. Somehow the cave has amplified your mind's negative energies."* My communication is an invader; my mind is like a computer virus infecting Kaylu.

Soul knows from having a computer at home that sometimes to clear a virus he has to shut down the hard drive. Soul has to shut off all forms of communication, in other words, "Be still!" Soul centers on me feelings for this new world with all the attention possible. Me mind gently and slowly enters a state of numbness like when my hand falls asleep underneath me. Soul remains totally aware of the environment; somehow, Soul is more aware than ever before.

Dandi shouts out, "He's responding! Hugh! Kaylu is coming out of it." Even though me body is standing right beside Dandi, Soul slips high above them, looking down not only at me two companions but also at me own body right beside them. Almost disinterested in the whole scene, calmness floods me consciousness; me body kneels and me arm reaches down to take Kaylu's hand. Upon touching

Kaylu, Soul again sees through me own eyes from me own body. Dandi helps Kaylu stand up.

We know now more clearly than ever our greatest adversary is truly ourselves. It is then we decide that mental discipline techniques are not to be trusted in the cave. From this point on, we will speak with our mouths, and I will no longer use the word Soul to replace "I."

I learned a lot about what Soul actually is and how different it is from the mind: not only in the mind's limitations but also as to what Soul strives for, versus the mind and its unlimited desires. This understanding came from the simple process of eliminating the word "I" and replacing it with Soul. I now feel a conscious relationship existing between the "I" and Soul; I must try to do what is necessary to keep this bridge open.

Chapter 17 ~
The Bridge

Dandi, Kaylu, and I march quietly by the light of me torch, each of us concentrating on our thoughts, feelings, and senses. The cave is proving to be an immense power conduit constantly expanding our minds; we feel its assault at every step. In doing so we discover our minds—like the cave—have many rooms. Some of these rooms are familiar, some not; some are warm and encouraging, some dark and mysterious. Staying in any one of these rooms too long can lead to a false confidence. False confidence leads to mistakes in judgment and creates illusions. If not careful, eventually we can drown in confusion and feelings of insecurity, which breeds fear and ultimately defeat. The cave's power seems limitless. We know instinctively that without warning its power can and will try to penetrate deep into our subconscious. Kaylu's experience taught us much. It's become clear that me mind is an individual entity surviving on its own. I as Soul am the instrument that's generating power, which the mind then uses to create and promote me personality; this personality then controls Soul's perception of what's supposed to be me own life.

Habits, pleasures, fear—sensual and emotional stimulation are running rampant within each of our minds. As much as the power expands our minds it also expands its control; each level of awareness I experience is like a double-edged sword. The cave enhances positive attributes of intuition, love, charity, freedom, and all the normal functions of the mind; however, it strengthens the negative attributes as well. One moment I feel as if I'm in total control, and the next moment I'm floundering—I'm being flung back and forth like a *ping-pong* ball. When I was out of me body and remaining objective, I experienced what's happening to me, but I was not overwhelmed. Slowly me higher self, the Soul, is learning to take back control of me mind.

We learned to be cautious from Kaylu's pain, knowing now that our concepts of right and wrong are not easily applicable to this realm. The secret in mind control isn't trying to out-think the mind but to rise above it! The only way to accomplish this is to be neither against anything, nor, for anything. Learning to experience this oneness and still maintain my individuality is the challenge.

As long as I'm not judging myself, circumstances or others, I'm safe. The moment I form an opinion, though, I again become enslaved by the mind.

Entering a huge cavern, the glow of the torchlight is barely penetrating the darkness; instead, its weak rays only accentuate the ominous shadows that flit across cavern walls. Giant pillars of rock emerge from the darkness as our torch dances off their crimson, blue, and black sides, making the cave even more treacherous-looking. The further we descend the smaller we feel: as we go deeper the cave swallows us deep into its belly.

I begin to sense living things in the cave. A movement from dark shadows catches me peripheral vision. I turn me head, and whatever it was is gone. Images are unclear and their movement swift. Even if I don't turn to look, I sense them creeping alongside the widening streambed or crossing low over the large jagged rock formations. These creatures are unnerving, to say the least. I feel for me sword hilt hoping I won't have to use it, but knowing if necessary I will. Stepping down to the bottom of the cave me friends follow. Torchlight flickers across the seemingly endless walls. "We'll rest here," I announce.

Between the constant effort of guarding our minds and the constant climbing up and down through endless caves and narrow passages, we are weary and rest is well-appreciated. None of us has any idea how long we traveled. Kaylu takes off his knapsack, then pulling out packets of food for everyone, we begin to eat. We still have a little water left, which is good because so far we haven't found any fresh water sources as Olgera had told us. Dandi makes a fire from the torch and some wood from his knapsack. We're tired and our heads ache; we only want to sleep. Dandi suggests we take turns sleeping so at least one person is awake to stand guard. I offer to keep first watch.

Soon I'm alone with the glowing fire. The flames form a circle of shadows on the wall that dance and disappear; I wonder if maybe these shadows are me own thoughts floating around me? I find a large flat rock overlooking me mates, and as I sit to take up my sentry duty, even the fire stills and the cave becomes quiet. In silence I reflect on me experiences since the accident with Mom. I want to remember me family, me friends, and life back in me own world, but I dare not, as the cave's power can't be trusted. Neither can me own mind be trusted, which is now intricately connected to the cave's energy.

All I can do is focus on nothing; this is easier said than done. At first I struggle in using me will power, but Will power is only another subtle way for the mind to gain control through desire. Somehow I have to allow the mind to run out of power, but new energy is continuously being created whenever me attention focuses on anything. By putting my attention on something I give it power, almost like creating life itself. Not giving thoughts or opinions to objects is one of the hardest disciplines to learn. The trick is to focus on something symbolizing a reality that the mind can't manipulate or control. This symbol has to personify something that is limitless, something eternal. I think maybe I should use God as me symbol, but very quickly I realize me mental concept of God is too limited to me human emotions and judgments. Me self-imposed limitations will only mold an illusionary image of the Creator, which the cave then creates within me mind. God, it seems, has many faces—or what we think of as God has many faces.

My mind spins in a myriad of concepts only confusing me further; perhaps thinking about love will lead me to stillness. But even love, I'm learning, isn't something easily understood by the mind. So instead I return again to a symbol or image I understand, which for the time being is Jotan.

Sitting on the flat rock overlooking our camp, I close me eyes and think about the child god. Carefully I place his image within me inner vision on the spot between me eyes; the eye of the Soul. Some call it the mind's eye or the single eye. I remember a passage in the Bible speaking about the single eye. I wonder if this is it? The little book <u>The Way of the Traveler</u> says if I start from this spot between me brows and use the proper breathing techniques, I can reach inside and find stillness. I keep staring into the inner eye and listen. At first, all is quiet and the process effortless, but then I hear a shuffle to the left of me, then to the right. A rock falls some distance away; the campfire crackles. Sounds echoing around me slowly begin to merge together, blending in me mind and then becoming one. I feel a slight pressure in me ear, then a popping sound as if I'm riding in a car coming down from a high mountain. I take several deep breaths and again listen. Sounds become clearer, sounding like a breeze whistling within me. Far off in the distance another sound moves closer. I focus my attention even more, and as I do, tinkling sleigh bells near. Listening intently I'm letting everything within me consciousness drop away; all that matters is the sound and looking at the image of Jotan. Pulsating vibrations spread through me body; me heart beats in response to the rhythmic pulse. Light within me inner vision moves inward with the constant rhythm of me heart. The jingling bells change to a slight buzzing sound. Beyond the bells, something is growing closer—gradually merging with the bells, creating an even higher note—similar to the buzzing of bees. Light becomes brighter, slowly fading as it swirls and separates from the center. The buzzing increases and changes to the single note of a high-pitched flute. I hold me attention onto the swirling image of intense light. The light separates and then merges again and again. As the flute goes higher, my awareness expands to follow the enticing sound.

Jotan the child god steps from the light into me full inner vision; a slight smile dances on his face, and his voice echoes within me mind. *"Very good, Hugh, you found one of the ways to contact me in your inner kingdom."* I keep calm, knowing instinctively that releasing any energy from my mind, emotions or body will end the communication. The boy with the gentle smile looks happy at my success, and he spreads his arms wide in a welcoming gesture. *"You contacted me by creating my image through the Light and Sound. None of this would be possible if you didn't have the discipline to shut down the mind. You are learning that your imagination is the key to creating the image my true self can fill."*

I force myself to stay calm.

Jotan continues. *"You have reached a bridge in your journey, Hugh; from here on in, you need to make wise choices and show courage in order to survive. So far, the darkness only tests you; it probes and searches to find a weakness within. Watch your mind like the cat watches the mouse, and remember! The greatest tool the mind will use to enslave you will be desire; it is imperative that you separate yourself from its dark clutches. In time you will achieve an attitude of non-attachment, but until then, remember, desire is the cause of all pain and all fear. It is a fact that when you begin to desire something you become a slave to it. When this happens, the dark power works its magic. If you are willing to give up desire, then you will pass through this cave effortlessly."*

For the first time I attempt to respond to this inner vision. *"How does one recognize desire when it takes on so many forms and feelings?"*

Jotan stares for a moment into me eyes then replies. *"A story in your world about St. Anthony of the Desert illustrates how this insidious desire works its illusions over the mind. St. Anthony fought against the demons of desire, but what he was really fighting were his own illusions arising out of his feelings, mental aberrations or*

mental pictures. St Anthony created his own demons from his own desires thinking that the desire was God's will. This is what you must be aware of, especially in this cave. These mental pictures appeared in St. Anthony's universe as attachments, just as yours will. All travelers who are seekers of truth must confront this same power sometime in their journey. For each it is different, but for all it is the same energy, creating false realities from your loves, your losses, and from your passions—but most of all, from your fears. Do not forget what has been told. There are forces that do not want you to attain your goal and will fight you to the end, but if you are persistent and practice looking within, you can pass through their traps."

Jotan's eyes smile as his words echo deep within me mind. *"The greatest weapon you have is love. Use it. This is the first and most basic lesson taught to all travelers journeying to find their kingdom. It is the safest way for the traveler to follow. This cave has many names, one of them is 'The Dark Night of the Soul.' It is a feathery world that is shaped according to the one who controls the power. The darkness can make it fearful or perhaps make it warm and inviting; whatever way it uses this power, the cave's objective is to catch you off-guard. If this happens, the cave's subordinates entrap those foolish enough to believe their fear-driven whisperings. Keep your attention on the melodies that emerge from within you, these sounds and others will assist you at every turn if you allow them.*

"The Sound Current is your life stream and acts as a power center to all existence; it will light your way when all else fails. The cave has power, but it is power directed by your thoughts and images. The cave is the veil that separates an ignorant man from his divine destiny; in some ways, it is so subtle that even the highest and finest thought cannot pierce it. Yet the veil is also the primitive base desires in man, which you must learn to strip away to experience true freedom for yourself. It is the mind's illusions that bind man to his material world. Do not assume illusion cannot hurt you; on the contrary, within its own sphere of influence it is deadly and can cause great harm and even death. Beware at all times!"

The Light and Sound fades, and just as Jotan's image disappears, I feel a sudden jerk as if someone's yanking me head back. For a few seconds I feel as if I've awakened suddenly from a dream. Suddenly, I hear a groan and a rushing sound to me left; I tense and spring back, and as I do, I draw me sword and steady myself. Instantly, a crushing weight falls on me back, and putrid hot breath assails my nostrils. I pitch myself forward and roll, trying to get whatever it is off me—the hateful creature hangs on, digging its claws into my chest and thighs. As it tries to tear at me throat with its snarling black mouth, I manage to stand up and thrust myself backwards, slamming the creature into the rough rock wall. Screaming, it finally lets go, and I turn and face the foul thing bent on killing.

Eyes like a snake are staring at me.

The nose of a lizard folds back and forth as the thing snarls. Its high forehead curves down over its back like a reptile; its body is black except for shades of drab green and pale yellow under its chin, arms, and legs. The eyes have a look of madness as it stares at me. Standing five feet tall on man-like legs, its long arms flex, and its tail flips in anger. The beast crouches getting ready to spring; it curls its upper lip exposing jagged, yellow and gray teeth in black gums. I gag on the smell of this scaly being. The creature tenses, getting ready to leap, and without thinking, I kneel down on one knee as the creature springs.

The sword takes on a life of its own, moving faster than the creature's leap; with a vicious slice it crosses the beast's stomach, spilling its organs and dark blood on the cavern floor. The thing utters a guttural moan and falls at me feet. For a few seconds I'm just looking at the beast as its tail waves and pounds the ground while life slowly seeps from it. The beast is dead, but even as I stare into the lifeless reptilian face I feel the presence of more foul, smelly creatures. To me left from the dark recesses in the cave's wall I see their snake-like faces staring at me with a look of madness flashing in their eyes. I turn and sense movement to me right; I again assume a fighting posture. Me heart is that of just a boy, but the sword somehow wrenches the innate primal warrior from deep within me to the conscious mind—survival is all that matters. I tense, me heart beats faster and eyes search; all me senses are heightened. I feel the creatures creeping closer, preparing to attack, and instinctively I back against the cave wall; the stench from the dead creature along with the live ones is suffocating. Holding the sword in front of me I bend slightly at the knees; the sword again takes on a life of its own, glowing dark crimson while it moves back and forth searching for more blood. I stop thinking about what to do and surrender to the sword's power, all of its fighting talent drains into me. I neither think nor feel—me every move is from pure instinct, the mind at this point is only in the way. The sword continues to search for more victims, its action a total contradiction to me prior experience with it. Before, the sword was a vehicle for knowledge—almost wise at times—now it's merciless. Once drawn from the scabbard for war, its nature becomes that of a master warrior; if drawn for blood, the sword has only one goal: to slay any opponent foolish enough to attack.

The creatures gather, forming a half circle; crawling closer, tongues slither from their vicious mouths. I ready myself. As I stare at the beasts me mind fights to assert itself. Doubt creeps into me thoughts, manifesting seemingly from nowhere and whispering death. The cave's power feeds on thoughts and feelings buried deep within me, the mind unleashes them so fear can take control. Me muscles tense even more, me heart beats faster. More of the creatures crawl from behind rocks, a horrible feeling in me gut surges through me body. The sword in all its magnificence wavers: slowly, gradually, it is losing its bright crimson glow. My arms weaken as fear filters its way deep into me heart. Instead of the warrior's ability flooding me mind from the sword, the cave is drawing out fears buried inside a scared four-year-old boy in a dark cave in Scotland. Fear feeds its way into the hilt of the deadly weapon; the creatures smell it. They creep closer for the kill. Sweat drips from me forehead, the hilt of the sword feels slippery in my grip; anxious eyes dart to the left and then to the right, there is no escape. Backing up even tighter against the cave wall, I hadn't realized this maneuver leaves me little room to fight. For the second time in me life, I feel sheer terror; my traumatized mind screams in panic.

It c-can't end l-like this!

What about M-Mom, me f-f-friends Ka-Kaylu and Dandi? They w-will all die because of me c-co-cowardice. The beasts are close, ready to make their kill. I try to block out the fear, but it only increases; my mind's totally out of control. Just then, a loud shout from behind the creatures startles the beasts; they hesitate and scatter, leaving an opening in the middle of their death circle.

Dandi jumps from behind a small dirt mound behind the beasts and plunges into their midst, swinging an enormous stone club with a growl. The beasts howl with fury, scatter, and then regroup behind the raging giant.

I slide into a sitting position against the cave wall, barely able to hold onto the sword. Dandi turns and faces the cave creatures with fire in his eyes, his club held high. Me head's swimming, clouded with despair and fear; the beasts continue to close the gap. At least a dozen of the beasts are crawling on their bellies, others leap on two legs. Dandi yells with loud words, "Get up, boy! Stand by me. Don't let them kill us! We can fight, and we can win, but you need to face them—it is our only chance!" Me mind screams in desperation; no, it's over! A-All is lost, we c-can't fight these odds! I try to still me mind but to no avail. Me arms go numb, me legs are like limp strings as I huddle against the cave wall whimpering like a coward; and then something happens…. I see it! At first I think it's a trick of me mind, but there he is. Kaylu, my companion, me little furry friend who is so gentle, so peaceful, and who always respects life, is running over the small dirt mound carrying a lighted torch, yelling aloud as he runs.

"Hugh! Stand up! Fight! Don't give up!"

I watch me little friend wave the torch back and forth as he scurries toward Dandi. The cave creatures scream in terror at the fire. As they back away, Kaylu rushes into their midst, and something breaks free within me. I watch as me friends try to defend me unconditionally, with no fear, no terror. Their courage, love, and devotion is breaking the mind's hold on me, and power again surges from within; me own fear fades, me only thoughts are to defend me friends.

The sword glows!

Standing up, Soul grips the sword tightly; me heart fills with the confidence of a warrior, I step forward to take my place next to Dandi and Kaylu. Staring down at the writhing black creatures, I raise my sword and feel power surge into me. The beasts hesitate. A few start to creep backwards, but others poise for the attack, intent on their kill; I look at me friends and nod. Instead of waiting for their attack, the three of us move as one into the screaming mass of slithering monsters.

I can't remember much after that: it's a mixture of blurs as I dodge, slash, stab, and cut without mercy. Kaylu scatters a few of the beasts with his torch while Dandi charges into the pack swinging his stone club. Two of the monsters jump Dandi from behind, but he overpowers them without mercy. My blade is deadly and me determination even deadlier. Grabbing one of the creatures as it leaps for me throat I hold the beast in me grip strangling the life from it as I swing me blade and dispatch another one. Dandi reaches behind and pulls off the smelly creatures who have seized his neck and back, stomping them as he clubs another attacking him from the side.

Several of the beasts scurry into the darkness, terrified of Kaylu's blazing torch.

It's over quickly.

I stand on a small mound surrounded by mutilated bodies, severed limbs, and badly wounded beasts. The ten-year-old boy is gone. For the moment, a fierce young warrior stands covered with not only his victims' blood, but also his own.

I nod for me friends to follow. We set off again into the darkness of the cave.

I will never be the same again.

CHAPTER 18 ~ MY
FATHER'S BATTLE

Clark Bailey is a man used to business complications, unsecured promises, clients pulling out of deals, and lack of performance from constituents or corporations, banks, or even government entities.

His career is built on a foundation of solving problems and overcoming barriers threatening his livelihood. His work seems to specifically create situations that constantly threaten to destroy the meticulous and sensitive transactions he relies on. His business life is constantly buffeted like a small boat adrift on the ocean with no oars. Ever since the accident, his focus has been on Ann and Hugh; the most important thing, he thought, is to learn how he can help them in some way. It has been a few months since Ann and Hugh entered the hospital. The primary auto insurance for his wife and son is running out; during the past ten weeks, the constant care and operations have eaten away its value almost to depletion. The medical insurance for his family is from the same company that carries his auto insurance, Allied Equities—a subsidiary of Alliance Insurance. The medical insurance covers an additional $250,000 for each family member. However, the medical insurance becomes secondary if the insurer is in an auto accident. Combined with this coverage is the trucking company's insurance, since as far as Clark surmised, the other driver was responsible therefore they are liable. So far, Allied Inc. representatives are the only ones in contact with the trucking company's insurance carrier. This morning, however, Clark receives a letter from Saturn Insurance:

Mr. Clark Bailey
Claim Number: BT65032
Insured's Name: East Coast Trucking

Dear Mr. Bailey:

We have been notified that Mrs. Ann Bailey and her son Hugh Bailey were involved in an accident on 7/1/14 with our insured. The claim has been assigned to my division for handling. Without claiming responsibility or liability, we are notifying you that we are investigating the accident to determine who is at fault. Please use the claim number referenced above on all correspondence and keep us informed of any change in your address and phone number. The statute of limitations for bodily injury to an adult is two years from the date of the accident; for a minor who is injured, there is one additional year.

    The driver for East Coast Trucking was killed in the accident and now we are informed that Mrs. Ann Bailey and Hugh Bailey are both in a coma unable to communicate. It is unfortunate that there are no witnesses to the actual accident as well. The police report does not indicate which driver was at fault. We will notify you once the investigation is completed. Thank you.

    SATURN INSURANCE COMPANY.
    David Harding
    Claims Adjuster
    Sept 30, 2014

    He reads the letter twice.
    This is unbelievable!
    His wife's car was crushed in the rear; the large truck had only front-end damage. The truck was found on its side off the road, but paint and parts of his wife's car were embedded underneath the front of the truck. How could there be any question of fault? He assumed the trucking company's insurance would have to accept responsibility and pay the hospital bills. Since his auto insurance is almost-depleted, he'll have to depend on the medical insurance to take over. At the rates the hospital is charging, this secondary insurance will also be gone in a few months. If Ann and Hugh don't come out of the coma by the time the policy's value expires, the decision to disconnect the life support could become a real threat. Normally, if the patients are conscious and receiving treatment for injuries that would be expected to heal, the treatment continues no matter what. In Ann's case—and possibly even Hugh's—there is no certain outcome. When patients are on life support, doctors can't predict what will happen, and their approach varies widely; some feel it's hopeless, while others keep up life support until the insurance runs out. For the trucking company to take over as the primary carrier, it will need to be proven that their driver was responsible for the accident. If either his son or wife awaken, there will be an eyewitness and Saturn will have to pay. However, if neither wakes up, Saturn Insurance could—and likely would—battle the claim in court, which could take years to settle.
    Clark is at a loss about his options; he doesn't know enough about the legal circumstances surrounding insurance claims. In Ireland, he never had to be concerned about medical care since it was just provided for the citizens through their taxes. He realizes he needs help, and he needs it fast. Ambulance chasers are on every corner, but what Clark needs is someone he can trust, someone who will fight for the client, and not just for his fee. What savings he has is enough to get things started, but he will need someone who will take the case pro bono or on contingency and stick with it no matter what! Between trying to learn how to communicate with his son, taking care of Melody, and being there for his wife, Clark has his menu full. Now to add to these burdens, he will have to fight his own

insurance company, find an attorney, start legal proceedings with the trucking company's insurance, and prevent the hospital from taking his wife and son off life support. He has only two weeks left before he will have to start work, because if he continues to ignore business, he could lose his clientele as well as the funds he invested as seed money for two projects that are almost ready to close.

The more he thinks about the whole situation, the more depressed and doubtful he becomes: how is he to handle all of this? He is only one person; the odds are against him, and he knows it. Not only does he have to deal with all of these problems, but he also has to do so while suffering from heartache so heavy and gloomy that it seems like a dark cloud hanging over his head.

Preparing for bed that evening he barely has the strength to get undressed. His mind won't shut down; the constant reminder of all that's at stake fills him with a deep fear and sadness. No matter which way he looks, he sees no way out. Ann, Hugh, and Melody are all depending on him; if he fails, all is lost.

As he lies on his back staring up at the ceiling in the darkness, his mind persists in not letting him sleep. He tries thinking about the meditation exercises he has been studying, remembering one of the techniques about calming the mind. He must concentrate on something he loves, which he chooses to be Hugh. His mind races wildly as he fights to keep his attention focused. Bit by bit, as he thinks of his son, his mind calms, and as he drifts off to sleep, he imagines sitting with his son in the tree house, looking into the stillness of the great tree.

As he sleeps, he dreams.

He knows it's a dream; he knows his physical body is in his bed, yet somehow here he is, very aware of who he is, and fully understanding what is happening around him. It's strange at first, but as he grasps the significance of being awake in his own dream, he begins to experiment. He's alone, it's daylight. He has just climbed the rope ladder and is pulling himself into the tree house. Seeing familiar objects again remind him that his body is still asleep in his home. Looking around the tree house seems to be important for some reason. His attention falls on the contents of the room. The more he looks, the more he realizes that each item he sees is actually a reminder of a period in his life. The old sofa, the hat rack, along with the old throw rug he used so many years ago: each item brings back not only a memory, but also a feeling. It dawns on him that each object in the dream is actually a part of his personality. He identifies which part by the way he feels at the very moment he sees them. Staring at the items he feels they are the most important things in his life. His mind holds vivid memories of not just the items, but the feelings associated with them during certain periods in his life. The old throw rug makes him feel useless, rejected, but why? For the longest time, the rug has been in the attic and forgotten, no longer having a purpose or a reason to exist. He sometimes feels like he's something everyone steps on; like the rug, he's being used to satisfy the dreams and goals of others, but he himself has no purpose in his own life. He's forgotten why he has come into this life in the first place. Over the span of his life he's stuffed his true goals deep into the attic of his subconscious. When he looks at the hat rack, he feels life has defeated him. Why? Mainly because all the wonderful dreams and goals he had when he was young now just hang like the hats somewhere in his mind—forgotten and unused. The old sofa makes him feel content and satisfied with life, even though he never achieved any of his dreams. Like the sofa, he sits around, letting whatever happens, happen…always being the effect instead of the cause…always hiding his dreams away under its cushions… each failure the result of fear and lack of decisiveness. These feelings are laying bare his whole life. If he continues to live and act the way he always has, and makes the same choices based on his current feelings and his limited perspective of life, then any new dreams will also become nothing more than past memories. He could lose everything by allowing his attitude to stay the same. This becomes clearer when he looks out the window.

The window edges melt into the tree's interior. Branches stretch, growing longer reaching, expanding and changing. Clark can't pull his eyes from the changing scene. He steps closer to the window. As he stares out, his awareness changes; it expands and reaches deep down to an unknown part of him. A surge of energy rushes up to his consciousness; his mind fills with new thoughts. The window becomes a portal, an entrance to a lost part of him. As he stares out, a great knowingness gently fills his mind. A simple understanding awakens within him. Love sweeps him through the portal that is his mind, the living tree swiftly becomes a part of him. Limbs reach out, touching life. He is no longer a husband, a businessman or even the father he once was; for a brief moment, he is something more. He discovers that this new self isn't entirely unknown to him; as feelings grow, he gets the strange sensation that he is going home. Once he was lost, his mind concealing his true self. For this moment, he remembers. The tree serves as a focal point revealing an open door to Soul. The limbs gently pull his thoughts and feelings together. As they do, he feels his life is so loved, so free and so deeply filled with purpose. Staring deeper into the tree, colors shimmer and shift as his awareness grows. Brilliant colors pass through the tree, the sky changes colors continuously. Unable to pull his attention away from the amazing sight in front of him, Clark feels himself changing even as the tree changes. Just as quickly as this realization begins, it begins to fade. He tries to hang on. He doesn't want to go back to the prison his mind has created. He wants to stay free. Freedom is what allows him to remember who he really is. Even wrapped in this dream, he realizes the experience is mystical, similar to what he has been reading about; he is a part of the whole, a part greater than before, but still limited in time and space. The belief that he is something separate is gone; this belief of separation created a prison within his mind. He must free himself from this mental prison permanently. This can only be done by embracing himself as a part of the whole existence within spirit.

His prison bars have been created over the years from his fears, doubts, passions, desires, and attitude within his mind. Negative habits are his guards, but even more than this, he knows the warden who constructed this prison will never let him go as long as he lives with the same limitations, desires, and doubts: he will stay trapped forever.

Feeling himself being sucked back into his mind, a lingering thought follows him. No one but he has the keys to the prison door; the warden doesn't have the keys. He knows that the warden is his own ego; the personality that mind has created over the years from his fears and desires. Yes, this ego is what controls his entire life.

His eyes open; he's back in his bed, wide awake! Wonderfully alive.

This waking is a moment of joy and gratitude, full of anticipation—the way life is supposed to be. It's late morning and even as the dreams slip away, the residual leaves him with a deep feeling of gratitude. He's no longer the result of his body's passions, desires, fears or ego; for in this moment, he sees life only as pure freedom. Never again will he bow to the fears and limitations his mind creates from the past or react to others' fears, other people's sorrows, doubts, and desires. There is a perfectly simple plan for all life, and he assures himself that he isn't about to lose this childlike trust or simplicity again.

Clark Bailey has finally understood that if he stops letting his mind get in the way of his life and its choices, then help will arrive. He can't always choose the type of help, but if he trusts in life, if he trusts in himself, then everything will work out. The mind isn't who he is; the mind is only a tool. Up to this point, mind has dictated and selected what he thought, what he did and how he reacted; this routine is over. Clark knows now he is more than mind. The dream reminded him of who he really is, and somehow he knows the essence of his real self is linked with freedom, simplicity, wisdom, and love. Whatever comes into his life, he will accept and deal with. This new warrior attitude will not allow defeat to be a part of who he is any longer.

CHAPTER 19 ~ HUGH'S UNEXPECTED CHALLENGE

Kaylu and Dandi pack up their gear to continue their trek through the cave. I lead as we leave the huge cavern and enter one of the cave's narrow passageways. Following a small dry streambed, I can see and feel it changing; it's getting moist with small pockets of water oozing out from long cracks.

Kaylu watches from behind as they are walking. The boy's walk is different; it's bolder, more confident—each stride strengthens his determination. He notices other changes, too. Hugh is no longer the lost bewildered boy who found him by the river's edge. His skin is taut, his muscles are lean, and his face is losing some of its boyish features. His eyes no longer reflect the innocence of youth. Instead, they are deep-set and look like the eyes of someone who has seen and experienced too much of life. Dandi notices these changes also, and wonders if they are because of the cave's influence. Hugh's no longer hesitant; he's direct and precise not only in his actions, but in his mannerisms and communication. He no longer asks but commands: not harshly, but like a leader who is in control.

The streambed's damp mushy sand sticks to our boots, making our progress slippery and slow. As we turn a bend, we hear flowing water. I stop and turn, and forgetting I'm supposed to use words, I project spontaneously, *"We must be careful; Olgera told me that once the streambed starts to get moist, the underground river is surfacing; as the water gathers on the surfaces, some areas can be soft and deep—in other words, quicksand."* I continue walking, testing each step carefully, especially whenever crossing any damp areas or small water pools. Me torch burns low. The other torch is in Dandi's backpack; we'll have to use it soon. As the streambed widens we are crisscrossing over more water bubbling to the surface. Pools merge together forming a stream that flows for a few yards and then disappears back into the sand. Dandi's great weight hinders his walking. His feet sink deeper as even more water bubbles to the surface. A long period has passed since we left the large cavern where we camped. We're getting hungry and need to rest. As the streambed descends at a steeper incline, I finally stop and aloud I promise, "Once we get on level ground, we'll eat and rest. I don't think we need to worry about quicksand as we descend, so let's pick up the pace." We push forward, anxious to get off this steep downward slope.

Not only is it hard to walk on, but the water is now constantly flowing, which forces us to walk to the side, slightly above the stream. We climb over large rocks trying to avoid little waterfalls pouring over the rocks. I'm trying not to think too much about the danger of the cave's power and what it can do to the mind, especially when thinking excessively. It's a constant battle to keep my mind blank. Most of my attention is on me feet: where to place them and keeping me balance, watching out not to slip on the wet rocks. The ground finally levels off and the streambed becomes a small river. We walk briskly beside the flowing waters. Sometimes we have to either jump or traipse around little jetties created by fast-rising currents.

As Kaylu and I turn a bend, we hear Dandi yell out. Looking back, we watch in horror as our friend struggles to free himself from a sand pool that's sucking him under. Dandi wiggles and weaves trying to move to dry land. We both run back, at the same time pulling our ropes off our waists; tossing Dandi our ropes, we try pulling him from the muck. At first our pulling seems to help, but it soon becomes obvious that no matter how hard we pull against the wet, cloying sand, the giant's weight is too much against us; eventually, we'll have to either cut the rope or get pulled into the muck ourselves.

Watching Dandi's thrashing and desperate attempts to move forward, I send a thought to him, *"Be still! The more ya' struggle, the deeper and quicker you'll sink."* Dandi stops struggling; he tries to be perfectly still as Kaylu and I tug furiously from our end, still to no avail. Even though we are slowing the sinking process, we aren't stopping it; if something isn't done quickly, Dandi will be pulled down into the dark sand hole and be lost forever. We only have moments to figure out what to do to save him…

From out of nowhere, a rope suddenly appears from the rocks above; seconds later, another rope falls from the cliff ledge. I cast about; looking above, I see two ropes dangling over the edge of a precipice. From above us a voice calls out. "Throw the ropes over to your friend; we have secured them to a boulder. That will stop him from sinking." I grab the two ropes and toss them to Dandi, and immediately after the giant ties the ropes around his chest, the sinking stops. Small pebbles begin rolling down the steep cliff as someone or something starts climbing down. Dandi pulls on the ropes, hand over hand, slowly using his great strength to extract himself from the dark sandy muck.

The voice from the darkness again calls out, "You should be more careful walking by these waters." As I turn in the voice's direction, from out of the cliff's darkness a girl emerges into the dim torchlight. I stare for a moment—somewhat surprised—but before I can say anything, another voice calls out, "Many a soul has been lost to the deep sands of this cave." A second girl, who appears about the same age as the first, steps out from the shadows.

By this time, Dandi has pulled himself free and is shaking off the clinging gunk. He lumbers exhaustedly over to where I'm standing. Kaylu stays hidden in the shadows behind us. The two girls walk out from the darkness as comfortably as if they belong to the cave itself. Both are beautiful. One has flowing light red hair with deep green eyes shining brightly in the torch's firelight. The other is just as stunning, with long dark hair cascading over her shoulders in deep curls. Her eyes are crystal blue and her dark eyebrows enhance her pixie-like face. The girls stand side by side; both are the same height; both have curvaceous figures clothed in dark brown tunics that wrap around their tiny waists and end about six inches above their knees. The girl with red hair speaks.

"My name is Karla; this is my sister, Loren. Who are you?"

I'm silent for a few seconds, and then regaining my composure, I reply, "My name is Hugh, this is Dandi; thank you for your help." The girls exchange glances. Karla steps closer and in a mocking whisper asks, "And who is the silent one, hidden in the shadows behind you?" Seeing that Kaylu is exposed, I motion for him to step forward. "This is Kaylu of the Wuskies; we're traveling through the mountain to reach the Land of Light and Darkness." The girls again look at one another and then walk over to where their ropes are lying. Both begin to pull the ropes, wrapping them in loops around their shoulders. Loren replies, "Not many have the courage to travel through this mountain; most are lost before they ever get this far." I step closer and shrug my shoulders, "Our need is great: we've been fortunate so far, and your help was greatly appreciated."

Dandi also steps closer to the two girls; they both look tiny compared to his great bulk. Stretching down, he bows slightly and places his hand on his heart. "I thank you for saving me; are you in this cave by yourselves?"

Both girls take the now coiled ropes from around their shoulders and stuff them into their packs. "We were with our father and his guards trying to reach the Land of Light; one by one, we lost our guards. Then with only our father and us remaining, we three kept traveling along the river; our hope was to find the other side where we were to meet with others. But then our father, too, was lost. The cave dwellers ambushed him. We have been alone since then. Our camp is just over those rocks up ahead; that location seems to be the safest. At least it's free from cave dwellers."

I was surprised and suspicious, so I ask, "How have you survived by yourselves?"

Both girls start to say something at the same time, and then laughing, just Karla speaks. "Our camp is just a short walk from here. We have the provisions our guards were carrying and water is plentiful. We also have fire starters."

I can't believe these two girls—who are not much older than me, in this new form—are surviving in these caves alone! I never had much use for girls back home, but these two did save Dandi, and they obviously seem to know their way around this part of the cave. If their story is true, then they'd be invaluable, since they came from the direction that we are heading.

Kaylu emerges and greets the girls with his joyful smile and trusting eyes; the girls are excited to meet him, as if he's something new and wonderful. Karla asks, "Is the furry little one from the Land of Light?"

I nod. "Yes, he's helping me in my journey. He isn't used to being around many people so he'll probably be as curious about you and the land you come from as you are of him!"

Both girls reach out and take Kaylu's hands. Karla whispers to Loren; "He's so cute; the light in him is bright and strong."

Loren kindly asks, "Would you and your friends like to come back to our camp for food and rest?" All three of us nod and start picking up our equipment.

As we are walking, the girls talk in whispers, without ever seeming to complete a sentence, glancing back occasionally as if to make sure we are still following. My attention is drawn to the girls' exposed legs and rounded curves;

little is hidden with the short tunics each wore especially since the two females walk directly in front of me. I'm embarrassed and confused by me reaction to them.

It isn't long before we come upon a flat area encircled by large rocks and cliffs, and a river flowing lazily past the camping area and beyond. A small inlet draws a gurgling channel of the river into a secluded pool surrounded by rocks and a small sandy beach. To the right of the pool, a small waterfall splashes down softened rock cliffs, eroded from years of wear. A small tent stands a few yards from the river's edge.

Two fires light up the waters; one burns brightly between the tent and river, and another by the pool glows by some means unknown to me. The girls hurry ahead and begin opening packs of breads, meats, and fruits. We're already hungry, but seeing the assorted foods reminds us how long it has been since we had last eaten. Olgera gave us plentiful food but with no variety; some bread, some sort of pudding substance, and some dried fruit. The girls' fruit is encased in hard shells, which keep it fresh and sweet. The change of diet is welcomed, and soon we are eating a wonderful meal. The drink is cold, the meat preserved in salt is flavorful, and succulent fruit is a fitting end to the meal.

Once we finish, I look at me companions, and realize all three of us are covered with mud, sand, and clay—even dried blood from our battle still cake our arms, legs, faces, and hair. Our clothes reek with the smells of our battle and journey. I'm embarrassed again...I fully realize how foul we must look and smell.

The girls insist we are their guests, and quickly walk over to gather our plates and clean up the dining area. Looking over at the pool of inviting water, I send a thought to me companions, "*Let's get cleaned up. We have unused clothes in our packs—this would be a good time to use them.*" Both nod silently in agreement.

I explain aloud we would like to go swimming in the pool to clean up, and both girls smile and heartily agree. Picking up our packs, we walk behind large rocks surrounding the pool. Stripping down, we dive into the clear sparkling waters. The water is cool and refreshing. The little waterfall makes a perfect shower to rinse off; it isn't long before we are diving and splashing like school boys. I climb the rocks just above the falls and dive deep into the clear pool. The water not only washes the mud and gunk from me body, but clears me mind and refreshes the spirit. Upon surfacing I hear a splash behind me. Quickly turning around, me mouth falls open and a spray of water is shot in my face. Choking and gasping, I tread water as I watch Karla and Loren swim toward me. What's troubling me wasn't just the fact that I'm naked, but both girls are also stripped down to nothing, and they are swimming quickly in my direction! As the boy I am inside, I've always felt indecisive, nervous, and somewhat disinterested in girls. If anything, I was just plain shy. Girls are not something I had on my mind much. Now with this older body, I feel it responding to their nakedness; me mind and body collide. It's as if two people are inside me: one is the shy ten-year-old boy while the other is a young man with the body of a seventeen-year-old raging with hormones and energy. The girls are close now. I duck down under the water to try to swim away. Me body is saying yes, but I'm saying no. I have to make it back to shore.

The girls are adept at swimming and soon they are immediately behind me. The waters are clear; I look behind me and see the two naked girls in a light haze. Kicking strongly, I come to the shore and quickly run for me clothes. My embarrassment will know no end if they see me in this condition!

Behind the rocks I'm slipping on me shirt and pants just moments before they get to the shore. Giggling, they both run to the camp toward their lean-to. I take a little time before coming out from behind the rocks to make sure all is tucked in and I'm presentable.

Kaylu and Dandi both watch the entire scene from the cliff above the waterfall, and I sense their thoughts. Instead of thinking how embarrassing or humorous it is, they are confused at what they have just seen. To them, the interaction between the female and male species is as natural as eating, breathing, or just plain living. Codes of conduct, embarrassment, and morals are not a part of their reality. The natural responses of the body and propagation of the species, or just the joy of giving oneself to each other, is a natural part of their environment and behavior. My behavior was confusing to say the least; it's something I realize they couldn't understand.

I walk back to the camp, avoiding the giggling girls as they dress and comb their hair. Me body is still feeling flushed; my mind keeps bringing up images of their naked bodies running from the water, and the more I try to stop thinking about it, the more me body responds. I unroll me bedroll, lay down on me side and turn me back to everyone. Soon the camp is quiet. Only the steady breathing of my companions fills the darkness.

I awake to a strange sound.

Turning around, I see the girls pounding and dipping something into the river. I stand up and check me pack. I then walk over. "Hey, what're you doing?"

Loren looks up and smiles. "We are washing your clothes—the odor is more than we could stand. We hope you don't mind."

Looking back to me bedroll and then turning to face the girls, I ask, "What did you do with the book that was in me jacket?" Both girls point to me bedroll. I walk back and ruffle through me bedding; there on the bottom of the bedroll lies The Way of the Traveler.

During our hike through the cave there hadn't been enough light to read the little book. With the light provided from the girls' fires, I might be able to read a few pages. Walking to the secluded fire by the pool behind the rocks, I find a comfortable place to sit. For the first time since we arrived at the girls' camp, I look at the fire starters. They are actually a lot like the charcoal briquettes Da' uses for barbeques, except these burn brighter and longer. Taking a few of these rocks, I toss them into the fire, and within seconds they flame brightly.

Everyone is still sleeping or washing by the other fire, so I think I'm alone. Opening the little book to read, I hear a noise behind me. Loren walks toward me. She picks up the bag containing the fire starter rocks, and at the same time she cautions, "We must be careful in using these rocks. They burn for a long time, but we have barely half of what we started with. If the rocks run out, we are at the mercy of the darkness." I feel embarrassed about adding the rocks to the already burning campfire; glancing in the other direction, I change the topic. "Are you two still planning to go ahead to the other side of the mountain?" Loren steps closer. Looking up into my face she speaks softly, almost in a whisper. "We are not sure what we will do. Now that we have met you, we are wondering if perhaps we should turn back. If we proceed, we will be alone again. From what you have told us, the cave dwellers live in larger packs deeper in the cave."

The mere thought of the girls confronting a dozen cave dwellers makes me shudder. "I can't tell you what to do, but I can tell you this. The two of you are no match for what lays behind us."

Loren steps closer and placing her hand on me arm, she says, "Karla and I feel much better now that you and your friends are here, and we both appreciate your concern."

A warm energy rushes into me from her touch; I look down, then I try looking away. Loren's blue eyes shine like crystals in the firelight; her skin has a soft glow to its whiteness—never have I been attracted to a girl like this. Trying to hide me feelings only makes me more vulnerable.

Loren notices me nervousness and she steps closer, pressing her body up against me chest. "We both feel safer with you and your friends, and I for one feel we can be of great value to your journey if we decide to go back."

I take a quick breath; me body's senses are again churning deep within. Loren's pressing close as she reaches up and lightly touches me cheek, then she is tilting me face to hers, and me mind swirls as warm feelings grow, making me feel weird, but pleasurable. Before I can act, Loren presses her lips against mine and pulls me close into her embrace.

I close my eyes, feeling the softness of her lips against mine: she pulls me closer, and without thinking I let my arms encircle her. That's the only signal she needs. Slowly, gently, her lips again press against mine. I feel her body's warmth, and me arms slide down her back feeling her softness. Her small waist squirms as she nestles even closer into me arms. Following her lead, I slowly kneel down bringing her with me. Gently, very gently she pushes forward, slowly sliding deeper into my embrace. Lying on me back with Loren wrapped in me arms I feel her becoming more aggressive and more sensuous. Her soft tongue brushes against me lips gently parting them. I can't really think about what's happening—I'm too busy surrendering to the pleasures this beautiful girl and me body are creating. In response to her kiss, my lips part, and the kiss becomes a fire igniting me senses. Loren's body moves across mine signaling me body to respond. I'm confused, embarrassed, and excited at the same time; pleasures run though this body triggering basic instincts to respond. The boy I was is fading quickly from me mind. A new me has arrived at a different place, experiencing something I have never known, something that seems to have liquefied me into a sensuous pool of feelings, responses, and pleasure never experienced before. Loren continues moving as me hands explore the gentle curves of her body, her breathing quickens, she moves in a pulse of passion and begins exploring under me shirt; her touch is soft but electric. Me skin heats in the movements of her passion; slowly I'm being pulled into a deep sensuous arousal, me body moving to the rhythm of hers. Every touch, every kiss evokes new pleasures racing through this body. I'm no longer a shy, indecisive young man; me body has taken over, me young mind is racing downhill with no way to stop from drowning in a pool of pleasure and desire. Loren's tunic is now up and over her hips, quickly she slides completely out of it and I'm out of control, me body is on fire as I feel for the first time a woman's power. Hands explore areas that had before been forbidden, as I roll over holding Loren in me arms the soft firelight contrasts against her white skin and my lips touch her neck. Instinctively, I taste her skin; it's soft and moist. Her scent and taste carry me even higher as I cover her neck with kisses and small, playful nips. Loren responds by pushing me head lower. Feeling for the first time the soft roundness of a woman, I'm on fire. My mouth tastes her light sweat as she pulls me further into her embrace, and we are lost to passion as Loren's hands pull at me shirt sliding it over me head. Feeling her skin against mine, I succumb to the fiery pleasure growing in me loins. The beautiful girl pulls me over her body, her hands exploring untouched areas; I'm approaching a place that has no return—lips and hands are carrying me to the edge of a vast unknown universe. I pull her tighter in me arms, kissing her deeply as our bodies move in unison, her body urging me onward. Driven in the heat of passion I position myself over this beautiful young creature, watching her face blossom as anticipation fills her senses, and then Loren reaches out and pulls me even closer…

Without warning, a sudden loud scream rings through the cave.

I jump back, grabbing me shirt at the same time I'm looking around us, and Loren sits up holding her tunic to her chest. Again a scream rings out, filling the cavern with a sudden chill. Pulling me boots on, I grab my sword from its scabbard and race around the pool to the main camp. Kaylu and Dandi are standing with their backs to Karla, who is lying on the ground behind them. Dandi has his club held high while Kaylu holds a large rock. Half out of the river a head surfaces that to me looks like that of a large alligator, but the beast begins to rise out of the water on two legs instead of crawling. Me head is spinning from me encounter with Loren: now, I advance forward, sword drawn.

A deep growl rolls through the cave. I come alongside Dandi and Kaylu, and the beast stands even taller as it emerges from the depths of the river. As the beast comes closer, I see the creature's head more clearly: it is reptilian, without a doubt. Its eyes are on the side of the creature's head much like a horse. Completely out of the water, it appears to be about ten feet tall and is very clearly male. The creature thunders again, only deeper this time. Eyes flash as the reflection of the fire illuminates his face; he has no tail, and the body is built similar to a man's, except larger. His back and legs are covered in scales while its chest area and belly are thick bare skin, with a light grayish hue. His face is shaped like an alligator, but blunted and shorter at the nose, almost making it appear pig-like. His feet are webbed between what appear to be toes and claws. His claws are like small knives that form his hands. The beast's most prominent feature is his exposed genitalia; the creature is obviously aroused. My eyes dart across the scene, and I realize in an instant that he has one clear goal: Karla.

Karla must have been finishing the wash when the creature bubbled up from the depths; after screaming and backing away from the shore, Dandi and Kaylu had raced to protect the terrified girl, and now they have stationed themselves in front of her. With a slight stoop to his body, the creature strides directly toward them; I step forward, brandishing my sword so the creature can see what he's about to confront. However, the river man-beast doesn't hesitate; he's focused on one goal—the lustful look in the creature's eyes says it all. Dandi lets out a yell while rushing forward with his club, but as he reaches striking distance the beast bends his knees and leaps straight up and over the approaching giant! The beast is now just seconds away from Karla.

Guttural noises, combined with his heavy breathing are passion gone wild: Karla screams. I step between her and the river beast. My head is about level with the beast's stomach; he has no weapons except his massive arms, claws, and teeth...and the creature keeps coming. Not knowing why I yell, "Stop! Or you die!" Undeterred, the beast moves swiftly and leaps over me too; he is now standing over Karla. Kaylu holds Karla's shoulders and head up as he backs off, trying to drag her away from the grotesque body that blazingly exhibits his arousal. The beast is fast; it grabs Karla by the foot and pulls her closer to him. I turn and lunge, driving me sword into the back of the creature's leg. With a howl the beast swiftly turns and slaps me across me chest, sending me reeling a few yards away. Never letting go of Karla, the creature turns and heads back to the riverbank, dragging his screaming prize after him.

Dandi is ready this time.

The creature can't leap while dragging Karla behind him, so Dandi steps forward, and with a crushing blow, hits the beast directly under his chin. The river beast staggers, then dropping Karla for a moment he attempts to recover from the little giant's brutal blow. I jump forward, and without flinching, drive me sword deep into the creature's shoulder before it can recover. Again the creature roars with pain.

Wheeling around, the beast reaches once more for Karla, catching her by one leg and pulling her closer to the river's edge. Karla kicks and fights to be free, but the beast clutches her even more tightly. His left shoulder is useless, but he still has his legs and his right arm, so together with his vicious jaws he's still a deadly opponent. Reaching the river shore, he pulls Karla to his chest and wades deeper into the slow current. Karla is by now beside herself with fear; I rush into the river after the beast but it's too late. As I reach the spot where the creature had last been, I see the very top of his head sink beneath the clear waters of the river. I dive, swimming to where I'd seen the head submerge. I see Karla struggling to free herself from the creature's massive arms; if I don't reach her in time, Karla will either drown or be ravaged by this half-man, half-reptile beast. The river beast is so possessed by lust he is totally unaware of being followed. I swim deeper, trying to get close enough to strike. The creature's intent on Karla makes him vulnerable and blind to the danger pursuing him. He's so absorbed in the young female creature he holds, nothing else matters; I'm almost close enough to strike. Karla's struggling, while the beast is twisting and turning her into position for his passion. The beast is now in front of me, and for a brief moment, I see an opportunity. I quickly lunge at the creature's body and me sword sinks deeply; dark red blood spurts from the wound, joining the many sprays splashing up from the churning water. Karla is free! I see her swimming away from the wounded twisting creature. As I start upward, I look back at the beast and see the gaping wound. The creature's blood floats up like a scarlet ribbon toward the surface of the river; looking down, I watch the creature sink into the deeper waters of the river as blood flows from the wound I delivered. When I surface, I see Dandi helping Karla from the water. Swimming weakly toward shore, I find my footing and stumble up on to the beach. For some reason, I'm feeling sorry for the beast I had just slain. Crawling onto the sand, I'm too unsteady to stand.

Lying on the wet sand I try to catch me breath. Hardly able to move, I reflect on what just happened. Being with Loren had set loose a desire and pleasure that is more powerful than anything I ever imagined; me body and mind was focused on only one thing...to satisfy me desire. My body completely surrendered to this powerful feeling, and I would have followed it to its end if Karla hadn't screamed. The power driving me body forward in passion was no different from the passion driving the creature I had just slain. Although our actions were consensual, I hardly know Loren. Passion and lust had run rampant throughout our bodies, controlling our every move. This body is a powder keg of explosive pleasures and desires, just like the river beast, I succumbed to lust, totally losing control.

I understood the Beast.

This same powerful drive exists in all life, and if allowed to run wild, this power can destroy a person, or even a world. Connected to this power are all the emotions: selfishness, hatred, vanity, and anger, along with love, humor, gratitude, and desire—even happiness—all is linked to this energy.

Sexual power is the current that supplies all the passions of life. It's like a double-edged sword. The power is creative because it triggers the creative flow in man. This creative flow spreads throughout his being, even into the imagination, allowing man to create his world. But if this energy is not controlled through love and disciplined restraint, it can become distorted by the mind. The power gives the ability to create either a world of unfulfilled desires or a world that exhibits the virtues of the Creator. It's each person's choice. Neither aspect is good nor bad. This power can't be judged as man judges other aspects of his reality. The power is neutral, and isn't limited to merely the physical world. The power expresses itself in the lowest forms of life and even reaches up to the divine; it's up to each individual how he or she uses it. If not careful, the power will consume man until his reality is like that of the river beast. Used wisely, it will take Soul to the windows of heaven. Used without discretion, sex can drag man to the bowels of hell. Combined with love, this same power becomes a tool to uplift humankind to their highest potential. Used without love, without feeling, man can and does degrade himself to the level of a beast.

I lay on the wet sand of the beach as these thoughts continue filtering through me consciousness. There's so much to learn. I need to be even more on guard, especially in this cave. The illusion of sex and love can draw a person down into the most subtle of delusions, difficult to resist. Loren is seductive, beautiful, and loving, as any woman could ever be. Even more than this, Loren is a female who knows her power; this young woman has a way of making a boy feel like the man he is meant to be.

CHAPTER 20 ~ FINDING A FRIEND

Morning comes—hot and humid. Melody and Cody are playing in the backyard under the shade trees surrounding their property. Clark sits in the backyard under the patio umbrella, watching. He's thinking of his situation when the phone rings.

Clicking his cell, a voice comes over on the other end. "Mr. Bailey. Mr. Clark Bailey?" the voice anxiously asks.

"Yes, this is Clark Bailey."

"Mr. Bailey, my name is Brandon Lewis, I'm an attorney, and your name was given to me by Dr. Orvitz." Something in the man's voice made Clark feel a little nervous. Usually attorneys mean trouble.

The voice on the other end of the phone continues. "I understand you may have some problems concerning your insurance and the accident involving your wife and son."

A little annoyed, Clark answers sarcastically, "Whatta ya' been doing? Reading me mail? Tis for sure if something doesn't change soon, ya' might say I'll have some problems."

The voice on the other end ignores the sarcasm. "Mr. Bailey, it's of great importance that we get together and talk as soon as possible."

"What for?" Clark snaps, suspicious of this Brandon Lewis.

"Let's just say for the sake of your wife and son, it would be wise for us to meet," the kind voice responded.

Later that afternoon, Clark pulls up to a charming brownstone building that looks more like a small church or someone's home than a legal office. He parks his car and walks through the wrought iron gate. A walkway paved with used red bricks leads to the front porch. The little house is shaded by large trees growing on each side. The arched wooden entry door is stained dark brown with a black wrought-iron antique door handle and lock.

Opening the door, Clark enters a comfortable sitting room with a counter window to the right. A woman's voice speaks from behind a small arched window glass. "May I help you?"

Clark says a bit tentatively, "Yes, I have an appointment with Mr. Lewis."

"Your name…?"

"Bailey, Clark Bailey. I talked with him, um, I mean, I talked with Mr. Lewis earlier this morning."

"Please take a seat. It'll be just a few moments."

Sitting down, Clark picks up a magazine next to his chair and waits. Flipping through the pages, he acts as if he's interested in reading. A few moments later, a side door opens and a man in his late sixties or early seventies walks in. "Mr. Bailey? I'm Brandon Lewis, I'm so glad you could make it today."

With a nod, Clark looks the man over. His hair is a mixture of white and gray, and thinning at the top. He stands maybe five feet seven, and weighs about one hundred seventy pounds. He is wearing a black tweed suit with a vest, white shirt, and a maroon tie. He has a ready smile and a sparkle in his eyes. Shaking hands, Lewis says, "Come in, come in, we have much to talk about."

Brandon Lewis's office is unconventional, so unconventional it looks more like a museum instead of a lawyer's office. The walls are paneled with rich, dark Brazilian nutwood. The floor is a dark, highly polished ipe with a dark green square carpet in the center. Bookshelves lining the walls neatly hold hundreds of books arranged in perfect order. Paintings and posters of exotic countries and animals hang on the wall overlooking an ornate tigerwood desk. Statues of Hindu gods, animals, and angels stand in corners and bookshelves. Two comfortable brown leather armchairs sit in front of the desk.

A massive stone fireplace behind the desk chair sets off the rich ambience of a gentleman's office. Less commonly, crystals are distributed throughout the room; one beautiful blue crystal sits on the desktop next to a silver train that is crafted in great detail and is used as a paperweight. The large window on the far end of the office is covered in dark maroon and green striped drapes.

Mr. Lewis walks over, sits in one of the armchairs in front of the desk, and beckons Clark to join him. "Sit down, sit down, Mr. Bailey; here—let me give you my card. Can I have some tea or coffee brought in?"

Clark sits in the other armchair adjacent to the elderly gentleman. Prying his eyes off the details of the ornate office, he says, "I'm surprised to hear from you. Dr. Orvitz didn't say he talked with anyone concerning my situation." Brandon stares at Clark for a few seconds before he replies. "Doctor Orvitz speaks very highly of you, Mr. Bailey, and he has advised me of some of the details concerning the accident and future medical treatment to your wife and son. To be honest, it's the peculiar nature of your situation that has me interested in your predicament. You see, Clark—may I call you, 'Clark'?"

"Do call me 'Clark,' do that."

"Well, anyway, the way in which your son and wife are reacting in their comas reminds me of a case many years ago. Out of curiosity and hope, I'm offering my services to you."

"And what qualifies you to act on my family's behalf?"

"My specialty is insurance claims, medical or otherwise, but on this case I'll work pro bono. I don't work as many cases as I did when I was younger, but every once in a while a case comes to my attention that promises a challenge. Your case, I believe, is one of those."

Clark is quiet for a moment, and choosing his words carefully, he replies, "Mr. Lewis, I appreciate your candor and the honesty of your offer. However, I need a lawyer who will devote his full attention to this matter. Tis my son's life along with me wife's that depend on what we do: there's no room for mistakes. I don't want to entrust my family's lives to someone because of their curiosity or Bucket list challenges they are seeking. This is my wife and son's lives we are discussing, not some game of chance and entertainment."

Lewis remains quiet as Clark continues. "You must understand. I'm fighting for me family, and sometimes it may call for unorthodox procedures. My question to you is, are you ready and able to devote your time and energy to this—no matter how far out I may seem at times?"

Brandon stands up, walks over to the end of his desk, and points to the large bookshelves against the wall. "Mr. Bailey, I know one thing that possibly qualifies me to act as your legal representative more than anyone else, although it's not found within all these books of law you see before you."

"What might that be?"

Lewis walks over to Clark and bending slightly, looks into his eyes. "I understand the power of the human spirit. I know a father's love for his family. And finally, I know nothing is impossible!" Clark sits stiffly, not saying a word; Lewis walks behind his desk.

Opening a drawer, Lewis pulls out a large book and places it in front of Clark. The book appears ancient; symbols are carved into its well-worn brown leather cover, and in the center of the design are two words: Jivan Mukti.

Clark looks down at the curious book, and asks, "What's this?"

"That, my friend, is the closest I've come in this world to truth." Handing Clark his business card, Brandon explains, "This book is so powerful that it has led me to use its wisdom in almost all of the events of my life, and even more than that, it has taught me about the Inner Kingdom." Clark furrows his brows; he doesn't understand what the lawyer means by some "Inner Kingdom," but he does realize this man may honestly be looking at his case for more than just a legal fee; perhaps he does have more than mere interest in just dissecting laws for manipulation or advantage. This man may be just what he needs if he has the understanding of the underlying spiritual current in this situation. He may not only offer legal representation, but also a true understanding and guidance a friend could rely on. Clark reaches over and opens the old book. The writing is unfamiliar to him.

"The words are written in Latin and Sanskrit. I can read Latin, but my Sanskrit is not so good," Lewis says. "Most of the words are in Latin though, thank goodness. I've had this book for over forty years, and in that time, I only recently have learned to finally understand the truth that runs like a golden thread throughout its pages."

Clark closes the book. Looking over at the lawyer, he asks, "Mr. Lewis, do you have time to hear a story?"

Lewis comes back around his desk, and pulling the second armchair closer, says, "Call me Brandon, please, and I have all day if necessary. I want to know everything, every event, every detail you can remember."

Clark spends the rest of the afternoon going over everything: the accident, his feelings, his fears, every dream, and of course, the threats from the insurance company. The tree house and the unexplained insight Melody had about her brother. He stops occasionally to answer questions, and sometimes backs up and explains something he'd forgotten. By the time he's finished, daylight is fading.

Lewis has taken extensive notes, but already he has the entire story in his head. Twice Lewis has his secretary bring them tea.

Standing up and looking at his pocket watch, Lewis asks, "Are you leaving anything out?" Clark thinks for a few moments and then remembers the spiritual exercises. As he tells him about his experiments with meditation and the strange sounds he has been hearing, Brandon seems to be engrossed with every word. Finally, when the story's over, Brandon sits silent for a few moments. Sifting through the pages and reading to himself, he finally places his notes on the desk and stands up. Walking next to the window and peering out for a moment, he pulls a pipe from his jacket and lights it. Turning around, he smiles.

"Clark, I believe this is exactly the case I've been waiting for. Let me study my notes and do a little research, and I'll get back to you by tomorrow evening. Meanwhile, relax about the insurance situation; let me handle that. Continue to meditate and research the motives and whereabouts of your son. We'll work as a team in every aspect of this adventure, and believe me, Clark, this is an adventure. It's a journey, I suspect, that will have far-reaching ramifications as we explore the facts, no matter how far out they may seem. There are two things I want to do within the next few days. First, I want to talk to your daughter, and second, I want to visit the tree house."

"I can arrange both—you just say when." Clark stands up and shakes Lewis's hand. "I'll be expecting your call."

Following his visit with Brandon, Clark spends the next few hours visiting his wife and son. He tries to communicate his new sense of hope as he strokes their foreheads. When he arrives home, he sits down with Melody. His little girl seems to be maturing by leaps and bounds, and this puzzles him. Perhaps, it's too fast. "Melody, I want to talk to you a little bit about what's going on."

She sits down on the couch and says, "First, can I tell you about a dream I had last night?"

Clark moves closer. "Of course, go ahead."

Melody snuggles up to her father. "It starts out with me walking on a sidewalk in a neighborhood. I was alone at first, and couldn't find my way home. The neighborhood was nice, and I wasn't scared or anything. Anyway, as I walked, I came to this large old-style home—it was gray and white with big trees around it. For some reason I walked up the steps to the front porch, and as I got to the door Namo ran up to me, purring. And then I opened the door without knocking, and went inside. The house was really nice, with carpet, furniture, curtains, and flowers in vases everywhere. At first, I'm just walking around looking at all the pictures of people on the walls and smelling the flowers, and then, I hear some music coming from upstairs."

"What kind of music?"

"Oh, I don't know…maybe like violins, or I think maybe what's called a cello."

"Okay, go on."

"The stairway was wide and curvy before it reached the top floor. Namo runs ahead of me to the top, and then stops and waits. Walking up the stairs, the music becomes clearer and more beautiful, and soon, I'm on the upper floor in a long hallway. There are doors on both sides of the hallway, and I feel it's important to look inside each room. I open the door on my left; the room is empty and dark except for some light coming in from a window in the back. In the center of the room is a chair and you were sitting in it. At first, I was confused, and I asked, 'What's wrong? Why are you in here all alone?' You looked up at me and I see you're crying, but I didn't know why. I felt so bad; I turn and leave the room, slamming the door after me. The next door I open is to my right. I notice this door is a different color than the other one."

Her father interrupts. "What color was it?"

"Blue...a pretty blue, like a clear sky! I went inside and it was brighter than the last room. There was a small bed to the right, in the center of the room was a chair, again with you sitting all alone. I stepped in, getting closer to you this time, and I asked, 'Daddy, are you okay? What's happening?' You were writing something on a pad, and you looked up and said, 'I'm busy, very busy; come back later.' Then you started writing again, so I left."

"I was going down the hall again, and the next door I opened was also on my right side. This door was yellow. When I went inside, I noticed the room was painted a beautiful yellow with white trim. There was a dresser to the left, and a nice large bed on the right side. White curtains were around a large window that had lots of sunlight coming through it. There was a nice big chair sitting on a white rug in the center of the room. You were sitting in the chair reading some sort of old book; when I came up to you, you laid the book down in your lap and looked up at me and smiled. I asked, 'What are you doing?' and then you said, 'I'm waiting for you to tell me the secret.'

"I laughed and said, 'Daddy I don't know the secret.' You smiled and began reading again, so I left. The last room had a white door, and when I opened it and walked in, I see an old rocking chair in the room—there was nothing else. As I got closer, I saw someone was in the chair, rocking back and forth. As I got even closer, I saw who was sitting in the chair, and I screamed and ran!"

Clark asked hurriedly, "Why did you run? Who was it?"

"The person in the rocking chair was me; when she turned her head, she smiled back at me! I ran away in my dream, and then I woke up."

Clark has listened closely as his daughter described the dream. He's confused about what it might be trying to tell her, but he's sure it means something. "Honey, could you do me a favor? Could you write down the entire dream? Just as you explained it to me?"

Melody jumps off the couch, excited. "Oh, yes, you mean right now?"

"I do, I do mean right now—before you forget any part of it—I think it's important to the both of us."

Sensing its importance, Melody runs to her room to begin the writing project. Clark feels strongly that the dream is trying to tell them something, but at the moment he doesn't understand what.

Later that night, he gets a call from Brandon. "Hello, Clark. I have some information we need to discuss. Can we meet tomorrow? If all goes well, I will have some documents for you to sign, too."

"Sure, sounds good, but can't you tell me over the phone?"

There is a pause on the other line, and then Brandon speaks. "To try to explain it all on the phone will only confuse you. Believe me, it is something you need to see and understand; you'll also have to make a few decisions before we progress any further."

Clark agrees to meet and hangs up, wondering what Brandon has found. Instead of worrying about it, he figures the best thing to do right now is to read a bit, and then contemplate using the exercises he has been learning. He has a feeling that tomorrow is going to be a day to remember.

At ten o'clock sharp the next morning, Clark walks through the quaint arched door of Brandon's office. With him are the pages describing Melody's dream, a briefcase of documents concerning his insurance policy and the hospital's billing schedule, together with records and comments regarding Hugh's and Annie's treatment: past, current, and future.

Brandon is dressed casually today, wearing a beige tweed coat with a sweater underneath, brown slacks, and loafers. He's ready for a long day and anticipates enjoying it.

Brandon Lewis, Esquire is a seeker.

All his life he has searched for truth. Becoming a lawyer was part of his search. Learning about justice, laws, government, etc. was just one aspect of his life's journey. Religions have always fascinated him. He's studied the world's major religions and explored countless cults, secret teachings, and even the mysticism attached to Christianity, Islam, Judaism, Hinduism, and others. He'd studied the sciences; the quantum theory, relativity, the structure of the atom, the physics of light, and the nature of vibrations and sound in relation to each other. All this while practicing meditation, out-of-body experiences, and even lucid dreaming. Brandon Lewis fills his life by expanding his mental capacity. Within the past ten years, he has discovered something that seems to be just beyond the mind: something beyond his mental capabilities, and something he hasn't been able to touch. This something is what compels him to get up every day. It's what makes him a seeker, and what keeps him searching for miracles in the simple things of life. From his life's search, he's learning to appreciate simplicity, and within this simplicity, he's beginning to see reasons for life's events with a unique kind of wisdom and a deep perspective.

Clark walks into Brandon's office. "Good morning, Brandon. I've brought everything you asked for and a little extra."

Brandon's eyebrows go up when he hears the word "extra." "Very good, I've cleared my day and hopefully we can get a lot done. First, let's look at the insurance policies on you and your family."

The two men spend the next two hours studying the stack of paperwork. After a while, Brandon leans back in his chair yawning. "Clark, these documents tell me a lot about the company that carries your insurance. Mind you, they're a good company, but they go strictly by the terms and conditions of your contracts. To make them budge outside of their box, we may have to threaten public outcry, and hit them in their heart."

Clark snorted. "What makes ya' think they have a heart?"

"What I mean is there are some restrictions within the policy that are in gray areas. You might call them 'Catch-22s,' if you know what I mean."

Clark knows exactly what he means; some of the contract terms are vague and possibly conflicting. They require certain procedures to happen to open the next door before they assume more responsibility. The dark side of these policies is that usually the patient can't fulfill the requirements, and so the door is shut after a certain period.

Brandon explains, "Yesterday, I was in contact with both of the agents who sold you your policies. I also sent a legal brief to the District Court, which is in essence a stay."

Clark looks up. "A stay; what's that?"

Brandon pulls out a copy of the brief he outlined for Clark.

"It's a request for an extension on the time restrictions that your policy gives. The court will order the insurance company and the hospital to continue treatment until the case goes to trial. The insurance company will be compelled not to interfere with your wife's and son's treatment until after we meet in court. My job is to cause substantial delays in getting a court date. I do this by filing objections and demands to the insurance company. These demands will compel the insurance companies, lawyers, and the hospital to support with documentation their cause for termination. Just as their policy holds requirements for the insurer to respond, the law has requirements that insurance companies must uphold. In this type of case, the insurance companies' attorneys and the hospital know it will be a long drawn out process to prove why they should terminate. If needed, we at some point will go for public outcry."

Clark stares for a moment at the brief Brandon outlined for him to review. It held so many terms, so many reasons, and objections for delay, that Clark was a little overwhelmed at what the man had completed in just twenty-four hours. There's a lot of medical jargon involved with the wording, which makes Clark wonder just how Brandon could know the type of medical procedures, treatments, and all the other causes he'd outlined. After reading the document, Clark is even more amazed at how familiar Brandon is with his entire case. Clearly, he has underestimated this man's mind!

Brandon looks curiously at Clark, almost with an amused look in his eyes. "Didn't you say you brought something else besides the policies with you?"

Clark stops being amazed for a moment. "I did, I did. I mean, yes; my daughter Melody wrote down a dream she had two nights ago. I thought you might find it interesting."

Brandon moves some files from his desk to clear an area for the pages Clark was holding. "I hope this will be more exciting than all the legal documents we've been dealing with. But before we get into the dream, I need you to sign some documents for me." Brandon pushes two pieces of paper before Clark. The title of the two-page document reads "Power of Attorney." Clark picks it up, scans it, and then asks, "I'm aware of a Power of Attorney; I use similar documents in my business. Where I'm confused is, what do you need my Power of Attorney for?"

Brandon pulls a pen from his coat pocket and hands it to Clark. "There are going to be times when I'll have to make instant decisions concerning the next steps needed for stopping any unknown scenarios the insurance companies' attorneys may spring on us. You must trust me to make decisions concerning your wife and son. Normally, I'll consult you on every step I feel you need to be a part of. However, when I'm at the courthouse, or when I have to appear to refute or respond to a demand or answer questions, I need to respond on your behalf with all the knowledge I have and with full authority. If this means signing documents or anything else that has to do with the medical treatment concerning your wife and son, this document gives me the power to do so."

Clark thinks to himself for a moment.

Can I really sign this?

Can I let another person who I just met be a decisive factor in the lives of my family? How can I just let go of the control? Does he really know what he's asking? These questions race through his head.

Brandon stands up. "I'll give you a few moments alone to think about what I'm asking, but keep this in mind. If you can't let go of this situation, if you can't let go of some of the responsibility or give me the authority and your trust, then I don't think we can continue as a team on this case."

Brandon leaves Clark alone.

Deep inside, he feels Brandon is right. He asked God for help; he asked for a friend, someone who could help him through this maze of problems. Now his prayer has been answered. Did he dare refuse?

Taking up the document, Clark reads every word. It's standard except for a few inclusions that allow Brandon power to act on his behalf with the hospital, the insurance companies, and all court documents. What a relief it would be to shift the responsibility from his shoulders to Brandon's; he could feel so much lighter. But could Brandon handle it all? Clark purses his lips, straightens his shoulders, and placing the document on the desk, he signs it. He has to trust someone and let go of some of the emotional burden and fear that is building inside him.

After a few minutes, Brandon comes back into the office. Seeing the document signed, he gathers all the paperwork on his desk and places it carefully into a file drawer. Brandon then sits down and picks up the two pages describing an eight-year-old girl's dream, and with a gleam in his eye, calmly says, "Now, let's get to the most important work at hand."

CHAPTER 21 ~ THE GUARDIAN

All five of us—myself, Kaylu, Dandi, Loren, and Karla—discuss what we should do. Should we separate, and the girls go on their way to the Land of Light, and we three proceed on our way? Or should the girls turn back and accompany us to the Land of Light and Darkness? After weighing the pros and cons, the girls agree it is better to join us and turn back.

I pack me bedroll, preparing to continue our journey and determined to stay away from the girls as much as possible—no use in taking chances. We decide to leave some supplies behind. From what the girls describe, it will take two full sleep cycles to arrive at the entrance leading back to their world. Based on this and going over all the supplies, we decide to keep only the most valuable things such as food and the fire rocks. I'll carry some rocks in me pack as will the others, and each of us also carries as much food as he or she can. It's decided Karla will act as point; I'll be next, then Kaylu with Loren, and Dandi following up. Tis made sense sure enough, since Karla knows what lies ahead.

I now know that the cave's power enhances not only me mind, but me senses and feelings as well. The fight with the river beast reflected the power we are dealing with. Just knowing that the same great power within the river beast lies dormant within all humankind—including meself—puts me on notice if it happens again. The cave's power is waiting…waiting and watching, ready to spring forth and take control of me thoughts, feelings or even invading me own personality. Olgera warned me that the part of me known as the personality of Hugh will struggle constantly to maintain control. The power of the cave reaches into every atom of me being: every thought, every action I feel through the mind, before I even think it. Thoughts are relentlessly striving to divert me from my quest.

Leaving the beach and river behind, we move into the darkness. After a while, I notice the cave is becoming smaller, and our path climbs upward into a rocky terrain forcing us to climb over high embankments and huge boulders. Finally, we reach a flat plateau with several smaller cave openings. Looking closer they seem more like tunnels deliberately bored into the cave walls than natural openings; the question is, which one should we take? Turning to Karla, I ask, "Which one did your father take when you were coming through this way?"

She hesitates for a second then says, "I'm not sure…I'm a little confused. I wasn't paying much attention when we came out."

I feel my heart beating faster; pangs of hot anxiety rush through me body as I stare at the cave openings: which one? Then my arm acts; without thought,

I pull out me sword and point it in the direction of each cave. The sword locks on the middle one and glows. Taking the lead, I motion the group forward. The cave quickly narrows until it becomes nothing more than a long round tunnel. Karla points to some drawings on the wall; she rubs her hand across the drawing and says, "I remember paintings on a wall similar to these when we were coming through; perhaps this is the right way." The tunnel is easily wide and tall enough to walk through; our torchlight illuminates smooth rounded walls and a ceiling about fifteen feet high. Murals painted on both sides depict different characters, stories, and words written in some ancient language under the drawings. Water has run through this tunnel sometime in the past, making the walls smooth and clean. Holding the torch closer, the firelight glides over each picture. One painting depicts a hillside with an old house on top. Next to the home's doorway stands a small man with light encircling him; for a moment, I wonder what the meaning might be? For some reason I feel it may be important. The cave tunnel continues to stretch, it seems endless. The deeper we go, the narrower it becomes. Soon there is no room to stop and even sit; it's a tight fit just to turn around. The ground is soft dry sand, so walking is easy; still, the walls are getting closer. I try concentrating on the pictures stretching through the tunnel walls. Some of the drawings seem familiar, like memories rushing through me. One picture is just a large pair of eyes next to a picture of large ears. The paintings are extraordinarily detailed and realistic; the ears and eyes seem to jump out from the smooth wall. More symbols and runes are scrawled below each drawing. What they mean, none of us knows, but one thing is obvious: the power of the cave is getting stronger. I'm becoming aware of a vibrating noise as we progress deeper; slowly, the vibrating is changing to a buzzing sound—similar to the hum of some electrical high wires. The contours of the tunnel are enhancing the sound. Focusing on me steps to keep me mind from being distracted, I'm only too aware of how me own thoughts or feelings can subtly draw me into a delusion; the others also hear the sound as it vibrates and travels along the smooth tunnel walls. Everyone keeps together in a single line.

There's no talking—we add only the sounds of heavy breathing and footsteps to the peculiar tone as we march through the seemingly endless twisting tunnel. The noise is growing louder, sounding now more like a hollow whistling; no one says anything as we keep pushing ahead. The sound pulsates against me body. Me mind strives to follow the pulse without surrendering to it; constantly I have to pull me thoughts and energy back as me thoughts keep slipping into the vibrating humming. Going as fast as I dare, I ignore the ongoing paintings and symbols. I have one desire: to get out of this tunnel! Time has no meaning in this darkness; we have no sense of how long it has been since we entered the tunnel. Still, we keep a steady pace moving forward, all of us hoping the end is near. Suddenly, I stop; quickly reaching out both arms, I brace against the sides of the tunnel with all me strength. I shout out to the others, "Stop!"

A few feet in front of me the tunnel stops; it ends in a pitch-black abyss with darkness so thick that my torchlight is instantly swallowed up. The others behind me stumble into each other. Staring into the chasm, I feel a deep emptiness along with a slight cold breeze. A few more steps and I would have pitched headlong into what looks like a bottomless pit! I hold me torch up for my comrades to see the end of the tunnel; Karla and Loren are surprised. Karla looks at me and exclaims, "This wasn't here before!"

Gathering to look into the cavernous black hole, we stare silently. After a few moments, Kaylu picks up a large stone and tosses it into the chasm—no one hears the stone hit bottom. The girls have ropes, as do we, but even connecting all of them together wouldn't help. It's impossible to tell how far it is to the other side. Dandi reaches over the ledge and feels the smooth walls beneath us. "It's impossible to climb down; the walls are nothing but smooth rock."

What are we going to do?

I can't even think about turning back—that would spell disaster for not only me, but me family as well. At the edge of the tunnel, a slight widening allows us to sit in a small circle. Loren places a few fire rocks in the center and lights them; the light is swallowed up in the darkness. There are no shadows or firelight dancing off walls except behind us. If no one comes up with a plan, it would seem our journey is at an end. Remembering what Tomas said about The Way of the Traveler, I reach into me tunic and move closer to the fire. The pages capture the glow of firelight and I begin to read. The words as before materialize in me mind, much like when I'm communicating with Kaylu or Dandi. Somehow, the words move into me thoughts and whisper like a friend.

Within the mind lies the void. This void of nothingness exists as a barrier for those foolhardy enough to think they are ready to let go of the last tattered remnants of their humanity. For one to pass this void, he must be knowledgeable in the ways of Soul and its power. All Souls encounter this void at some time during their existence in the lower worlds of Matter, Energy, Space, and Time. Sometimes humans visit this void in their dreams, or sometimes in meditation, or even upon death; occasionally, a Master Traveler may take Soul to this dark chasm, but no matter how they arrive, very few ever go any farther. The void is endless; its vastness alone discourages seekers from trying to cross without the proper experience and wisdom. Crossing the void expands the awareness of Soul, releasing great power to the one fortunate enough to make it to the other side. This power allows the traveler to navigate his journey without further hindrance from the mind. To cross the void, one needs only to stop thinking, stop feeling, and become one with the essence of what the void actually is; this is the only way!

Concentrating, the words manifest in me mind like I am wearing a pair of headphones and I'm listening to a recording. The instructions are direct, but not hard to understand; I continue reading.

> Crossing the void is ultimately a necessity for Soul, but following instructions with the mind is difficult for one must drop the mind in order to cross over. Learning to drop the mind with the mind is as difficult a task as any man can encounter. The human consciousness has divisions: several minor ones and two main ones. The void is the last major dividing point separating the conscious from the subconscious mind, and it is truly the "Dark Night of the Soul." Any attempt to cross the void and mind will create the illusion that all actions of the mind, emotions, and body are the most important part of Man's being, and forsaking them means death.

I close my eyes and listen as words continue to flow into me mind.

> Most of the senses are fooled by illusions, and our reliance on them acts as survival techniques in the ordinary man's daily life. Among these survival modes exist desires that clearly establish the type of person an individual eventually becomes. Most people believe the results of these sensory and emotional traits form the real self, but this is part of the illusory apparatus projected from the mind. Man is so consumed in living his desirous life that his only goal is to develop only his mind and personality; in doing so, he soon forgets himself as Soul. The void's purpose is to remind Soul of its true potential and its original source. Right thinking, contemplation, discipline, and most of all, Light and Sound, help erase any illusions that hold the mind back from knowing the true self. Soul is the only being capable of crossing this void which exists in every mind.

I continue listening, going deeper into the words and their meaning.

> The subconscious mind is linked directly to the universal mind and its power, which is itself connected to all existence within the parameters of time, space, energy, and matter. Because of this, the subconscious is unlimited in its creative power in comparison to the conscious mind. All

forms, images, ideas, and experiences already exist within the universal mind. A person's mind, his world, his universe, and his very existence are nothing more than faded facsimiles of the original truth and cause. This truth and cause exists on the other side of the void.

Access to the higher divine images, ideas, and concepts on the other side of the void await those capable of drawing them through the subconscious and subsequently pass them to the conscious self. Once these images, ideas, and so on cross the void and enter the subconscious mind, they come into contact with matter, energy, space, and time; this solidifies them in humankind's personal reality. Some Souls consciously tap into this subconscious storehouse and take these ideas and concepts from its meticulous filing system in the mind. Uses for these images and thoughts are to enhance their physical life; this also happens in dreams or during contemplation.

It may seem these types of people are artists or geniuses, but actually everyone has the potential to do the same; he only needs to learn how. Emotions, actions, feelings, and thoughts—even our physical existence—come from this vast subconscious storehouse of energy. Everyone is subject to this subconscious command center; how one uses it determines a person's awareness and reactions to the "reality" that exist within. Upon reaching the worlds below this dark void, inexperienced travelers think they have reached heaven or paradise. They look at the void as finality, believing that nothing more exists; therefore, the inexperienced traveler will not leave his world of paradise and explore the nothingness.

Nothing could be further from the truth, however, for the void is the raw power of the universal mind. It is such a force of pure power and awareness that few go beyond it and discover the true reality existing on the other side. Some believe the void is the end of time, and rightly so, for beyond the darkness, time ceases to exist as do matter, energy, and space. Beyond the void are Light and Sound, combined with a higher, deeper, and unlimited experience with what we call the

Creator. To cross beyond this area of darkness, one must leave the mind behind entirely. Each Soul must deal with this mind energy as an individual experience. Very few are ready to deal with the full potential that the subconscious can share with us. Those in the past who have tapped into its potential are called Spiritual Giants, Masters, Savants, Saviors, Prophets or Saints. In Soul's spiritual journey to its true home, it must at some time confront this part of its being. When this happens, one realizes a giant step in its own evolution is near.

Fear is the one factor that will cause the seeker to fail when attempting to cross the void. Fear is the cause of the longest and deepest groove carved in the brain; this one groove creates most aspects of the personality. Fear creates all the limitations and controls of the mind. When weakened by fear, people can be manipulated and dominated by others, too fearful to challenge the concepts and rules of others or rise above their own doubts. This fear spreads throughout humanity like a virus; humanity has become what it is because of the patterns of fear carried from generation to generation. From fear, mankind creates leaders claiming they will lead the way to a better world. These leaders are not immune to this virus, however; in most cases, they become the strongest carriers for this universal disease. Fear causes such doubt and loss of hope that in the end, without eliminating fear from the conscious mind, man is doomed to failure. Not only are the fearful incapable of crossing this vast chasm of nothingness, but because of fear's trickledown effect, it further dooms humankind to failure in the physical life as well. Trust in the Creator and yourself; this is the only way to cross the "Dark Night of the Soul."

I'm absorbing as much of the teachings from the book as quickly as I can, but at certain points, I am so moved that I have to stop reading so I can reflect on what has just been said. One thing is for sure—when it gets down to the bottom line, I realize that I'll have to deal with me oldest enemy again: fear.

Returning the book to me tunic, I sit still, allowing the information to fill me thoughts and feelings. According to the book, I already possess the knowledge; it's just up to me to use it wisely.

I look about me. The others are lying down, trying to get a little sleep before they start what they expect will be the journey back. I relax against the cave's smooth wall, staring into the firelight against the endless background of darkness. I close me eyes, and me mind ponders how I'm supposed to become a part of this essence or void: it's fairly simple to contemplate in the abstract and focus on the stillness within me, but how am I to maintain this stillness while up and moving around? This is what has to happen if we are to cross the void, isn't it? I have to overcome my attachment to the mind for a few moments; if not, it will do everything in its power to keep me trapped within this cave's own reality.

I still hear the constant vibration we heard in the tunnel; me sword is pulsating in harmony with the humming sound. Letting my attention be absorbed into the sound, me mind eventually stops resisting, and the humming begins to change, slowly becoming a melody, and then very slowly, it transforms into the sweetest music I could imagine. Looking through me inner eye and relaxing, my awareness merges into the strange melodies that are sweetly playing. Like Sirens calling me to join them, the sound changes to an even higher, more urgent note as me thoughts follow its vibratory wave. I hear sounds of a gentle wind, like when a breeze rushes between tall buildings or trees. Letting me thoughts glide with the wind is a lifting sensation. I gently feel meself being carried away. The more I absorb myself into the sound, the more me mind can let go. I'm soon aware of only the sound moving around me. It's becoming like bagpipes, breathing a constant melody that reminds me of who I am; then the sound floats closer toward me, gradually becoming louder. It's a lonely sound. Lost and forlorn feelings flood me mind like some distant dream; these feelings of loneliness bring to mind images of barren hills and desert plains. A gray sky with billowing overcast clouds blocks out any brightness. A soft wind whistles and blows through me; still the bagpipes sing their plaintive melody enhanced by what sounds like a heavy stringed instrument, like a weeping cello. The melody is entrancing but haunting; it's pulling at me awareness. The deep bass cello music is blending in perfect harmony with the bagpipes. I'm not afraid, and me thoughts clear and gently slow down until they settle into stillness. The sensation is like being put to sleep, but oddly, something within my consciousness is stirring, becoming more aware. Being aware without thought is a weird and strange sensation; more images appear in me inner vision. Brown bare mountains stand as if in silhouette against the pale whitish and dark gray sky, the scene enhances me feelings of loneliness—it isn't a negative feeling, but more of a soulful feeling with deep profound gratitude.

Gentle winds become warm breezes. Scents flow within me as breezes brush me face. New feelings are bubbling up from within; with this bubbling feeling, wonderful blessings are coming to me.

There is something else.

Stirring deep within me, the gnawing feeling of loneliness lingers as a barrier of something that I have created in me past and am constantly still creating from me mind; awareness overwhelms me, I expand, and I swirl gently around stillness. I'm thinking it's because maybe I am the actual stillness. I see clearly how me mind is always taking for granted all the little things in me life. By taking for granted life's magic, I see how my attitude is leading me down worthless paths; these paths seem so important at the time but really never are. The ordinary magic of just being alive is growing stronger within me consciousness; so much more of life exists without the mind blocking life's full meaning. Choices have been, and always are me own. Always my world was—and is—of me own making; Light and Sound slowly and gently begin to show me another way. Moving closer to this larger truth, I realize I have always been alone and will continue to be so. No one can touch or know the deepest part of Soul, no one can invade the center of me own being. Softly, realizations are erupting within me mind, they are showing clearly that in the end Soul must build its own path, this is necessary if Soul is to move through the loneliness that all travelers must pass through…Deeper feelings swirl within me; then like a wave they are crashing against me consciousness.

Oh my God…There's so much love in my life! It has been so easy to forget all the blessings and love that plant their seeds within. I've ignored them in the past, now I can see how they are growing in ways I never dreamed possible. My heart opens even more, allowing further surrender to the Sound Current. Moments become demonstrations of the power of truth, every experience is an open door to a larger and more beautiful world, and every person, thing, or event I have ever experienced, met or will meet or attend only adds to me blessings and joy. All this has always been in the simplest of things.

Me awareness expands further…the sound carries me deeper into this barren world lifting me on vibrating waves of soft musical sounds. Joy spreads, assuring me for this moment that I'm safely and surely led to a faraway place existing only in dreams. I no longer feel me body. Only the Sound Current—with each and every chord, beat, and movement—flows in and out of me awareness, an integral part of me own being. I become a musical wave flowing through worlds of light and darkness, seeing worlds that are as much a part of me as me own thoughts. Loneliness is also part of these worlds, but as lonely as it feels, I know I'm moving toward something divine and wonderful as I swirl and float within the sound. I'm being absorbed in something divine and holy; it is recreating me. Eternal unconditional love is touching parts of something I'd forgotten, trust pulls me further into a vast ocean. Who I had been is lost in a mystical, musical wave of sound that's creating a yearning desire to want only to follow the sound. Cellos sing somewhere in the distance, and a terrible yearning hunger grows within me—it isn't intrusive or invading so much as it is nudging at my memory and somehow growing more and more familiar. This is an ancient companion, something I'm just on the brink of remembering, yet can't quite identify.

Quite unexpectedly, the sounds cease and all is still. No movement: nothing except a tremendous feeling of peace and oneness combined with the feeling I get when I have returned home after being away for a long time, only intensified a thousand fold. A soft presence nudges me from within, then something penetrates me being, probing, growing, moving, and making itself known. It's barely touching the outer rim of me consciousness, and then it flows back to the center of me mind.

Then, it happens!

With one mighty rush a presence explodes within me heart followed by a vibratory wave rumbling through me entire consciousness. The sound of Hu flows effortlessly from within. The sound is clear; it's me own name calling out from the center of me being, a voice within me whispers with surreal clarity.

The voice is ecstasy, freedom, and joy all as one. *"I am what you are. I am what you were. I am what you will become. I have waited eons for you to return and remember; now you are here."*

The whispering voice seems familiar; it feels and sounds like meself! The communication isn't a projection or telepathy, but me own words coming out from within me own being, and it's with me own understanding and accent.

"We are the power! We are the truth! You are I, to know me is to know yourself. You have searched for me throughout the ages. Sometimes on mountain tops of old, but still I wasn't there. You searched for me in battles lost and won, but still you couldn't see me. You looked for me in the deserts and in a babe's eyes, you have searched your lover's heart, but still I eluded you. I have always been here, always watching...always calling our name in the darkness, always reaching out to you in your dreams. I have tasted the tears of loneliness with the bittersweet feelings of lost love. I've felt the power of success and the fear of loss and isolation. I have felt the joy of living through our every breath, and in this joy I have seen our creation through your eyes, walked with your feet, listened through your ears, spoken with your lips, and loved with your heart. Never were you alone but still you did not know me. You have given these gifts of living freely, and now it's for you to take another step closer to me; in doing so we leave the pangs of sorrow behind. No longer will you be the effect of illusionary worlds for as we further merge as one, our understanding and wisdom grows. To cross the void, all is left behind. Listen to me voice in the Sound Current; look for the great light within it will guide you to your True home. Give all, and all will be given unto you, nothing else matters.

"Can you trust yourself? Can you forgive yourself?

"I am all that you have been and all that you will be; I'm at your side forever.

"I was with you at the Wisdom Pool and I am seen through the image of Jotan.

"I was there when you fought your passion in the form of the river beast.

"I guided you to face your fears in the form of the cave dwellers.

"I am the tree in the meadow, and the little boy lying in a coma. Some call me the Creator; some call me God; others know me as Soul.

"I am none of these; and yet, I am all of them.

"I guard the doorway that allows access through the void, because of this I am also known as the Guardian. All this and much more am I, however know this Hugh. In me purest form I am you, nothing more, nothing less, in me humblest form I am love. Long have we traveled, now you stand at the door to eternity will you enter?"

The voice coming from within is mine, but deliciously rich, quiet, musical, and deep with an echo that resonates within, holding me as if enchanted. The Guardian continues. *"It is your choice, for in crossing the void all that you have been and all that you are attached to will become but an atom existing in the one living truth. All you know and all you have learned will become less meaningful compared to what awaits you on the other side."*

I again feel the tug of the Sound Current; the music is like food for a starving man, every atom in me being wants nothing more than to see what is waiting across the void. The voice now whispers. *"We have been like the servant serving his masters; to break these bonds of servitude you must realize you are no longer the servant, but the prince. Are you bold enough? Are you strong enough? Do you love enough? Can you trust yourself to take the step and become that which you already are?"*

Me consciousness is swirling— the sound is obsessive and enchanting—I feel meself stepping out—inching across the dark chasm—and as I move forward, I feel power!

The deeper I go, the more power I summon; the voice from within bubbles up within me consciousness. *"Only true sons and daughters can pass the void; but even as you cross, the masculine and feminine attributes blend and become one, this blending is the true meaning of Soul mates. Soul is put back together in such a way that it never feels the blending except as an increase in awareness, once Soul is whole again it knows itself. This knowing is an experience that has no words to describe it. Soul from this blending is now ready to know its Father.*

"Soul is a most precious part of the Creator, for in its true form, it is a perfect replica of its Father. Soul can never be the Creator in its entirety, but it is now divinely aware, and a conscious part of the divine existence. IT has learned to be a part of this existence within the constructs of the Creator's own reality. Soul has always been and always will be. Its existence is a pathway to experience that enhances itself and its source."

As the strength of the Light and Sound increases, a feeling of unbridled freedom bursts within me, a freedom filled with power; no, I'm becoming the actual power of freedom itself! My joy grows, pushing/pulling me further into the unknown; faintly, I sense something else tumbling through crashing/competing waves of energy, unboundedness, and music. It's distant, barely perceptible, but I concentrate on its frequency, and from out of the noise, it becomes more clear… voices!

Someone is calling out from somewhere: very distant, very insistent. Are these voices from deep within me, and I am simply asleep and dreaming? Or are these voices coming from outside, penetrating deep within me?

"Hugh, wake up! Hugh! Are you all right? Wake up, please! Can you wake up?"

The faint voices are calling me, but for some reason, I can't communicate properly; I release only a slight shudder in response.

The overlapping voices grow louder. "Hugh! Come back! Don't leave us!"

I now feel overwhelming anxiety… I can only merge my emotions and worries and desires into a mishmash of feeling outwards, reflecting my desperate need to return to help my new friends and to find me mom.

The voice within falls silent: utter emptiness, no thoughts even of not thinking.

Then a massive tidal wave of love and power breaks within me heart and absorbs me entire consciousness. The divine voice again is manifesting within me. *"You cling to the warmth of living, Hugh. This is a reflection of the great love inside you...So be it."*

A loud explosion—like several cannons bursting at once—erupts inside me. I feel a surge of movement, and then I'm back on the ledge; Kaylu is shouting out loud and shaking me body.

"Hugh! Wake up!"

I open me eyes and look around.

Karla, Kaylu, Loren, and Dandi are all standing over and peering down at me with anxious looks on their faces.

"I'm okay," I mumble as I slowly stand up.

Looking around at my friends, I turn and squint into the dark abyss. Walking to the edge, I gaze over the darkness and quietly state, "We're turning around. I've come the wrong way."

CHAPTER 22 ~ THE ORDER OF DREAMS

Brandon is on his way over to Clark's home for several reasons.

First, he wants to meet Melody, and then he wants to see the tree house Clark and Hugh built. Finally, he wants to clarify the meaning of the dream Melody had about her dad. Brandon knows that in trying to interpret dreams one has to take care when helping extract meaning from someone else's dreams for dreams can be interpreted on several different levels; Brandon wants only the truest meaning of Melody's. He certainly doesn't want to give his own interpretation of the dream, which is easy to do if he isn't careful. He hopes, by using tools learned from many years of experience and study, he may be able to help Melody and Clark discover the true meaning of hers.

Turning onto Dogwood Circle he's struck by the quaint beauty of the narrow country road, an old stack fence on both sides of the street blends with the trees running the entire length of the street. The fall foliage is just beginning to break, and tints of red, yellow, and orange are peeking through the green branches overhead. Large limbs from both sides of the road stretch, touching each other above the road. Morning sunlight chases myriad shadows on the road.

Within a few moments he's pulling into the long driveway of the Baileys' house. As he opens his car door, a yellow Labrador wags his tail in greeting as he rushes from the bushes along the driveway. Reaching down, Brandon lets Cody sniff him, and then pets the excited dog; he's made a new friend.

Clark walks down the steps from the front door and calls for Cody to be still. "Morning, Brandon, glad you could make it. I have breakfast ready and Melody is anxious to meet you. I hope you brought an appetite."

Brandon immediately feels comfortable in the Baileys' house. The dining room is large with the back interior wall made from glass that opens to the balcony and deck. The room's focal point is the view; it sweeps across the entire back yard and the surrounding trees.

Melody's already sitting at the table when Clark and Brandon walk in.

"Melody, I'd like you to meet a friend of mine; his name is Brandon."

"Hi, Mr. Brandon..." Melody greets him shyly.

"Hi, Melody. Please just call me Brandon."

Melody's a little shy meeting new people, but Brandon's smile and the sparkle in his eyes soon win her over, and before long, they are talking like old friends. Breakfast rushes by, and before they know it, Clark is telling Melody to get her shoes—they are going to the tree house. Cody jump back and forth; he knows they are going for a walk, his favorite thing.

The country road is shaded by tall trees, and soon they step onto the trail leading to the meadow. It's a beautiful morning. Patches of white clouds scatter throughout the blue sky, while in the distance birds sing, the meadows are dressed in green, tainted with gold. A background of surrounding trees explodes with leaves of yellow, orange, reds, and green. As they walk, Brandon recalls memories of youth as he watches Cody skip and dive through the meadow grass. Cody joyfully frolics and springs about, finally disappearing into the dark shade of the woods just ahead.

Entering the woods it's as if they are in another world, a stream flowing on the other side of the tree line gently splashes against small rocks sounding like natures music. Within moments the three enter the glen where the tree house stands.

At first, all they see is the giant maple standing in the center of the glen with its huge branches, some areas are showing patches of yellow, orange, and red. At last standing under the huge tree, Brandon looks up and finally makes out the tree house perched deep in the tree's center on its large dark limbs; multicolored leaves mixed with green succeed in keeping most of the tree house hidden. Brandon admires the workmanship, and he knows this was built from a father and son's love. Looking over at Clark, he nods and comments quietly, almost reverently, "This is a very special place. I can understand why you love it so much."

Clark stares up into the branches of the tree and says, "This glen reminds me of Hugh more than any other place. I feel his presence wherever I am, but here it's different, more intense you might say.

Melody's already halfway up the tree when she yells down.

"Come on up! Wait until you see the inside." Gesturing for Brandon to step up, Clark's right below him making sure he doesn't slip.

Climbing through the floor entrance, Brandon crawls into the structure and Clark follows. Melody's standing to the left next to the far wall; she hasn't opened the window covering yet. Clark steps over, reaches for the tarp, and pulls it open: light rushes into the little room while the tree's interior unfolds before them. Brandon just stares. Never has he seen anything quite like this; the depth of the limbs and color are enchanting. Walking closer to the window's edge he stares into the tree's hidden interior; long, twisting, leafy limbs cross each other, forming miniature canopies while patches of blue skies peep through the foliage. Sunlight pierces the darkness of shadows while splashes of bright orange, red, and pale gold highlight brown limbs stretching to the sky. Birds flutter from branch to branch, and various iridescent insects skitter through sunlight beams. Squirrel's jump from limb to limb chasing each other, the fragrance of someone burning leaves blend with subtle scents of autumn, it's as if a bit of heaven dropped right down into the bosom of this tree. Clark also feels somewhat overwhelmed, every time he comes to the tree it has changed.

Melody takes Brandon's hand, and pulling him away from the window, she seats herself beside him on the couch and asks, "Can we talk about my dream now?"

Brandon feels as if he is already in a dream; he pulls his eyes away from the tree's interior and smiles at Melody and Clark. "I've brought the description of your dream, so let's see if maybe we can find what it's trying to tell you." He pulls the slip of paper from his pocket, then getting comfortable, he looks at Melody and says, "Before we start, you need to understand the way dream interpretation works. I have studied dreams for years, and experimented many times with my own dreams, and the most important thing I've found is that the dreamers always are the best interpreter of their own dreams."

Melody puts her hands on her lap and gives all her attention to the elderly man.

Brandon continues, "Images we see in our dreams don't always mean what they seem. Images usually are created to extract feelings from us, and these feelings are then carefully pieced together to form a message either about ourselves—our lives or someone or something in our lives. Do you understand?"

Melody nods; at the same time, she's looking at her dad who also acknowledges his understanding.

Brandon continues speaking. "Everything in dreams usually means something; even colors of objects have a message to tell. Colors bring out feelings but they can also tell us what senses the dream is touching. For example, black can bring out fear or maybe red can bring out our anger, but be careful; colors can be deceiving, especially when they are colors of objects. Colors also tell us if the dream is of a physical nature or maybe emotional, it can even show our spiritual progress. Dreams can also be a past memory dream or what we call déjà vu."

Melody frowns for a moment, clearly showing she doesn't understand.

Brandon explains, "Déjà vu is the expression used for times when something happens that feels as if it happened before, but like the wind, the memory quickly and quietly disappears."

Melody's eyes open wide, and she responds excitedly, "Oh, yes! I have that happen all the time! One time I walked into my class on the first day of school, and it seemed it had all happened before. I knew I had never been there, but for a moment it was like I had, I was trying to remember, and then the memory was gone."

"Yes," Brandon nods, "we all have these types of things happen to us, but most people don't know how or why they happen."

Clark interrupts for a moment. "I know what you mean: I've been in conversations with someone, and they say something that triggers a fleeting memory, like all this was said before, but I can't place the time or event. It leaves me with a weird feeling; what causes that?"

Brandon continues. "To those who don't know, it is strange, but there's a simple explanation. Sometimes when we sleep, we as our higher self or Soul enters into different levels of awareness. Some people think these experiences are other dimensions, or different states of consciousness. Most of what we experience while we sleep seems like it is lost or we only remember bits and pieces of the experience when we wake up. Because we can't remember, it doesn't mean the events are lost."

Brandon shifts his position on the couch. Leaning closer to Melody, he says, "When we dream, sometimes we travel as our higher self, or what you might call 'Soul.' If we go deep enough in the dream, we sometimes experience a loss of time and space, and when this happens, we escape time and peek into the future."

Melody's eyes widen, as do Clark's.

"Time is another dimension—as are matter, energy, and space. Each represents a different dimensional reality that overlays our three-dimensional physical reality. Space and time are so closely related that, at times, they seem as one."

Clark sits down on the other side of Melody.

"Some believe gifted persons can predict the future or an event that eventually happens. This gift is more dominant in some people than others, but let me tell you this! I believe all humans have this same ability. For most, it only surfaces when they're in the dream state. When we experience events that happen in the future, we—unknown to us—store this information in the subconscious mind, or what I call the mind's filing cabinet. Our minds have a vast storage area where we store all events that we experience. All this information that's absorbed is kept safe and nothing is left out; we use this ability constantly in our daily lives. It's called memory. Without this remarkable ability to store information, humans couldn't remember one event from another, or think in a continuous stream of thought. We couldn't even calculate two plus two."

Brandon pauses for a moment and then explains, "Most of the time, the mind blocks us from consciously accessing these filing cabinets stored in our subconscious. We use only about ten percent of our total memory, which is what we normally use in our everyday lives. What people fail to realize is that vibrations trigger the opening of these vast memory files. Vibrations are sensitive and subtle; everything that exists—including mental images—are made from vibrations or basically sound."

Melody again frowns, clearly not understanding.

"Let me break it down a little simpler. All life is active, or moving. Our movements, our thoughts, and all our words are creative in sound. This is clearly demonstrated in nature, where everything is constantly active and changing. This activity creates vibrations, even the basic building materials of this reality; I am speaking of atoms."

Brandon puts his arm on the back of the couch and says, "Everything is made from atoms which are constantly moving—either clockwise or counter clockwise—and the speed of their movement determines the mass of any object. Some atoms move faster, others move slower; water, fire, our bodies, plants, and rocks all move at their own vibratory rate, but all are made of the same thing... atoms."

Sensing he might have lost Melody, Brandon tries to give her an easier example. "Let me give you an example. When you strike a tuning fork against something, what happens?"

Melody's face lights up. She chirps, "I know, I know! We did that at school! The fork makes a humming sound, and it vibrates real fast."

"Exactly! That's a perfect example of sound and vibrations heard and seen together, while visually being one and the same. This same process happens at every level of movement throughout existence. Most of the time in the higher sense of creation, this vibration is working at such a high tone that our human ears can't detect it. Even light is made from these high frequency waves, I call them wavicles."

Clark startles. He speaks slowly, "You know, now that you mention it, you're right. We have a dog whistle we use to call Cody sometimes; we blow on it, but can't hear anything. When Cody is around, he hears it and comes running."

Brandon looks pleased and nods. "Yes, another example of how sounds work at different levels of vibration. Now getting back to the mind's filing cabinets, this is how it works. Every dream, every event or experience in our lives is recorded and filed away separately within a single vibratory wave; this vibration is a lot like how computers file away information on a microchip. Even now, scientists have figured out how to store images and sounds in a laser light, so you see it's not inconceivable for our minds to do the same. Since our minds are far more advanced than a computer or even light waves, we can and do file events as vibratory chips; in fact, this is done constantly second by second in our everyday world. The mind sees these sound vibrations in the form of light waves especially during meditation.

"We're all familiar with radio or TV stations that broadcast on wavelengths—when you tune a radio to a station, you pick up the wave vibration the station is broadcasting on and can access it. Our minds work on the same principle, but instead of a knob to turn we use our attention as the tuner. When you walk into a situation that you previously dreamed, your attention focuses and your subconscious—unknown to you—identifies that experience as the same vibration stored within the mind when you dreamed it: that's what we know as déjà vu. When you remember the inner experience by seeing the same outer experience, the filing cabinet closes as the vibratory wave dissipates. When this happens, you can't bring the memory back, which leaves most folks perplexed about what just happened.

"This is only one kind of dream we have. Dreams have so many functions, and work on so many levels, that on the surface, it can be very confusing. Dreams are either trying to tell you something about a negative habit that is possibly harming spiritual growth, or possibly it is a message from your own higher self. Some dreams are designed simply to organize all the events you see or experience during waking hours into a balanced category for future use. Again, just like your computer, which has to shuffle all the bits and files into a proper order, your mind does the same, most of the time in the dream state. When this happens you have dreams that don't make any sense; they're not in order and have no real meaning. This happens while your mind is trying to organize itself. If this type of sorting dream doesn't happen, a person can become disoriented and depressed: he can't perform at his peak abilities. This is why it's important to get the proper amount of sleep so the mind can balance and organize itself, which in turn allows you to function well the next day.

"Other types of dreams have to do with past lives, and some can be traveling dreams, which allow the soul to travel free beyond our ordinary mind, and to experience higher realities. These dreams help make the person more self-aware, and seem to always enhance the desire to know more about spiritual matters.

"Remember, it's not important whether the conscious mind remembers the dream or not. Over time, the information will trickle through, and help to build the person's character and personality.

"Okay, now if we're ready, let's discuss Melody's dream and see if we can help her bring out its meaning. But at the risk of being redundant, let me make one thing clear. I need Melody's input to properly interpret her dream's true meaning, so before we begin, Melody, try to focus on how you felt during each event in the dream. Colors are important, so don't leave out details as to what color items in the dream are."

Clark feels a nervous anticipation, knowing that they are about to take a critical journey into the complex dream of his vulnerable little girl: a little girl who has gone through so much in the last few months, and desperately needs answers.

Hopefully, this journey will help solve the riddle to Hugh and Annie's situation.

CHAPTER 23 ~ THE SECRET WAY

I pick up me gear and start back through the tunnel, leaving the dark abyss behind. The others follow, but are clearly puzzled about where I'm going. Although I don't offer an explanation, me companions can sense that something has happened. I'm not confused anymore. In fact, if anything, I know exactly where I'm headed.

Kaylu watches Hugh carefully; again he notices a change in his young friend. Hugh no longer has the look of a young naïve boy, or facial expression of a determined warrior…There's something else, something that just happened. Hugh's shoulders and back are straight; his walk is casual and intent, and somehow less forceful. His face is relaxed, his eyes calm, and his demeanor seems older; wisdom and nobility radiate from his whole body. Every step and every gesture Hugh makes are for a reason; occasionally, he will smile and look back at his friends. Whenever this happens, Kaylu is certain Hugh is keenly aware of each of them, almost as if he were a protecting father. Even though he is in a young body, his friends feel Hugh's concern and love for each of them generates from an older, more protective way.

It seems like hours before Hugh finally stops. Facing a cave wall and without saying a word, he reaches back and pulls his sword from its scabbard. Holding the sword in front of him, he watches as the sword glows. Cocking his head gently, he listens for a moment and then straightens up. Without making a sound, he strides straight toward the wall. His companions are startled; has he gone mad? But just as it seems Hugh would bash right into the stone, he takes a step sideways and disappears! Dandi gasps and rushes forward; Kaylu follows. Just as they reach the wall, Hugh steps out from what seems to be the wall itself. With a grin, Hugh says, "This wall is an illusion. If you look closely, you can see another cave entrance carefully camouflaged so it can't be seen as you walk by." Dandi and Kaylu step closer and see for themselves how the trick is done. The wall is shaped in such a way it makes the parallel wall alongside the cave invisible. This other wall is the entrance to another cave. As the girls approach to follow Dandi and Kaylu's example, Hugh takes Loren's hand and guides her into the new cave, Dandi, Karla, and Kaylu continue just behind.

Hugh explains further. "The sword revealed the secret. I felt it vibrating as we were walking in the old cave and realized it was trying to show me the direction."

The new tunnel is small and a tight fit for a few minutes, but soon it quickly expands until it is a large cave with another streambed running through it. There is no light, but the reflection of the torch illuminates the shiny cave walls, giving them more than enough light to see by. The cave floor is mostly soft sand. The stream is not as large as the one in the previous cave, and seems to run straight through. Hopefully this one is pointing the direction they must go in.

It isn't long before Hugh decides it is time to stop and camp for a while; they have all been hiking a long time, and although Hugh himself is neither tired nor hungry, he senses how the others feel. Loren and Karla build a fire, open their packs and pull out food and drink, as the others unroll and arrange their bedrolls around the fire. Kaylu looks steadily at Hugh, and then speaks. "You have changed, Hugh. What happened before we woke you at the void?"

I remain quiet for a moment, thinking of the Guardian.

I look one by one at each of me friends, and then I pull the little book from my shirt and place it carefully, even reverently, in front of us. Carefully choosing me words, I explain.

"While sitting at the void's edge, I began reading a few pages from <u>The Way of the Traveler</u>. Like in the past, I was assuming the words would be sent to me via thought projection; instead, its words melted into me mind and somehow carried me off to a place deep inside the void. At first, I thought it was someplace else entirely, but soon I realized the whole experience was revealing a part of me I never even knew existed; I think the void is actually a part of every living being. I can't go into all the details of the journey, but during this time I was actually crossing the void."

Dandi and Kaylu both look at him with surprise. Kaylu breaks the uncomfortable silence, saying slowly and gently, "We were there, Hugh; you never left the cave. In fact, you were so still, it looked as if you were about to die."

Hugh put his hand on his friend's shoulder. "It is because of you and the others that I came back. The void we saw was only an illusion; sort of like a sign pointing the way, and showing what exists within each of us. The exterior version was never meant to be crossed—it's only a reflection of the great void existing in each of us. It is one of the last barriers we must pass as Soul in order to know the secret way."

Kaylu and Dandi exchange glances, now looking even more confused. Kaylu shakes his head and insists, "But we didn't cross any void, we only sat there on the ledge watching you."

Hugh shifts his position and looks into both of his friends' faces; thinking for a moment, he again tries to explain. "Crossing the void is not a physical movement. It's a journey within ourselves that when completed, allows us to overcome one of the deepest barriers that separate us from being what we truly are. For me, the barrier is fear. By leaving me fears behind, I was allowed an opportunity to cross part way over, and gain a greater understanding of not only myself but the Creator as well. Mine was a journey to remember who I am, and why I am here. I can't tell you anymore. Please trust me as I must trust each of you."

Kaylu and Dandi are silent for a moment, then nod their agreement.

I must be careful not to reveal all I have learned: it may cause confusion and delay the completion of our quest, not only for me, but for me mates as well.

Clearly, their help will be vastly important at the right time. I know beyond a shadow of a doubt that for me to be successful, I will need help from the others.

Loren and Karla walk over with the food. Sitting next to me, the girls pass the bread, fruit, and meat to each of us. For a while, we remain silent as we eat our meal. I eat a little of the bread along with some fruit. I'm not very hungry but know I will need the energy later on. Once we finish eating, I watch as each lies down for a needed rest. I need to think and be alone for a while, not rest, so after walking a short distance from the camp, I find a place to sit.

I simply have to find a way to communicate with me family, especially Melody. My experience with the void made me realize how every person in me life is going to ultimately be affected by my actions; the only way for me to succeed is to make the right choices and perform the right actions at the right time. But what is the right action? Here in this cave what seems right may be wrong; what seems wrong may be right.

After a few moments pondering and worrying about taking a misstep, I realize that one thing I know for sure is that something in the cave's environment enhances my emotional, physical, and mental capabilities such that I am far more advanced than I could have ever imagined. So while I'm being empowered in this way, I should take advantage of this unusual situation to somehow communicate with Da', me sister, or both; I can't squander this opportunity.

At the same time, I must be careful; I can't allow the cave's raw power to corrupt or control me. By itself, the power is neutral, and has no direction of its own; it grows from me own feelings and thoughts, and especially me imagination. Once it connects to me thoughts, senses, emotions or feelings, it goes in the direction that they desire. Imagination, I'm finding, is the strongest way for this power to express itself in me. If I am not disciplined, then my mind will stray and my body's lower desires will influence everything I do; if I do not use it correctly, then the power will cause as much harm as good.

Pieces of me mind and the many revelations I have experienced slowly stitch together. Staring into the cave's vastness, I realize that even though I had risen above fear during my experience at the void, I haven't eliminated it. Possessing a body, I still have attachments, desires, and emotions. I'm still susceptible to being brought down like anyone else. I must not allow meself to be foolish enough to think that I have beaten the traps in me mind, and I also must not allow meself to underestimate what I'm capable of.

Thinking about the little boy who is lying in the hospital somewhere on Earth, I now know that this whole adventure has been created out of that coma. The person I am now is nowhere near who I was as that boy; yet the truth is that it's that little boy who is controlling this entire event. The child known as "Hugh" is only another reflection of what I am, and yet it's that reflection I have always thought was truly real. The very concept of what I thought was real is truly in the power of me own imagination. This world where I am now—is it even real? Is this body—this older body wearing this tunic and boots—real? From what I've experienced, it's possible that all of this is just some sort of dream…what some call a waking dream.

But this reality seems much more real than the reality I felt when I was—am?—a boy in his tree house.

The more I try to figure out the mechanics of this reality, the more confused I become. My thoughts jump and move, like a game of mental gymnastics. My thoughts are like monkeys in a cage, bouncing from one side to the other, fighting each other for dominance.

Sighing, I walk back to the campsite and lie down; perhaps some sleep will help to reorganize me thoughts after all. Closing me eyes, I try to bring into focus a mental image of me home and family. I see our house, sitting on its small hill, surrounded by azaleas and willows. Da' stands at the front door, thin and dark-haired; he smiles down at Melody, who's petting Cody furiously on the lawn, her bright blonde hair and Cody's pale yellow fur reflecting streaks of sunlight.

Slowly, I drift off to sleep.

As I sleep, I dream.

Distorted and blurred images passing through me mind's eye…nothing is in continuity, nothing in logical order: just images, hundreds—perhaps thousands— of images, all passing through me inner vision, like cards being shuffled impossibly quickly, and somehow disappearing into oblivion, as if by a magician. The images finally slow, and at last, stop altogether. I feel me mind relaxing as I drift on the edge of consciousness. Thoughts become still, distant voices come drifting around me; as I listen they become clearer. Gently, I force meself to concentrate, and the voices become more discernible. I think I can make out who they are; one of the voices sneaks up closely, and I recognize it. There's a shift and a pull, and suddenly, I'm looking down at me Da', Melody, and someone else I don't know.

I am just a pair of eyes, I have no body, but I feel myself responding upon seeing me family. I'm in the tree house, together with Da', Melody, and this stranger. It's morning, and sunlight pours through the open window; my sight shifts again, and I focus in on Melody. She is sitting on the couch in the tree house, and my first impulse is to reach out to let her know I'm here, but I sense she can't hear or see me. I feel me heart thumping in my chest. I feel all the things I normally would with a corporeal body. I try to stay calm and listen to what's being said, and the rumbling noise begins to take on familiar patterns, and I can finally figure out that the older man is talking about dreams. As I listen, I become more aware of what is going on around me. Emotions are bubbling up from being so close to Melody and Da'. Quickly, I take action to suppress my feelings, because somehow I know that if I do not control them, I risk losing this connection and getting nothing from this experience.

The man is still talking.

"Dreams are a doorway to communicate with our true self. To understand what our dreams are trying to convey, we must look at them not from a mental or emotional point of view, but from a spiritual viewpoint. Most dreams display meanings at all levels, whether it be psychic, emotional, physical or spiritual. It is up to each person to approach their dream's meaning from the highest viewpoint available within himself. If the person is spiritually inclined, then he will see the experience's deepest meaning; if he isn't, then he will see the meaning from whatever level of awareness he views life from. Unfortunately, in most cases people do not see any meaning at all."

I can see the speaker shifting in his seat as he says, "Everyone experiences life from a very personal state of awareness, you see; people tend to see many different meanings from the same dream, but still, each sees it at his own specific level of awareness."

I'm listening carefully, and as I do, I consciously summon feelings of love, and try to transmit them to Da' and Melody; will they feel my presence?

The older man continues speaking. "Melody, your dream starts out in a neighborhood that you feel comfortable in; do you remember feeling anything else, besides feeling comfortable?"

Melody shakes her head up and down vigorously in assent. "I was walking on the sidewalk when I came to the big house; I went up the steps thinking that I needed to go inside."

The man interrupts. "Okay, let's take this one step at a time. Usually, in dreams a house can symbolize your own consciousness. In other words, the house is the place where Soul lives, which is the mind. The way you enter this house, and the condition of the house, usually indicate the dreamer's state of mind. For example, a house that is dark, run down, and in disrepair, or with tattered furniture and broken windows, feels scary or sad. That kind of house could symbolize that the dreamer is in a negative phase of life. There may be addictions, moral problems, or perhaps too much attachment to the body's desires, maybe financial problems, spiritual decline or relationship problems. On the other hand, if the house is organized, well-kept, with nice colors, comfortable furniture, and a warm feeling, then it may indicate this person is in better shape mentally."

I'm listening closely to this man's words. Focusing me attention, I find myself suddenly right next to my sister. The elderly man continues. "You say that this house has an old style: this may tell us that you are what some would call an 'Old Soul,' and someone who leans toward traditional values. If the house in your dream had been modern, it might have been representing the opposite."

"I can't be an Old Soul—I am just a little girl," Melody objected, shaking her head and crossing her arms.

The man slowly shakes his head and explains to Melody in a soothing voice, "I'm sorry, I didn't mean to call you 'old' at all; being an 'Old Soul' doesn't mean that you are older than other people; it's just an expression that says you have had a lot of deep experience in the ways of this world—probably by what is happening to you currently, and especially, I think, through your past lifetimes."

Melody smiles and nods with understanding. I see the man's face relax as he continues to explain how they might understand her dream. "Your dream's interpretation also depends on what you do in the house, or maybe how many rooms it has, or the sounds that you hear. These things help tell us about your spiritual growth, and possibly, other aspects of your life."

Melody considers his remarks carefully for a moment, and then replies, "This house was big and it was painted nice. When I walked up the steps, the double doors were beautiful. When I got inside, I noticed pretty flowers, fancy pictures, and nice furniture everywhere."

The man nods. "Okay, the fact that you walked up steps instead of down shows that you were entering a higher state of consciousness where the lesson has to be learned. Since the house is organized, with nice paint, flowers, and furniture, it shows that not only are you prepared to experience the lesson, but you are also going to learn a positive lesson from this experience."

I watch as all three seem to pause to let these statements sink in.

The man then asks Melody, "How did you feel when you entered the house?"

"I felt fine; it was a warm feeling—safe and inviting."

"Good, tell us more," he encouraged her.

"Once inside, I could hear music coming from somewhere. I walk upstairs to follow the sounds, and I notice my cat Namo is at the top of the stairs, running back and forth. He seems to be impatient; I think he wants me to follow him and keep moving. When I reach the top, I notice a long hallway with doors on each side."

The man interjects, "How did you feel when you saw all the doors in the hallway?"

"I was curious; I felt like I needed to search for something in these rooms behind the doors."

The man nods and then explains, "Walking up even more stairs shows that you're progressively ascending to an even higher awareness. The doors may be pointing to a spiritual decision you must make."

After a moment, he gestures at Melody, and she continues. "I open the first door on the left and walk in. The room is dark and empty, except for a chair in the center of the room; Da' is sitting in the chair. I feel sad and a little frightened when I look at him."

Brandon leans forward and asks quietly, "Why?"

Melody squirms a bit, glancing shyly at Da', and looking down at her shoes. I sense her discomfort. She says softly, "He seems lost...he's very sad...and I can tell he's been crying...It's as if he doesn't know what to do. I run out of the room, and I feel alone and scared by myself."

Da' rubs her shoulder in support and struggles to smile.

The man is quiet for a second, then suggests very gently, "Melody, what you thought your father felt may mean something else. It may have come from your own search to uncover why this tragedy has happened to your family. The empty room may symbolize the empty feeling you have felt since your mother and brother's accident. You went to your father for answers, but when he could not help you, it made you realize that even he—the person you have always depended on—can't give you the answers you are searching for. His crying and seeming to be lost seem to be a classic example of you projecting your own feelings about your own life at this time: you are sad and feel lost."

Melody squints at him for moment, "Projecting?"

"I mean that maybe the feelings you saw on his face are really your feelings, not your dad's."

Melody brightens, and says excitedly, "Oh, like face-swapping in Snapchat?"

Confused, the man looks over at Clark, who nods and explains, "It's an app, Brandon; it allows you to switch faces with your friend, or to put one celebrity's face onto another celebrity's face. So yes, it is a little like that."

I now know the man's name; Brandon asks her to continue.

"Well, after I see Da' and run out of the room, I go back into the hall and walk over to the other side. I open the door to my right, and as I walk in, I notice the door's a pretty blue. But Da' is in this room, too; he is sitting again in a chair right in the center of the room. Sunlight comes through a small window, and it shines onto the room's only chair, the one my dad's sitting in. He's writing and writing, and I can tell he doesn't have time for me, so I leave. I just feel confused, since my dad was in the other room, too. And so I go into the next room, and there is my dad again, this time reading a book! This room is different, because it has a bed and chair, and it is lit up better. When I step over to Da', he closes the book and smiles at me. I ask him what he's doing, and he says he's waiting for a secret that I will tell him."

Brandon puts up his hand and asks, "So here he speaks to you, and he wants a secret from you? How did you feel this time when you enter the room and see your dad reading? How did you feel when he told you that he is waiting for you to tell him a secret?"

Melody shrugs her slender shoulders and says, "I'm comfortable this time, but a little confused, mainly because I don't know of any secret to tell him. Da' seems more peaceful. The book he's reading on his lap seems very important to him. I feel he's learning something important, and whatever it is, it's making him happy."

Brandon thinks for a moment, then comments, "This part of the dream may be showing your father is learning what he needs to know, but it is not what you need to know. In other words, what it is you're looking for is different from what your dad is looking for. You are looking for something only you can discover for yourself. The room being in better condition and having a bed show that your father is getting things in order. He's finding his answers, and they're his, and nobody else's."

Melody and Da' both nod in agreement; Da' has listened attentively to Melody's story of her dream and Brandon's interpretations. I can feel that he somehow knows that this dream interpretation is very much meant for him as much as for Melody. She continues. "Once back in the hallway I go on to the next door, which is painted yellow. When I open the door, the room is empty except for a rocking chair in the center of the room. This time, instead of Dad being in the chair, I see me! The Melody in the chair looks at me and smiles. Then I woke up."

"Tell me," Brandon asks slowly, "what did you think or feel when you saw yourself?"

"I felt confused at first and a little scared, but then I sort of felt satisfied, sort of like I had discovered something."

Brandon stands up and steps over to the window looking into the center of the tree. He pulls his pipe from his shirt pocket, nods his head slowly, and says, "Melody, the last room may be showing you again that you must find your own answers by yourself. Neither your father nor I can give you all the answers you seek, but your father can and will help point the way. That last room indicates that you'll discover your personal relationship with Soul, that you will find your true self if you continue as you are doing. The answers you seek are all within yourself."

Disembodied, hovering in between worlds, I can somehow listen and watch these events taking place as clearly as watching the tele. This older man seems to know what he is saying; the more I hear, the more I like him. He might be just what Da' and Melody need to establish some sort of communication with me.

Apparently having second thoughts about smoking, Brandon puts his pipe back in his shirt pocket and says, "Both of you are moving forward in the right direction. It seems you are traveling parallel paths but the answers for each of you are different. Yes," he nodded his head, "I think you're going in the right direction, and will be very helpful to one another."

Da' joins Brandon over at the window and says, "I am amazed at how the pieces of the dream fit together once the feelings and symbols are clear; learning what I did from the dream makes me feel more comfortable with what we're doing."

I can feel Da's profound respect for this man after this dream interpretation. He extends his hands onto and over the window's edge, and leaning in, he stares into the tree's interior as he asks, "Are all dreams as insightful as this one?"

Brandon chuckles. "Oh, some can be far more revealing, and then others can be far more confusing than we can ever understand. I only lent my knowledge of universal symbols and reminded Melody of the way she felt each time she opened a new door. It is her own insight about what she was feeling and searching for that revealed the answers: not only for her, but for you also."

I feel meself and the scene both fading. Upon hearing the dream interpretations, I know within me heart that Da' and Melody are to be a part of my journey in ways that I can't even begin to imagine. I just see the three climbing down from the tree house when the scene dissolves completely, and I'm back in the cave.

****

Once the trio arrives back at the house, Brandon declines their offer of more hospitality and excuses himself. "I have to get some paperwork done that needs filing by the beginning of the week. I also want to do some research; if there's any chance we can find some way to establish communication with Hugh, we need to get going and find it."

As Brandon strides away from the house, he realizes that he is becoming ever more convinced that Clark's son actually is traveling the inner dimensions searching for his mother. At the same time, perhaps Hugh is trying to contact with either or both his dad or sister; if so, it would be of utmost importance that this boy know that a third person in the outer world is trying to help.

CHAPTER 24 ~
ANOTHER LAND

When Hugh and his comrades awaken, they discover that Karla and Loren have disappeared, taking their bedrolls and backpacks with them. Their footprints point in the direction of the stream.

Hugh, Dandi, and Kaylu begin searching in three different directions for the girls. Hugh wonders, "What could have happened? Why had they left with no word? If the girls wanted to leave, they could have simply said so and left; there's no reason for the secrecy of their departure." After a short search with no results, each begrudgingly heads back to camp.

Dandi is the first to arrive.

As he waits for Hugh and Kaylu, Dandi hopes that one of them might find the girls. He decides to pack up not only his own gear, but that of the other trekkers as well. Stuffing the backpacks, he thinks about how he has been stuffing his own feelings lately, packing them deep down inside himself. This cave seems to be swallowing him bit by bit. At first, he felt this journey was what he was supposed to be doing—the experience at the Wisdom Pool clarified his destiny for him. Now he isn't so sure.

He sees great changes in Hugh. The boy he met on the dock outside the city of Jotan barely seems to be any part of this new person. He's almost the same size, and he wears the same clothes, but Hugh's face looks markedly different. It's not that he looks that much older so much as he looks more grown up. Hugh is quieter, his expressions more serious; he walks gracefully with dignity. But his eyes are the most different; they seem to have an intensity and noble power that can draw a person in. At the same time, they reflect a cooler detachment offset by the warmth of an impersonal love that reaches inward first and then extends outward into an endless time of unlimited experience.

To Dandi, this transformation is unnerving. He knows the cave can do strange things to the mind, but the change in Hugh extends beyond him, too. Whenever Dandi is near Hugh, he begins questioning himself. He feels ashamed, guilty, undeserving for what life has given him. Has he given back to life? Have the bad deeds he has done in the past caught up with him? He shakes his large head with disbelief. For some reason, Hugh's presence brings out questions in him about his own self-worth. It's as if the boy's presence demands that others' nobility should show itself. Does he even have any noble attributes to express in the first place? Maybe the girls felt this strange feeling as well? Perhaps they too felt feelings of incompetence; could this be the reason for their leaving? Dandi walks over to the stream to wash his face. Kneeling on the sandy shoreline he stares at his reflection in the clear, slow moving water. The huge grizzled face staring back at him looks like a stranger. Dandi's mind whirls with strange energies and thoughts.

Why?

Why is he here with Kaylu and Hugh?

Where is he going?

What will he do once he arrives?

These and a hundred more questions keep rushing into his mind, but never with any answers. Each time a question surfaces, he looks within himself, wandering deeper into his mind trying to search for meaning. One thing for sure—it's becoming clear that it's getting harder and harder to stay with Hugh. It's like Hugh peers into his Soul, and can see the fear and confusion, but he never says a word. If this is who Hugh is now, what will he be like once they leave the cave and enter the Land of Light and Darkness? Dandi slams his fist into the stream, shattering his image, and then stomps back to camp.

Kaylu and Hugh have returned—without the girls. Silently, they pick up their backpacks. Dandi swings his pack across his back and falls in behind Hugh. The group starts following the streambed as it flows deeper into blackness. Soon their only light comes from the torch that Hugh holds aloft. Unlike the first cave, this one has a breeze; it isn't constant, but each waft carries a promise of fresh air and freedom from the dreary cave that all of them have grown especially weary of with the departure of Karla and Loren.

The walking seems endless. Hugh's mind wanders.

How many hours?

How many days?

I can't tell; there's only constant blackness and the unchanging vastness of the cave itself.

I don't seem to be affected as much as Kaylu and Dandi, judging by the drudgery of their slow steps. In fact, most of the time I remain quiet, which would have been unusual for the old me. When I do say something, it is just information concerning what is approaching us or what we just passed. We don't stop much for sleep, either. We all have but one intention: to get out of this cave and leave the darkness behind us.

Dandi is the first to notice. At first, he thinks it is a figment of his imagination, but then he knows that he actually sees it: a bluish light faintly illuminating the cave walls. Dandi's heartbeat quickens as he walks faster, brushing his hand along the wall. The light does not come from an external source, but is the glow generated out of a bioluminescent moss lining one of the sides of the cave!

Now all three can see the faint, blue-green glow, and walking further the moss is so thick that it lights up the entire side of the cave in a diffused fluorescent glow; it's so bright they can almost see without the torch's help. The blue light outlines the cavern walls, showing ledges and smaller caves above their heads.

I slow down, gesturing for the others to follow; I've gotten use to using caution as me guide when walking into unfamiliar areas. Walking deeper into the blue glow the landscape changes.

Kaylu is entranced by the blue light. Moss grows on the ceiling of the cave and along both of the walls, creating a light source that is almost like normal daylight, except it is wrapped in a blue misty glow: even the stream is turning a fluorescent bright blue.

Dandi looks about him; his delight with the blue effervescence surrounding them begins to fade again. How had he ever been coerced into taking this quest? Here he is, lost in this alien cave, whose strangeness can only distract momentarily before giving way again to his depression and uncertainty; how could he have let this boy talk him into journeying with him? What is he to gain? Would he even survive to see the outside world again? His thoughts carry him deeper into the spiral of depression; his mind rebels against the idea that he is on a quest for truth, or that he's there to help this boy find his mother. Besides, what business is it of his? He is putting his life in danger, and for what? Dwelling on the stupidity of his motives and actions, Dandi's anger grows, stimulating his emotions to almost a point of rage.

Hugh signals his companions to stay behind him as he enters a passage where the stream appears to tunnel underground. After just a minute of exploration, he steps out and turns to face them. He smiles and opens his mouth as if to speak, but before he utters a word, he notices the weird expression on his friend Dandi's face. Hugh purses his lips, holds up his hand, and says calmly, "We stop here; the stream flows only a short ways further, ending in a lake. The moss grows even thicker along the sides of the lake and the cave's ceiling."

Then I motion for me mates to follow. As we emerge from the short tunnel, we see a waterfall cascading from the right side of the lake reflecting in the churning waters. The blue glowing effect generated from the moss on the lake bottom gives the whole scene a surreal, ethereal look. A light blue haze shimmers within the mists, churned up from the lazy lapping waters then spreading out into a great halo. There is no shoreline to walk around it, nor materials to build a raft or a floating device of any kind. How are we to cross?

I pull off me backpack and walk closer to the shore of the huge underground lake. There has to be a way to get across—surely we don't have to turn around again? The sword did not vibrate or make a sound: aren't I going in the right direction? The lake's too wide for us to swim. The walls of the cave are too smooth to climb. Kaylu and Dandi walk up alongside me; all three of us stop and stare out across the hazy blue waters. The lake seems to be motionless; neither a ripple nor wave breaks its surface.

Silhouetted against the bluish light, our three dark forms stand staring over the thickening mist rising from the water like ethereal misshapen forms. Taking a few of the fire rocks and lighting them with our torch, we sit down to warm ourselves.

Dandi walks back and retrieves his backpack. Tossing it down beside himself, he fumbles inside it, rummaging for any kind of food. Luckily, we still had the food Olgera gave us; the girls had taken all the supplies they originally had with them.

Kaylu unrolls his bedroll and pulls some of the paste bread from his pack. I roll out me own bed and sit down. Through the firelight, we see the mist wafting on gentle breezes. The blue glow of the cave has intensified, giving off an intangible but definite feeling of foreboding. No one says anything for a long while. We just sit, each of us thinking, each of us wondering what to do, each of us questioning himself. Then from out of the silence a slight whispering sound escapes. At first it is barely audible, but it slowly builds up. The lake waters begin to stir; small ripples brush against the shore, and as I watch, the ripples gradually skip faster across the surface. As the breeze picks up and becomes a constant wind, the ripples gradually change into small waves. Our fire dances in the wind; Kaylu pulls his blanket tighter as the air takes on a chill.

The wind is steadily growing; soon we can hear it whistling loudly through the cave. The waters rush faster and grow larger; the wind howls through small tunnels above us, keening like wolves on lonely mountain tops. I stand up, listening to the wild call.

Stepping closer to the shoreline, I watch the misty haze swirl on the lake surface as it spirals off in different directions. The wind screams and the chill factor drops—cold blast of air drills deep into our marrow. Dandi listens to the ominous mournful wind cry. Disjointed thoughts cartwheel through his mind like litter pushed along the gutter by an angry wind; his frustration grows with each blast of cold air. Spray from the ever-growing waves knocking onto shore soak us; there is nowhere to hide, nowhere to escape from the wind and spray.

Dandi yells at me, but the howling wind drowns out his voice. When he stands up and strides over to me, at first I think he's trying to help me get out of the wind, but when the little giant grabs me by my shoulders with his huge hands and lifts me like a rag doll, I know how wrong I am. I glance up at the fiendishly distorted face staring back at me, and the blood in all me veins freeze: I can't even feel my heart beat. Dandi's eyes blaze in maniacal hate; his neck muscles bulge as he lifts me high above his head. I find my lungs with a start and let out a howl as the giant tosses me onto the ground. The sand cushions me fall, but the breath is still knocked from me body...other than this, I'm all right—for the moment. Dandi curses and lunges at me, but I'm too fast; quickly I roll out of his reach and stand up.

I yell as loud as I can, straining against the wind. "Dandi! What's wrong?" My voice is nearly indistinguishable from the growling wind, and he can only feel rage coursing through his blood. His mind is on fire with hate and anger. Dandi's crazed thoughts scream at him for being so stupid; he is convinced that he is worthless and deserves an ill end.

Dandi lunges at me again; I pivot, throwing Dandi off balance and into the water's edge. He stumbles trying to stand, but between the wind, the waves, and his own wrath, he falls back again, this time further from the shore into deeper waters. Struggling to stay afloat, Dandi never was a good swimmer, and his struggles only carry him further into the lake. Shocked, I stare open-mouthed for only one panic-stricken moment before coming to my senses, and I dive into the lake to save me friend.

After just a few strokes, I have closed the gap between us; how can I help my giant friend back onto shore? The cave's inexplicable power is fueling the growth of some anger normally hidden deep inside of Dandi. As the giant thrashes, he curses and reaches out to grab me; if I get too close, I'll be pulled under along with him.

Dandi sinks beneath the waves. At first I think he will surface again, but after several moments, I only see waves pushing me further from my friend. The wind howls and echoes even louder throughout the cavern with a loud and deafening *Huuuu...*

I dive under the water, and am surprised how calm it is beneath the surface. Light from moss growing on the lake bottom lights up the water, making it easy to see Dandi's massive body struggling to rise up to the surface. For a moment it seems the little giant will make it, but then he's struggling again and begins to sink.

Pulling me scabbard off me back, I swim closer to Dandi one-armed and reach out, nudging him with the scabbard. I kept the sword still encased in the scabbard, so it's rigid enough for Dandi to grasp, and as I hope, he reaches out and grabs it. I pull with all me strength; the water helps to lighten the giant's weight so it's somewhat easier to pull him as long as he holds onto the scabbard. Pulling and kicking as hard as me muscles can, I desperately swim upward, and then as if by magic, me head breaks the surface and I use both hands to pull Dandi toward me.

The giant's head breaks the surface, gasping for air. We both struggle toward the shore; every movement is a fight to pull the giant back to shallow waters. When I think I can't move another inch, me foot grazes the bottom of the lake. Giving one more tug, I feel the giant stagger to his feet and then stand up. I release the scabbard; it's all I can do to struggle toward the shore myself.

I'm exhausted, and even though my feet can just touch the lake bottom, the waves and the wind's intensity keep me from moving forward, and I feel myself slipping, pulled down under the relentless waves. Just as I'm sinking, a huge hand dips into the water, grabs hold of me waist, and lifts me up; Dandi half-carries me as he trudges against the wind and from out of the water onto dry land. Dandi places me down on the shore and Kaylu rushes to me side. Standing stiffly on wobbly legs, Dandi looks down at me with a confused expression on his face; releasing his gaze, he stumbles a few feet away and plops down beside me. I take a few deep breaths and then raise me head with a start: me sword! I breathe a sigh of relief as I realize that the scabbard is still tied with a thin cord to me waist, and lies close by in the shallow waters of the lake. Struggling to stand, I stumble over to Dandi's side. Placing me hand on his shoulder, I ask him between long breaths if he's all right.

With his head resting in his hands, Dandi stares at the ground. The winds have died down and the water is rapidly quieting, and Dandi's mind grows still. He looks up at me and says, "I think so—I can't remember all that just happened. I only know that I hated you and wanted to destroy you before you destroyed me."

I shake me head. "Dandi, it was the cave; it's stirring your emotions and bringing out some kind of deep fear or anger lying deep inside you. Once you were thinking or feeling it, it grew and eventually overcame you."

Dandi sits silent for a moment and then looking again at me, he asks, "Why did it make me hate and fear you so?"

I pull in the cord wrapped around me waist and then finally grasping the sword, I attempt to explain. "The best answer I can give is that me presence or me energy is magnifying in this cave. It's radiating out, and intermingling with your own energy or aura; it's like what happened earlier with me and Kaylu. Instead of our thoughts intermingling, it's our emotions being affected; these emotions cause your reality to become unbalanced, almost like punching holes in you. Once the barrier broke within you, it released deep hidden pockets of negative energy. This energy can sometimes manifest as hate, fear, or something else, and since I was the cause of the disruption, naturally you focused it on me. These thoughts of suspicion, anxiety, hate, and fear kept growing inside you, enhanced by the cave's power; they became a destructive force so intense that they had to be released. I think the wind storm was caused by this energy. Once you were submerged in the water, the energy dissipated into the lake, cleansing you. You've hidden this anger away so well that even you weren't even aware it existed."

Dandi hung his head in his massive hands. For a few moments he is silent, and then he looks up.

Tears trickle down his cheeks. Through those tears, I see a look of peace and nobility that wasn't there before. I help him stand. "Dandi, this is a great thing that's happened to you. It's cleansing you of something that's always delayed your own growth. We both can be thankful for the experience, never feel guilty or ashamed of what happened here."

Dandi looks deeply at Hugh, and for the first time, he sees his pure unconditional love. Hugh has grown before his very eyes, and now is partly responsible for him reaching an awareness that has eluded him throughout his life. Hugh's patience and kindness along with his courage helped cleanse his past and bring peace, grace, forgiveness, and finally freedom to his mind; for this he will be eternally grateful and never doubt himself or Hugh again.

The three build a new fire and dry their clothes. A quick meal makes them feel better, but silently the trio knows they are lost, and have no way to cross the fluorescent blue lake.

CHAPTER 25 ~
MEDICAL JEOPARDY

Anxious energy floods Clark's mind as he enters the main doors of the hospital. Brandon is waiting at the information counter in the center of the lobby. Grasping Clark's extended hand, Brandon says, "Clark! I'm glad you could make it on such short notice."

Clark responds, "You said it was urgent. What's wrong?"

"We have a surprise meeting in a few moments with the medical staff and insurance representatives."

Clark stops abruptly. "Why?"

Brandon's face flinches. "I'm not sure, but whatever it is, you know it can't be good."

Both men enter the supervisor's office. Seated at a table are several people in medical white coats, presumably doctors, and some in business suits.

Dr. Orvitz stands up and gestures toward two empty seats. "Mr. Bailey, I'm glad you made it so quickly. We have a situation that demands our immediate attention." Dr. Orvitz then introduces the rest of the people in the room. "To the right is Mr. Larry Hauerbach, the claims examiner for California Insurance Guarantee Association. To his right is of course Dr. Stepp, who is the medical representative for Alliance Equities. And, finally, Mr. Harding from Saturn Insurance, who represents the company whose driver was operating the truck that was in the collision with your wife and son. Ladies and gentlemen, this is Mr. Bailey and his attorney, Brandon Lewis."

Both take a seat. Dr. Orvitz continues. "Without getting too deeply into who's right and who's wrong, the first thing we would like to address is the reason for this meeting. Alliance Equities is the medical insurance company for Mr. Bailey and his family. Currently, they're responsible for the billings connected to Mrs. Bailey and her son Hugh. Dr. Stepp is the medical examiner for Alliance. Mr. Harding's from Saturn Insurance and is representing his company, without taking responsibility for liability at this time. Sitting next to him, Mr. Hauerbach represents CIGA, which is the guarantor for Saturn Insurance Company based in California. I'm turning this meeting over to Mr. Hauerbach to explain further the circumstances that have arisen in the last few days. Mr. Hauerbach, please take over from here."

"Thank you, Dr. Orvitz." Mr. Hauerbach stands up. A thin fellow, about sixty years old, wearing a black suit, Mr. Hauerbach has gray thinning hair combed back to try to hide more serious balding spots. His narrow eyes are framed by black horn-rimmed glasses. "Ladies and gentlemen, I'm here to advise that I am now the adjuster assigned to handle the afore-mentioned file. Please allow me to finish before responding." He then pulls some papers from his folder and proceeds to read.

"Pursuant to an order of the Circuit Court of the First Circuit State of California, Case number S.P: No: 09-1-0776. The Saturn Insurance & Guaranty Company was declared insolvent on September 21, 2013. The Insurance Commissioner of the State of California is appointed as Liquidator. All Claims and files that were previously handled by Saturn Insurance & Guaranty Co., including this file, have been transferred to the California Insurance Guarantee Association (CIGA) for review and further handling under the guidelines of the California Insurance Code, section 1063."

Mr. Hauerbach places the file down and looks at Clark. "I need to make something very clear, Mr. Bailey. I represent a division of the California Insurance Guarantee Association, which is not an insurance company in the traditional fashion. This division of CIGA issues no policies, collects no premiums, makes no profits and assumes no contractual obligations. CIGA's sole duty is to pay what is defined in the Insurance Code Subsections 1063.1 and 1063.2 as 'covered claims.' CIGA was created to provide only a limited form of protection in the event of insurer insolvency. Furthermore, covered claims are not co-extensive with what the insolvent insurer's obligations under the policy would have been. What I am saying is that CIGA does not stand in the shoes of the insolvent insurer for all purposes. CIGA's role is to be of the last resort. Because CIGA is a fund of last resort, we can't indemnify you or your family for the injuries they sustained as a result of the above-mentioned loss."

Clark's face freezes; a rush of fear shoots through his body. Without saying a word, Brandon reaches out and holds his arm.

Mr. Hauerbach continues. "It's our understanding that Alliance Equities is currently assisting you in your medical bills. Alliance Equities is considered other insurance in this claim and as stated, CIGA is governed by Statute Section 1063.1, which states in essence that 'covered claims' do not include any claim to the extent it is covered by any other insurance of a class covered by this article, which is available to the claimant or insured, nor any claim by any person other than the original claimant under the insurance policy in his or her own name. I am to inform you that Section 1063.2 states, 'If damages against the uninsured motorists are recoverable by the claimant from his or her own insurer, the applicable limits of the uninsured motorist coverage shall be a credit against a covered claim payable under this article.' In other words, CIGA is refusing liability because Alliance Equities and your own automobile insurance take senior liability, which leaves Saturn Insurance free of liability and recourse due to its bankrupt status."

Clark can't stay silent any longer. "You bastards! Me wife and son are lying in this hospital fighting for their lives, and you're throwing statutes at me and refusing to take any financial responsibility for their injuries? What the hell is that all about?"

Mr. Hauerbach calmly looks at Clark and says, "Of course, you have the right to file a lawsuit against the person you feel responsible for the loss, which is the trucking company directly, but we feel that's a waste of time, and the time element it takes to file would be beyond any current assistance that's required now."

Brandon holds Clark's arm, steadying him. Calmly and resolutely, Brandon says, "We understand your position, Mr. Hauerbach, and we will take into consideration all that you've said. However, we are not in the state of California, so how do you take presence outside of California?"

Hauerbach picks up some papers and begins to stack them, and without looking up, he replies, "The Saturn Insurance Company has offices not only in this state, but its main office is in California as well."

Before anything else can be said, Dr. Stepp blurts out, "While we're all here stating our respective positions, I wish to declare the intention of Alliance Equities. Since we were eventually going to pursue damages against Saturn for our clients' injuries and medical bills, it is now obvious this is highly unlikely. Therefore, I have to advise that we now intend to reach a final settlement with Mr. Bailey. Upon reaching a settlement, we will then legally move forward in court to get approval to disconnect the life support system that is currently maintaining the body functions of his wife and son. Please keep in mind, Mr. Bailey, your policy limits expire within two weeks at the current rate of billing that we're receiving. It seems clear now that we can no longer participate in keeping two persons connected to a life support system when they aren't showing any improvement from a medical standpoint. Dr. Orvitz, you'll receive documents that mandate you fill out for submittal to the court for a cancellation of the stay that Mr. Lewis previously filed." Ms. Stepp looks over at Clark. "We're sorry for the inconvenience, Mr. Bailey, but our rules mandate that we protect our interests. In two weeks, we will no longer maintain the financial burden, and you must find other sources. With this said, I think this meeting is over."

Clark pauses for a few seconds trying to internalize what he's being told; then suddenly he bangs his fist on the table. "Over! Over, ya' say! The hell it is! Nothing is over! Nor shall ya' be murdering me wife and son for your convenience!" Jerking his arm away from Brandon, he puts both hands on the table, and he looks angrily at Brandon. "Tell me now, my fine barrister, how is it ya' just sits there and says nothing? Tis not the time now to shut your gob! All this blather they give and not one of ya' gives a smidgeon about two human beings! Tis a bunch of banshees ye' are, with hearts as dark as night!"

Putting his hand on Clark's shoulder, Brandon firmly replies, "Clark, calm down! This is not the time to throw a tantrum. Nothing is over, trust me!"

"Tantrum, you say! Are ya' all daft? What you are seeing is only a sure smidgeon of a tantrum, me trusted barrister!" Everyone except Brandon, Clark, and Dr. Orvitz quickly stand to leave. Clark is beside himself; he isn't about to let them kill Annie and Hugh. Who do they think they are? Anger sweeps through him like a dark storm; it's all Brandon can do to keep him seated in his chair.

Brandon talks quickly and calmly. "Clark, stay down! This is not over! Anger will not help the situation. Believe me, my friend; we will not let them proceed without a fight. We'll act on this first thing in the morning; we have a minimum of ten days before they can do anything, so let the doctor and I talk this over. You have to trust in me, Clark, more now than you've trusted in anyone before. I'll need your help, but in the state you're in, you're only making things worse."

Brandon knows the insurance representatives are mostly bluffing, but to explain this to Clark right now in front of the others would not only be unwise but useless: Clark has to calm down first.

Clark takes a deep breath; his heart is beating furiously, and he feels nauseated as if he's going to vomit. His chest is tight; his mind won't calm down, but he knows he's powerless at the moment. He has to let Brandon handle it.

Walking out of the room toward the hospital exit, Clark has to get away to think and calm down. Abruptly turning around in the hall, he walks toward his wife's and son's room. Maybe, just maybe, being with them will help. Entering the room, he goes to Hugh's bedside.

Staring at his son and thinking about what's happening, tears moisten his eyes.

Hugh's just a lad, not even a teenager; just a small lad, and yet he's trying so hard to save his family. Where does he get the strength? He's so pale and so small in the bed with lifelines hooked up to him. It seems impossible he could be capable of doing anything. Yet Clark knows his son is somewhere doing whatever he can to find his mother. Clark has to trust in his dreams and what he's learned in the past few months. Turning to Ann, he stares for a moment. She, too, is pale and small; she looks as if death has already come if not for the tubes and bandages. In her stillness she is as beautiful as the day when they had first met.

"Where are ya', Annie? How can I help? What are ya' going through that keeps ya' so silent, so still?" he whispered. Taking his wife's hand and closing his eyes, he thinks of a better time, a time when she was vibrant and young, full of life and promise; he misses her so much, his torment is the empty feeling in his soul. Without Annie, life doesn't seem to have any purpose. Without his son, there is no promise of the future.

He stays for hours just sitting in the darkness, watching, hoping, and praying that Ann will show some little gesture of life—anything—but it doesn't happen. In his solitude, Clark feels alone and defeated.

Next morning, Brandon calls Clark and asks him to be at his office by three o'clock. Clark barely slept during the night; his mind wouldn't stop worrying over what the previous day's meeting unveiled. No matter how hard he tries, he sees no way out. It's quite possible that less than two weeks from now his wife and son will die. How could society let this happen?

Insurance companies are supposed to take care of these things. How could laws be created that allows them to take people's money and then fail in their responsibilities to take care of people?

Why does this government allow this to happen?

In Ireland, medical aid is given freely to the citizens; perhaps he should go back, possibly for the rest of his life. With his dual citizenship, he might be able to take Annie and Hugh back to Ireland, but then again, they might not even survive the trip. For years now he has paid enormous premiums every month, not once using any of its benefits beyond paying for a checkup or two. Now, when it's needed, the law allows the insurance company to shirk its duty. He had to admit he had been naïve about medical insurance when he got to the states, but he had no idea what they could and couldn't do. It appears that there is no regard to human life or the suffering this is causing. It is, and has always been, only about the money! The bottom line is the hospital, the insurance companies, the government, and others all create rules and laws to wiggle out on their obligations to the citizens. The world is dedicated to making a profit, and to hell with human life and suffering.

Clark never thought in these terms before, but now he's seeing a part of life that probably has always been there, but he avoided it.

Now it's consuming his entire being.

CHAPTER 26 ~
PRISON OF FEAR

Freezing winds blow across barren mountains.

Gray skies with black shades of drifting clouds move swiftly across black granite mountains menacingly projected from a black ocean. No life, no growth, nothing; only a stark contrast of blackness against the dark gray sky. Wind whistles through slices of crevices and pointed outcroppings standing out like daggers defying anything to come into their embrace. At their top, one mountain stands out from the rest, wearing a crown of jagged peaks. Fierce winds, crashing waves, and other violent cataclysms over endless eons formed this treacherous land. The keen observer, though, feels something else.

A dark foreboding emanates from this equally dark land.

Energies of despair, fear, and hopelessness; but even greater is an energy reeking of death. The ocean surrounding this sad land is dark, turbulent, and full of swift currents, funnels, whirlpools, and furious ravenous creatures. Fear from the dark side of life holds this land together. No one living as humankind knows life survives here. As vast as the dark island is, it's a lifeless wasteland. No soul ever goes willingly to this place, yet deep within its center is the power and energy that under the right circumstances draw countless Souls to its black heart. Over billions of cycles this power was formed, and through its dark images it creates an energy point that sends its power outward to infect all it comes in contact with. Within these barren black mountains that rise above dark, depthless waters, Ann Bailey lies as a captive deep within this black prison.

The negative power has complete control over all illusions especially those formed in her mind from hopelessness, fear, anger, and attachments. Once the auto accident happened, Ann's spirit drifted in a temporary adjustment state, trying to gain consciousness. Ann is overwhelmed by her fear of losing her children, her husband, and of course, her life. The depression that plagued her all her life ultimately took control and dragged her spirit down to this unholy place. A surge of negative energy carved out a dark place within her Soul, damning her to this black, barren wasteland. Once in its grasp, the poisonous energy overwhelmed her with a fear so loathsome that its very essence created her prison and its demons. These demonic images are born from her dark feelings which then give substance and power to Ann's self-made prison. Not only is this prison keeping her trapped but it's also beginning bit by bit to consume who, and what she is and would ever be. It's a slow process. Most Souls fight back...but eventually all succumbs to their own mind's treachery. Once totally consumed, the Soul still exists, but only as a form of energy that feeds an evil darkness. All that they were, all they had become, is forever lost. Eventually this hideous self-serving power will consume what is Ann Bailey, but before this happens, the power must emotionally and mentally prepare her. This preparation is the most insidious part of the entire process. Combined with Ann's own energy, the power grows, keeping her locked in a hell of her own fears. Each fear grows as the dark power feeds and nourishes the negative seed within her.

Eventually, the power pulls Ann into itself. She will cease to exist as a life form composed of love, compassion, wisdom, awareness or any other virtues humans are capable of. The power entraps her like a spider's web; invisible strands grow thicker, stronger, binding her closer to its center.

Her greatest enemy is and always has been herself.

The power has many names—Maya, karma, hell, Satan, sin, purgatory, and hundreds more—that describe the hardships of living within a body of flesh that's responsible for all its thoughts and actions. Blinded by fear, Ann cannot see that the freedom she craves is still within reach. She only has to let go of the very thoughts she has held for so long and still perceives to be her reality. Without help, without something intervening in Ann's struggle, she will eventually sink into the blackness of fear and hopelessness, and all will be lost.

CHAPTER 27 ~
ESCAPE FROM THE
MOUNTAIN CAVE

Dandi, Kaylu and I sit together looking across the vast lake shimmering with misty blue light.

To get out of this cave, we need to cross the lake; but none of us can figure out how. I've been quiet for some time, trying to clear me mind and let me higher awareness come up with an answer. However, time keeps passing, and still I haven't thought of anything. Dandi and Kaylu remain quiet, letting their own thoughts wander, hoping to come up with a plan that would work.

Dandi looks up at me. "Do you still have the little book Jotan gave you?"

Startled, I feel a jolt of energy. "Yes, of course! I have it here in my tunic. Why didn't I think of that? I bet the book has the answer."

I pull the little book out and open it; the soggy pages are stuck together, so I carefully pull them apart. I begin to read.

> *The sword will point the way, but the boots will carry you there.*
>
> *If all else fails, then one must follow their steps, one in front of the other with total faith and knowingness that each step is closer to the Creator. Nothing exists that can stop Soul from meeting his goal if he fills himself with courage, faith, and above all else, love. Leave the past behind and keep your attention in front of you. These attributes alone will carry Soul forward.*
>
> *Having the knowledge of how the tools that have been given work is the second requirement that assists in finding your destination. To not use your gifts is like the lover searching for his lost beloved in the dead of night; in his hand is the lantern to light his way, but he does not light it. This omission is folly and will keep him searching aimlessly until he recognizes what has always been there.*

I look at my companions, and then continue reading.

> *To travel across barriers, sometimes one must confront the mind with its ocean of thoughts that arise from its depths. Past wisdom rises to the surface of the mind and provides stepping stones to success.*

I stop reading. "Of course! I've had the tools right here all the time. How could I have been so blind?"

Standing up, I look down at me feet, and I put one foot in front of the other. I try to be confident that the boots will show me how to cross the waters. As I stare at the boots, I walk to the left, toward the side of the lake. Each step takes on a life of its own. I don't lift up my eyes to see where I'm going; I focus only on the boots. Dandi and Kaylu follow as I get closer to the edge of the lake near the cave wall. The boots keep going toward the water, always pointing to the wall. I don't waver from me trust even as the boots take me to the water's edge; I calmly step into the lake.

The waters are lit up near the wall due to the increased growth of fluorescent moss covering not only the wall but the lake bottom as well. Water splashes over me boots and the lake gets deeper. Large flat rocks maybe an inch below the surface appear in front of me. The boots move toward the flat rock which is just large enough to stand on. I step on the flat surface and instantly another flat rock appears in front of the first. Taking a step out on the second rock, I see a series of rocks, each rock laid out in front of each other. Each rock is taller than the previous one, so that even though I am going deeper into the water, I don't sink any deeper than the depth of the first rock. Dandi and Kaylu follow; the rocks behind Hugh are easy to see now in the clear water.

From a distance it must have looked as if we were walking on top of the water. The rocks are spaced just so to form a perfect underwater bridge, allowing us to walk as easily as if we were on land. Soon we are far out in the middle of the lake. The rock steps are still just an inch below the surface, but now I can see that the rocks are tall pillars disappearing into the depths of the lake.

We are about a half mile from the shore and still have another half mile to go. Keeping me eyes on me boots, I carefully place one foot in front of the other. I suspect that if I take me eyes from the boots even for a moment, the pillars might not be there for the next step. This is confirmed when I see flat rocks rise to meet each forthcoming step as if directed to do so by my gaze. Due to the enormous depth of the lake, the columns of rock rise just in time for my next step.

This process makes walking somewhat unnerving. To Dandi and Kaylu behind me, it seems that the rock steps are already in place. I, however, have to be careful not to get dizzy or off balance; I must stay focused on each stepping stone as it rises to meet me next step. We walk slowly as we approach the opposite shore. As the waters become more shallow, I'm able to walk without watching as carefully and the columns are shorter with each step; consequently, I feel calmer and more balanced. The shore is quickly approaching; we see the other side clearly. Taking my last step, I jump to the shore, glad to have my feet firmly planted on solid ground.

We are elated to have crossed over this seemingly impossible obstacle. Looking about eagerly, this side of the lake is similar to the side we just left, except now there's no stream to follow, and shafts of sunlight with dust motes floating within them beckon us onward. We walk briskly toward the light's source. Fresh air floods our senses; it's slightly damp and the aroma is salty. I lead my friends toward the cave entrance; the closer I get to the fresh air and light the more excited I become. The cavern floor begins to climb upwards with boulders jutting on both sides of the sandy pathway. Light pours into the cave as we move closer and then I see it. At first, it's just a small patch of light blue; then light breaks onto our faces. The mouth of the cave comes into view; we scramble like thirsty men running to water. We stand there silhouetted against the light; behind us the darkness of the cave disappears along with the darkness that attached itself to us. Our minds become clear; something is leaving us, fading back into the unholy darkness as more and more light pours onto our faces.

I see a sandy beach below us. The cave's exit is on the side of a mountain with a pathway heading downward toward to a small flat area adjacent to the beach. Brown sagebrush and rocks spread out onto the sides of the mountain; a few trees dot the scenery. It looks a lot like the home I come from.

Beyond the sandy shores lies a vast ocean with white waves crashing on the shore.

Even with the pristine beach right in front of us, and me feeling my mind becoming free, nothing could compare with the huge pinkish orange sun that is setting on the horizon. Slowly changing to a bright yellow orange, the huge ball of light touches the edge of the ocean I can't imagine anything more beautiful as the sky begins to change, preparing itself for twilight.

Dandi and Kaylu stand still, not saying a word, each transfixed by the world that spreads out before them. Never in their wildest dreams could they have imagined something as strange and beautiful as the scene before them. I had talked of the great ball of fire in the sky that brought warmth and light to my world, but until this moment, neither quite believed it could be real. Now, in the brassy glare of this huge sun with the ocean lying below, it is as if they had passed into an enchanted land. They both could now understand the shock I experienced when I entered their sun-less world.

I quickly turn and look at them both with a huge grin on me face, and then with a shout, I'm running down the pathway toward the shoreline and the blue ocean; my mind and thoughts are free and I feel like the boy I really am, and so I shout, "C'mon, mates; let's go!"

CHAPTER 28 ~ JOTAN'S PROPHECY

I reach the bottom of the hill first.

Entering a small grove of trees, I stop and wait. Dandi and Kaylu are scrambling down the last little ridge when I call out. "Over here under the shade trees." Both see me waving and hurry over.

I'm excited. The child within me is taking back me heart. I look around, absorbing the landscape unfolding before me; almost skipping, I start in the direction of the ocean.

As we near the shore the ground changes to thick sand. Dandi moves more cautiously as his feet sink a few inches in the moist sand. We clear the trees and come into the open sunlight. Large waves are crashing on the shore. Neither Kaylu nor Dandi have ever seen or imagined such vast waters and such huge waves advancing, one after the other.

I'm bursting with anticipation, calling out as I sit and pull me boots off, then run to the water's edge. I let the waves wash over me feet; when the waves recede I feel the power and energy rushing back into the ocean's grasp. Turning, I wave for me comrades to join me.

Kaylu walks up beside me; he feels the pull on his feet from the sand and water rushing back into the depths. Kaylu whispers, "It feels as if the water's trying to pull us into its depths." With a jump he jerks back, grabbing my arm in his excitement.

I have to laugh. "You don't have to worry, Kaylu, the ocean won't harm you."

Dandi walks up and with awe watches the larger waves crash against the beach. Dandi listens to the loud crashing of the waves as they explode so close to us; this was way beyond anything he'd ever imagined. The water's salty odor and fine spray blow on our faces as wave after wave moves forward, crashing then receding into the dark blue waters.

Kaylu asks anxiously, "I cannot see the other shore; what kind of a lake is this? What is causing the water to be so angry?"

I think for a moment. I'm assuming this world is similar to my own, so I try to answer the best I can, recalling my research about oceans, the Caribbean and snorkeling for our family vacation.

"This is an ocean, not a lake. The ocean is a body of water much larger than any land mass; so as this world spins, the pull between this world and the moon creates a gravity force that keeps the ocean moving forward; when it encounters land, it's forced to back up. This is the pulling feeling you get when the waters recede after each wave hits the land."

Kaylu looks up at me and with a blank look on his face then asks, "What is a moon?"

Right then I realized I could tell them anything and they would probably believe it. I don't know enough about the relationship in this world of the ocean, gravity, the land and the moon to be sure of any facts anyway, so I just say, "Wait—tonight you'll see."

Dandi reaches down and scoops a handful of water and puts it to his lips, and just as quickly he spits it out, making a frowning face. "The ocean tastes awful. What is this stuff? Certainly it's not water?"

Trying not to laugh again, I reply, "You can't drink it—it's saltwater."

Both look at me blankly and at the same time ask, "What is salt?"

Thinking about how I can explain the ocean without confusing them further, I begin to formulate an explanation. "Salt is what is inside the ocean. It allows millions of life forms to live in the ocean. The water is not for drinking like fresh water. Without the salt the fish and other creatures that are in the sea couldn't live."

I realize that the more I talk, the more confused they become, so I just say, "While we're here, I'll try to explain bits and pieces of this world as we go. I'm not sure if this world is like mine or not, but it might be. Meanwhile, let's follow the shoreline and see where it goes."

Kaylu and Dandi shrug their shoulders and agree; after all, who are they to question things they don't understand, and who am I to explain something I'm just guessing about anyway? Maybe it's best to just explore this strange land a little bit at a time. The sun is almost gone from the horizon. This also puzzles them, but instead of asking more questions, they just follow me and we all explore this strange new world as best we can.

As the last bit of sunlight vanishes from the darkened sky, stars begin to appear. To me, it is the most natural and beautiful thing I had seen in a long while. To my two friends, it is simply awe-inspiring; so much so, that when I try to explain planetary systems and that some of the stars are actually suns with many other worlds spinning around them, they again can't grasp the idea. Kaylu then says quietly, "If I look at the stars as if they are the suns of many other worlds, it sort of takes the magic and fantasy from the beauty they project."

"I have to agree," I nod.

In this world I communicate with words as do Kaylu and Dandi, but the understanding of what is being said is more limited than the ordinary projection communication that we are used to. Still, it doesn't diminish this world's beauty or their fascination. To Kaylu and Dandi, this is a divine gift from the Creator and nothing less. The breezes from the ocean warm us as they caress our faces. One thing is for sure, we're getting hungry and thirsty. Walking inland a little bit, we sit down under what looks like pine trees and I pull me backpack off. We filled our water bottles before leaving the cave and each of us has a little food left from the journey. I build a fire from the last few fire rocks, and we sit on the sand to eat and rest awhile. Lounging around the fire listening to the ocean waves and feeling the wind gently blowing, I suddenly point across the other side of the ocean and exclaim, "Look! Here comes the moon!"

As they turn their gaze to the direction I'm pointing, both of their faces freeze into a stunned silence: a monstrous, huge, white glowing ball is beginning to rise from the far edge of the ocean into the darkness.

As we silently watch, the moon becomes larger and brighter; Kaylu and Dandi become more and more amazed. It's a full moon, and even I have to admit that it seems as if this moon is larger than what I remember back home. As the white globe rises from what seem to be the depths of the ocean, Dandi and Kaylu both are transfixed; soft moonlight spreads across the waters of the vast ocean.

Kaylu finally speaks. "This is one of the most beautiful things I've ever seen, I can't take my eyes away from it."

The moon rises even higher. Its bottom part is just above the ocean. We see light gray patches across the front of the huge, bluish-white globe. With the contrast of the dark ocean below and the twinkling of bright stars in the night sky, it's a scene that will imprint on their minds forever. I sit and watch me friends, recognizing myself in their faces. When I first visited their world, my reaction was similar. The wonder in their eyes makes me appreciate the natural beauty of what has become commonplace back in my world. Even the simple everyday events of life hold great beauty, but it's so easy to take for granted. I see now how we can get so lost in our minds that we block out the beauty of what seems ordinary acts of nature. Every feeling that Dandi and Kaylu feel, as they watch the wonders of this reality, become my own feelings. We stay up late that night as I try to explain the laws of nature existing in my world, hoping they are close or the same in this world. My two friends find it all fascinating. Eventually though, as the moon raises higher in the night sky, one by one each of us falls asleep, listening to the crashing of the ocean waves. For me, it's the first undisturbed sleep I can remember for quite a while.

As I sleep, I dream.

Upon waking the next morning, I vaguely remember parts of the dream; bits and pieces fall like rain drops from me mind as I try to make sense of it. The one part that stands out more than anything else is an image of Jotan saying, "You will need a ship in order to save your mother."

And I wondered; where would I get a ship? Would it be needed in this world, or somewhere else? Having learned not to prejudge things, I keep my mind open.

In the morning we walk down to the shore to watch the sun rise. To Kaylu and Dandi, the sun is not only a beautiful experience, but a puzzling one, since last night they had seen it sink beneath the waves of the vast ocean, and now it's rising from behind the mountains to their backs.

The three of us walk along the shoreline. As the sun rises higher, Kaylu notices small creatures living in the sand where the waters race across the shoreline; the curious things run sideways and some burrow quickly into the wet sand as the water rushes back to the ocean. But as interesting as these were, nothing prepared them for the huge round sea turtles coming ashore. Waves carry hundreds of these creatures to the shores where they emerge slowly crawling onto the beaches. Dandi and Kaylu find these creatures certainly odd with their huge shells and paddle-like flippers. I explain they are coming ashore probably to lay their eggs, which they bury deep into the sand until they hatch.

Dandi shakes his large head, and says, "This world is getting stranger by the moment. There seems to be no end to the wonders that constantly crosses our paths."

After traveling for most of the day without seeing any type of town or village, we look for some type of shelter and perhaps food for the evening. Nothing eventful happens and I'm beginning to wonder where this world's citizens are.

As the sun dips behind the waters again, we decide to walk a little further before settling down for the night. The night sky is dark and to our surprise, no moon rises up from the ocean as it did the night before. I would expect at least a waning moon like back home, but there is nothing. I have to remember this world probably is different from home in more ways than I know. Not having the moonlight left the night in total darkness, only the twinkling of stars light the night sky. Because of the lack of moonlight, the stars are intensely bright; none of us can believe the enormous number that shine in the night sky. Just as we come to the top of a massive sand dune, we see a cluster of lights in the distance; the town or village illuminates the shoreline like a small constellation of stars. I want to keep walking until we reach the village, but we knew that we would not reach the town for quite some time, so instead, we decide to set up camp and get an early start in the morning.

What little water and food we have makes for a meager dinner, but having found no other source of food we settle for what we have. We're weary from the day's traveling so after our meal we soon fall asleep.

Morning light is diffused from overcast clouds gathering in the distance. I rise first and try fixing breakfast for the three of us before the others awake. Breakfast is heated bread rolls and some water: not much, but it helps wake us up. Soon we're ready to continue our journey.

Walking down past the sand dune where we camped, we see small streams of smoke coming from the village. Dandi figures we'll arrive long before the mid-day meal; to me this meant about two hours traveling time. The landscape gradually changes as we draw closer to the village. The surrounding ground is covered with soft brown grass. Scattered bushes and trees dot the countryside.

We find a pathway that looks to be a narrow road heading in the direction of the town. The sun climbs the midmorning sky when we come within sight of the town. The smells of smoke and the ocean stirs our senses. The town is larger than we expected; most of the buildings are made from wood, and they bear an old European look about them. A small river runs through the town with a quaint bridge connecting the town to the shoreline. The first residents of the village we encounter are busy at their chores or walking along the same path that's now much wider and paved with some sort of brick. The people give us curious looks as we walk deeper into town. The street opens wider, roads attached to the main highway weave their way throughout the village. Most of the structures are similar to a Tudor design. Some are two-story buildings, others are small shops with wooden sidewalks that line the brick roadway.

The curious looks from the people increase as we approach what looks like a town center. The people are wearing colorful clothes: the men mostly in smocks and the women in heavy gowns. What children we see are wearing shorts with short-sleeved shirts and no shoes.

Flocks of sea birds squawk as they dip, dive and soar about the tops of buildings. People mind booths in front of their shops with all sorts of merchandise on display. There didn't seem to be a lack of produce, including fruit and leafy vegetables. I smell the sea along with a slight hint of what I assume is fish. Spices and smoke blend with other odors leaving me with the feeling of being in the midst of ocean commerce. The town is a seashore village, some of the booths have fresh fish for sale and others display linens, tools, nets and ropes along with freshly baked breads. Overall, the entire town seems prosperous and the citizens happy.

What an odd picture we must make. Dandi, who is much larger than probably any one this village has ever seen, with his craggy face and huge head, walks alongside Kaylu, who, though small and hairy, has a presence about him that must be odd to these people. Kaylu's large eyes grow even bigger as he stares at the variety of people and buildings and what seems an endless display of merchandise. I wasn't aware of it then, but I had an unusual presence about meself also, causing people to stare and wonder who we are.

We continue walking through the village without being approached by any of the curious merchants, children, or passing citizens. Soon we are close to what looks like long wharves and docks, and at long last, two men walk out of a shop or office building and approach us.

"Greetings, friends. Are you lost?" asked the taller of the two.

"We are new to this area and looking to stay perhaps a day or two; can you direct us to a place to stay?" I respond. The man smiles in return, but with a look of concern on his face, he replies, "There are several inns on this road in the center of the town, but pray tell me: why are you carrying that sword?"

I hadn't even thought about me sword; I take a quick glance around and notice no one else has one. "I got it as a gift from a friend. We just came from a cave in a large mountain a few days walk from here; I used it to defend ourselves."

"A cave, you say? Is that the cave that goes through the mountain to another land?"

"Yes, it's taken us a long time to get through, and we are strangers to this land, so we are looking for maybe some work to pay our way."

"I see. Well, we just wanted to make sure you are not looking for any trouble. We are a peaceful folk and try to keep things simple and peaceful. You are welcome here. If you want some work, you might try at the docks—they are always looking for help. From the looks of your large friend here, he might come in real handy with unloading and loading of the ships."

We thanked the two men and continued on in the direction of the wharfs.

The village lies alongside a large harbor providing access to the open ocean. Buildings clustered along the wharf cater to the ships that are docked along the harbor. Ships of all sizes and shapes are constantly unloading and loading crates; some are lifted by ropes and brought to the wharf by long poles and then guided to their landing spot. More ships are anchored in the harbor while others are moving out to the ocean for ports unknown. Most of the vessels look like old clipper ships I'd read about and seen pictures of; they look as if they have been taken out of one of my history books, although I have to admit they are more intricately designed and seemed to be built for speed and carrying cargo. Some larger ships are beautifully designed with carvings and have what looks like large cabins, possibly for passengers.

The masts are tall. Their huge sails are rolled neatly across the cross mast. Other ships move across the harbor with white billowing sails dancing across the water. The activity is contagious—it makes you feel like an endless journey is just waiting for those brave and bold enough to live the life of the sea. I walk over to the end of a long wharf. Dandi and Kaylu are busy looking at the spectacle of sea birds swooping and then landing on the ships, docks, and wharf. All of this is something they'd never seen or dreamed of, and such hustle and bustle! The smells and sights are intoxicating. Dandi is a boatman and so of course knows a great deal about his craft. However, he and our companion Kaylu know only those boats that are used to traverse rivers or to cross gentle lakes. Some could carry passengers, but none was built as elaborately or as large as these marvels. The contrast of the ocean, the wharves, and the vast blue sky with the sun, combined with the bustling activity, was almost too much for them to comprehend. Dandi and Kaylu will have to depend on me for direction, since this world is so far away from their own reality they could never fathom how to proceed or even communicate to others in a way that wouldn't cause suspicion or concern.

"You there! Watch out! We are coming through!"

I wheel around abruptly to see several men carrying a large crate toward where I'm standing. The crate is heavy, and even with the four men wrangling the load, I can see they are about to lose it. Quickly, I move aside and reach out to help balance the box, and together we carry it to the wharf's edge and lower it onto a net lying next to a ship. Setting the crate down in the middle of the net, I can tell that whatever is in the crate has great value, for each man is exceedingly careful not to drop his end down too hard. Once the crate is settled, the men step back. One of them holds his arm up and twirls his hand; immediately six ropes attached to the net from above pulls the net tightly together. When the ropes are together, another man carefully climbs the net to where the ropes meet and pull them tighter with a chain at the neck, and climbing down, he yells out, "Away!"

The long wooden arm holding the net lifts the crate about ten feet off the wharf and then swings it to the middle of the boat, where several men are waiting to store it. I watch as the crate is secured, and then I turn to face the man who secured the ropes to the net. He gives directions to the other three men and turns to me. "Thank you for your help, son, for a moment I thought we were going to lose it."

"No problem, I was glad to help."

The older man is tall and heavy-set; he has a short, gray, grizzled beard and shoulder-length white hair. His eyes are blue as the sea, and his skin is tan and leathery.

I gesture toward Kaylu and Dandi and say, "My two friends and I are new to this town and looking for some work for a few days, is there anything available?"

The man looks at them and replies, "Well, actually I have a large load of crates like the one you just helped us with. Your large friend there looks as if he could carry the boat itself. If you're willing to work, then work is available."

I nod my head, "Yes! We would really appreciate whatever work we could get."

The sailor smiles and gruffly says, "Okay! Go to the end of the dock and give your names to the cargo chief; tell him Pascale sent you." I thank him and walk over to Dandi and Kaylu.

"My friends, we have jobs!" Kaylu and Dandi turn to face me and both ask almost at the same time, "Why? And what can we do? Both of us have sailed or paddled small crafts, but never anything like these. We don't know anything about these type of ships."

I smile, and soothe their worries. "Don't be concerned. We're going to be dockhands, which is nothing more than carrying cargo on to or off of the ships."

Kaylu appeared genuinely confused. "But why are we doing this?"

I realize that Kaylu and Dandi have never lived in a system that required them to make a living. "We're going to need money to buy food and lodging while we gather information. Besides, we need to make contact with people who know this world and this area."

Kaylu looks up at me. "Why don't we ask the leaders of this community for assistance? Surely, they will provide us with whatever it is we require. After all, we are guests in their land."

"Well," I reply, "that would work in your world, but here, I think, it's different. If you want something, you must pay for it, usually by working for it. Food, lodging, clothes, and anything else all need to be bought with money."

Kaylu looks at me again with a confused expression on his face. "Money; what's that?"

I think for a moment and then explain, "Things here...I don't think are free. When you want something, you exchange it for something else. In this case, the people have created a system of exchange that's common throughout the land. One of the components of exchange is something I call money. With it you can purchase things you need."

"I have heard of that, but never experienced doing it. How do you get this money?" Kaylu asks.

"We work for it. For example, we help load cargo crates onto or off of the ship, and in turn we receive money for our work." Kaylu was trying to grasp this new concept. He then asks, "Why don't people just help each other for the joy of helping and sharing?"

I take a deep breath; I heard a lot about these questions on the news. "Some folks want more than they need; they accumulate things and have large dwellings. They have other people do things for them. They desire prettier clothes, more food and don't want to do some types of work for themselves. The more they have the more they want. You experienced this in the cave when you saw a glimpse of my world. When some people have more than they can use, they feel like they're better than people who have less, and they may even resent just giving to others who ask them for something without getting anything in return."

Both Kaylu and Dandi again had that lost look in their eyes. I shrugged, knowing I was again confusing them.

We come upon a small building and join a line of workers waiting to speak with a man sitting inside at an open counter window. The clerk efficiently takes down the name of each man in front of us, and after looking through various charts, quietly confers with each. The line moves quickly. I stand patiently waiting with me comrades until our turn comes up. Walking up to the window I say, "Pascale sent us to sign up for loading."

The clerk asks our names, records them, and then gives each of us a pair of gloves—and it took a fair amount of searching for him to find sufficiently flexible gloves that could stretch over Dandi's huge hands. Pointing to a ship behind us, he says, "Go to that ship and see the foreman; he'll instruct you. He is the tall man in blue, holding the charts."

Thanking the clerk, I turn away and smile at me friends. "This will be fun! We can get more information while we're loading the crates."

We walk over and approach the foreman. A large man, he gestures for us to come closer and with a look of awe, he stares up at Dandi. "My word, man, you look like you could carry the loads by yourself! I've never seen such a large man."

Dandi grins and says, "You point to what you want carried, and I guarantee that you will be happy with my work."

We are assigned as a crew of four; rounding out our team is a young man about my age and size who's standing by himself. He stares for a moment at Dandi and then introduces himself as Davy. I introduce meself along with my friends, and then we listen to our instructions.

Our first job is to load a crate that is almost as large as the crate I helped with before. Stepping up to it, Dandi reaches down and picks up the crate in its entirety and hoists it up over his shoulder. I rush to place myself in front of Dandi, making sure to clear a wide path to the ship for him. With perfect balance, Dandi follows me, calmly walking toward the end of the wharf where the ship is waiting. People turn their heads and stare in disbelief as Dandi ambles by with his huge load, followed close behind by Kaylu and Davy.

After identifying which net our crew was assigned, I work with Kaylu and Davy to straighten it out and Dandi carefully places the crate in its center; I lift me arm and twirl my hand, instructing the ropes to be pulled as I had seen Pascale do. The ropes tighten, pulling the net together. I whisper to Kaylu, and in a flash he's up the net, pulls the chain to close the neck, and then he's right back at me side. I shout, "Away!" The long arm lifts and swings the crate to the waiting crew on the ship. Our crew quickly walks back to our loading site. I instruct Davy to carry a small crate, then picking one up meself, I watch Dandi again lift one of the largest with Kaylu following behind. We quickly walk back to the nets. Between Kaylu scampering up the nets to secure the neck and me and Davy carrying the smaller boxes while Dandi carried the large ones, we soon have developed a smooth and efficient operation of loading, so much so that soon others begin to stare. Dandi and Kaylu are greatly enjoying the brisk work together, and within a short time, Davy has caught on to their energy and begins to enjoy the work, too, feeling as if he has joined a great team in a competition.

We finish our work and return to wait in line for our pay. When our names are finally called, Pascale steps up and asks if he might talk with us for a moment.

Taking us aside, Pascale shook his head and said, "I have never seen a more efficient crew load as much as you all have; because of you, we're way ahead of schedule! Your crew loaded three times more than any other crew on the wharf. The crew that loads the most qualifies for a bonus: you and your friends have earned it easily." Pascale pulls out his wallet and gives each of us a few coins.

Pleased with the pay and even more with the recognition, we promise Pascale to return early next morning, the four of us then head back to the town center to see about acquiring quarters for the night and some food. Our new friend Davy acts as our guide; he knows the best places to eat and which places are reasonable for sleeping. The inn he guides us to is on the main road in the town center. It's clean, comfortable, and the food smells great—we haven't had a full hot meal for what seems like ages.

Looking at the samples of the food being served, I decide on what looks like chicken along with bread, cream sauce, and some leafy vegetables combined with a small red fruit looking a lot like strawberries. Dandi orders a huge portion of what looked like porridge and a side dish of fish, vegetables, fruit and a half loaf of bread. Kaylu is less adventurous and orders some soup, bread, and fruit.

The pretty waitress offers us some ale, which is made right there at the inn. I sample a bit; it tastes sweet. Curious, I order a round for me friends and meself. The innkeeper builds a roaring fire in the large fireplace and announces the entertainment will start soon. Soon we are all, including Davy, feeling content; our stomachs are full, and the ale helped us relax. We all decide to stay up for a while and enjoy the entertainment. The fire burns a little lower and most of the patrons have eaten. The tables are cleared, and another round of ale is sent to our table. From a door behind the bar, two figures with scarves covering their faces emerge and move in front of the firelight. The first girl sits down on a high stool and begins playing an instrument that looks very much like a flute. She plays a melody that drifts across the room evoking a feeling of peace and warmth to the atmosphere. The other figure drops her veil, turns her head and begins to sing. Her voice floats throughout the room in perfect harmony with the beautiful flute music.

Davy and I start to talk and get to know one another better. Out of the corner of me eye, I see something familiar and I turn me attention away from Davy to peer more closely at the singer: me eyes widen, and me mouth drops open as I stare into the beautiful eyes of Loren.

As I'm watching her, she steps down from the stool and strolls from table to table singing to each patron. As she approaches our table, me heart beats faster; remembering our moment of passion, I feel me heart pounding and yearnings surface. I'm staring and listening to her song and the words move me feelings. She floats like mist; approaching our table, she is soon standing behind Davy, singing her song.

Turning toward me, her voice slows and then wavers for a second as she looks into my face. Quickly catching herself, she smiles and sings with the flute music flowing around her. Her eyes light up and she brushes her hand across me cheek. I smile and reach out my hand to take hers, but she just smiles and drifts away to the next table, letting her hand barely touch me fingers as she moves away.

I don't know whether it's the ale, or just me heart feeling a natural response to Loren's beauty. What I do know is that I'm glad to see her and to know she made it safely out of the cave. Looking over at the other figure playing the flute, I realize it's Karla; she is just as beautiful as before, even more so perhaps as she closes her eyes and becomes one with her music. Like coming out of a spell, I feel a slight nudge. Dandi's looking at me; he, too, has recognized the two girls, and has also noticed my reaction as I realized who they are. Loren moves back to the stage and ends her song with soft fading words. The audience applauds as the two girls leave the stage. Dandi and Kaylu continue watching me. Finishing our drinks, I then suggest we end the evening.

Davy lives across the strand and has a little walk to get home. Saying his goodbyes, he promises to see us in the morning before work. Each of the rest of us has his own room. As we climb the stairs to our quarters, I'm feeling a little dizzy, so Kaylu and Dandi help me into my room. The ale has made me feel a little too relaxed. Kaylu whispers, "We will be up bright and early to get down to the wharf, so get as much sleep as possible." They then leave me sitting on the bed.

Feeling dizzy, I look around and see a washbowl with a large towel hanging next to it. Splashing some water on me face, I lay back down on the bed, but sleep is something that isn't easily found. I lay there thinking about what just happened.

How could we have chosen the very inn the girls are working in?

What are they doing here? Would I see them again? And where are they going?

Is this their home, or are they just passing through?

These and many more questions race through me head; I'm staring at the ceiling watching it slowly spin when a knock at the door brings me back to the moment.

Wondering what Dandi or Kaylu had forgotten, I swing open the door and freeze. Me face flushes and mind ceases to function: Loren stands in the doorway like a vision from heaven. Her dark hair flows over her shoulders and her eyes sparkle in the soft candlelight. She smiles and steps forward; her cloak dangles across her white shoulders.

Almost in a whisper she asks, "May I come in?"

CHAPTER 29 ~ THE TWAIN SHALL MEET

Brandon sits in the comfortable chair behind his desk. A low-burning fire behind him warms the office. Reading over his notes on Clark's case, one thing is becoming more and more clearer. The Baileys' tragic story isn't what it seems to be. Careful study of the insurance policies for not only the Baileys but also the trucking company and the CIGA group reveal various hidden implications within their rules and regulations. One of great interest is the health benefit section in the policy that insures the Baileys. Clark is due in his office today at three o'clock; Brandon wants to have his legal response ready when he arrives.

As important as it is to complete the legal briefs, even beyond the legal ramifications is a far more complex reason for what's happening to this family. There's an intricate pattern of cause and effect. The legal side is a mundane battle that has to be endured, but the legal element is only a reflection of a larger battle. He knows he's being drawn deeper into a journey that at this point is unpredictable, but this journey also seems to be designed in accordance with issues reflecting events happening on a scale unparalleled to anything he has seen, read or experienced in his lifetime. His secretary's knock at the door stirs him from his musings.

"I'm sorry to disturb you, sir, but Mr. Bailey called and said he would be a few minutes late."

Brandon straightens up the notes and thoughts he had written down.

"Emily, come in, I'd like you to put these drafts into a legal summary before Mr. Bailey arrives. All the points of law are highlighted along with my thoughts and a brief history. This is a priority, so let's start at once." Emily takes the briefs and leaves Brandon to his thoughts.

By the time Clark arrives, Brandon has two copies of the legal briefs set in front of him. Clark drops into one of the chairs in front of the desk. Brandon can see that this man is worrying himself ragged. He's losing weight, his clothes are disheveled, and he's unshaven and slumping in the chair. Clearly, this situation is taking a toll on his emotions, body, mind, and psyche. Dark circles line his eyes, and his concentration is scattered, hardly focused.

What Brandon is about to show him will hopefully calm him down enough so he can refocus his attention. "Clark, I have some documents I'd like you to review, especially page forty, section four, third paragraph in your policy."

Clark picks up the brief and casually flips through the first several pages as if he's bored, then he stops and sits up. Slowly putting the pages back down on the desk, he leans over and studies the section that Brandon mentioned. He reads and re-reads section four, then finally looking up at Brandon, he asks, "What does this mean?"

Brandon smiles and leans over in his chair. "It means we have grounds to stall Alliance in denying further benefits for your wife and son."

Clark sits back, puts his hand over his forehead and exhales deeply, and then asks, "Does this apply to both Hugh and Ann?"

"Not exactly; it's a gray area with regard to Hugh, however, for Ann it's one hundred percent. My plan is to adapt it to Hugh through some rather unorthodox legal maneuvers and then we keep our fingers crossed. The doctor's medical statement concerning Hugh will help also, but, for right now, we have enough to give a cause for delay on the termination date we're facing."

Clark's shoulders suddenly feel lighter and looser. For the first time in days, he can think and actually relate to another person. Ever since the meeting with the insurance companies, he has constantly worried about what to do, but here again Brandon comes to his rescue. How do you thank a person who has done so much? If he hadn't trusted Brandon, the help he's getting wouldn't have happened. It's a big lesson to let go of his pride, his anger, fear, the sadness and especially control. He realizes how these emotions quickly destroy not only himself, but also put his family in jeopardy.

Brandon sits back in his chair and smiles, then looking intently at Clark, he says, "Clark, I need you to focus. Forget about the insurance and forget about the hospital; I need you to keep your mind free...if you don't, there's no way I can begin to help. It's essential that you trust what I'm about to tell you, because it could mean win or lose in the journey we're embarking on."

"Your reactions during the meeting a few days ago are exactly what we don't want to happen when the pressure is on. You must be calm and receptive in order to receive any direction, from not only your higher self, but also from Hugh." Clark nods silently and pulls his chair closer to the desk.

Brandon calls Emily and asks for some coffee and tea for the two of them. It's cold outside—one of those late fall evenings that promise the coming of winter. Neither Brandon nor Clark has anything pressing for the evening. Melody is staying the night at one of her friends and Emily's getting ready to leave, so it's just the two of them. Brandon brings out a bottle of brandy and places a log on the small fire behind him. Emily brings the coffee and tea and then leaves for the evening. Pouring some coffee for Clark and some tea for himself, Brandon adds a small shot of brandy to each cup. He then holds up his mug in a silent toast, and nods.

"We need to talk a little, Clark; do you think you are up to an old man's rambling?"

Clark takes another sip of his coffee and says, "Go ahead, I'm all ears."

In a crisp voice and with a gesture of someone about to give a lecture, Brandon begins.

"What I'm about to say is important, Clark; if you have any questions or comments, please feel free to jump in at any time." He takes a slow sip of his drink and then sets it down on the desk. "I need to discuss with you your reactions to the situations that keep unfolding in your life. It's imperative at this stage of the journey that you learn to control your reactions. I will do my job as your attorney, so don't worry about what you may think is happening, for in most cases what you are seeing is what the other side wants you to see, and not reality. If you believe what they show or tell you, then it is possible we will have lost before we even begin the battle. I don't have to tell you that only you are responsible for the consequences of your actions; what you think, say and feel really does orchestrate the future. Perhaps it's hard for you to see how your thoughts and actions have consequences beyond even yourself, but believe me, they do. It's pretty easy to see the effect of existing consequences because you're suffering from them right now, but you must understand that only you control your present and future life. You control it by making choices."

Brandon pauses. Taking a sip from his cup, he continues. "Sometimes it's necessary to discover how the consequences affecting us currently are from choices we've made and felt in the past—believe me, they're all connected. The point is if you don't like what's happening in your life, if you aren't enjoying the daily events or even the moments, then try to find out what choices you've made that are responsible for the consequences you don't like. If you do this, you can transform your life. You can't just look at certain areas of your life that you think aren't working and expect to figure out what went wrong; you need to find all the places where you deceive yourself. Our lives are a manifestation of our personal choices, but if you can transform the events of your personal life, then you become the Master!"

Clark starts and asks, "Master...Master of what? And for that matter, what is a Master?"

Brandon's quiet for a moment as he thinks, then he says, "A true Master is simply someone who has learned to create a masterpiece of his life. This is a challenge to us as humans because most have become slaves to their past choices. A Master is someone who does not react, but only acts and lives in the present only."

Clark interrupts. "What does that mean? Why do we constantly seem to choose all the stupid things? Why can't we choose properly to avoid negative events that befall most of us?"

"Good question, let's see if I can answer it." Brandon sets his cup down again and pours another shot of brandy into his tea, then begins. "We are all programmed from birth to make choices that are formed from limitations. These limitations are manifestations of our programming from parents, society, religions and government. Almost everything in this world is designed to program us with failure, fear or limitations. In order to escape this programming, we must confront the seed of these limitations, which is the energy that drives fear. Once fear is seen for the illusion it is, you learn to master it: you're no longer the victim. Until we deal with the root cause of this emotional fear and pain, it can and will return to consume our thoughts and behavior. From experience I have seen that most of the human race tries to mask their fears with work, drugs, sex, violence, anger, family, emotional stimuli, shopping, blame, attachments or complete withdrawal. Choices that are made with fear lock us into a never-ending dream of redundancy. In your case, Clark, you've been forced into a situation that mandates you learn to create a new dream; this dream is where everything is possible including escaping from the illusions of the mind. When you become the master of transforming your attitude, then you will know illusion when you see it. You need not fear it but instead simply learn to play in this world knowing it is an illusion. You must be to the mind as the cat is to the mouse, watching every action and reaction, this isn't easy. You'll have to work with yourself every moment, always watching your actions and reactions."

Clark interrupts, "Yeah, I hear what you're saying, but trying to remember this when anger or fear creeps in is not so easy. Any ideas on how to see it when it happens?"

Brandon nods. "Normally it takes a lot of time, patience, heartache, and courage; this is because it's easier to take things personally and react the way you always have. This is the redundancy I was speaking about. Our reactions to fear only generate more fear, and this fear increases the drama, and from this drama more illusions and fear grow within you. When you learn to control your reactions, especially on the emotional level, then you begin to see things for what they really are. The mind uses all its previously stored behavior programming from its past, not only from this lifetime, but from previous lifetimes as well; all these things form the beliefs we hold dear."

Clark finishes his coffee and brandy and then says, "You are me attorney, and I respect your expertise in legal things, but don't get preachy with me. What is it that makes you so sure about what you're telling me?"

Brandon sees that the brandy is starting to affect Clark, so he patiently waits a few moments, letting his feelings sink away before he continues. "You know, Clark...my only expertise on this matter comes from watching hundreds of emotional court proceedings with my clients and the opposition's clients; this includes my own mistakes. Most of what I'm saying is just common sense. Not judging people or events allows me to respond with controlled impact. Not controlling how your emotional self reacts means what you perceive you automatically judge within your limited programming, that is, your emotions or fear. Our judgments are always made according to our core beliefs; when our emotions get in the way, our judgment becomes distorted and then the illusion increases: sometimes to an intensity that's beyond our control."

Clark pours himself another cup of coffee, adds a squirt of brandy, and then says, "You know, when something is going on and it's not what I want, I just react—I can't control it."

Brandon finishes his tea and pours himself another with a small shot of brandy. Then looking at Clark, he says, "When something happens in your life, you have the choice to decide how you are going to feel. You can get mad, or be happy, sad, and calm, or even feel humiliated. You also have the choice to simply ignore it. With practice, this ability to choose how you feel develops direct impact, which becomes a part of who you are. If you don't work to control your judgments, then you stay who you are, and your reactions will continue to come from beliefs that are kept alive with emotional energy. Because of this, the way you react repeats itself thousands of times. It becomes routine for you. Changing your beliefs about yourself alters your belief about reality. Most of us thrive on emotional highs; we dwell in the drama of the world, addicted to the politics, morals, entertainment, cultural values, and the illusion of greatness from others. Sadly, through this form of celebrity worship we get caught up in the world's emotional drama. This poisons not only us as individuals but society as well. If your choices don't produce what you want, then change them, if necessary, repeatedly until you finally get the desired result. You must learn to master the greatest relationship you have: the relationship with yourself. No one grows for us, we must each grow for ourselves. This intelligent growth consists of our increasing recognition of the universal laws and ourselves as Soul."

Brandon shifts in his chair and continues. "Granted, things are bad for you right now, but with the proper attitude, you can make this whole event a learning experience for you. How? By learning that we're not the body we care for every day, nor are we the body that reacts to other people's poisonous energy on a constant basis. Remember this, Clark: we are not humans going through a spiritual experience, but Soul going through a human experience. We are simply the life force that activates our bodies, and this force is life itself: free from fear, free from emotions, and free from other mundane human traits. People gain great power with fear, with this power they spread their poison to all those they can infect. You see this every day in the events of the political world: the wars, weapons, religions, media, diseases, and money, along with lies, terror, and the constant loss of basic human rights that are our birthright. We lose these rights through fear-driven illusions created by those we put our trust in."

Brandon sips his tea, which has cooled but still has the warming effect of brandy. Clark nods slightly.

Brandon leans closer to him and speaks again. "Those who are in power know how an illusion can be woven from greed and fear. Don't ever think it's not used on a grand scale throughout the world. When a person sees through the illusion and discovers how it is created and how deceitful it can be, then he begins to emerge from enslavement and eventually becomes his own Master. When someone reaches mastery, they begin to perceive a different world. His heightened senses allow him to penetrate deeply into reality itself; from there he builds different beliefs. He experiences alternate truths that exist without illusion. These different realities don't respond to the limited human reactive state. This is where I'm sure your son is right now. Somehow, Hugh has pierced the veil of the mind, and is leaving the human condition behind. I believe Hugh is journeying to another existence, one that's revealing a different set of beliefs…beliefs that form a reality that's drawing him closer to an unlimited state of awareness. Each of us is searching for this same bliss, but most don't know it. How he accomplished this, I don't know, but I do know he has accomplished it, and that in itself creates hope for all humankind. Each of us, perhaps, cannot travel the exact same path, but we can take the journey and experience it in our own individual ways. The way is narrow, but it's true.

"Most of humankind can believe in a Creator that is great, magnificent, and all powerful, and the Master of all. But humankind has a problem believing that such an awesome God can personally love each and every Soul created. The mind just can't accept such a love that is so enduring and so personal to each of us. This doubt about the personal interest that the Creator has for its children allows us to think in mundane, limited concepts that create chaos in our world. Why? Because we react to our own personal fears and limitations, which are created by these world fears. We react to the world's elite and our leaders' fears and their power-crazed illusions of power. Our reaction to this whole worldly drama is what impedes our journey."

Clark has a smirk on his face when he asks, "What are you doing now? Getting political on me?"

Brandon calmly responds. "Whether it's religious, political, or otherwise doesn't matter; we as humans have a habit of becoming a virus on this planet. Because of this, through emotional choices we have created the type of world we live in. It's up to us to create our personal universe within us. It needs to be built from unconditional love and the understanding of true spiritual laws. If we do this, then we are the Master of ourselves, which is all that matters. Please don't misunderstand what I'm saying; being human is an act of kindness from the Creator. It's a gift we don't totally understand yet. Our emotions and feelings are rooted in the Creator's own essence; they're divine functions. We as humans allow the mind to reconstruct these divine functions to a limited distorted energy, which is guided by our judgmental attitudes toward all we experience. We tend to react to the body's senses sometimes without our emotional yardstick and discrimination to guide us. When this happens, the mind begins to create an illusionary sense of self. This illusionary self survives by creating a personality that's generally one of fear, worry, pleasure, limited joy, and unyielding anger, thus taking us deeper into an area that ultimately blocks out our memory of who we really are and why we are here in the first place. We as humans have forgotten why we have bodies and why we exist in this reality. This forgetfulness is part of the illusionary self/personality that's in control, which is known as the ego."

After listening intently to Brandon, Clark responds, "I remember many times when I felt sadness or fear, and many other times when I was angry and blamed someone or something for some situation, sometimes even blaming God. The more I think about what I was doing, the more I realize how much damage I was inflicting on not only myself, but my family as well. The insurance companies aren't responsible, nor the government nor even God. I, Clark Bailey, am responsible, maybe not for what happened, or what they're doing, but absolutely for my attitudes, feelings, actions, and choices. I would sometimes challenge fear and act as if I were confronting it. I even created the illusion I was defeating fear; nevertheless, in the end it always came back, and each time it returned, it was more powerful. This situation with my family is very real, but it isn't what it seems. I'm beginning to understand that perhaps I can be happy again—maybe there's hope after all."

Brandon listens thoughtfully as Clark speaks. He can see Clark beginning to understand what he's trying to show him. He nods sympathetically, and then says, "Clark, you can stay calm and make decisions that aren't clouded with fear. But in order to do this, you must learn to scrutinize every reaction. No matter what happens, you must remember: you have the choice either to be the effect, or to be the cause through your non-reactive attitude, which ultimately determines the circumstances of your choices."

Brandon stays silent to allow Clark time to absorb what he's trying to convey.

Brandon is a little surprised at what he is saying, too. In his mind, he intended to convey a simple message, but as he began to speak, a door seems to have opened in his mind, releasing a deeper flood of information that actually increased his own awareness and understanding as he spoke. It's true, he thought to himself; we usually teach what we need to learn ourselves.

Clark looks like he feels guilty. His demeanor is as if he's thinking about the many times he reacted in anger or fear. Even in his moments of sadness, he sees how he created barriers that impeded not only himself, but Melody and Hugh. Is it also affecting Annie in some unknown way?

Brandon barks out, "Clark! Snap out of it! You're doing it again!!"

Clark grimaces, shaking his head.

Brandon continues. "Clark, please, don't feel guilty about the past! It's only another trap of the mind. The mind will spin every conceivable negative attitude it can to keep you involved with its illusion. Guilt is one of the keys to its survival. Your mind is devised to keep you from realizing the deadly camouflage that covers your true awareness."

Clark looks up and asks, "What 'camouflage'?"

"By 'camouflage,' I mean the current life you've created around yourself. All of it is created from the mind to distract you. All past experiences and all memories are only dead images; dwelling on them with negative emotion holds you back from allowing new beliefs, new thoughts, and a new awareness to grow within you. This type of thinking stops change."

Brandon claps his hands once. "Now! Now is the only true reality that exists! However, most of us live in the dead images of the past or desired events hoped for in the future. The future is still flexible, and can change in an instant with the right attitude, right choice or right action. Guilt from past dead images is a powerful tool that holds you back, so let it go! If you do, you'll allow a new awareness to grow in your consciousness. This is our purpose, this is the meaning of existence—simply to unfold to the limitless being that each of us really is."

Leaning closer, Brandon places his hands on his knees, and continues in an almost whisper. "The mind cannot exist as it is if you don't give it the attention it thrives on. Your attention is a form of energy that allows the mind to exist as its own entity. Attention also gives it the ability to project images that affect the senses and the emotions; this attention on negative things from your past and attention on illusionary worries in the present are together the insidious trap for Soul. Without the power of attention, without this one element, the mind ceases to be your master. Instead, it becomes the tool it was originally designed to be. It was never designed to create or to make judgments based on the senses and feelings of a mechanical brain. All creating and all decisions should come from Soul. The mind is a vehicle for transferring Soul's power into what we know as the human consciousness. This consciousness is then supposed to appear as a reflection of the Creator's essence using us as vehicles for the divine power.

"The problem for us as humans is a common one. It's similar to what happened to the original concept of the United States. Through the original leaders of our country, a constitution with a bill of rights was created. Soul inspired these documents. These documents were supposed to act as a map or a guide to operate, protect, and run America. Unfortunately, over the centuries they've been distorted and misused. This Constitution was to act as a map or guide designed for each American to have rights and freedoms so they can experience the best life possible without interference from government. Elected officials were to be servants and custodians of the Constitution. Over time, the servants corrupted their positions and eventually became corrupt leaders that have—and still are—distorting this original map or concept. This is accomplished by burying the rights given by the Constitution under laws and regulations that are contradictory to its original concept. Eventually, through tactics of fear and lies, the leaders add confusion to the basic rights people are born with as citizens of this land. Before you know it, crime, greed, wars, culture invasion, drugs, degraded education, inflation, and other negative factors are woven into the fabric of the leaders' power. The citizens as individuals forgot what the United States originally represented and what its true purpose was. They forgot everything but survival. Eventually we're forced to depend on our leaders, the former servants of the people, for our survival. This is our greatest downfall.

"The leaders we put in office only have power that we the citizens give them. This is the same as the mind. We, the original masters of this country, now bow down to the servants we put in place to serve us. The leaders and elite create power from their own personal desires and fear; eventually, they enslave the people to the leader's own personal reality. Instead of each experiencing their own reality, we become focused on the government's problems, so we lose our private sense of what our country originally represented.

"This example is a perfect replica of what the mind does to Soul. Originally, Soul had a set of intrinsic laws that were basic, simple, and allowed the real self to unfold on its path to discovery. These divine laws are imprinted onto our Spiritual DNA; they represent the exact same laws that exist within the Creator, or what many call spirit. Over eons of time, the mind clouded these basic universal laws of existence with fear, confusion, false promises, desires, pleasures, greed, and attachments. We desperately try to survive as the real self, but because we forgot our true purpose we became lost in societal laws, moral codes, religious laws, war, fear, dogma, rituals, attachments, pleasures of the body and all the mind's illusions. Finally, Soul begins to totally depend on the mind for survival.

"The mind—our former servant and tool—becomes our leader and Master. This is Soul's greatest downfall. What is happening in our outside world is only a reflection of what has happened within each of us as individuals and as a society. Religions are but a faded memory of those forgotten divine laws. Even they have turned to the corrupt illusion that keeps us shrouded in ignorance and fear; they do this for their own survival. Each of us as individuals must someday pierce the mind's illusion, and in essence discover again these divine laws. When you accomplish this, you become a spiritual giant, such as Jesus, Buddha, Krishna or Milerapa. These are only a few of the many men and women who have attained this exalted state."

Brandon stands and stretches. Leaning down, he pushes a small charred log closer to the flame in the fireplace. He straightens up and gazes for a moment directly into Clark's eyes; the light from the fire throws a warm orange glow over his features.

Then abruptly he says, "Remember this! Each human who reaches this divine state operates contradictory to the laws of the mind. This is why society rebels against these Spiritual Travelers. Of these basic divine laws, love and freedom are the most powerful of all. From love springs freedom.

"Clark, the mind is so vast and so complicated that we could talk about it forever...herein lies the trap. By losing ourselves in the mind's vastness, we lose our true selves; this again is one of its tools. I call it the spin. We as humans have the ability to see deeper than our mental powers can fathom. We must sharpen our intuition and see this reality as a whole, instead of complex individual units of matter or scattered, random thoughts and theories."

The fire is burning low. Brandon kneels down and begins to tend the fire. Without turning around, Brandon continues. "I've been talking a while, I know, but let me just say this. It's through the Creator and our ability to give unconditional love that allows us to receive love and give love. From these attributes we are propelled to our original reality or back to the original source to what we call Heaven. Love in its purest form is staggering in its simplicity; so much so that the mind can never comprehend this simple oneness."

Clark quickly asks, "Why do you say that? It seems to me that the simpler something is, the better. My mind always responds to something that's simple: so much more than complicated issues."

Brandon stands up, placing his hands on his hips. Turning to Clark, he nods his head. "You'd think so, wouldn't you? The mind operates within the reality of two energies: the negative and the positive. Without these two energies working together, matter, energy, space, and time would cease to exist, as would the mind's ability to function. The mind must and can only experience events in the context of opposites or duality. Unconditional love, the Creator, and true freedom are always experienced as oneness. It is not something we experience, but something we become."

Brandon sits down and leans back in his chair. The fire is nearly spent and it's dark outside.

Clark feels his own mind straining to ask endless questions, but he fights the urge; what has been said is more than enough for him to ponder. "Thanks for your time, Brandon. I'm going home to let this sink in. Let's talk on Monday about the next step to take."

Brandon smiles, knowing Clark understood the message. "Sure, I'll call you late Monday and let you know the outcome of the legal briefs. Take a copy with you for your files, enjoy the weekend, and keep a calm attitude. Perhaps you may have something to tell me when we next talk."

Clark shakes Brandon's hand, and walks out into the chilly night.

The stars seem brighter than usual. The aroma of fall permeates the air. City lights brighten the streets.

As he starts his car, he thinks what a beautiful evening it truly is.

CHAPTER 30 ~ A NEW POINT OF VIEW

I open me eyes to a dim cloudy morning light. The covers are warm and soft. Slowly rolling over, I look into Loren's face. She sleeps with a slight smile on her lips. Long dark curls wrap her shoulders; her skin is soft and fair.

Last night was like a dream; never in me wildest imagination would I have thought such feelings could exist. As soon as Loren came into my room, the liquor gave me the courage to demand that she explain why she and Karla left us. She was hesitant, but seeing that I would only be satisfied with the truth, she opened up and told me their reasoning for why they had left us. For quite a long time, she and Karla had sensed something felt wrong. On reflection, they both concluded that the cave was magnifying and distorting all of our emotions, thoughts, and senses. While we were all together, the cave's strange powers would continue to manipulate our emotions and heighten our physical desires, fears, and anxieties, causing tremendous conflict between the five of us. It took constant effort to maintain control over our minds and emotions; it would be better to separate to stop the mind games. Since they were already familiar with this portion of the cave, the girls felt safe enough to go on without them. Why not at least tell us that, I replied angrily. She softly answered that they simply had to leave without a word. Even raising the issue would have resulted in some kind of conflict, unloosing storms of anger, paranoia, fear, and possibly even danger among us.

They were right.

After hearing her explanation, I knew they had made the right choice. I knew firsthand how devastating the Dark Cave's power could be. Just after they left, Dandi nearly killed me after his dark thoughts, fears, and other emotions were warped by the cave's infernal influence. Who knows what could have happened had they not left us?

Last night with Loren had been a milestone for me. I felt love mixed with passion, and upon surrendering to it, I discovered something else, something that I could never have known in the cave. Making love with Loren awakened powerful feelings; but even more important, I felt that a piece of life's puzzle was revealed last night that had eluded me since this journey began. I was standing amid crashing waves of emotion. I always had these feelings, but they were hidden, submerged in the mind and body of a young child. When they did surface, they moved into me heart in a natural and wonderful way, not forceful at all. Reaching over, I touch her cheek, lightly brushing a dark curl from her face. She's so beautiful.

Last night I opened myself to an ecstasy I never imagined. Beyond the pleasure there had been oneness with this seductive creature. Perhaps that oneness is the attraction that brought me to this seaside village; after all, nothing happens by accident, and there are no coincidences, no dumb luck. A strict law of cause and effect connects all things, doesn't it?

Loren opens her eyes. Looking up and seeing me, she smiles and sits up. Yawning, she says coyly, "Morning is here already?"

I lean over and kiss her gently on the cheek. "Yes, morning's here, and I must hurry. The others and I have to be on the docks early for work." I throw the covers back and jump from the warm bed. That's when I notice I'm not wearing anything. Blushing, I scramble and stumble to get dressed. Loren enjoys watching as I clumsily grab me shirt and boots.

She laughs and calls out as I open the door to leave, "Karla and I have another performance tonight; will you be there for dinner?"

Looking over me shoulder as I step out the room, I call out, "We'll be there as the sun sets."

Loren lies back on the bed, wondering whether last night was a good idea. Strong feelings run through her mind for this young warrior—stronger than any she has ever felt before. She is deeply attracted to his determination, the look of wisdom in his eyes, and strong discipline. But she also felt a foreboding. She senses a darkness of something she doesn't understand; the very things that attract her could be the same that destroy any future she might have with Hugh.

****

I'm waiting downstairs. Today, I have to try to find information that will point us in the direction to find mom. Soon Dandi and Kaylu come down the stairs, ready for their new work assignments. We're walking in the direction of the wharf when we see Davy jogging from up the road. Out of breath, he's calling me name. We stop and wait for him, and then the four of us continue on together.

Soon we are standing in front of a magnificent ship that came in last night. From bow to stern, the ship is at least three hundred feet long and its masts tower with flags blowing in the wind. Several people carrying small suitcase-like bags disembark across a long ramp.

The ship is built of long split logs, each one planed and sanded, all shaped to exactly fit the log next to it. Below and above the light beige stained logs in the middle was a line of dark stained logs every five feet or so. Toward the stern of the ship, a higher deck was built into three levels for apartments reaching high above the other decks. Each apartment has carved wooden shutter windows in the rear. The middle deck displays a rear balcony attached to it, with the top deck enclosed with railings that go around the entire upper deck in a horseshoe shape. A giant helm is at the front of the top deck, to the rear behind the helm is a brass carved pole standing straight up with a huge crystal affixed to its top. The lower apartments are level with the main deck and placed just under the apartment with the balcony. On each side of the cabin deck's entrance are two large golden unicorn statues, both standing on their hind legs with fierce expressions as if guarding the entrance.

The middle and front of the ship have three large mast poles from stern to bow; they are painted a dark green with light brown ropes wrapped around the bottom. Lines attached to the top of each mast connect to large white sails. Stairs lead from the lower deck up to the top forward deck where benches line both sides of the outside rail. On the second front deck are two compartments that look like some sort of barracks: possibly quarters for the crew. Up on the top bow, benches line each side. An intricately carved silver throne sits in the center of the top bow. The throne has strange carvings and designs studded with precious stones. The galleon is more beautiful than any other boat I have ever seen; I can only imagine how expansive the view must be from one of those crow's nests.

A lower door opens on the bottom of the ship, and a huge ramp slides out from the lower cargo area. Two men attach it to the wharf locks, and then a large man waves me and my friends forward. "You're early. You four are assigned to this ship. We have a large load in the hull, and it may take two entire days or more to completely unload, but until the other crews get here, we can't get at it."

"That's okay. We'll just wait here until you call us. How long do you think it might be?"

The ship foreman looks at me with a funny look on his face. "If you mean when you will start," he said slowly, "that's obvious: when the other men get here." For a moment I wonder what he meant, but then I remember that attention to a specific time is uncommon here. I turn and say to my friends, "Well, guys, it looks like we have time for a little rest before we work. Let's find a place to sit."

As we stroll along the wharf, Dandi notices some stray piling remnants lying near our ship's bow. Wordlessly, he chooses a short stub—maybe eighteen inches long—and placing it upright like a stool, leans on it to fix it firmly into the moist soil. He quickly creates seating for more than just the four of us, eventually setting up a dozen piling stools so that they formed a small circle right at the waterfront. We sit quietly, enjoying the morning, and soon, a few other men show up along with a few women. They, too, are told they will have to wait. One of the men approaches and asks if they can sit with us. I notice a guitar-like instrument strapped to his back and gesture with a nod and a smile for him and companions to take a seat and rest. Sitting down, the sailor lifts the instrument around his head and places it in his lap. I admire the detail and care someone has given the instrument, and I ask, "Can I look at your instrument?"

The man asks, "Do you play?" and I reply, "A little—I haven't held a guitar for some time and I miss it terribly."

Placing the instrument across me lap, I strum a few strings and can't believe the quality of the sound. Not only is it rich in tone and pitch, but each time I strum the music lasts far longer than normal, or at least what I remember to be normal. By this time, a few other people are gathering around and listening to my strumming. Remembering the joy I had playing me own guitar back home in the tree house, I strum the instrument a little more, and as I do, a melody begins to emerge.

I think of me remarkable journey in this wondrous land and idly strum an old Irish melody. As I do, I sing a haunting lyric about me travels in this strange land: a land full of new friends, wonders, and exciting experiences. I have always liked my singing, but now with this older version of meself, me voice is lighter and richer. My Irish accent takes over, and I sing about truth, and about my friends, and where I wish I could be. I soon lose myself in not only the music, but also within memories and the thoughts of what may come. Finishing the song, everyone applauds. I hadn't noticed so many others gathering around us.

Just then, the foreman from the great ship shouts for all crews to report to their designated areas; it's time to work.

When Dandi steps up on the ramp, the foreman stares in awe at the towering giant; the ramp even bends a little under Dandi's weight. We follow Dandi as he disappears into the gaping entrance leading to the hull. Lit torches with glass shades line both sides of the interior walls. The soft light exposes large crates and wooden boxes that are stacked and lined up on both sides of the ship's hull. Walking deeper into the ship's body, I see hundreds of wooden boxes, wrapped stonework, furniture, and sealed metal crates stacked from floor to roof. Staring at the crates, I wonder what they all contain. Some are light while others are so heavy that four men can barely carry them out.

The foreman points at a steep stairway rising up from the middle of the hull lit by shafts of daylight streaming downward. "There's more cargo on the lower deck, and some still in the upper apartments. After you clear the bottom hull, we'll go up on deck to finish."

I exclaim to Dandi, "We'll carry what we can, but Dandi, you're in charge of the large crates."

Dandi reaches up, selects a large metal crate, and lifts it as if it's made of tissue paper. Placing it on his shoulders, he ambles toward the exit door. As he emerges, those on the wharf turn in disbelief as the little giant steps onto the ramp. The rest of us grab smaller boxes and trundle after him.

Dandi walks up the wharf a ways and places the crate on the back of a huge wooden wagon hitched to four large horses. Following his lead, I'm then hopping on the wagon, pushing crates toward the front to make more room.

The work seems endless; each time we take down one crate, another higher up replaces the one just taken. But by working non-stop until noontime, we empty half the hull and fill ten wagons, which are then sent away to deliver the cargo to its final destination. The foreman is amazed at the volume of work we are doing. If we keep this up, he remarked, the hull will be empty by the latter part of the afternoon.

Taking a break, I ask Davy a few questions about other towns, their culture, and the ship we are unloading.

This land is known as Thorndike. The coastline is dotted with numerous seaside villages, which subsist on trade with other lands. The village we are staying in is called Outbound; the population's large as Thorndike villages go. The ruling classes are wealthy merchants who depend on the people for not only their wealth, but also their survival. They take good care of the villagers by providing employment, dwellings, and entertainment. The people don't pay taxes; the merchants use a portion of the profits generated by the sea trade for all municipal upkeep. The people are satisfied with the wages and comforts provided by their work and the merchants. They form what seems to be a perfect symbiotic relationship allowing both classes to exist in harmony. It seems that none of the merchants is after excessive power or riches. Among their duties, the merchants must negotiate contracts, have ships built, and organize the shipping and receiving. They hire accountants and collectors to make sure debts are paid by the purchasing parties, which is then disbursed according to contracts. Contractors who work under the merchants oversee the physical work along with sailing the ships, supplying crews, and guaranteeing the pickup and delivery of cargo. Without every level working in a coordinated effort, problems would arise. Within this streamlined working relationship, groups of coordinators constantly review the mechanics, financials, and all other aspects of the businesses. Crime seems not to exist. If any quarrels do come up, the parties involved usually handle it, and if not, a board of citizens is chosen at the time to settle that particular quarrel.

A merchant from another land owns the ship we are unloading. He's moving part of his family to this village to establish a balance. When the population of a village reaches certain numbers, some members of one village will move to another to keep balance. This is purely a voluntary selection; family members who make the move are honored to accept a new responsibility in another village. This keeps balance, and avoids poverty or unemployment. When a new area is found to be conducive to building a new village, then reviewers from select villages hire landscapers, carpenters, as well as wharf and dock contractors to build the basic structures. Once they complete the buildings, people from different areas volunteer to become the new inhabitants. These newcomers eventually become the leading merchants. It's known that this is a much-desired opportunity for those who want to take on more responsibility and build a new village that someday will be a port for trading goods.

This has been the way of this land for eons, and it seems to work well. The people are content with the way things operate.

I asked Davy how large the ocean was. "No one really knows; no one has ever found its end because it's so vast, and ships only sail along the coastline bordering our continent. There are a few islands some ships dock on, but to go to the other side of the entire ocean isn't considered important."

These people don't know about electricity or modern types of transportation or communication. Nor do they seem to be concerned about creating new inventions, especially anything that might harm or pollute the land or ocean. The way the system works is just fine with the citizens. Their food is fresh from the sea or from organized farms outside the village. They also grow some food in their own yards.

Toward late afternoon, we move from the hull to the first deck. The sea air gusts are a welcome treat. Gulls swirl around ship masts while crewmen go down into the hull to begin the cleanup. A different ramp is pulled out to accommodate the deck and apartment cargo. The deck cargo is light and easy to maneuver compared to the hull cargo. We soon approach the apartments, and I run me hand over the detailed carvings on the ship's rails.

Neatly devised compartments are built into the sides of the ship to store food, water, clothes, and other miscellanies. The deck is a beautiful stained hardwood that's buffed to a shine, but even with this luster, the floor has a rough non-skid surface texture that makes walking easy even when damp. We climb to the upper deck to clear it of any leftover cargo. The ship is both a cargo and passenger ship, and one of the finest in a fleet owned by a wealthy merchant and his family. The top decks are apartments for as many as twenty-five to thirty people. Each apartment is richly adorned with exotic woods, curtains, carpets, and furniture providing only the best in comfort. Hauling large chests, I can only imagine the wealth stored in these metal and wooden crates; they look like a pirate's treasure chests.

As I enter the final apartment, I encounter a man storing away the last of his belongings into a chest with its lid still open. The chest brims over with vast amounts of gold, jewels, and exotic cloth similar to silk trimmed in jewels and gold thread designs. Some of the precious stones in the chest are huge: easily as large as my fist. Diamonds, emeralds, rubies, and other gems sparkle in the dimming sunlight.

The man nods and smiles at me. "I will be done here shortly. Could you take the chests alongside that wall while I finish up?"

I beckon Dandi to take the largest chest while Davy and I take two smaller ones. When we come back, the other chests are already closed and ready to be taken away. The man doesn't seem nervous about the treasure chest as Dandi lifts it up and places it on his shoulder. I climb the stairs to the top deck to make sure everything is gone. Reaching the top, I take a deep breath and walk to the railing. I'm at least seventy-five feet high over the sea level. The view of the ocean with the sun setting is as beautiful as anyone could imagine. Walking toward the helm that faces the entire length of the ship I marvel at the details in every part of the ship.

Looking up, the sight of the lookout's nest another fifty feet up makes me feel warm and excited. I imagine being on the open seas moving with the wind on this magnificent vessel; from where I stand, the bow of the ship seems far away, and yet I can see the entire village from me perch. My imagination allows me to almost feel the ocean wind in me face as the ship flies through the waves.

The ship has three masts and its white sails tightly wrap around the cross masts. Ropes hang down from above and seem to be everywhere: some secure the sails, tied off at railings; some run through pulleys; others are fashioned into ladders for climbing up down the mast poles. Water barrels, life boats, the helm, and the gentle rocking of the ship—all these things make the ship somehow more surreal. I wonder what it is like being on the open sea, feeling the wind and sun against me face, while looking into the horizon and beyond.

My imagination fires up; I remember stories and movies from my old life back home. What must it be like to sail from port to port, even to points beyond "where no one has gone before?" Deep into my fantasy, I hear me name being called out. Shifting my thoughts back to reality, I climb down the deck ladder to the lower level.

Somewhere deep inside of me, I'm still a ten-year-old boy with a child's fantasy and vivid imagination. I clearly see the scene in my mind's eye, and feel the excitement in me heart...I shake me head and shrug. Oh, well, I doubt I'll ever have such seafaring adventures. My life seems to be meant for more serious business. Besides, even when I find me mom, I have to learn how I'm going to free her. Traveling over the ocean is just the childish boy in me dreaming a fantasy. Then again, what did Jotan say about a ship?

I reach the bottom deck where Dandi and Kaylu are waiting for me below.

Both have big grins on their faces. Dandi asks, "You were dreaming about sailing this great ship, weren't you, Hugh?"

I cover my surprise with a little laugh. "Yeah, I guess I was—what a great time it would be to sail across the ocean in search of amazing adventures."

Dandi nods. "We heard and felt your thoughts. We, too, feel your excitement. It would be an adventure worth taking; too bad it is not possible, though." We look at each other, chuckle, and walk down to the docks.

The sun is setting, and Davy's waiting on the wharf. All four of us are ravenous, but before we can eat, we have to be paid for the day's work. When our names are called, we walk up to the pay office. The paymaster asks us to come around through the side door into the back office. We look at each other with puzzled expressions.

Opening the back office door, a kind-looking elderly man wearing a fine velvet jacket and holding a wooden cane with a silver knob on its top welcomes us inside.

The man is a merchant, and his mannerisms and demeanor show he's an educated man of wealth. "Greetings friends; My name is Albrecht. I'm sorry to inconvenience you, but I wanted to thank you personally for your exceptional work on Soultraveler today."

"Soultraveler?" I ask.

"Of course, of course, you do not recognize the name; I should have known. Soultraveler is the name of the ship that you four so expertly cleared out for us today. Normally, it takes two days' work to unload the hull itself, but you four not only cleared the hull, but the rest of the ship, too. You have saved us one or even possibly two days' work and time. This is very valuable for us, and not only that, none of the cargo was damaged or lost."

"Thank you, Mr. Albrecht, we try to do our best for the day's wages."

The elderly man grins and exclaims, "Day's wages! My boy, you have earned far more than wages today! It is not often that we see work done so well and with so much humility. Let me show my appreciation by taking you all to dinner and discussing further opportunities that may interest you."

"I'm sorry, but we have a dinner reservation at the inn where we are staying."

"No matter. If it is all right with you, I'll accompany you and pay for your meal out of gratitude for your work today." We all agree happily. After we are paid our normal wages, as well as large bonuses, we all set off to the inn for dinner.

When we arrive, Albrecht asks for a large dinner table close to the stage. The innkeeper recognizes the merchant and happily obliges; he knows which side his bread is buttered on, and thus orders his best table and chairs brought to the front. I sit next to Albrecht with Dandi and Kaylu on the left. Ale is brought in with mugs for all. Albrecht declines the ale, but asks for some of the innkeeper's finest wine, and soon mugs and glasses are raised. Albrecht stands and says, "A toast to the future and to new friends." A maiden brings bread, and cheese soon follows. The entrée orders are given, and the party begins in earnest.

After a while and a few drinks, Albrecht inquires where we're from. I'm thinking I need to be careful at what I reply. "We're from the other side of the great cave in the large mountain, a few days travel from here."

Albrecht's eyes widen. "The cave, you say! My word, boy; that is remarkable! Very few have entered the cave and lived to tell about it." He continues asking questions about the cave, and even more about the lands or worlds on the other side.

"Dandi and Kaylu are from the other side; they can tell you more than I."

"Ah, this explains their odd appearance. Are you from the Land of Light also?"

I didn't think it wise to tell the entire truth, but I don't want to lie either. "I'm from a land called Earth. It also exists on the other side of the cave, but far away from where Dandi and Kaylu's lands are."

Albrecht accepts my answer and asks, "So where are you going when your work here is completed?"

"We're on a mission to help members of my family," I answer.

Albrecht thinks for a moment and then leaves it alone. He knows there is more to the story than what he is being told, but he also respects privacy. He doesn't want to put us in a position that will cause ill feelings or embarrassment to either of us. I shift the conversation and ask Albrecht about his business.

"Ah, well friend, I am in many different sorts of businesses, but mainly I am an importer and exporter of exotic cargos. I ship to many ports along the coast. I usually carry only precious cargos for the wealthy from one family member to another. Currently, I'm bringing cargo for my brother, who I have not seen in a long time. He was last seen at this very inn. I received a message from him to bring a rich cargo of furniture and wealth for his children, who are going to be setting up his business here in Outbound. Along with their personal cargo, I brought some other wealthy families that are headed for different villages along the coast. It's a long trip to get here, as I had to stop at many ports and drop off these clients and their cargo before finally landing here at Outbound. My ship is empty now, and the last of the families are settled. I'll be looking for cargo to take back on my trip homeward."

I listen to Albrecht's story, but all the while thinking about his magnificent ship.

"Does Soultraveler belong to you only?"

Albrecht smiles and, shakes his head, he replies. "No, it is only partially mine; the ship was built specifically for our family, and is to be used for transportation of not only our family but other wealthy families also. A handsome price is paid to travel on Soultraveler, for it is the mother ship of all the fleets along the coast. It is not only the fastest, but also the smoothest and safest ship afloat. I own a portion, and my brother and his children own the rest."

Dinner is served, and we eat and drink until we are full.

As the table is being cleared, the innkeeper announces the entertainment is about to begin. Lamps and candles are dimmed, the crowd quiets down, and the curtain parts.

Karla steps out on the platform.

Sitting on a high backless chair in the dim candlelight, Karla begins playing her flute. The music wafts like a warm breeze throughout the room. Patrons become lost in the sounds floating from the girl on the darkened stage.

The side curtain opens slightly and Loren steps onto the stage.

Dressed in a white tunic dress with a diamond necklace around her neck, she is stunning. A white veil drapes over her face, allowing only her eyes to be seen. Then she begins to sing.

Loren's voice floats throughout the inn capturing everyone's attention. The song sounds like a Celtic ballad from me mother's CD collection; it's a story of a young warrior on a quest to save his beloved. As she continues to sing, she walks from table to table starting with the left side of the inn. Moving closer to the center table where I'm sitting, she flutters a silk scarf over the patrons' shoulders or faces, playfully teasing each as she walks by. Stopping at our table, she finishes her ballad and bends down to caress me face. Slipping the scarf over my shoulders, she moves to me other side, and then bending down, she drops her veil and kisses me softly on the cheek. Turning her head, she looks into Albrecht's eyes and whispers, "Hello, Uncle."

Albrecht's reaction is immediate; he reaches out and takes her into his arms. "Loren! How glad I am to have found you! I only arrived last night, but what is this? Why are you singing in this inn? Where is your father?"

"Oh, Uncle, there's so much to tell you, I hardly know where to start." Looking back to me she takes my hand, tugging at me to stand up.

"Uncle, this is Hugh, my very good friend."

Albrecht presses against the back of his chair and says, "I've had the good fortune to have already met Hugh, but how do you know him?"

"I can't say right now; let me finish my performance and then we can talk." She slips away to the next table and begins a new song.

Albrecht nudges me. "I should have known there was more to you than what the eye can see; how is it that you know my nieces?"

I pick up my ale and take another drink. The ale gives me confidence and unselfconsciousness, so I answer honestly and directly. "Your niece helped me in the past. Since then, we've become close friends. But only now am I beginning to understand why we have crossed each other's paths. Let's wait until Loren comes back, and then we can bring you up to date about our relationship."

I lift me mug of ale again and turn to watch Loren complete her performance. As soon as Loren finishes, Karla plays background music on her flute.

Bringing an extra chair to our table, Loren slides in between her uncle and me.

"Uncle, I have much to tell you, but you must know the worst news first." She hesitates a moment, and then with her voice cracking, she gently says, "Father is dead." Albrecht's eyes widen, and sorrow fills his face as Loren begins to relate the story of the cave—how her father had taken a crew along with Karla and her to explore the possibility of going through the great mountain to the Land of Light, but eventually met his death there.

Albrecht stops her for a moment. "Why did he take you and Karla with him?"

Loren pauses for a few seconds. "Father planned on completing the journey to the other side, and we all agreed that we wanted to be together." Her eyes fill with tears as she relates the circumstances of her father's death. Finally, she comes to the part where they meet Hugh and his companions, and Albrecht listens carefully as the story unfolds, including when the girls left us in the cave by ourselves. From there, I take over.

I explain the cave's power, how it magnifies our mental capabilities, senses, and emotions, and finally, how we eventually came together in this village. Albrecht takes a drink of his wine, then carefully takes Loren into his arms and expresses his sorrow at the loss of his brother and her father. He then stands up and takes me by the shoulders. "Thank you, son; if not for you, I don't believe I would still have my nieces here with me now."

I reach out and take Loren's hand. "I'm just beginning to learn how special your nieces are, sir. Loren has already taught me so much; I hope this is only the beginning of our relationship." Albrecht motions for us to sit and then waves over to Karla to come and join them. After greeting her uncle, she sits down next to him. Her eyes are alight and she keeps her arm wrapped under his arm as he speaks to them about their future and his present plans.

"First, I know you, your music is one of your passions, but neither of you have to work here for your supper any longer. I have brought your father's wealth, and of course, his ship. You both should be aware that ownership of over eighty percent of Soultraveler is passed on to you both. The ship is empty now, so there is no need for you to stay here at the inn. Cabins are available for not only yourselves, but your friends as well if they wish. The wealth I brought with me from your father's village will easily take care of you both for the rest of your lives. The rest of our ships are working steadily; I have rented most of them out to wealthy families that will ensure an income for all of us long into the future. If you wish, I will gladly operate Soultraveler for the importing and exporting of goods and people to the coastline villages. Due to your father's faith in me, I have acquired great wealth of my own. What I am saying is, the future is free and open; it is your right to choose what you wish to do."

Both girls look at each other and then at me; Karla is the first to speak.

"Hugh, without your help in the cave, I would not be here right now. Both Loren and I would like to try to repay our debt of gratitude." I look over at me friends, remembering what Jotan told me—what he predicted is now happening. I keep silent for a moment, and then, taking Loren's hand, I ask if we might be able to move to a cabin on Soultraveler while we are here in the village. Her eyes brighten and open wider.

"Oh yes! If you had not asked, I would have insisted on it myself." We take up a mug of ale and then toast to our good fortune and to everyone's reunion.

Davy looks around feeling a little out of sorts; these new friends and coworkers seem to be moving in a different direction. How fortunate he felt to become a part of such a great working team; now something else is brewing, and he wants to play a part in whatever it is, but doesn't know how to approach Hugh.

As if reading his mind, Hugh looks over at him and asks, "Davy, do you want to stay on Soultraveler with us?"

Davy looks at the group, and with a huge smile he raises his mug and says, "Thank you, thank you; I would be honored to stay on Soultraveler."

That evening we move our meager belongings to the great ship. It's late, and by the time we settle in, we only want to sleep. There is a cabin for each of us, so saying goodnight, I enter me cabin.

My apartment is on the middle deck, with me own balcony that wraps around the ship's stern. The cabins are large in comparison to the small room I had at the inn. The rich wooden walls are stained and shellacked smooth as glass. An exquisite down quilt and richly designed sheets and blankets cover the queen size bed. The floor is some sort of hardwood with throw rugs scattered about. The cabin has an adjoining small room, which back home, sailors called a head; there's also a sink and a shower, plus shelves for toiletries. In the main part of the cabin, a small desk and a comfortable chair sit beneath a square window with leaded glass. Double French doors open onto the balcony deck.

A large candle on the desk lights up the room with a soft brassy glow, its flickering flame reflects off the dark stained wood. I open the doors to the balcony and step out to get some fresh air. The ship is silent and still; the harbor waters barely move in the stillness. Leaning against the brass railing, I gaze out over the sea. Stars shine in the night sky, brightly glinting on the still waters, ocean smells fill the air. A breeze carries odors of cooking fires from the docks. These familiar smells fill my head with thoughts of home and me old life. I wonder what me mate Billy is doing? I wonder if Da' and Melody are thinking of me? If so, are they worried ? What are they doing? Have they given up on me?

Somehow, I know they haven't. I know they are doing everything they can to help. Da' wouldn't ever give up on us, not as long as any hope existed. I miss them a lot. Memories float along like a silent river in me mind. Me family and friend's laughter emerge from the dark waters around me, and I feel homesick; if only Billy could be here with me.

I reach up and take hold of a cable attached to an iron lock embedded on the top of the balcony rail. Staring over the ocean, I hear a low humming whose vibration pulses to the beat of my heart. The heart is that of a ten-year-old boy, who is slowly merging with me mind. In my innocence and in me heart, I'm living the fantasy dream that I always imagined, but something is missing. Feelings that Loren released in me through her love and passion are strange to my mind. This older version of me responds not only to her touch, but her mere presence makes me feel warm and happy. Feelings of loneliness are soothed when she holds me.

With all I've gained—the wisdom, the found courage, the confidence, new friends, and even this new awareness—I still feel as if I am losing something. Life in this reality reaches out like claws from the darkness, dragging me through my childhood far too quickly, and far too roughly. How I wish I could be at the tree house with Billy, where the only thing to be concerned about was where to fish the next morning, or hoping to grow a few more inches before school started. How can I ever go back to my old life with all that I'm experiencing from this journey? For now, these are questions I can't answer, and perhaps never will. If I'm to help mom, I have to stay focused on the journey at hand no matter what.

I can't allow me feelings for home or desire for Loren to distract me from what awaits. Is this great ship meant to become a part of my journey? Will Loren allow me to use it? And if so, how am I to operate it? I know absolutely nothing about sailing even a small boat, let alone this great vessel. I close my eyes, letting the ocean breeze whisper its freedom to me. I must trust in Soul. Soul alone knows nothing is impossible if it's meant to be; if it is, then all will be provided. Worrying about what might go wrong or what I don't know is senseless. I can only draw on my experience and have faith I'll be guided in the right direction at the right moment.

I'm beginning to realize that what I'm thinking at the moment usually sets the stage for whatever happens in me near future.

The next morning I awake to the patter of raindrops. I walk out on deck, and the sky is a dark gray. A cool breeze blows across the stern, and Albrecht's just emerging from his cabin above me.

"Good morning, my young friend." Smiling, the elderly man climbs down the stairs onto the same level as me. "The rain isn't hard, but strong enough to wash the dust from the deck." Albrecht pulls on some riggings. Tying them to a pole at the end of the stairway, he asks, "Are you hungry, or would you like a little tour of our ship?" I turn and look down the long deck. "A tour would be nice."

Albrecht points the way, and as we are walking, he begins telling me about the ship.

"This ship is larger than most, and can carry quite a load when necessary. As you can see, we have three main masts with three sails on each one, and a lower sail attaches to the boom rising to the front and fourth mast. We have fifteen cabins for officers and guests, and quarters for another twenty crewmen."

Walking further toward the bow, he shows me the life boats mounted on each side. Then pointing up, he explains the reason for the crow's nest.

"Those are placed high in order to see other passing ships, landmarks, storms approaching or any other bits of information that can only be seen from such a high point. The watcher in the crow's nest constantly looks down on the ship for any problems with the riggings or sails. Usually a good watcher can spot a problem before it becomes dangerous to the ship or crew.

"There are three nests, one on each mast. On some occasions all three are filled, but in calm seas either the far stern or the bow nest is used. The middle nest is for caution most of the time. If necessary, we can store enough supplies for a six-month journey, and with hatches down, we can weather out any storm that comes our way."

Looking up, Albrecht points to the bow. "You see that throne in front of the boom? It's usually used by the captain or someone of great importance. Primarily, it is a status symbol, and allows the person to see in greater comfort how the workings of the ship are maintained on a daily basis. The benches sitting on each side of it are for advisors, wise men, family or perhaps discussions or lectures that allow teachers to discourse on varied subjects."

Pointing to a gold unicorn placed on the boom in front of the ship, he continues, "That is not only for design, but it also provides a service. It is mounted on a stand that pivots to the right or the left; using the right measurements and applying directions from the stars, the unicorn can be used as a directional finder. Only the single unicorn on the bow is functional; the other two on each side of the cabin entrances are for anesthetics only."

I look past the unicorn at the great crystal tipping the end of the boom which extends over the bow. "What's the crystal for?" I ask.

Placing his hands on my shoulders, Albrecht turns me around toward the stern of the ship. "You see that other crystal behind the helm on the brass pole?" I see a second large diamond-shaped crystal tilting a little downward. Albrecht then turns me back to the crystal on the end of the bow. "When necessary, and when the sun is at our backs, those crystals harness energy from the sun and align them together into a great power that can propel this ship not only faster than just the sails, but also provide her with far more control. This crystal power is used only in case of emergencies, and at times when great speed is required. The crystals can even be used when the sun is blocked by overcast clouds, such as today."

The more I see of Soultraveler, the more impressed I become. The ship is a marvel in natural technology and engineering, using the wind and sun not only for movement, but navigation, too. Albrecht says, "You can't possibly see everything on the ship in such a short time, but perhaps another time I will show you the hull and how the guidance system works."

Albrecht and I walk back toward the stern and meet up with Loren and Karla, who are both standing on the high deck waiting for our short tour to finish. Dandi and Kaylu sit next to Davy, who is looking over the side of the ship by huge water barrels. When Albrecht asks if any of us would like some breakfast, we all eagerly assent.

We follow him down the plank and begin threading through the docks as we head toward the village. As we pass along the colorful shops and streets of the little hamlet, Albrecht asks me, "So, Hugh, what is your story?"

I think for a moment, wondering how much I should say. I begin to explain about me mum and the quest to find and free her; by the time I'm through, we have entered a small café and are waiting to order our food.

Albrecht remains silent for a few moments, and then turning to Dandi and Kaylu, he asks them, "You two have stayed with Hugh from the beginning. Why?"

Kaylu looks curiously at Albrecht and replies, "Hugh is our friend; we, too, have a mission to fulfill from this quest. Dandi and I are accomplishing something that will bring us both something we have sought for a long time."

Albrecht looks intently at them both and replies, "And what is this something you have been seeking?"

This time Dandi answers him. "Some call it higher awareness, some call it Soul. We search for answers not only about life itself, but of ourselves. Since traveling with Hugh, our journey has become one of discovery in ways we can hardly explain. I come from an ancient race that is older than anything you can comprehend, and yet I wish to discover something more than what I previously thought myself to be."

Kaylu then speaks up. "I come from a race that seeks to discover the Creator's plan for not only ourselves, but for all life, and on every level of existence."

Albrecht shakes his head. "You are a strange group, I will admit. You have lofty goals; most men seek wealth or physical happiness, but with you, it is different. From what I have heard so far, Hugh's journey demands that he move forward, always searching, always growing…and most of all, always taking high risks; somehow, my nieces are caught up in your journey. I, for one, do not think there is anything I can say or do to persuade them to leave you. I do not know if I would even try."

Loren looks up at her uncle. "I am glad to hear you say that, Uncle, because there is something I have been thinking about, and wish to discuss it with you." Loren chooses her words carefully. "If Hugh will agree, I would like to use Soultraveler to assist him in his search. It seems clear to me that his journey will require him to sail our oceans in search of information about his mother's whereabouts; he has both knowingly and unknowingly helped us. We can now help him and his companions, and since the ship is not in use now, Karla and I both wish to use some of our wealth to assist him in accomplishing his quest."

I start to say something, but then think better of it; I've learned to accept help when it presents itself, especially when it is help of such magnitude.

Albrecht remains silent for a while, and then looking up at the travelers, he says, "To be successful in such a journey, one must know the direction he needs to go; at this point, I do not think either Hugh or his companions have any clue where they are supposed to go next."

I look up with a startled expression, but I realize that he's right. At this point, I have no idea where to go. The only thing I do know is that at some point, I'll need a ship to find me mother.

Albrecht is quiet for a moment as the truth sinks in, then leaning closer to me he offers a way forward. "There is someone who might be able to help. He doesn't live here in the village, but his home is only about two days away by sea."

Loren reaches over to take her uncle's arm. "We can take him there, Uncle. Just tell us who he is and where we can meet him!"

Albrecht looks at the faces around the table and then turning to his niece, he says, "It is a short journey by ship down the coast toward the east. The person you will be looking for has a peculiar way of finding or already knowing things that are normally beyond the ken of our normal minds. Nevertheless, if you decide to go to him, it is not necessary to take Soultraveler."

Loren asks him how that can be so and Albrecht explains, "I will authorize a smaller vessel to take Hugh where he must go. Meanwhile, my nieces and I will begin to outfit Soultraveler for the forthcoming journey."

I take Albrecht's hand, and with a firm shake, I thank him, and Dandi and Kaylu do the same.

And so it was that within just a short while, Albrecht has booked us on a small sailing vessel; we leave today.

****

The vessel that Albrecht charters is swift and sturdy, and is ready to sail before nightfall. Albrecht pays the boat's captain handsomely for his time, because the Captain has had to cancel his earlier plans. Before I know it, I'm on my way to the village of Narupai to meet with a person that Albrecht considers a sage. Supposedly this person not only gathers information, but also in some cases foretells what events could transpire in the future; I'm dubious, but keep an open mind, for I have already seen and experienced things that normally would have seemed fantasy to the little boy I used to be, and I'm not nearly as judgmental or opinionated as I once was about what is possible and what is not.

The captain keeps his ship within eyesight of the shoreline; we sail swiftly on ocean currents guided by the experienced helmsman. The craft is nothing in comparison to Soultraveler. We share a small cabin that is cramped and sparsely furnished, with only one large bunk and a bench to sit on. I spend most of my time outside the cabin watching and asking questions concerning navigating the little sailing craft.

The trip is uneventful other than the education about seafaring that I receive from the willing captain. Two days pass, and by the time we pull into Narupai, it's dawn. The little ship sails into the harbor and docks at the wharf, which is tiny compared to the wharves in Outbound. We step ashore and begin searching for the sage—his name is Morleck.

Albrecht told me that any inn or shop could point me in the right direction to the sage. In the market square, people are busy haggling, buying, and trading wares. Fish, fruits, vegetables, and other goods are abundant. The morning sun begins to heat up the little village, and we enter the nearest shop, whose trade is selling tools and farm equipment. A short man wearing a white shirt with a brown leather vest fitted tightly to his stocky frame mans the counter. I walk up to catch his eye. Edging closer to the counter, I place a few coins on the counter and stay silent. The shopkeeper looks up.

"What can I help you with?"

I whisper low, "We're looking for someone, can you help us?"

The shopkeeper leans over the counter and replies, "That depends on who or what you are looking for; does he live in this village?"

I lean closer with me hands on the counter, and pushing the coins toward him, I say, "He goes by the name of Morleck, and he is supposedly well-known in this area."

The man raises his eyebrows and remains silent for a moment before replying, "Yes, I know him. He's known quite well throughout the village, and it's no secret that he lives just outside the village in a cottage atop the hillside on your right." I step back; that was simple…I had thought there had to be an element of mystery to this person if he could do all the things Albrecht said he could do, but apparently I was wrong!

The shopkeeper picks up the coins on the counter and smiles, "I would have given you the information for free if you had just asked." Feeling foolish, I motion to Kaylu and Dandi and we walk briskly out into the street. I thought to myself, maybe I've watched too much TV.

We walk toward the end of the village and soon leave the noise of the marketplace behind us. I see a large hill about a half-mile ahead; pointing it out, we step up our pace. The morning sun is getting higher and the temperature getting warmer; by the time we reach the hill, we have worked up a sweat, especially since I'm still wearing the sea jacket provided to me for the trip on the sailing craft. As we approach closer, I can see a pathway leading up to the side of the hill paved with flat rocks and an occasional small stairway rising to the next level. I see a small ancient-looking structure perched atop the hill; smoke floats from a stack on the roof, and a small creek runs alongside the home and then down the side of the hill.

I remember the pictures in the cave; they seem very similar to this scene. Could this be the same place depicted on the cavern walls?

The large archway door has a bell-type mechanism on the side, which I assume is the way to get the inhabitant's attention. The bell is melodious with a long chime echoing after the initial ring. I hear the latch being lifted and then the door opens. A little man standing as high as my shoulder appears in the doorway. He has a white beard and a small cap on his head.

"Welcome! Welcome! I have been expecting you," he says loudly and graciously.

The door swings open invitingly, and I walk in with Kaylu following; Dandi hesitates for a moment, and then bending almost double, he ducks into the darkness of the hill house.

Soft beams of colored light stream in through a stained glass skylight just over our heads, illuminating the larger than expected cool chamber. The air is pungent with spices and herbs; a small fire burns in the hearth, and a pot dangles just above the flame. Rustic but cozy, Morleck's chamber is filled with well-used furniture: a thick-cushioned sofa, armchair, dining set, and a comfortable-looking bed nestled in the corner. A small dog snores in front of the hearth, utterly unfazed by our entrance.

The little man pulls some tiny tin cups from a cupboard. "Sit down! Sit down! We have so much to discuss. Would you like something cool to drink?"

With a nod, I accept his offer, and the little man opens a metal door embedded in the side of a stone wall. Pulling out a goblet, he pours a little of its clear liquid into each small cup. We all position ourselves as we can on the small chairs, and he smiles a bit as he places a cup in front of each of us. After he seats himself atop a comfortable cushion on a wooden chair next to the table, the little man asks, "Now, what do you think I can do for you fellows?"

I introduce myself along with Dandi and Kaylu. The little man nods and responds, "My name is Morleck. I knew you were coming, but I don't know why."

I'm thinking about how I can approach him with my story and then explain what it is I'm actually here for, but Morleck seems to know my thoughts more clearly than I do. Before I can say a word, he smiles and kindly says, "Just start at the beginning, I have plenty of time. If I am to be of any assistance to you, it would be best that I know the entire series of events that have led you to my door." I feel I can trust this little man, so I begin my story from when I was a little boy in Bristol, and then quickly move on to the building of the tree house. I tell him about Da' and me mum, the accident, and all the events afterward in these new strange worlds. When I'm through, Morleck just sits there, sipping his drink. I hadn't even picked up my cup yet; my mouth feels as if a dust storm had settled in it, so I take a sip of the brew. Sweet with a slight fruity taste—although what kind of fruit I can't say—it's cool and refreshing.

The little man sets his cup down, furrows his brow, and strokes his beard.

"Strange tales in my lifetime I've heard, but never anything as fascinating as what you just described. So if what you are telling me is true, then just a short time ago you were but a little boy, and now you are thrust into this adventure, becoming not only a Traveler, but a warrior as well?" Morleck continues to pull at his beard as he stands up from his chair. "Interesting. Never have I heard such a story, and never have I ever encountered one such as you, let alone the strangeness of your companions! I need a little time to absorb your story, then maybe I can give you information to help you on to the next step of your journey." Without saying another word, the little man retreats to a corner of the room, crawls onto his bed, and promptly nods off to sleep.

We exchange hurried glances; none of us knows what to do. We simply keep sitting there, uncomfortable in the fact that our host has abandoned us, and that we have little other choice than to await his reappearance. I am uncomfortable and fidget a bit. Hunched on top of the small kitchen chair, Dandi is both uncomfortable and confused; he keeps looking around the room as if he's trying to understand where they are. Kaylu, however, seems undisturbed. He quietly sits there sipping his brew, watching me. I find the silence nerve-wracking.

After perhaps a half hour, Morleck calls out, still lying on his bed with his back to us, "Is there a book involved in this adventure?"

I jerk me head up and answer. "Yes, I was given a book by Jotan; I keep it in my tunic pocket."

The little man turns over and sits up. "May I look at it, please?"

I hesitate, and then I remember Jotan's caution, *"You can let others read this book, but no one who is not ready will understand it."*

I walk over to the bed and Morleck carefully takes the book from my outstretched hand. "Ah, yes, I can feel the power in its pages."

Morleck sits up with a start and shifts to his rocker. I watch as Morleck carefully opens it and reads the words, delicately turning each page as if it were fragile and precious. Within a few moments, he places it down carefully and looks up at me. "You have had the answers you seek all the time; the book quite simply explains your eventual destination."

Opening the book, I scan the words for the answer to mother's whereabouts, but after a few pages I look up at Morleck and say, "I don't see any directions or explanation as to how or where we are supposed to go."

Morleck laughs lightly, then reaching out he takes the book back and places it on the little table in front of us. "You must read between the words. This book speaks of wisdom and describes events. Sometimes this is in riddles, but for those who can see deeper into its meaning, the words and riddles project themselves directly into their mind with the true meaning."

I remember all the times I read the little book before; the words were written as if they were me own thoughts, and each time the meaning was clear. Sometimes there were rare moments when I actually experienced what the book was trying to show me. Now Morleck tells me that the book has an even deeper way of communicating...if one is ready for it.

Morleck motions for me to come closer and read alongside him. The page he points to describes negative entities that exist in the lower worlds. Morleck reads aloud as I follow along:

There are certain types of beings who live in various places, but always remain close to an energy portal. These portals are conduits used to disperse the negative energy that is needed to create matter, space, and time. Close to each portal is an energy point where the power is the most concentrated. These points are home to entities that feed on negative energy, not only from the portal, but also from Souls that get lost, caught in their own negative energy. Souls can stay trapped within a negative mode such that their lives eventually becomes controlled by unbridled passions, fear, sadness, hatred, or other habits of self-destruction. Such a Soul can become a receptacle for this negative energy, endlessly drawn down into and affected by these power portals, whether in dreams, death, or other ways.

The closer he comes to this area of consciousness, the more negative he becomes; eventually, a lost Soul may even be absorbed and lost in the internal source of negative energy.

In some cases, a person's body can be separated from the Soul with just a small string of consciousness left to keep the body alive. This connective consciousness is called the silver cord. When this happens, the Soul can be trapped in one of these power points and not even be consciously aware of it.

There are two main portals for every plane of existence in the lower creation. One is the portal for the negative energy waves to flow out, and the other is for the positive energy waves to flow in. People themselves act as minor portals to either create positive energy or negative energy through their actions, thoughts or emotions.

Power itself is neutral in its original state, but once it flows through the human consciousness, attitude is what determines whether it becomes constructive or destructive. It's wise to avoid the types of people who create only negativity and spread it to others. When the two waves of positive and negative energy merge, they create matter, which provides existence for all physical life in the lower worlds. For a Soul to journey to either one of these points of power is not easy; to be successful, the Soul must have a highly developed sense of spiritual intuition, as well as genuine knowledge that supersedes faith or trust in personal beliefs about himself and his relationship with the Creator. Each portal exists in opposition to the other: not only in qualities, but also in location. Whatever it takes to get to one portal requires the opposite maneuvers to reach the other. Man is always noisily searching outward for the negative portal; few look in silence to the positive source within.

Morleck hands the book over to me, and I continue reading, looking or trying to find the directions to the place where my mother was held prisoner, but the more I read the more confused I become. Something I'm doing seems to be creating circumstances that put me in conflict, stopping me from realizing where my destination lies.

Morleck reaches out and closes the book. "You must stop analyzing every word! You are blocking the directions."

I become frustrated and angry. I can't seem to decipher the meaning and discover the directions…why? Dandi and Kaylu just sit quietly; both know that if we are to find out where to go, it has to come from me.

Morleck pours another drink for himself. "Hugh, you cannot force the book to give you the information. Your love for your mother and your desire to help her are the arrows that point the way. The book takes these feelings and tries to elevate wisdom and energy in you. The book takes your feelings, transmutes them, and then sends back from its pages what you need."

Morleck pats me on the shoulder gently and continues, "So long as you do not have the knowledge or understanding of how to withstand the power you would be up against, the book will not create the map you are seeking. Don't you see? If the book simply gives you the proper directions, and you follow them without realizing how to protect and preserve yourself, then you will surely find failure and possibly entrap yourself and others in a pit of negativity that you know as hell."

I stare at the ground for a minute and then stand up abruptly. Waving my hands in exasperation, I reply, "I read that book! Still, I don't understand. What do I have to do to see the way?"

Morleck wants to tell Hugh to calm down, but he thinks better of it. Hugh's mind is trying to defeat him. He must let his true self surface and take control, otherwise he will never understand. Morleck knows Hugh's love for his family, combined with his experiences so far, have stirred deep emotions and feelings that are just now beginning to surface. These factors are blocking his understanding, and only Hugh himself can override them.

Looking away from Hugh, Morleck stares down at the book, and says softly, "Soul has to read the passages in the book. The words are written for the authentic self, not for the personality or for the mind that mixes emotions and feeling with thoughts and attachments."

Morleck sits quietly for a while, and then folding his hands together, he says calmly, "I believe that in the beginning of this new journey, you will need a guide. At some point, you will discover the final path to your journey's end, but until then, if you wish, I can be that guide."

I turn quickly from me pacing. "You would do that? You are willing to go with us?"

Morleck smiles, "I am old and need one more adventure in my life! I can start you out on your journey, but believe me when I tell you that you must eventually finish the quest alone."

I feel overcome with relief, and I grab Morleck by the shoulders. "Of course, of course, but with your help, we can at least begin the journey! I'm sure at some point I'll find the way, and be able to do what I need to do alone."

And so it is agreed. Morleck will travel back with us, and assist with his knowledge of not only this world, but of the mysterious portals.

It is almost evening before we are ready to start back to the village. Morleck busily patters back and forth, identifying the necessary items we must tote in large canvas bags, and locking away all the rest of his belongings. Patting his dog on the head, he whispers to it to be a good boy; it barely raises an exhausted eyelid in response to his bemused owner. Then carefully locking the door to his hillside home, Morleck stands up and chuckles, "We will have to stop in the village to let someone know I'm going to be gone for a while and to leave a key so they can take care of my ferocious dog."

As we four march together back to the small cargo ship, Morleck explains that he is bringing many scrolls, maps, and charts that he believes will be needed on the voyage to point us in the right direction.

Once we are on board the small ship, Morleck asks to be left alone in one of the small cabins so he can study the charts and make sure they will not only be headed in the general direction, but also to study the signs and dangers they are to encounter on the way.

That night, under a starlit and velvet sky, our small cargo ship finally pulls into the little harbor. Closing in on Soultraveler, I sense something wonderful is about to happen.

Albrecht and the girls have not been idle while we have been away. Food was transported into the hull along with tools, clothes, water, and weapons, as well as three cases of his finest wine. Each cabin was cleaned and outfitted with new blankets. The old sails were replaced with new glistening white sails that are even stronger and bigger; these will provide better performance and speed for the journey. New ropes are outfitted on the mast and riggings. Replacement sails are stowed in the hull along with extra ropes, masts, and other parts that may need repairing during the journey.

The crystals on Soultraveler shine like diamonds in the moonlight. The decks are polished along with the rails and helm. The cleaned cannons have stacks of new ammo placed in their adjacent gunnery boxes. The outside of the ship was scrubbed free of any barnacles or salt water corrosions, and then polished with a new coat of light brown stain. Every inch of the ship was inspected and brought up to the highest standards.

Albrecht arranged for an excellent crew as well; he took pains to hire on a favorite cook he used for important passengers on special trips, and he selected an expert navigator and a crew of twenty specifically chosen from among the finest ships docked in the village. To recruit the best men, and to entice them away from the ships they were already on, Albrecht promised these selected crewmen a bonus along with their unusually high crew pay.

Soultraveler is already known for its beauty and durability along with its speed. Together with its unusually qualified crew and recent overhaul, even the legend that Soultraveler has already enjoyed during its short life is greatly enhanced. No other ship is as large, or as strong and beautiful. The railings on the rear balcony shine like new brass; the newly shellacked wooden floors reflect the images of those who trod them. Each portal has its brass trim polished. Flags wave at the top of each mast as firelight from the shore reflects off the two giant crystals: Soultraveler is captivating.

Tamping down our excitement, we are quietly welcomed onboard. I show Morleck the quarters where he could stay, and then we surrender to our cabins and all go to bed.

The next morning at sunrise, Albrecht stands on the wharf, admiring the ship's perfection. A sudden blast on the longhorn signals the ship's readiness. In seeming response, a steady sound of heavy footsteps from a distance rattles the wharf. Six armed men with shields march onto the wharf and stop in front of the ship. With just a glance, one could tell these are not ordinary men. Their shields are embedded with a huge faceted crystal stone that covers the entire front of the shield. The crystals shields constantly change colors as sunlight dances across their surface. I was told later that the crystals are unbreakable; nothing can chip or shatter them.

For eons, these ancient shields have been handed down, father to son. If a son isn't worthy, then the shield is stored away until someone who deserves such an incredible defensive weapon is born. At the moment, only six men prove worthy to own one, although I have learned that there are actually fifty crystal shields in existence.

Hiring these warriors is expensive, but cost is no option when it comes to the safety of his nieces, Albrecht muses to himself. During his many journeys, Albrecht had learned of these elite warriors, and he feels now is the precise time to use them. Each warrior has a specialty that he trained for since childhood. Their orders on this mission are to protect and serve not only the Captain, but also to ensure the safety of the entire crew in any way deemed necessary.

The forward plank is pulled, and the six great warriors step onto Soultraveler.

Even to them the ship is inspiring. They have seen many wonders in their chosen life, but Soultraveler is something they never imagined; Albrecht makes a point of introducing himself to each warrior and remembering his name. The respect he has for these men is unquestionable; their fame is legendary throughout this world. And importantly, these warriors have chosen to be here, and not because of the money Albrecht will pay them.

The deciding factor for each is the opportunity to blaze new trails. The challenge to explore the oceans and beyond is a quest none could refuse. All six felt honored and humbled to be chosen for this journey. Once all their gear is stored away, the orders are given for all crew and warriors to rest, and be present at sunrise tomorrow, ready to sail.

Blood races in me veins, my heart beats faster. Stepping on the dock, I feel something in the air; the swirl of activity around Soultraveler catches the attention of the townspeople as they gather on the dock to watch the activity.

That night I stand on the upper deck looking down on the ship. The moon is rising and its silvery light reflects against the silhouette of Soultraveler. The two giant crystals glisten and polished brass railings sparkle. The unicorn statue stands out against the moonlight like a protector pointing the way. The helm stands like a beacon on top of the upper deck with the mounted crystal gleaming behind it.

I walk into my cabin, still sensing the great energy and work accomplished in my absence. Before retiring for the night, I say goodnight to Kaylu and Dandi, and make sure that Morleck is comfortable.

The smells of newly varnished floors, brass polish, and incense drift about me in my cabin. The double doors to the balcony are open, allowing fresh sea air to drift into the cabin and blend with the other aromas. Laying my bundle down on the bed, I walk through the double doors out onto the balcony again.

The moon lights up the ocean with multifaceted reflections, casting off lime green phosphorescent waves rolling to the shore. I move forward, noticing a soft glow reflecting off polished brass. A few ropes stretch down from above, connecting to hooks bolted to the railing. The scent of jasmine from the deck above floats to me senses; vines hang from above, framing both sides of my arched doorway. Someone has lit candles around the flat railing overlooking the ocean.

A movement to the left catches my attention; slowly my eyes adjust to the darkness, and there in the corner of the balcony where the railing curves stands Loren.

I step closer—silent and breathless—as the golden moonlight and amber candles flicker all about her. Loren's full hair flows over her bare shoulders and slender arms as the wind playfully tosses her soft curls. Her sleeveless gown's low, draped neckline perfectly sets off her elegant porcelain neck. The sheer, diaphanous panels of seafoam green are cinched by a matching satin belt that accentuates her tiny waist. Loren's stunning beauty and the intensity of her eyes quietly searching the waters are so great that I am struck with the thought that in ancient times, lonely seafaring men might have mistaken this creature to be a goddess.

I stare amazed. First, I am struck by the vision of this beautiful young woman scanning the ocean; second, I am astonished that this lovely person is waiting for me to come back to her. Finally, I allow myself to inhale, and I draw near to her. Me heart beats faster, a warm feeling spreads in my stomach. She turns and smiles; her eyes shine like twin diamonds. A small silver bracelet glistens around her left wrist. Gracefully, she moves forward and takes me into her arms whispering, "I missed you so much, are you really here?" Still speechless, I assure her that I am by tenderly kissing her.

We both move to the balcony's edge and look at the moonlit ocean. My arm rests around her shoulder as her arm encircles my waist. There's nothing to say; we both feel the love and happiness of just being together, and we share the happy anticipation of our forthcoming journey.

I gaze into the night sky, thinking that all of this seems so unreal. Here I am, standing on a breathtaking ship, holding a girl who is even more breathtaking—and she becomes more beautiful every time I see her. I am about to embark on an adventure no storyteller could tell, not only to save me mom but to save myself also. The responsibility of people's lives and their futures has been placed in my care. Am I strong enough to accept this responsibility and to succeed in such an adventure?

My new body is strong; warrior's blood flows through me veins. My new mind is strong; adult thoughts, self-awareness, and confidence flow through me brain. My old life in Bristol is surreal, like a past life, or a dream. Just as I have become accustomed to my new height, strength, and stamina, my mind is no longer that of a ten-year-old boy either. These new thoughts and feelings are as natural to me now as walking, sleeping, and eating in this new body.

Love flows freely from my heart: a love from a deeper part of me that seems to have no ending. I remember an old song and I smile to myself. Yes, the more love I give, the more love I get.

Loren's whispers to me, "Hugh, let us go inside; we have much to do tomorrow. This may be our last night on this ship alone."

Looking into her eyes, I reach out to touch her cheek and whisper back, "You have given me so much; you truly are one of the miracles in my life. It's like we've known each other forever. Is it destiny that we're together?"

Loren smiles; reaching over she places a finger against my lips. "Shh, don't ask and don't try to analyze; just accept what we feel now, and go with the moment."

We turn and look at the ocean waves crashing on the shoreline past the village. I take her hand, and we walk into the cabin. My heart beats faster, and a familiar warm feeling spreads in my stomach. She turns and smiles; I marvel at her eyes—they really do shine like twin diamonds.

CHAPTER 31 ~ A DECISIVE MOMENT

The hospital room is painted a sanitized whitish blue. White sheets and blankets cover a little boy on a small twin bed. Breathing tubes and oxygen lines snake from his mouth and nose. IVs feed him while monitors track his vital signs. He lies there with eyes closed; although short and shallow, his breaths are continuous. He is thin: far too thin. His light brown hair needs cutting, and he looks to be about six or seven years old, but in truth he's ten. This is the shell known as "Hugh."

Each day his body is washed and examined. Each day the question is, "will this be the day life ends, or the day life starts again?" To those who love him, and understand what the little boy is going through, Hugh represents more than just a son, a brother or a friend; he is the connection that forms the circle that is a family. This sick small child—whose pallor is almost as white as the sheets that keep him warm—is the keystone holding the Bailey family together. Clark looks upon his son with a mixture of emotions: feelings of awe, sadness, inspiration, grief, pride, and love; and feelings of that ineffable bond between father and son that no one can understand except the two of them. Clark knows bits and pieces of the struggle his son has chosen to endure, and if he knew the entire scope of what his son is experiencing maybe then he could see that life truly does exists in a far greater reality than anything he ever imagined.

Melody sits next to her father watching her brother. In the innocent wisdom of a child, she knows Hugh is going through something far more significant than what they see. She feels a powerful warm energy transmitted through Hugh's frail small body. Not mentally understanding everything she is feeling, she intuitively knows the importance of what her older brother is trying to do for them. Reaching out, she holds his small still hand. If only he would move or squeeze her hand just to let them know he was still partially there…but there's nothing.

Four long months have passed. Clark and Melody have waited and watched while life around them still progresses. School is open again.

Relatives and Hugh's friends occasionally call or stop by the house, sometime summoning the courage to ask if he is going to be all right. Clark and Melody both wonder how the world keeps moving ahead while their world is on hold.

In the four months since Hugh's accident, his friend Billy has shot up about two inches, leaving him thinned out and beginning to look more like a young teenager. He still goes to the tree house and sometimes borrows Cody for long walks in the meadow. The few times he was allowed to visit Hugh, the experience was really rough for him. To see his best friend lying in a coma and seeming to shrink a little bit more each time he sees him became more than he could endure. He prefers instead to visit the tree house. Billy feels connected with Hugh when he sits in his wooden sanctuary, pondering what Hugh might like added, thinking about how it can be improved, and discovering minor flaws and working on their repairs; when Hugh comes back, it will be perfect.

Billy's long walks with Cody, and sometimes Melody, are opening his eyes to how deeply Hugh treasured the meadow and woods. Yes, Billy is indeed growing through this experience. Quiet moments at the tree house allow him to stop and ruminate on his friendship with the boy who from what Melody has told him is determined to save his mother.

Melody has taken time to have long talks and explain what she and her father are discovering about Hugh and his mother's accident. Prior to the accident, Billy never really thought about life and death. Life to him meant having fun, going to school, and fishing. Now, he feels a drive to learn and explore some of the things Melody tells him. He pays more attention to his dreams now, and he has learned to become quieter around others. He seems to have become an observer in life, which suits him fine. He is getting accustomed to being alone, looking within himself for answers that either nobody else cares about or wouldn't, couldn't, know. For the first time in his young life, Billy is discovering that the only true answers for his questions are those that bubble up from within his quiet moments and his times of observation. One thing he realizes is that to learn or to walk the path of truth it takes a two-step process. First, he has to know the way, and second, and most difficult, he has to walk it alone.

One night after Billy spent most of the day in the meadow with Cody, he lay sleeping in his bed when he started to dream.

At first, the dream doesn't make sense; he had gone to sleep thinking about Hugh and what he was going through in the hospital, but in the dream, Billy finds himself on a great ship similar to the old-style clipper ships. However, this ship was somewhat different—it wasn't just large; it was also beautifully crafted in every detail.

Billy finds himself stationed at the ship's helm, steering this wondrous ship out across the ocean, he feels a rush of freedom and power alongside warm breezes continually brushing against his face. As the ship rolls and moves across the waters, he hears ropes creaking and the great flags on the mast flapping. The sky is blue and the sun is warm. It's a beautiful day, and the ship glistens as it sails through the blue calm waters. Then Billy begins to wonder.

How did he get here?

Where is he going?

What is he supposed to do when he gets to wherever he's going?

What if he gets lost?

Will he ever find his way back?

As his worry grows about all these unknowns, the sky is completely transformed. The sun fades behind dark threatening clouds until it is altogether masked, leaving an angry gray skyline before him. Despite his worries, he sails farther out into the open waters, and the sky and ocean turn even darker. The great ship plows through ever-growing waves; his face is pelted by slaps of salt-water. Now he is fighting the helm, and as he tries to keep the ship on a straight course, desperation claws itself deep into his heart and mind—he's losing control of the ship. The more he tries, the fiercer the storm becomes, and the greater his fear grows. The waves batter the sides of the great ship, and cold stinging salt water soon soaks his clothes. Dripping and shivering at the helm, he fights to maintain control. Suddenly, thunder claps announce heavy sheets of rain; winds howl while the ship pitches and heaves, fighting its way through swirling waters that seem to be trying to reach out and drag its prey into its dark depths.

How has he lost almost complete control of the ship so quickly? At that exact moment, when he thinks perhaps all is lost, a young man suddenly emerges from a narrow stairway leading up to the helm. Billy senses something familiar about him; the man looks like someone he should know. The stranger reaches out and takes over the helm. With a mighty turn, he begins to maneuver the ship away from its perilous path, almost as if from sheer will.

Turning to Billy, the stranger shouts into the howling wind, "The right way to take control of your ship is to put everything into the hands of the Creator! Help me, Billy, and we can steer your ship to safe waters!"

Setting himself alongside the stranger and grabbing hold of a part of the helm, Billy takes the man's lead and pulls as hard as he can. Between the two of them, they gradually manage to move the ship out of the destructive currents and finally into calmer waters. Releasing the helm, the young man steps back and tells Billy to take control. Billy guides the ship into smooth blue waters.

Putting his arm around Billy's shoulder, the young man says, "Billy, the person you are now is entirely different from the child you were not long ago. You are not the same person because you have developed a different capacity to give love. This greater giving opens you from within and allows you to receive greater love; this changes your perceptions and life itself. True loving allows you to understand that the greatest concept we can have of God is the greatest concept we can have of ourselves. Remember, Billy: the most secret part of you resides in a heart that is driven by a love for all things."

The young man takes a step back, and then in a familiar voice Billy clearly knows, he says, "Thanks for taking care of Cody."

Billy wakes with a start; the dream is vividly clear in his mind.

The strange young man is someone he thinks he knows—there's no question about it—he has been with that person before. But where? And when?

After this dream, Billy's attention and awareness begin to expand rapidly. He now sees importance even in the very smallest of things, including those that in the past he would have likely ignored. Now, even in the most private parts of his life he sees meaning he never noticed before. Just as his dream cast him as its main character setting out in a great ship on a daring journey that is simultaneously exciting and dangerous, Billy decides to undertake his own journey in his waking life, searching for something, taking control of the direction of his life. True, what he's searching for he doesn't really know; but he does know that life holds greater beauty, significance, and depth he had never understood as a child, and now he wants to find and explore it all.

****

Clark and Brandon arrive in the courtroom early.

A hearing has been called to decide whether the judge will honor the request to go to trial over the potential discontinuance of Ann Clark's life support. The insurance company decided it was best to address Mrs. Bailey's case alone instead of Hugh and her together; if successful, they could then bring their case against Hugh's life support.

The four legal representatives from the insurance companies are seated opposite Clark and Brandon. Thumbing through their briefs, they look busy and important; to them, this is an obvious, minor case, and all of them are confident that they have prepared their case so well that the judge will without a doubt decide on their behalf. The mountain of paperwork in post office bins beside their table is rather impressive. The judge looks serious, but distracted. Brandon is calm and he smiles as he hands a few pages of a rebuttal to the judge. The judge looks up for a moment as if in surprise, and then taking the pages, he lowers his head, adjusts his glasses and begins to read.

Walking back to his desk, Brandon smiles at the opposing counsel, who scowl and grimace sarcastically in response. The informal hearing is due in part to the persistence of Alliance Insurance Company's pressure on the court to hear their case and allow them to end what they believe to be a futile attempt to keep Ann Bailey on life support in hopes of eventual recovery. Their claims are based on their firm belief that Mrs. Bailey will never come out of her coma; their law briefs are thick with legal jargon, statements from well-paid expert witnesses in past cases, and medical summaries saturated with dire prognoses that manipulate words in such a way that the outcome seems inevitable. Hundreds of pages detail previous cases, in each of which the patient never emerges out of coma. This is a slam dunk.

Brandon doesn't seem to be disturbed about their strategy, or if he is, he isn't showing it. The judge proceeds to read over the pros and cons of the case. Both parties know the judge received copies prior to the court date, but judges like to make a ritual out of reviewing the cases and any last-minute filings on the bench.

Looking inside his briefcase, Brandon seems more interested in his lunch bag than the hearing. Noting this curious fixation, Clark is nervous. The lives of his wife and son are at stake here; surely Brandon could be more professional, or at least act serious about the proceeding, couldn't he?

After about five minutes of this legal foreplay, the judge places the briefs down and calmly asks if there is any additional information concerning this matter. Immediately, the Alliance's main attorney rises.

"Your Honor; on behalf of The Alliance Insurance Company, we would like to make our oral summary statement to clarify our position."

The judge sighs and looks at the lawyer intently. "Counsel, I don't think I need to remind you this is a preliminary hearing only, not a trial; what you say here must be within the realm of discovery information to determine if this should even go to trial. However, the rules are more relaxed in this sort of hearing, so I am willing to be a bit tolerant."

"We understand, your Honor, and we promise we will be brief."

The judge looks over at Brandon. "Do you have any objections, Mr. Lewis?"

Brandon smiles and waves his hand. "No, your Honor, let them talk." Clark looks over at Brandon incredulously. He is shocked by Brandon's calmness, and wonders why he is not raising any objections. It is as if he's completely uninterested in the whole proceeding. His detached attitude is unnerving for Clark, to say the least. The insurance's legal staff smile with a smug, confident indifference as the lead attorney stands up to speak.

"Your Honor, the defendant's wife, Mrs. Ann Bailey, has now remained on life support systems for over four months. Alliance Insurance has continuously and generously paid out all the past and current bills, not only for Mrs. Bailey, but her son Hugh Bailey as well." At the mention of Hugh's name Brandon looks up, and with a small tight smile, begins writing on his notepad.

The attorney continues. "It is our contention that we have proven beyond a reasonable doubt that medically, morally, and financially, continuing treatment for Mrs. Bailey is not going to improve her current medical condition. In fact, your Honor, we have submitted medical records that show Mrs. Bailey's current status is deteriorating on a daily basis."

The attorney asks to approach the bench, then hands a small folder of medical records that are underlined on the most important examples of the doctors' comments.

"We understand the sadness and distress this accident has brought upon the Bailey family; however, neither our client nor the medical experts can see any projected improvement in the case of Mrs. Bailey and her son." Brandon continues to write, trying to get every word that's spoken, especially when Hugh's name comes up. The Alliance attorney continues. "Our financial contributions have fulfilled the contractual agreement that the health insurance provides. To keep Mrs. Bailey attached to a mechanical system that supports only her biological functions makes no sense, for it is only prolonging the inevitable, which morally conflicts with a person's right to die. We hereby request that we be allowed to go to trial with the existing evidence shown here today with the intent that the trial will serve to determine if Alliance has fulfilled their responsibilities according to the terms of the plaintiff's policy."

The attorney takes his seat.

The judge is quiet for a few moments as he reviews the medical charts and comments attached to each page. Finally, he looks up at Brandon and asks; "Do you have anything to say on behalf of your client?"

Brandon puts his papers back in his briefcase and stands up. "Your Honor, it is my understanding that the defense has outlined a medically qualified file that shows to their satisfaction that my client's wife, Mrs. Ann Bailey, and her son, Hugh Bailey, are in a comatose state, and they assert there is no chance of recovery. Is that right?" The judge looks over at Alliance; the lead counsel quickly stands up. "Yes, your Honor; that is exactly our stand on this matter."

The judge acknowledges their claim. Brandon then steps out from behind the desk and simply states. "Then I have no further questions or objections at this time, your Honor."

Clark's head jerks up. "No! What?! What are you doing?!"

The judge bangs his gavel. "Silence! There will be no disruptions here!"

Clark, now standing, looks at Brandon. "What's going on? Why did you betray me?"

Brandon walks back to his desk, and putting his arm across Clark's shoulder, he sits down and whispers, "Trust me. Remember what we discussed; have a little patience."

Clark fights for control. All his emotions—all his anger and frustration—are exploding within him like a super volcano; his guts feel as if a shearing knife is twisting inside of him. Trust! Clark is flabbergasted; how can he trust him when he just signed his wife's death warrant?

Fighting to regain his focus, Clark closes his eyes and lets his mind drift. Let spirit take all the anger, all the emotions, fear, and mistrust, and carry them away. Control begins to grow within his thoughts, and then his emotions; calmness fills him as he stops thinking of what is supposedly going on. For once, he has to have faith! Total blind faith! He has to trust this man he barely knows, but even more importantly, he has to trust himself. He has chosen Brandon and given him his trust to make these legal decisions; now he has to trust his own choice and to trust God.

The judge takes out some papers and prepares to sign his name.

"This is an order and acknowledgement that due to the medical severity of the comatose patient it is this court's decision to allow this case to go to trial." The Alliance lawyers all shake hands and proceed to close their briefcases. Brandon quickly stands up and addresses the court: "Your Honor, before you sign that order, can I have a moment of the court's time?"

"What is it, Mr. Lewis?"

"Your Honor, I have here a written demand that requests that Alliance Insurance immediately enact and compel the hospital to not only maintain the current life support system for Mrs. Bailey, but to comply with and extend all provisions of the contractual policy that Mr. and Mrs. Bailey purchased in good standing to their son Hugh Bailey."

Before Brandon could say another word, the Alliance attorneys all stand up.

"We object! The court has made its decision! Indeed, the fact is that his request is in absolute contradiction to not only our evidence, but the court's decision that you're about to sign!"

The Judge looks over at Brandon. "Mr. Lewis, I stated in the beginning of this hearing that this was an informal hearing and the normal rules of trial don't apply, but even with that said, I understand we're dealing with two lives at stake here. So what is it that compels you to make such an extraordinary request?"

Brandon pulls from his briefcase a thick copy of Clark's health policy.

"Your Honor, I am only clarifying the policy in question. May I approach the bench?" Brandon steps forward and presents a copy of the policy to the judge. The Alliance attorney steps up to the bench with Brandon.

Brandon continues. "Before I begin on contract policies, I would like to add a little background information on what is called 'Persistent Vegetative State,' also known as PVS."

The judge looks over at the Alliance legal and then back to Brandon; before he can respond, the Alliance head attorney barks out in frustration. "Your Honor, the case has been decided upon. The defendant had the opportunity for their say and their chance to present their evidence, but declined."

The judge is quiet for a moment then carefully choosing his words he asks. "Why did you wait until this moment to bring this information forward?"

"I needed to have the opposition completely clarify their beliefs and statement of facts before my information would become pertinent and vital to this process. I know it's not normal legal procedure, but then again, this is an informal hearing, and as you said, the fact remains that two lives are at stake."

The judge looks somewhat confused, but after a moment's pause, he nods and says, "Proceed, but make sure it's pertinent to this exact situation." Brandon exchanges glances with Clark and then turning back to face the judge, he begins.

"Persistent Vegetative State, also known as PVS, is a condition of a patient with severe head damage whose condition has progressed to a state of wakefulness without detectable reactions. There's strong controversy in both the medical and legal fields as to whether this condition is irreversible.

"This syndrome was first described in 1940 by Ernst Kretschmer and later expounded in more detail in 1972 by New York Hospital-Cornell Medical Center Neurologist Fred Plum, who again labeled this illness as 'persistent vegetative state.' At the time, it seemed as if only 'vegetative' brain functions like breathing, waking, and blinking were working among their patients. The higher functions commonly associated with consciousness seemed to be lost. The brain-damaged areas that were especially noteworthy were the thin outer rind of the skull called the cortex and the thalamus, a pair of walnut-size lumps in the brain's central core. Along with the neural fibers that connect these regions, these areas of injury are also known as cortical death. Patients in a persistent vegetative state are usually considered to be unconscious, unaware and unresponsive to external stimuli, except possibly pain stimuli. The consensus was that semiconscious brains do not heal—especially not months or years after an injury—so research and aggressive treatment were deemed futile.

"However, an associate of Dr. Plum, Nicholas Schiff, discovered something much different. During his first month as a resident at New York Hospital in 1993, he was examining a patient: a woman who had suffered a stroke more than six months earlier. When Schiff examined her in 1993, he found no sign of consciousness, as expected. Three years later, on a visit to a local rehabilitation, he ran into this former patient again. Not only was she awake, but she spoke to him. He remembered saying, 'I was shocked; I remember the visceral feeling of having seen somebody come back from the dead. It seemed truly surreal.'

"Unlike comas, in which the patient's eyes remain closed, patients in a vegetative state often open their eyes. The PVS patient experiences behaviors that can be construed as arising from partial consciousness, such as grinding their teeth, opening their eyes, swallowing, smiling, shedding tears, grunting, moaning or even screaming, all without apparent external stimulus. Many patients emerge from a vegetative state within a few weeks, but those who do not recover within six months are said to be in a Persistent Vegetative State.

"The chance of recovery depends on the extent of injury to the brain and the patient's age; younger patients have a better chance of recovery than older patients do. Generally, adults have a fifty percent chance and children a sixty percent chance of recovering consciousness from PVS within the first six months. After a year, the chances that a PVS patient will regain consciousness are low, and most patients who do recover consciousness experience significant disabilities. The longer a patient is in a PVS the more severe the resulting disabilities will be.

"Some authorities hold that PVS is in fact irreversible and that any reportedly 'recovered' patients were not suffering from true PVS. This conclusion is in dispute, however, as there have been cases where patients have awakened from the PVS and led perfectly normal lives."

Brandon continues, taking a moment to glance at the Alliance legal staff and back to the impassive judge. "Now, your Honor, I want the court to know that unlike the comatose state, PVS is not recognized as an illness in any known legal system. This legal gray area has led to several court cases involving people in PVS. The pros and cons of this type of illness are as follows.

"One group feels the patient should be allowed to die, and then there are those who are equally determined that if recovery is possible, care should continue.

"Well-known cases include Paul Brophy, Sunny Von Bulow, and Tony Bland, whose case created a precedent in the UK, and of course, the highly publicized case of Terri Schiavo in the United States. The Schiavo case involved disputes over a diagnosis of PVS given by several court-appointed doctors; the husband prevailed in that case, and care was discontinued. Mrs. Schiavo died shortly after. It is my client's stand that all patients have the right to professional and careful medical treatment throughout life and at its end. He legally should have the right to decide for his wife the nature and scope of her medical treatment. The doctor must respect the right of self-determination of the mentally competent spouse or next of kin. The doctors must not carry out any medical procedure against the patient or against the wishes of the person legally empowered to make decisions for said patient. Medical or nursing staffs violating this right of the patient or persons responsible such as Mr. Bailey for his wife Ann are acting unlawfully, and must be held expressly liable to prosecution for physical injury. This also applies to measures to prolong or save a life. The withholding or discontinuation of medical care which leads directly to the death of the patient, even when there is every prospect of improvement from the medical point of view, is unlawful. As a precautionary measure, to cover the possibility that a patient may not remain mentally competent, citizens are entitled to make a living will. A living will is valid and is regarded as the expressed wish of the patient. If the particular medical measures desired or rejected are set out in concrete terms, then compliance with the living will by all those involved in the patient's management is obligatory unless there are concrete signs that the person concerned no longer wishes it to apply."

Brandon stops speaking for a moment as he rummages through his briefcase, and then pulling some papers from his bag, he separates two copies of each file, giving the judge a copy and the Alliance lawyers a copy. "Gentlemen, before you are two forms; one is the living will of Ann Bailey giving all decision power to her husband, and the second is a very current doctor's report, in fact current as of this morning. The medical report says that Ann Bailey has indeed opened her eyes."

Seeing the trap, the Alliance legal staff rush to speak at the same time in a state of panic.

"Your Honor! We have nothing in our file to verify this. In fact, this is the first we've heard of this new condition."

Brandon smiles. "Boys, it just happened this morning. I got a call from the hospital and sent a runner to pick up the report." Brandon then turns to the judge. "Your Honor, we must make our decisions concerning Ann Bailey from the viewpoint that she is suffering from PVS, not from an un-induced coma, which is the diagnosis that the opposition's case is solely based on. In addition, we now have a legal statute that we must address, which is that our client has not been allowed the required six months for basic recovery, Alliance turned their bulldogs loose on her, ignoring the PVS requirement.

"Moreover, we have to consider the living will, which engenders a completely different set of legal issues that must address. In addition, I bring to your attention a clause in the actual policy Alliance wrote for the Baileys. Note page forty, section four, third paragraph."

The judge rifles through the policy until reaching page forty, and the prosecution quickly does the same.

The judge scans the paragraph and then looks up. "Gentlemen, I will read the clause pointed out by Mr. Lewis for all to hear."

The silence was surreal; the attorneys for Alliance seemed like statues in their seats.

The Judge intones in his deep voice:

> *If the treating doctor or a court of law determines that the patient may have a permanent disability, even if the extent of the disability is unknown, the insurance administrator must begin extended payments of a permanent disability indemnity within forty-eight hours after termination of normal benefits. These payments must continue until a reasonable estimate of the disability has been paid.*

This disability has two sections of payments.

One: If the insured has missed continuous days of work since the disability occurred, then the rate of payment is calculated as total disability and all medical bills plus a percentage of the insured's wages must be paid. (A maximum of two-thirds of the weekly wages is to be disbursed.)

Two: If the insured is determined to be in a terminal medical condition then the calculated amount of how much the insured would have earned until age sixty-five is to be paid to insured's designated beneficiary. All medical bills past, present, and future, which may be undetermined, are to be paid until said natural termination occurs.

Brandon smiles and turns to walk back to his table. The Insurance attorneys all start talking at once; finally, in desperation the lead attorney calls out, "Your Honor, since we have already concluded the first phase of termination of this case, we feel we are not responsible for any further obligatory payments since the decision to go to trial is already decided."

After listening in total awe to Brandon's defense, Clark feels a surge of hate spiking through him; he wants to jump and tear the Alliance attorney's head off, but just as fast as the anger appears, he lets it go, saying nothing. He just watches as the lead legal representative tries to wiggle out of the trap Brandon has so elegantly laid out. Not only did Brandon create the trap, but he had allowed the other side to give him the tools to make it escape-proof. The insurance company's legal team themselves had argued that Mrs. Bailey's condition was terminal and there was no hope of recovery. In addition, they pulled Hugh's name into the court, which allowed Brandon to include him under the umbrella of protection the section called for.

Brandon whispers to Clark, "Alliance may re-enter a case against Hugh, but now this case is the precedent that sets the standard for the Clark family in any future medical cases against you by Alliance or anyone else."

The judge is quiet for a few moments. Without looking up, he begins to state his views and findings. "Based on what has been presented to the court—however in an untimely manner—" here he does look up for a moment and raises an eyebrow at Brandon for a second before turning back to the document, "it is the court's decision that the findings in the first point of action taken earlier today are invalid. Alliance by its own contract and by their own legal opinions have fully established their obligation and responsibility to provide payments for the continued medical treatment of Mrs. Ann Bailey.

"It is further ordered by this court that Alliance Insurance begin immediate disability payments to Mr. Bailey, which are to be retroactive, starting from the date of the accident and continuing to the present. Each weekly disability payment will be in the amount of two-thirds of Mrs. Bailey's weekly earnings prior to the accident.

"It is also ordered by this court that if Mrs. Bailey should die while under the medical care provided, then a lump sum payment is to be paid to Mr. Clark Bailey. This lump sum will be calculated based on the same wages Mrs. Bailey would have earned had she lived and continued working from the time of her accident until the age of sixty-five.

"This court is adjourned."

Brandon puts his hand on Clark's shoulder and says quietly, "Do you trust me now?"

Clark smiles sheepishly. "You could have told me what you were plotting. I nearly went crazy for a while there."

Brandon laughs. "Well, my friend, if I had told you, then the reaction I wanted the opposition to see would not have been there, now would it?"

Clark stands up, muttering something under his breath. Looking over at the insurance attorneys, he smiles. "Actually, I learned a great lesson here today. For the first time in my life, I faced a grave challenge, and I chose how I wanted to feel. When hatred and fear started to overtake me, I fought it off. Instead, I wanted to feel calm and detached, and I did. I saw the opposition fall apart—not in a physical sense, obviously, but it seemed that fear and anger along with frustration were crawling all over them. They no longer even seemed a threat; in fact, I almost felt sorry for them!"

Brandon pats Clark on the back. "No need to feel sympathy for them, my friend; they're only suffering the effects of their own choices, and the consequences are fair and fitting. I hope they, too, will have learned a few lessons today."

Brandon walks behind Clark over to the opposition table.

Shaking hands with the four stunned attorneys, he casually makes a comment. "Fellas, if you or Alliance think that in the future you want to contest what happened today, I feel it's only fair to warn you that I will then file suit for denial of liability on the part of Alliance; as you know, that type of case will run into the millions. Please pass that on to your bosses."

And with that, Brandon and Clark leave the courthouse. Both have won a great battle today.

Now it is time to turn their attention to deeper matters—matters that aren't as easily manipulated as the laws of man.

CHAPTER 32 ~ THE DEPTH OF COMMAND

Morning comes quickly.

I blink as darts of sunlight move through the cabin; Loren still sleeps. Blue satin sheets wrapped around her body make me catch my breath. Last night surpassed all I had known about love, feelings, passion, and stimulated senses. I'm left stranded in corridors of the unknown. Whatever I thought I knew about love has never come close to the warmth and trust Loren gave me last night. Our bodies, minds, and Souls blended as one, carrying both of us to feelings I never dreamed existed.

Quietly slipping into me clothes, I step onto Soultraveler's deck.

I marvel at this amazing ship that is sparkling from the highest mast to the brass unicorns on each side of the guest quarters. Salty air rushes to my senses; a few gulls squawk in the distance. Not a cloud in the sky, and my view of the ocean is spectacular. Empty wharves stand silent excepting for a few boys setting things up for their employers. Leaning over the side railing, I'm surprised at how high I am on the deck—it makes me feel small.

As I'm looking over the ship from bow to stern, I hear a light thumping sound. Steady rhythms like muffled drums are getting louder. Are my ears playing tricks on me? The rhythmic beat continues to get closer.

Standing on top of the railing I hold onto ropes suspended from above to get a better look. The noise drifts from the north side of the village. The sound increases.

Hearing something behind me, I jump and turn, at the same time bumping into Davy, who is also looking toward the beating sound.

"Morning, Davy—you hear it, too?"

"Aye; I was wondering what it is."

"I guess we are about to find out. Do you have everything ready to take with you today?"

"I was born ready for this adventure. My wildest dreams could never come close to what you're allowing me to be a part of!"

"It is my pleasure to have you come along. You'll earn your way. As you say, no one before has explored this ocean. What we find out there might make our hearts grow, but it may also test us to the very center of our Soul."

Davy climbs up on the railings next to me and says, "Aye, that's what draws me to you. You somehow bring out the best of me. I'm just grateful to be given this opportunity to sail with you."

The pounding is so loud now that it is the only sound we can hear. It begins taking on a familiar beat, blending more in unison with each moment. As the sun rises from behind us, we see six men marching in step in two rows of three coming from the village toward the wharf. Marching as one, the six approach Soultraveler. The first row of three slows down and shifts to their left, and as the second row passes, all six fall in line creating one row facing Soultraveler.

The Crystal Guards Albrecht hired stand in their magnificence before us.

The sight of the Crystal Guards is captivating. All six wear silver-tipped gray boots and brilliantly polished silver blue helmets that partially hide their faces except for their blazing eyes. Their dark blue uniforms are bisected by a huge sword sheath strapped to their backs. Two warriors have quivers of arrows mounted on their backs next to the sword sheath and hold a bow almost as tall as the man himself. One warrior carries what looks like a round mandolin strapped to his shoulder. Sunlight glistens off their helmets, but their shields are the most eye-catching: each man's left hand grasps a glorious shield, glistening from the polished brass frame encircling it and punctuated by the multifaceted crystal filling its center. Every time a shield moves, it catches the sunlight and shimmers; the intensifying morning rays make their shields grow brighter by every moment. Never have I seen anything as striking as these men standing motionless in front of me like stone statues.

Albrecht emerges on the lower ramp of Soultraveler. Walking up to each Crystal Guard, he acknowledges them. I notice how tall and muscular the guards are compared to Albrecht.

Albrecht looks up at me and shouts out, "Good morning! Can you slide out the upper deck ramp for us to board?"

I look over at Davy, and our eyes meet; both of us are new to this ship's operation, and are unsure what to do. Fortunately, we catch sight of the ramp slot at the same time, and we place the long wooden ramp on the ramp slot and push it outward toward the wharf. As it hits the dock shore, we lock it in two round clamps. I open the gate above the ramp to Soultraveler's deck. Albrecht motions the six men, and then follows them. Davy and I flank each side of the ramp gate as the soldiers file by, one by one. No doubt about it, they are an impressive sight, not only for me and Davy, but also for the villagers gathering on the dock. Once on board, Albrecht introduces us. Davy's somewhat shy, but his curiosity quickly overcomes his reserve. I learn each warrior's name and shake his hand; Davy follows my example. Dandi and Kaylu appear from the stairway above us. Walking across the deck from the stern, their eyes widen.

Morning light hits the shields causing each to sparkle with purple, blue, pink, crimson, yellow, and green. Colors interlace as a blazing white light pierces each color for a brief second making the shields glitter and swim. As Dandi appears from the upper deck, all six men turn at the same time. Never have they seen a man such as this. Indeed, the warriors look small and feeble next to the giant. Their splendid shields, helmets, and uniforms blaze, but Dandi dwarfs their magnificence by his sheer size. He walks from man to man, examining their clothing and shields.

Albrecht takes me to the side and explains who they are and why they are accompanying us. He makes it clear the six warriors are under my command; whatever I need, they are to obey, even if their very lives are in danger. I feel a little overwhelmed, but then suddenly I am distracted by other men who start boarding; these men are the crew reporting for duty.

Activity begins almost immediately. These men know what to do, and take no time in getting the ship ready for sail; riggings are lifted, water barrels and more food are being taken in, along with more supplies than I ever thought necessary or even possible. Each man has his job. Crew captains are responsible for their areas of the ship and bark out commands to their own crews. Within a remarkably short time, Albrecht announces all is ready.

Huge sails lift halfway up the mast, the top of their white cloth reflecting dawn's pinkish light. Morleck appears from his cabin wearing a light gray robe; he climbs the stairs to the helm, and Albrecht follows him.

For some time, the two sit and discuss. The familiarity in their gestures and quick easy laughs suggest they know each other quite well. I'm guessing they are talking about the ship, weather, and responsibilities. As the village awakens, Albrecht stands and steps over to my side.

Placing his hands on my shoulders, Albrecht smiles and says, "It's time for me to leave."

I freeze for a minute.

"Wait! You're going with us...aren't you?"

Albrecht tightens his grip on my shoulders and shakes his head. "I can't. I have to stay here and look after our family's business. You have the most capable crew money can buy, plus six of the most able warriors in the world. You have supplies to last you half a season, plus the most powerful and swiftest ship ever built, and if I may say, the most beautiful, too.

"Take care of my nieces, and take heed of Morleck's wisdom; watch and learn from the crew, but understand one important thing: you are the Captain. This is your ship and your journey; learn the ways of the sea wisely, and show the proper attitude in commanding such a special ship. Follow your instincts, but also, use the gifts given to you, for what lies out there will challenge you to the very depths of your Soul! Loren will help, and so will Karla, as will your three friends. When you come to the middle of this experience, Hugh, you will at some point discover that you—and you alone—travel this path. You have to make the choices."

I'm listening somberly, but at the same time I find it difficult not to scream out, "But I'm just a little boy!" I shake off the urge to get off the ship and start running. For a moment, I'm as motionless as I am speechless.

How can I be the Captain of such a ship?

Can I direct and give orders to men that have vast more experience? I think of Jotan, who although appearing as a little boy, was the most powerful being I ever encountered. Within all his power and wisdom, there was still a childlike attitude that dominated all other aspects of his greatness. As I'm thinking of the child god, small realizations pop up like bubbles into my mind. The bubbles start breaking, and then I know!

This is the only way! I have got to control my own journey.

Reaching out, I embrace Albrecht and thank him for his many gifts. I vow to return both Loren and Karla safely. Albrecht walks down the ramp to shore and two crewmen pull the ramp onto the deck. I hear someone shout, "Blow the sails!"

Two middle sails fly to the top of the mast. Wind catches, and they balloon like giant clouds.

The rear sail billows out along with the bow sail. Ropes are pulled in; mooring lines are released from the dock. Other loading ramps are pulled in. Soultraveler begins to creak and groan as it slowly pulls away. I look at the helm. One of the crewmen is guiding Soultraveler into the open harbor. From the upper bow a musical sound floats across the ship. One of the crew is playing an instrument much like bagpipes. The music is rousing and encouraging as the great ship slowly moves away from the village. Dandi and Kaylu stand at the railing, watching the wharf growing smaller as we slowly edge further away beyond the harbor and into the bay off to open sea. The skill of the men directing the ship is amazing; my confidence soars and stronger feelings of excitement flow through me. The next phase of my journey is at hand; and now, I'm the Captain of me own ship!

I walk to my cabin to waken Loren, but she's already up and dressed. Wearing a white long-sleeved blouse and gray pants stuffed into long black boots, her black hair falls over her shoulders. Her natural curls frame the sides of her face, and she's looking every bit the sailor's dream. She takes my hand and we walk onto the cabin balcony and move over to the edge of the railing. We stand side by side silently as we watch the village grow smaller, and the great ship moving deeper into the bay toward open seas.

Breaking away from the view, Loren turns to me and then asks, "Well, Captain, how about some breakfast?"

With so much activity going on, I hadn't thought about food, but when she suggests breakfast I realize I'm famished. Taking her hand I walk out to the ship's open deck. A new kind of excitement is flowing through me; it reminds me of how I used to feel on Christmas morning, but this sensation is even more powerful. I look up at the great masts and huge sails blowing in the wind; I see crewmen running everywhere as they adjust the sails and tie ropes to riggings. Gulls squawk and my excitement grows as smells of the sea air fill up my senses, slow, melodious bagpipe music floats around us. I watch Dandi and Kaylu exploring the ship like two kids discovering a new toy.

All of this is mine to command. I'm the Captain! I'm the one everyone looks to for direction; the man in charge! Ah, this is going to be great!

Turning to Loren, I ask, "Which way is it to the kitchen?"

She looks up at me and grins. "The 'kitchen'! Hugh, on a ship, it's called the 'galley.'" She's giggling as she takes my hand and leads the way. I feel myself blushing a bit as she says, "You have a lot to learn, Captain."

After breakfast, I feel more alive than ever. Leaving the galley, Loren and I step out toward the upper deck at the bow. The midmorning sun creates a backdrop soft orange light; streaks of blue and yellow move across the horizon. White and gray sea birds fly overhead, looking for food scraps from leftovers. Climbing further onto Soultraveler's upper deck, Loren points out all the different parts of the ship and explains their functions; every facet of the ship is a marvel. Walking to the bow, we stand behind the silver throne overlooking the main deck. The great brass beam jutting out from the bow divides the waters with every thrust and forward motion of the ship; I feel as if I am in a dream. The boy's heart within me fully appreciates this journey I am starting.

I am Captain of this great vessel and I have the most noble—almost mystical—warriors under my command; even more amazing, I have Loren at me side. What more could a kid ask for?

We hear a noise behind us...turning, we find ourselves facing an odd sight.

Morleck ambles up the small stairs leading from the main deck to where we are standing. He carries several large scrolls tucked under his arm, and wears a gray robe and a dark hat that looks like some kind of version of a French artist's beret.

Reaching the bow deck, he calmly sits down on the throne, dropping most of the scrolls. He then proceeds to pull out a pouch from under his robe.

I step from behind the throne. "Good morning, Morleck!"

He looks up, smiles and nods. He then begins to unroll the scrolls and charts in front of him. Loren walks up and introduces herself. "Good morning, sir; my name is Loren. I don't believe we have ever met."

Morleck peers up at the pretty girl, and a twinkle in his eye and a wide smile appear on his face. "Why, good morning! I believe you are right, we haven't met."

Putting my arm around Loren's shoulders I say, "This is Loren; she's with me."

Morleck looks at me oddly for a few seconds, then chuckles and replies, "My name is Morleck; I'm here to help Hugh navigate this great ship, and hopefully assist in finding his mother."

Loren takes Morleck's proffered hand. "I am so glad you are here. My uncle has told me wonderful things about you."

"Don't believe everything you hear, my dear." Morleck grins. "Sometimes people create a more colorful picture than what is actually true. Come, sit here on the bench; let's get to know each other a little better."

I immediately take a seat to the right of Morleck, and motion Loren to sit on the edge of the bench to my right. She is so close to the bench's end that she must wiggle very close to me, as if she can't get close enough.

Morleck can't stifle a laugh before he shakes his head and leans over me to ask her, "I understand this great ship belongs to two young women; are you one of them?"

"Yes, our father left it to us. He died in the Dark Cave in the mountain leading to the Land of Light."

"I see," whispers Morleck.

Loren continues, leaning over me to speak with Morleck more clearly. "Yes, Karla and I were traveling with Father, and soon after he died, Hugh and his friends helped us escape from the Dark Cave. We are happy to help Hugh on his journey. He is now the Captain, and must learn all about running a crew and commanding a ship."

Morleck nods. "Yes, yes, I am sure he will, dear, for if not, then I suppose failure will be his new companion instead of this ship."

I look anxiously to my left at Morleck, wondering why he would say such a thing. Looking forward over the bow to the open waters, Morleck calmly says, "The ocean is a good teacher. To some, it is the great master; to others, it is a hungry wolf waiting for the ignorant to wander into its jaws. There is much to learn from the sea. In fact, there is very much one can learn about himself from these wide waters."

I interrupt, "What do I need to learn from the sea in order to survive the journey we're taking?"

Morleck continues to stare across the ocean as he speaks. "As a person begins to understand the nature of the sea, he need also begin to understand his own nature. For how can you possibly understand or relate to the great mysteries of the ocean if you do not even know the mysteries of whom, or what, you really are? Most men never learn their true power, only because they never learn the mechanical parts that make up their lower nature. Not knowing these things can trap a man in his lower nature, or within what is also known as the lower worlds."

I think for a moment and then continue. "I've learned a great many things about the power that exists within...and its connection with the Creator's love. What greater wisdom could a man need?"

Sitting back against the throne, Morleck remains silent for a moment; mesmerized by the ocean. He continues staring across the open waters as he speaks. "The wisdom you speak of is important, and ultimately it will serve you well, but you must also learn the mechanics of your body and the mind, for they are tools that help navigate not only your life, but help in understanding the nature of other men and where they have reached in their life's journey. Knowing the limitations of others and how they react is a yardstick to measure your own growth in this world. Studying another man's reactions to things that happen tells much about where this person's awareness is, and how much trust and responsibility he can handle; that is the making of a true Captain. Being the captain of this great ship does not mean you are solely in charge of everything that happens. What it really means is that you must learn to evaluate and decide what your crew is capable of. If you know your crew and know what each man can handle, then you will know what your ship can and cannot respond to. Knowing how each man's mind functions is invaluable to a leader."

I am a bit embarrassed and annoyed by his comments. "But how can I know how other men are thinking and feeling?"

Morleck pauses and then smiles. "All human minds work basically the same; they all have great potential. Each individual must determine for himself what he can and what he cannot endure. The closer you get to understanding your own true self, the more you will understand others."

Loren and I listen carefully to the old man's wise words. His manner of speaking, demeanor, and precise articulation are almost spellbinding.

I ask, "What's the way that a man can determine who and what he really is, or what he's actually capable of?"

Morleck is quiet for a brief second, and then he relates a story.

"I remember once hearing a story about a young boy who would often go fishing with his grandfather. One day, the boy asks his grandpa, 'What makes some men good and others evil?' The grandpa looks down at his young grandson, and he replies gently, 'A long time ago, when I was a young man, I discovered there are two beasts living inside each of us. To me, the beasts are wolves.'"

Morleck slowly turns his gaze from the ocean to look intently at both of us.

"The grandfather said, 'One of the wolves is always angry, always hungry, always searching for food. This Dark Wolf is lonely and full of fear and hate. It never stops howling, for it never has enough. There is another wolf that also lives inside of us. It is a Noble wolf, who is brave, patient, and a great hunter. Due to its nobility and love, it shares its bounty with others. The Noble Wolf has great power and uses its power to hold back the ravenous Dark Wolf. I found that, for me, I had to decide which wolf I would set free.' And then the boy asked, 'How did you decide which wolf to set free, grandpa?' The grandfather reeled in his fishing line and set his pole down. Then walking over to his grandson, he places his hand on the little boy's shoulder, and at the same time he leans over, looks deeply into the young boys face, and says, 'I decided to feed only one of the wolves, and the one I fed was the one I became.'"

Loren and I are quiet for a few moments. We both are thinking about the story of the two wolves. The story seems somehow familiar to me; I know I heard it before—maybe I heard it back in Bristol?

Finally, Loren asks, "How and what did the grandfather feed the wolf that he chose to become?"

Morleck turns to gaze across the ocean again, and then says softly, "Most men feed the Dark Wolf; they feed him with greed, desire, temporary pleasures, sadness, pride, material possessions, fear, and anger. The more they feed the Dark Wolf, the more it wants. So these men live a lifetime serving the hunger and passions of the Dark Wolf, which like our own human desires, are never satisfied.

"Then there are a few men like the grandfather, who feed the Noble Wolf. The Noble Wolf is fed with freedom, discipline, kindness, courage, joy, patience, and a love for others and himself. His happiness is in giving and loving, and eventually, the Noble Wolf shares these qualities with others. When the sharing begins, man gains wisdom and becomes noble. At just the right time, just when Soul is ready, man steps out of his wolf skin and meets his Creator as a true son and co-worker."

Morleck falls silent for a moment; he gazes upward at the sails slapping in the wind, pushing the great ship forward. The sounds of waves splash against Soultraveler's hull; Morleck listens for a moment more before continuing.

"The mind, my children, is not self-aware. It has no power of automation or initiative. Like the two wolves, it reacts both because of its basic nature and by the food that feeds it. The human mind's nature is like the wolves' nature; it is simply that of a machine, much like this great ship is merely a machine. The mind, of course, is much more highly refined and more sensitive, and extremely powerful when motivated by the true self, or what is commonly known as Soul. When seen as a machine, the mind can be made to do what it was intended to do, and just like any other machine, it will never do anything different from what it was designed and trained to do. It is trained by what you feed it. The mind is automatic in all its actions; it reacts to your will. This is important to understand…probably the most important fact we can learn if we are to know how the lower nature or the Dark Wolf functions."

Morleck rolls up one of the scrolls on his lap; as he does he continues to speak.

"Most of us are taught from birth that the mind has the power of origination and initiative, but that is because most men do not know better. What happens is that people confuse the mind with spirit or the true self. You see, the mind works only when it is activated by Soul; learning and truly understanding this one truth can mean the difference between an eternal life of freedom or a laborious, never-ending journey of redundancy. Very few ever find or know the difference between the mind and Soul. Soul and its instrument—the mind—is something that must be clearly understood in order for you to know the spiritual psychology of not only ourselves, but also of humankind. The fundamental difference is that the mind by itself cannot will, cannot love, and cannot create original thought. It cannot remember, nor suffer nor enjoy, to do any or all of these things Soul must activate and participate.

"Every activity that exists in every universe in every reality is carried on by the essence of the Creator, which we know as spirit or Soul; this essence is intricately linked to the mind. The mind, being made from matter, is just like this ship, except infinitely more refined. It stands next to Soul in all of its fundamental qualities, except in the mind, they are in a limited form. Mind's supreme function is to serve and act as a tool for Soul, and to make all of its conscious and unconscious contacts within the physical and psychic worlds. Some compare the mind to fire, a powerful and useful tool for man. But if the fire gets out of control, then it destroys all in its path."

Morleck looks at me and Loren, making sure we understand, then continues. "Soul must learn to control the mind, because if not, then all the dark passions consume man's own personal universe. Mind is your servant, nothing more than a tool. But if the mind becomes the master, it may speedily bring about chaos and disaster. Mind does not reason, even though you are taught it does; in reality, the mind acts with an automatic precision exactly as it is stimulated to act. The mechanics of this stimulation are the key to the secret workings within itself.

"You will find that mind can and will carry on deductive processes, but it really has no power over the induction process. To simplify, the mind reacts to causes within its orbit of experience. The reactions are usually judgments based on pre-programmed feelings, facts or assumptions. The mind is never the creator of the cause itself: this is done by the God power given only to Soul. Soul creates the events that mind either rejects or accepts. These choices of rejection or acceptance made by the mind determine humankind's life's journey. Discriminate choices are processed through the induction processes of Soul, while un-discriminated choices are processed through the deductive powers of the mind. It is the rare man who uses the deductive and the inductive powers to the benefit of Soul.

"Most of humankind makes quick choices based on the superficial feelings of any given experience, thereby bypassing the discriminating process. This lack of inductive process by the mind is demonstrated daily in the worlds of mass manipulation through governments, media, friends, family, and religions. These all create guilt, desire, fear, pleasure, worship, false security, and violence. But they also create family, relationships, emotional love, and joy, rituals, and feelings of security.

"Give the masses certain premises—no matter how absurd they may be—and you will find large percentages acting upon such premises with automatic deduction. To a large extent, the masses do not use their powers of rational induction nearly enough. This is such an obvious fact one only has to observe a small subset of the actions of people the whole world over to confirm its truth. People everywhere act more like out of control machines than rational beings. Soul alone has light within it; spirit alone works independently and rationally.

"The main contributors to this mental manipulation begin their work from the moment a person is born in the physical universe. Each is taught to act according to the rules of their culture, their race, their sex or their parents. They obey rules and laws of a government and society that exists mostly to satisfy its Dark Wolf. It is the rare individual who thinks independently and actually acts on it; when he does, it is because Soul has to some extent become emancipated from the domineering control of the mind."

Morleck leans back on the throne and looks out over the ocean.

"This subject is important, Hugh, so we must spend a little more time on it. It is crucial you know the functions of the mind, for at some point, the mind will use its power to try to ensnare you even more deeply than it already has."

I lean forward looking intently at Morleck and ask, "'Even more deeply than it already has'?"

Morleck turns his gaze from the blue water, and then staring across the deck, he continues. "The mind, as I have said, is a highly refined and finely tuned machine, but without spirit or Soul to activate it, the mind is useless. The mind is a reactive entity; this reactive feature is not only deceptive but is mind's most powerful hold on humankind. You are aware that over time the mind has created the personality of what you call Hugh; this creation is a tool for the mind to use, but in its use, it manipulates the mandatory reciprocal actions of Soul."

Loren asks, "What is 'mandatory reciprocal action'?"

"Basically, mandatory reciprocal action means whatever you put your attention on will eventually be attracted for you to experience. Whatever Soul receives from life experiences, it is mandated that it must reciprocate or give back even more to all life. Due to its divine creation, Soul acts in accordance with natural physical and divine laws, which are imprinted into its Spiritual DNA. Soul in its purest form exists within these laws as if they are a part of it. Whatever Soul receives, it gives back. This reciprocal action is the same action instilled within the Creator itself. When Soul exists within the guidelines of unconditional love, it is a fact that the more it gives the more it receives. Living within this law of unconditional love, Soul becomes enlightened or spiritually evolved. If this law is not perverted, this reciprocal action allows the personality to become aware of its divine self.

"This is accomplished through four different levels or functions of the mind. You might call these 'inner modes of action,' or the 'four primary attributes,' or 'four divisions' of the mind. These are what you must become fully acquainted with.

"The first part of these divisions is called the brain. It is the part that has mechanical flesh, which receives and registers impressions through the senses of smell, taste, hearing, sight, and touch. The most powerful stimulant of these is taste. Mind tastes, relishes, and enjoys different types of stimuli or rejects what it doesn't like. Touch and taste are practically the same thing; all of your reactions to taste and touch are normally automatic.

"When the mind enjoys and accepts a certain taste or touch, it moves forward almost instantaneously to experience more; what it does not like, it avoids or rejects these reactions. This is where mind's greatest power lies, and this is why. Within every thought, event, action, conversation or experience in life, there are four primary automatic functions that appear to happen simultaneously and instantaneously. Mind receives and tastes; it feels. It sees form and beauty, or ugliness; it perceives. It then discriminates and decides; in other words, it chooses. It then executes orders and acts. It is either active, as the cause, or reactive, as the effect. These four functions seem to us to be instantaneous, but this is the illusion perpetrated on man. If you bundle these functions together as the mind does, then you have impulse reaction. But if we separate out each function, viewing it objectively, then we have what is known as discrimination.

"Soul knows only freedom, unconditional love, charity, joy, wisdom, and power. Divine power is the result of discrimination. Soul uses feelings to create emotions, which it uses to express and communicate through its physical body. This reactive function of the mind is necessary for man in his bid for survival. If you touch something hot, you react instantly; this is good and right. But when a higher, more complex action takes place, causing man to think, then this reactive function must be controlled. It is these impulsive mental feelings or actions of the mind that leads man to his troubles.

"Any one of the four previously mentioned functions can become disarranged, abnormal, or perverted. If this happens, they become destructive modes causing perversions of these normal faculties. This happens due to the constant negative impulses from the illusions the mind constantly creates. These illusions take the normal faculties described and turn them into habits and addictions, causing the release of the Dark Wolf from within. This happens when we react from habit instead of discrimination and common sense.

"As odd as it may seem, the Creator allows the mind to have basic impulses that can pervert and distort normal uses of the four functions, making them abnormal. They may become so perverted through misuse that they become destructive instead of constructive; this again is the Dark Wolf.

"Meditation, contemplation, and the Light and Sound can teach a person to watch his reactions with a sense of detachment, like the cat watching a mouse's every move. The Dark Wolf changes good to evil or positive to negative if allowed.

"I call these the destructive passions, but the main point is that we learn to understand them. I sometimes think of them as diseased conditions of the mind. By contrast, the Noble Wolf changes the negative to positive; this is done by attitude, which is determined by what we feed the Noble Wolf.

"For all their seeming darkness, these functions or perverted passions have a deep spiritual function, which in most cases is to force us to learn discrimination. Man needs only to put his attention on these four children of the mind in order to control them, thereby controlling his reactions. In other words, when you are stimulated by these functions, don't react without using Soul's induction power. This will allow you to make choices that are from Soul, thus avoiding the chaos of the mind. Even when these normal faculties are the least perverted, these destructive modes can take control of the mind. As long as Soul controls the mind, the four faculties perform their proper function and the Dark Wolf cannot manifest itself. Always keep in your thoughts that when the mind runs wild, out of control under the influence of the Dark Wolf and its passions, it almost always leads to destruction. Do not condemn the Creator's plan, but try to obey the normal functions of the mind. To tame or control these functions takes practice.

"Patience, discipline, discrimination, tolerance, and a non-judgmental attitude—these are your tools to use. This is only one of the ways how the Creator teaches us these higher qualities; life can be our best friend if we first learn to obey the natural laws that are created for Soul's growth and experience. All pain and all suffering, whether mental or physical, that men are ever called upon to endure, exists to drive us toward a more perfect relationship with the Creator. There is practically no limit to what the mind can do when properly awakened, trained, and vitalized by Soul; this, Hugh, is what your journey is about."

Morleck turns back to the ocean and becomes quiet for a few moments, then without looking back he says, "This is enough for today. There is much more to discover about the mind, but these discoveries will come through direct experience and from other teachers who will help you awaken and remember. If you cannot remember all I have said this morning, then remember only this: Your survival depends less on what you feel than on what you know.

"Whatever bears the quality or character of any of the destructive evil passions, or in any way hinders or delays Soul in its progress toward spiritual freedom, is the Dark Wolf. Whatever changes or raises the consciousness for growth is the Noble Wolf. The Noble Wolf lives in mankind's heart; the Dark Wolf always resides in the mind."

Morleck stands up, gathers his scrolls, and walks down the small stairway to his cabin. I am unsure of myself, and as I stand and walk behind the throne, I look out to the still rising morning sun and feel grateful that Loren's still by my side.

I turn to her and say quietly, "I had so many questions I wanted to ask."

Loren snuggles closer into my arms and says, "Perhaps that is one of the reactive traps of the mind, Hugh. The mind automatically seems to want to ask unending questions, like the howling of the Dark Wolf, but if we allow the mind to calm itself, perhaps all will be given at the right time and place."

For a brief moment I think about the Noble Wolf and the Dark Wolf; looking back at the sea, I nod and respond, "Perhaps you are right."

At that precise moment, I feel pangs of my father's love diving into my heart and I sense his hand gently touching my face; and then he was gone.

CHAPTER 33 ~
BRANDON'S DECISION

Clark's world changed in the last forty-eight hours.

Brandon's expertise in the courtroom a few days ago gave him a new perspective on what was happening to him and his family. No longer did he see the past events as something dark and evil imposed on his family. His studies and nightly contemplations have taught him how to open his mind to a deep new feeling of gratitude and hope. His relationship with Brandon has become more than just a lawyer and client; he also sees clearly a change in his own attitude toward the daily trials that come his way. His visits to the hospital are no longer filled with sorrow and guilt alone; now when he sits next to Annie, he looks into his inner vision, and he sends her power and love. The comfort of not having to worry about whether she was going to be disconnected from the life support or whether the hospital bill is going to be paid gives him the energy he needs to become more confident in trying to help his son's journey into the unknown.

Clark knows Hugh is his only hope in finding Annie and bringing them both safely back to this world. He sits next to his son as morning light streams in from the hospital window. Reaching out, he holds his boy's hand, and for the moment all he can see is the pallid frail body of a small boy who is somewhere trying to save his mother's physical life and possibly her Soul. He's so young to face such a challenge, and yet Clark realizes that this is Hugh's decision; he has chosen this life, this family, and this experience.

Holding his son's hand tighter, Clark closes his eyes, and then looking deeply into his inner vision, he sees Hugh's image. He sends him his love and strength; he pours all the strength and love he can summon into his small son's frail form. As he holds the image in his inner vision, he feels a rush of energy flow into his body and burst through his inner eye, vitalizing the image of his boy.

The image within becomes clearer, and Clark focuses his attention on the inner picture of his son, not wanting to let it fade. The image emerges from within a soft light moving in and out of his vision. Clark tightens his grip on his son's hand. Holding his emotions in check so as to not distort or destroy the image, it gets clearer, and he sees Hugh in a sitting position wearing strange clothes.

At first, Hugh is as Clark remembers him, but as the image enlarges and becomes clearer, the boy's features change. He's larger and his hair is longer and lighter. His skin is tanned and his face is more mature. He bears a strangely detached look of determination, and his crystal green eyes bear a look that only experience and age can produce.

Even though the image of Hugh is still young, Clark notices he is far older than the ten-year-old boy lying in the hospital bed. The image grows clearer and then widens. Clark makes out ropes and what looks like a ship's masts in the background. The sky in the distance is deep blue.

Clark keeps himself calm. This is his son, but he has changed so much! He watches as this older version of his son stands up and walks toward a railing to look out over a vast ocean. As Clark stares at the image, courage and power rush into him. The boy turns his head and smiles, looking directly at Clark…and the vision fades. As it fades, he sees the look of determination in his son's eyes and nobility in his face.

Clark opens his eyes and stares at the still child in front of him. Who was it he saw in his inner vision? Was it really Hugh? Could it possibly be his son? If it is, what has happened to him? He's so different from the little boy lying in front of him. No. the young man in the vision was his son—he's sure of it! But the Hugh from his inner vision exudes power, and has such a powerful look of determination about him; how can that be?

****

That evening, Brandon drives to Clark's house. He had received a message that Clark needed to see him as soon as possible. He wonders; what could be so urgent for him to almost demand that he come out tonight?

Melody answers the door. "Oh, hi, Mr. Lewis. My dad's expecting you. Come in, he's in the den."

Brandon walks into the den to find Clark reading The Path of the Masters, a book written by Dr. Julian Johnson back in the 1930s.

"Brandon! Glad you could make it. I have so much to discuss." Clark pats the seat of the chair next to him.

Brandon sits down on the leather recliner and sighs. "Well, tell me. What is it that's so urgent it couldn't wait until tomorrow?"

"I have so much to discuss with you, I don't even know where to start."

Intrigued, Brandon crosses his legs, leans forward, and says, "It's always helpful to just start at the beginning."

Clark pulls his chair closer to Brandon's.

"This morning, something happened to me—I can't fully comprehend it. I went to the hospital to see Annie and Hugh as usual, and while I was sitting next to Hugh, I tried one of the contemplative techniques I found in this book you gave me. I was holding Hugh's hand and thinking how brave he was to choose this experience he's going through, and when I closed my eyes, an image of Hugh appeared in my inner sight."

Brandon's eyes open a little wider and his interest is piqued as Clark proceeds to tell him of the vision. Clark pauses for a moment and then says very seriously, "I have been reading this book that you loaned me. In The Path of the Masters, the author talks about how when someone becomes spiritually developed, he can travel in other planes of existence, and their body can take on new forms.

I was thinking maybe my vision of Hugh shows that he is somehow growing up spiritually in another world. Listen to this passage, on pages 211 and 212." Clark begins:

> This world is the theater of intellect. At least this is one of its fields of operation. It is the play of the mind. In this field science has made many a conquest and will doubtless make many more. But there is a vast field far above and beyond the play of the mind, where the developed spirit alone may enter. It is into this higher region of the spirit where the Master goes, and it is there where his real achievements are made. Entering there by methods well known to him, he finds that this earth-world is nothing more than the mud-silt of Nature's vast and complicated structure. Above and beyond this world of shadow and pain lie innumerable worlds of intense light. They are real worlds, full of beauty, color, rhythm and joy. Escaping for the time being the limitations of the body, the Master travels in those higher worlds, in full consciousness, and then he returns to report what he has seen and heard and otherwise experienced. He knows, among other things, that death is only an appearance, an illusion. When a man leaves his physical body at the time of what we call death, he simply steps out into other and higher worlds. He takes with him a finer body, which he now uses unconsciously, and on that higher plane, he uses the finer one just as he uses the physical body here. Going about wherever he pleases, clothed in a god-like vesture of light, wisdom, power and beauty, the Master explores the higher regions, wholly unknown to the common earth man. This is but a glimpse of the real Master. To understand a real Master fully, one must oneself become a Master. Can the insect comprehend the man?

Clark leans forward and asks, "What do you think?"

Brandon thinks quietly for a moment; then taking the book from Clark, he opens it and begins searching through its pages.

Brandon stops searching and looks up at Clark. "I agree with you on one thing; I think Hugh's journey is much more advanced than what I'd previously thought. Having an older body tells me he's living through events and tests only an older, stronger man could hope to survive, but then again, I'm probably only seeing the tip of the iceberg. From what you said, you saw a person of nobility and determination that only maturity and growth in a higher region of the spirit could create. If this is true, then your son is living a lifetime of experiences most people could only dream about. If, indeed, he's trying to free your wife from her comatose state, then he may be battling forces we as humans barely understand; we're just the proverbial insect, as Dr. Johnson puts it! In other words, it's reasonable to believe he's growing and advancing in some way that to us is happening with incredible speed; what's happening to Hugh could be happening within a time frame that to our spiritually advanced Hugh may seem normal, but to us seems to be happening in leaps and bounds."

Clark asks, "So he's growing into an adult in that higher realm within the few months he's been in this coma?"

Brandon nods. "I think that right now, time doesn't have the same meaning for Hugh there as it does for the small boy lying in that hospital bed that we know as Hugh. Hugh is on a spiritual journey. What he experiences in just one day there could be a month or even a year to us. If this is so, then the past several months he's been in a PVS could mean that in this other realm, Hugh may have bypassed his childhood and entered young adulthood."

Clark's face betrays his fear and confusion. Brandon continues, "This is probably only one of many phases of the journey he's taking. He also could be going through experiences on an even higher sub-consciousness level that would facilitate his becoming a very highly evolved soul, not just in terms of mental or physical maturity on a normal human scale, but especially spiritual levels, too."

Clark shakes his head. "Unbelievable! Let me ask a stupid question. What happens if Hugh comes out of this PVS, but he still has this mental maturity and expanded awareness of God knows what? How is he going to live again in this world, stuck in a boy's body?"

Brandon stares ahead, focusing on nothing for a moment. Shaking his head, he replies, "I don't know, Clark. I honestly don't know. This is something beyond me; honestly, I've never thought or heard of anything like this happening to anyone I actually knew."

Brandon opens the book again and looks at it with admiration. "Dr. Julian Johnson wrote this back in the 1930s, and decades later, the book is still a classic. I remember reading something in The Path of the Masters about what we are talking about; it's a passage that may help us understand what type of person Hugh may be turning into. Let me read it to you."

Brandon thumbs through the book and then stops. "Here it is—let me read this from pages 434 and 435." He clears his throat and begins to read aloud:

If the Master wishes to leave this earth plane, he simply sits down and concentrates, and by his own will leaves the body, and goes up to whatever subtle world he may wish to visit. Arriving there, he visits with the inhabitants there, looks over the country, and then returns here when he chooses. The going and the coming are not difficult for him—no more than stepping from one room to another here. And he remembers his experiences while up in those higher worlds, although it is often very difficult for him to tell about them on account of our lack of sufficient language and mental imagery. Thus the Master goes and comes at his own will and keeps in touch with any and all of the higher worlds, just as he may wish to do. When his work here is finished, he simply steps out of his body and leaves it.

Brandon looks up from the book and smiles. "Hopefully, as Hugh travels through these new worlds, although he might find many things that will test his inner awareness and strength, he can return to his body as the Master can; we must hope that he has access to wise teachers who can help him on this journey!"

Clark interrupts Brandon from his reading. "Do you think Jesus, Mohammed or Buddha or other spiritual beings had trips like Hugh?"

Brandon shakes his head affirmatively. "I think it's highly likely, but then again, look at Rasputin or Milerapa. They sort of went crazy in trying to relate what happened to them." Brandon closes the book and studies Clark for a few moments; Clark tries to grasp what he has just heard.

"Clark, listen to me. The book says a lot of things; this doesn't mean that Hugh is going to be like anything described. There are many ways to imagine how Hugh may be when he returns, but we just don't know. How can we say what to expect when it's Hugh's journey? It is an experience that will come about by what he does and by what he's going through. How he accepts his experiences will determine his relationship with this world. I feel the advantage we have here is that Hugh started this journey as a child and can in some cases possibly overcome, or what you might say leap frog over, the mind and its many traps. His childlike attitude is his greatest power, and when it comes down to it, I feel he'll be all right."

Clark stares at Brandon for a moment and then says slowly, "We really don't know, do we? He could come back a raving idiot, a zealous fanatic, or some kind of Jesus or Buddha." Clark stands up and takes a few steps, then turns and looks at Brandon again. "I'm not going to think about his future prognosis. I can only hope he succeeds in doing what he set out to do. Whatever happens after that, we'll have to see."

Brandon stands up and paces around the room a bit before stopping in front of Clark. "Clark, do you have the courage to take this to the next level? Do you wish to go deeper into Hugh's journey and attempt to help him?"

Clark looks up at Brandon. "I don't know what you're getting at. I've been trying to help in any way I can, but it seems we can only go so far."

Brandon sits down again, and leans closer toward Clark. "Believe me, my friend, when I say we can go deeper. It seems Hugh is going to go wherever it is he has to in order to find his mother, but we're not as limited as you might think. The thing you must understand is this. If we attempt to go further with this, then we ourselves are going to have to begin the exploration of not only our own inner kingdoms, but to some extent, go deeper into the inner worlds themselves."

Brandon stares at Brandon. "What are you trying to say?"

"I'm saying it may be possible to develop the ability to travel into the inner worlds, but to do this we must put our resolve in front of all other things. Traveling in the inner worlds is one thing, finding Hugh is entirely something else; but I, for one, am willing to try if you're willing to help."

Clark was struck for a moment with the idea of traveling into the inner worlds. "If my son can offer himself as he has, then so can I. What is it we have to do?"

Brandon reaches for the book again at the same time replying, "You just did it. The very fact that we've decided to pursue this on a deeper level is the most important step we must take. There are certain spiritual principles we must not only learn but also actually use before we attempt this journey. It's highly possible we may make this journey and not even be aware of our success in this waking world; we are going to try to avoid that outcome."

After leaving Clark's house, Brandon thinks about the admittedly bizarre decision he had just committed to. Here he is, in his senior years, chasing after a boy in a coma who supposedly is having some kind of inner mystical journey; and then to make matters worse, he has never even met Hugh. What in the world is he thinking?

All his life, Brandon has pursued truth in some form or fashion, and now he has the opportunity to be exposed to a living person who's actually traveling in these so-called inner worlds. Yes, he has read about them and has experimented with various techniques in his younger years. He even experimented with certain drugs, but for what experiences he gained, none satisfied him. None could be proven true.

Now he is presented the opportunity to go far beyond all his studying and experience: even possibly touch the robe of God.

Does he have the courage and faith?

Does he have the stamina at his age to hold true to the discipline he knows will be needed? This could be his greatest challenge; it could also prove to be his last opportunity to know truth for himself.

Seeing this whole event from a higher viewpoint, Brandon knows in his heart that this is truly a godsend, for Hugh can act as his focal point of the journey. Without him, there would be no proof, no image, no direction that he could focus on to reach the goal. He feels in his heart that what's happening to Clark and his family is real, and for some reason, he is being granted the gift of becoming a part of their journey. In reality, this experience is what he has always searched for throughout most of his life.

An ordinary person might laugh or scoff at the idea that someone could travel to the afterlife or other worlds while still living, but Brandon isn't an ordinary person.

All his life and throughout all his travels, he has tried to live and breathe truth, and in doing so, he has witnessed many strange and wonderful things. All this and more shaped him into becoming a ready vessel prepared for just this sort of quest. Brandon is a planner; he studies facts, always sure of every move. He calculates the odds, but for the first time in his life he will have to start with nothing more than faith and trust, for these are the true attributes that transform a planner into a Seeker. He must trust that Hugh is actually traveling in the inner worlds, and he must have faith in spirit to guide and protect him as he steps into the unknown. Having read so much about people in the past who allegedly have taken these inner journeys in other dimensions, now it's time to prove it to himself: beyond all doubts and beyond all illusions. After all, didn't the past spiritual giants speak of these inner places? Jesus, Buddha, Kabir, Rumi, and so many others; even some Roman Catholic saints—such as Padre Pio and St. Francis of Assisi—either spoke outright of them or hinted at the possibility, so now it's his turn to take that final step and determine it for himself.

That night as Brandon prepares for bed, he anticipates something important awaiting him. He can barely fall sleep, as his mind keeps tossing out his faith, fostering doubt within him. Focusing on what he learned in the past and what he knows of the Baileys' experiences, he finally falls into a deep sleep.

As he sleeps, he dreams.

He's in darkness. It's obviously nighttime, and he's in a forest standing by a line of trees. A vast starry sky stretches out, reflecting images of a gigantic mountain silhouetted in the darkness. An orange, yellow, and blue variegated light burning just beyond the bushes in front of him catches his attention. Moving closer, he can see that the burst of colors come from a campfire. A young man is feeding some wood to the low flames. He watches as the boy or young man stares into the small fire. Figures lying to the right of the fire apparently are asleep. Moving closer, he stands behind a tree and watches. The young man looks around him, and then stares in Brandon's direction; it is silent for a moment, and then the boy puts his hand on his sword and bends into a fighting stance.

The boy calls out, "Who's there?"

Brandon feels strange, but keeps silent. Looking down, he sees that he's wearing a dark blue robe and holding a staff in his hand. For a moment, it's as if time itself froze. He feels a presence, not outside, but within him, and words form in his mind.

"You wish to be the Traveler! Well, behold—that is what you are."

The voice is strong, clear, and precise. "To speak with this boy, you must allow all your thoughts, all your feelings, and even more than this, all your fear to dissipate into the nothingness they come from."

Brandon thinks for what seems an eternity, and he's realizing this dream has become something far more than just a dream; he is fully conscious of everything about him. Staying calm, he allows his thoughts to drift away and he listens to the voice within him. Words again form within his mind.

"We have waited for this moment since the beginning; now it is upon us once more. Yes, you have been here before; not in this place, but in this understanding. Do not try to remember the past; it is gone, buried, in the illusions that have held you imprisoned for so many eons. There is much for you to know, but for now, we must address this boy's needs. If he is to survive, you must place the personality of Brandon aside and become who you really are."

Brandon fights to control his response; he has wanted something more all his life, but now that it's nearly upon him, fear strikes, seeking to tear him away from his goal. He stares at the boy by the campfire who sits silent and still as if frozen.

The voice again pushes softly in his mind.

"Time is short; we must prepare quickly! Know this, we or you are known as Shakti. Remember what and who you are: this has always been a part of you. Your seeking for truth throughout your life is only a reflection of Soul trying to remember *what it has attained throughout the ages. In your mind, it has taken countless eons to gain the awareness you have exhibited as the human Brandon. Now, in this moment, you will see and know what has to be said to the boy you know as Hugh."*

Brandon wakes up, shaken! Sweat soaks his pajama top. His mind tries to hold onto the experience. Sitting up, he wipes his forehead, and then swings his legs over the bed, trying to think clearly about what just happened.

"My God! It's true," he repeats to himself. He tries, but he can't remember all that just happened; he remembers a brilliantly colored fire, perhaps a flaming torch? There was the name Shakti, and the image and name of the boy by the campfire...?

Hugh! Yes, that's right; it was really him. No more illusions, no more doubt; it has become so clear—and now it's gone.

Or is it?

No, no...It isn't gone. Brandon knows that there is something else, something much more now. He knows for certain, both in his mind and in his heart, he is at just the beginning.

CHAPTER 34 ~ IT BEGINS

It's hot, it's humid, and not a sound can be heard, not even the slightest breeze can be felt this evening. Soultraveler floats silently, anchored for the evening in calm waters.

Standing on the balcony rail, leaning against a support cable, I watch for stars to come into view. The sky slowly fades from orange sunset to light gray and then to darkness. Thinking about what Morleck told me this morning, I watch. Lately it seems I'm always watching. I'm always looking for any sign or circumstance that might point me in the direction toward me mum, or more likely, a lurking danger. Traveling across this unknown ocean with primitive latitudes and longitudes, I'm just hoping they are pointing us in the right direction. A journey like this makes a person grow up quickly; in the excitement of traveling on Soultraveler and sailing with me crew and guards, I'm beginning to find a balance within me. It's time now to focus on the critical matter at hand: finding my mom.

Kaylu and Dandi are adjusting splendidly to being sailors on such a large ship. Davy works as an assistant to Morleck and me. He is doing just fine, although lately, most of his attention is on Karla, who is returning the interest. Loren and I are glad that Davy and Karla are getting to know one another better. As for myself, I haven't taken time yet to get to know the Crystal guards, but this is to be corrected quickly.

Many things have changed since we left the mainland. The excitement in the beginning had turned my attitude and enthusiasm back to that of a young boy again. Morleck thought it better to let the newness of the ship and its functions wear off a little so that a more adult me could present myself as a mature captain. I'm more than ready to begin.

My job as Captain is to listen to me mates and companions, and keep Soultraveler going in a direction that I feel will lead us closer to me mum. Perhaps I don't apply all the rules of regular seamanship, but I know one thing for sure. If I give the same respect and attention to each crewman that I would want for myself, then I know the day will come when each man will become not only a comrade, but also a brother in arms.

The night grows blacker; dark clouds hide the stars. The blackness reflects in the dark waters of the ocean. As I'm watching, even more deepening darkness drifts onto Soultraveler. The blackness reminds me of the black void in the cave. I often think of that abyss of darkness. I had been almost ready to cross that blackness until me friend's cries drew me back. The feeling of freedom and power at that pivotal moment was something I've never forgotten: the joyous feeling of being pure freedom itself!

Tonight, I reflect once more on my experiences with all the souls I've met, all the new thoughts and feelings that are slowly changing me, and the danger that is always close. But something else is also close: something, mysteriously awesome, something all-powerful, and somehow all-loving all at once.

This journey has been like a puzzle, and I wonder. Each teacher I meet and learn from seems to be a part of the puzzle, from the Wisdom Pool to Jotan, the Council, Olgera, Morleck, and all the others who have giving their wisdom, love, and guidance. All appear to fit together into some kind of cosmic plan that, for now at least, eludes me. This world is truly amazing. These people, even though they are of all races and all species, work together in harmony. Their leaders all respect each other. They are always offering their wisdom and love to assist in whatever way they can. All the things happening to me feel as if it's happening in a sequence of events that aren't coincidental, but almost as if they are predetermined.

I once heard it said that what some call coincidence others say is the Creator; I'm starting to agree with the latter. Each experience sets the stage for the next scene. An unknown force seems to be creating and directing this entire journey for me.

Thinking about how much I've grown, I can see that although most of me development has been in leaps and bounds, through it all, I've never let go of me child's attitude of open-mindedness and wonder. It's not even a struggle to let me childhood survive; in fact, at times it seems to be the greatest asset of my awareness. The new wisdom I'm gaining is constantly weaving its way into every particle of me being.

When waking in the mornings, I sense something has gone on during me sleep. Things are simpler, clearer, and more real than anything I have known before. I'm discovering through this process that intuition is intricately linked with this childlike demeanor. From what I've learned so far, I know my intuition will have to be sharp like a razor. It's my responsibility to keep the mind from creating incorrect feelings. If fear becomes any part of a decision I have to make, then I need to step back and reexamine the situation until the right solution presents itself. Fear spawns many children, and I have to guard constantly against the insidious attacks these nagging children of darkness can inflict. Sometimes my decision seems wrong at the moment, but with time and patience, it almost always proves itself to have been the right one; this is how I must guide Soultraveler—only with pure thoughts about the men, ship, and ocean.

In the brief time of my contemplation, I notice that an ever-increasing and thicker darkness has drifted over and encircled Soultraveler. I realize, too, that this darkness pervading throughout the ship isn't just an absence of light, but a void of silence, too. The ocean waters are uncharacteristically silent and still like glass; not a ripple, not a single movement. Not even the small waves that usually slap against the ship's side can be seen or heard. Soon I can't see the railing I'm leaning on, I cannot even see my hand stretched before me.

Turning carefully, I feel my way back to the cabin to light a lantern. Finding the lantern is difficult enough, but finding something to light it with proves to be a near miracle. Finally, the lantern's light fills the cabin with an eerie yellow glow. The glow only extends about five feet or so, and then the blackness again takes over. Opening my cabin door, I look out onto the deck. It's getting late. Still, I figure someone must be on deck doing something, but there's only silence.

I sense something in the silence. I hear a noise; I try staring into the darkness, but still I see nothing. The blackness is becoming a thickening mass, and no matter how hard I try, I still can't see. I hear a noise again, then out of the darkness, Morleck abruptly steps into view, carrying his own lantern. Walking toward my light, he calls out in a loud whisper, "Hugh, is that you?"

"It is! It is me, Hugh. Come toward the light."

Stepping in front of me, he gestures for us to enter me cabin; we both set our lanterns on each side of the table so there is a ring of light about us.

"Morleck, what is it? What's happening?"

Morleck sits down at the table waiting for me to sit as well.

"I am not sure; I have never seen such a fog—if that's what this is—in all my years. This darkness is something else. It is enough to put fear in any man's blood. No, there's a strangeness about this night; something more is happening here. Can you feel it?"

I nod and sit silently, feeling the room about me. I try to extend my concentration beyond the glow of the ship's lanterns.

At first, I feel nothing, but then I recognize something different. Yes, there is something. Something in the air is alive—it is dark and loathsome. It feels thick and heavy, similar to an invisible black curtain. I can't touch it, feel it, or smell it; I only sense its darkness and its efforts to penetrate me mind. Something or someone is watching us. It's subtle at first; I barely sense it, but as I focus, its presence increases.

Light feelings touch the rim of my subconscious. Next, I sense a complex set of interlapping emotions entering my awareness: a feeling of disappointment mixed with sorrow, sadness, anger, and a hate for all life, especially for those walking in truth.

These dark feelings infiltrate my thoughts. It's a conniving presence: powerful, shrewd, scared, and angry. All these attributes and more are blending and working together as one, single, mutually reinforcing power that continues to grow in strength.

"Hugh!" Morleck whispers. "We are being invaded!"

I lean down closer to Morleck and whisper back, "By what?"

"This is a thing; it is the concentrated essence of the entity that distributes the negative energy throughout existence in the lower worlds. It has many names. I call it 'Abaddon.'"

"What is it doing here?"

Morleck closes his eyes and is silent for a few moments. Then, opening them and gazing intently into my eyes, he explains, "It's probing us, trying to find out why we are here and who we are. And it's searching for something."

I look around, and then slowly I return to face him and ask, "What's it searching for?"

Morleck cocks his head, and then straightening to look me dead in the eyes, he replies in a hoarse whisper, "It's looking for you."

My blood turns cold. Me?

Morleck puts a finger against his lips. "Shh! Do not react! Keep quiet. It has not concentrated all its essence yet; it is spread out, like a thin layer of gravy on a piece of bread. It's searching now and is being drawn toward emotional reactions. It thrives on a person's fear or passions, so keep calm, maybe we can turn this situation to our own advantage."

Morleck motions me to pick up my lantern and follow him. We creep silently across the deck toward the guards' quarters. Their cabins are dark and silent: nothing moves. Morleck opens their door and slips into the darkness with me following. Before any wary guard could pounce on us, Morleck directs the light on himself so they can see he is friend, not foe. Putting his finger to his lips, he signals for them not to speak.

Setting his lantern on the table in the center of the room, Morleck clears his throat.

"Warriors, listen to me. We are being invaded. This invasion is not by anything of flesh and bone that might be laid waste by your weapons. No, our uninvited guest is quiet, dark, and evasive; we cannot capture it, but I believe that we can possibly learn from it."

Morleck asks the warriors to push the table to the side and give him some space. Joining three lanterns he collects from the guards cabin, he arranges all five in a small tight circle in the very center of the room. He then instructs the warriors to position their shield about four feet away from the center. Once the two circles of lanterns and shields are complete, Morleck turns up each lantern to its fullest intensity.

The effect is brilliant!

Lantern light reflects off the shields, illuminating the room many times greater than that provided by the lanterns themselves. But far more significantly, each crystal field on the shields is unique, and so it reflects these diffuse emanations of varying color spectrums according to its own character, powers, and resonance. Together, they focus the lights into multiple beams of higher intensity, and by crisscrossing the six shields, the beams radiate a beautiful and protective light mandala formed of sacred geometric patterns.

We stand transfixed by the shocking sight of this divine light. Morleck composes himself and sits down cross-legged on the floor. He reverently bows and then motions the warriors and me to enter the circle of light. As we take our place within, we sit cross-legged in the same fashion as Morleck. I am struck by how eerie we must appear: six noble warriors, Morleck, and I sit amid a protective light field generated by circles of shields and lanterns, and just a few inches behind our shields, complete blackness.

Morleck speaks in a low voice, just loud enough for all to hear. "The black essence you are sensing is known as Abaddon. This being has no strength except what we give it, and it becomes powerless within the light. But we can discuss now how to use this opportunity to our advantage."

I sit amongst the six elite guards, all of whom are as calm as Morleck. Morleck explains what this blackness is and what its mission is. Then he begins instructions on how they are to assist.

"The light keeps the essence away, but it also keeps information it has away from us. We must first use our greatest mental and spiritual resolve to force this evil back into the blackness it comes from. Next, one of us must enter the blackness to uncover the information it conceals. To do this, we must turn the lanterns off and face the darkness together."

The guards look at one another and then at me. Morleck continues. "Once the light is gone, the blackness will totally envelop us. Physically, it cannot hurt us, but its real power lies in its insidious attacks on our minds. To block its assaults, we all must concentrate on something that all of us can identify with: some type of symbol, either verbal or an image. Once we have focused on this symbol collectively, we must take on an even greater challenge. The one who enters the blackness will need each of us to conjure and send him those mental forces that we have all been practicing containing all of our wisdom, good will, power, and courage, and most of all, a detached, unemotional, and unconditional love.

"The one who enters must be our symbol. The black essence cannot discern what the image will be, as long as it is being created from within our own individual imaginations. It cannot place where the vision is coming from, because it will be coming from eight different states of consciousness. Now all we have to do is decide whose image to use."

The warriors look around amongst themselves, but Morleck has a different idea. "Brothers, we all are here because of one person. He is our Captain, and even though you do not know him personally, you all must know this: Hugh is a noble Soul. He is looking for his mother. He is brave and honest, and he has the heart of a child, but the courage of a warrior at the same time. If it is acceptable to all of you, we should use him as the image for our focused power."

The warriors look at me; then, without saying a word, each nods in agreement.

"It is settled then; the lanterns must go out. As soon as we shut off the light, we each must close our eyes and look into the Tisra Til."

I blurt out, "Wait a minute! What's the Tisra Til?"

Morleck smiles and points his finger to my forehead right between my brows. "You know it as the third eye, or as it is written in your Bible, the single eye."

I wonder momentarily how Morleck would know anything about the Bible, but I begin to breathe easier. "Oh, okay. I never heard it called by that other name, that's all."

Morleck continues. "Create the image of Hugh in the center of your third eye, and begin to weed out all other thoughts. Place within your thoughts feelings of power, nobility, courage, patience, wisdom, omnipresence, and love, and send them into his image. Do not deviate from what you are trying to accomplish. The focusing of your energy on his image will give Hugh the power he will need to ward off the blackness and to travel within it."

Morleck looks around him, and nods; then he turns the lanterns off, one by one.

Total blackness falls upon us. None can see anything, not even his hand in front of his face. Nor can we sense anyone else around us. The silence is surreal. The blackness closes in even deeper. I focus my attention on the Tisra Til, or the third eye.

I never imagined me own image before; this is going to be something new. Staring into the blackness of my inner vision, I keep creating the image of myself within the darkness. The warriors are trying to do the same. The black essence grows thicker. I taste an oily substance on my lips. As Abaddon focuses more of itself, it condenses even thicker, now making it difficult even to breathe. The black fog penetrates each man's mind, trying to fill him with hopelessness. I keep building on the image of myself; trying to see the older version instead of me as a little boy. Morleck feels the power of the blackness growing thicker; he knows the guards and I are battling to create and keep my image within us, but he also knows this might be the most important battle any of us ever fight. If successful, the ramifications for me could be beyond anything I ever dreamed.

Darkness closes in like tentacles touching, feeling, and probing each man's mind. All feel the eyes of Abaddon upon them. The warriors keep creating an image of their captain but the black essence still penetrates deep within each, pushing into our minds, searching our fears, our sadness, and our passions. The six warriors fight to maintain control over their minds, but even as they do, the darkness redoubles its effort. Faint cries of fear or a moan of sadness comes from the darkness. The essence pulls and twists our thoughts, confusing our thinking and taking us to the edge of despair.

I feel again the pain of the car accident; I see my father's pain—even more, I feel it. It becomes me own pain as it sucks me into an abyss of loneliness and fear, twisting and knotting my brain as if a huge, frightening, thick fist was squeezing me thoughts together. My brain feels tight, almost suffocating.

I fight to regain control, trying to keep me image within my inner vision. But for all my effort, I can barely keep my mind from falling into a widening black pit of fear and defeat. The warriors are fighting their own battles; each falls deeper into a thickening darkness of helplessness that may soon swallow them into madness. Morleck fights his battle, too, using all the wisdom and calmness he possesses.

I feel myself reeling as the essence negates all the images I'm trying to create. The only images I see are those the black consciousness wrings from my mind.

Fear drips from me subconscious like drops of water from a twisted rag; each drop explodes in me conscious mind like splatters of darkness against light. Darkness is pulling all of us into its web of illusion, using our own fears as its weapon.

Morleck struggles to maintain his sanity; he knows the battle will be lost if he doesn't do something. He tries to say something. At first, it's just a whisper, but as he yanks his thoughts closer, he stammers in a hoarse voice, and the sound grows and strengthens. Each warrior hears the sound, and in a last, desperate attempt, each echoes the old teacher's chant.

Initially, the sound can't be understood; it sounds like just a deep humming or moaning. As Morleck increases his volume, so do the warriors; their chant then crystallizes into clarity.

Faintly I hear a melodious but eerie vibration. The warriors' voices strengthen one another. As I struggle harder to listen, at last I make out the sound clearly. It's my name, or something close to it! The sound reverberates from within our small circle, bouncing from shield to shield.

I feel almost embarrassed to have my name used in a chant, but finally I, too, start to intone the word. I can only draw it out slowly at first, but I quickly gather strength and become more comfortable, I say it with power, as does each warrior. The men's voices are deep as I join them in repeating, *Huuuu...*

The sound resonates within the confines of the crystal shields, becoming deeper and deeper; rolling within our minds, it drowns out insidious images and thoughts.

The warriors chant louder, fighting Abaddon shoulder to shoulder. The room becomes an echo chamber; each chant is unyielding, rolling into a never-ending sound. Each man picks up the chant as the next leaves off. The room fills with one sound that is reverberating off the shields and penetrating each man's awareness. I begin to relax.

My efforts at creating my own image are succeeding. At first, the image I conjure is fuzzy and distorted, but it eventually clears, becoming the center of my attention. I begin to tremble as the HU rumbles through my entire being; the others must also be having success, because my image becomes bright, filling with energy and clarity.

I see me for the first time as others see me.

I look older; maybe twenty or so, with a tanned face. I have filled out, although I'm still slim and youthful-looking. However, it's the look in my own eyes that holds me spellbound. Me eyes are light green, glinting like crystal glass set deep into my face; they are the eyes of a warrior. The features are strong, determined, and intense. The hair is several shades lighter than I remember, but there's no sign of a beard. A noble look of wisdom comes through those eyes…Those eyes! Oh, my gosh! These are the eyes and face of the young warrior who came to me in the dream at the tree house sleepover; they are the same!

The chant continues. With every deep rolling HU, the image becomes clearer and stronger, radiating light so intense that me inner vision lights up. The sound of my name is rolling like thunder, rushing through me body. Just then, a deafening explosion within the inner world of each warrior erupts just as our consciousness penetrates into the darkness. Like a pebble being dropped into the center of a still pond, waves of energy ripple in a circular motion. An opening appears in my inner sight.

Focusing on the light, I feel myself moving forward, melting into the brightness itself.

I gaze at a dark and turbulent scene.

Images are off at a great distance, but as I continue to stare, they grow larger by the second. An island appears with large mountains in its center. Black seas surround the land and their angry waves batter the rocky shores. Whirlpools spin while huge shapes can be seen diving in and out of the black waters. Dark clouds hang over tall mountains. I struggle to stay calm, and the island continues to come closer.

Moving like a pair of eyes only, I proceed toward the black rocks guarding the mountains. I see a cave entrance deep within the center of the tallest mountain. The vision shifts. The force of my attention pulls me inside the cave. I see a form moving just ahead of me. My eyes go deeper into the darkness; I see it again. There's no doubt; someone or something is just ahead. It's moving as if suspended in mid-air.

Then I see it!

Yes! Now I can make it out; it's….it's me mother!

She's being held by what looks like strands of a web. For a moment I feel her fear; I hear her moans while she twists and turns within strands of the grayish-black webbing. The cave's surroundings are black and rocky, like inside some kind of rocky tunnel or pit. More alarming are the movements around me mum's body.

Black glowing blobs are rotating all around her, methodically sucking her life energies away. The more they attack, the more she moans in terror! Me emotions take over. I can feel her terror and pain! I cannot help but scream out, "Stop! Stop hurting her!"

Immediately I feel a sucking sensation; the vision dims as I'm pulled back into the blackness. The last thing I see is two burning eyes watching me from within the darkness.

Opening me eyes, I see the other men sitting in a circle, still chanting.

The blackness is gone. Beyond the shields, I can see all the rest of the room. The intense feelings of loneliness are gone; no fear or hopelessness remain, all is as it should be. The rolling HU dies down and becomes a whisper.

Morleck opens his eyes and sits quietly. One after another, the warriors stop their chanting. As the sound ceases, each man opens his eyes. Morleck stares at me closely.

I still see my mother's form twisting amid the webs while dark blobs whirl around her. I again feel the pangs of fear and hopelessness she feels. For the first time, I know what true hatred feels like. I want to scream out, 'I hate those dark creatures who torture me mother! What kind of being is this that weaves webs of terror, sucking the life from its victims?' But I keep silent.

Morleck blurts out, "Hugh, what did you see?"

I look at the old man; tears glisten me eyes. I whisper in a shaking voice. "I saw her. I saw me mum…"

Morleck stands up and motions for the warriors to remove the shields.

"Sit up, boy! Quickly! Come to the table and tell me everything you saw." Morleck motions at one of the warriors near him. "Get me a pencil and paper!" The young man hurries over to his bunk and brings out a pencil along with some rolled up paper. Morleck then glances over and nods his head. "Quickly, boy, tell me everything while it is still clear in your mind."

I tell him about the island, the dark ocean and the rocks leading to the cave. As I speak, Morleck writes every word as fast as he can. When I finish, Morleck looks up.

"This has turned out better than I thought! Hugh, you have done well, as have you, men. Without your help, we could never have penetrated as deeply as we have."

Confused, I ask, "What just happened?"

Morleck rolls up the parchment and with a gleam in his eye, he calmly elaborates. "My boy, you entered the belly of the beast! We turned the tables on the negative force through the power of the Sound Current, or what some know as the Audible Life Stream. We just found our first clue to where your mother is. I'll have to study my maps and charts, and decipher the signs, of course, but from what you have just told me, it appears that your mother is being held somewhere near a portal of negative energy."

I was stunned! "Are you sure?"

"Absolutely! She is being held in another dimension, one that is a mixture of the essence of Abaddon. You could not have pinpointed the whereabouts as you have if it were not accessible. I'm not sure where she is yet. However, with my charts I am confident that I will find the direction, and when I do, we need to sail."

I feel a rush of hope flowing through my veins. The vision had been dark, but at the same time, it held out a light that might show the way. This new direction comes with new feelings of confidence as well, and a bond of camaraderie with the warriors who I have not even taken time to know yet.

I turn the light of the lanterns to a warm glow. Turning to face the six men who aided me, I exclaim, "Men, I thank each of you. Tonight, you have given me hope and courage in more ways than any of you can imagine." Walking up to each, I not only shake their hands, but also give each an exuberant and genuine hug.

"Tonight, let's talk. I want to know who each of you are, and I want to give you the opportunity to know me."

One of the men pulls out a bottle of wine, and with a smile says, "There is no reason not to end our first battle with a cup of wine and good conversation." All agree and pull up to the table with their clay cups. A cup is put in front of me, and I say, "This evening I will get to know all of you, even if it takes all night."

The youngest warrior who gave Morleck the pencil and parchment pulls up a chair next to me. "Captain, my name is Baylor. I want you to know it's my honor to serve you."

The rest of the night I talk to each man, getting to know their past, what they believe in, what they want out of life, and many other personal things that help create friendships between people.

By the time the sun is about to rise, I know these men as comrades. No longer are they strangers; each has a story, and now I am a part of his, and he of mine.

Lucas and Corwin have families; Elias and Shawn are alone. Paul is the oldest of the six and a teacher. Baylor is the youngest. All are astute in the mystic teachings of the Light and Sound; it's a requirement in order to carry the Crystal Shield. Their fighting skills are known far and wide, but what many don't know is there's so much more to each of them than just being a swordsman.

In order to carry the Crystal Shield, each man must go through an intensive training and testing period. The many diverse tests are a combination, assessing fighting skills, mental preparation, ethics, and bravery, as well as demonstrations of their ability to grasp the truth about their purpose. Each must have deep spiritual wisdom to enable them to use the ancient art of seeing within. In some ways, the shields are their diploma.

Rarely do they journey together. Although they are prepared as fighting men, they are also educators. Usually they live in their own country or realm, teaching those ready to listen. Some instruct adepts in fighting skills, which incorporate the spiritual discipline that undergirds such skills. Several tutor others in the Light and Sound and more mystical teachings of the ancients: all are elements of the truths about how man can live in harmony.

I was amazed at the depth of each man. They are warriors so that they can right wrongs in their physical world, but they are also warriors for the Creator. To these men, the very act of getting together to journey on this quest is far more than a means to make some extra funds; to them, this was their destiny.

To be together on a great ship like Soultraveler sailing into uncharted waters of their world is the chance of a lifetime. When the warriors hear the story of my world and the events that brought me to them, they are more convinced than ever that theirs is a mission of destiny and even divinity. I'm somewhat embarrassed by their servitude, but I revel in the respect and friendship they give me.

When I leave the guards' cabin just before sunrise, not a cloud is in the sky. All is calm. A warm breeze slowly wafts the ocean's salty aroma across the decks, and a soft gray light from the approaching sunrise lends the ship a surreal atmosphere. Just as I'm turning toward me own cabin, I hear a noise near the bow of the ship. Carefully, I climb the steps to the top deck by the ancient throne.

From me perch, I see Baylor's dark silhouette against the gray sky.

A few mast ropes are dangling in front of him as he sits on the rail bench looking out over the horizon. I'm about to say hello when I hear the plucking of a string instrument. Silently, I creep closer. Baylor is holding the strange instrument that I had assumed earlier was a mandolin. I listen as the young man strums the instrument. The tuning soon turns into a soft melody. Baylor clears his throat and then begins to softly sing.

> I'm traveling on my way back home again
> The way is clear, I'm getting near the end
> With all the guidance I've received
> And all the love I have known
> Life has been a blessing of love
> A blessing of love from the truest of friends
> A blessing of peace I have found within
> And so I say, knowing you'll understand
> I love you, my friend
> Now I dedicate my heart to eternal love
> A pleasure I'm truly worthy of
> With all the joy I have known
> And all the love I have shared
> Life has been a blessing of love
> A blessing of love from the truest of friends
> A blessing of peace I have found within
> And so I say, knowing you'll understand
> I love you, my friend
> I love you, my friend.

Baylor's voice is soft and clear, the melody's entrancing. My throat catches in gratitude and awe as the young man sings. Just as he's about to finish, the sun tips across the horizon; colors of fiery red, bright orange, brilliant yellows, and soft blue grays burst over the smooth waters. Baylor is singing from his Soul to the one friend he loves and trust, the one friend who will never forsake him: his Creator.

The silhouette of the young warrior as the morning sunlight dawns is mystical. Not wanting to disturb him, I back down the steps and head for my cabin, the words of the little song repeating in me mind.

****

Loren slept in her sister's cabin last night, or else I would be telling her about last night for hours. All I want at this moment is to get some rest. Within minutes of reaching my cabin, I am fast asleep.

I'm wakened by a gentle kiss on me cheek.

Opening me eyes, Loren is lying next to me with a mischievous smile on her face. "Hi, guy. You finally decided to wake up?"

I mumble something about a dream I was having about Soultraveler and my friend Billy. Loren stands up and pulls me up after her. "It's a beautiful day. Karla, Davy, and I want to do something fun."

"Fun! What can we do that's fun?"

"Come see!"

I stagger while at the same time Loren pulls me outside. Pointing across the railing, she shouts, "Look! Over there!" I see a large island with high mountains in its center about two miles away. A few other mountains stand to the side of the island like guards watching over the ocean. Soultraveler is moving closer toward the island as sea breezes puff out the sails like huge clouds floating over the horizon. Loren slips her hand into mine and beams up at me. "Isn't it beautiful? It looks like paradise. I want us to stop and explore it."

"Of course, Loren; let me just check some things first. I'll be right back."

I hurriedly climb the stairs to the upper deck and discover the helmsman looking straight ahead. "Is that island on the maps or charts?" I ask.

He peers down on his navigation chart for a moment and looks up, shaking his head, "No, Captain, not anywhere that I can find."

I stare out at the island again and then ask, "Can we take her in and see what this island is about?"

The helmsman stiffens. Looking at me curiously, he replies, "Captain, this is your command. You can do anything you please. We are paid to take your orders; if you want to anchor in and explore this island, then that is what we'll do."

My cheeks redden for a moment. Feeling more than a little embarrassed, I hastily give the order to bring us in as close as possible and drop anchor. Climbing down the ladder, I shake my head and laugh a bit at myself. The helmsman's right. I am not a sailor. I am not a cabin boy. I am the Captain, and I have to start acting like one.

Joining Loren, I tell her I arranged for us to explore the island as she wished. Smiling, she thanks me and says, "Now tell the crew leader to get two of the lifeboats ready to depart, but first, let's have some breakfast."

Puzzled again, I ask, "What do we need two lifeboats for?"

Loren smiles, "One lifeboat is for crewmen and guards."

Morleck steps out of his cabin and hurries over to us. "What's going on? Why are we slowing down and changing direction?" I point out the island and tell him we want to go ashore for a short time. Morleck looks over the railing at the island, squints, and replies, "This island is not on our maps; maybe we should think about this first."

By now, Davy and Karla have joined Loren. I look over at them; all three want to get off the ship for a while and feel dry land under their feet. And after last night, I feel the same way; hiking through an unexplored island seems like the perfect diversion for all of us. Still, it pays to be careful. I look at Morleck and ask, "Why don't you go with us? We can make a map and add this island to your charts." Morleck is quiet for a moment, and without a word shuffles off to his cabin, apparently to change his clothes and ready himself for the hike.

Four guards will go with two crewmen on one boat, and Kaylu, Dandi, Davy, Loren, and Karla will join Morleck and me along with two crewmen on the second lifeboat. The boats carry up to ten men with no problem, so there's plenty of room for the nine of us. We finish breakfast just as all is readied.

Soultraveler anchors in a quiet cove two hundred yards from the white sandy beaches. Both boats are launched from the side of the ship into the clear blue waters. As we pull away, I look back and can't help but admire the beauty of the great ship. The sun is high, and light sparkles like fire from the two large crystals. The sails are dropped, and Soultraveler stands by itself in the lagoon, like a sentinel waiting for its orders.

Both boats are quickly carried along by the current and the crew's steady rowing. My boat lands first on the beautiful beach of a lagoon. Before long, we are out and heading toward the woods. The other boat arrives within moments; its two crewmen and two warriors jump out and secure the boat.

Catching up with us, one of the warriors pulls off his helmet; it's Baylor.

"Captain, we'll go ahead and signal if there is a problem."

Noticing Baylor's mandolin in his hand, I ask if I might borrow it. Baylor places his instrument into my hands, "Enjoy, Captain." I nod for Baylor to take the lead and then turn and call to everyone our plans.

"Look, people; we will divide into two groups to cover more ground. Each group will have a scout in front of them. We will all meet back here when the sun is directly overhead." It's decided that Morleck, Dandi, and Kaylu together with one guard will go to the right, while Davy, Loren, Karla, and I will go to the left with Baylor acting as our scout. The remaining men will stay with the boats.

As the two groups move out, I can't help but sense my friends' excitement. Approaching the wooded area that outlines the beach, scents of exotic flowers, large trees, and the rich aroma of earth and sea mixed with herbs tantalize our senses. Walking deeper into the woods, the beauty of the island is revealing itself ever more with each step. A deep dark cobalt blue sky with ribbons of scarlet pink fading in and out around the mountain tops opens it arms to us.

The surreal mixture of the cobalt blue and pinkish streaks of light give the island a mystical effect. This, combined with the meadows, waterfalls, and streams, gives us the feeling we are in an exotic paradise.

The island conveys a deep feeling of peace. Shy wildlife stalk us, fearful yet curious about the newcomers. It makes for an excellent adventure.

As we move inward, a large meadow comes into view covered with rippling green grass. It reminds me of my home in Bristol. The meadow strangely resembles the one by me tree house. For a moment, I feel pangs of homesickness. I can almost see Cody running after a deer, or Billy rushing ahead of me to reach our tree house before me. Then, I remember me mom and what I saw last night in the dark cave. For a moment, I feel a dull ache in me stomach.

Loren catches up with me and takes my hand. "Look, Hugh, over there!"

Turning to where she's pointing, I see a tall waterfall plunging down the center of what looks like a huge, split granite mountain covered with snow. The waterfall isn't very wide, but it cascades from a great height, creating little arcs of rainbows as the water refracts the sun. Me sadness fades as the mist sprays out across the meadow, moistening my face and watering the flowers and grasses. Loren takes my arm and presses her head against my shoulder; we amble across the green grasses. Davy and Karla linger a little behind us, marveling at a flock of large white and blue birds flying just over their heads. Baylor's about fifty yards ahead, just approaching the border of woods.

Thoughts and feelings of me home again enter into me mind, especially that last day when me and mom took our first trip together to the tree house. Looking down at Loren, I whisper, "I'm sensing that maybe Davy and Karla would like a little time to themselves. What do you think?"

Loren giggles and looks back at her sister. "I think you're right. Let's see what we can do about that." Turning around, Loren shouts out to Karla and waves them to come over.

Davy's like a little boy as he and Karla run up to us. The excitement in his face isn't only reflecting the island's beauty, but the freedom he feels just getting away from the confinement of the ship. However, there's something else, too; something I suspect that has to do with Karla.

As I look at Davy, I think of me mate Billy. Wouldn't it be something if Billy were here right now? What times we could have exploring this exotic island!

Davy has hold of Karla's hand; she's radiant in the morning sun. Her red hair lights up in the sunshine like strands of auburn silk. Her green eyes flash like twin emeralds. Both she and Davy are in love; it's so obvious that I'm sure Loren sees it, too. I put my arm around Loren's shoulders and suggest, "Listen, guys, why don't we split up for a little bit and meet later back at the waterfall?"

Davy and Karla both grin at the same time. "Sounds to us like that is an excuse for you two wanting to be alone, not some favor to us," Davy teases.

"Well," I reply, "we thought it might be fun to explore the meadow a little, and then rendezvous with Baylor in just a little while." Karla and Davy both agree at the same moment.

I signal to Baylor. The warrior is at our side within moments. As I tell him of our plan, Baylor nods in agreement, smiling. "Aye, sir, I'll go to the waterfall and wait until you arrive."

Our group then separates. Baylor finds a secluded spot where he can meditate to the sound of the falling water and the wind blowing through treetops. As we walk to one side of the meadow, Davy and Karla walk to the other. They soon find a small grassy area close to the tall waterfall; what an enchanting place for them to get to know one another better.

As Loren directs us toward a spot under a large shade tree, I still can't help thinking of that meadow at home. For some reason, this meadow and woods give me the same feelings I had when I walked to the tree house with Billy and Cody. She sits down, and I hand the mandolin-shaped guitar to her. Reaching up with one arm, I grab a low branch of the shade tree. Both of us are glad to have a few moments alone with each other, especially in this beautiful setting.

Loren looks up at me for a moment and then says, "Hugh, I don't know why, but sometimes you remind me of a small boy, especially in your facial expressions and attitude. I wonder why that is?" I simply smile in return.

I can't bring myself to tell her I'm really only ten; after all, I'm Captain of Soultraveler and her lover! Still, deep inside, I also feel like the boy I used to be. It is strange that even with all the wisdom I've gained and the battles I've fought, there's still a part of me that stays ten years old. It is that boy who is the one who holds on to the memories of home and me family. That boy is also the one who chose to take this journey in order to save his mother, and it's that boy now who feels again the pain of last night with memories of me mum trapped in the dark cave.

At times, this older part of me—the warrior—doesn't want to feel so young, and wants instead to totally become the man and warrior he feels destined he will be. This is the subtle battle within me, and I know that at some point I will have to confront it. However, for now, I'm content to be next to Loren under the shade of the tree and sit in this beautiful meadow on this island.

Loren looks up at me and asks, "Can you tell me something of your world?"

Reaching with my other hand and grabbing the limb above me, I lift myself from the ground with both hands, doing a chin up. "There's so much to say, but really it might only just confuse you." Loren smiles, but she is persistent. "So try me. I really want to know more about where you come from."

I let go of the branch and fall to the ground.

"I really don't want to think much about it; but if you insist…In my world, there are many different countries. Some are poor; some are rich. Many of them are at war with each other, and some are even at war with themselves. They fight over land, ideas, religion, and power, but mostly they fight because of the greed of their leaders. Then there are those who make war over their God. In my world, it seems young men are always dying in battle ditches; dying is somehow what they believe freedom is all about. The old men keep sending the young men to fight and die for their cause. This is the way it has always been. We sacrifice the young people to feed the tired dreams of yesterday. In the end, they achieve nothing but the destruction and the death of themselves, their women, children, and their future. But still, they think dying will lead them to glory, so they constantly strive to carve tomorrow from the tombstones of their sons and daughters. The battlefields of destruction serve as the baptisms of fire that my world has chosen to create. From these wars, so many viewpoints, so many different sides…They create so many different worlds, all within one. Lately, it seems that the bad outweighs the good…But honestly, I don't want to talk about that. Right now I only want to be with you. And if you like, I will sing a song about my world and my life with you."

Loren smiles and while clapping her hands, she urges him on, "Oh, yes, please do.

I take up Baylor's mandolin and began to strum a few notes, and then gently I begin to sing. The song is true, and Loren weeps at me words. When I finish, I sit down and take her into my arms. She snuggles…clearly wanting to get amorous, which is just fine with me. I realize I need to give Loren the intimacy she craves by sharing myself with her emotionally, not just physically. Although I don't want to tell her about my ten-year-old self, I want to—I need to—tell her about the Hugh who I am now. With my arms around her, I tell her about the black essence that had enveloped me, searched for me, and threatened me last night. I describe the great circle that the Crystal Guards, Morleck, and I formed, and the brilliant protective light mandala. My voice breaking, I described the chanting and image projection and how Morleck helped me open my mind so that I could travel to the mysterious island and see me mum, struggling and in pain.

Loren reaches up and touches her hand to my face; for a moment, I sense she can peer through my disguise and see the young lad who I truly am. She reaches out to comfort me, and I feel such relief and gratitude that she so gracefully accepts me for what I am now: confused, uncertain, and raw. As she brings me into her embrace, my body responds, and I allow my mind to surrender to the passion.

Loren's dark hair captures the sunlight as it dances around her shoulders. Embracing me tighter, she brings her face close to mine. For a moment, I am distracted and amused by puffs of wind playing with her hair.

Like the wind, for this moment, I don't have a care. Why can't it always be just like this?

Breezes gently cool my face, reminding me of Soul's true freedom. My thoughts begin to fly to my journey and what may lie ahead. Somewhere, I know there's a star…somewhere off in the distance…a star that is always leading me to someplace; where it is leading, I don't know, or even why I should follow it. Soul, however, keeps urging me onward, always trusting in the Creator.

Loren again commands my attention. Our lips touch; I feel a tingle rush throughout me body. What a wonderful thing love is. Yes, all is right with the world; this island is the perfect paradise for reflection and for love.

Little did we know that our paradise was about to expose another side of its nature.

CHAPTER 35 ~ DISCOVERY

Sipping his coffee carefully, Brandon thoughtfully blows steam off of the hot brown liquid. How has his life become swept up in such peculiar circumstances? For reasons unknown to him, either Hugh or some other power is communicating not only to Clark, but now to himself as well. Brandon stares into space, his hands cupping the brew warming his face. How can he figure out that dream—or that vision, or whatever that experience was—the night before? Never would he have imagined the possibility of his subconscious self or Soul existing at higher levels of reality while "he," Brandon, wanders through his earthly life. Events from his past that before he couldn't explain are now starting to make sense: at least on a spiritual level. In his youth, Brandon felt a driving need to study in depth not only the history of mystics and religions, but also to broaden his viewpoint and expand his experience throughout diverse fields, including archaeology, law, travel, medicine, writing, and teaching. All that preparation has contributed to who Brandon is now.

Brandon's own subconscious probably guided these interests for reasons he's only now just beginning to understand. As a young man, he assumed they were done partially out of curiosity and partially out of expectations for eventual financial gain, or perhaps partially to satisfy his ego. Now, after this single experience in his dream, he wonders. Perhaps every field of endeavor he has learned is for a higher purpose; life is now weaving all these knowledge quests together, forming a bridge to connect to a larger part of himself he had never known. The keystone to this growth appears directly linked to Clark, Hugh, and their situation. This realization of the higher self is quickly establishing itself in his awareness, thereby changing his perception, attitude, and conscious life. From what he can remember, this other part of himself—Shakti—is working at a level of awareness that allows Soul to influence his tangible self more directly, but he has not been able to reciprocate until now.

As he finishes his coffee, he realizes he can follow this stream of thought only so far. If he attempts to take it further while still mired in a limited understanding, he will only confuse himself, and possibly demean the entire experience as something fabricated from his own fantasies and desires.

Brandon now understands the impetus for his discovering, studying, and practicing multiple contemplative techniques for so long.

Contemplation helps an individual build a bridge to the higher self; Brandon's mind begins to race. Any person can find a suitable form of contemplation, so why doesn't everyone take advantage of such useful tools? If they would, then man as Soul could become a co-worker with the Creator as was originally designed. Each person can be understood as an individual subculture within their own society's culture; these individual subcultures influence the outer culture, and in most cases, man's perspective on life. People are the product of their societies, sex, and race, but more importantly, people are products of inborn spiritual laws that frame all existence. Therefore, each person is either knowingly or unknowingly building the bridge to their higher self during mortal life. If he doesn't catch the ultimate truth in one life, he will have the opportunity to get it later in another. This eternal unfoldment is accomplished by allowing Soul to lead the will or mind. It does this through attitude, perspective, courage, dreams, and forgiveness, plus spiritual experiences.

When the café waitress stops by again, Brandon orders another cup of coffee.

When man has built out sufficient lengths of this bridge that links his conscious self to his unconsciousness or higher self, Soul then begins to help in completing the final phase. Religions, philosophies, and spiritual teachings are all merely one of many building blocks in this construction. However, through each life and through man's current existence, the human psyche absorbs the effects of wars, acts of evil, goodness, charity, families, and all the trials, emotions, relationships, and tests of life. This is necessary so that someday a person will be strong and aware enough to eventually experience the other side, or the kingdom within. This experience of living in the earthly body eventually allows an individual to take control of his destiny, and ultimately merge with Soul. All past lives, every experience, and every personality Soul has created are all parts of the puzzle to the pathway of self-realization.

After settling his bill, Brandon steps outside and slides back into his car. He pulls away from the coffee shop and merges onto the thruway. His jumbled thoughts also coalesce, merging as if into one brilliant thought, merging as if into one sublime emotion, and finally merging as if into one ultimate realization.

The most important part of building this bridge to Soul is love! Not the limited human love or emotional attachments to this world, but the love that frees Soul and allows it to step away from mundane human reality and move forward to complete man's connection to his true self and ultimately to the Creator.

The simplicity of this sudden awareness explodes within Brandon's mind like a wave of light crashing into his consciousness, filling him with a warm, compassionate understanding of his fellow man. Life's purpose is no longer hidden. Humans aren't here to just learn about love; their true purpose is to become love. What power in this simple statement! If only life in this world would grab hold of this simple, holiest of understandings! Brandon relaxes in the afterglow of his sudden enlightenment.

Understanding the ramifications of what just happened within him, he struggles to contain himself; for once in his life, he feels like shouting out to all who would listen. What a simple victory that's waiting for each man, woman or child! If only humankind could let go of its limited concepts, which separate us from our source—the same source that creates and sustains every second of our existence. Instinctively, Brandon knows this realization is meant only for him; it's deeply personal, and exists as a gift from spirit directly to his mind and heart.

Humankind's highest ideal allows each person to journey on to his true self, and thus again become pure Soul. The path is constructed from the same qualities and understanding as everyone else, because all are traveling to the same source, or what is called the Creator. In other words, as Brandon—a man with a limited mind constrained by attachments to duality—he can never know the Creator in its entirety. The best he can accomplish will be to complete his journey and join with Soul, who will then continue the journey into eternity ultimately growing into the oneness of the Creator, while still maintaining its individuality. Just as Soul allows a part of the human self to survive when merging with it, so the Creator allows the Soul to maintain its individuality upon completing its journey. The key to understanding the survival of the personality (or at least the best part of a person) is understanding the Creator's perfect plan, which allows no Soul to escape its divine destiny. Each Soul, or drop of love that manifests itself as life, ultimately finds its way back to its origin. There might be delays for some…There might be dark tests for those who have lost their way…But in the end, Soul cannot fail to connect at some point and move forward to complete its spiritual purpose. To Brandon, it is as clear as if it were written into a Spiritual DNA code.

Soul, as an individualized part of the Creator's consciousness, has within it all of the Creator's characteristics and capacities. Some say we are actually God, but this is hardly true; in reality, the Creator is us. Our purpose is to know ourselves as spiritual beings, each with a personal relationship to the Creator. Realizing this ultimate truth can be a lifelong goal. The power that enlivens all creation through its nurturing is a power that we all must learn to respond to.

Brandon collects his thoughts; he needs to meet with Clark as soon as possible. After a quick call, he convinces Clark that he has new information that may help them connect to Hugh on a more conscious level. They agree to meet again at 8:00 that night. After hanging up, Brandon knows what they need to do to help Hugh, but he also knows their help will only be effective to a certain point. Like all souls, Hugh must finish his journey on his own: this is the only way.

When Clark arrives at Brandon's house in the early evening, Melody is with him because he couldn't get a sitter.

Still feeling the afterglow of his earlier discovery, Brandon smiles and greets both of them warmly as he directs them into the great room. The Tudor house is large and has the ambience of a home from European architecture a hundred years ago. Even though the house is only a few years old, it is decorated to fit his personality, which gives it a worldly look and feel.

A large fire burns brightly in the stone fireplace. Tea is brewing in a silver teapot; the large, overstuffed, dark green corduroy couches are soft, inviting, and comfortable. Brandon motions them to sit as he pours them both a cup of herb tea. Sitting himself in a large matching chair, he raises his cup and toasts to their friendship and to the success of their journey.

Clark is a little puzzled.

He has never seen this side of Brandon, and wonders what brought it about. He's even more surprised when Brandon reaches out and touches him on the shoulder and says, "I want to thank you, my friend, for allowing me to be a part of your family's lives. My gratitude is beyond words; I just wanted you both to know that if not for you, I may have been delayed in a very important goal that I've pursued most of my entire life."

Brandon's warmth and love are so sincere and so gentle that both Clark and Melody are captivated. Brandon then reaches out and taking Melody's hands in his, he says, "Child, you're about to become part of something that will enhance your life beyond your wildest imagination. I want you to know that you're one of the main components in this quest, and I want to thank you for that, too."

Unable to contain herself, Melody reaches out to Brandon, and gives a hug around his neck and then whispers something in his ear. Brandon's eyes open wide for a moment. Melody gives him a tighter hug then, and looking into his eyes she puts her finger to her lips. Clark can't hear what she is saying, but clearly he notices the warmth and love Melody is giving so freely, and for this he's glad. Melody releases Brandon and sits back down on the couch with her father. Suppressing his surprise, Brandon stares for a moment at the little girl, and then sits back and takes a sip of his tea. Clark asks, "Okay, where do we start?"

Brandon then tells them about the dream he had two nights before. Both listen spellbound by the sudden revelation about his not only seeing Hugh, but also about his merging with his higher self. Brandon doesn't share about his spiritual name "Shakti," however.

Clark sits for a few moments trying to fathom Brandon's dream; his attorney's story sends him spinning into thoughts that before this meeting didn't exist—at least not to him. If he is going to be of any help, he must understand what was just told him. Coming out of his shock, he asks, "If what you're saying is true—which I have no doubt—then each of us is living a spiritual existence as well as living our earthly lives at the same time?"

Brandon chuckles, "Well, you're partially right. In fact, I thought the same thing earlier today. However, you have to adjust your mindset a little when it comes to the concept of time. Are we living two lives at the same time? I doubt it. Remember, the time frame changes as we grow in consciousness or awareness, eventually disappearing altogether. I agree to this, though; our mind convinces us we live in the illusion we're leading two separate lives. This realization of the higher self in the beginning seems to be composed of two lives, but as you adapt and grow, it clearly becomes one."

Clark sips his tea and then asks, "What does that mean?"

Brandon thinks for a moment before answering. "Well, it's difficult for the mind to comprehend life outside of time, but the simplest way I can describe it is in the way a carpenter said it two thousand years ago after being nailed to a cross. He said, 'It is finished!' What I now believe he was saying is that creation in this world and all worlds within the reality of time and space is already a completed part of the total creation. We are merely walking through an aspect of this finished product."

Pausing to let his words sink in, Brandon continued. "To our eternal selves, the Soul, creation in the lower worlds is already done. Soul is living as one, but it has lower states of consciousness or awareness that exist within it. This lower self just hasn't caught up with the higher self yet. The same applies to the Creator;

Soul just hasn't caught up with it as of yet. To humankind, it seems as if our daily lives are different moment to moment, but now I see what's really happening. Time is one of the illusions that conceal the fact that we're trapped in a limited awareness, and that we all are merely walking through a device created and designed to purify each of us, no matter what."

Clark interrupts. "Are you saying we're living in a predestined reality machine?"

Brandon shakes his head. "Well, yes and no; let me explain. As long as we humans live under certain guidelines that we accept as reality, and as long as we live according to the laws of matter, energy, space, and time, we're subject to the physical laws of nature. One of these is that for every action there is an equal and opposite reaction. Some call it reap what you sow, cause and effect, or karma. So, we could say for every evil we cause, we eventually will suffer the repercussions of that particular concept of evil. The same idea works with humankind's concept of good also. This concept isn't exact in the whole process that we can see, but just another part of the purifying process we know as creation. In the realm of the mind, it is exact, and this is why it is important for man to come to know it. Making daily choices forms the events for tomorrow, making it seem that we are living in a predestined reality. Once a man becomes aware of his higher self as Soul, then everything changes. Humans rise in consciousness above the normal everyday drudgery and mundane karma. Mankind no longer is the effect of the lower illusionary laws, he now begins to live and create within the aspects of 'Here and Now,' which means he's no longer under the laws of cause and effect or whatever. He now lives according to the Creator's divine constructs, so he is free!"

Brandon can tell Clark needs a bit more coaching. "Remember, Clark, the human concepts of creation and duality only exist within the confines of matter, energy, space, and time. This conceptualization simply doesn't apply to the higher levels of creation that the mystic calls paradise or heaven. The trick is learning to rise above our human conscious reality. As one travels through this purifying process known as life, we are in the lower worlds, and we're subject to basic laws and concepts that propel us always forward—sometimes slowly, sometimes quickly—to the next stage of purification, which is known as evolution. So it's true, we start as untried Souls in the lowest forms of creation, which is the most basic—and actually the entry—part of this purifying machine. In what our mind thinks is the beginning of Soul's journey, we inhabit forms that are the building blocks of life itself. After eons of time and experience, we eventually come to experience the human consciousness. We are, and have been, battered by this cause and effect, from our very first sojourn into this universe, almost completely at its mercy. However, there comes a time in Soul's journey where it reaches a crossroad in its existence in the lower worlds; when it reaches this crossroad, Soul must choose wisely. If it does, then it's no longer controlled by cause and effect. In other words, Soul becomes pure cause, thereby changing any concepts of predestination to choice. Soul no longer lives totally in the completed parts of creation. This is a crucial time, for this is when Soul begins to grow spiritually in the human state of consciousness, and begins to experiment with its own creative powers. This increase in spiritual awareness allows humans to peek into the higher levels of reality with full awareness. In other words, your head is in Heaven, and your feet are on Earth."

Clark asks, "How does Soul get to the human stage of development, and then progress from there?"

Brandon nods. "Prior to Soul unfolding in the human consciousness, it works its way through the myriad forms of lower consciousness, or what we know as existence. As Soul progresses in these lower vibratory forms, bit by bit it grows beyond the limited laws that govern each of the lower states of consciousness, such as the atomic, biological, mineral, plant, and animal, eventually arriving at the human state of consciousness."

Clark asks, "Are you saying that I was once a rock, a plant, or maybe a monkey?"

Brandon again chuckles. "Well, that's the concept of most Eastern religions, and many cult teachings, but in truth, no—you were never any of these things."

Brandon stops for a moment to let Clark process that last thought, and then smiling, he begins again. "The Creator gave birth to you as Soul in its exact image. You are your Father's child in every way, a perfect replica but in miniature form. You did, however, upon entering this universe, like all humans, take on a body. These are nothing more than shells created to protect you from the harsh vibrations that exist here in this universe of positive and negative energy. Each form you inhabit is created to not only protect Soul, but also to assist it to take in certain bits of knowledge and information to store within its consciousness. Soul absorbs all the information that comes from each form during the period we call a lifetime. Then it graduates from that form to still another. Each new form is less limited than its predecessor as far as its potential to absorb and store data. Each body Soul inhabits is better than the last, so even though Soul climbs this evolutionary ladder, getting better and better flesh bodies, it never is the body itself. It only uses that body as a covering to survive in the lower worlds as it builds its own consciousness, or its own inner kingdom."

Clark watches Brandon closely, and notices a change coming over him. He is no longer speaking like Brandon. His words seem to have changed; his tone is becoming more direct and authoritative. His facial expressions are also different; there is a serene and noble look about him. Clark notices, but doesn't interrupt.

"As Soul continues to take on more powerful and complex biological bodies or coverings, it begins to learn how to get rid of useless information, and only keep the best from each lifetime. Soul then carries this information to the next body. This process is based on two factors. First, Soul must carry over only the very best of the cumulative experiences it has already experienced from its past lifetimes. Second, Soul uses its past knowledge to incorporate these past experiences into the experience it requires in its next life for higher spiritual understanding. This divine process allows Soul to grow in awareness with each lifetime. This expansion in consciousness is a major step, and necessary in the purification process, for it eventually brings Soul to a giant leap in its evolution. This leap is when the mind is about to experience what we call love. The entry of conscious love in Soul's journey begins from the emotional level. For now it's ready to take on a biological life form that not only feels but expresses itself on the emotional level. When this happens, love comes into the individual's own universe as feeling. Up to this point, love has expressed itself only as an act of procreation or survival. Now at this juncture, the whole purification act takes on a new reality; Soul now ascends to a higher level of purity."

Clark rolls his eyes. "Oh boy, here we go again. I swear, the more I try to learn about this spiritual stuff, the more confusing it gets. Are you sure God created all this complicated stuff? And if He did, why is it so damn difficult to understand?"

Brandon's quiet for a moment and then asks, "Clark, do you want to hear this or not? I know it isn't simple stuff to understand, but it does have a purpose, and ultimately, there is a point to this."

"Go ahead; I'm sorry. I'll be quiet."

"Okay, now where was I—oh yes, I remember. For the first time in its journey, because of love, Soul cares for its young, and protects something other than itself. It nourishes and feeds its offspring. As it does, this same action nourishes and feeds its love with feelings and affection. As love grows, it prepares Soul to get ready to enter into still another higher body of expression. Soul continues to work in this way, until it's ready to operate the human state of consciousness. We see glimpses of this lower kingdom growth in animals that we call pets: the animals that cohabitate with humans. You need only observe these animals while they watch almost every move we do. They begin to respond to us with higher love, usually on an unconditional basis."

Clark asks, "Our pets Cody and Namo—do you think they're getting ready to move on to the higher state of human consciousness?"

"Well I can't say for sure, only because I don't know what they have experienced in their lifetimes. But usually, you can tell they're ready when they begin to take on some of the traits of their owners, such as love, patience, and behavior that's either gentle or non-violent, etc."

Melody blurts out, "I know Namo and Cody are ready. They are always giving love to me!"

Brandon smiles and nods. "You may be right, Melody, but I have no way of knowing for sure. I just know that they, too, are traveling on the road back to our source."

Leaning forward, Brandon becomes very serious. "Now this is most important, so listen carefully. All states of consciousness in the lower worlds are operated on a mechanical level. This means that without all the previous knowledge, preparation, and experience that Soul gains from its journey through the lower forms of life, our spiritual evolution would not happen. We couldn't even begin to operate the power of the sophisticated human mind on a mechanical level; it needs all this previous input and experience if we are to grow spiritually. Without the previous experiences of numerous lifetimes, it would only manage to trap itself within the millions of programs that are genetically engineered into the human experience. Therefore, when Soul first operates the human mind, it makes mistakes.

It pushes the wrong switches, you might say. It picks up habits that slow it down and make its thinking process inefficient and unproductive as far as surviving in this world and conducting itself in accordance with the laws of society. This happens constantly here in this world, which is why we have so many different states of awareness. These different states of awareness cause major conflicts due to feelings that are incorporated into a lack of expertise.

"When Soul takes on its first human mind, it might operate it for only a short time, and then translate, or experience death. When this happens, it leaves its old body host and prepares to come back again into the human experience again. This continues until it finally works out how to function and operate the human mind in a society or culture that is approximately the same as its own awareness. This explains why there are so many different cultures and individual experiences in this world. All the starving children, wars, religions, hate, disease—they are all intricately linked to the cause and effect process that allows Soul to unfold and the mind to evolve."

Brandon gets up and walks over to get another log for the fire. He has a lot to tell Clark, but he also realizes that if he gets too mental, Clark won't keep up with him. Brandon knows that keeping the spiritual works simple and easy is the best way for it to be accepted. He must continue, but try not to become too mental or boring. "Our world will never see global peace; the purification machine is not designed that way."

Clark raises his eyebrow, leans over, and says, "That's a pretty pessimistic attitude, don't you think?"

"Well, it may be," Brandon responded, "but this is a warring universe. Can you tell me a time in history when we've had universal peace?"

Clark leans back. "No, not really, but you'd think that maybe in the future it'd be possible."

"That would be nice," Brandon agreed, "but logically speaking, and given our past history and the current state of the world, it isn't feasible. Remember, we live in a world of opposites or duality, so in the end there cannot be total peace. Our journey home to the Creator is where true peace and total freedom exists. This physical universe is temporary; an illusion. One of the redeeming values for Soul in the Creators plan is that eventually each individual will have to chart his course alone. Humankind at some time is forced to consciously rely on the Creator for his existence. He may have assistance from family, religion, science, and teachers. Nevertheless, in the end, he must stand alone, naked in his purity in front of the Creator. The Creator isn't waiting to judge us when we're finally ready to recognize it as our Father. The Creator is there waiting for the sole purpose of accepting you into its kingdom."

Clark asks. "Why do we have to wait to be accepted? Why can't we just be there with the Creator from the beginning?"

Brandon takes a sip of his tea and then says, "The individual Soul's purpose is that it must learn how to create its own kingdom within the framework of the Creator's divine laws. In other words, Heaven is made in the image of the Creator's own reality. Our personal reality, or kingdom, or consciousness must be the same. Creating this kingdom is done through discipline, proper attitude, compassion, detachment, love, experience, and freedom."

Brandon pauses, waiting for the furrows in Clark's brow to smooth down as understanding dawns. "Once Soul passes through the lower parts of this massive purification machine called life, it reaches the point where it's finally ready to exit. Remember when Jesus said it's harder for a rich man to enter the kingdom of Heaven, than for a camel to pass through the eye of a needle? What he was saying is that to get to the point where the individual can leave the human state of consciousness, he has to let go of all the materialistic and emotional desires he has accumulated while being human. When Soul reaches this stage, it begins to sift through the knowledge and experiences it has gathered during its sojourn in this universe. It keeps only the simplest, most compassionate, and detached part of its experience, plus the wisdom of common sense, charity, freedom, love, and power. Everything else is rejected, including the mind with its concepts of duality, matter, energy, space, and time. When this is accomplished, Soul attains the wisdom that up to this part of its journey is likened to a person about to receive his master's degree. Generally speaking, Soul must let go of its childish ways, and must discipline itself, but more than anything else, it has to let go of the one thing that will hold it back from graduating, and that is where the real battle begins. Soul's greatest adversary is from within. This adversary has been its closest companion, and even though it has assisted in getting it this far, it now turns on him like Judas did the Christ. This traitor, of course, is the mind."

Clark nods, and Brandon begins again. "Remember, Soul only takes the best virtues from the mind, and leaves the passions, rules, fears, ego, attachments, morals, and limited human concepts behind. These passions and habits constitute the lower part of us, and without these passions, the mind ceases to exist as the master. So it's necessary for the mind's survival to hold us back, to always keep us within its human ways. Humankind has forgotten that the mind's divine function is for expression of Soul and storage of information only. Once Soul is ready to ascend, the individual must clear his mind of any baggage that will hold him back. The mind must be emptied so it can receive the divine wisdom. Once done, Soul uses this wisdom as a springboard to the universes beyond matter, energy, space, and time. No one knows for sure when man reaches this point in Soul's journey, but it is known that it comes in many forms. For those who are fortunate enough to foresee his journey's end, he'll strive harder than most. However, for those not aware of the forthcoming enlightenment, it sometimes takes a great event in his life to break through the mind's grip. This is what has happened to us. This is why we're together. This is why Hugh's circumstances have become the dominating experience in our lives."

Brandon becomes quiet. Sitting back, he sips his tea, and stares into the bright fire. Then looking at Clark and Melody he asks, "Do you have any questions so far?"

Clark thinks for minute, and then says, "All this information is incredible. Trying to digest it is something else entirely."

Almost as if reading Clark's mind, Brandon says, "Listen, I'm telling you a lot tonight; it doesn't matter if you understand all of it or not. The seeds are planted; they'll grow quickly and help in what has to be done. Don't be concerned about understanding every word or phrase—the mind records all whether you consciously know it or not."

Clark then asks, "Tell me something. As interesting as this is, how is understanding this going to help us assist Hugh?"

Brandon takes another sip of tea before answering. "By you building a foundation for a new consciousness within yourself, you're opening the door to communicate with your son. This knowledge is merely the first step to the discovery of who you are. It is up to you to either reject or accept what's being revealed to you. When man accepts truth, he becomes fertile ground for the seeds within. Being ignorant of truth makes man infertile to the divine seeds trying to grow, thereby slowing your own growth. Each word, each sentence, is but a small part of one simple realization that you will experience in your own time and way. Before we can help Hugh, it is necessary that we must help ourselves."

Clark nods, and Brandon elaborates. "Actually, one simple sentence can explain the entire purpose for existence, but the mind's censors won't let us understand its simplicity. This is why we're taking a few twists and turns to reach the inner you. Remember, the mind is always watching, always looking for ways either to confuse you or to pull you in the opposite direction, especially when truth is given. Going back again to the carpenter more than two thousand years ago, didn't he say, 'We must be wise like serpents and innocent as doves to know truth?' Well, this is exactly what we're doing; have patience, understanding will come."

Brandon pauses for a moment, and then resumes. "Remember, Clark. This is not our home; it's only a temporary respite for the lower states of consciousness or the mind. Remember your Bible studies? 'Foxes have holes, birds have nests, but the son of man has no place to rest his head.' I believe this was referring to foxes and birds as examples of lower states of consciousness that exist in this universe. For these lower states of consciousness, this is home. But for the true son, this is not where we should build our eternal homes, for man has the ability to recognize his divinity, and grow spiritually to ascend to Heaven."

Puzzled again, Clark shakes his head. "Let me ask one question, and please try to give me a simple short answer."

"I'll try," Brandon responded.

"Why was all of this created in the first place? I mean, if we're created in the image of the Creator, why were we sent here to go through this purification machine. What are we being purified of?"

Brandon offers Clark another cup of tea and then pours himself a cup.

"Excuse me; my mouth gets dry with all this talking." Taking a sip from his cup, Brandon looks at Melody and smiles. The glow from the fireplace reflects off the wood floors and huge oak mantle. Sitting in his big chair, sipping on his tea, Brandon projects a comfortable ambiance that gives Clark and Melody a warm homey feeling. Setting his tea down, Brandon continues. "Clark, that's a good question, and yes, I can answer it short and sweet, but I wonder whether you'll understand the answer."

Clark snorts in response. "Try me."

Brandon picks up his tea and leans over. "The answer is in one simple word."

Clark leans closer, as if to better hear this wonderful word.

"Identity."

The room goes silent. Clark looks at Brandon in disbelief. "Identity? What's that supposed to mean? You already said we're supposed to let go of our minds, our passions, our attachments, and God knows what else. Why would we be sent here for identities?"

Brandon picks up his tea and leans back in his chair and says. "You wanted a brief answer. Well, you got it. Now what are you going to do with it?"

Melody jumps down from the couch. "I know! I know! Can I tell him? Please? Please!"

Brandon coughs and almost spills his tea. He's too surprised to speak for a second. Then, looking at Melody, he sees she's sincere. "Go ahead, dear." He looks at Clark and says, "This should be interesting."

Melody walks over to her father, sits in his lap, and puts her arm around his shoulder. "Daddy, don't you remember? When God made us, we were just like him, but smaller. We weren't in these kinds of bodies. We were made of light. But we didn't know who or what we really were. God couldn't just tell us who we were, because we wouldn't understand: just like when Brandon told you the answer and you didn't understand. It's like Aunt Fran's new baby boy. He's just like us, but he doesn't know it. He doesn't know he has the ability to talk, crawl, or even change his clothes. Someday her baby will read, write, and drive a car, and do all the things you do, but right now he doesn't know this. In fact, he doesn't know his name, or even if he's a boy or a girl. These are the things he has to learn in order to understand who he really is. If I gave Aunt Fran's baby a computer video game, he would only break it or spit on it. But if I give him a rattle, he plays with it and has fun. So when we were created from God, if we were given the body and mind of a man or woman from the beginning, we wouldn't know how to make it work. That's why we start with the littler minds like plants, insects, rocks, and other stuff; they're like blocks and rattles. As we grow, we get to play with better toys like human minds. I don't think Fran's baby could work a computer like I do. And I don't think I can work a computer like you do. I'm not ready to work with something so complicated. For us to help God, we have to know who we really are, and how to use our minds in good ways like the Creator. Someday, we can be God's grown up children as Soul. If we don't grow, then we hurt ourselves and others with things like wars, pollution, selfishness, and other bad things. It's like me trying to drive our car. If I did, I would crash it or run over someone, and maybe hurt myself. But I know how to ride my bike, and this will help me learn so someday you can teach me to drive a car. This is why we must learn in steps what we really are, and what we can really become. Do you understand now, Daddy?"

Clark sits there staring at his daughter thinking, who is this person?

Can this possibly be my baby girl? How can she take a one word answer like identity and turn it into such a simple analogy of the most sought-after question in the world? However, because it is so simple, Clark understood. He realizes the eternal quest. Taking Melody into his arms, he says. "Yes, honey, now I understand." Melody giggles and then returns the hug. Sliding off Clark's lap, she reaches out to give Brandon a hug, too. In a moment of shock, he feels the child's pure love, and then returns the embrace. Snuggling up to him, Melody whispers softly in his ear, "I love you, Shakti," and then she sits back down on the couch next to her dad.

Brandon stares at the little girl, wondering how she could have known this secret. Taking out his tobacco bag and pipe, he begins to fill it. Clark leaves the couch, pulls up a smaller wingback chair, and sits down in front of the fire, watching Brandon. Lighting his pipe, Brandon takes a few puffs and exhales. The smoke has a rich aroma, like a smooth whisky touched with the aroma of apricots.

"Clark, my friend, there's much for us to still learn. One of the things you must understand is that we have more than just the physical body, and what we call the spirit. Indeed, we actually have five bodies according to some Hindu teachings and Sant Mant writings. Most occult teachings say we have physical, astral, causal, and mental bodies, and then there are a few teachings that talk about the fifth body of man, or what they call the Atman or the pure Soul."

Clark again gets that blank look on his face. Brandon chuckles and takes another puff on his pipe.

Frustrated, Clark has to ask, "If I have all these bodies floating around, how come I never see them or even feel them? Wouldn't the world and heavens get messy with all these bodies moving around in the universe? It's bad enough to try to maintain one body, let alone five!"

Brandon looks at Clark with his eyes half open. "If you're finished, perhaps you'd like to listen to what I have to say about these bodies and their function." Brandon puts down his pipe. "Clark, it really isn't so confusing if you're ready, but actually, it isn't even necessary to know all these metaphysical mental gymnastics. However, because of our circumstances, it might behoove us both to try to grasp the real picture of what Hugh is going through. Doing so may perhaps allow us to go into areas most men can't even speculate about, let alone visit."

For the sake of his son and wife, Clark becomes quiet. He's determined to focus on what Brandon is about to say; he knows it's important, but it seems every time he learns one new concept, there's another waiting around the corner.

Brandon stands and paces slowly; he needs a few moments to think before he speaks again. He could easily lose Clark in the mental gymnastics of the mind; Melody has shown that very clearly, and he isn't about to get caught in the same old mental trap that the mind loves to use. If he is to be of any value to Clark and Hugh, then he will have to show Clark in a simple, precise way how spirituality is actually caught, not taught.

While thinking about how to simplify the mechanics of Soul travel, Brandon can't get out of his mind the fact that Melody knew his spiritual name Shakti. He's sure he hadn't mentioned it, and yet somehow she knew. He sits down and turns toward Clark. For a moment he just sits there staring.

Sitting in front of the cozy fire, Clark has fallen sound asleep.

Brandon shrugs and shakes his head. There has to be a lesson here…

CHAPTER 36 ~
PARADISE LOST

Loren and I walk across the meadow toward the waterfall. Spending time alone together is helping strengthen our feelings for one another. Loren has an easy way of showing me things about myself I never knew existed. She's also a reminder of how important human love is.

Jotan, Morleck, and others say that human love is limited, and that it will eventually have to be left behind; I don't agree. Love is love, and whether it's at a human level or a divine level, I can't see any difference. The way Loren makes me feel is almost divine itself—her gentleness, her caring, her alluring ways, and incredibly strong confidence—these qualities and more are something I need to learn, and she's a generous teacher. I don't want to change anything about her, and I hope she feels the same about me.

I think the failure of most human relationships is because people constantly try to change their mates, their children or even their friends. This causes almost every problem and misunderstanding in any relationship. It's hard enough for a person to change himself or herself without the burden of someone else trying to change them to what they feel is a better image of who they should be. Yes, it's true that some people can't get along with others, but in trying to change these people without allowing them choices sometimes leads to unspeakable retaliation. It's better to avoid these people and let them work out their issues in their own way. However, for those who are supposedly good people and fall in love with someone who is generally good, for those it seems that in the beginning of the relationship they both love each other as they are. After a while, they try to change little things about them. This happens gradually over time, and eventually results in resentment from both parties. So far, Loren and I accept each other for who and what we are, and we allow each other the freedom to express ourselves in our own special way.

When we arrive at the waterfall, Baylor is sitting on a rock above the serene pool. As soon as he sees us approaching, he points his finger toward the pool. Loren and I look over at the pool and see Karla standing with her back to us in the serene waters. She's like a painting. A light mist surrounds her like a gentle white fog. The pool is a silvery turquoise blue, shimmering in the shadowing light. I call out, "Hey, where's Davy? Are you guys going to stay in there all day?"

We hear giggling, and then we see Davy as he dives into the deeper part of the pool from the other side. After surfacing, he swims to a hidden corner, and we hear him slip out of the water to get dressed. Karla swims to the same corner, and soon both are coming out from around the large rocks hand in hand with grins on their happy faces.

Loren smiles back and says, "Well, it looks like you two have had fun; are you ready to leave now?"

Davy waves his hand and shouts out, "You two should have gone swimming. It was wonderful and quite refreshing."

I think he's right; a shower and a swim would have been nice. The sun is almost directly overhead and Morleck and the others will be here soon. "Maybe we'll have time later," I respond.

Within minutes, a rustling from the bushes behind us announces the arrival of our other friends. Morleck is carrying flowers and plants, and Kaylu and Dandi make a path to the water's edge to get a drink. Morleck approaches us and says, "This island is the largest treasure trove of exotic plants and herbs I have ever seen, but I am tired, and ready to go back to Soultraveler. Why don't you take Kaylu and Davy to explore the interior of the island? Baylor, Dandi, and I can go back to the boats with the girls. I'm sure they are explored out anyway." It is decided that Baylor will bring back a few supplies with Dandi's help and we will meet them both at the base of the huge mountain in the center of the island.

After saying our goodbyes, the three of us begin marching deep into the interior of the island paradise. It will be a while before we will reach the mountain, but since the day is warm and the breezes cool, it should be an enjoyable hike. As we reach the jungle part of the island, the going gets a little rougher than expected. Thick vines and thorny bushes block our way. It becomes a slow process getting through the thick foliage. I still see the tip of the mountain above the trees; the view of the mountain is the only directional marker we have. We have our swords, so we begin hacking through the ropy vines and bushes. If Baylor is going to find us, we will have to continue in the direction of the mountain.

I notice the sky beginning to cloud up, and the wind picking up a little also. Soon the sky looks threatening and is darkening quickly; we're in for a storm. Hoping to get through this jungle before the rains hits, we plow through as quickly as we can.

Morleck and the girls have already arrived at the boats and are in the midst of rowing back to Soultraveler with the crewmen when they notice the sudden clouds. As they finish packing up supplies, Baylor and Dandi turn the second boat over so that water won't fill it from the rain. Gathering the backpacks and some food, they head toward the direction of the mountain. Baylor feels a moment of doubt when he rethinks his decision to hand over his shield to Morleck to take back to the ship so that he could walk more comfortably with the supplies.

Kaylu, Davy, and I finally break through the jungle and reach the edge of a grassy plain. Except for one or two trees, the plain is covered in long grass and rolling hills. The walk isn't as hard, but it's difficult to see over the tall grass surrounding us; Kaylu can barely see in front of him because he's so short and the grass is so tall. The top of the mountain is still visible, so we keep going in that direction. After just a few paces on this plain, the rain starts. When the rain starts, it starts hard! Soon sheets of water driven by fierce winds make it difficult to trudge forward—we are soaked to the skin. The ground is quickly saturated and becomes like a bog; every step is an effort as our feet sink in the mud. The sky darkens, and the wind howls like banshees wailing and screaming. We hear whistles through the blades of grass. I wish we had gone back to the ship with the others; this definitely isn't fun.

Finally emerging from the tall grass, we find ourselves on top of a rolling hill. A few miles away lies the base of the mountain. A small pathway leads downward from the top of the grassy hill, and we start moving along it. The grass is no longer tall, but the three of us move quickly to reach the shelter of the mountains and the nearby woods.

Dandi and Baylor reach the jungle as the fierce force of the wind gets even stronger. Thunder claps and the sky grows dark. The jungles seem alive; vines swing in every direction, and branches with thorns whip across their bodies. Dandi's in front, and his large body acts like a shield for Baylor; he takes the bulk of the wind, rain, and slapping vines. Both try to keep their eyes on the large mountain that's disappearing in the darkness. Dandi, being the taller of the two, can still make out the darker mass of the top of the mountain, but Baylor can only see Dandi's backside and follows the best he can.

Dandi knows if he loses sight of the mountain, he can easily get turned around in the jungle and end up somewhere other than where they're supposed to be. The earth trembles as the force of the wind steps up.

Baylor wonders if maybe the storm will turn into a hurricane at the rate it's growing. Dandi has never experienced such ferocity in the weather; in his world, the weather is normally calm and pleasant. Even the rain is gentle; this is something he never experienced.

The ground shakes with every bang of thunder, and the wind increases to gale forces. The jungle becomes a nightmare. Every step, even for the little giant, is an effort. Baylor can barely stand as the wind rushes against him. He falls down every few steps, and each time, it is more difficult for him to stand back up, even with Dandi's help. Vines entangle them as they plunge deeper into the jungle—this jungle has surely come alive and is determined to stop them!

Finally, they have to stop; it's no use trying to go forward. The wind, rain, and the jungle together form a barrier even Dandi can't penetrate. The two find a ledge under an embankment where the rain and wind are partially blocked. Huddling down, they decide to wait out the storm rather than risk injury or getting lost. The ledge acts as a blind against the wind, but water runs over the rim like a small rushing waterfall. Both are helplessly stuck, and have to bear the wetness as best they can.

My two friends and I are not much better off.

We manage to reach the forestland below the mountain, but still have to contend with rushing wind and blasting rain. No matter where we look, we can't find shelter. Thunder cracks above us in the tall pines. Lightning could strike us any moment if we don't find cover. Running through the trees, Kaylu can't believe this type of weather exists. Thunder again shakes the ground, while lightning lights up the trees then hits the ground just a few feet from us. The wind howls and pushes

Kaylu off his feet. For him, this is a nightmare. I take his hand and pull him along as we run through the storm. Darkness closes in as we get closer to the mountain. Soon the only light comes from the repeated lightning which allows us to briefly see. I can only imagine what Soultraveler is going through; I hope they have a little protection from the cliffs around the cove where the ship is moored.

Davy yells and points ahead; a few feet from us is a semicircle of large boulders forming a barrier against the storm. We run to the boulders and find a small ledge we can crawl under. There's nothing else to do but wait the storm out. It's hard to believe it's still just early afternoon; the sky is almost black with storm clouds, and instead of the balmy warm air and sunshine, it's cold and wet. The horrific storm continues to blow around us.

Loren and Karla watch the storm through a porthole in Hugh's cabin. The ship is battened down, and most everyone is inside. Waves fiercely crash against the ship as the winds carry the water over the lower deck. The girls have to hold tight to prevent themselves from being thrown about the cabin. The ship pitches back and forth like a toy as lightning cracks, bursting open the sky. The roar of waves crashing against the ship even drowns out the thunder. The cliffs and reef afford some protection, but further out, the open waters create giant waves that toss back and forth, then crash against the small cliffs that protect the cove.

Loren and Karla both stare in utter disbelief; they can't believe this is the same beautiful, gentle island they had played in just a short time ago. They wonder where Hugh and his crew are, and they hope they have somehow found shelter from this frightening storm. Surely no one could survive this battering without some sort of shelter?

As we sit under the ledge, I can't help but worry about Baylor and Dandi. I hope they haven't tried to find us in this storm; maybe they got back to Soultraveler? Watching the might of the storm break against the surrounding boulders, I think about some of the storms back home. Once we had a hurricane slam against the coast very close to where I lived. I remember seeing television clips of trees being lifted out from their roots, and cars being tossed around in the wind. I hope this storm won't reach that power.

It seems like hours before the storm starts slowing down. The rain still pours, but we are relieved that the wind is softening, the rain slowing, and the sky growing lighter; we lean out from the muddy little enclave that protected us and look about.

Bushes and small trees are scattered everywhere. Trails of water are running off small ridges. The grounds are muddy and pools of water dot the forest floor. I crawl from the protection of the boulders and wonder why I decided to go to the mountain in the first place. The sun gradually comes out, and the clouds are nearly gone. I want to get a fire going and dry off, but there's no dry firewood. Now would be a nice time to have some of the fire rocks we stored in our backpacks!

"Let's wait here, at least until we find out where Dandi and Baylor are. Davy, can you find an area a little dryer than this mud hole?" The boulders that surround us are protection from the wind, but they sit in an indented area where the water accumulates, making a muddy pool. Kaylu climbs to the top of the highest boulder and stretches to see if he can see Dandi and Baylor.

I take off me shirt and begin wringing it out when I hear Kaylu shouting. "There they are, coming over the ridge of the grass hill!" I'm relieved; just knowing they are safe takes some of the pressure off of me mind.

Running from the surrounding trees, Davy shouts, "I've found a great spot to camp; it's at the top of that little hill. It's flat with bushes and trees surrounding the entire area. It's almost already dry and the trees don't obscure the sun, so we might have some dry firewood by nightfall."

The three of us walk the short distance to the little hill and begin clearing out some of the windblown bushes and debris from the storm. In no time, we have a semi-dry area where we can build a fire. It isn't long before we hear Dandi climbing the little hill. Kaylu runs to the edge, waving his arms and calling to them. Dandi and Baylor are soaked and covered with mud, thorns, and bits of vine. We open the packs they brought, and soon have a small fire going from the fire rocks. We sit around the fire, warming up, and drying drenched clothes. Dandi and Baylor have already removed their shirts and are wringing them out and brushing off the debris and mud, trying to get their shirts as clean as possible. Everyone agrees with my plan to spend the night and head back to the ship in the morning.

We go to work to transform the area into a campground as best we can. There are enough supplies in the four backpacks to give everyone extra blankets. Baylor finds a lantern, some packets of food, and a few serving dishes. Davy finds some good size stones that he makes into a perfect fire ring. Adding some more fire rocks, soon we have a large fire burning. Fire rocks will only burn for several hours, so we gather some small kindling and put it by the fire to let dry for later.

As the sun slowly sets behind the mountain, the sky grows clear, and the smell of the burning fire combined with the wet pine trees is comforting.

After looking through the food supplies, Baylor begins to heat up some of the beans and meat the girls had stuffed in the packs. A pot of hot tea is already bubbling on the hot rocks. Blankets are doubled over so we have a comfortable place to sit.

Settling down in the twilight, we begin talking about the powerful storm and what happened to us while we were separated. Kaylu's excited; he loves the outdoors, and to him, this is great fun! Dandi, too, is relaxed. After we finish eating and the clothes are dry, one by one, each moves away from the fire to settle into his blanket and drift off to sleep.

Kaylu and I soon find ourselves alone by the fire. Kaylu's throwing little bits of wood into the fire, enjoying himself almost like a little kid on his first camping trip. Looking up at me, he asks, "Have you read from the book lately?"

Looking over at me little friend, I reach into me tunic and pull out The Way of the Traveler.

"No, I haven't, but thanks for reminding me." Kaylu moves closer, pulling his blanket over his legs. "Could you read aloud so I can listen?"

"I'll tell you what. I'll skim through the pages; you say when to stop, and that's where I'll read from." Kaylu smiles and watches closely as I turn the pages. Finally he says stop, and I begin reading.

The words come alive in the light of the campfire as I softly read, almost in a whisper, so I do not disturb the others.

> The way of the traveler is often riddled with tests and obstacles that are constantly put in his way. Some of these obstacles are placed to bar his way from moving forward, and some are there to test his strength, spiritual stamina, and discipline. Not all these barriers are placed by the same entities.

As I read the words aloud, I notice the words don't form in me mind as they normally did. Somehow reading aloud prevents the internal dialogue; I continue.

> During the normal expansion of the new traveler's awareness, he will meet individuals who come in the guise of teachers. Some of these teachers may not even be aware they are teaching; there are even times when a teacher does not understand why he is placed within the new traveler's orbit. However, this does not diminish the teacher's ability to impart wisdom to the neophyte, nor does it limit what may be shared; the neophyte understands he is listening to information that is directed by spirit, and in some cases has nothing to do with the person who is giving the wisdom.

> A true traveler never allows himself to become attached to the teacher. The neophyte traveler is only concerned with the words that are spoken and the examples the teacher may give. Because spirit is directing the teacher's words, a teacher is placed at the right time and the right place for causing certain events or sharing certain wisdom.

> In almost all cases, the traveler will already be at the threshold of understanding, so when a teacher appears, it is to act on behalf of spirit to bring about appropriate opportunities or bring relevant ideas to the new traveler's attention. A true traveler will thus absorb and understand the teachings that are transferred almost effortlessly.

A true teacher exists and works at many different levels of awareness. For example, a student traveler may have an experience with a teacher at the ordinary human level of awareness only to later have an experience with the same teacher at a psychic level or dream level, and sometimes even up in spiritual planes.

In all cases, it is the traveler's faith and belief in the teacher that allows the teacher to teach the student at every level of awareness. Someone in the dream state may meet a teacher and have a friendly and complete conversation with him, and then later meet the same teacher in the physical world and find that the teacher has no recollection of the dream teaching or even recognize the student.

Reading this book is an example of spirit using written words as the teacher in an alternate vehicle to communicate with the student. Spirit does not limit itself to restrictive forms or bodies in teaching Soul the ways of the Creator. A teacher can be a child or an old man sitting under a tree, or even this book. Spirit uses nature, music, society, laws, stories, poetry, song, and thousands of other expressions to reach Soul when it is ready. You who read The Way of the Traveler may be teaching those who are your companions, family, and co-workers and vice versa. The Creator never limits itself in its ways of communication or the conditions. The Creator can reach deep down to the bowels of hell or up to the highest heavens to touch those who need uplifting, which in reality, is all life.

I close the little book and look over at Kaylu. "Well, what do you think?" Kaylu smiles.

Taking a stick, he draws something in the dirt by the fire. Without looking up, he says, "It seems I'm your teacher at times, and now you are my teacher. I wonder when it will become my turn again." He stands and gives me a hug around the neck. "I am going to sleep now. Thank you for reading to me."

I'm left alone, thinking how odd life is.

This adventure is moving me into areas I never would have imagined or created with me mind. But in reality, that's exactly what I have done. It seems as if I'm traveling in a circle, going through experience after experience, and then coming back to where I started, only to set out again on the same path, but somehow each time it's different. This difference becomes clear as Soul perceives its life experiences each time with a deeper awareness. After completing the previous circle, hopefully I have grown. If Soul goes through similar experiences as before, then it must see them from an expanded viewpoint, and therefore react differently. The reaction determines the next step in me training in this never-ending circle of life. I wonder; when will I finally get off this wheel and begin to experience something beyond it?

Gathering up some of the wood to feed the fire, I look around at me sleeping friends. The camp is surrounded by tall pines with a view of the starry sky directly above. Smells of pine and smoke fill me senses. All's quiet except the crackling fire. I start thinking of the storm we came through today.

Fighting our way through the storm was a striking parallel to the battle I've already fought and am still fighting within myself. Then there's the island's meadow. Why does it remind me so much of the meadow back home? I've never been here before, but somehow it all seems like a distant memory.

Looking deeply into the fire, I feel a sense of expectation—as if something is about to occur, something I have waited for all me life. This journey has shown me unexpected revelations that have shattered my normal patterns of thought. Events leading up to this moment are like an unfathomable story, but I know this is real, so very real, in fact, that everything else in my entire life seems unreal in comparison. All time, space, the Earth, home, and even my family are sometimes like a dream.

My thoughts continue to wander, when suddenly, I have a prickly feeling of being watched. I take a deep breath; something in the trees moved!

Maybe it's a trick of the campfire or the deep shadows surrounding me, but my intuition says otherwise. Something or someone is just beyond the line of pines that encircle our camp. My vision adjusts to the darkness; a figure fades in and out of the shadows.

Reaching slowly over my shoulder to grip my sword, my breathing becomes shallow, my body tenses, and my senses become alert. I call out in a half whisper, "Who's there?"

For a moment, all is quiet...then a figure moves from the darkness into the glow of the firelight. The shadowy figure speaks: "Release your sword, Hugh; I am a friend. There is no reason to fear—I will not harm you."

Standing above the campfire, I peer closely into the dark...for a brief moment, it seems as if time is standing still.

A robed figure emerges from the pines and comes closer. I can barely make out his features, but he's tall, and has dark hair except for a few streaks of silver on the sides. His hair is shoulder length, and is brushed back to reveal a strong face. He doesn't appear particularly handsome, but he isn't plain either. In fact, I know that there's nothing plain about this man.

He carries himself with grace and spiritual nobility, a quality that I have come to recognize.

His voice is strong but gentle. He carries a staff in his left hand, and wears a dark blue robe with a rope tied around his waist. The robe falls just below his knees; the material might be wool, but I notice that it also has a strange shimmer as he moves closer to the fire. He wears sandals that lace up around his ankles, and there's a hood laid back over his shoulders. A shadow of a light beard barely shows against his brown skin. The man looks to be in his middle forties, but it's hard to tell. The most remarkable thing about his appearance is his flashing gray eyes, sparkling in the glow of the campfire.

The robed figure looks around the camp area. His heavy black brows contrast sharply with his eyes, giving him a look of power; however, it's more than just power that he radiates. There's a confidence, wisdom, and strength of presence that normal men hardly ever possess.

His eyes take in the surrounding area, and his gaze stops when he looks at me. A smile spreads across his strong square face. Perfect white teeth and narrow lips accent his smile even more. I gaze into those flashing eyes made even brighter as the firelight exposes them more deeply. The man speaks again.

"Release your sword, Hugh; I am a friend. There is no reason to fear—I will not harm you. I am Shakti...I am here to help you."

CHAPTER 37 ~ THE MIND OF GOD

The hospital's quiet in the early morning. Clark and Melody just arrived. Both are standing on opposite sides of Ann's bed, watching. Numerous tubes protrude from Ann's body.

Seeing her mother kept alive by devices and machines creates dismal feelings deep inside for Melody, but what's even more dismal is seeing Ann's eyes wide open, staring into emptiness. Her frozen features reflect the grotesque emotionlessness of her condition.

In the courtroom, it was announced she opened her eyes, thus helping to change the court's decision in Clark's favor. Nevertheless, to those who love her, to those who sit with her day after day, Ann's eyes are a window to her nightmare. Sometimes tears slowly trickle from her staring eyes; sometimes they close.

Even though her eyes open at different times, nothing has really changed. She's still locked in the prison of her mind with deep shadows reflecting a death mask upon her face.

Melody wants her mom to wake up so much! She always tries to feel a response when she holds her hand and brushes her hair. Most of the bandages are gone now, so Ann seems normal, except that she lies dressed in a hospital gown, accompanied by the constant beeping and gasping sounds of support equipment, constant reminders that she isn't really there. Her body's there, and signs of life can be detected, but the woman, the wife, and the mother is gone: locked away someplace far away.

Clark tries to control his emotions, but even after all he has learned, he knows that he can't be completely calm when he's with Annie and Hugh. It seems every time he and Melody visit them, both are shrinking away more and more. Dark shadows under Hugh's eyes and the white pallor of his skin seem to confirm that this deathly stillness reflects his grief. Neither Clark or Melody or even the medical staff, can understand why Hugh remains in a coma. All their medical experience combined cannot explain the condition of this little boy; his injuries are healed, but still he sleeps, still he hangs on somehow. Perhaps it is his youth that keeps him alive; perhaps his youth, combined with his family's love, feed him the energy he needs to keep going.

Both Clark and Melody know the secret. Both know that somewhere, deep in another reality, Hugh is searching for his mother. But knowing this still doesn't lessen their fear and sorrow. Holding Annie's hand, Clark hopes in some small way to feel her life force or perhaps to see where she is, but even though he tries the spiritual techniques he's learned, he can't detect even a tiny amount of consciousness coming from either of them. Melody's just about to take Hugh's hand when the door opens.

Brandon walks in, and he says softly, "I'm not disturbing you, am I?"

Clark turn's his eyes away from his wife and replies, "Of course not, we just got here a few minutes ago ourselves." He stands up to shake his friend's hand. With a puzzled look on his face, he asks why he's here.

Brandon walks over to Annie's bed and then says, "This is the first time I've seen them, Clark." He stands for a minute looking at the woman he so desperately defended. "She's as beautiful as you said." Reaching out, he strokes Ann's face; her unblinking eyes stare at the ceiling. Desperation and sadness hang like a cloud in the room. Brandon bends forward, looking deeply into her eyes. A tear forms and trickles down Ann's face; for the first time, Brandon's heart feels the fear and pain this woman and her family are going through. Up to this point, he has felt sympathy, concern, and sadness; now as he stares into her eyes, he feels himself being drawn into the cycle of energy and pain in this family. He now knows and feels the horrible darkness that Clark, Melody, Ann, and Hugh are living in. His hand trembles as he wipes her tear away. He turns and looking down at Hugh, he asks, "Can I sit with him for a while?"

Clark sits back down with Annie, and looking at Hugh for a few seconds, he responds, "Of course, take all the time you want."

As Brandon approaches the little boy, something happens; a surge of energy that can best be described as warmth penetrates his being. He stops for a second to steady himself. What's going on? He takes another step toward the little boy, and he can't help himself. Never before has he felt such a powerful rush of emotion surging through his body; a lump forms in his throat, and tears moisten his eyes. Staring down at Hugh, Brandon wonders how this can be the same boy he saw around the campfire in the previous night's dream. The child before him looks like death has taken him already. But Hugh's physical appearance doesn't fool him; he feels the power, and even more, the love. Love on so many levels emanates from this frail little child. Controlling himself somewhat, he whispers, his voice cracking as he tries to speak. "My God, the love—it's so powerful."

Melody looks up. "You feel it, too?"

Pulling up a chair, Brandon sits beside Melody and takes Hugh's small hand in his. Melody watches closely as the elderly man closes his eyes and becomes quiet. Softly, he begins to chant Hugh's name. Massive waves of energy immediately form a soft light within his inner vision; the power is coming from Hugh. This realization gives him an even warmer feeling throughout his body. As he continues the chant, he concentrates on listening, and slowly, gently, his voice merges with the Sound Current. Although distant, the inner sound comes closer as he continues to chant.

Taking several deep breaths, he calms himself and again chants the word HU...this time longer and deeper. His head bowed, he continues softly chanting; his dream from the night before comes to his thoughts. He remembers the entire dream.

Visualizing the older version of Hugh around the low campfire, he focuses on Hugh within the light. As he stares, he remembers an ancient Tibetan exercise used for reaching those who have passed to the other side. Still holding Hugh's hand, he reaches up with his other hand and places his forefinger and thumb gently against his closed eyes until he feels a slight pressure; he watches a soft light swim and churn deep inside. The light grows brighter as gentle waves of light form within his inner vision.

He continues chanting HU. At first, the light looks like hundreds of small lightning bolts bursting within his mind; then the bolts coalesce to form a round light directly in the center of his vision. Patterns of intense yellow and white light blend in and out, forming a pattern similar to a Mandala.

Easing a little of the pressure with his thumb and forefinger, he relaxes. The light grows and expands, getting brighter as it enlarges; concentrating on the pattern, he looks directly into the growing light and sees a black pinhole emerging in the center.

Keeping his attention focused, the light shifts, changing from a perfect circle to the shape of an eye, the dark pinhole expands in the center, like the pupil of an eye, except it's totally black. Drawing all his attention to the light, he removes his hand from his eyes.

The effect is brilliant; the light explodes!

Swift as thought, doors previously hidden within the shadows of his mind fling open. Wisdom of his true self slowly flows.

These shadowy doors exist in all humankind; once man chooses to enter the light, the shadow doors fade. This ultimately leads to the discovery of the secrets of Soul. Some doors are more difficult to open than others. Some are false realities controlled by one's own unknown psychic powers, or what some call magic.

These doors of the mind share one common denominator; eventually, they all lead to experiences required for growth. Brandon watches the light within merge as sound reverberates through his entire being.

He feels something within changing.

A sucking sensation moves him deeper into the light. The doors fade, and Brandon feels himself slipping away. He leaves his thoughts. He leaves the hospital and little girl sitting next to him. Brandon then leaves his body, and then he leaves his very humanity.

Staying calm and still concentrating on the dark spot in the center of the light, he hears a clear, high-pitched ringing in his inner ear. He focuses and keeps his attention on the light and the sound. Like a clear breeze that is blowing sharp as a whistle, the sound penetrates the light. As it does, it changes to the clear shrill signal note of a flute. The black hole expands further, enveloping his consciousness. He again feels a shift—like a pause—in reality. Then almost undetectably, he finds himself standing in a pine grove in the darkness of night.

Remaining calm, he looks about.

The young man from his dream is poised over a campfire with his hand on the hilt of his sword staring into the trees. Awareness again fills Brandon's mind. The boy is Hugh! But now he is no longer just Brandon. The true self blends and merges deeper within his mind; Brandon allows himself to become that which he really is.

Calming himself once more, he takes a few steps forward into the glow of the campfire. Then, without hesitation, he speaks. "Release your sword, Hugh, I am a friend; there's no reason to fear. I will not harm you." Brandon gazes intently into Hugh's eyes. "I am Shakti...I am here to help you."

Hugh pauses, stares for few seconds, and then says, "H-how can that be? No one knows we're here, or that we were even coming here."

Shakti/Brandon slightly smiles and replies, "I have always known of your coming, but let us sit...I will explain my purpose and pass on to you information that is needed in order for you to proceed."

Hugh hesitates a moment, then he decides to allow Shakti to speak.

Lowering my hand from the hilt of me sword, I gesture for Shakti to sit. I cautiously squat by the fire, ready for something. What? I don't know, but something. Shakti sits directly across from me in a cross-legged tailor fashion. Laying his staff down beside him, he picks up a pine branch lying next to the fire, and begins peeling off small twigs from the branch. He gazes into the fire for a few moments as if thinking about what he's going to say.

Finally, I speak up. "Would you like some bread or cheese? We haven't much, but what we have we can share." Shakti smiles, looks up and says, "I am not here to eat your food, Hugh, but to give you food. The food I offer is not for your stomach, but for your heart and mind; it can even feed the Soul!" I gaze into the man's face, then I make eye contact; a rush of joy explodes within me.

Shakti smiles. He, too, knows the joyous feeling rushing through me blood. Shakti speaks again. "You see, my friend, you already have the appetite and hunger for more of my food." Brushing the dirt away in of front of him with his stick, he continues. "I am here at your request, even though you are not aware of having asked me directly. The wisdom I pass on to you will help take you into the Mountain of Light. There you will gather additional experience that will assist you in completing your task. Are you ready to listen and weigh my words? If so, I will proceed."

I'm silent for a moment, and then I nod. Shakti puts down the pine branch and begins to speak, his words flowing effortlessly, filling the silence of the night.

"There are countless kingdoms within the mind of the Creator; within these mysterious realms, lie each of our own personal worlds. Entities exist in these kingdoms in a way mankind cannot comprehend. Their existence is nothing we as humans relate to as the meaning of life. Not all of these entities are here for our good, but know this! These entities cannot do anything harmful to humankind as long as we not partake of their dark existence. However, if allowed, they can and will use the senses and passions of man's mind to distort and capture him. They do this through humankind's own willingness.

"As long as we have a mind and body, we are not safe from these creatures; they are always at work, constantly searching for those among us they can use by exploiting attachments, fears, and the desire for power. This is their means of survival, and so they can and will manipulate and turn humanity against itself in every way imaginable if allowed."

"It is known by the Travelers that humans in their natural state as Soul have more kingdoms within themselves than all other life forms. These kingdoms are also known as states of consciousness or levels of awareness. These kingdoms are the reason these entities constantly seek to entrap humankind."

I interrupt. "I have encountered some of these entities in the past, especially when I was in the Dark Cave. Why do they attack us so viciously?"

Shakti stares into me face and smiles. He flicks one eyebrow upward, and then says. "They attack the human consciousness because their very existence depends on how deeply they can attach themselves to the psyche of man. Man's psychic energy to them is like food to a starving man; they survive by capturing the inner kingdoms of those humans who are weakest and at their most vulnerable state. However, they cannot touch those who have surrendered to the higher self, or what you call Soul.

"For this reason, and this reason alone, you as a Spiritual Traveler must commit yourself fully to something higher, something greater such as the Creator itself. To understand what this means you must understand something else first, something that few people ever realize."

The Traveler picks up his stick and pokes at the fire again, and then leaning over, he looks deeply into me eyes and says with his voice reverberating like an echo in me mind, "When the masses of humanity think of a Spiritual Traveler, they think of attributes that have very little to do with the actual act of being one.

"Man tends to conceive of the Traveler as a man who has reached the spiritual heights of God. He believes these Travelers can create without effort the mystical experience of God. To compound this belief, they think the Travelers can do this without any effort or cost. Even if this were true—which it is not— these people rarely stop to consider the real cost the Travelers pay to become enlightened in the first place.

"The spiritual giants, the great Travelers—those who are still remembered, such as Buddha, Lord Krishna, Rumi, Lao Tzu, Jesus, Apollonius, and others—didn't involve themselves in the great science of the Light and Sound for the benefit of personal rewards. It wasn't the fame, the wealth or power that carried them down through their long journey to what they finally became. It was the experience itself: that wonderful thing that sets them apart from humankind and leaves them alone as they absorb themselves in the art and science of creation."

The wind stirs slightly from out of the darkness, momentarily brightening the coals of the low-burning fire. The Traveler's voice doesn't change, yet I feel Shakti's words gently penetrate from within echoing from a faraway place, somewhere deep within the deepest part of Soul.

The voice continues. "It is now of utmost importance that you gain some understanding of the price one pays to become the Spiritual Traveler. To become what is a true Traveler, the cost is everything! All we have become is what one must give so that they will learn; the greatest cost of all is the great loneliness."

"Loneliness?" I exclaim with surprise. "How can one be lonely with the great freedom and love that I thought was part of being a Traveler?"

Shakti pauses for a moment, and then replies, "Humankind will at some point learn that no matter how close we may become to our fellow humans, ultimately we must live alone within ourselves.

"Even you, Hugh, will at some time pay the ultimate price; when you do, you will then understand this great loneliness, for it will be your only companion while you journey the long road home."

Shakti pauses a few seconds while looking up at the starry sky, and then he says, "The Spiritual Traveler feels this loneliness even more than those who follow behind him. He becomes like a recluse who withdraws into himself so that he may be alone with nothing: nothing but that which lies beyond illusion. Have you ever wondered why someone would do that?"

Shakti looks intently at me; I remain silent. Turning his face upwards, the firelight accentuates his serene features. He then says, "It is the love! It is the glorious love and freedom of spirit that picks him up and carries Soul to its own paradise. This freedom and love instill in us a desire to rise above the mundane life of humanity and all other things. We all strive for it, but in different ways and at different levels. Some create it from their families; others, from their work, and even more from their passions. Then there are those who give their entire life over to the Creator, and from their surrender, a great loneliness comes into their lives, for they who serve the Creator at some point must depart from the average person. They are known as the Spiritual Travelers.

"That which the Traveler loves most leaves him no room for the things of humankind, so we become different. The true Traveler is apart from man's world—we are within it, but apart from it—most of us, at least." Shakti again leans over slightly, looking at me with fierce and blazing eyes. Then lowering his voice, and with words like daggers penetrating me very Soul, he asks, "Do you feel that it is worth it?"

Is it right or even fair that I should leave behind all the ordinary responsibilities and human experiences in order to remember who I truly am? Without giving me time to answer, he answers for me. "For the most part...the answer is yes."

Shakti sits back and continues. "Nonetheless, because we exist in a mind and a body, which we possess until we translate, the memories and hunger of what we had and lost never leave us. Instead, they leave a lingering wish and attachment. It is these attachments the dark powers try to exploit. The lower powers and passions are like the hound that hungers when it is on the scent of the hare. We, the Travelers, in a sense are similar, except our hunger is not for possessions, passion or power, but for the Creator; so we become the 'Hounds of Heaven.'"

The Traveler looks away from me, shifting his gaze to the fire for a moment, then turning back to me, he continues, "Even you, young sir, know what these attachments are. You know this from your many lives in the lower worlds."

The Traveler pauses again. I look away from those intense gray eyes that seem to penetrate to me Soul; Shakti stares deeply into the fire thinking of his next words, and then he says, "Remember this, Hugh. The dark powers always promise that you shall have greater pleasure, greater riches and more power. From these false promises, man turns against his brother, family, and his fellow man, but even more than this, he turns against himself. These promises are the mind's deception to the Soul. Even with the greatest of Travelers, this hunger for what we have given up becomes the price we have to pay. This hunger lingers as long as we remain a part of humankind; it becomes the window of darkness from where the hands of desire may enter, and it can happen even to the best of us.

"Those closest to the Creator, those who already possess such great power and wisdom—to them the strongest of temptations come. Even though they already have much in the form of wisdom, power, and love, the mind and body still desires more. Their battle is constant. This is why some cannot make a truly great Traveler, for they are bound too deeply to the world outside of themselves, bound by worldly attachments that exist within them." The robed figure again looks up to the sky and then turns his gaze back to the fire.

Quiet again for a few moments, he lifts his eyes and looks into mine and continues. "I have to admit, it is within my own kingdoms I am weakest, for even my kingdoms are sometimes overshadowed by the mind and senses that exist within my temple of flesh. To others, it seems I've won my freedom. They never know about the never-ending battle that I must constantly endure to recapture the essence of the Creator and allow it to direct me in my journey."

The Traveler isn't looking at me anymore; he's staring down at the fire, hesitating. It seems he's thinking about his own life and the many battles he has had to endure. Even though his words are sharp and concise, it's almost as if he considers it petty to waste words that don't take the listener to the true meaning of what he's saying.

As I watch Shakti, I realize what he is feeling. I understand how a true Traveler is never a stranger to failure—perhaps he knows that sometimes the words he gives are even greater than the man who speaks them. The more I listen, the more my mind opens up.

From this opening, I ask questions. "Traveler, what is the difference between my will and the Creator's will?"

Shakti chuckles good-naturedly, and then says, "When you say, 'I do this or that in God's name,' you do not realize you are trying to force your own will on the Creator. Or when you say 'let God's will be done,' what you are really doing is telling the Creator to actually let your will be the power. Why? Simply because the Creator has no will, because it has no desire! What you are really saying is let your own desire be done. God has no will; it is always your own will, your own desire.

"Man cannot fathom a God who exists outside the realm of desire, but nevertheless it is true. The Creator will never say 'let my will be done'—this is in exact opposite of divine law. Man constantly confuses the nature of God with what he thinks is the desire of God. God only gives, it never wants or takes, and therefore the concept of the will cannot exist in the true Father and Creator. If something or someone wills something to happen, then it is a want or desire that they are using to accomplish their supposed needs."

I stare at the embers of the fire, trying to grasp this unsettling revelation. I then ask, "Then what is my will?"

Shakti pauses a moment.

Again he is looking deeply into the fire. He then says without hesitation, "Desire only! Without desire, there is no will. Actually, in a spiritual sense, man seeking divine truth should use his will only once: when he desires freedom. When man says, 'I want freedom. I want to be free;' this becomes what the travelers call divine will. Use the will only for this purpose; using the will or desire for freedom will fulfill your purpose and ultimately form within you the Nature of God. The Nature of God does not ask, nor plead or assume. The Nature of God just is! The fallacy that man has free will or free choice is actually true, but only in the lower realms of the mind. Soul of itself does not need what you know as free will, for it is created from a desireless condition called love. Some use the term 'Just Be' to describe this pure condition of the true self. Do not forget, Hugh, for the true God Seeker, it is of no use using your will to chase this thing and that; love, power, wisdom, and true freedom only come from within your own kingdom, which already exists inside of you."

I throw a stick on the fire; sparks explode upward, disappearing into the darkness. I'm thinking to myself how this man does not hold back. His answers are bold and daring—somewhat unnerving—but I feel truth and power within his words, so I ask, "What is it that pushes us to want freedom? Is this not the will?"

"Actually, young friend, in its highest sense, it is the accumulation of love and your own divine nature. This love is accumulated by right thoughts and right action, which builds your capacity to give even more love. When this love builds to a certain level within your being, it begins to express itself by letting free your own divine nature; this divine nature yearns for freedom from the human consciousness, which exists only in the lower kingdoms, and is opposite to Soul's true nature. This divine nature is what mankind calls divine will. Its purpose is to fulfill its one sole mission: for Soul to desire the Creator or freedom in such a way that nothing else matters. If you miss it in one life, then you carry over to the next life, until you have built this mountain of love…"

I reflect for a moment and then ask, "But isn't this love or right action involved with time and emotions, and therefore created from the mind?"

Shakti looks again into the fire, pausing for a moment before replying. "Yes, but since you possess a mind that is still in control of your reality, it is the only way this can be explained to you. When you cross over into the beyond, then others or the direct experience itself will speak to you in a different form. For now, accept the truth in the form it is given, for this truth is designed for the higher mind, and is one of the keys that allows Soul to escape the mind's limitations."

I look over at me friends who are sleeping a short distance away. I wonder why they are here with me. What compels them to endure the danger and hardships? They know something dark and unknown is about to engulf their lives, but still they stay with me. I turn back to Shakti and ask, "Who is journeying to freedom?"

The God Man smiles; a large grin shows nearly perfect teeth. He replies, "Those who strive for freedom are the ones who are already free. They need only to let go of the concept that they are separate from the Creator. You must understand Hugh...that you return to what you always were. This journey will take you home if you allow it; as a Traveler I will not push you to any new kind of dimension, for you cannot become or be what you really are by the choices of others. You have to be that which you truly already are in the true waking state, which is where you now exist; there is no difference between man and all life, be it animals, fish, energy or even rocks. All are of the total being. This waking state is the jumping off point where Soul begins its conscious journey through the Mind of God!'"

Me legs are getting sore squatting like I am, so I push down with my hands shifting me position so I'm sitting on the ground comfortably. Shakti picks up a branch again, using it to enhance his gestures as he continues speaking.

"Listen carefully, for now we are going into profound truths that exist deep within each man and woman; these truths are not for the masses." The traveler stirs the fire with his branch, then leaning over as sparks float upward, he gazes deeply into the firelight. There is a still silence as he stares. Then he says, "Hugh, do you understand that most of the human race is asleep?" Shakti again sits back, but continues to stare into the fire; pulling his robe tighter around him, he continues. "For those who are awakening, freedom becomes their hunger. When you or others aspire to freedom, the hunger subsides; the whole cosmos then joins with you. By keeping free of any thoughts except freedom, you are helping the world to wake up. When your world is saturated with wars, poverty, disease, and greed, then the masses will cry for peace. Whether they are aware of it or not, all are actually already crying and yearning for that freedom which is the key to becoming what they already are. Most of the world still sleeps, all dreaming. When they start awakening—as you are—they discover duality is removed. It is replaced with the wisdom of unity. Remember! Duality exists only in dreaming, when you wake up nothing exists outside your true self; this is total freedom. Freedom is the essence of the Creator. Spiritual freedom allows you to look into and understand 'The Mind of God.'"

I keep getting lost in what he's saying. I have to say something. "What do you mean, the 'Mind of God,' what is that?"

"The Mind of God is the entire existence that abides in the reality of time, matter, energy, and space. It is composed of the energy and power of unlimited suns and stars, endless dimensions, galaxies, gravity, time, black holes, and nebulae. All of these are only mechanical, working functions of this One Mind. When you look into the universe, you are looking into the Mind of God. When you look into your lover's eyes, you are looking into the Mind of God. Look into a dying face, and you will see the Mind of God. Every flower and every life form is moving and acting as functional parts of this omnipotent mind that creates life as we know it.

"Human emotions and feelings animate your kind; these are also functional parts of God's Mind, for they are the connecting fibers that weave our existence into a divine journey. Our journey is mapped in such a way that it ultimately leads to the simplest of understandings. Without emotions, we would be on a worthless journey. Emotions are for humankind to explore their five senses and to work side by side with the two divine senses: inner sight and sound. Disasters, illnesses, wars, joy, happiness, and sadness create emotions that are all a part of the great transformation."

"Great transformation?"

Shakti reaches out and grasps the staff lying by his side and then answers. "It comes in many ways, mostly undetected, but make no mistakes about it, my young friend: it is coming. This transformation is taking the human consciousness from just five-sensory perception to multisensory perception; it is what all mankind is striving for."

I'm totally focused on what Shakti is saying, and again I interrupt to ask, "What does this mean? I mean, for me and my family?"

"It means everything, my young friend. Everything that you see and experience, including all life, is in a scope of immensity that can't be described. It means that your ability to experience life is going to be far beyond anything that you have ever imagined. All life looks into the Mind of God and wonders, but as each Soul wonders, they at the same time see the Mind of God in their own way.

"When you look at a serene scene of nature, you are looking into the divine Mind. When you stare at a cataclysmic volcano erupting, you are seeing the Mind of God. When you see the universe in all its glory, you are looking deeper into the beauty and mechanics of the Mind of God...Look deeply, young Traveler, for within your own mind, you can perceive a replica of divine Mind: only in miniature. Your mind is created from the same map and materials that the Supreme Creator created the Mind of God with. Using divine Mind, the Creator has come into these lower worlds with its children. It has always been here, connected to each of us through a divine science called the 'Light and Sound' or simply love.

"The Mind of God has endless functions. One that is a most important function to you and to mankind is that it adheres to human thoughts and feelings; these two human traits are intricately connected to divine Mind, and they send messages to its center constantly. So man has inherited his Father's power, but the problem is that man fails to understand its real use and purpose.

"Many names have been given to this divine Mind—far too many to mention here. At no time can man turn away from the Mind of God, for all is a part of the Supreme Creator's greatest gift to all life. When man begins the transformation into a God-Man, his emotions will carry him only so far, and then he must embrace his higher senses, the spiritual ones. When this happens, then man relies on intuition to guide him deeper into divine Mind. If you complete your journey, your transformation will be an example for mankind to emulate. This transformation is not far off in the future; it is beginning to appear even now in your world. This change will be the most profound and important change in mankind since the beginning of human consciousness; you, my young traveler, will be one of many torch bearers.

"In this time of transition, old ways will drop away as they are doing now with you. Mankind will begin to align their spiritual selves with their personality. This all begins with the power of intention. When you use the power of intention with the mind, the universe will assist in every way to bring about this remarkable change. Your intent is powered by choices; these choices give you the opportunity to act and either create with fear, or create with love. For now, Hugh, you need to know and understand that this instant, this moment, this here and now, is outside the concepts of time. By keeping your attention on 'Now,' questions disappear. 'Here and Now' is your true home, your final abode, where nothing appears and nothing touches it. The wisdom of the unknown is empty, nothing is there; no wants, no needs, and no desires. This is peace; this is your own self. You do not have to attain the transformation, or achieve it or acquire it by methods whatsoever described by either Man, Preachers, Priests, Rabbis, Mahdis or even Gods. No effort is needed to reach this transformation and freedom; for it is the easiest of all to know who you are. You don't need to travel to find freedom, for you are already free."

The Traveler pauses, the silence grows deeper, and the fire burns low, throwing out an orange glaze across me and the traveler's features, transforming our faces. Shakti pulls his hood up from around his shoulders and covers himself. Standing up, he looks to the stars and raises his arm, pointing outward toward the sky, then he looks at me and says, "If you see the mountain, then you will know your journey's end."

I look upward into darkness where the traveler is pointing; within the starlight the black sky reveals a tremendous mountain in the distance. Above the pines, against the starry sky, I see my destination.

Shakti picks up his staff and turning halfway as if to go, he turns back and says, "You must go alone, Hugh; no one can do it for you. The way is not a beaten track where someone else can lead. You do not need any help and there is no path. All worn and beaten paths are only reflections of past rules and fears. Do away with all paths and have no one lead, for all paths are merely the imagination of your past and future; remove the past and future, and you will be there. I again speak in riddles, but to the true seeker, there are no riddles for all things point to truth and freedom. Humankind is like the fishes in the river who cry they are thirsty. Awake! And accept the water that feeds the real self. Soul exists in an ocean which is the Mind of God. Awake! Accept my water that feeds Soul! The journey exists in your mind, so it is only fitting you see what the mind has carried with you for eons, life after life after life. Tradition prescribes that to discard the ego, you must obey the teacher.

"Nevertheless, know this! The teacher is none other than your own true self. It's often said you have to obey that which you are seeking, however, a true teacher does not expect obedience from anybody. Whatever you perceive the teacher to be, the mind will create that form for you. Soul and man need a symbol to focus on; this symbol can be anything that exhibits divine attributes. The source or Creator is too fathomless for the mind to comprehend, and Soul of itself needs to gradually grasp the reality of the Creator. Soul in its purest form has the light of a hundred suns flowing from it. But even in this form it is pale to the actual experience of what the Creator's reality exists as."

"My mind is still having a hard time understanding Shakti's words about teachers," I say, shaking my head.

Shakti steps back to the fire and squats down on bended knee; he leans a little on his staff and says, "Because most of humankind is not brave or bold enough to accept that they are the true self, the Creator or even the teacher. Soul compensates for the mind's lack of faith and experience by taking on the image or form you decide is acceptable…Soul takes your highest ideals of truth or the highest ideal of a teacher and manifests an image within yourself, for if you think of an ideal or truth concerning Soul or the Creator, then Soul will conform to that ideal; this is done so as not to disrupt your concepts until you are ready for a higher and truer concept. When you finally drop all concepts, then the self emerges as who you always were. The teacher is gone; in its place is you."

Leaning heavily on his staff, Shakti stands and takes a few steps backward. He raises his hand in farewell and says, "The next step in your journey, Hugh, is one of exploration. You will discover the secret of temptation within the Mountain of Light. Keep the wisdom you have received close to your heart, for it will form an attitude that will expand your awareness and allow you to enter this most holy domain. If you falter, if you fear or succumb to temptation, or lose control in any way—then all is lost. Stay calm. Empty your mind of all thoughts and let the self or Soul take charge. Remember, my young friend, man thinks it is natural for him to think thoughts and then follow them through, but in reality thoughts are a byproduct of mind energy. It takes effort to create thoughts; you must learn to perceive reality effortlessly."

Shakti grows silent. The only sound is the crackling of the embers burning in the campfire. As I stare into the embers, I feel and hear a sound moving within, as if me blood is calling Soul to its source. I know that for me to succeed on this part of my journey, I have to leave my friends behind. When I leave my friends, I also have to leave my feelings, concepts, ideals, and me dearest values. To see truth, I have to leave my very mind behind me without remorse. I look up just in time to see the Traveler disappearing into the shadows of trees. I stare into the night, pondering the words of the robed stranger. Then leaning over to reach some dry wood for the fire, I notice the drawing Kaylu had etched out earlier with his stick.

My blood freezes as I recognize what Kaylu wrote:

Shakti

CHAPTER 38 ~ THE MOUNTAIN OF LIGHT

I stare at the word Kaylu wrote in the dirt.

How could he have known?

The name is clearly printed, yet I myself had never heard the name Shakti before this evening.

I want to waken Kaylu and ask him, but a nagging feeling keeps me from doing so. Instead, I start packing some gear in my backpack. Grabbing my cape from the pack, I attach it to my shoulders. It's late, and if I'm to do what has to be done, now is the time. I creep away silently from the dying campfire and me friends. What I have to do now is for me to do by myself. Half-running, half-walking, I fade into the darkness. The mountain Shakti pointed at looms ahead, beckoning me to come closer; I walk deeper into the night toward the great mountain.

Stars in the night sky are brilliant, and are getting brighter as I go deeper into the darkness. I have no idea where to go except toward the mountain, which if I thought it through, doesn't make a whole lot of sense. The mountain is so large, I can easily get lost at just the mountain base. The stars are brighter and more numerous once I'm away from the campfire; I easily make out the ground by starlight alone.

As I'm walking, I start thinking again about my entire journey, from the time I entered through the realm of mist to the last few moments with Shakti. So many things have happened: not only outside of me, but also within me own mind and Soul. This journey is like a book of many pages, which is still being written, and not by this new-found warrior part of me, but by who I really am: the little boy back in Bristol, the one who lives in a house on a small hill with his family. The boy who sometimes gets lost in swirls of events that threaten to obliterate who I was before the accident.

As I walk deeper into the darkness, I feel the child and not the warrior. It is like I have different parts to who I am, and each has a deep purpose in this adventure. So many things I have learned that are supposed to help me in this quest to find me mom; but in some ways, this knowledge seems to be stalling or hampering me from reaching her. Me mind is full of so many foreign and new ways of looking at life that I have to keep reminding myself of who I am, and why I'm here in the first place. If not, I might lose myself in the warrior self that I have created.

Loren has an alluring way of holding me close to her; not that it's bad, but it does have its distractions. Sex is something I used to think about back in Bristol, but it never occurred to me that I would experience it so soon. This warrior body enjoys all the pleasure of love, but Loren gives me something more. Closeness, love, trust, and friendship are not to be underrated. Still, as much as it is enjoyable, maybe it's distracting me from my ultimate goal. The little book Jotan gave me warns of allowing things outside of myself to hold my attention. Have I allowed the wonderful physical feelings and our emotional love to overwhelm me? Have I really let it all distract me? After all, isn't what I'm doing right now the effect of all I have experienced, including my relationship with Loren? Have I not developed a love for my friends also? Surely the way I feel for Kaylu and Dandi is a bond of love; are those bonds distracting me as well? There has to be a simpler explanation, and I think it has to do with being true to myself and not allowing the grown-up part of me, the warrior I've become, to carry me away in its fantasy of glory and adventure. I have become good at acting the part, but if I'm not careful, I will become the part; after all, in my own personal reality I'm still a ten-year-old boy, and something about being that boy contains the power to ultimately free me mum.

Walking deeper into the woods, these thoughts and more carry me into the silence of the night. A slight chill mixes with the scents of trees and plants; their freshness is a part of the quietness. I feel myself inexplicably drawn into a mystical reality as I move forward, almost as if in a dream. Reaching deep into my backpack, I feel for what I stored away at the beginning of this journey. I pull the little packet out and open the cloth, bringing out the now dried flowers from the meadow. Kaylu said that these flowers have the power to release memories of the past, so I close my eyes, gently press the dried flowers carefully to my nose and inhale the light aroma that remains.

Instantly, I am transported to my life before the accident.

I clearly see me with my family, with Cody, and my friend Billy just as if it is yesterday. I remember me school days and me friends Paul and Matt; Saturday mornings eating breakfast with the family while watching Dagwood and Blondie movies.

For a few brief moments, I'm there and savoring every detail—all the feelings and all the different things that make me the child I am. It's almost as if I'm watching a big screen TV within me mind.

While memories unfold, I become the image I'm watching. I'm home with me sister Melody; her cat Namo is on her lap; my Da' is reading a book; the whole family spends a quiet evening together.

True, it isn't as exciting as sailing the ocean on Soultraveler, but it leads to another kind of feeling, one that reminds me of who I really am and why I'm here at this very moment. I put the flowers back into me pack. I feel even more like the boy I was—so much so that this older body seems strange and foreign; the world around me slips into a dream as I move closer to the mountain.

The love for my family that I feel at this very moment brings about a tremendous flame of homesickness that erupts inside of me. The world I have created with Kaylu, Dandi, Loren, and Soultraveler, along with the teachers and experiences, is just that: it's something I created. No matter how I look at it, all of this is merely a byproduct of my mind, imagination, and emotions. What is its purpose? Is this getting me closer to me mum, and if so, how? I think for a moment, and then realize something that hadn't occurred to me before. Why is my mind reaching out? Why does it keep striving for answers that aren't important? I only have to accept who I really am and be happy with that; using this body and having my new friends to help are the tools I have been using to get to this point. I realize the circle is complete; I've come back to who I was when I started this journey, but this time something is different.

I see things more deeply, and I don't react like I did as the ten-year-old boy. The experiences I've had and the warrior person I am now are all part of the total awareness of me. This journey is a self-created pathway home that is being created from within; if I'm not careful, the new knowledge, warrior body and friends will in some way separate the child from me. Even the world back on earth is part of this self-created path to my true home, in trying to find Mom and get back home I'm finding freedom in accepting myself as that ten-year-old boy. From this moment on, I will use the tools around me with gratitude and I will respect them, but I have to remember that the tools are to help me find Mum without losing who I really am. It's like a game of hide and seek; losing myself in this adventure and then finding myself again, my new friends are all teaching me by being examples of things I need to learn.

Dandi offers common sense and strength, combined with love; this is a part of what is deep inside of me. The same applies to the unconditional love and courage Kaylu has shown. This, along with every teacher and even Loren—all are parts or expressions of my own expanding awareness. This changing consciousness is a part of Soul, a part of me!

I continue putting it together. The abilities, personality, and characteristics I need are constantly being shown through my friends and the experiences they are having and the ones I'm having.

Without courage, could I have withstood the onslaught of the cave dwellers? Without patience, discipline, and trust, could I have made it through the Dark Cave with all of its mind expansion energy affecting me? Without strength, could I have helped Dandi in the misty lake when it attempted to drag him down in anger and rage? Without Loren and her gentle but devoted love assisting in my growing maturity, could I have understood and trusted the love I am touching within?

The answer to all these is no.

All these events and more were all necessary to prepare me for what I still have to face. Nevertheless, with all of this, I now know I must face whatever lies ahead alone and as the boy I really am. The conversation with Shakti about not being afraid to accept yourself as the Creator now makes sense. How many times back in Bristol did I imagine having a body that was bigger, more muscular? How many times did I imagine myself as a hero carrying a sword and winning the beautiful girl?

How many times did I imagine myself on a great quest? Well, here I am, now living as my imagined, more interesting self. Still, the circumstances here are somewhat different, although the danger, the adventure, and the mystery are all here. I'm experiencing sad and frightening things, and at times these make me afraid of not only losing Mom, but my entire family as well; I continue walking toward the mountain while my mind still tries to figure it all out.

Kaylu told me in the very beginning that one appears in this world with the best body and mind so they can cope with whatever experiences he's about to encounter. I see myself not only as the Creator, but also I am a part of all the characters in this journey as well. However, more important than anything else is me remembering and realizing that being a ten-year-old boy is the best adventure of all.

With this expanded consciousness and adult responsibilities, me mind wants to figure out everything, but the awareness of my child-self catches the mind, stopping its wild figuring and allowing me to "just be."

I'm closing in on the base of the mountain.

The sky's dark; the starlight is intense and breathtaking. The stillness around me is as much a part of me as the trees and rocks; all are a part of me own awareness. The mountain reaches up into the darkness like a monolith, yet at the same time, it feels like the center of my Soul. Stars twinkle and shimmer in the mystical sky above the great mountain. I've no idea where to begin looking, or even what to look for. The mountain is so vast with steep sheer cliffs on three sides. As I get closer I see a crevice that snakes its way up the middle between two cliffs. Following a narrow path along the crevice the trail eventually breaks away and leads upward toward the center of the mountain. The climb is easy at first, but as I get higher the mountain begins to narrow, becoming steeper and more treacherous with every step. Looking down from this great height I see the entire island. In the distance the great ocean wraps itself around the shoreline; under the starlight I see Soultraveler sitting in the quiet cove waiting for our return.

The mountain trail is disappearing, forcing me to climb upward from one ledge to another, being forced to grasp any small roots or protruding ledges I find. The higher I climb, the harder it is to find hand- or footholds to support me; sometimes rocks slip as I grab for support to boost me upward. Looking down is dizzying. I begin to feel stupid for putting myself in this situation. My anger at my stupidity turns into a slow, creeping fear of whether I'm even going to survive. Looking down again, I realize I can't go backwards; the only choice is to move forward, which only takes me higher and deeper into the mountain's grasp.

Sweat trickles down my forehead. Inch by inch, I pull upward, my hands becoming raw from the sharp rock ledges cutting and tearing my skin. It seems like hours since I began this treacherous climb, but there's nowhere else to go but up. The cliff wall is so smooth that in some places it's like glass. Every minuscule ledge crumbles when I grab it; still, I climb.

The faint light of dawn spreads gray light over the ocean below. Stars disappear one by one and still I climb. Pressing against the wall of the mountain, my fingers are constantly searching for some kind of hold to gain another inch or the next foot.

I find a small ledge extending from the wall about two inches. I boost myself up on the small lip of rock and pull upward again, only briefly glancing down; the jungle's a carpet of green, and any details are invisible.

As the sun rises above the horizon, a deep red blanket spreads over the ocean and island; the river far below flows like a trickle of blood. The stars are gone, and the sky fades into a soft, brassy orange, and still I climb.

Using all my strength I pull upward gaining a few inches at a time. Looking up, I see a large precipice jutting outward from the cliff wall. The familiar feeling of fear flows through me, but if I am to reach the ledge above, I have to let fear go. I clear me mind and ignore the screaming in my head.

Finally, my hand touches the bottom of the precipice. Searching for a strong handhold, I pull myself up and place my foot against the rock I just had my hand on. Desperately, I try pulling upward, but just then the rock under my foot shatters. I swing and grab the bottom of the ledge; I am now dangling under the precipice—only my right hand saves me from certain death on the rocks far below. I twist my body and bring my left arm up and over to grasp the lip of the ledge, pulling with all the strength this warrior body can muster, and then with my feet against the cliff wall, I desperately search for small niches to balance myself. Finally, I wedge myself securely and with a last mighty pull, I position my stomach against the lip of the precipice, and then heave myself over to safety.

The ledge appears to be a flat solid rock standing out from the cliff like a beak. There's enough room to sit on, but above it the mountain is sheer cliff with no place to climb. Below lies the wall, the un-scalable wall; the only way down is to climb back under the ledge, like Spiderman on all fours.

I'm trapped!

I sit down to catch my breath and to let my muscles stop twitching. I'm beginning to realize how tight the trap is: no one knows where I am; there is no way down and no way up; no matter how much and how creatively I think, there's no way to escape this prison. Sitting on the ledge, I let my muscles and lungs recover. I watch the sun rise even further above the horizon and the ocean. The sky changes from orange to yellow, and then from yellow green to light blue. I sit watching the spectacle unfold. Light shimmers and twinkles from the two crystals on Soultraveler; my friends will be awake by now and wonder where I am...I could kick myself that I didn't tell someone. When I left, it seemed the right thing, and besides, one of them—or even all of them—would have insisted on going with me, and after Shakti's sermon, I was convinced this was something I had to do alone. The waters turn a light turquoise blue as the sun rises ever higher. The island takes on the assorted colors of its meadows, flowers, lakes, and waterfalls. All this grand beauty blends with the greenery of the jungle and the great forests that are bordering meadows and lakes of the island paradise.

I have my book, The Way of the Traveler; maybe it can help me.

The book has never failed me before, and now I need its wisdom more than ever. I pull the book from me tunic and thumb through the pages. They are all blank. I'm staring at the empty pages, hoping somehow the writing will appear or I will hear the wise words of confidence and wisdom, but still there's nothing. The book for some reason is empty: no words, no print, nothing! I'm beginning to seriously worry; realizing the gravity of the situation, I look again over the beauty of the valley, and I begin noticing something. The view of the island and the cove where Soultraveler waits is shimmering as though I'm looking through intense heat waves. The landscape and its colors are melting together, and then soon enough they are clear and distinct again. I wonder, is this coming from me, or is it really wavering?

When walking in the meadow with the others yesterday, I saw the colored ribbons of light floating around the top of the mountain. These appear to be the same, except now I am seeing them from the other side. Watching these ribbons of light reminds me again of the aurora borealis, except these are more intense and colorful; waves of light move in and out from the mountain as if the mountain itself is a conduit for the energy waves.

The surreal scene becomes stronger; it's as if I put on colored sunglasses, except that the colors are constantly changing. The ocean is purple for a minute and then changes to green, pink, or red. The same thing happens with the lights sparkling from the crystals on Soultraveler.

I sit on the ledge and watch, feeling as if I'm floating in some mystical land, but then the lights pass and everything is clear for a brief moment. I shake myself and close my eyes, focusing on the spiritual eye; a similar display of lights unfolds within.

I begin to feel strange and my attention begins to scatter. Then for a brief moment, my inner vision becomes clear. My body feels heavy and groggy, then like a wave moving through me I feel tired, but this tired is different. More as if the body feels weak because it weighs a thousand pounds. To focus on me inner sight is like having me thoughts dragged through thick mud or tar, leaving me feeling sluggish.

Me inner vision clears and a brilliant cluster of colored lights appear.

Staring at the brilliant mystical lights, me consciousness withdraws, like being sucked backward deeper into the farthest reaches of my subconscious. The feeling fades, and suddenly I'm spinning outward, as if shot by a slingshot directly into the lights. Briefly I become lost in a swirling universe of light. When I open my eyes, my sight is unfocused, which makes me dizzy. I stand up and turn around; looking at the side of the mountain cliff, I see a dark shadow lying against it. With effort, I drag myself closer toward the shadow. When I'm nearly upon it, I realize it isn't a shadow at all; it's a dark doorway leading into the side of the mountain. How strange; a few moments ago, I would have sworn there was nothing there. Moving closer, I cautiously take a step into the opening; if I can't go down the mountain, or up the mountain, then I will go in the mountain.

Stepping into the darkness, the opening closes behind me.

I'm trapped again!

Remembering what Shakti said, I don't panic; I figure this is better than being stranded on the ledge. Taking a few steps further into the mountain, I see a faded light in the distance, and as I move forward cautiously, the heavy feeling of me body lifts.

As I'm walking through a dark passage, I try to make out what's on the walls. The light's getting bright enough to see, and I notice the ground is covered with some kind of smooth tile and the walls are painted with strange, beautiful designs. The passage ends at an opening to a large room. The room is sparsely furnished with only a round black marble-like table and four wooden chairs. Looking around further, I can just make out four open doorways. In the far corner of the room is a lectern like those used for giving speeches. Other than this, there's nothing much to look at. The room is clean, there are wall paintings depicting symbols of some possible ancient language, or maybe they are just designs. They are colorful and seem to symbolize the many hued ribbons of light outside. I walk closer to one of the exits; my sword begins to vibrate.

I pull it from me sheath and point it toward the nearest doorway.

The sword hums. I move toward another door; once again the sword hums and vibrates. At each door, the sword doesn't differentiate. Puzzled, I walk back to the center of the room and pull one of the chairs out from the table. I lay the sword down, and as soon as it touches the tabletop, it begins to glow. The sword becomes brighter, glowing a light yellow, almost white, and then changing subtly to a crimson red. Reaching out to touch the hilt, a voice manifests in me mind. *"Leave the sword behind; it can no longer serve you."*

Then the sword vanishes!

I leap up and look around, but see no one. The voice again projects in my mind. *"There is no wrong exit, for all are of value. Follow your true self and the next step will reveal itself."* Backing away from the table, I look around; surely there's something I'm missing?

Peering around at the four doors, I can see they all look the same. Then something in the opposite corner catches my attention.

I see a large framed mirror on carved legs standing against the wall. Leaning in to inspect the mirror more closely, I see my reflection. For a moment I just stand there looking into the mirror. The image staring back isn't the adult warrior I had grown accustomed to; it's someone I know very well.

Standing there facing me is the ten-year-old boy: the skinny kid with jeans, a red tee shirt, and tennis shoes. I look closer at the reflection, and think, how can this be? I'm back in my own body! What's become of my warrior body? I step closer, looking at me child-self, and I notice the mirror also reflects one of the doorways. Looking behind me and then back to the mirror, I realize that this has to be it! Why else would the mirror be here, other than to show my true reflection and to point to the true door? As if to answer my question, the reflected image of myself turns and walks into the reflected doorway and is gone. I stand there staring for a moment, then walking over to the same doorway, I step inside. Immediately, a flight of stairs appears. I begin to climb them upward.

After a good amount of time and a great many steps, the stairs end. A long red-carpeted hallway stretches before me. The walls are paneled on both sides with dark polished wood. Lamps are mounted on both sides of the hallway every fifteen or twenty feet, with framed pictures between each.

Walking down the hall, I stare at the pictures as I pass. Each picture is some other era in time, each with a person in it. I stop at every picture; I get that prickly weird feeling that I know the person depicted in the painting. Some of the paintings show a vastly different era, such as during the days that Greece ruled the civilized world or during the times of the Spanish Inquisition or medieval days.

Walking farther down the hallway, pictures continue to depict different eras, and even times that are recent, possibly during the Earth's World Wars. Sensing that somehow these pictures are connected to me in some way, I wonder at the different feelings flowing through me from each one. Some of the characters are female, others are male. In every picture, the figure is shown in action, not posed, such as the picture of a soldier lying in a battlefield, and another of a man working in the fields. I don't know if these are people I'm descended from, or if they might even be me in previous lives. Approaching the end of the hallway, I see another mirror like the first, except this one doesn't show me my reflection; this mirror reflects another world: a world I'm very familiar with.

I turn around to look behind at the reflected world and only see some heavy red curtains at the end of the hallway. I move closer to the mirror and then step through; instantly I find myself standing on a country road lined with a wooden stack fence and maple trees growing on both sides of the wide path. The tree branches touch each other from the opposite sides, forming a beautiful canopy of colored leaves of oranges, reds, and golds. Various animals such as deer, squirrels, and birds move within the trees. As I step on the small road, I see a bicycle leaning against a tree parked to my left. Recognition kicks in: my bike! It's me own bike! It looks brand-new, but it's definitely mine. The candy apple red paint with the black racing seat and the three-speed gear shifter on the lower bar are all there. The sprocket is chromed like new, and the tires even have red-wall stripes on them. I inspect it for a moment, and then swing my leg over and push away to begin a ride down the little country road. The bike rides smooth as glass. For a moment, I feel like I'm home.

Riding down the little lane reminds me of all the times Billy and I rode down the roads around Bristol with Cody trying to catch up. The feel of the wind and the smell of autumn freshness in the air are exhilarating. All the struggles, all the challenges are left behind as I pedal the bike down the lane. The foliage reflects the bright fall colors. The small unpainted wooden stack fence lines both sides of the little country road; leaves fall like rain as I pedal down the country road.

Even though I'm thoroughly enjoying myself, I know this is all happening for a reason. Finding the bike, riding down a familiar country road, right in the middle of fall—this is just too wonderful to be for nothing. Shortly, I turn at a bend in the road. A small wooden gate appears to the right with a little pathway leading away from the road. Stopping, I open the gate, roll the bike inside, and start riding down the path. A pond to the left of the path appears; it looks similar to Amity Pond back in Bristol.

Passing the pond, I come to a park that actually resembles the town square back home, except this one is planted with more flowers and trees. The only structure I can see is a small chapel which is almost hidden from the trees, bushes, and flowers blooming as if it were spring. Pulling up to the path that leads to the chapel, I stop and get off. Laying down the bike, I walk through the bushes and find myself going toward the steps of the little building.

The chapel is white with a tall steeple on top, and a pathway leading up to a double door entryway. As I walk up the path and near the wooden doors, I hear the faint sound of organ music playing in the distance. Pushing open the doors, I walk in.

The room has five rows of dark wooden bench seats on each side; a green carpet is laid down in the middle aisle leading up to a pulpit; scattered leaves are strewn about. The pulpit stands on a stage just above the seats. Behind it, to the left and right are two empty balconies. In between the two balconies on the rear wall is a large stained glass window; it has mysterious inlaid symbols instead of religious figures. Walking up the aisle, I truly feel as if I'm in a church, since the organ music is now louder.

As I walk up the aisle, I stop at the steps leading to the pulpit. I turn; I could have sworn I heard something move behind me, but I see nothing. Turning around again, a woman is standing behind the pulpit. She's tall, in fact she's extremely tall, and beautiful; she's wearing a magnificent, tight green dress made from woven leaves. Some parts of her dress are woven from a thick, spider web-type material sewn together to form intricate designs. A dark sheer netted hood covers her head. I'm cautious but not afraid. Taking a few steps forward, I hesitate in front of the pulpit. Looking up at the woman, I ask her, "Excuse me, but can you tell me where I am?"

Although the woman's face is behind netting, I can still see her features. She smiles and answers me in a high musical voice. "You have entered the realm of magic, young master; we have been waiting for you. Now you can rightfully inherit your true power."

Looking around, I see no one else. Undeterred, I ask, "What kind of power are you referring to?"

The woman steps from behind the pulpit, and then taking a few steps to the side she lifts her netted veil. "I refer to the greatest power in existence, the power of magic!" I say nothing, and then she continues. "With this power, you can accomplish all your dreams and all your goals."

Something inside makes me nervous about this woman. I ask, "What do I have to do to get this magic?"

"Do? Why, boy, you have already done it; the power is yours. It is your right, and with this magic, you can control anyone or anything you desire. Your mere thoughts will carry you to the greatest wealth, the greatest pleasure, and assist in finding truth in a way entirely unknown to you at this moment." With a wave of her hand, a table appears in front of me with all my favorite foods: cakes, pies, hamburgers, chicken, and roast with fruits of every kind imaginable. Drinks and breads are in abundance. The woman smiles, "You will never go hungry again! Or perhaps you like pleasures of another appetite."

Instantly, two scantily dressed girls appear near the sides of the food-laden table; each takes a piece of fruit and offers it to me. Their eyes are large and innocent, golden curls flow around their faces as they smile and offer the alluring fruits: theirs and what's on the table. I step back. "What's going on here? Why are you offering this to me?"

The woman smiles again. "Dear boy, you have come so far; now it is time for your reward. The courage and patience you have displayed is uncommon to your kind. He who climbs the Mountain of Light and survives gains the rights of kings and princes. You have suffered much in your journey. Should you not be given what you have earned?"

I stare at the tempting feast. The enticing girls dance in front of me, flirting shamelessly. Surely, this has to be a trap; nothing the veiled lady has said makes any sense compared with what I've already learned, so I ask, "Can this magic lead me to my mother and help me free her?"

There's silence for a moment, and then the woman speaks again.

"Magic can do many things in helping one gain power and control over his life. If used properly, your mind will expand beyond your wildest dreams. Rescuing your mother cannot possibly be more important than learning the secrets of this universe and all below it. Once you learn to use the magic, then your mind will show you ways of freeing your loved ones and much more."

My surroundings seem to be trying to distract me. The organ music seems to be getting louder; the dancing girls move suggestively closer. The symbols on the colored glass window subtly move, changing into ancient languages long forgotten. I want every opportunity to help me find mom; however, this woman only seems to be selling her magic. I don't want to control everything in this realm and below, or expand me mind. She doesn't mention the Creator or the Light and Sound, so can I trust her? "Answer me this. Why am I not in my warrior's body right now? Why am I here in my younger form, without my sword? And why does my book show only blank pages?"

The woman turns and slides her hand along the edges of the pulpit as she walks toward me. Looking down, she replies, "You ask so many questions. Do you not want the gift you have earned?

I say nothing. She continues. "Very well, in answer to your three questions, understand this! You can only receive the magic in your true form, not one created from illusion. Your sword is powerless here, as is the wisdom of the book you cherish; neither is formed from the power of magic. For once, Hugh, take the power offered and use it to conquer not only all who resist you, but your mind and emotions as well. Can't you see? The feeble power you possess has no way of entering this domain? With magic, you can have power over the elements, over energy itself. All life will bow to your greatness; you only have to command it, and it serves. When you infuse your passion with the magic of the mind, you accomplish so much more than with mere love."

The woman takes a step closer and stares into my eyes, then asks, "Does not hate make you strong? When you desire something, is it not that very desire that gives you what you want? When one hurts you, does not vengeance satisfy the hurt? All of these passions can be enhanced a thousand fold, and be at your beck and call. Is this not the goal of the leaders in your world? The religions, the commanders of wealth and power! They all strive for power! Control! Pleasure! And possession of humankind's destiny! Do they not beckon for the attention of the masses so they can bend the will of man? This is magic in only one of its many forms; it is the magic of the mind! The magic does not want to be treated gently or kindly; it demands brutality, it demands control...and it will fight to get it and keep it. It uses violence and war, but it also uses pleasure and love. It is satisfied with nothing, for it always demands more. This is why those who have bits and pieces crave more. It is truly the eternal quest of man. Sometimes it demands blood, but often it demands a man who can rule it. The magic needs someone to subdue it for the sake of submission only. Your religions use it for enlightenment, not realizing that for giving a little knowledge of creation, it commands their servitude. You, having accomplished so much, are now at the crossroads in your existence that demands you choose. Are you to be the servant or the master? For when the world becomes your slave, there is nothing you cannot have. The sole purpose of creating life is so that life and power becomes your servant. This is truth, whether you accept it or not!"

Listening to the woman is very gently and very slowly putting me in a light trance. The thought of control and the image of creating a better world according to my desires capture my imagination and spins images of glory and happiness beyond anything I ever considered.

Her magic spins its web of illusion around me in such a way that I begin to feel as if I'm the chosen one. I'm the special person who is being handed a gift that can forever change my life and the lives of all those I love. The more I listen, the deeper the magic bores its tempestuous images into me mind. I'm succumbing to the allure of magic and all its promises and pleasures.

Somewhere deep within, I know this isn't the path I should travel, and despite all that's being offered me, I sense something else, something deep down, something not part of the magic. As I continue to listen to her promises, I feel myself being cradled in the arms of the woman in green. I'm feeling powerful! I'm becoming more through the power of magic, which I alone control.

Suddenly, a voice deep inside softly whispers my name; the voice calls me from the deepest recesses of my being, even further beyond the illusory spells the witch is casting. However, the magic is strong, and the mind responds to the false images of glory and power. I respond to feelings far more than soft words so I follow the magic. The whisper becomes louder and more direct; then the words change to a warning.

"Hugh! Listen closely." The voice is familiar; Shakti!

"Hugh, this is the way of magic; it is a weaver of false promises. You are as susceptible to its calling as anyone else. Entire worlds live under its spell, for magic uses our desires, our passions, and our imagination to create a world of unnatural cravings. It is the seed of sadness and false hope.

"Magic fools us to trust the leaders we put in charge of our lives. Magic tricks us into worshiping false idols in the form of celebrities, symbols, religions, and wealth. Magic works in every conceivable facet of our lives. Even the world's religions spin webs of dark magic by using guilt, fear, emotional love, and attachments with promises of a better life after this one. Religions ask you to put your trust in past spiritual giants whose true spiritual teachings have been twisted into lies and woven into the events of history as divine destiny. This is magic at its worse!"

Trying to listen to Shakti's cautions while trying to pull away from the witch's clutches, I find her power to be too much, and I feel myself sinking deeper under her spell.

Shakti persists.

"*Even when magic is used for the good of man, it fails us. For magic is a distraction from Soul's real goal. It sends us spiraling onto paths that take us back to the realms of illusion. Never can magic of any kind show us the way to the Creator; it simply is not designed that way! How can an illusionary power take Soul back to truth? Whatever magic offers is false, for how can you benefit if you gain the whole world but lose your Soul? Magic is the tool to create a prison for Soul. Hugh, you have been warned; your experience with the mind has shown you that man cannot defeat the mind with the mind, and magic is only another aspect of the mind power.*"

The power of magic is blending all things together in my mind. Humanity, the universe, all events—even other life forms—are becoming a part of my experience. I can hardly tell the difference between me and everything else in existence. I feel myself being cradled in the arms of the woman in green. I'm feeling powerful! I'm succumbing even deeper to the power of magic. The organ music becomes louder, seemingly trying to drown out the inner voice. My mind swirls as the music penetrates every fiber of my being.

Half opening my eyes, I watch the beautiful girls dancing around me. The woman dressed in leaves holds her arms in the air with her eyes closed, swaying and dancing to the tempo of the melodious organ music. My mind feels drunk; heavy thoughts swirl like feathers in a storm. I'm falling further into the net of darkness being spun around me. I feel myself falling deeper into a calliope of colors.

Then a faint voice calls from the wilderness of my darkened mind. The voice is chanting my name. The voice seems to be that of a child. Thoughts disrupt the cry, and I float through this magical world of desire, power, passion, and darkness. Then the child's voice becomes clearer and closer, stirring the darkness within. The voice rings out within me Soul, and as I concentrate, the chant begins to ring clear: *Huuuu…*

The child's voice grows…like angels bursting from sunlight, breaking darkness into shattered pieces of light, I recognize the voice.

Melody!

Yes, I'm sure of it!

My mind captures and hangs onto me sister's voice. I struggle while trying to come to me senses. Opening my eyes my vision clears, then I see clearly the illusion that is being foisted on me. With a shout, I yell out, "No! I don't want it!" I stumble to the double doors, bursting them open. I run into the sunlight. Clumsily I run down the path, grab the bike, and pedal to the gate.

Passing the little pond, I approach the road. A man that looks to be in his sixties is standing by the side of the fence. Braking hard, the bike falls, and I slide off in front of the closed gate. The man is leaning on a shovel; he's wearing a light blue button down shirt, with long sleeves rolled up on his arms. He tips his cap, smiles, and swings the gate open. He then says, "That was a close call, son, but it seems you made the right decision. Where ya' headed now?"

I squint at the man; he has a soft twinkle in his blue eyes. Not knowing whether to respond or ignore him, I pick up me bike and push it through the gate, and then I reply, "I'm going back to where I came from, down the lane a little. Who are you?"

"I'm Paul, the gardener." He looks very serene. "I just try to keep things growing and in order. I think you're making a wise choice by going back; this place is not for you."

I study the man's face, which seems to be relaxed and at peace. He has a slight southern drawl mixed with something else. Paul is short, but emanates a tremendous energy just through his smile. He points to my bike and says, "By the way, that's a mighty fine bike you have there. Do you know how to shift it?"

"I have one just like this back at home. Me Da' showed me how to use it."

Paul leans his chin on the shovel handle and with a grin says, "Well, when you are riding down the road, try shifting the gears; you'll find the ride a lot easier."

I look again at the short man, and for a second, his eyes twinkle as he smiles. Then I jump on the bike. I start to ride...my mind is still groggy but quickly begins to clear. I yell back to him, "Thanks, I'll try it out!" Then speeding off, I head back the way I came.

Melody's voice still faintly rings in my mind. I keep playing this close call repeatedly in my thoughts. How did Melody do it? I wonder; but the point is, she did do it! And it probably saved not only me, but also possibly Mom, too. Riding down the path, I also think about what Paul had just said. Reaching down, I shift the lever to the next higher speed.

The pedals move easier, and the bike speeds forward, but something else happens also. My mind relaxes; I feel a surge of warmth enter my body. My vision clears completely, and me ears pop as if I was driving down a mountain to a lower elevation. The sound of the wind blowing in my face becomes melodious and cool against the skin. The leaves are brighter, the sky is bluer, and I feel stronger. About halfway down the road, I reach down and shift the lever again to a higher speed. The tires spin free, and the bike again jumps forward. At the same time, my mind clicks into a higher awareness as a feeling of gratitude sweeps over me. All the teachings I've received are rushing into my conscious mind; Jotan, the Teacher in the park, Olgera, the Wisdom Pool, Morleck, and all the others rush into the mind as one great understanding. Their knowledge is no longer just words or feelings; they are becoming a part of who I am. Their knowledge turns into my power!

The simplicity of who I am doesn't need the mind to make it known; the value of who I am is again exploding within me heart. No thoughts, no contradictions, just oneness, not only with what I am observing, but with who I really am: Soul. I'm flying down the country road. The bike moves as if it has wings. With a wide grin, I reach down and shift the lever all the way to the last and highest gear. I hear the clicking gears engage and the bike begins to vibrate; a finely tuned vibration emits a low humming sound. My heart feels as if it's going to explode!

The realization that I as Soul am a child of the Creator fills me entirely with love. As I absorb the power of enlightenment, an explosion of Light and Sound reverberates within me. I close my eyes and feel love penetrate every atom of me being. At the same time, I'm feeling and hearing the rolling thunder of the Creator's voice echo within me. A tremendous shudder runs through me and then: stillness.

I open my eyes and then I open my heart.

Greater feelings of gratitude are still growing within me. Before me is the beautiful island with its rivers and lakes. Meadow flowers are bursting with color; the contrast against the emerald green forest is spectacularly beautiful. I'm back on the ledge. Looking around, I have to smile.

Dancing ribbons of colored lights play in front of me like rainbows dancing to Soul's whim. The ledge offers a perfect view of the blue waters of the great ocean, and Soultraveler sitting in the cove as magnificent as ever. Clarity and oneness are part of this deep mystical experience.

As far as I'm concerned, I can stay here forever, for within my heart, I feel the Creator sending waves of unconditional love. I feel like I have to sing or burst. Looking out over the vast valley, a song of gratitude and love floats within my mind. Then I feel myself fading, fading into the brightest and most beautiful light I've ever seen.

My back is against the cliff wall; I'm back in the warrior's body. The sword's back in its sheath, and The Way of the Traveler is securely tucked in my tunic. Contentment and confidence flow through me. The effortlessness of being Soul generates the Creator's love and power through my consciousness. From this love, I know all will be done in its proper time. Right now, I'm on this ledge at the top of the world, watching and just being Soul.

For the moment, nothing else matters.

I'm like a pair of eyes. My awareness is razor sharp. I am the eagle watching the world unfold around me; at the same time, I'm completely detached from everything. The only thing important is the wave after wave of love flowing from within, and then gushing outward to all existence.

As I perch on the ledge observing my domain, a push deep within my mind manifests, a voice with the clarity of night stars bursts within me mind. *"Hugh! Where are you? We are searching for you. Use the mental projection technique to direct us toward you."*

I send a thought outward.

"Ah, Kaylu! I knew you would find me. Look up, me friend. I'm above you, on the great mountain's ledge. I'll wait here for you." Closing me eyes, I watch the light within flow like a great river from one end of the universe to the next, engulfing all existence, and then receding back into my heart.

****

Unknown to Hugh at that moment, the experience of Soul travel he just endured has given him the great love he is experiencing. This love transfers a life-changing awareness into his consciousness, filling every atom of his being with a power that fuels each cell of his body with its own sense of being.

CHAPTER 39 ~
WORLDS COLLIDE

Brandon Lewis opens his eyes; a tingling sensation vibrates throughout his entire body as if it is waking up; slowly, he becomes aware of his surroundings. His hand is still holding Melody's, whose other hand holds her brother's in turn.

He looks at the young girl sitting with her head bent down; a low humming sound is coming from her lips. Slowly pulling his hand away the little girl stops her chanting, and turns to look up at him. For just a brief moment it is if they are one, sharing their thoughts, feelings, and emotions; then it's gone. Melody leans over, putting her arms around his neck; Brandon hugs her back and smiles. He knows her feelings and she knows his. "Thank you, Shakti," she says simply, and then she walks over to her father who is still sitting next to her mother. Clark, still holding Ann's hand, assumes Melody has been doing the same with Hugh.

Brandon leans over Hugh and touches his forehead with his fingertips and whispers, "You're doing fine, son, don't give up. We're learning as fast as we can." He then walks over to Clark and Melody. "Clark, we need to talk, including Melody."

"Fine, let's go to my house; we can have some supper and then think over our strategies."

They walk out of the hospital into a pouring rain; it's late afternoon and a strong wind blows raindrops against their faces. Running to their cars, they head for the Baileys' house. On the drive home, Clark looks over at Melody who is strangely quiet. "Is there something I need to know?"

Melody looks up at her dad and replies, "Brandon and I just helped Hugh, that's all."

Assuming she means they helped when she and Brandon simply sat with Hugh at the hospital, Clark nods agreeably, and says, "That's great, honey," and asks no more questions.

Arriving at the house, Clark puts a frozen pizza in the oven to bake and the three of them go into the living room. Rain is still falling hard outside. Clark throws a few logs in the fireplace and gets a cozy fire going. Brandon sits in the big armchair, while Clark sits on a padded footstool close to the fire. Melody's lying on the carpet with Cody.

Brandon's staring at the fire as he talks.

"Clark, something happened in the hospital today, something that has again hurled me into an area of experience I never dreamed existed. Not only did I experience something beyond my mind, but I also shared this with Melody."

"With Melody? What do you mean?"

Brandon looks at Melody and Cody playing on the rug and smiles. "It seems your daughter has started on a little journey of her own."

Clark looks over at Melody rolling with Cody and asks, "What do you mean, 'a little journey of her own'?"

Brandon tells Clark about how he again merged his awareness with Shakti, and how as Shakti, he was able to meet with Hugh and explain certain principles and ideas to help Hugh stay on the right path to his goal. Brandon then turns to Melody and asks, "Melody, do you remember anything strange that may have happened while we were holding Hugh's hand at the hospital?"

Melody grabs Cody around his neck and says, "Hugh was in trouble, sort of like he was lost, so I called his name with my thoughts hoping he would hear me and come back."

Brandon nods and exclaims, "That's it! That's what I heard as I tried to tell Hugh to avoid the magic. Somehow Melody was there with me, calling her brother back from the psychic magic that was trying to trap him." Brandon then went on to explain to Clark as best he could how both he and Melody helped Hugh get through a trap.

Clark looks first at Brandon and then at his daughter. He's having a hard time believing what he's hearing. How could both of them communicate at the same time with Hugh? Were they actually assisting Hugh? How can this be?

A distant beep surprises the group; Clark stands and goes out to the kitchen to get the pizza. Clark returns with the pizza and some plates and napkins. Setting their dinner down on the coffee table, he encourages everyone to grab a piece. Brandon picks a slice up and takes a bite. Still chewing, he says thoughtfully, "Apparently, I have another existence that I'm only now becoming aware of." Looking again into the brightly burning fire, he finishes chewing and tries putting his thoughts to words. "This is all beginning to make sense to me now. Throughout my life, I remember many instances when I would sometimes doze off, or sometimes in my meditations seem to experience another life.

"At the times when this would happen, I would awaken, feeling as if I had just been somewhere else doing something totally unrelated to this life, but I could never quite remember what it was. Sometimes, I would even have dreams about this other life, but again, I just couldn't remember events, circumstances, or people; just a fleeting feeling, and then it was gone. Now I remember everything. It's like slipping through a crack of another reality for a brief time and then coming back. This other realm or plane where I am Shakti is just as real—if not more so—than this world."

"But how?" Clark asks.

Brandon shakes his head. "I'm not sure about the actual mechanics, but I do know I can attribute some of this breakthrough to our desire to help Hugh. When I'm in the consciousness of Shakti, Hugh's quest is supremely important to not only me, but others as well. Somehow my higher self has completed a bridge between worlds, using Hugh as the catalyst for my mind. Melody's having a similar, but somewhat different experience. Her inner world seems to be melting into Hugh's, giving her the ability to communicate with him even though she isn't totally aware she's doing it. And yet she does remember helping, and she seems to know what to do at the precise time, so that is different from my experience. I am not sure, but all three of our worlds seem to be colliding: Hugh's, Melody's and mine."

For a moment, Clark feels a bit left out, but then he remembers what Brandon said about precise timing. This coincides with what Melody told him that day in the meadow when she mentioned her dream about Hugh and when to tell their father. It's all about timing! If he is to help Hugh, then it will be according to Soul's timetable, not his. Clark thinks to himself that he should just be grateful that Brandon and Melody have been able to help Hugh, and he's still making progress on saving Ann.

Grabbing a slice of pizza for himself, Clark responds, "You know, Brandon, I don't really understand all this metaphysical stuff, but it doesn't really seem to matter. For example, look at Melody. She doesn't study and doesn't seem to be searching for answers, but still she's growing spiritually in giant steps and she's just being a person that's taking more responsibility."

Brandon thinks for a moment. "You might be right. From what I can see, it really has nothing to do with how much the mind learns or about how much the individual thinks they know about God, religion, secret teachings, rituals or whatever. I think it's based on how much love a person has to give, and if they can give it unselfishly. I know for most of my life I put myself above others because of my supposedly superior mental abilities, but from what I've recently learned, I totally agree that the seeking, the reading, and all the things I've learned and experienced, may have actually hindered me from knowing the one thing I wanted most of all. It was my faith and belief in what you told me about Hugh that opened the door for me."

Brandon reaches out and pets Cody. Chuckling, he rubs the dog's ears and pats him on the head. "I wonder how close Cody is to 'Soul'?"

"What do you mean? You think animals have souls, too?"

"From what I've experienced lately, I'm one hundred percent convinced they do. It seems we each have a mission, and we each fill a special place in the Creator's plan: whether we're human, animal, insect, plant or spirit. It doesn't matter if we're Jewish, Muslim, Christian or whatever. It only matters that we learn to give of ourselves with unconditional love like our friend Cody here. Surely, the mind has an important role in arriving at the door of spiritually, but once its role is played, it has to be discarded just like a bad habit.

"We keep the love and joy of life stored within the mind's limited memories, but as far as knowing Soul and eventually the Creator, the mind is not the ultimate answer. We use the mind merely as a tool to get along in this world and with others; it's like a stepping stone to soul. As we grow and go deeper within, eventually we have to forget all the junk we like to think is so important. I firmly believe that mental and emotional trash isn't allowed in the higher, more pure parts of what we call Heaven. Can you imagine taking attitudes about war, killing, rape, stealing, greed, selfishness, gossiping, vanity, fear, and so many other negative human habits into the pure heavens of love, joy, power, and total freedom?

"Why, with the power we're given as Soul, would we retain the negative habits, or even all the worldly knowledge we think is so important of the mind and our immature emotions? Holding onto all that, we would destroy not only ourselves, but also everything around us. The time for judgment is gone, for then one knows each particle of life is important, and will continue to exist; no matter what shape or form it happens to reside in at the moment."

Brandon stops speaking for a moment to let his thoughts sink in. He then continues trying to explain this. "Soul will eventually learn its lessons, and then forget the evil that infected it for so long. When that happens, Soul will step into the arms of the Creator with great power, love, and gratitude; these are the keys to the freedom that awaits all of us. Hugh is pointing the way. It's up to us to follow the best we can. Personally, I feel blessed to be Shakti, who my higher self created as an expression of itself. What a wonderful gift knowing each person has a kingdom within that's ruled by the true self, and that all is in order. All is just as it should be because each individual kingdom is merely a part of the Creator's kingdom."

Clark watches Brandon talk in such a simple, loving manner. He marvels how much he has changed since the day they met in his office; it's almost like a miracle. For someone like Brandon, who seemed at one time to be so detached, to now open himself up and allow love to be such a dominant force in his life is a great miracle in and of itself.

Melody stands up and walks over to her dad. Looking him right in the eye, she whispers, "Remember the secret in my dream, Dad? Now I know the secret, but I can't tell; it's not time yet." Puzzled, Clark decides not to prod any further; for the rest of the evening, they hold their conversation to less heady stuff. That night, Clark sleeps deeply: no dreams, no disturbing thoughts, nothing. He didn't even wake up in the middle of the night.

Awakening to a refreshing morning, Clark decides that he, Melody, and Cody should get away to have some fun today and not worry about how everything might or might not turn out in the future. Maybe it would be good to take a ride up to the lake, he thought. Smiling at the image of the three of them enjoying a relaxing visit, he wakes Melody, telling her to get dressed and to put Cody in the car for a ride to the mountains.

As they drive up the steep mountain road, Cody hangs his head out the window, loving every minute of the car ride. The fresh air and the wind in his face are intoxicating, and he aims to enjoy every moment of it. Melody's having a great time, too. Just to climb up and away from everything below feels like ascending to Heaven. Clark keeps an eye out for a place to have breakfast and maybe rent a small boat to take on the lake. Soon they find a café nestled in a grove of trees just a few miles from the lake. He pulls the car into the little parking lot.

"Here's a good place, let's get some breakfast."

Clark checks out the menu and orders for himself and Melody; he also orders a to-go order of French toast for Cody, who's waiting in the car. The server is a kindly woman, perhaps in her mid-fifties. She's chatty, and after a few moments, she begins telling Clark some of the history of the mountain and how she came to own the little café. Clark listens intently to her story. As he does, he begins to feel a connection to her. Her story is important to her, and for some reason she feels comfortable telling him a little about her life. They are the only customers in the café, and since it's still early, there's no interruption in their conversation.

The waitress introduces herself as Grace. She's been on the mountain for more than twenty years. Her husband died ten years ago, and she's operated the café alone ever since. Her children are grown and moved away, so the high point of her day is visiting with customers. Melody is sitting next to her, and she eases herself closer to the woman, listening intently like her father.

"I've been told there are legends about strange things that happen up here in these mountains. In all the years I've been here, I must admit things have occurred that most people either wouldn't believe or wouldn't understand."

Intrigued, Clark asks, "What kind of things?"

A sparkle flickers in her eye for a second and then she continues. "One night about ten years ago, I was walking along the ridge beyond the woods behind the café. You got to see the view. Once you get beyond the trees, you can see the valley and lake below; it's so beautiful! Well, anyway, on this particular night it was a full moon, and the moonlight spread itself across the waters highlighting the mountains and stars surrounding the lake. It looked like a picture post card. I was standing on the shoreline just watching the moon as it rose higher over the lake's horizon. Mind you, I wasn't drinking or nothing, just thinking about Bob—that's my dead husband, you know. Anyway, I felt this cool wind brush my face. I closed my eyes for just a moment to feel the breeze when I hear something. At first, I think it's my imagination, but as I listen, the sound becomes clearer."

Melody asks, "What was the sound like?"

Grace thinks for a moment. "Well, it was like a high shrill whistle, sort of like a teapot when it gets hot, but not as loud. At first, the whistle was far away, and then it got closer; I look around to see where it's coming from, but couldn't see a thing. I stare out over the lake listening when the sound begins to change. It wasn't abrupt, but more of a melting from one sound to another. I listen closer as it begins to sound like high notes on a flute. The sound had a rhythm to it, going higher and higher. Standing there listening to this real pretty sound and looking over the beautiful starlit lake, I forgot my loneliness for a moment. Then, just for a minute, I feel Bob next to me.

"Now, I know what this sounds like, but believe me, I'm not crazy. I've always been a Christian, and I believe in Jesus as my savior, you know, but just for a little while, Bob was with me. I had that man in my life for thirty years, and I know what it feels like when he's around. All I could do was whisper his name and listen to the sounds that are now coming from me! Yes, I know it sounds insane, but the music was actually coming from inside me."

Clark asks, "Had anything like this happened to you before?"

"No sir, never have I felt anything like this. Suddenly, the flutes stop, and I hear a rushing wind, but there's no wind. The breeze had stopped, but still I hear the wind blowing as if it's rushing through the trees, but when I look around, the trees aren't moving. The lake waters are calm and smooth."

Grace stops talking for a moment, remembering that evening as if it were last night. She grabs a towel and stands up.

"I'm sorry. I don't know why I'm telling you this. You must think I'm crazy. Let me check on your breakfast." She starts to turn when Clark reaches out and touches her hand.

"Grace, please continue; you have no idea how much this means to my daughter and me. Believe me, we want to hear the rest of your story."

Grace rubs her hands in the towel and with a nervous look on her face, she sits down. "Are you sure? I don't know what possessed me to start jawing like this. I've never told anyone this before; I always figured they'd lock me up or something."

Clark smiles, then reaches out again and takes her hand. "We don't think you're crazy, and we both would love to hear the rest of your story."

Grace looks as if she might cry, but then looking over at Melody, she smiles and continues with her story. "Well, I didn't hear or see or feel nothing more, so I walked back to my cabin to go to bed. That night, I dream about Bob and me. It wasn't like any dream I ever had before. Bob was in this beautiful park and looked so handsome: just like he did the day we got married. I felt good myself. My bones didn't ache; I was slimmer and felt like a young girl again. Bob took my hand, and we walked for a while around the park. I noticed other people walking around also. Bob tells me he misses me, but he's all right and waiting for me. He took me over to this circle of people who were sitting down on the grass listening to this beautiful older lady who was talking about some kind of sound and light or something. I can't remember it all right now, but at the time it seemed pretty important. After a while, Bob turns to me and kisses my cheek."

Grace reaches up and touches her cheek; she's quiet for a moment as she is remembering, then she continues. "He took my hand and said it was time for me to go back. He said I was supposed to remember as much as I could about what the lady talked about. Then he whispers in my ear a name and then I woke up."

Melody asks, "What was the name?"

Grace thinks a second.

"The best I can remember, it sounded something like Joe Tan. I can't be sure, you know, it was about ten years ago, and to tell you the truth, I hadn't really thought about the last part of that dream until just now while telling you the story. To make matters crazier, I don't even know why I told you about any of this!"

Clark pulls out a small pad and a pen from his shirt pocket. "What was that name again?" Grace says it more slowly this time.

"Joe Tan, I think, 'tan' like the color."

Clark writes it down and then invites her to join them for breakfast. He has a story he thinks she might find interesting.

"Give me a minute to get your food ready; I'll be right back."

Finally, all three of them are sitting in the café and chatting as if they've known each other all their lives. Clark tells her about what's happened during the last five months to his family.

He tells her about Hugh and his journey to try to save his mother and about Brandon and the court battle, even Melody's dreams; Grace just sits there spellbound. When he's through, she has tears flowing from her eyes.

"I don't know why we met, Mr. Bailey, but I think there's something about my story that hopefully will assist you down the road. I know one thing for sure. After hearing your story, I want to thank you; I don't feel alone anymore, and I don't think I'm crazy."

Clark and Melody stand up to leave. Reaching for his wallet to pay the tab, Grace puts her hand up. "Your money's no good here. You two have a wonderful day at the lake, and I hope we can see each other again soon."

Grace gives her phone number to Clark and asks him to call her once his son and wife get well. Both Clark and Melody give her a big hug, then taking Cody's order with them, they leave the little mountain café, glad to have met a new friend.

CHAPTER 40 ~ JOURNEY OF NO RETURN

The mountain looms ahead. Kaylu and Dandi have now connected with me and they are trying to locate where I am on the mountain to identify exactly where I'm trapped, but the blazing sun overhead is so blinding that both of my companions can only turn away and blink furiously to restore their sight. How are they going to get me down? Kaylu can climb the steep cliff, but to what end? Once he's with me, how is he going to get us both down?

Kaylu thought he could simply climb up to the precipice with some rope, then tie it around something and let them both down, but there's nothing to secure the rope to on the ledge.

I'm sitting near the edge of the precipice wrapped in the cape I took with me the night before. My sword is strapped to my back; I'm kind of oblivious to the dilemma unfolding below me. I know it's just a matter of time before I will be free from this mountainous perch, and so I leave the details to my friends below.

The heat becomes more intense as the sun climbs the heavens; it shines directly on top of me and the ledge I sit on. Pulling my cape over my eyes to shade me from the brightness I glance down to the small ledge I'm sitting on. A slight sparkle where the sunlight hit the ledge catches my eye. Bending over to see better, I see a small tiny light penetrate the rock I'm sitting on. Taking my sword, I scratch the surface of the rock. The sparkle of light becomes larger. Curious, I scrape some more through the loose rock. As I scrape, more sunlight sparkles through the stone. Soon there's a large patch glistening as the sun's rays expose what looks like glass or crystal of some sort.

The more I scrape, the more the light is exposed.

Scraping and clearing more of the thin surface, I eventually expose an even larger area. The light is reflecting from a crystal rock. In fact, the entire percipience is actually a huge crystal that over time has been covered by dust, sediment, and dirt, eventually solidifying and covering the crystal. I wonder whether the entire mountain might actually be one giant crystal growing from the earth below. That would explain why the cliff face had been so hard to climb.

Continuing to clear the loose rock off the rest of the ledge, I soon find myself standing on a giant flat crystal blazing with light and color. Ribbons of light dance before me and around the mountain. It intensifies as the crystal becomes more exposed. I now understand the source of those mysterious lights; they're reflections of tiny exposed areas of the mountain that the naked eye can't see from below. Uncovering the ledge exposes the light as it expands and dances in front of me. Dandi, Kaylu, and their two companions watch from below.

As they gaze from below, the light intensifies. Kaylu sends a question to me. *"What's happening? Hugh, are you all right? Where is that light coming from?"*

I think for a moment, then pushing my thoughts in reply, I explain quickly what I've discovered, and then I ask, *"Dandi, can you take Baylor's sword and cut into the cliff?"*

Dandi strikes the side of the cliff and then scrapes away where he has cut; immediately, light glistens from the incision. As he scrapes more vigorously, more and more crystal becomes exposed.

It's true. The entire mountain is a giant crystal behemoth that over the ages has been covered with the elements, losing its glory and luster. I can only imagine what it must have looked like before it had been concealed!

Kaylu sends me a suggestion. *"Read The Way of the Traveler to see if it can show you a way down."* I don't really think it will do any good, since the pages are blank, but to my surprise when I open the book, it is back to its original form again. Every page has writing on it! Opening the book at random, I begin to read. The words manifest in my mind as before.

> Man is a unit of power existing for creation purposes only. Within his personal universe, there exists the awareness and power of creation itself! In his ignorance, man has forgotten the power that allows Soul to take responsibility for his actions, deeds, thoughts, and words. Due to their unnatural way of life, humankind has adapted; they live only to survive in the darkness of their limited mind and universe. They are unaware that lying dormant within their own being is something much greater. The world of humankind has always been a part of the Kingdom of God, but mankind over time has forgotten this important element of their existence.

> Not understanding that the world that man and woman live in is a part of the divine Kingdom, they also don't remember what is beyond, and so they think only their world is real. This is humankind's greatest mistake, for in forgetting they are part of a much more expansive Kingdom of God, mankind no longer applies the natural laws and divine laws to their existence. Instead, they apply their own emotional and mental concepts bestowed by religious and political leaders.

> Until Humankind takes responsibility for their thoughts, they will live with no true direction, just as the

shipwrecked sailor who is lost on the ocean in a boat without oars. Man does not believe that every thought coming from the human mind must by its own nature crystallize into forms somewhere. Until he learns this and how to direct his thoughts correctly, the crystallized forms will manifest within his own universe, creating barriers, habits, and illusions that man perceives as real. These forms appear to humankind in their dreams; they haunt him in his nightmares, and eventually in his relationships, and his outer world.

One of Humankind's greatest barriers to discovering their true nature is the millions of thought forms crystallizing constantly within his inner and outer worlds. These thoughts cause chaos, fear, and loss of control. This loss of control includes not only his emotions, but also the very outer world where he believes reality exists. The great Saints from man's world—such as Hafiz, Shams-i-Tabriz, Maulana Rumi, Kabir Sahib, Buddha, and Yeshua Ben Yosef (aka) Jesus—all had to shatter the crystallized thought forms that bound them to their earthly embodiments. None of these Saints was orthodox in his teachings. Their greatest gift to humanity was not derived from any fixed and organized religion. Their gifts of truths were always given from mouth to ear by true saints who themselves experienced it.

Religions base their authority upon one man or one book or one tradition. If a man or woman disagrees with that single source, then the teaching fails to indicate another way for man to gain the same truth and the same spiritual eminence. Thus, they fail to meet the most urgent spiritual needs of humankind. In light of this principle, all world religions will be found wanting. Only the science of the Light and Sound can meet the inflexible demands of this principle.

A true teacher does not tell you how to live among your fellow men and then inform you that if you so live, you will go to heaven when you die. On the contrary, a Spiritual Traveler tells you that if you live rightly among men, and then devote yourself to the practice of the Word, or Sound Current, you will enter the Kingdom of Heaven while still living in the body. This teaching constitutes a world of difference between the spiritual science of the Spiritual Travelers and all religions.

The followers of mainstream religion have accepted the ideology that they should not go beyond what is written in their holy books. This is a drastic mistake. Devotees do not realize how limiting their choice is, and they would probably resent the suggestion to go beyond what is written in their holy books. This has always been the case with formal religions in which a teaching shows just what to believe and that it is laid down in a written form; unfortunately, very few can go beyond the book. Their thoughts crystallize in their beliefs and progress ceases. How can it be otherwise?

As soon as man joins a formal religion, he ceases to look for anything new or better; he is bound. It has always been so, since the earliest days of civilized cultures. There has always been a tendency to systematize religious thought, and finally to write it down in a book as the very last word to be said on a subject. This inscribing results in stagnation, and eventually ossification.

This tendency to idolize their book has within it another deadly menace, for often devotees believe the next logical step is for them to try to compel all men and women to accept what is written in their religion. Persecution and murder follow in the name of God.

Can history show a more ghastly tragedy?

Usually, when people accept a book as the authoritative word of God, they assert that all revelation is closed. The last word has been spoken; all must believe it or be damned.

This has been the supreme tragedy of Mankind's history.

No matter which holy book, whether it is what the Earth world knows as the Vedas, the Upanishads, the Shastras, the Gita, the Zend Avesta, the Torah, the Bible, the Koran or any other religious scripture, each teaches that it is to be worshipped and obeyed. People declare their Scriptures as the inspired word of God and it is the duty of all men to accept and believe these books.

No matter how good they may be in and of themselves, at some point each becomes a fetter to intelligence. They all become fetters because their followers insist that all revelation is closed. All spiritual instructions are finished.

Instead of listening to a true teacher and learning to experience one's own inner kingdom, the followers use their respective books and consider them to be the infallible word. Crystallization of thought always walks before moral stagnation. As soon as religion becomes fixed, static or crystallized upon a foundation, a corrupt priesthood is established and at once the whole thing begins to decline into an insipid formalism.

This is history. It is no theory.

Each man must find his own truth; if you fail, then it is your own fault. You have shut the door against your kingdom and barred yourself out. The man Jesus said. 'The works that I do, ye may do also.' Herein lies one great truth that can assist man in shattering his crystallized thought forms, for in this statement lays the key to man's own divine destiny.

There is no monopoly on the path to the inner kingdom of heaven. The doors always swing wide to all who give the right knock. However, the doors swing inwardly; since the door within swings inwardly, the more one pushes to open the door, the harder it is to experience his truth. The door is closed only to the unworthy.

All great teachers instruct that the kingdom of God is within you, and that whosoever seeks shall find. The Spiritual Traveler does still more; he always shows his disciples the exact way to enter the kingdom that lies within each of us, the teacher shows through the Light and Sound, and for a very important reason. One must not only learn and practice the techniques of the Light and Sound, but one must pass through the experience of shattering his preconceived ideas of himself, his society, world and most of all, the Creator Itself.

At some time in Soul's journey, Soul must confront these forms, which have solidified into one great mountain within him. This mountain bars him from his ultimate quest. Once confronted, the Traveler must be prepared, for now he must use the wisdom he has gained like a sword and shatter the chaotic mass of stored negativity created over the eons of his sojourn in the world of the mind. All must be paid. The debt is accrued and awaits each Soul to pay it in full.

Once these past thoughts are cleared, then the crystallized mountain of solidified thought is shattered. In its place, a mountain of love balances the Soul's obligation, and only the Creator's divine love is left.

No one consciously encounters this debt that has taken eons to create, but when he does, the complete debt is now ready to be paid in full. Until this happens, the mind goes on creating more debt. Sometimes the debt is paid down, then it builds up again as man falls back to the seductions of the passions and habits of the mind. It is not the thoughts themselves that are so destructive, but rather the attachment the mind uses from its own web of illusion.

One must be ready to strike when the golden opportunity displays itself, for by shattering the old stagnant crystallized forms, Soul can move as a free agent, no longer hampered by the mind's downward pull into the worlds of duality.

The words of the book stop projecting into my mind.
I close the book, pondering the meaning of this latest transmission. Looking about, all I can see is the brilliant light reflecting off the slab of crystal

I have uncovered. Could this be it? Have my thought forms and negative energy crystallized into this tremendous mountain?

Surely not! How could I shatter a mountain such as this? Looking about, I am convinced of the impossibility of shattering the entire mountain. But then again, maybe I'm not supposed to shatter the entire mountain; maybe I am supposed to destroy only the part that holds me prisoner, the one part that traps me from going forward in any direction.

Carefully, I take my sword and scrape around the edges of the crystalline ledge that holds me prisoner. The ledge from the wall of the cliff is joined with the actual crystal slab I'm sitting on. As I clear around the edges, I see that the crystal slab itself forms an octagon shape. Scraping closer to the cliff side behind me, a small part of the ledge I'm standing on seems to be made from some kind of metal similar to lead or pewter. Carefully, I refine my scraping. When I finally have the edges of the actual crystal defined and traced, I'm left with about two feet of space against the wall behind me to stand on. The rest is a giant eight-sided octagon shape made of crystal. Stepping back, I kneel down. My cape drapes over my shoulders and falls around me on the pewter ledge. Raising my sword, I grasp the hilt with both hands and hold it directly in front of me just above my head.

Looking down at the crystal, which is glimmering and shining like rainbows embedded in glass, I aim for its center. Just as I'm about to strike, I send a quick thought to Dandi and Kaylu warning them to back away from the mountain. Then I strike downward with all my strength into the heart of the giant crystal. The sword drives deeply, embedding itself within the center of the octagon crystal.

I hold on to the hilt, trying to keep it steady as the ledge begins to shake. At first, it's just a small vibration. Then, it actually begins to shake back and forth; I clutch tightly with all my strength. The light within the crystal becomes more brilliant as the trembling increases. Holding onto the sword and clenching my teeth, I close my eyes just as the sword begins to glow. The ledge shakes violently as I push the sword deeper into the crystal. I hear growls and rumbling as rocks fall from above.

The rocks below the crystal begin to break off and fall down the cliffside to the valley below. Struggling to maintain my hold on the sword, I feel the ledge wobbling, falling apart piece by piece. The crystal octagon stays intact as one piece, but it vibrates and shakes as its foundation begins falling away. Keeping my eyes closed and focusing through the spiritual eye, I concentrate on the light within. My muscles ache as the vibration grows in such intensity that I feel as if an electric shock is continuously shooting through my arms and shoulders. Never have I felt such force or pain; I'm enveloped in a shock wave that reverberates throughout my body and mind. I'm not prepared to endure the power coming from the cleansing of my consciousness. Holding on to my sword, I feel myself drowning in wave after wave of electric shocks generating from the crystal. Somehow I know that the power flowing through me is actually life's energy being stepped up to such a high vibration that it seems to be burning my very cells. This process sets my body's systems to a higher frequency, forcing my metabolism to speed up. The cleansing is purifying my consciousness, preparing it to see life with a higher and deeper perception. I hear the mountain behind me roar and shake, as does the crystal. Rocks fall all around me, but I manage to hold on. The sword is my lifeline to maintaining my resolve and strength; it helps keep at bay the fear that so desperately is holding on to the last remnants of my humanity. Somehow I know that a new birth from the Light and Sound is taking place. This new birth is subjecting me to a spiritual cleansing that religions only scratch the surface of at in their rituals.

With a mighty roar and a few last shakes, the power flow ceases. I hear a whisper push into my mind; it says two words: *Crystal Destroyer.* I hear the last few rumbles of falling rock.

I lift my head and open my eyes.

The sky's still there as blue as ever; the valley is laid out below me, but the sword is suspended over thin air. The crystal is gone! I'm kneeling on a ledge of gray pewter-colored rock; my knees are inches over the ledge. Falling back against the wall, I clutch the sword to my chest. As I lean back, I see that the mountain behind me has also changed. No longer is there just a blank wall. To my right and left, I see two gray columns that together form a horseshoe arch above me. The arch is embedded into the mountain with a thickness of about three feet protruding outward from the mountain. Looking at the columned arch, I notice engravings carved into the metal.

The arch reminds me of the one on the TV series, "Stargate," which is a huge circle of metal with runes or symbols engraved into the entire ring. This arch is similar, but it isn't a complete circle. This is just an archway that frames me as I lean backward against the cliff wall. I look down, not by leaning over but by straining my neck and eyes to see below me. Then turning my head, I see the carving of a cave dweller to the left. It's the same type of image as I saw in the Dark Cave except this one has wings and its head is shaped like the river beast. Taking a deep breath, I send my thoughts outward to Kaylu.

"My friends, are you all right?"

Within seconds I feel the familiar push. *"Yes, we are all fine. The avalanche cut away part of the mountain below you; it's formed ledges we can climb on. If I bring a rope, do you think you can make it down?"*

I look around and breathe with relief as I see places I can tie a rope to around the archway.

"Yes! I can't move much, but you can tie a rope here to one of our old friends with no problem."

Kaylu remains silent for a moment, probably wondering what I mean by "old friends."

Soon I hear a noise, and before I have a chance to move to look down, Kaylu appears at the ledge to the right of me. His eyes widen as he sees the archway above me. I smile with relief and say out loud, "Boy, I'm glad to see you."

Kaylu acts quickly. Before I can move back farther against the wall, he jumps from the ledge, first to my right and then to the left. Tying the rope to the neck of the cave dweller statue, he hands the rope to me, then jumps to the other side and waits for me to begin my descent. In no time, both of us are at the base of the mountain joining our comrades in a joyous embrace.

Backing away from the mountain base, I look up to see where I had been trapped, and I can just barely make out the archway formed by the destruction of the crystal. Baylor's eyes are wide in amazement. "How anyone survived that I'll never know, but if someone can, it could only have been you, Captain."

I pick up my backpack and respond, "Our journey is beyond the half-way point; there's no turning back when we leave this island. Let us head back to Soultraveler; with the Creator's blessings, we should be back on the ship before nightfall."

The journey back is indeed quick. The weather is pleasant and before nightfall, we are rowing back to Soultraveler. Once on board, Loren and Karla come running from their cabins. Taking me and Davy into their arms, their relief is obvious. Then they embrace Kaylu and Dandi along with Baylor.

That night, a lightning storm flares for hours as a grand dinner is prepared.

Kaylu and I stand on my cabin balcony watching powerful bolts of lightning strike the island paradise. The giant mountain shimmers in the flash of lights that blast its sides and top.

Morleck seems to be in a much better mood than usual. This night, he makes an announcement. "I have finished my maps and translated the symbols from Hugh's experience with the Dark One; tomorrow morning at sunrise, Soultraveler will no longer sail for parts unknown. We now have a firm direction. We now know for certain we will soon arrive at the Dark One's domain."

I sit at the head of the table watching my friends and comrades enjoy themselves. None could know that as I sit here with them, I'm also exploring across the great waters searching as Soul for the Black Island that holds not only my mom, but also my family's destiny. With the destruction of the mountain crystal, all my thoughts, all the previous experiences, all I've read and have been taught, have been purified.

They are now coalesced into one awareness that merges with the conscious personality and heart of a ten-year-old boy, creating a shattering state of awareness that expands beyond the mind's grasp.

Soul can now travel at will as pure spirit while simultaneously maintaining my warrior's body. With this new ability, my sense of freedom magnifies a hundredfold. I understand now how Soul receives spiritually more than it gives. This is truth for every state of consciousness. For me to receive this ability, my consciousness had to be prepared first to receive it.

Up to this point, my whole journey has been nothing more than a journey of preparation. The Light and Sound are now conscious parts of my total being. If I had been desperate and grasping at straws, then there would be no opportunity for the fulfillment of this gift. If I had sought the Light before I was ready for it expecting miracles would have been futile. However, by allowing the Light and Sound to create circumstances that put my awareness into a state of preparation, I received the one glorious true miracle: a changed consciousness. Extended consciousness can only be experienced through Soul travel, which is beyond the mind and thought. Soul traveling reaches far beyond the frontiers of primal thought; it actually moves Soul into the realms of esoteric experience through inner vision and the Sound Current. The language of feeling replaces Soul's language of words; the language of feeling is then replaced by visual symbols from within, which ultimately are replaced by the Sound Current in which the vibrations of Light and Sound combined becomes oneness to Soul.

In other words, I'm now "The Spiritual Traveler."

CHAPTER 41 ~
MELODY'S SECRET

It's a New England fall morning deep in November. Melody wakes to sunlight streaming through her window. Last night, she dreamed she and Hugh were together again. Hugh was different; he looked the same, but he seemed older, wiser, and far more distant than how she had known him before. Even with these changes, she felt a great love from him as he walked hand in hand with her in a beautiful dreamland.

Getting dressed and grabbing a banana, she tiptoes into her father's bedroom and finds him still asleep. Leaving a note on his dresser, she quietly creeps to the living room where she finds Namo. Soon she's walking the path to the meadow feeling the warm sunshine on her face.

The morning is beautiful, with all the trees dressed in their fall foliage. Some are scarlet red mixed with bright yellows and deep oranges. Leaves fall like raindrops when the slightest breeze wafts through their branches. There's something special about a fall morning; the air is crisp and energy sizzles around her. The ground is covered with fallen leaves that brightly litter the pathway as sunlight scatters its beams through the tree branches. Squirrels run through leaves playing tag; scooting up the tree and then scampering down, they chase each other in a flurry of speed and noise.

Holding Namo so she won't chase the squirrels, Melody walks carefully through the meadow's high grass. Meadow flowers are gone, but sunlight still glistens off dew drops tipping the grass's golden tips and faded green stems. Together with the surrounding colorful trees, the meadow looks like a scene from a Norman Rockwell painting. The grass reaches a little higher than her waist, which makes walking a little slower, but she's in no hurry. There's so much to investigate as the grass folds beneath her feet. Walking along the familiar path, she notices the brook running faster and fuller than normal; the rain from the past few days probably filled the pond where the brook is born from. Burbling waters make a happy sound as the rivulet flows into the meadow and other areas before joining a larger stream deeper in the woods. Flocks of turkeys squeal and with a rush, fly to the lower branches of an aging chestnut tree; the startled birds watch nervously as she passes. All these things mix with the abundant life that lives in the woods; these wonderful vibrant, living things are what she loves most. Her enjoyment never ceases when she walks through a natural setting and observes its beauty all around her.

Namo manages to wiggle free and jumps to the ground. The turkeys excite her, and she isn't about to miss the opportunity to scout out the noises and smells. Just as she lands Melody hears a loud sound to her right. Something's pushing through the tangle of bushes and branches on the opposite side of the brook. Not knowing what to expect, she chases after Namo, trying to catch her before she gets into trouble. A flash of yellow fur scrambles out from the bushes heading straight for Namo. Her heart skips a beat until she recognizes Cody rushing through the dense cover of leaves on the forest floor. He playfully chases the cat up the path toward the tree house. Like a bullet, Namo darts ahead with her tail raised high; she's in no danger and she knows it, but the thrill of the chase is enough to make her rush toward the tree house trying to outrun Cody. Laughing and shouting, Melody joins the race to the giant maple. The ground under the giant tree is ringed by almost a foot deep of colored leaves.

Climbing the ladder, she enters the tree house with Namo following close behind. Cody decides to roll in the deep bed of leaves below the tree. Drawing back the window covering, morning light streams through. With a small broom she finds left in a corner, she sweeps out the dust and cobwebs that seem to constantly appear from nowhere in the corners and crannies of the single room. When all the dust is wiped away, she steps over to the large window and sets her arms on the wooden sill, with her chin resting on her hands.

The tree's coming alive.

Sunlight bounces off thousands of bright orange leaves lighting up the interior of the tree with a brassy glare. Light moves slowly across limbs and leaves, Melody notices animals beginning to grow active again as each recovers from their instinctive freeze caused by her unexpected appearance. Gazing into the brassy light, she slowly closes her eyes and sees the same light within her mind; she watches in her imagination as a scene unfolds.

She thinks of being with Hugh, and the last time he took her fishing. He was always trying to get her to stop being afraid of the worms and hooks, and of course the fish when he caught them. But even though he tried, it didn't help stop her from being scared.

More images in her memories flow, and then blend into the light within her. At first, they are puzzling, but then they began to take on a life of their own: like watching a movie. The more carefully she watches, the more intense and detailed it becomes. She becomes lost in the images unfolding within her mind.

She finds herself hovering above a great ship, the kind of ship she has seen in movies or read about in her books. She's high above the deck looking down from a round box-like perch. The ocean smells clean and refreshing as she looks about her. The wind blows against her face, and she feels the swaying of the ship as it moves through the water, the wind blows, and flaps against huge white sails.

Watching below, she sees men scurrying about tending to the needs of the ship. A young man stands on the upper deck talking with an older man in a long gray robe. The young man looks familiar, but she can't figure out who he is. Feeling the freedom of the open seas, she feels almost intoxicated with the view and energy flowing through her.

Her head jerks up!

She's back looking into the tree from the tree house window; the ship and other images quickly fade from her thoughts, but one image remains: the young man talking to the man in the robe.

What just happened?

Was it just a daydream? But it felt so real! She can still feel the wind and smell the fresh sea air.

A chipmunk creeps to the windowsill looking for a handout. Her attention's still on what had just happened. It was so real; for a brief moment, she felt like she was there. Namo jumps up to the windowsill, and the chipmunk scampers away. The cat rubs her cheek against Melody's shoulder, nudging her as if she was trying to tell her something. Melody picks her up and sits on the couch, thinking about what had just happened. Could the body she was in on the great ship be another part of who she is?

She considers; Brandon said that's what was happening to him; is it possible for me, too?

Lying down on the couch with Namo curled in her arms, she soon falls asleep in the warm sunlight.

As she sleeps, she dreams.

She's watching herself standing in front of a little wooden hut made from sticks and small logs in a grove of trees. Suddenly, she's not watching herself, but she is actually approaching the hut's entrance, and as she does, she feels something warm and wonderful softly diffuse within her heart.

Walking inside the hut, she sees a dirt floor with a mat rolled out to sit on. Hearing a noise from the doorway, she turns around. A boy about her age walks in; he's wearing light brown shorts, and has no shirt or shoes.

"Hi, Melody. I'm Jotan; I've been waiting for you!" A warm feeling passes through her as the little boy sits down on the mat and crosses his legs. "We have a lot to talk about, and some of it concerns your brother Hugh."

Sitting down on the mat opposite Jotan, she looks around the little hut, noticing what looks like models of ships, castles, and assorted things; all of them are made from tiny sticks of wood.

"Those are my toys. I like to build things; maybe someday we can build some things together."

She looks into the small boy's face framed by his light blonde hair, and marvels at his penetrating eyes that seem to look into her very soul. As strange as it should have been, this whole experience felt quite natural to her, almost familiar, especially his name. Then she remembers what Grace in the cafe had told them about a word or name; "Joe Tan."

"Do you have any questions before we begin?"

Melody is puzzled for a moment.

"Begin? Begin what? What is going on? Where am I?" Jotan is quiet for a moment, then looking at her with a thoughtful expression on his face, he replies, "Right now you are in the tree house dreaming, and I'm your dream."

Melody shakes her head, "But where am I?"

Jotan reaches out and points around them. "This is my house; this is where I play."

Melody is quiet for a few seconds and then she presses the issue. "Okay, I can see this is a house even though it's tiny, but if I'm sleeping in my tree house, then how can I be here?"

"Can't you guess?" Jotan smiles.

She thinks for a moment, and then shaking her head she responds, "Is all this inside my head?"

"You are getting warmer, but no, it is not just inside your head. It is inside your imagination, which you as Soul are creating. I'm a part of your creation, as you are mine. Now, let us play! I have a wonderful game we can do together if you are willing." She sits watching the little boy. Even though he's only about six, there's certainly something oddly grown up about him.

"Okay, how do we play?"

Jotan scoots a little closer. "This game is about questions, and us talking and guessing the answers. It's also about your brother."

"Then you know Hugh? Is he all right?"

Jotan reaches out and takes Melody's hands in his. "Yes, he's fine. I was with him some time ago when he was first starting his journey to find your mother. He is not as you remember him though, he has adopted a different body, one that is him, but at an older age. This is necessary to complete what he is attempting to do."

"Where is he now?"

Jotan looks down at the mat and then smiling he looks up into her eyes.

"Hugh is on a great ship called Soultraveler; he's the captain, and he is getting closer to your mother. He is having a wonderful adventure, and he is helping others to grow just as he is growing. He has been very brave so far, but soon he will meet his biggest tests, and he is going to need help from not only his friends, but his family, too."

"What kind of tests?"

"Well, so far, he has fought black demons in a dark cave, and conquered a huge monster called the river beast. In fact, he has even traveled within an evil darkness itself while searching for your mother."

Melody's eyes widen. "Hugh! My brother? Hugh is so nice; it's hard to believe he'd actually fight anyone or anything."

Jotan shrugs. "Well, he is getting pretty good at it. Recently, he climbed a giant mountain, and escaped from a witch who was trying to trap him with magic."

"My goodness! How could my brother do all those things?"

Jotan picks up on her excitement and replies, "He even has a girlfriend."

Melody's mouth drops open. No way! "Hugh's scared of girls; he's so scared of them that when he gets around even my friends, he stutters even more than usual."

Jotan's eyes widens as does his smile. "Oh yeah, I forgot to tell you; he doesn't stutter any more either. He talks like a grown up."

Melody can't believe what she's hearing; her brother with a girlfriend, not stuttering, fighting demons, monsters and witches? It sounds like an enchanted tale.

Jotan continues, "What Hugh is doing is what all Souls eventually go through in one way or another, just not in the exact same way. All must confront the same power, and all must overcome their own demons. Hugh is fighting all the darkness, fears, and temptations that exist in his own inner worlds. By defeating these images, he is getting rid of what has always held him back."

Melody stares at Jotan for a few seconds, and then almost afraid to say anything, she asks in a quiet voice, "Hold him back from what?"

Jotan's eyes sparkles as he replies. "That's part of the game I want to play with you. The game is called, 'In My Soul I Am Free.'"

"How do we play?"

"It's easy. The game is about losing oneself in illusions and then finding oneself, which is like waking up."

Melody's silent for a moment. She then replies, "It sounds confusing; I don't think I'm smart enough to be any good at this game."

Jotan laughs out loud. "Smart enough! Listen, Melody; the smarter you are about life, the farther away you are from it. So-called knowledge exists only in the lower worlds. Sometimes it can be the barrier that separates the seeker from knowing truth. That's why you will do well at this game. The game has two parts, an inside and an outside. The inside is composed of nothing; it is empty. It offers you freedom because of its nothingness, which means there are no limitations to it. The outside world you currently live in is full of images, changes, illusions and questions. The idea is to lose yourself in the outer and then find yourself in the inner; it's like a game of hide and seek. But the great part about this game is that it has no beginning and no end."

Melody scrunches her eyes in a look of confusion. "I know how to play hide and seek, but how do we hide in this game?"

Jotan thinks for a moment and then replies, "The game of Soul is like a movie or a play in which Soul is not only the actor, but the audience as well. So as we lose ourselves in the outer world, which is the stage, we at the same time watch ourselves without being drawn in emotionally into the actual events. In other words, we are the observer and the participant at the same time. The awareness of watching the outer world comes from your inner world, for it is really Soul that is watching."

Melody claps her hands. "Oh I see! It's like when I play with my dollhouse and dolls. I make the dolls do things, and they talk to each other like a real family, but all the time I'm looking from above creating everything they do, knowing that it isn't really real, only make believe."

Jotan jumps up on his knees. "Yes! That's it! Now you have it!"

Melody laughs and asks, "Okay, when do we start?"

"We already have."

Jotan reaches out and touches her softly between her brows, telling her at the same time to close her eyes and look inside.

She feels the small boy's fingers touching her brow. Just that instant, a soft surge of energy seems to press its way up and against his fingers on her forehead. Her inner vision separates as light divides within her, and then she finds herself looking at herself sleeping on the couch in the tree house with Namo in her arms. Not understanding exactly what was happening, she stares.

"The child sleeping on the couch isn't who you are at this moment," Jotan explains.

"When Soul is ready, secrets are revealed. The secrets are an almost unknowable wisdom, for it can only remain within those who are ready to receive it until they give it away. Humans are like marionettes being pulled here and there by the invisible strings of their passions, fears and their higher selves. Sometimes these strings get tangled; this entanglement causes chaos in that person's life.

"As the tangle of life's events knots us to our passions, we desperately try to untangle ourselves through the limited powers of the mind; most of the time it becomes even more tangled within itself and other's life events. The trick is to carry this higher detached consciousness you are experiencing this moment into the outer reality of your human awareness. Living life as pure Soul will allow you to build life from the inside to the outside, instead of in the reverse. How this is done determines the winner of the game: mind or Soul."

Melody then feels Jotan's voice project within her mind.

"Hugh is learning to live as Soul, but his experience is different from yours or your dad's, and now he's closer than ever before. Not only is he close, but he is carrying others with him who are also getting ready to remember their true selves. With each new discovery, the meaning of true freedom becomes more apparent in their consciousness.

"You see, Melody, all Souls are on a journey to discover their personal relationship with the Creator, but before Soul can accomplish this, it must go through the ordeal of fire, which in essence is what all Souls are already doing by living their human existence. A new force is entering Hugh's awareness; it is this force that draws those he loves to his sphere of influence. It doesn't matter whether he is living in the same house or light years away in another dimension or distant universe. The force affects anyone, anywhere, for it is not limited like the mind is. As Hugh grows, spirit begins to enter into the play of his life in a more powerful way. Once this happens, there is no telling what will be in the future. Spirit operates by its own light; mind must follow, whether it likes it or not. This statement is without qualification; it is literally and universally true."

He pauses to give Melody a moment to understand.

"Light, awareness, harmony, plus beauty, wisdom, love, and morality—all come from Soul. They are derived from spirit and imparted to mind by spirit, just as the electric current gives power to the light bulb to make it incandescent.

When Soul goes into the lower worlds, where your corporeal body exists now, it often works under a serious handicap."

Jotan becomes silent for a moment, then looking deeply into Melody's eyes, he says, "You see, Melody, the world you live in is not Soul's true home."

Melody stares at Jotan, trying to understand what he is saying. "Why isn't the world our home?"

Jotan scrunches a little closer and then says, "Soul is obliged to work under and through a series of coverings; one of these coverings is what you call the mind. Once wrapped within mind and body, Soul finds it exceedingly difficult to express itself and have its own way. The more fit the mind, the finer Soul can work through it. However, the mind can become as diseased as the body can. When this happens, Soul is helpless. It can only sit back and watch as catastrophes appear, and suffer in silence. Your earth world is home to the body, but not your true self: the Soul."

Melody blurts out, "Wait a minute. You're going too fast, I still don't understand. Why isn't the earth world my home?" She has a blank look—oddly similar to the look on her dad's face when Brandon talks too much and too fast for him to grasp.

"The earth world is created for Soul to have experiences that will remind it of where it really comes from. The body you have is only a temporary house for your Soul. The body is a form of protection. Your true home is not in the body, but in the reality that the Creator and you are building together."

Melody's quiet for moment, and then speaks. "Sometimes I don't follow everything you are saying, but somehow by you pushing the words into my mind, the meaning seems clearer. If I don't understand, I'll stop you and ask. Just go a little slower, please."

Jotan nods, and begins speaking more slowly and gently. "It is your simple attitude that prevails over my words; not many have the awareness to comprehend what real truth actually is, but let's do continue. The reality being created as your true home is constructed through divine love, which is what you are learning while in the lower worlds. Divine love and its powers are something you have to experience so that you will understand.

"Everything your brother has been through and will still go through is designed to shatter the false images his mind has carried for eons into life after life. Nothing Hugh is experiencing is by accident or coincidence; everything is generated from his own personal universe within him. This applies to you and every Soul that exists, too.

"Soul, the real self, is using the mind's stored images, feelings, memories, fears, longings, and thoughts to create the journey that Hugh's mind is experiencing. This is done by the power of divine imagination. You might call his journey 'The Land of Hugh.' Right now, his mind is desperately trying to escape the control of Soul. If Hugh is not careful, at any moment, his mind is likely to stampede and run away. If this happens, then it may run madly to its own destruction.

"The Soul sits in the innermost chambers of the mind like the captain of a ship. From this place in the mind, Soul controls his ship or his body. This control depends upon his ability to keep the lines of communication open with all parts of his ship, and the control also depends upon the instant response of his crew to its every command of the ship/mind, and the body.

"Remember this, Melody. When existing in the lower worlds, Soul is always in enemy territory. Soul is surrounded by those faithful servants of the negative power, the passions of the mind. These faithful servants are as addicted to intoxicating passions as the drunkard is addicted to alcohol: maybe even more. If allowed, the mind's passions can mislead Soul and the mind. This makes trouble; it's the passions' reason to exist. The worst part about this setup is that the mind rather enjoys being swayed by the passions. You see, once tasted, the passions form a close fellowship with the mind. This fellowship lends a ready ear to all their whisperings. Together, they constantly stir up rebellion, all the more so when one of them—or all of them together—become intoxicated with some new temptation; it is then they all cooperate to send the senses and faculties of the mind into a whirlwind of rebellion against Soul, the real captain of the ship. This explains how the story of Adam and Eve came to exist.

"Man and woman once held the God consciousness within their minds, but temptations from outside sources, such as the passions, senses, and pleasures of the external world, drew humans down from God consciousness deep into the consciousness of the body. So, in a way, it is true that man and woman lost a paradise, but this wasn't a physical garden of Eden, but rather a great state of awareness. They lost this state of awareness by succumbing to lower pleasures, and drawing their awareness down to the level of human consciousness as it is known today. Now, each and every human being must struggle to reach the exalted heights again. The mind and body passions cannot enter the holy chambers of Soul if they are guarded by the Holy Word, or the protection of what is also known as Sound Current and Divine Light. The ship that Hugh now sails is a reflection of his inner self. He is learning to take command of his own mind. If he fails to do so, he will be like the man rafting along a treacherous river current, heading for a large waterfall, and with no oars to help steer away from danger. If he succeeds, he will be like the eagle that soars above all life guided by spirit. Freedom will be his call, and love will be his duty. This is how one becomes the Spiritual Traveler."

Melody sits quietly listening to Jotan, absorbing as much as she can. As he speaks, somehow she can see what he's saying in images, which makes her comprehension far deeper than normal.

She says, "There is so much I don't understand, but when I think of any questions to ask, they all seem silly. I wish so terribly much that I could be with Hugh! I miss him so much."

Jotan moves in much closer, until his face is just a few inches from hers.

Melody looks deeply into his eyes; her vision begins to swim. She feels a surge of warmth and love rush through her heart. Jotan's eyes are like two clear pools of water that one drops a small pebble into; waves of circular energy emanate out from the depths of his eyes, pulling her into a vast pool of unconditional love. Jotan's childlike voice reverberates with incredible clarity throughout her consciousness.

"Melody, always know this…You have been with Hugh every step of the way."

She feels as if she's falling into a great ocean of love and mercy. All thoughts stop. Only love is left; only love matters. A whisper like the wind brushes against her ear, moving deep within her mind.

One word, one name, echoes within the recesses of her heart…Kaylu.

CHAPTER 42 ~ SEAS OF DANGER

Soultraveler moves away from the island. The sun's rising as the ship drifts from the misty cove and heads out to open seas. Kaylu and I are on the bow looking back at the isle that nearly cost us our lives. As the sun breaks over the horizon, beams of light radiate over the dark sea; a rocky shoreline is barely visible. As I look at the island, I see something incredible.

"Kaylu, look there in the center of the island."

Kaylu turns, and just as the morning light spreads its way over the island, the Mountain of Light that I had been trapped on lights up like a giant jewel rising from the darkness. The lightning storm from last night apparently sent bolts of lightning into the great mountain, shattering the remaining covering of dirt, rock, and sediment that had accumulated for so long. After the following rain, the mountain now gleams in the morning sun, sending waves of shimmering light in various colors out across the sky. The sight is magnificent, even from a great distance. The mountain shines like a beacon in the middle of the ocean, and as Soultraveler sails off further, the Mountain of Light remains within sight for most of the morning.

Once we are far out into the open seas I meet with Morleck to go over the new maps he has made. He rolls out each map on a large table in his cabin, and one by one, he explains what he's created.

"There are many signs pointing the way to your mother; we must look carefully for them."

I pore over and study the meticulous drawings, admiring the detail the old man has patiently and painstakingly drawn out. How he has determined the directions and entered what's lying ahead for us is beyond me. According to the alchemist's maps, we must head north. Along the way, we will be confronting dark areas that holds who knows what. Dangerous areas are defined by shadows. What lies within the shadows, no one knows, but they are plainly marked alongside currents and small islands that dot their route to the far north. Supposedly, the negative portal waits for anyone foolish enough to come into its area. I'm not so foolish as to think that because of my new ability of Soul traveling, I can penetrate the darkness and defeat mom's captors. In reality, if I'm careless or foolhardy enough to try to penetrate the darkness as Soul, I could very well become trapped within the portal's power as well. We will have to play this game inch by inch; each moment will only reluctantly reveal what danger lies in wait. The only advantages these maps provide are to make us aware of the direction and that danger is certainly waiting.

Abaddon's power grows stronger as we sail closer to its domain. If we aren't careful, it will infect us in numerous ways, especially if strict discipline is not applied to not only crewmen and friends, but to myself as well. I must take care with this newfound ability to travel beyond my body as pure consciousness; if used carefully, it will assist me greatly in making sure the ship doesn't fall prey to the dark passions within men's minds—and those I, too, might generate.

While the sun's still high, I arrange a meeting with Morleck, Dandi, Kaylu, Loren, Davy, Karla, and the six crystal guards. We all gather together in the ship's great room, which is designed as both a meeting hall and dining area for formal meals, important trade meetings or other business dealings. Once everyone arrives, I take my place at the head of the table, and when all is quiet, I stand to speak.

"We're here to discuss how to navigate the rest of this journey. Before we start, I want to say something to all of you." What I have to say is important to me; it clarifies my feelings with each and every one of you. I'm quiet for a moment while I look into each person's eyes before I continue.

"I count you as my friends and comrades, and to each of you, I give my greatest love and respect. Without your support, I would never have gotten this far, and for that I am grateful. In order to successfully complete this quest, we all must come to a complete understanding about the discipline and rules we must abide by. We are about to enter a domain that is controlled by forces beyond our understanding. What we do know is that the darkness seeks cracks within each of us so that it can enter and overpower us. We experienced this when we were attacked by the darkness earlier. From that confrontation, Morleck, the guards, and I have tasted what's to come. For us to not be overtaken by this insidious force, we must apply all the principles of discipline the Creator has given us. It's through these disciplines that Soul will control the mind and body. Control of the mind, body, and environment is essential. This control will depend on the strength and understanding we have in our awakened consciousness."

Nobody says a word; all remain silent intent on listening. I feel odd; the way I'm speaking and my words seem as if someone else is talking instead of me by myself. I continue.

"Each man and woman is different from one another; their differences are in accordance with the law of karmic evolution. This is purposefully designed, as a process which reflects the continued unfolding of the individual spirit in alignment with whatever individual habits, feelings, and weaknesses to which they are bound. Abaddon will try to encourage and take advantage of any of these individual weaknesses. We must let go our attachments, and not only to things outside of us, but to our inner attachments as well. Our emotions are going to be one of our most dangerous weaknesses. To prepare for this challenge, for the rest of this journey we must continuously try to react from a higher state of awareness. This awareness must come from Soul and not from the mind. If we are to succeed, we must surrender totally and unconditionally to the Creator's direction. This is easily said, but what does that actually mean?"

I pause for a moment, taking the time to gaze into each person's eyes again, and somehow forge a direct connection to each. "It means that in the past, we have been seeing the world only through our minds; in doing so, we are preventing Soul from being 'what it is.' Each of us must come to realize we're living in a perfect universe with perfect ideas. This perfection appears to us more clearly as we harmonize with it. As you praise and bless everything in the world, you dissolve negativity and dispel discord. This tactic allows you to align yourself with the highest frequency...love. We love because we are love. We seek joy because we are joy. We thirst for truth because each of us is an expression of truth. Soul exists in the eternal now, which contains truth alone. Love and wholeness fill me, and they also exist perfectly within each of you. From the moment I came into this new world, I have been taught how to do this and how to do that; and I have absorbed most of the wisdom that has been given me. At the Mountain of Light, however, I had a truly transformative experience and a new realization, which together have given me the power to use my new wisdom correctly and at just the right time. From the experience on the Mountain of Light, I can perceive eternity; I see it through an inner sight, hearing, and a deep knowing—most especially, by a simple and deep knowing.

"This new knowledge reveals to me that I am not special. Each of us has access to this knowingness of the oneness that Soul has been attempting to find through its inner senses. This knowingness creates a deep understanding of what has been seen, heard, and known in all things you experience. As Soul, I recognize or realize my relationship with the Creator through mind-realization and self-realization. This is not to say that I have reached the peak of Soul's awareness—far from it—but I do have control over my lower kingdoms, and my lower passions don't rule me. Without your help, I would not have attained the attributes that I now have, nor be this close to helping my mom; I sincerely thank you for this. Through my experience of Soul traveling, my view is no longer limited to just human consciousness, and somehow I know that each of you is also at the threshold of your own realization and choices. From here on, your conscious choices will determine your destiny throughout eternity."

I pause for a moment, letting new thoughts and words manifest within my mind and then I speak again. "I came to this world as a child: bewildered, frightened, unaware, and lost, looking for my mom. But in reality, aren't we all like frightened children? Lost and looking for our parent? I encountered Souls offering their hearts and taking me under their wings to nourish and protect me. They then began to see the lost child hidden within each of them, and from that realization, they now strive to grow as much as I have. We are on this journey together for a purpose. It isn't coincidence we're together, for each of us has been a part of each other's lives many times and in many ways. We must know and understand that we are brothers and sisters of the same creation, and when we help each other, it stands to reason that we're helping ourselves, too. So what I ask of you will be difficult, but with proper understanding of what we stand for, and who we really are, I know we will succeed, because with our very attempt and with proper understanding, we have already won."

Anticipating their question, I ask, "What is it we have won? The answer is simple: freedom! My mother is one of my symbols of freedom; she is the person we seek to free. In your quiet moments, focus on her and the Creator. By doing this, we can free ourselves from the mind's tyranny and from the limited and biased concepts we perceive as our existence.

"I know now that each of us is so much more than what we are commonly taught. Once we let go of the barriers that our attachments cling to, such as fear, anger, envy, vanity, and other mindlessness, we begin to understand our own divinity. Our ascension shows how simple we as children of the Creator really are. We must control all emotions, and also the mind from this point on, and subdue all the passions that might arise within us. By drying up all fear and leaving our past behind us, we are free to just be Soul. Gone are our perceptions of who we were in the past; whatever we were yesterday, we are not that now. We are all so much more in the eternal present. We are all 'Swordsmen of the Creator,' each with our own inner shield and our own sword of power. These weapons can only exist by surrendering to the Creator as Soul. Our limited awareness of the mind is gone, evaporating like a mirage in the hot desert sands. In its place stands an entity with no limitations. Soul no longer watches you, but has become you...So as each of you look about, know that you are all brothers of the Hu, for that is the secret name of our father, and within his name lies our power."

Hugh then stops and again looks intently and deeply into the eyes of each person at the table before he sits down.

Loren stares at him as if transfixed. What just happened? Where is the naïve young man she met back in the cave not so long ago? Who is this stranger, who not only takes command of others effortlessly, but also employs his words as if they are razor sharp knives, each word cutting into the depths of the Soul? Each person feels not only the power in his words, but they also feel the expansion of their own awareness. As he carefully outlines the necessary behavior for success, Hugh is no longer the young warrior ready to follow, but the man destined to lead.

While Dandi stares at Hugh, he, too, thinks about the boy he first met, and he wonders how in such a short time, Hugh has grown so much. He is now very clearly the Captain; of that there is no doubt. Dandi can't help but feel proud about Hugh's willingness to engage with and learn from the difficult and harrowing experiences that he has encountered. Having survived and succeeded in each test, the young man before him has become a great leader.

Morleck watches Hugh closely. Ever since his return from the island, Morleck has sensed something different about him. Hugh's eyes reflect a strength that most men can only dream about, and his face reflects an ageless wisdom that even intimidates him somewhat.

Kaylu also feels something different about his friend, but the change he senses isn't so much in the confidence and power that now exudes from Hugh. Rather, what Kaylu feels most intensely is Hugh's humility and love. And even more important, Kaylu feels how his friend not only has transformed himself, but his presence among them is changing all those who come into his orbit of influence.

Hugh looks out over his comrades. As he settles into his chair, he wonders how he can tell them what he is really seeing and feeling from each of them. Do they know that each of them radiates a light of shimmering colors from within? That each of them feels like a part of his self? That each is a powerful entity with endless purity and power? Hugh sees and feels this and so much more; the recognition of their true nature humbles Hugh, and he feels a profound sense of gratitude for their loyalty and trust.

That night as I prepare for sleep, I wonder what Loren's doing. I feel it would be wise to avoid any temptation of sex while we travel in dangerous waters; no sense in tempting the fates. As much as I wanted to be with her, I know opening myself up to even the most miniscule of emotions could have deeper ramifications, especially if the Abaddon is anywhere near to take advantage of our passion. No, it is far better that she stays with Karla while we sail into enemy territory. The experience with the Riverman and the witch remind me how treacherously the magic of passion can pull a person down the road to ruin. With the Abaddon's ability to exaggerate and enhance our physical responses and emotions, even the slightest slip could prove disastrous.

All night, Soultraveler sails deeper into the darkness, following Morleck's carefully charted map that is so clearly drawn and notated that it allows the helmsman to even sail by just the stars.

Morleck stays up most of the night, watching and contemplating what they are about to encounter from his perch on the bow's throne. He knows their degree of success will be measured by how well the crew and their leaders resist the Abaddon's powers.

The waters grow darker as Soultraveler moves closer to the borders guarding the portal and its dominions. Morleck's confidence in me is immeasurable, but I know the mission's success isn't just about me. Every man and woman onboard is susceptible to the dark force's power which can bring out our lower natures. Once someone is under the Abaddon's control, it's anybody's guess as to the destructive evils it could release. In reality, each person is nothing more than a miniature portal; what flows from each of us could very well destroy Soultraveler and the entire mission. On the other hand, if a person is disciplined enough, he can act as a vehicle for the Light and Sound and counteract the negativity flowing within. Tomorrow morning, Morleck and I will need to have a discussion with the crewmen about what lies ahead, and how they must guard themselves in their daily activities.

****

The next morning, I'm up dressed and ready to go just as the sun breaks the horizon. Walking out on my balcony, I stare out across the vast waters.

The ocean has changed.

No longer is it a bright, clear turquoise blue with a surface like glass. The waters are a dark, brackish, green/blue; its currents do not flow synchronously, but rather crisscross each other, causing small, choppy waves and whitecaps. Faded light reflects on its darkening surface as it fights to break free out of dark clouds. As Soultraveler speeds through the troubled waters, huge dark gray and brown thunderheads roll out across the heavens; there's a sharp chill in the air that makes me wrap my cape around my shoulders to ward off the cold. Lightning crackles in the distance.

Looking into the depths of the waters reflecting the sparring storm clouds, I feel as if I'm staring into my own mind as it fights to take back control from my doubts, passions and—more than anything else—fear. I remember something similar to what Shakti said: "Even those who others see as having gained so much in wisdom, power, and freedom still fight daily to hold onto what they have gained." And so it seems, for even now I feel the ceaseless battle raging within me, similar to the battle being played out before me in the sea and the clouds.

By focusing my attention on fighting these passions and fears, I only give them life and let their will dominate. To counter this, I decide to force my attention on things that I must accomplish and only those things that don't take advantage of my trust. My father, Melody, this quest, and the dire situation my mother is going through—all are part of the battle within myself. They also constantly keep pushing me forward. Within all of this mental chaos lies the foundation I've built from love, trust, and faith in the Creator. Whatever comes forth, I know that the Creator has bestowed within me the power to rise and eventually overcome any attack from the Dark One. The trick is to not get sucked back down into the lower consciousness; if that happens, then I will be controlled by the mind again. I feel a touch at my shoulder; Loren stands beside me. We look out over the threatening sky in silence. I stretch out my arm, opening my cape to shelter her from the first drops of rain as they begin to fall. I feel the warmth of her courage, and I feel comfort in the confidence and trust she has given me. Together, we will confront whatever is out there waiting, with the strength of not only our love, but the wisdom and power from the depths of our Souls.

CHAPTER 43 ~ THE CALL OF SOUL

Ann Clark trembles in her dark world.

Her hands won't be still, nor will any other part of her drained body. Her sense of time and space is distorted; what are weeks or months to others is at times just a moment to her. The insidious side effect of this distorted concept of time is that she sometimes experiences a jolt of pain that seems to extend on like eternity. Nothing is right, nothing is permanent or temporary. In this environment, it's impossible to collect her thoughts or feelings. The negative force never lets up; it's the only constant reality in her existence. Ann senses she is losing herself in this new world of pain and darkness. Distorted images and alien feelings seem to be thrust into her consciousness against her will. In a long, extended silent scream, she shouts, "Why is this happening? Where am I? Is there no escape?" Death would be a blessing over what she's experiencing. Her struggles are useless in fighting this force; her mind only binds her more tightly into a sticky web of fear and loss of self. For brief seconds, Ann thinks of her family, trying to focus on the memories of something lost, something she hadn't appreciated to its fullest when she had it. Most of the time, these memories are distant; they pop up like just a glimmer in her mind, and then as suddenly as they have arrived, they are gone. Within the chaos of her torture, a flash of the love her family feels for her breaks through her consciousness, and for these rare, brief moments, she observes the feelings as they crash into the evil that fights to subdue her. These brief respites are her life support; she hangs on to these feelings while everything else that is human seems to be sucked from her and dissipated into the darkness. Tears are useless; they only whet the appetite of the evil that continuously feeds on her life force. Ann Clark pleads for a miracle.

****

Unknown to Ann, salvation is hidden deeply within her own mind. Her belief in yesterday's God, who punishes her for the many mistakes she has made in her life, is only one of the prison bars in her mental cell. The moments of happiness and growth in her past are all but buried by her feelings of sadness, loss, guilt, and fear; she has become the victim of her own mind. Doesn't her God have mercy, as it says in the Bible? Is this hell? Is she even alive, as she understands living? Ann would give up completely if she knew the beliefs she holds about her God are actually the perpetrators of her misery.

For even though she knows her God as a God of love, she was brought up as a child and young adult to know this God is also wrathful. He demands vengeance, and He judges her according to her very thoughts, actions, and beliefs. Her God of yesterday does not punish her just once, but over and over. This is her belief system, and by accepting this agreement, the mind creates what she agrees to and then keeps her attention trained on it. Her mind constantly summons these illusory images and concepts and graphically portrays these destructive creations in her mental visions.

She doesn't understand that her believed negative experiences and thoughts are as if chains of iron, and they can hold her body, and the things she sees as good or right are chains of gold that hold her Soul.

The waking dream of life she has ascribed to throughout the years now helps keep her trapped in this dream of hell. Mind quietly builds up one's inner kingdom based on those concepts and feelings that each person accepts as their own; Ann's inner kingdom has been built out of a sense of guilt, sadness, fear, anger, betrayal, emotional love, attachments, strict morals, and rules about acceptable conduct within her society. Her God has emotions and feelings of His own; it's no wonder that the trap holding her is so successful. After the auto accident, her mind awoke trapped within her own imagined afterworld. Just as her own thoughts have created her God, so has it created this unique prison. There is no escape as long as she clings to her intractable concepts, such as the attachments and beliefs she holds about herself and God. Ann's beliefs act like a blindfold to the one great truth hidden deep within her being. Soul can only observe, and with great effort, send light into her darkened consciousness. What little influence Soul does have, is love. Ann feels this love in those rare moments when she lets go, either when dreaming or during those brief moments of recognition of her real self. When this happens, she feels and sees the warm light, but then the darkness screams a howl of vengeance, and strives harder to twist her in its negative magnetic grip. Ann feels the force respond more aggressively as it twists her thoughts and feelings; the light fades. However, for one brief instant, when she's thinking of Hugh and the rest of her family, Ann feels a brief respite; the evil isn't invulnerable! It has a crack in its armor of darkness where love penetrates as a warm light. With tremendous effort, she calls out her son's name, remembering their last moments at the tree house.

As she cries out her son's name in her mind, the dark force shakes her unmercifully, but still she holds on. Her son's name is her sword; she sends it forth again, long and drawn out, *Huuuu…*

The darkness responds with screams of madness. The darkness responds with vengeance. Further screams erupt from the Dark essence as the vibration of Hu ripples across its being. Ann barely has the conscious strength to repeat his name again, but she does. The force again screams its rage and terror, spitting out multiple layers of images, each more malevolent and revolting than the next; distorted bizarre faces of fury and hate crash down into her mind. Weakly, she sends out his name again: *Huuuu…*For just that moment, Ann feels release as Hugh's name echoes within her inner kingdom; then everything collapses back again, fading into the darkness.

The black force manipulates itself bit by bit to regain control; it shrugs off the positive vibrations Ann had summoned that sent electronic shocks throughout its malevolent essence. The battle for her soul continues as the darkness regroups to renew its efforts to feed on and drain all hope from the astral body of Ann Clark.

CHAPTER 44 ~
DREAM MASTER

Clark lies in bed. So far, it has been a restless night.

Tonight, his mind has a life of its own. The more he tries to sleep, the more his mind races taking his imagination along with it. Pictures, words, worries, dilemmas, and memories run the gauntlet within his brain before colliding with thoughts of his son and wife.

Lying in the dark, he tries to concentrate on the humming in his ears. According to Brandon, this sound is part of what he calls the Audible Life Stream, or the Sound Current. Even though it's merely a humming sound, if he uses his power of attention and focuses on its vibration within his inner ear, the sound will change to higher frequencies that can lead to higher states of consciousness. The Bible calls it the Word; other teachings have called it the Bani, Logos, or Music of the Spheres. The Koran calls it Kalma-Ilahi. It is the NAD of the Vedas, and the Saut-i-Surmad of the Sufis.

The sound has so many names and is so prominent throughout the history of Earth that it's amazing that the masses today ignore this most vital, simple, yet powerful teaching. Clark has felt its effects in the past, but not to any particular extreme. He knows with discipline and patience, the spiritual senses can open up to these higher sounds. According to Brandon, once a person learns how to use it, the sound will assuredly lead a person to a more expanded awareness, and possibly even spiritual enlightenment. Many teachings use echoes of this original sound in their prayers, meditations, or songs. Some say it is the essence of God or the voice of God. The chanting of sacred words such as Aum, Om, Alleluia, Love or Hu are sounds that help the mind to focus and experience the spiritual aspects of this holy sound.

Clark continues to listen to the humming.

Slowly, his mind begins to calm down and he focuses his attention on the inner eye.

The inner or spiritual eye has the unique quality that if a person concentrates on it, he can still the ramblings of the mind. If persistent, a person can actually open the door to the realms of heaven by concentration on the inner eye. The Eternal Journey back to the Creator actually begins at this third eye or inner door. From this point, Soul moves inward eventually leaving all material bonds behind; even the mind itself is eventually left behind. Through ancient spiritual exercises, the seemingly impossible becomes possible. The finer senses or the spiritual senses become active, and by their correct use, they can be transformed. At first, the Sound Current is weak—often imperceptible—but with faith and continuous practice, eventually the Music of the Spheres is heard. Once experienced, it becomes easier each time the techniques are practiced. The sound is unsurpassed by anything else; divine music literally pulls Soul inward on wave after wave of Sounds, like a magnet drawing Soul inwards toward its inner kingdom.

As man's consciousness expands, it ascends. Soul ultimately becomes purified from all negative attributes learned during its sojourn on Earth. Combined with this sound, the inner light actually forms energy in the form of vibrations that allow the seeker to open the secret inner door and explore personal inner kingdoms or what Jesus called, "mansions" in his father's house. This energy/vibration is in reality the essence of the Creator sometimes called spirit.

The first step of the journey to God has always lain hidden within each person's own body. These secret spiritual sciences are what all great teachers have used and taught.

Jesus, Apollonius, Socrates, Tolstoy, and others all have affirmed that the Kingdom of Heaven exists within. This is why the body is referred to as a temple; if people will just open themselves to understand that they possess spiritual senses along with their physical senses, this world could become paradise.

Clark's thoughts seem to be plugged into some kind of spiritual notebook; everything coming to him keeps bubbling up from within, like a fountain overflowing with words. Things that he had wondered about in the past now make sense to him from a spiritual viewpoint. Keeping his attention continuously on his inner eye, he slowly falls asleep.

Unknown to Clark, together with the help of the Sound Current, his thoughts are forming a new matrix within his mind. This matrix is being filled with new spiritual insights through which he can dream in a higher level of awareness.

As Clark sleeps, he dreams.

He watches himself sitting on a flat rock overlooking a large pool of water encircled by giant trees. Waterfalls drop down over huge branches before splashing into the waters below. The sound of the water tumbling off the large branches is almost melodic. A fine mist brushes against his face. For a few moments, he looks around in amazement; at the same time, he notices numerous tiny details around him. He notices small rainbows forming circular patterns where the falling water splashes in the pool; he notices that the rhythm of the water cascading from above reminds him of a favorite song's beat. These little observations plus a multitude of others depict the whole scene so completely, so fully, that the brilliant experience touches his mind and heart in a way he never felt before.

Gazing across the pool, he sees a stone arch bridge extending from one end of the pool to the other. Looking about, he becomes aware he's dreaming, but is this only a dream? This isn't like any previous dreams he's ever experienced. He read somewhere about lucid dreams; is that what he is having?

For the first time, he's in total control of his thoughts while in the dream-state. The dream continues to unfold around him; never has he seen such beauty with such clarity. He can't recall when he has felt more aware or alive than at this very moment. Carefully stepping down off the rock, he moves down a small pathway leading to the stone bridge, its edges lined with dark green ferns and flowers. The aroma of the water and the trees smell familiar: jasmine, pine, and sandalwood, all blended with honeysuckle. Walking the pathway by the pool, he steps up on the bridge to cross over. For some reason, he feels drawn to the woods on the other side. Realizing that his physical body is asleep in his bed back home gives him the sense that this is much more than just a dream.

A movement catches his attention.

Stopping for a moment to see what it is, he discovers a shadow moving up ahead. He can barely make out the dark form standing behind the great trees. Moving closer quickly, he reaches almost the middle of the bridge. Peering closely into the trees, he catches a glimpse of the figure moving out from the dark shadows of the woods. As the figure walks from dark into the light, Clark takes a few steps back. A young man steps out upon the bridge from the other side. He's wearing a dark maroon cape draped over his back, concealing a scabbard with a sword hilt slightly protruding. His boots are light brown, almost tan, and they have etchings on them. His shirt is white with small lacings tied together instead of buttons. What stuns Clark even more is the resemblance this man has to someone he knows so well.

The young man calmly walks into the light; the look on his face is almost regal as he approaches. Half-way across, his steps quicken, and a smile appears on his face as his eyes twinkle brightly. The young man begins to half run, half walk. As he gets closer, he calls out in his excitement, "Da'!"

A surge of love bursts within Clark; Hugh! "Oh my God…son, is it really you?"

The young man falls into his outstretched arms. "Da', it's me! You're here! I can't believe it! I've missed you so much!"

Clark holds his son, who is now as tall as he; his eyes mist as tears well up. A second surge of love rushes through him. "Son! I can't believe it; it's really you!"

Hugh steps back, still holding his dad's arms. "It's me, Da'; older, but still me."

"How is this possible? Look at you, you've grown up!"

"Da', there's so much to tell you, but now isn't the time. I'm just so glad you learned how to contact me. We have a lot to discuss and very little time to do it in."

Clark stares at his son and then asks, "How is this happening? And where are we? Are you all right? Where's your mom?" Clark is just bursting with questions and excitement; between his feelings for his son and the excitement of actually seeing him, emotion overwhelms him. How much he has changed! His son is a young man; but there's something else, something different, something uplifting about Hugh. Clark feels confidence and power exuding from Hugh's presence.

Hugh tries to explain to his Dad what's happening.

"Da', somehow you've opened yourself to the Light and Sound, which has brought you to this place. What you're seeing right now is a projection of what I look like in this different world. My body is really in contemplation on a great ship called Soultraveler."

Clark interrupts. "But how did you find me?"

For a moment Hugh becomes quiet. Father and son stand in the middle of the arched stone bridge with waterfalls falling around them. Rainbows of light project patterns of color above and below, while long hanging willow branches sway just above them. "I was contemplating when I felt your thoughts and feelings. Then using the Sound Current, I followed your thoughts here. Right now we're both using our astral bodies for this meeting."

Somehow Clark didn't think what Hugh was telling him was so strange. He remembered what Brandon said about each person having several different bodies, each at a different vibration existing within us. Each body exists as a state of consciousnesses. Our attention is what gives it energy, which then gives it form. The body moves by this energy and is an image of our thoughts, but for Hugh to reach out and find him as he dreamed was unbelievable!

Hugh walks his Dad to the edge of the bridge overlooking the pool and says, "Da', right now you're in a place similar to where I was earlier in my journey. I think the reason why we've met among these giant trees is so the shock would be lessened. The waterfalls you see are coming from rivers and streams high above us on a mountain behind the trees. I'm on the other side of that mountain on a ship in the middle of a great ocean."

Clark looks bewildered as Hugh quickly explains how they came together. Hugh hesitates for a few seconds, and then says, "Da', I think I'm getting close to finding Mom. When I reach her, I believe you and Melody will need to help me. This is why I'm here with you now. There are things you must know if you're going to help."

Hugh quickly gives his father a brief overview of his journey. Then he explains that through what he's learned and experienced, he has gained the ability to contact those he loves, no matter what the distance, and even through their dreams if necessary. This ability only works if the one he's thinking about is receptive to him.

After catching Clark up to the events leading to this meeting, Hugh says, "Da', you must believe what I'm about to tell you. I assume that you're learning like I am, and will recognize truth when you hear it. If you hadn't, you wouldn't be here. First and most important, believe this—Mom is alive! I'm not sure exactly where she is, but I know I'm close, and I know there's going to be a battle. This battle will be for the very Soul of not only Mom, but you, Melody, and me as well."

Clark is puzzled. "How are Melody and I involved?"

Hugh is quiet for a moment as he looks deeply into his father's eyes then he says. "We—meaning Mom, you, Melody, and me—have been together far longer and closer than you know. We have chosen to be together again in this lifetime to help each other find spiritual freedom."

Clark listens closely. What he's hearing seems impossible, but after all he has confronted and experienced, he knows that nothing's impossible any longer.

Hugh continues, "Through her depression and fears, Mom has created not only a prison for herself, but she has also created conditions that are allowing us to manifest this entire experience in such a manner that we will either win our freedom, or we will lose all we've gained throughout our journey in the lower worlds. There's a dark power trying to stop us from our finding this freedom. It cannot destroy us as Soul, but it can wrap dark and powerful illusions around us so that we forget what we've gained. If it succeeds, then a fate far worse than what we call death awaits us. Only now are we just beginning to understand our true nature as Soul. This understanding has been expedited due mainly to what happened to me and Mom in the car accident."

Hugh places his hand across his father's shoulders. "Da', one thing I know for sure. I'm learning in my own way as you and Melody are learning in your own ways, but no matter how each of us learns, and no matter how far away we seem to be from one another, it's important that you realize that as Soul, we have chosen this course of action together. We're bound by invisible cords of unconditional love."

Clark replies, "I know, son; the last few months have been lessons beyond anything I could ever have imagined. But even though it's been a nightmare at times, I see now that it has helped advance me and your sister's own growth."

Hugh nods. "Da', this learning comes from the Creator's love, or what is called the Sound Current. It's actually the divine essence—what we call spirit—coming from God the Creator. It flows from the Creator and is the binding force that not only creates everything, but also holds all creation together. It's the same power that makes a small child smile; it's the energy and intelligence that make the flowers bloom in spring. It creates, unites and ties us all together as one great family of the Creator. This Sound Current teaches that love is the only thing that really matters. Because when all else fails, love is what Soul falls back on and then finally becomes. I wouldn't be here right now if it were not for the Creator's love, and neither would you. The greatest truth I've learned is that Soul exists because of the Creator's love for it. Because of the way Mom was brought up in this lifetime, and because of her move from Ireland to the States, Mom has forgotten her own way, she has unknowingly created dire situations by accepting concepts of a yesterday's God. Her concept of what she believes God is, has unknowingly grown into this dangerous situation.

"Her bringing us to this point makes also what happened a blessing in disguise. From the mind's point of view, this is a sad, terrifying and horrible situation. That's the way the mind sees almost everything that threatens its survival and control. Fear is mind's greatest tool. And believe me, Da', the mind will ferret out negative situations in anything it wants to control. If successful, it then infects other minds to believe its lies and manipulations. This infection has a trickledown effect that allows what I call the Dark One to gain control of vast worlds and universes throughout the Creator's lower kingdom."

Clark's eyes grow wider.

"It's important we keep practicing the Hu with our contemplations, for doing this will build our power and our love. It is also the vehicle we communicate with, no matter where we are. Your calling my name with love is what builds the matrix within you for the higher consciousness you're now experiencing."

Clark reaches out and grasps his son's shoulders. "Son, I am sorry to interrupt, and I don't know how you know all of this, but I feel our time is almost up. I want you to know that no matter what, I will be there for you. I am so proud and I feel so blessed to have you as my son. Both Melody and I will do whatever is necessary to help you, but I have just one more question I need to have answered before I go."

Hugh puts his hand on the ledge of the bridge wall and stares over the glistening pool of water. He doesn't want to leave his Dad again.

Clark continues. "I was given a name by a lady who had a remarkable story. Since then, I can't get the name out of my head, and I thought that maybe you might be familiar with it."

Hugh turns to his dad. "What is it?"

Clark looks over the waters, and then exhaling he says, "Joe Tan."

Jotan!

"I know the name well. Jotan is a Spiritual Traveler who has helped me throughout this entire journey. I first met him when I had barely arrived in this world. I was trying to find mom, but didn't know where to look. Jotan was the one who not only pointed my way, but also gave me my sword, my boots, and what some would call my Bible." Hugh reaches in his shirt and pulls out the little jeweled book. "This is it; it's called The Way of the Traveler."

The book's cover sparkles as light strikes its embedded jewels. Clark stares; light radiates each gem and they blaze into his consciousness. His vision begins to blur; the world around him fades. The book is the last thing Clark sees before he awakens to find himself in his own bed back home.

****

I watch as Da' fades and then vanishes. Realizing the visit is over, I think about Soultraveler and within seconds I'm back sitting on my bed in the cabin.

Opening my eyes, I feel very alone.

Seeing Da' for a few moments reminds me even more how much I miss my family. The ten-year-old boy inside me wants my Da' and family to be together again more than anything. The empty feeling of homesickness spreads throughout me mind. Even with all the discipline I've learned, even with all the wisdom I've gained, all of this can't stop my tears as I think of Da'. I brush them away. Now isn't the time to be caught with a bad case of homesickness. It's very early, and Morleck and I are scheduled to address the crew this morning. Washing my face, I look into the mirror at my reflection.

As I'm staring, I notice something; my face seems a little older. It isn't so noticeable at first glance, but as I look closer, I can make out slight lines around the corners of my eyes, and for the first time, my face feels slightly grizzled, indicating a light growth of fuzz on my cheeks and under my nose.

I no longer look eighteen: more like twenty-three or so. Brushing hair from my eyes, I realize I'm growing and aging faster in this body. I wonder how long it would take before I'm too old to complete my task?

Walking out on the cabin's balcony, I watch the gray skies. The ocean waters are blacker than yesterday. Huge dark clouds move across the rough sea. Waves roll and pitch as Soultraveler cuts through small valleys and hills of rolling water. Whitecaps form as waves crash against each other. Even though the waves are relatively small, I sense intense energy building in the air, gradually getting thicker. A knock at the door interrupts my thoughts, and with a shrug, I turn to meet the day.

I find Baylor waiting for me as I step out from my cabin. Then I discover with a start that the entire crew—including my comrades and the crystal guards—is fully assembled and waiting for me.

Morleck steps forward. "Captain, we called the crew together to address what we must do in the coming hours to prepare for whatever is awaiting us."

I look over at Morleck and say a bit underneath my breath, "I hadn't expected this, Morleck; I was figuring that I would stand by as you gave the crew new directives and whatever protocol that's necessary."

Morleck leans over and whispers in me ear. "I thought it would be more effective if they're addressed by the Captain, rather than just an old alchemist."

"I see. Thanks a lot."

Loren and Karla sit on a bench just to the left of me; the crystal guards stand in a straight row to the right; Kaylu and Dandi stand on the deck just above my cabin. I look at the crewmen one by one, effectively catching their attention and quieting everyone down. The quiet gives me a moment to think about what I'm going to say.

"Men, as you are aware, we're approaching the realm of he who is known as Abaddon. As you can see, the ocean and sky are already reflecting his dark power, and based on what I've seen in the past, we can expect far worse than what we see here now."

I pause and clear my throat. "This Dark Power is quiet and insidious. To defeat its prey, the power turns its victims' own minds against them. This is what we must defend ourselves from; each of you has feelings, expectations and passions along with various desires as all normal men have. The Dark One's power lies in manipulating these natural and normal functions. If allowed, it will turn any one of them into uncontrollable, exaggerated feelings, and hallucinations, sometimes with deadly results. No one, including myself, is immune to this evil. Our first and foremost defense lies in our trust in the Creator. Our second defense lies in our trust in each other, and third, the disciplined techniques we will teach you. These techniques will help you focus your attention on something immune to Abaddon's power, which will become one of your greatest strengths.

I pause again, scanning the faces of the stoic crew. "Men, we are all on a journey of mystery, growth, courage, and freedom. There is nobility and meaning in just being a journeyer, for every journey is important. We must all care for one another, and we must also care for ourselves, and we must be careful in our decisions, relationships, and statements. We must avoid becoming victims."

I stand silent for a moment again, looking at each crewman's face. My words shimmer with personal relevance even though they are directed to each man. I continue.

"Before this journey, I never had the chance to realize the strength human beings must have to simply endure their own unique journey. Our path is both simple and difficult at the same time; the Creator simply wants us to grow up. Each of you has been chosen because of your skill and integrity, not only in your work on Soultraveler, but as individuals with honesty and courage. Each of you will be tested before this journey's over, so look to the man beside you. Remember who he is and what he stands for; remember him as a friend and a trusted comrade. Now is the time to put aside any ill feelings about anyone on this ship, for those feelings are what the Dark One seeks to use to destroy us. Any disgruntled man will open himself to self-destruction at some time during this battle if he continues to hold onto this type of attitude. Remember, men! Each and every one of you is Soul; each possesses the inner power of creation itself! You have no limitations when you act and think as Soul."

I'm silent for a moment; their silence and nods show they understand, so I continue.

"If you allow negative and uncontrolled thoughts or feelings to overcome your mind, the Abaddon will attack; it will build a delusional world of fear and desire within you. For those whose minds are overtaken, the result can easily be death. Our primitive drives are exalted by boasts and over-confidence that convert these basic drives into illusionary heroic ideals. In this depraved state, man can murder others; if this happens, something dies within us, too. We cannot lower ourselves into the turmoil of primitive instinctive drives. If you do, the Abaddon can and will create the illusion that you're killing your ego, but in reality, you may be surrendering your own inner self to the darkness.

"Without taking care, the darkness can and will debase the level of your consciousness to that of a primitive being, and if your consciousness is diminished in that way, it is relatively easy to succumb to ideas of primitive magic, rituals, sex, anger, and the basic fears that still survive in our natural primitive drives. By regressing to a primitive stage, you kill something pure within each of you. If this happens, the wisdom, self-awareness, and everything that Soul has gained is lost. Wild, rampant emotions can kill an individual just as sudden fright and bodily shock can cause a man to die. Abaddon's greatest power lies in its illusion of lost hope. It doesn't need any weapon to do this; instead, it uses your own desires, emotions, and even your mind to accomplish its goals.

"Remember this one thing, men. We must help each other in dire moments. The Creator doesn't condone self-destruction in any form. Each of you may come under attack; if so, to do this unthinkable act of suicide is to defeat everything you are and possibly to doom your shipmates as well. If you see this despair in your comrade, then help them! The suicidal trait is instilled within the human consciousness; this suicidal tendency is infectious, because it arouses the suppressed, self-destructive inclinations in each of us, if we allow it. Each of you must become the leader, if not of others, then of yourself. In becoming the leader, you must fix your attention above the awareness of the brute. Do not speak out of vanity or deceit; avoid thoughts of unhappiness and do not criticize the actions of others, or blame others for wrong doings.

"Do not quarrel, fight or inflict injury on each other. Try to be respectful and courteous to others and always show the greatest compassion and understanding you can muster, but most of all, be patient. Your greatest power lies in humility. Hatred and insults may seem curious weapons, but they can be toxic and dangerous; the Dark One will snare the one that becomes boastful and exhibits vanity. At the time when the Abaddon passes over and through us, we must use prayer and contemplation. Mental acrobatics or tortuous, complicated rituals are useless. Still the mind and always act in the name of the Creator. For our purposes, use the holy name of Hu as your chant to defend yourselves. The Creator's truth is too simple for the mind to totally comprehend; when not disciplined, the intellect will always create problems, and then make the rest of us miserable trying to solve them. Abaddon will magnify these problems a hundredfold if you allow it. Remember...truth always expresses itself with the greatest simplicity.

"The truth of Soul will give you the power to resist this Dark Power's insidious attacks. The Abaddon can attack you during your waking moments, and also during your dreams. What the Abaddon does to us physically is only a fraction of what it can do with our minds, emotions, and spirit, so always be on guard."

I pause, and then I say, "For the rest of the day, I want the guards to take you in groups of five and teach you the defensive exercises that are necessary to escape the Dark One's clutches while we are in its realm."

I'm again quiet for a moment, looking over the crew. Then raising my voice a bit, I finish with one last statement.

"Each of you is a warrior, whether you know it or not. I thank you for your courage and strength. Know this! True freedom is within your grasp! By changing your vantage point from the low level of the physical to the high level of the Soul, all things will appear in a new perspective within your own inner worlds. This level of awareness reflects the degree of each man's own development, experience, and the love he gives. This is a unique opportunity to experience something far more beneficial for you than anything you ever imagined; each of you can actually enter a different kind of reality, even a different world—the world of the Spiritual Travelers, the world of being where eternity dwells."

Walking to the stairway to me left, I climb to the top deck next to Kaylu and Dandi. I turn back toward the group and say, "If any of you have questions, ask them now; all too soon, it will be too late." The men look at each other; no one asks anything. Apparently they understand the daunting task that's about to be thrust upon them.

I smile down at the crystal guards and I end by softly commenting, "So it begins."

CHAPTER 45 ~ VENGEANCE IS MINE!

The tree's last remaining leaves float down gently to gather beneath the tree house. A chill fills the air as gray clouds gather; Melody wraps her coat tighter, winter is coming, slower than usual, but it's coming.

Since her experience with Jotan, Melody's dreams have become more consistent—or maybe she's just remembering more dreams. Going to school every day gives her little release from the thoughts and feelings that seem to never end. Even when she lies down to sleep, her dreams are like some type of education. This teaching isn't about ABCs, math or history; no, it's far more subtle. Most of the time Melody can't recall what she's learning, but during the day her mind releases new thoughts and feelings from her subconsciousness; it's a little unnerving at first to know something just minutes before she had no idea even existed. Feelings flow from her growing new awareness, and flood her young mind; all these strange sensations and emotions together solidify the information transfer into her consciousness. She no longer relates to other children in the same way. Things they are interested in don't matter much to her anymore. Friends ignore her and leave her alone, which is okay for it gives her the time needed to sort out the new information and to familiarize herself with her new feelings caused by her dream experiences.

Talking to her father about what's happening would be nice she thinks, but he seems preoccupied. Besides, these new experiences aren't harming her. When they fade away, they leave feelings of peace and happiness.

Brandon told her that sometimes when someone connects strongly to the inner self, spirit will come to them in their dreams and lead them to spiritual temples. These temples provide valuable information and experiences that the dreamer may or may not remember right away, but they will still be retained deep within the mind, and maybe the next day, week, months or even years later, the gift emerges into the individual's consciousness. This process must follow its natural course when the individual is ready to take another step in their spiritual evolution.

Melody has strong premonitions that what is coming is about Hugh and her mom. Many times overpowering thoughts about Hugh or her mother rush through her mind, leaving her with feelings of urgency and concern. As Melody sits silently in the tree house, a feeling of great impending change floods her mind and heart. This feeling is simultaneously warm and sad, lonely and mysterious. She can't describe it: not even to herself, let alone to someone else. Sometimes the loneliness seems to be trying to carry her away somewhere to a place that is happier, brighter, and simpler.

Something is about to happen: something huge, something so important that when it happens, she wants to be ready. Instinctively, she knows she is being prepared. She knows intuitively she is about to play an instrumental role in the journey Hugh and her mother are on.

As she walks home in the late afternoon, gray skies sprinkle soft raindrops on her. She starts walking faster—the last thing she needs is to be caught in a downpour. As she's crossing the meadow, she notices a few green patches of flowering weeds. Low rolling thunder suddenly vibrates through her and her eyes widen as lightning flashes in the distance.

Suddenly, a loud crunching noise by the edge of the woods causes her to turn. Two large bucks face each other; both stand with heads bent, then without warning they crash head-on into each other. The sound reverberates throughout the meadow with a loud cracking sound. Antlers entwine; both deer push against each other, trying to win the battle with sheer strength.

Melody sits spellbound as the deer shuffle and push. She can't tell where one deer's antlers begin and the other's end. The battle becomes a test of wills. Both break away and step back from each other.

Too astounded to move, Melody watches as the deer circle. Then the battle is on again; this time, both are on hind legs striking out not only with heads, but with front legs also. One deer jumps sideways and with a vicious thrust impales the other in the side; the wounded deer moans and jumps back into the brush. The victor stands still, watching. Melody hears the injured deer move through the thicket, and then it is gone. The large buck stands facing her with its front legs spread and head lowered. The deer stares at her for a few moments and then relaxes. The buck takes a step toward the thicket, and then stops and nibbles at a few leaves on a bush as if nothing has happened; nonchalantly, it chews on small branches. Melody relaxes and turns to walk in the other direction. As she strolls across the meadow, she thinks about the battle she just witnessed. Apparently, the wounded deer was threatening the large buck's territory and his doe's. How odd to think that even in the peaceful meadow there's always fighting.

Whether it's between two people, one country with another, or just an act of nature—battles are constantly being fought. She thinks of the battle she and her father are in the midst of. Isn't it sort of like the deer, fighting to protect its territory and family? Isn't her dad fighting a battle inside himself to protect his home and family? Isn't Hugh fighting a battle somewhere for his family? And Dad just finished a battle alongside Brandon in court for the very life of Mom and Hugh?

No matter where she looks, the world's in a constant battle with itself. It's as Jotan said, there will never be peace in this world because humankind creates and lives in a warring universe. How odd that we humans are destined to battle one another or even the elements of nature...even our own beliefs create battlefields between us, and if that isn't enough, we have the constant battle with crime, diseases, and the ceaseless struggle of our own minds. It doesn't really matter what the battle's about; just the struggle itself seems to be some sort of mandated act of survival. It's like the experiment in school with the emperor moth.

The students in her class had been divided in half, each side given a caterpillar still in its cocoon. The students were to observe how long and in what way the caterpillar turned into a moth and eventually freed itself. It took almost the whole school year, but one day the other half of the students saw movement in their cocoon. The moth wiggled furiously, struggling for its freedom. The students bet each other which cocoon would open first, and each half was sure of its victory. Then, the cocoon Melody's half was watching also started to move. The kids watched in fascination as the race for freedom unfolded in front of them. It soon appeared as if Melody's side would win. Then something strange happened. Two students on the other side grew impatient, and started cutting their moth's cocoon, trying to help it free itself. Once the cocoon was cut, the moth emerged from the sack. It didn't move much as it slowly crawled from its cocoon. Something was wrong. The moth hardly moved as it wiggled and stumbled trying to stand up. Crawling across the table, within minutes the deformed creature died.

The other moth continued its struggle to leave the cocoon for most of the day. Struggling furiously for several hours, it finally emerged. Unlike the other moth, it was strong and beautiful. It was no longer the little caterpillar but a large fully grown emperor moth. As it dried itself by moving its huge wings back and forth, it grew stronger. Then finally it expanded its wings and flew around the room.

The teacher explained that the struggle to free itself is part of its required growth pattern. By "helping" the other moth as those kids did, they inadvertently halted the cycle of growth it needed in order to be strong and to develop to its full potential. The actual struggle to be free was what helps transform it into a beautiful creature.

So, even in birth, struggle and hardships are keys to survival and growth.

Melody understood the lesson. Each of us must confront our own inner struggles and overcome them. This is what causes us to change and eventually grow into the best we can be. The battle to grow is one we must fight alone, because the ultimate battle is one we fight within ourselves.

Melody's nearly out of the meadow when she sees the big buck and his does run behind her and cross the meadow. She watches their white tails flicker and vanish within the thicket. At the same time, she thinks about her own mind, and how lately she feels like she is in a constant battle with her own thoughts. No one can really help in her struggle, because the battle within is the very tool that can take her to the next phase of life, just like the emperor moth.

Rain drops pelt her and she begins to run; just as she gets to her house, it begins pouring. Bursting through the door, smells of delicious cooking confront her senses; Dad must be making a late lunch. The aroma reminds her how hungry she really is. Clark is in the kitchen heating up some soup when he notices Melody. "Hi, honey, want some?"

Melody nods and steps over to the fire cheerily burning in the den. Rain is coming down hard, rattling against the roof. Looking outside, she sees the wind picking up and rain drops beating against the window glass.

"Dad, is Cody inside?"

Clark walks in with a TV tray and places it in front of her.

"I think so, maybe he's downstairs. I'll check."

Walking downstairs to the family room, Clark sees Cody curled up in a ball sound asleep. A gust of cold air hits him, and he turns to find the sliding glass door to the patio open. Pushing it shut, he notices how windy it is becoming.

A crack of thunder explodes outside, startling Cody. The dog trembles as the sound rolls through the house, and Clark reaches down and pats him on the head. "It's all right, c'mon upstairs with us." Cody runs ahead to the stairs with Clark following. Thunder again rumbles across the skies, followed by a bright flash of lightning.

Once upstairs, Clark throws a couple of logs on the fire. Melody smiles and points to a steaming bowl of soup on the TV tray that she set up for her dad. "Thanks honey. It's getting pretty nasty out there, huh?" Melody nods as she sips her soup. Rain's comes down in sheets, the skies grow blacker as clouds boom with thunder and lightning flashes. The phone rings and Melody answers. Looking over at her dad she whispers, "It's the hospital."

Taking the phone, Clark feels apprehensive. "Hello, this is Clark."

"Mr. Bailey? This is Dr. Orvitz. I think you'd better come down here immediately."

Clark's blood froze. "Why, what's happened?"

"It isn't what happened; it's what's happening right now!"

"What is it? Tell me, what's going on?"

The phone is silent for a moment. Dr. Orvitz—obviously restraining himself—says, "We don't know exactly, but something is happening to Ann." Clark's stomach sends a rush of pained energy through his body.

"What is it? Is she all right?"

"Listen, you need to get down here as quickly as you can. You'll see for yourself; she's reacting to something, but we don't know what." The doctor's voice lowers. "Clark, you need to be here."

Clark takes a second to pull himself together and says quietly, "I'm on my way." Hanging up the phone, he turns to Melody and cries, "Hurry, get your coat. We have to go to the hospital: now!" Melody runs to the foyer and grabs her jacket; both are immediately out the door and into the garage.

Pulling out onto Dogwood is a nightmare; rain is coming down in buckets, and the skies are almost black. Winds blow fiercely; tree limbs are scattered everywhere. Clark heads toward the hospital driving quickly but cautiously; all he needs now is an accident, he thinks to himself. He is nervous, but controls his emotions. He strains his mind to remain calm and hold back feelings of panic—not only for himself, but for Melody, also.

"Dad, what's the matter? Is Mom all right?"

"I don't know, honey. The doctor said something is happening, but he didn't tell me what."

Normally it takes about ten minutes to get to the hospital from their house, but due to the storm, it is almost thirty minutes before he pulls into the hospital parking lot. Running toward the door holding hands and crouching under the flimsy umbrella held by Clark, they enter the hospital lobby soaking wet.

Both dash up the hall to Ann's and Hugh's room, and pushing the doors open, they rush in to see the doctor standing over Ann injecting her with something.

"Doctor! What's going on?"

As Doctor Orvitz steps aside, Melody and Clark see something neither will ever forget for the rest of their lives. Ann's moving, but it isn't normal movement: massive convulsions make her body twist and turn; her chest bounces up and down as her legs shake; her head jerks back and forth as she utters strange, guttural, moaning sounds.

Clark's eyes widen as he sees his wife writhing in some kind of nightmarish dance. Melody screams, "Momma! Momma!" Struggling to get to Annie's side, the little girl has to be held back by a nurse. "Let me go! Let me go! She needs me!"

The nurse holds the girl tightly in her arms, and Clark turns to the doctor. "My God, Doctor; help her! What's happening to her?"

Doctor Orvitz checks the graph and heart monitor along with her life signs. "We're not sure what's happening, but whatever it is, it's something we can't control or manage! It's as if she's being attacked by something. I've just given her a sedative to stop the convulsions so we can take further action."

Clark has seen people with epileptic seizures before, but never anything like this. Annie's eyes roll up into her head showing only the whites of her eyes, and guttural groans come from deep within her body: she looks possessed. When an alarm bell goes off behind them, Clark turns and sees the buttons on Hugh's monitor light up. The doctor rushes to Hugh's side; monitors register activity, but in a way that puzzles him. Hugh isn't moving and he looks the same, but his vitals are erratic. The doctor bends over the boy, and with his stethoscope listens to the frail boy's heartbeat. Shaking his head, the doctor removes a medical penlight from his breast pocket, and opening one of Hugh's eyes with his thumb, he shines the pen's beam into his eye. "He's not dilating—his heart is beating too fast—his blood pressure is climbing and he's sweating profusely!"

Clark tries to control himself but he's beginning to lose it. Not knowing what to do, Clark gathers Melody up in his arms and pleads, "Doctor! Do something, please!" Melody holds onto her dad and tries not to cry out as she watches her mother continue to convulse; her brother's life support machines make loud ringing and beeping sounds, and a nurse is using a damp sponge to wipe the sweat from Hugh's forehead. The whole world has gone mad! A loud crash booms outside: thunder rolls and a second crash follows before the first even ends. Lightning flashes outside and rain falls even harder! To Clark and Melody, it seems the world is ending.

Clark's mind is racing. For all they'd suffered, all the tears, the prayers, the battles, and now? Everything is crashing down at once, nothing makes sense; what the hell is happening? Why is this happening?

Neither Clark nor Melody know about the entity that is seeking to disrupt their efforts to help Hugh and Ann; it is on the offensive, and attacking with vengeance. The power of Abaddon isn't limited to just the psychic or dream worlds. The Dark Lord's power can invade all the lower kingdoms, including this small planet known as Earth!

The Abaddon had noticed Hugh's approach, and sensed underneath his aggression a deep concern for his mother. The darkness followed his concern as it reached into the thoughts and emotions of Ann Bailey; it was then able to track her thoughts like a roadmap until it found the body she used in this world. Once the Abaddon discovered Ann's body, it seized upon the spark of life left in it without mercy, fueling it with enough negative energy to overwhelm her lower body functions, and now it sought to cause her higher functions to fail eventually and kill her. Whatever torture Ann is enduring with her astral body is now reflecting through her physical body; and when the darkness found Ann, it also discovered Hugh's mortal body to be within range of its influence. However, to its dismay, the Abaddon discovered it could not take control over Hugh as effectively as it could Ann. Even though Hugh is not in his body, a protective consciousness acts as a shield against the Dark One's power. Due to the high state of awareness Hugh has attained, he has created that shield from his subconscious power. The effect the Abaddon has on Hugh's body is concerning, but not life threatening; by contrast, the Abaddon's power isn't limited in its attack on Ann. If it kills Ann's body, the Abaddon will also destroy her spirit being held in the black mountains.

At first, Melody reacted in panic like her father, but as she watches the doctor's work on both patients, she begins to calm down enough to realize this situation must be what Brandon meant when he told them that at some point they both would need to help Hugh. Remembering what Jotan had said, Melody knows this is her own battle as well as her mom's. If she is to be of any help at all, it will have to be right now. Looking up at her dad, she tugs on his arm. "Dad, Mom and Hugh need us now! We have to do something now or Mom will die; if she does, then we lose Hugh, too!"

Clark knows she's right. This moment is what he feared would come in some form or another; now it is here. Does he have the strength and courage to deal with it? Taking Melody's hand, he walks over to Ann's bed, gesturing to Melody to get on the other side. He pulls up a chair for himself and Melody does the same. They take one of Ann's hands in theirs, breathe deeply, close their eyes, and concentrate on the inner eye. Straps hold down her body, but Ann still shakes and twists; guttural moans rumble from her throat as white saliva drools down the corner of her mouth. Tears fall like rain from her whitened eyes as her face contorts in anguish and pain. Tears well up in Melody's eyes also, but she keeps all the attention she can muster on the small inner light within her vision. Clark feels the grip of Ann's hand tighten on his own as he focuses on his inner eye and begins to think of Hugh.

At first Clark's and Melody's attention is scattered. Their minds flood with nonsensical images and fear stabs at them. Nevertheless, as they focus on Hugh's image they begin to chant. The sound drifts from their lips as just a whisper at first, but as they gain more control of their emotions, they chant louder and with more determination. The sound becomes piercing; as they sing the HU longer and higher, the little girl's voice raises itself in perfect unison with her father's deeper song. Ann's body twitches with rage and the guttural moans change to a howling as she clashes her teeth together; Melody and Clark hold on. Within their inner visions, they both sense a name resonate and reverberate within their thoughts: Jotan!

Both almost at the same time change their chant from HU to Jotan, pronouncing it …Jooooooo-taaaan. The sound floats throughout the hospital room. A presence nudges Melody's mind; not knowing what it is, she remains neutral toward it. The nudging persists in trying to push into her thoughts and feelings. Melody can't tell where her mind begins and this nudging force starts. A violent surge erupts within Melody, and as the presence gushes up, it seems to explode painfully within her young mind, like a knife suddenly cutting into her. The presence is dark, loathsome, vicious, and full of hatred and fear; it grabs hold of her young mind and twists her feelings and thoughts to those of its own. Melody gasps! Taking several fast short breaths in panic, her chest heaves as she tries to take a deeper breath. The force is evil: the same evil that's trying to kill her mom.

Clark feels the same darkness flow into his mind. Visions spread within his mind of Annie being held in blackness while being sucked into pockets of darkness filled with hate. He holds Ann's hand tighter, and the force twists his mind with its power of hate, evil, and longing for perverted passions; a loathsome fear and hopelessness staggers his senses. Melody and Clark are frozen as if invisible arms have reached out and tightly wrapped themselves around them. Clark feels the power enveloping him; it's as if he's caught between two magnetic poles of the same polarity, unable to move in any direction, and what's worse, he feels his mind caught in the same frozen fear. Words and feelings whisper to his mind, gripping more tightly as it invades his deepest being. Ann screams out in a heart-wrenching moan of pain and terror as the darkness pushes deeper into her physical body, trying to break it. Melody and Clark both struggle to continue chanting Jotan's name—the battle is in full force!

Within Clark and Melody there is a blackness and fear that's taking them over completely. Sweat pours down their faces as evil stretches its hand into their Souls, squeezing their consciousnesses, blocking any love from penetrating their hearts; only fear, terror, darkness, and death filter through their minds.

Melody breathes hard as the insidious attack buries itself deep within her young mind, exposing her imagination to frightfully evil feelings of despair and hopelessness; evil spills over into Clark's mind, submerging his efforts with its venom and dark foreboding. Somehow both hang on, however; both continue chanting Jotan's name. Clark and Melody know they are engaged in a battle not only for their earthly selves, but also for their Souls. In the next hour, they will both defeat their enemies and survive, or the Bailey family will surely be lost forever.

****

Soultraveler pushes through darkening waters; angry waves slam against the great ship's sides, pushing it off course. The waters are as black as the skies, which thicken with huge, dark, billowing clouds. Since yesterday, the crew has coordinated their shifts to allow half to be engaged in spiritual training while the other half sail the ship. Now all hands are at their posts working the sails, tightening the rigging, and batting down any portholes or hatches to the interior of the ship. Rain pelts us as do the gale force winds.

Morleck stands by the helmsman, directing the ship through the ever-threatening waters. Dandi, Kaylu, and I stand opposite of Morleck on the bow; we direct the men the best we can. I know we're dependent on the skills of the crew. At best, we can only be there to encourage them as the waves grow more threatening. Loren and Karla are in their cabin. All they can do is pray and hope the ship will stay together as the winds howl outside their windows. The crystal guards move throughout the ship, directing and encouraging the men; they know the ocean's attack is only the beginning of the battle, and they try to prepare the men and themselves for the even more insidious attack that soon will be upon them.

Morleck turns and looks into the dark sky.

Stepping over to the large crystal behind him, he reaches for a small round wheel attached to the pole the crystal rests on. Turning it to the left, the huge crystal starts to tilt. I look over at the other crystal on the end of the boom, and I notice that it, too, begins to rise; the brass boom lifts inch by inch. From the dark sky, a shaft of bright orange light shoots from the heavens directly onto the pole, hitting the crystal; the blaze then travels up through the bow's other crystal on the raised boom and back up into the sky. The brilliant effect looks like a fiery upside down wishing bone: twin lights are coming from the single light beyond the clouds! The effect on Soultraveler is immediate. The great ship shoots forward, cutting its way despite growing waves and bracing wind. With an astounded look on his face, the helmsman directs the ship by following Morleck's pointing arm. The old alchemist stands fearlessly against the wind, revealing the ship's path as the light and energy harnessed from the light through the rear crystal shoots to the front crystal on the boom. The ship is encased in an electric blue light as it continually bursts forward.

The crew shouts out in amazement as the ship maneuvers its way through the giant waves and hazardous currents that are crisscrossing each other. I watch dumbfounded; never would I have believed what I'm seeing, or that it was even possible. Nevertheless there it is...my ship charging forward as if oblivious to the winds and raging seas.

Climbing down to the main deck I watch crewmen hold their posts courageously facing the storm. Soultraveler moves deeper into the blackness ahead, and I send me thoughts outward trying to detect when the Abaddon's attack will increase; like a sea anemone that curls inward when touched, my thoughts touch the evil ahead and recoil. I feel the power and instantly withdraw me probing thoughts. I shout, "Prepare, men! Our enemy is almost upon us; each of you pair off—watch and take care of your partner, for by giving of yourself, it will lessen the attack." The crystal guards have diligently prepared everyone. Each man now partners up to prepare for the onslaught. I look out and see the intense blackness ahead as Soultraveler advances, carrying with it the blue light from the twin crystals into the darkness. As the ship speeds closer into the thickening darkness, all eyes are fixed in the same direction. Their mood is solemn and filled with uncertainty; a foreboding anticipation of danger pervades their shared silence.

A movement from the guard's quarters snaps me attention back to the present. The crystal guards calmly gather and face the approaching darkness. Kneeling down, each guard tilts his shield toward the beam of light projecting from stern to bow. The beams from the six crystal shields reflect into the oncoming darkness. I run to get a better look, and I see the six separate crystal beams of light merge into each other forming one large brilliant blue beam penetrating into the darkness; the sight is truly amazing.

As the merged crystal light strikes the roiling mass of darkness, it splits horizontally in two directions; racing over the edges of the dark mass, the two beams break into billions of small brilliant sparks of light. The darkness stops advancing and recoils; all six guards kneel, holding their shields steady. Soultraveler moves onward, advancing its charge as the light clears a pathway. Morleck stands on the upper deck, his white hair tossed all about from the powerful winds. He holds to the helm's edge, still directing the helmsman to advance forward. As the force of the waves slightly lessens, so the wind's power decreases. The darkness ahead regroups, throwing its mass upward above the ridgeline of the light, but the guards attack again, tilting their shields, projecting the beams higher into the center of the dark mass. As light hits the dark mass's center, the winds howl and the waves erupt in a surge that lifts the black mass even higher into the atmosphere, like an erupting volcano that forms a black boiling cloud. Lightning breaks out savagely throughout the billowing black mass and the guards continue to focus on its center; beaming their light directly into the heart of the darkness, the black mass swells even higher.

As Morleck watches, the darkness expands high into the atmosphere, and it suddenly dawns on him what the darkness is doing, but it's already too late! The dark mass shoots even further upward until it succeeds in blocking any sunlight, thus destroying the concentrated beams refracted from the six shields. This thick, black boiling cloud is so great that it is too much even for natural sunlight to penetrate. The guards back up; their shields are now useless. The lower swath of the darkness moves like a rolling black dust cloud, across the waters toward Soultraveler. I shout for the men to prepare, and running to the girls' cabin, I burst open the door to warn them. "Get ready, it is attacking and we can't stop it!"

As I run back onto the main deck, I pull me sword from its scabbard and point it toward the rushing darkness. The sword glows as I lift it high, and every man on board watches their Captain try to stand his ground. The sword radiates a bright blue light in a small circle reflecting off me face. The blackness overwhelms and envelops the entire ship. Kneeling down on one knee, I place the tip of the sword into the deck, and then holding its hilt perpendicular to the floor with both hands, I bow me head and focus on the inner eye. The light of the sword throws out a hazy translucent light that's not enough to see by; still, I kneel with me head bowed in a deathly stillness. Everything becomes dark—the entire ship becomes engulfed in blackness—and the petrified silence radiates a crackling fear and hopelessness throughout every living soul onboard.

Within the center of blackness, the small pale light is the only sign that within the dark are hearts of men fighting the demons of their fears for the survival of their Souls. The silence is surreal; not a breath is heard, nothing but black stillness. From the darkness, a flash of lightning followed by a rumble and then a tremendous clap of thunder rolls across Soultraveler. I feel weak; my body isn't reacting as before. I'm nauseated. Me heart races, sweat pours from my body, and me mind screams out! Something's wrong!

This attack is somehow different from before. In the last attack, my body wasn't affected; the assault had only been on me mind. This isn't the case now.

Feeling weak, I lean heavier on the sword for support, and while the blackness grows thicker, I feel it penetrating me mind, heart, and body. I strain to maintain consciousness—what's happening? I'm barely breathing, my body's starting to feel numb, and me inner vision is overloaded by a deep, blood-red light. I feel sucked ever deeper into a universe of death and despair; nothing makes sense! I feel myself sinking into an ocean of a bloodlike, sticky gelatin, thickly drowning me in dismal thoughts and feelings of hopelessness.

I thought I knew the type of attack the Dark One would thrust upon us, but I was wrong. This attack is affecting my physical body as well as me mind, and I feel meself slipping away into the darkness...Numbness creeps its way up my legs, moving like a million stinging ants crawling over every inch of me body. My breathing becomes shallow, and a thought flashes across my mind: Is this death?

I try to think as the tingling numbness marches across me chest, continuing to climb upward. I can't feel the lower part of me body any more. My mind releases me senses; like a bird might molt its feathers, each sense seems to be unattached and left dangling, only to float away into the darkness. I wonder... was all this happening to everyone else? If so, how can they withstand this type of onslaught? I had been so wrong in my description of the attack; how will they defend themselves from this intense power? I struggle to stay conscious. I think back on my journey, beginning from the moment of the car accident and then on to all the different realities, new friends, wise teachers, and extraordinary experiences with Loren. All of this couldn't have been for nothing, could it? My whole goal is to free me mom, and now I am not sure if I can save myself, let alone save her! As I think of me mother, I can almost see her body writhing in the black cave as her essence is agonizingly drained from her. Was what I'm going through the same? Was it like this for her?

My mind slows; thoughts barely move within me—I feel that the battle is almost over. Again thinking of mom, I feel myself falling headlong deeper into a dark universe, diving into a bottomless blackness. A loud rumble of thunder again rolls across Soultraveler, making the whole ship shudder. Lightning shatters the sky, and a voice rings out as the thunder fades; at first, the voice is soft and slow, but quickly it grows, and is soon followed by the sound of a string instrument.

Baylor! The young warrior's voice rings out in the darkness, singing words of hope, strength, comradeship, and home. His voice floats across Soultraveler, giving succor and hope to men who have all but given up as the darkness penetrates their minds with its vicious, twisted evil. The song is a call to brothers at arms. Slowly, moment by moment, his steady voice lifts the spirits of the crew as each struggles with the fingers of Darkness insidiously trying to block the light from within their hearts. I flail about, attempting to reach out with me mind, to grab hold of something, anything, that might stop this endless descent into blackness. With me last thought, my mind feebly whimpers, "Why h-have you f-forsaken me?" And I continue to fall farther and farther away. Baylor's voice fades to just a small, slight whisper within the rumbling cacophony of thunder, until now there is only quiet darkness. I'm conscious, but there's no thought; I feel nothing nor sense anything.

I'm quietly adrift in a dark softness defying limitations or description. A flutter, almost like a gentle wave, moves through me. The wave feels curious; it moves back through me, leaving me with a sense of wonder. Thoughts no longer are real; I'm only feeling my attachment to Mum. Concentrating, I feel a jolt and then I hear a sound like a cork being pulled from a wine bottle; in a sudden rush, I abruptly pop into a bright room and I am looking down on a white bed where I see a small pale boy lying with tubes penetrating his body. A man in a white coat and a woman in a nursing uniform are bending over and tending to him. Concerned, I move in closer and I recognize the tiny pallid child: ME!

The whole scene is surreal; I watch with fascination and shock as the doctor tries to revive me earthly form. Noticing movement next to me, I move up closer to the ceiling so that I can have a wider view of the room.

Melody and Da' are both sitting opposite each other holding me mum's hands. She lies in a bed similar to the one me body is in. What happens next sends a cold wave of nausea through me. Her body starts convulsing and twitching; her eyes blacken with streams of sweat pouring from her forehead; however, what really captures me attention even more, is the black mass of oozing darkness I see engulfing her body—the ooze penetrates the very fabric of space, tearing it open! Within its blackness are countless tiny bits of light that look like stars. As grotesque as it is, it also holds an uncanny beauty that hides its insidious goals. Da' and Melody are sitting with their eyes closed, chanting something together.

I listen and soon make out what they are chanting: Jooooootaaaaaaannnnn.

Blackness creeps over not only Mom's body, but it's also swirling around Da' and Melody, and I see the same blackness hovering over me own frail body.

So that's why I reacted physically back on the ship! The Dark One is attacking not only me astral form and Soul, but my physical body as well; no wonder I felt the way I did on Soultraveler!

I think I know what I have to do.

Soul has use of a power the Dark One can't defeat. Even though this power is available to all, very few know how to properly use any one of its many facets. To misuse even a single aspect can set off dangerous repercussions. The trick is to discover how to remain completely open and vulnerable, allowing this power to flow into me and thereby use me as its vehicle. Stepped down and deployed properly, this omnipotent essence acts as a shattering force that nothing can resist. It is always there just waiting; just as love is the foundation for creation itself, this same energy is the foundation for destruction.

I'll have to let go of all my worries and fears if this is to succeed. I place my attention on the scene below me, and at the same time I send out a wave of detached, unconditional love. This love has to flow through me without attachments to outcome. The more I focus on the scene below, the more concentrated the love becomes; I'll be powerless once the essence begins to flow. To try to use it at my command would be useless, because once called upon, it becomes a force of its own doing.

Nothing seems to be happening for a moment.

Then, I feel it!

A presence emerges from within and a familiar voice projects within me. *"I am here, Hugh..."*

Jotan!

The presence grows stronger; as it intensifies, it voices inside me, *"Continue opening yourself, for love is the power that I move through."*

The presence of the Spiritual Traveler is overwhelming, despite having no image or form; it emerges only as a presence of great power. I again focus my attention and I soon send out a stream of unconditional love to me family. Jotan taps into me and uses my love as a conduit through which he pours his power into the little room. By its own nature, the divine essence begins to balance everything within its directed sphere of influence.

Da' and Melody are almost drained; they are succumbing to the Dark One's power, and their chanting is becoming feeble and faint. Jotan infuses their consciousnesses with our transformational power and slowly they re-energize and grow stronger; their voices become more clear as they chant the child god's name.

Together, Jotan and I open a channel for the power of the Creator to enter, and I feel its force rush through me like a mighty wind.

The Creator's power engages the Dark One; the dark mass recoils, backing away from its victims, then it rebounds and attacks them again. I wonder at its power; how can it persist and fight the Creator? Then I remember my single most important lesson: the kingdom is within!

I have to contact Da' and Melody! It's the only way!

Directing all my attention to my family, bit by bit I begin to feel my thoughts approach the edge of their consciousnesses. I sense the terrible evil that coats their minds like black ooze—it's twisted and full of hate and fear. I persist, and suddenly, I'm through! *"Da', it's me, Hugh! Listen to me, Da'. Tell Melody to direct her love and attention to Mom's spiritual eye; this is the only way! Mom has to win the battle herself!"*

A startled look crosses me Da's face, but he recovers quickly, and whispers to his daughter, "Send your love to her; your mother has to win this battle herself! Just keep sending her your unconditional love!"

Melody thinks for a moment, and then remembers the emperor moth! She focuses on her mother's face and sends pure love directly to her. The Dark mass moves upward, enveloping mom's entire lower body; the rest of it spreads its insidious gloom into Melody and Clark. Just then, Jotan helps strengthen my resolve so that I can become a pure vehicle for the Creator's essence; in that very instant, I am infused with spirit and I allow it to take over completely. My unconditional surrender provides the Creator a direct way to enter into me mum's heart.

For a moment, a serene look crosses Mom's features and the dark shadow on her face fades. A translucent glowing light then emerges on her face and begins to creep down toward the dark, ugly mass. As the light approaches, the Dark mass begins to shrivel, like a drop of water sprinkled on desert sands.

This Darkness has dominated my family with fear, sadness, and illusion for far too long. Finally, for once its power is beginning to shrink and fade, losing its hold in this world. Mom's face calms; her body stops its convulsions and twitching. Da' and Melody stop sweating and both begin breathing normally as the feeling of the Creator's love flows through each of them. I watch the blackness evaporate, dissolving into just a tiny spot, and then suddenly, it's completely gone.

I, too, am suddenly carried away at that same moment. The pitching of Soultraveler brings me back to me senses; the great ship is drifting in darkness.

The Dark One's power no longer affects me physically; my mind is immune to its attacks of fear and hopelessness. No longer am I a part of its lower kingdom; no longer is the limited mind master of my destiny. As I gaze into the darkness, I lift the sword in front of me, and summoning all my strength into its hilt, the sword begins growing brighter by the second.

The sword's light shines victoriously amid the retreating darkness. I see men lying on the deck, some crumpled and cowering, and others holding on to each other as the blackness fed upon their hidden fears and desires. As I step forward, the sword becomes more brilliant. I call out, "Stand up! The Dark One is an illusion! Look at the light, focus your attention on me!"

One by one, each man feebly turns his head; some stare blankly and others hold up their hands before tear-stained faces to protect their eyes from the glare of the sword. I walk among them, chasing the darkness from their hearts, and then I move toward Loren and Karla's cabin.

Kicking the door open, I walk in with the sword guiding me. Loren and Karla clutch each other on the bed, smothered in the Dark One's black embrace. As I enter the room, the black mass recedes and vanishes. Karla and Loren have looks of anguish and pain etched onto their faces.

I lay my sword against the wall and assure them, "It's all right. It can't hurt you any longer!" Both girls jump off the bed and run into my open arms. Loren's voice breaks, "Oh, Hugh, you can't imagine what it was doing to us!"

I hug them both, and reply gently, "You both have done well. You held on, and defeated its attack! It's gone, and you are both all right. Now come help me." Taking both girls outside, I ask them to attend to the men.

"But what can we do?" Karla asks.

"Console them, touch them, and give them faith to go on. Your love and compassion will do more than anything else can." I break away from the pair and begin searching for Kaylu and Dandi. I find both on the high deck toward the bow sitting on a bench holding their heads.

The blackness moves away at my approach, and when both look up, I see that Kaylu's face is as calm as Dandi's. "Well, my friends, it seems you've held your own against this assault."

Dandi stands and responds, "We encountered this before in the cave."

"I see; can you help with the men? I'm afraid they haven't been as fortunate as you two. Karla and Loren are tending them, but I am sure they could use some more help." Both Dandi and Kaylu climb down from the upper deck, and then together with the girls and crystal guards, they mingle amongst the men, helping them to stand up and encouraging them to resist the Dark One's power.

I motion to Baylor and say, "Take up your instrument and sing something that can help bring courage back to men's hearts." Baylor climbs the steps up to the bow and begins to sing. Soon the ship is clear of the dark mass, the seas are calm and the skies are less threatening. As some of the clouds part, I catch a brief glimpse of a huge dark island with cloud-covered mountains looming ahead, but then the clouds shift and the island disappears from view. Looking up, I see Morleck manning the helm. He nods, acknowledging that he, too, has seen the black island.

The sails are raised, and Soultraveler speeds forward.

CHAPTER 46 ~ CHARTERS OF FREEDOM

Even though it's impossible to see through the darkness, I sense the island is near. I feel the presence of evil; it's like touching a hot fire. My mind recoils whenever me thoughts get close to its source. Watching Morleck as he stands against the background of dark skies, I wonder about this wise old man, alchemist, wizard, traveler, eccentric teacher, and philosopher. Who really knows what this man has seen, experienced, and knows? To me, he's foremost a guide, and just one of many; but there he is—standing a little taller perhaps—pointing the way for the helmsman. His image reminds me of the movie "The Ten Commandments" when Moses stands before the Red Sea, just before raising his staff and allowing God's power to work through him to part its waters.

Morleck looks over at me and motions for me to meet him at the stern. Quickly, I climb the stairs to my teacher's side. Morleck instructs the helmsman briefly and then motions me to sit on the rear bench atop the stern deck.

"Tell me, boy," the old man asks, "what happened during the Dark One's attack?"

I describe finding myself in the other world and the attack on mother and me physical body. I explain how my family and I prevented her death and my own with Jotan's help.

The wise teacher looks at me kindly and says, "My boy, we are approaching something that is as hard to grasp as the wind itself. You have felt the beginning of its power, but believe me—that experience is nothing compared to what you will experience on the dark island. We are about to enter the very jaws of the beast itself! Make no mistake in thinking you have won the battle; no, all that you have accomplished is to allow the Abaddon to analyze your strength and resolve! It will adjust and adapt to another form of trickery and evil."

Morleck paused, and then nodding his head, he looked into my eyes and says, "But no matter what, always know this; the Creator is spirit, and where spirit exists, there is freedom. This freedom is self-existent and self-propelling. Never doubt that it can overcome any situation, however dire, for being pure freedom, it has no limitations. Once you realize this freedom, you can express it in its truest meaning, which is through your true nature. Spirit will always lead you from the unreal to the real, taking you from darkness to light. Greatness is achieved by building your inner world and reconciling it with your external reality, whatever that might be.

"You are at the threshold of the greatest discovery a man can find, which is entirely due to the rarest of occasions; your earthly form lives in the outer world, yet you can communicate as pure Soul to the outer world. Do you know what this means? Simply stated, the spiritual part of you can sit together with the physical part of you at the foot of the spiritual mountain which symbolizes the God self within you. With just you and your humanity merging to form Soul's completeness, thereby allowing only the spiritual to remain. In other words, you have the opportunity to become whole again. When this occurs, just to live is holy."

I look out over the darkening waters and ask, "To become holy is one thing, but at what cost to me and my family? I really don't understand what I am about to face other than it is evil and very powerful."

Morleck puts his hand on me shoulder and replies, "You are approaching a darkness that cannot stop you from knowing it. Once this darkness is known, then you must dream it into a new image. This image must live and exist as Soul's true nature; for how can it resist its nature, especially when you dream this lower nature into the higher oneness of the Creator? What you are about to confront is the deepest part of your mind that has ruled over you for eons. Remember, my son; you can never trust the Creator too much. Those who fail are ones who have no trust either in God or in themselves. So I say to you, whatever you ask, believe you will receive, and you will have it. The power of your belief sets the limit to your own demonstration of a principle that is without limit."

I listen quietly all the while, thinking that Morleck's words seem contradictory and yet somehow powerful; I must remember them.

Morleck continues. "With trepidation I watch you walk into the demon's clutches. You must know the Dark One's limitations and weaknesses, for in learning your adversary's shortcomings, you will know how and when to strike, and most importantly, when not to strike. Always remember this; the greatest fighting ability is worthless if it does not serve creativity in shaping the cosmos. You are building and shaping kingdoms with every step you take, just as all life is doing. The Creator's greatest pleasure is to give you the kingdom that exists within. Even the deepest darkness of the spiritual system is saturated with divine ideas and populated with spiritual forms. The wisdom you have gained is your tool to prevail over the madness you are about to encounter. Through the many events of life in billions of different voices during a trillion different moments, the Creator was and is always there. Your quest is one of these momentary events.

"During your darkest hour, the God/Creator of your understanding is with you. Even now in this hour at this precise moment, you have reached the stage where the Creator is ready to welcome you whenever you are ready to come home. Your realization of the Creator within governs your existence from this moment on; what you have seen, what you have experienced, is no longer a valid history of who you are. From this point on, you are to only experience and express the Father. Remember, son, for the survival of who you are at this moment depends on this realization. You need no longer search for the kingdom of Heaven, for you are living in it now as you always have. As a child of the universe, you are in store for wondrous surprises in the greatest happiness you have ever known, and the grandest experience you will ever have! Be a leader not only of yourself, but also of those who will follow. Know for certain, that when you enter Abaddon's domain, you will again be with all who have held a place in your heart.

"You cannot win this battle alone. Others, whether you know it or not, are as equally involved as you, but from different perspectives each is moving forward toward the moment when the Creator reveals its breathtaking creation. However, before this happens, each must confront who they really are and become the glorious self as each was originally created. For this to unfold, you must use the events of today to create the promise of tomorrow and your experience of 'beingness' to set free your eternal self. There is no other way. If you are successful, then your whole world will change. This I can promise you; the world in its entirety will begin its remarkable transformation within each man's heart. For it has been said that at the point of each man's eternal unfoldment, it will reflect to some degree on the entire cosmos. This reflection creates a doorway to the wondrous, changeless heart of the Creator."

The old man's words are wise, profound, deep, powerful, and true; but I know Morleck isn't telling me the "truth." He's telling me <u>his</u> truth. For each man holds within his kingdom his own truth, which reflects his core. Scores of religions proclaim themselves to be the sole source of truth, but there are as many truths as there are individual forms in existence. The best any of us can hope for is that another's expressed truth will point the way to our own. In the end, each Soul will eventually find its unique personal relationship with the Creator in its own way. This is how life is designed, for in truth, the Creator and life itself are the same.

But one thing he said I must question.

"You say the Creator's heart is changeless; can you explain this?"

Morleck stands up and walks to the railing at the rear of the ship. Looking across the storming sea, he replies, "The Creator in its purest state is changeless because it is perfection. Something that is perfect is changeless, for how else could it be?"

I think for a moment on his words and then I say, "For myself, I have to disagree with you on that particular subject."

Morleck smiles, and turning toward me he asks, "What is it that you disagree with?"

I reply, "The Creator is not changeless. If it were changeless, none of us would even exist." Morleck remains silent; the look in his eyes encourages me to continue. "The way I now understand life's purpose and all of existence, is that growth involves constant change. A short time ago, I was merely a small child living with me family, and not concerned in the least about God, love, and life's purpose. The only change I was concerned about was me own physical body, or going into junior high school. But through what has happened to me, I have changed, and that change comes from experiencing life in a way that mandates that I grow. Are we not each inseparable from the Creator? Aren't all of us connected through the Light and Sound? If so, then what affects each of us to some degree affects the Creator, who is our true Father. What I'm trying to say is that if I can change, and if you can change, and all other aspects of life grow from change, then the Creator is changing also. My mind cannot conceive what those changes are, but my heart tells me this is so. As each of us grows into the understanding of who we are and what the Creator is, this growth feeds into spirit, which it then must pass to the Creator in whatever way it has devised. The most wonderful thing about life is that we are growing and changing, always for the better, so why would the Creator not enjoy the same growth in its own way? I firmly know that when each of us reach certain stages of growth in such a way that it is noble, fearless, loving, and free, then these qualities and others act as an energy that enhances the Creator's beingness to some degree. Soul's existence is a reciprocal action, as is the Creator's. The more love we share with others—including with the Creator—the more love the Creator and others give back. This constant giving and taking is actually causing change."

Morleck remains silent for a moment. Moving slowly toward the railings, he turns back again and says, "I have never thought of perfection being anything but changeless; if it changes, then it must lose its perfection and therefore it was not perfect at all in the first place."

I shake my head. "But perhaps we should consider another concept of perfection. Maybe the Creator is a being that is always changing by its own choice; maybe what we see as change is only expanding what already exists into something greater; maybe this is what perfection actually is."

Morleck reaches up and takes off his beret. Scratching his head, he reminds me of Da'; then looking into the darkening sky, he says. "You might be right, Hugh. If most things are not constantly changing they end up becoming stagnant. So by saying the Creator is changeless, as all the great thinkers and scriptures have said, then perhaps we are saying that the Creator is stagnant also. The God of any religion can then be seen as a God of stagnation when its followers choose to refuse the freedom to change their individual perspective of what they conceive as God."

Crossing over to the railings closer to Morleck, I ask one more question. "How do I defend myself from this creature you call the Abaddon?"

Morleck shakes his head wearily. "I have no weapons to give you, Hugh. There is no sword, there is no cannon, there is no power in the universe that can harm Abaddon. The greatest and only weapon that exists is within your very heart and Soul. In the past, during your darkest moments, you have sometimes had to confront situations alone. I tell you this now; you are to trust in your comrades, your family, and most of all in your God, however you define it. For in trusting your inner knowingness, together with something outside of yourself, you will find a consolidation that provides the greatest weapon at your disposal. Take heed of these words, Hugh, for I do not say them needlessly to those who cannot use them wisely."

I look at me friend, and for just a brief moment, I see a multitude of images flash across his face: Jotan, Shakti, Olgera, the witch woman, the old man at the gate, Kaylu, Dandi, Loren, the Guardian, the Riverman, and so many more. Then, I know! All are me teachers. All, even me enemies, are teachers. Those I had once seen as evil, I now understand are really giving me lessons to learn from. All are reflections and aspects of me own self. Even Abaddon is a part of who I am. All are pointing the way to something far greater than me limited concept of good and evil. The vision is instantaneous and then gone; in its place is a simple pure wisdom that leaves me speechless.

Morleck stares into me face and smiles. "Now, you know."

****

Clark sits at his wife's side brushing hair from her face; Melody holds her mom's hand.

There is for the first time a look of peace and comfort on Ann Bailey's face. She isn't conscious, but it doesn't matter. Both Clark and Melody know something wonderful has taken place. Both felt Hugh's presence and something even more.

For the moment, Ann is showing stronger signs of life. For the first time in months, hope has become a part of her recovery. The doctors and nurses are still in shock from what they had seen. One moment a woman is having what looked like a seizure from hell, and then after stepping back and allowing her husband and daughter to intervene, the woman recovers. All her vitals are strong; color rushes back to her face, and she lies in a peaceful slumber.

The staff heard the chanting, and saw Clark and Melody take her hand and perform what looked to them like a prayer. Yet there was more: something none of them could explain. They all had felt the room filled with some kind of powerful energy.

Dr. Orvitz checks Hugh, who seems to have also recovered from the unsettling and unorthodox events that just occurred. Hugh's vitals are normal; his temperature's at a safe level along with his pulse and heartbeat. To the doctors, it's as if both patients had simultaneously recovered from whatever it was that nearly killed them.

The door flies open and Dr. Stepp rushes in. "I heard there was an emergency. Is there anything I can do?"

Nobody says a word for a moment, and then Clark stands up and replies. "Yes, there was an emergency, but it's over now, but thank you for your offer."

Dr. Stepp looks around; no one moves or says anything else. She looks uncomfortable as she walks over to Hugh's monitor and checks his vitals, and then stepping over to Ann, she does the same. The expression on her face changes to what could only be described as surprise, shock and bewilderment all at the same time. "H-How is this possible? She looks incredible!" Then again checking Ann's support monitor, she becomes even more at a loss of words. "Th-This is impossible! She shows no sign of a deep coma; it's as if she's sleeping!"

Dr. Stepp looks over at Clark; horror rushes into her face as she realizes what her previous actions had almost done. "Oh! Oh my God! What have I done? I was wrong!"

She lets out a cry and a whimper as the reality of what has happened sets in. Clark stands up and tries to soothe her. "It's all right, everything is all right. In fact, everything is just fine. You couldn't have known. Hopefully, you have learned from this situation like we have."

Perhaps it was the residual energy from what had just happened, or perhaps it was the realization of how much damage her actions may have caused, but whatever it was, Dr. Stepp was no longer acting like a detached doctor in her relationship with these clients. She stares into Clark's face. "How can you treat me so kindly? I almost killed your family. I was so sure of my facts I let my ego make judgments based on anger and self-righteousness. I don't deserve your kindness! I don't deserve your forgiveness. I don't deserve to be a doctor!"

As Clark looks into the woman's face, for just a moment he sees anguish, and then he sees what he should have seen from the beginning. This woman is living mired in her fear, and unknown to her, she has been suppressing this fear with her position and the little power that was given to her as a doctor and representative for the insurance companies. Betrayal is written in her eyes; this woman was hurt badly sometime in her past. The emotional damage from that hurt infected her and eventually consumed the loving person she truly should have been.

Clark knows the look and the feeling well; he was also once a captive of the same fear, and he knows the insidious way it filters into the mind, and distorts the sense of right and wrong. How can he judge or condemn this person when she is a victim just as he was? Gently he takes her hands in his, looks into her eyes and softly says, "You have so much to offer life; don't let past circumstances stop your greatness or define who you truly are. If you do, then that's the only real wrong. You have grown just as I have. There's no need for forgiveness from us but only from yourself, for no one here judges you, and most of all, no one condemns you. Forgive yourself, let go of the past, and most of all, love yourself."

Clark releases the doctor's hands with a compassionate look of understanding, and then gently smiling, looks down at his wife. Putting his arm around Dr. Stepp's shoulder, Clark continues, "A great doctor once told me that there are miracles happening in the medical field all the time. I think it's time we accept them with acknowledgment and wonder."

Dr. Stepp looks at Ann Bailey and weeps, not tears of shame but tears of release and gratitude.

****

I walk into me cabin with Davy. "My friend, I need you to gather our comrades and have them meet me here as soon as possible."

Davy looks confused. "Who do you mean, Captain?"

I reply, "I mean assemble everyone except the crew itself—they'll need to hold the ship once we make our move on the island."

One by one, me friends begin arriving.

Loren, Karla, Dandi, Kaylu, the crystal guards, and Morleck; the cabin's getting full. I stand under the double door entryway to the balcony with the sea and dark gray clouds as my background.

Finally, all are present.

"Friends, I've gathered you here for the sole purpose of discussing what we are about to attempt. The Black Island, which is the domain of the Dark One, is close. I feel it's better for us to discuss and confront this situation together. If there's any among you who don't wish to join in battle, then let them leave now, for only the strong of heart and conviction can withstand the power we're about to confront." There's a moment's silence, but no one moves.

The clouds behind me are changing rapidly, and I'm silent for a few seconds. The skies are getting darker, and the wind moves the billowing clouds into a great swirling mass of gray, white, and black—the effect is surreal, even mystical. Standing in the dim light of the open doors, I watch as everyone's face darkens from the shadows moving furtively across the room. I continue, "There are twelve of us, so we'll take two boats to the island. Once we land, we'll stay together."

As I'm speaking, Soultraveler suddenly trembles as if some large hand were shaking it. Water heaves alongside the ship, and for a moment, everyone steadies themselves as the ship rocks and shudders. Then, just as suddenly, all is calm. I'm staring at their surprised faces as a dark shadow passes through the room. Suddenly, everyone facing me gasps and their eyes widen. Karla screams and points toward the ocean behind me. I swing around just in time to see a huge neck rise from the sea above the ship's balcony; following it up, I see attached to the snake-like neck the head of a huge serpent beast. The serpent sneers and glares at me, and then as quickly as the huge sea creature appears, it sinks below the dark waters back to the black depths it came from. I run to the edge of the balcony just in time to see the water churning and boiling as its huge serpent-like back disappears beneath into the ocean depths.

The crystal guards bolt from the cabin to the main deck. Baylor yells out, "If the crew sees such a monster without support, they'll lose courage and panic! They'll be useless in their duties."

I push me way out to the deck followed by the others. Just as I step to the side of the guards, the ship again shudders and shakes, swaying from side to side. Turning to the bow, I see that huge serpentine head emerge again from me right, but just as quickly, I see another head rise to the left of the ship. Two monsters are now hovering over the ship with their heads reaching almost halfway up the middle mast.

Some of the crew scream and sheer panic breaks loose when the starboard viper viciously thrusts forward, and seizing a man from the crow's nest, sinks back into the sea.

Before anyone can think the other viper strikes at the guards, taking Paul into its mouth; the man swings his sword against the gaping jaws, but the blade has little effect as ten-inch fangs clamp around him and lift him deeper into its gaping mouth. There was time for just one scream, and then he was gone; the serpent sinks beneath the waves, and all that's left is Paul's shield lying on the deck covered in blood. I stare in horror.

Never have I seen such viciousness and predatory speed! The realization that Paul is dead hits me like a club. I pull me sword from its scabbard and run to where he was taken. The ship again heaves and shakes, and the crew and the girls are in total panic. The crystal guards are on alert, forming a circle around Loren and Karla. Morleck moves close to me, and I whisper hoarsely, "What are they?"

Morleck has to raise his voice above the yelling and screams of the crew to answer, "They are the Black Island's second defense—they guard the Dark One's domain and heed his commands only."

I look across the black sea as enormous waves crash against Soultraveler; the water churns and boils as the sea monsters slither along the ship's edges. Everyone on board watches their massive coils moving in and out of the raging waters as they prepare for another attack. I call out to Morleck, "What do we do?" For the first time, I'm beginning to feel the panic that's overtaking the minds of the crew. This is for real! Death is at our doorstep, and no magic, no reasoning or guile can take us from harm's way.

I have only a moment before the next attack. I have to do something!

I feel a touch on me shoulder; swinging around in panic, I raise me sword but just before I can swing, I see Baylor by me side. "Captain, we have the cannons! They might be effective against the sea vipers."

The cannons! Of course! I completely forgot about them. I call for Dandi to open the deck doors and get the men down below. I grab Baylor by the shoulder and scream, "Get them loaded, now!"

Calling the rest of the guards to help, Dandi takes Loren and Karla down below. I rush to the ammunition closet where two guards collect powder and balls, while two others roll out one of the cannons for loading.

Just as they move the weapon into position, we hear a tremendous roar behind us. One of the dragon vipers raises its head behind the bow, and there's no time to load the great gun before the beast thrusts its head onto the ship, trying to reach past the first mast and its sails. It angrily grabs the mast in its jaws and rips it from its bolts, tearing the sails and pulling the guide ropes across the ship's deck. Ropes as thick as a man's arm whip out in all directions, themselves deadly to anyone in their way. The mast snaps and falls as the beast drags it over the side of the ship. I stare dumbfounded.

"My God, they're going to destroy Soultraveler!" I whisper in horror.

Elias moves the cannon to the center of the deck. It's loaded and ready, but not knowing where the next attack will come from, he's confused. He has to be able to turn it in any direction quickly. Dandi rushes to his side and stands behind the cannon. Elias has the flame and is ready, but only still waters meet our eyes as we search, trying to anticipate where the next attack will come from.

Kaylu scrambles up the middle mast and climbs into the crow's nest. Because of his size, he's practically invisible. Watching with eyes like an eagle, he stares at the waters below, trying to see where the monsters will surface next. Suddenly, he sees it! The water starts to churn toward the middle of the ship on the left side. Kaylu shouts, "Behind you, it comes; quickly, turn around!"

Elias pushes on the pivot, while Dandi heaves against the massive cannon and swings it in the direction Kaylu is pointing.

The attack is quick and staggering as both behemoths side by side rise up over our small group of remaining men. The one on the left rises even higher, keeping its eye on the crow's nest where Kaylu hides. Its tongue flicks, using sensors to detect a living body within the nest. Rising higher, it swings its massive head just above the nest, sensing Kaylu's warm body heat. The other dragon slithers over the railing intent on heading for our small group of men huddled by the base of the middle mast.

I yell out to Dandi, "Take aim! Go for the one in the air!"

Dandi ignores the approach of the second snake, which is moving across the deck toward us. Swinging the cannon upward, he points it toward the monster intent on grabbing Kaylu. Once in position, he screams at Elias, "Light the wick!"

Elias looks through the loop down the cannon to see where the ball will go, and grabbing a small wheel on the side of the cannon, he turns the crank. As he does, the cannon moves in the exact direction he's aiming for. Dandi's nervous; the monster is searching out Kaylu and is getting ready to strike. Elias locks the directional finder and lights the wick. Almost instantly, there's a loud explosion as the cannon fires the ball toward the dragon's throat.

At that very instant, I turn to see the second viper break through the second mast where a barricade of ropes and crates temporarily slow its attack.

I'm ready!

My sword is out and I stand with me feet apart to give me balance. The sword's glowing blood red as it stalks its victim. The sword and I are one with each other.

I'm not the same warrior I was back in the cave, where the sword had its first taste of blood at me hands. The warrior who holds it now has an almost unlimited source of power that the sword can tap into and bring it to a level of performance that has never been equaled. I bend me knees as the monstrous creature slithers toward me. I feel the power flow through me and down into the glowing sword, and then return again. It's like waves of confidence and ability pouring into me consciousness, bringing out the primal, intuitive survival factors lying dormant deep within. The serpent moves quickly, counting on an easy kill. As it nears striking distance, I leap to the side; the monster lunges forward. If it had been smaller and quicker, the strike might have worked, but to my heightened senses, the creature is slow and sluggish. I'm under the creature's neck instantly and with lightning speed I strike the giant's massive throat and slice across its jaw line. The viper hisses and raises its body upward, smashing the middle mast that Kaylu is perched on. Reeling back, it feels the sting of my cut and recoils.

I look back to discover that the cannon ball has ripped into the other viper's throat, mortally wounding it. Screaming in anguish from the gaping wound inflicted by the canon ball and squirming like a worm on a fishhook, the beast falls over the ship's side, with its attached lower half still lodged on deck. The body flips and writhes as death takes hold. The second viper, seeing its mate destroyed, moves back and dives over the railing back into the black depths.

The middle mast is resting against the sails of the only remaining mast at the ship's stern. Kaylu's holding onto one of the massive hanging sails, apparently unaffected by his ordeal. Soultraveler is sorely wounded. The great ship's railings are smashed, and two masts are in shreds with sails slung everywhere. Ropes and cross masts are lying over the helm. Thick pools of blood from the vipers soak the deck. Three life boats are smashed, with others slung across the damaged deck. Drenched with the viper's blood, I stare at the destruction and death surrounding me. Baylor walks over to Paul's crystal shield. Carefully picking it up, he carries it over to the water bucket and rinses off his fallen comrade's blood. Corwin walks over to assist, and together they ponder how their friend and comrade could be gone so suddenly and forever.

I am stunned as I take stock of our situation. I watch the unreal scene of two noble warriors carefully wiping the slain hero's blood off of his magnificent

W.T. LEWIS

crystal shield. Looking around me at the extensive damage done to Soultraveler, I finally understand in me consciousness what we are up against. Death is lurking with every step closer to the island. The loss of a good crewman and a great warrior casts a dark shadow over everyone on the ship. I hear the deck door open and see how one by one the crewmen begin to emerge from below to the horrific scene on deck.

Loren and her sister surface, and then like the others, momentarily stand still, stunned by the shocking wreckage on deck. Stepping over to me, Loren put her arms around my neck, embracing me fiercely as if this were to be the very last time. Holding her to my chest, I watch as the guards form a circle around the fallen warrior's crystal shield. Each kneels on one knee and becomes quiet as he silently says farewell.

Morleck climbs to the upper deck beside the helm to survey the carnage of Soultraveler. Placing his hands on the railing and looking down on the survivors below, he calls out, "Men, you have met the children of the Dark One and defeated their efforts to stop us. Take courage, for our comrades are not dead, nor have they ceased to exist. Each is now experiencing the blending of his mortal thoughts of existence with the spiritual existence of his God. They will no longer grope in the dark and cling to earth, for they have now tasted Heaven. The destiny and reward they were created to receive is upon them. Their lives are not lost but renewed. So let us mourn what we will miss and at the same time celebrate in their victory over their fallen shells. They would be the first to say, 'Let our fate be an example to all that life does not stop at the destruction of the shell that we have dropped; indeed, true life is just now begun.'"

I realize what has to be done and I know me duty as Captain.

"Men, let's repair the damage. Team captains, take your crews down below and find the replacement supplies stored in the hull. Deck leaders, clean up and prepare the ship for sail."

Taking their cue from me, the crew begins the arduous task before them.

I gather my comrades around me. "We must get rest, for in the morning we set out for the island. Each of you will stow your packs with gear and be ready when the sun rises. What we do from now on will be done in the memory of our fellow comrades who were taken from us this day." Then, after shouting their assent as one, the eleven remaining comrades separate to prepare for the next day.

394

CHAPTER 47 ~ NO MAN IS AN ISLAND

Except for the steady sounds of the crew repairing damages from the afternoon's battle, everyone else is silent and most try to get as much sleep as possible before morning. I spend a restless night wrestling with me mind. A constant parade of thoughts and images keep running through me head.

During this onslaught of thoughts I try to figure out a strategy for the next attack. All of my expectations have been shattered, and not knowing what to expect from Abaddon leaves me with little to go on. If I plan an attack based on what I already experienced, it will be to no avail. The treacheries of me own senses, emotions, and thoughts would be my worst adversary, especially if I lose control of my mind even for a brief moment. Finally, I fall asleep.

The first light of dawn breaks through the dark clouds and spreads its rays into my cabin. I open me eyes; I don't know where I am or who I am. For a moment, this confusion is intensely frightening. I'm lying on me bed. I look around. Ah yes, I remember now; the viper dragons killed my comrades.

I roll on my side, curling into a ball, and then flip on my stomach. Now I wait, and wait some more, for the blood to flow into my brain again and wake me up. I run through the basic facts, trying to place a stamp of reality on me thoughts and feelings.

My name is Hugh Bailey, and I'm ten years old. My mom's name is Ann. I live in Bristol, but now I exist in the body of a grown man in another world. If these are facts, then I'm crazy? I feel as if I have aged over night; all of me muscles are tight and sore.

Images of the viper dragons devouring Paul and the crewman keep filling me with deep emotions of sadness, anger, guilt, and sorrow. Stumbling to the head, I glance into the mirror. What I see makes me stare in disbelief. My hair is still light brown mixed with blonde, but now I can see some streaks of gray above my sideburns. Staring closely, tiny lines and creases around the edge of me eyes stare back. The dark stubble of a beard shadows my cheeks and chin. I look to be a mature man now in his mid-thirties!

As I continue to stare, I realize the most startling part of the image in the mirror isn't the gray hair or the wrinkles around me eyes or even the slight growth of beard. What startles me is that I'm staring into the same eyes, the same chin and the same nose as me father's face. I feel dazed and disoriented.

I hate this journey! I hate it with a dark passion and secretly I always have! Why me? I'm just a kid! I slide down on me knees. Please let this be over! But I'm not ready for it to be over. Confusion clouds me mind. I take a deep breath. Hate and fear threw me on my knees; love slowly coaxes me back up. I splash water on my face and then prepare for the journey ahead. After I finish dressing, I walk into the hazy light. A gray fog has settled over the ship during the night muting everything except for the occasional slapping of the sea against the ship's hull. Walking noiselessly across the deck, I see the deck crew has cleaned and repaired most of the damage. There are repairs still to be finished, but at least the ship doesn't look torn apart as it had after the battle. Soultraveler is wounded, even battle worn, but it's not out. A sound behind me makes me turn, and I find Karla and Loren emerging from the morning fog.

Wearing pants, boots, long jackets, and small capes with attached hoods, both girls carry small packs that they drop before me. Loren slips into me arms and looks into my eyes; a brief look of surprise crosses her face as she sees the changes in me features, but she doesn't say a word. Then, one by one the others appear like silent ghosts, ready if necessary to lay down their lives. Kaylu is the last to appear. He, too, carries a small pack. As he nears me, he steps up and takes me hand. I sense something different—something strange, but also familiar.

Kaylu looks up and solemnly says, "As you approach this final test, your awareness of unity will grow. You have remembered so much more of who you really are, and so it is with me also. So, brother, we go together now to finish our quest." I look down at the little Wuskie, and like a wisp of wind I hear a faint, haunting sound of flutes playing a forlorn melody in the depths of me Soul. It's a lonesome sound, but its very loneliness clears me mind. I know now for sure that my ideals of yesterday's God are gone; in its place is a new God, a God of tomorrow. Whatever I think I know washes away in a single, lonely wave of unconditional love exploding within me heart, like cosmic waves crashing against a distant galaxy.

For a few brief seconds, I as Soul stand on the edge of a precipice looking out over the created universe reflecting me true self. I look again at Kaylu, who has been with me from the beginning of this strange journey—and possibly will die with me in its end. A silent understanding passes between us.

I turn and call out to a crew leader.

"Lower two boats. We'll divide ourselves in half, with two guards going with Davy, Morleck and Karla, while two more go with Loren, Dandi, Kaylu, and me."

Boats are lowered; the calm dark waters only reflect the composed dread each of us is feeling. Before long, we are rowing silently into the gray mist, disappearing into the direction of the Black Island.

I think back to our fight with the viper dragons while on Soultraveler. If we were attacked while in these small boats instead, the fight would end before it starts, with us at the bottom of this black sea. A long rope is tied to the rear of our boat connecting us to the companion boat; we can't afford to lose contact with each other in this fog. Silently, we move through still waters watching for signs of more vipers or any other unknown monsters. Morleck navigates with a sure hand toward the island as if he has a sixth sense. The fog is far too dense to see through. None can tell which is north, south, east or west, but somehow, Morleck pushes forward, drawn to the vibration of evil surrounding the Dark One's abode.

I still haven't worked out a plan of action. Since I don't know what to expect, the plan that makes any sense at all is to trust in the Creator and accept that whatever happens is meant to be, whether it be failure or success. Me mum is on this island, and once found, Abaddon will do whatever is in its power to stop us from freeing her. However, instead of dwelling on that, I know that I have to get to her first, and this is where my thoughts need to center. Only the present moment is of any value. All me struggles, all the growing and startling revelations from the past, are now an integral part of who I am; these qualities are leading me to the next stage of me journey.

Staring thoughtfully into the impenetrable fog, I pull my cape around me as if to ward off the forthcoming battle; the fight will not be a war of swords, but a test of raw wills. Only one will survive, for Abaddon leaves no witnesses; all become its victims.

I'm suddenly tired.

I'm tired of loneliness, tired of searching, tired of fighting, but mostly tired of living. Who can know the true depth of what's inside me? Perhaps life is lived to be ultimately alone, always searching for what cannot be described. A voice from within gently fades into me mind.

"There is no promise to you that you won't be tired, Hugh. But know this. There's unlimited good waiting for you on the other side of tired. So get yourself tired, Hugh; for that's where you're going to know yourself: on the other side of tired."

Silence as thick as the fog closes in from the dreaded island. Morleck has one of the guards wave his torch to indicate the island is close and to prepare for landing. I reach behind me and feel for me sword, and then putting me hand inside my tunic, I feel the little book against me heart—although I know in the end it will not be a sword or a book that conquers the day.

Success has to come from somewhere within me; I have to do what works for me. Will it be understood by others? I don't know. But at the moment, I'll do what I must do. A nudge in my mind followed by an impression of feelings gently pushes its way into me thoughts. Kaylu and Dandi's energy merges in me inner thoughts; both are sending me their strength and love in a moment of incredible giving. No matter what the outcome, my friends are always there to support me. In the end, this is why they are here. Throughout the entire journey, their patience and care have taught me that when your life is no longer about you, and actually has nothing to do with you, but is about everyone else whose life you touch, then you've arrived at the entrance to the holy chambers of the true self. Love, growing, and freedom is what I live for. When all is said and done, so-called enlightenment has really nothing to do with what you do with the body or the conscious mind, for these are what we are trying to be free from. Enlightenment has to do with what you do as Soul. Wave upon wave of knowingness is flowing through me as if a fountain has been turned on, pouring into my being. I ask myself, what can I do? Then I ask again, what can I do?

A voice deep and clear rolls through me mind, saying something quite extraordinary: *"There is nothing you have to do."* After all this time, after all the challenges and tests, sudden overwhelming realizations hit me like gusts of wind. This quest isn't about books or sitting in meditation. It isn't about traveling to gain more wisdom or even meeting new friends that have become a part of me life. It isn't about swords, magic or any of that. It could be, if I wanted it to be; it could be, if that's what suited me. It could be, if that's the path I choose, but it isn't necessary.

True enlightenment knows there's nothing you have to do or be enlightened for. To achieve the success I seek, I have only to fully realize that I need do nothing at all, and in that nothingness is everything. My mind swims in this revelation. The boat abruptly hits the shore. My mind is empty, like a vessel turned upside down, nothing mattering any longer except for a deep sense of surrender that is pouring out from within me. Whatever me mind might conceive as a plan for defeating Abaddon is simply the Dark One's own plan in disguise. Mind can't defeat mind; this is clear.

I step from the boat. The others step out just as the second boat lands. Everyone gathers around as I walk toward the huge black mountain rising out of the center of the island. Black and gray clouds gather around the huge mountain with its crown of jagged peaks. A gray fog grows denser, swirling a few feet above the ground. We move deeper into the island's heart. Clarity and calm along with feelings of faith expand and intertwine inside me, crystallizing into knowingness. I cease to worry or try to forge a plan in me mind. Excitement and the glad expectation of a child begins to bubble from within me heart, merging with feelings of calmness. It's a constant energy, carrying me back again to me feelings as a young boy, the boy me mum knows and loves. Any sense of dread slowly dissolves as I move closer to the mountain's base. Anticipations of a ten-year-old boy gurgle from me stomach. Memories from home and me lost youth run through me heart. I can almost hear Cody running through the grass, chasing shadows in the meadow with me and Billy.

Isn't that what I've been doing? Chasing the shadows that me mind creates?

These shadows are born from anger, desire, fear, attachment, and guilt. These are the true enemies of humankind. The voice from within blends again with me mind.

"You as a human have always lived in a world built on shadows and fear. If you fear enough, you will give away your very freedom to be free from those things you fear. You will do it gratefully for there is only one thing the human consciousness wants more than freedom, and that is security. A sense of security gives humans the illusion of survival. Your world has lost its way in its false sense of security. For what is security without God?"

I continue walking even as the voice within continues impressing me with realizations that deepen me awareness. With each step, me concepts of yesterday's God continuously keep fading even more. A new expression of the Creator is filling me with a sense of independence. With this independence, come feelings of freedom and power. This freedom creeps deeper into my inner kingdom.

We move closer to the massive black mountain; winds howl as they rush through narrow canyons and gullies. A bitter blast penetrates our flimsy outerwear. However, our feelings of coldness aren't entirely from freezing winds. There's something else, something like fingers of ice grasping at us; insidious demons are screaming within each of us, stoking our fears. I can only feel the effects dimly, but I know the others are fighting for control of their thoughts and emotions as the frosty breath blows mercilessly against them. I stop for a moment to let my friends catch up to me. I stand on a jutting precipice overlooking a deep chasm that's covered with dense whirlpools of dark swirling clouds below.

As I turn to face them, huge clouds almost as dark as the black mountain gather around behind me. Looking at each man and woman, I send each an impression of confidence and love—the greatest weapons I have. These thought impressions I send act like powerful visual imprints that help stay the feelings of fear and uncertainty trying to gain control of their minds. Pulling me cape over my shoulders and lifting my hood to cover my head, only me eyes are exposed to my companion's sight.

Morleck stands well behind the group watching Hugh as he positions himself against the gray sky on the black precipice projecting over the chasm below. Hugh cuts an imposing figure as the gray fog swirls about his feet. Each feels his power, which lifts their hearts.

"Who is this Soul?" Morleck wonders.

Within just a short time, Morleck has seen a young boy evolve into this higher form of being, beyond even his own awareness. Hugh aspires to give his total self to others without ever thinking of himself. Morleck feels his power; he also senses emanations of courage and love mixed with a wisdom that forms a tremendous feeling of confidence and freedom. He's humbled—almost embarrassed—when he looks into Hugh's eyes.

Hugh steps down from the precipice, and continues leading the group along to the black mountain. For a brief moment, his friends feel relieved and encouraged. The mountain looms larger, the wind blows colder, and the sky grows darker; suddenly, Abaddon's power intensifies.

Loren's and Karla's minds are again in a state of panic; every conceivable negative thought and feeling attack their minds without mercy. Kaylu and Dandi are calmer; they have fought this battle many times since their journey, especially in the Dark Cave. This dark power is far more intense, but they have built the stamina and discipline required to control the self-betrayal of their minds. The crystal guards remain deep in contemplation, chanting the holy names of the Creator and the sacred Hu. What a mystical and eerie sight this peculiar group must be as they move along together toward the black mountain.

I continue marching toward the great mountain. Looking up, I stare for a moment as the sky darkens with angry boiling clouds. The battle has started; it's only a matter of time before there are casualties. The energy of the Abaddon is overwhelming here in its own domain, and anyone who thinks he has overcome it is only deluding himself and falling into another subtle trap of the Dark One's shattering power. Finally, we reach the base of the first mountain. Here the trail becomes a narrow footpath, forcing us to keep marching in single file. As we climb higher among jagged rocks, the thin trail zigzags like a long garland on a Christmas tree. Icy winds don't bother dispensing the thick fog at our feet, intent instead on chilling our Souls. If we aren't careful, any one of us could misstep to our death in the murk covering the chasms below us. Our marching slows to a creeping trudge; we test each step in the thick gloom. Keeping our hands against the cliff wall, we traverse our way higher toward the black mountain. Slow, cautious walking is all we can do to keep pushing forward.

I emerge first from a large turn of the lower cliff. I see the trail spreading out into what should have been a flat plateau. Instead, a bare stretch of gray land littered with rocks, deep crevices, and boulders sprawls before us; there's no plant life, just grayish black dirt and even blacker rocks before us. The scene reminds me of old TV movies in black and white. Giant mountains stand like sentinels above the flat valley. The topography of the land gently slopes upward as it nears the Jagged peaks and great boulders covering the entranceway to the mountain's cave.

I wait again for me comrades to catch up. Gathering in front of the dark stretch of land, a thick cloying mist swirls about our feet and then drifts over the land, hiding the black rocks and crevices that pepper the unholy terrain. Crossing the valley is the last visible obstacle before ascending the mountain. We are hesitant; looks can be deceiving, and this mist is a master at creating illusions. I press forward, me friends cautiously following trying to match their steps with mine.

Howling winds increase; so does the cold. Each step feels like a step closer to a frozen hell. We find ourselves wading deeper and deeper into a moist sticky fog, which gradually increases until we are totally submerged in a wet gray darkness. None can even make out a person right next to them. Each traveler moves forward with his or her own dark thoughts and fears mercilessly trying to subjugate them to their will. Then we feel the first tremor.

A deadly silence penetrates each of us.

Another slight movement—similar to a wave rolling beneath us—is followed by a tremendous echoing crash like thunder, only a hundred times louder and far more powerful. Instantly, the ground shakes, lifts then tilts. Thick chunks of fog are sucked into pockets of earth as the ground cracks open, groaning an eerie, thunderous howl. I try to shout above the terrible sound, but me voice is snuffed out like a candle in a hurricane. The ground shakes again and the fog clears for a brief moment. What we see freezes our blood.

Jagged boulders ranging from the size of a man's body to the size of our lifeboats are now plummeting and thundering down upon us! We hear just steps away another deep thunderous crash, sounding like a tremendous drum being beaten. With each rumble, the ground shakes and vibrates like rolling thunder. We are barely able to stand as the ground heaves and rolls. Out of the fading gloom, lightning flashes for a brief second. Rocks standing at the entrance to the mountain are crashing down and rolling across the low-lying valley directly toward us.

Boulders and smaller rocks the size of basketballs are flying by our heads and crashing around us. From out of nowhere, rock missiles are suddenly being hurled directly toward us; they are the most terrifying part of this unholy onslaught!

The eleven of us quickly separate, we fling ourselves away from the crushing boulders. Each of us is on our own as the attack continues. Loren desperately gropes around her, trying to find her sister, while at the same time dodging the deadly rocks. Just trying to keep standing as the ground shakes and trembles around her is a struggle in itself. Even as she regains her balance, she sees hurdling at her a jagged rock the size of a large basket. Before she can think, a body with a crystal shield jumps in front of her taking the full brunt of the impact! The body crumbles and falls. Sinking to her knees, she crawls toward the lifeless form. The boulder smashed into the man, leaving him twisted and injured almost beyond recognition. Feverishly but gently, she turns the man's head toward her; Elias's face is bloodied and broken. The courageous guard fulfilled his promise to protect at all costs the lives of the girls and Hugh. He paid the highest price. Holding his head in her lap, she caresses his face in a tearful goodbye as screams of thunder and howling winds fill the air. Elias's shield rises from his broken and torn body.

Lifting her face, she sees Hugh battling the winds and the rocks.

Kneeling down and reaching out his hand to her, Hugh shouts, "Come, we must leave this place before it's too late!" He quickly turns and raises the fallen soldier's shield in front of them. A boulder the size of a dinner plate bounces off the crystal facing. Without waiting further, he lifts Loren to her feet and quickly moves forward, half dragging, half carrying her.

Dandi scrambles forward on all fours, If he stands he makes a larger target for the flying rocks, so he must keep low. The wind screams as small rocks pelt his chest and face his thick craggy skin acts like a protective vest, but he knows if one of the larger boulders hits him, even he would be smashed. As he slumps and crawls forward, he prays he can find Kaylu; his mind screams, and fear rushes through him. He's beginning to feel like he will falter, then possibly he may even succumb to the hopeless situation. Standing up the ground continues to shake, jagged rocks careen off each other smashing into smaller pieces like exploding grenades.

Dandi falls again on his hands. Crawling close to the ground he slowly advances, foot by foot. Just as he is about to stand and move in another direction, he feels something brush against his hand. Pulling himself forward, he nears the object. As he reaches out to touch it, he sees through the fog the face of his dearest friend. Moving closer, he touches the body of his little friend, and then kneeling, he slides his hands under his friend's body, lifting him up off the ground. Staggering to his feet, a feeling of overwhelming sadness, grief, loss, and defeat smother his consciousness. Holding the torn, lifeless body of his wise yet childlike friend, he whispers, "Kaylu!"

Gently nudging the lifeless form, he whispers again. "Kaylu, don't leave me! Please God, don't let him die!" The ground shakes and gasps one last time, and then becomes still.

The pounding of rolling boulders cease, the wind stills. Dandi staggers aimlessly toward the mountain, hoping against hope to find help for the limp form that was once his dearest companion and friend.

A silence permeates throughout the fog—a silence that must be like death itself.

Out of the stillness, forms emerge as the fog fades. Jagged boulders and rocks of various sizes litter the flat plain. I sit on a large flat rock holding Loren, gazing over the carnage before us. One by one, my companions appear from the fog like apparitions. Together we are seven, leaving the fate of four unknown. Laying Loren down on me cape to rest, I walk slowly to a giant form that's moving into the clearing. I see immediately that it is Dandi, but what's he carrying? Quickly, I run down the slope. Me vision clears, and I see the small, limp body in the giant's arms. Stabs of emotion race through me as I run to Dandi. Although I recognize Kaylu, gut-wrenching disbelief overwhelms me.

The boy who has grown so much, who has learned so many wise lessons along the journey, the boy who controls his mind and holds his emotions at will—shudders and falls to his knees.

Kneeling down, Dandi places my friend's body gently on the ground in front of me. I'm not the man I thought I was; I no longer feel the great wisdom and love within me. In me heart, I'm still a ten-year-old boy, and that boy is being torn apart at the sight laid out in front of me. I can't take anymore; on my knees I cry out, "Kaylu, nooooo, not you!" Gently, I lift me friend's head into my arms and to me chest. Tears stream from me eyes; I feel totally forsaken and lost. Memories of the little Wuskie at the river's edge in the beginning of my quest flood me mind. Images race through me like the blood in me veins: Kaylu, running over the embankment in the cave carrying the torch to scatter the cave creatures; his laughter; his wisdom; his selfless sharing of his endless love and patience. I press myself to his broken body.

He's gone!

"Dandi! Tell me, what can I do?" My pain drowns out any clear thoughts. Only pain, sadness, and grief are left. Kaylu was always there for me; now I can do nothing for him. Guilt, combining with shame, fear, and loss of me dearest comrade all attack me mind vigorously. Wave upon wave of horrible sadness generates from deep within me.

Dandi rests his hand on my shoulder. "Be strong Hugh. Kaylu would not have wanted us to react in any other way. For his sake and his memory, focus on the joy of who he was, and what he has meant to all of us. The Creator's plan is just, and playing out for each of us. If Kaylu is meant to begin his own journey in a different way, then we have to allow it to happen without our grief and sadness clouding his way."

I look down at me dearest friend's face. His eyes are closed and for a moment it looks as if he's just asleep. I turn to see a withered hand reach out and rest on Kaylu's chest. I look up into Morleck's eyes.

"Let me hold him," the old man gently murmurs while lifting the small, limp body into his arms. Morleck carries Kaylu over to a small area surrounded by boulders. There he has laid some blankets, apparently preparing a soft spot to lay Kaylu upon. Just as Kaylu's body is laid down to rest, Morleck feels a movement in his chest; he touches Kaylu's forehead. For a moment there is only silence, then turning toward us, he looks at me and says, "He's alive!"

I rush over to the old man and ask, "Are you sure? I mean, I can't see any signs of life! How do you know?" Morleck takes my hand and places it firmly on me friend's chest. For a moment I feel nothing, but then I feel a faint movement. Focusing even more, I feel another beat.

"His heart...It beats!" I beam at Dandi and shout, "He's alive! Dandi, he's alive!"

Morleck opens his pack and pulls out containers of powders and herbs. "Quick! There is not much time! Get me some water and start a fire!" A small pot is soon boiling over a fire lit with the fire rocks.

Shaking varied smidgeons of powder into the water, Morleck carefully sprinkles in some of the herbs. He then stirs the brew until it bubbles. Pouring a small bit into a cup, he adds some cold water to cool it down, and then pours a little in Kaylu's mouth. He waits a moment and pours some more. He does this a final third time.

Then, laying the little Wuskie down, he covers him with a blanket.

"He will sleep now, and while he rests, hopefully his body will begin to heal. I've checked the rest of him, and he seems to have a fractured arm along with a terrible bruise on his chest where I am assuming he was struck by a rock...I cannot guarantee anything. His chances are slim, but he may make it. The main thing is that he should not be moved and that he be kept warm as the mixture helps heal his internal injuries."

I kneel next to me friend and pull the blanket up over his chest. "We'll do whatever is necessary for him." Standing up, I look at the haggard group. With Dandi and Kaylu, that meant nine have made it out. Two are still missing. I know Elias is dead, but who else is not accounted for?

I then hear Loren call out. "Karla, where are you?" I turn to see her frantically looking for her sister. I also search the area, and then walking toward the edge of the misty valley, I begin calling out too. There is no answer. Loren runs to me side. "We have to find her! She could be hurt or lost." I nod and reassuring her, I take her hand.

We walk over to the men and I say, "Brothers, we have a grave situation. We have one seriously wounded comrade, and we have lost another. If you don't know already, Elias gave his life to the duty he swore to uphold. I have his shield, which is what he used to save Loren. Now, Karla is lost or possibly hurt in the attack. In either case, we have to assume she's alive. That leaves just the eight of us who are in good enough shape to take on the responsibilities needed at this time. Morleck, Loren, and one guard will stay here protecting Kaylu; that leaves five of us. Three guards and Dandi will begin the search for Karla. Dandi, you'll be in charge of the search party; be thorough, and leave no corner of the valley untouched until you find her. I will continue alone to the mountain to find my mother by myself, and I swear that I will not return unless I have my mother with me." Everyone agrees and begin to prepare for their duties.

Morleck fusses about Kaylu, making sure there are plenty of fire rocks to keep a warm fire going at his side. Dandi begins organizing the three guards, discussing directions and the perimeters of their search. Loren and I walk a short distance away from the others. "This is not how I had planned this, but it seems that everything has come down to each one of us facing our own mission. I don't know why this is happening, but I do know one thing for sure. Don't give up on Karla, and don't give up on me. Take care of Kaylu; but more than anything else, let the Creator control the situation."

I choke up a bit and rub my wet eyes.

"Based on what I just experienced—my grief caused by my assumption of Kaylu's death—I can see I'm not as in control as I thought I was. What I'm trying to say is this: I can't say what's going to happen or even how it's going to happen, because when I make plans, it seems the Creator's plans override whatever I'm thinking, anyway. I'm giving myself totally to this mission. I will be a vehicle for the Creator, and you must also be so. We can't fathom the true meaning of things happening right now, that's for sure. We can't always change some things in life, but this doesn't mean we're powerless. All things are teaching us, whether it's a breeze on the ocean, or our love for each other. All, everything, is exactly as it should be; even though to our minds it seems to be in chaos. Our lives in corporeal form are just a blink in the eye of the Creator, so if we lose each other today, know that we'll be together again someday, no matter what."

I take Loren into my arms and kiss her for what may be the last time. Turning away, I walk toward the mountain with just one thought in me mind: to allow the Creator to use me as its tool to accomplish whatever its plan will be. I fully understand now, with no doubt whatsoever, that I, as a man, can't ever completely control the mind with the mind. Only my true Father's power can accomplish this.

I must totally surrender to that power. Looking off into the distance at the tall mountain, I begin to feel the loneliness Shakti talked about.

CHAPTER 48 ~ TO BE TRUE TO ONESELF

The last part of the journey to the mountain is narrow, guarded on both sides with black misshapen rocks that even after the earthquakes still cling tenaciously to the mountains sides. I watch every step while still trying to maintain a sense of balance within. This isn't happening the way I expected. For one thing, I thought me friends would be with me. Never in me wildest imagining did I think I would be confronting the Dark One alone. I keep thinking of Kaylu and Karla; I can only pray both will be all right.

The closer I get to the cave's entrance the narrower the path becomes. Clouds are again gathering together, becoming darker and threatening a downpour any second. I see no plants to speak of; the ground is only a dark gray clay, not dirt. Gruesome-shaped rocks squeeze closer as I climb toward me goal. My mind calms down a little. Pausing for a moment to catch me breath, the inner voice again gently speaks from within.

"Make no mistake, Hugh. It is neither the mountain nor what's inside that you are conquering. It is just yourself that you must face." The voice becomes silent again, leaving me to ponder just what those words really mean. Walking alone on the trail gives me time to reflect on what my life has become and where it seems to be going.

A few short months ago, I was just a boy enjoying me family and friends. My greatest concern was putting on a little weight and preparing for junior high. Compared to now, I realize how small but precious that world was. I look back to those simple times with me sister, Cody, Mom, and Da'. Life seemed so easy! Here I am in the body of a grown man, a captain of a great ship, a warrior and a lover, on a spiritual quest confronting that which Morleck calls the Dark One.

The Dark One; who is this being? Why is it holding me mum prisoner? How come the Creator ever created it, or even still allows such a being to exist?

The concept of unity and oneness clarifies that life is an extension of myself and vice versa, and even the need for positive and negative forces makes sense. Nevertheless, what can I possibly learn of value by confronting this unknown being that apparently is the foundation and seed of evil and misery within the entire universe? If the Creator doesn't halt the Dark One's malicious behavior, what chance do I have in doing so as a mere mortal?

Rain starts falling, making it almost impossible to walk on the slick clay. The trail climbs higher; I catch myself from slipping by grabbing onto rocks on the side of the trail. Rain falls harder, and wind whips drops against me face. Pulling up my hood and cape doesn't help protect me much. As I turn a narrow bend, the path finally widens; I see a strange mist moving in front of the black mountain's gaping mouth.

****

Morleck carefully watches Kaylu, hoping that the brew he administered will help his companion sleep while his body repairs itself. The chances of Kaylu's survival are small, and Morleck knows it. His internal injuries are extensive, and only God knows whether they will heal; the brew has restorative effects, but it's ultimately up to Kaylu's own will to live.

Loren nervously watches through the sodden fog, looking for either the men searching for her sister or for Karla herself. Turning back to Kaylu, she also senses that for the little Wuskie to live, he must summon great internal strength. She remembers her father once telling her that life is not the way it's "supposed" to be, but is simply the way it is. The way each of us copes with it is what makes the difference in the end. We each alone must fight our battles. At this moment, Kaylu is fighting his own battle for his life. Struggling to maintain her faith and hope, Loren worries about her sister, Hugh, and Kaylu; all of this is testing her to her very Soul. Karla must also be battling her own fears, as well as trying to find her way back. Loren ponders, remembering something else her father repeated before he died in the cave. "Hope exists in all life. Hope is when dawn touches the sky, or a bird spreads its wings. Hope is what happens when one first sees a light—even if it is just a distant small star in the darkest night." Many times he warned her never to give in to the darkness. Her mind fights Abaddon as he seeks to drain her of any hopes of ever seeing her sister again.

Abaddon tears into her thoughts, blasting horrible images of Kaylu's possible death, and stoking her fears that she might never see Hugh again. Gloom ravages her mind and heart, driving her toward darkness. Feeling nearly void of hope or love, she tries to reflect on her sister's laugh, her honesty and bravery. Her mind shifts then to imagining a future without Karla. Hopelessness creeps into her even deeper. As the darkness slowly swallows the light within her, she remembers what Hugh told her one night while lying in his arms. "What lies behind us and what lies before us are but small matters compared to what lies within us. Out of what we see as difficulties, grow miracles." She reminds herself that she has to hold to her faith, not only in herself and in Karla's return, but most of all, in the Creator.

As she summons these thoughts over and over, a small sliver of peace begins to grow in her heart, and she clings to it. Knowing only the present moment is real, she focuses on helping Kaylu however she can. Kneeling over her little friend, she caresses his childlike face. Quietly, she begins to sing. She sings about life, joy, love, and glory. As she sings to her friend, the tiny light within her heart grows.

****

I pull myself over a slippery ridge, steadying myself as I stand. The cave's mouth beckons me to come closer. Within moments, I'm almost at the entrance. Rain begins to fall ferociously and the wind howls around me as I run the last dozen steps and stoop just a bit to enter the cave. All becomes eerily silent. Walking a few steps inside, I pull me sword, and the blade immediately begins to glow, lighting my way. The sword senses evil; evil is as thick and dark here as the wet gray murk outside. I walk deeper into the belly of the black mountain. As I turn a bend and enter another section, a gentle breeze wafts around me. Fresh air fills me senses, and a pleasant scent of sandalwood drifts through the cave.

The cave becomes wider and deeper; it's huge inside, almost like a valley within itself. The walls aren't as dark as I had feared, because some strange source of light illumines the passages and walls. I try to keep me senses alert, but not knowing what to expect keeps me off guard.

Descending further into the cave, the ceiling becomes higher, and the odd light becomes brighter. The walls dazzle like the sparkles when fierce sunlight hits calm, flowing waters. Approaching the wall, I see embedded within it jewels of different shades.

Each gem reflects light in tiny sparkles of different colors. In its mysterious way, this cave is as beautiful as it is hideous. Between each jewel, the black mountain's walls acts like a prison, capturing as much of the brilliant light that it can from each stone struggling to be free. Following the cavern's path, I enter deeper into the heart of what seems to be a living mountain. The further I go, the more brilliant the cave's walls become; light dances all around me.

Turning a bend, the cave takes on an even more mystical quality. A waterfall is flowing from a gap in the wall up against the cave ceiling. Several gigantic black rocks studded with jewels frame both sides of the waterfall. Light emanates from the jewels, and the falling water form a dazzling pattern of colored lights like a twinkling rainbow. As the cascade tumbles into a dark as midnight blue pool, the waters churn and bubble, misting the black cavern walls. Glimmering lights dance on the ever-changing surface of the pool. Eerie, dark, and mystical, the sight grips my attention much like a deer caught fast by approaching headlights. For a moment I am still and silent. The surreal scene sparkles and shimmers. I shake me head to clear me mind, and I walk around the edge of the pool. A slight draft of air from behind the falling water brushes my face.

Curious, I step closer and I see a small natural rock path along the edge of the wall disappearing behind the cascading waters. Hesitating for a moment, I watch the sword's reaction; it points under the falls.

Cautiously moving forward, I take a few more steps and then I see an opening. I duck and walk through a small entrance, finding myself in a short walkway whose presence is protected by the curtain of tumbling water. After just a few steps, I see the entrance to a huge room whose walls are like the rest of the cave, but somehow even more intensely lit. Leaving the water-draped entrance, I walk in and am stunned to see that the walls are as black as coal and studded with countless jewels, larger and more brilliant than the others I have seen so far. Each is sparkling with an almost blinding intensity; their light spills all over the entire cavern. Light sparkles, overlapping and mingling, at times creating the illusion that the jewels cast just one light.

In the center of the cave sits a dais rising above the cavern floor by about two feet. It looks to be made from solid black polished marble. Lights from above coalesce into a united shaft of soft, defused green light surrounding the pedestal. On the pedestal, under the light, I see a dark shadow. Within the shadow stands an image of someone or something; the image is distorted and is as still as a statue within the shadows. I step closer. My vision clears as the light becomes brighter. The image becomes more distinct, and then the image turns. It is a hooded man: a very, very old man.

The wrinkled face has no noticeable beard; he's wickedly thin. Heavy dark gray eyebrows sit high on his forehead, intensifying his eyes. He's wearing a long dark robe and he keeps within the shadows, making it difficult for me to see him. His hands are thin and boney with dark—almost black—finger nails. His face turns just enough for me to see his eyes peer out partially from the shadows. The one eye that I can clearly see is vicious. I take a few steps forward. As I approach, I feel an intense net of energy all about me.

At first the energy seems to probe, but then with a rush, it fuses itself within every cell of me body. Instantly, I feel heavy as if I had just gained hundreds of pounds. I try to step forward, but the effort is nearly beyond my ability. I struggle again, trying to take a few steps before having to stop. The closer I come to the dais, the harder it is to move; even to raise an arm is impossible. The heaviness reminds me of dreams I have had in the past when I would try to run, but the more I would try, the heavier I became. And so here I am now, but this isn't a dream. A harsh crackly voice filled with power projects itself into me mind.

"So, Traveler; you have arrived!"

The voice fills every part of my mind, saturating even me body. Words again push into me mind.

"I am Abaddon. I am that which you have always known, but never met. I have been waiting for you."

I want to respond, but know it's useless to try to speak. My muscles are like concrete; my voice is frozen. I suddenly realize, however, there is nothing stopping me thoughts, so with a push I send out a question. *"Where's me mum?"*

There is a deathly silence for a moment…then words again spill into me mind.

"Patience, Traveler. There is a time for all things. Surely you have many other questions to ask before we get to that one?"

I send out me demand again, but more firmly. *"Where's me mother?"*

The old man remains silent. I stare at the silhouette, waiting.

The shadowy form suddenly thrusts his neck forward from under his hood like a vulture and freezes his pose. With a hoarse chuckle, he projects his voice again and says, *"You didn't think it would be so easy, did you? After all you have gone through, and all you have learned, did you really think you could merely demand what you seek and it shall be given? This is not how real truth works, young traveler. You above all should know this. Somehow through persistence, patience, courage, and desire, you have reached this far, but do not think you have won! Before you cry success, you will confront your greatest obstacle, and that, young master, is where your defeat is assured."*

I concentrate on Abaddon's words; the accent and meaning of each word is seductive and manipulative. The voice twists and turns each word as if he's cheering for me but at the same time counting on me failing. Looking directly into his partially covered face, madness shows deep in his eyes.

With a powerful projection, I demand an answer. *"I have traveled far and fought hard to be here; now tell me, where is me mum?"*

For a moment, the shadowy face stares back, then twisting his neck to the left, his insane face contorts. Faded green light mixes with the dark shadows falling over his features. Dark eyes flash as he studies the warrior in front of him, then with words as hollow as the cave and as rough as the gravelly sand, he replies, *"I am old, young seeker, older than man, older than known creation, even older than time. I have been created for a purpose."*

I'm silent for a moment, then again with a powerful push from me mind, I reply. *"From what I have seen and experienced, you are filled with hate and fear; you inflict evil on life itself, so for what possible purpose can you exist?"*

Abaddon leans his head forward, studying me like a snake before it strikes its prey. *"Fool! Without me, you as man would not even exist! Without me, not even your puny universe that flows throughout creation as matter, energy, space, and time would exist! You will listen, Soul, for this is the moment you were created for. You will listen, and listen well!"*

I again try to break free of the heaviness, but to no avail.

"I exist in many forms, for I adhere to the power of the universal mind. When man uses his feeble brain to think, he creates waves of energy from every thought. Each wave is a vibration attached to a particular sense, desire, feeling, thought or passion. It really doesn't matter what the energy wave is actually born from, for each wave must pass through the mind, and when it does, it becomes subject to my will. It is not very often that pure thoughts with none of the mundane human attachments come through me; but when they do, I'm powerless to manipulate them.

"As the ocean wave travels on energy, so do thoughts and feelings from your mind. The ocean wraps the energy with water; man wraps his mental energy with images, desires, feelings, and sometimes—but not often enough—love. These patterns and waves of energy must pass through the universal mind in order to eventually manifest back into the world you call reality. Every thought is balanced with a reciprocal wave going back to the sender. I currently exist in this form because

this is what you have created, just as I manifested in the form of the dragon vipers. You expected something evil so that is what you received. Whether it is a violent storm, a cave dweller, a black mass of evil darkness, a pretty witch woman or even a child god, it doesn't matter; as long as I can use your thoughts and images to keep you enslaved, then I'm fulfilling me purpose. To keep the mundane human consciousness trapped in mind's illusions keeps my purpose ongoing.

"What the human race does not yet understand is that for most people, the truth is a lie, and the lie is the truth, and I am both of these. For countless ages, man has built his world from his fears, desires, his joys, and even his lust and greed. From his limited beliefs, he creates his devils, his gods. From his religions, he creates even his own heaven and hell. Material, sensory, and emotional attachments enslave his senses and mind, so guilt, fear, and desire become the inspirations used to create most of his personal reality.

"In search of security, humankind creates governments and then uses them to enslave the masses. Once enslaved, the leaders then make war on their fellow Souls—contributing to poverty, ignorance, disease, famine, and ultimate corruption.

"In trying to create from love, mankind confuses it with desire, and so fails miserably; 'I' then make manifest your desires in the energy of your expectations—but not necessarily always with the desired effect, for that is inflected by man's own lack of faith and wisdom. Man provides the energy, feeling, and form, and I choose the matter in how it is used according to one's limited beliefs.

"Mankind gladly gives his wealth, greed, adoration, fear, and power to his adversaries and leaders, and then viciously murders his Saints, Saviors, Redeemers, and Divine Teachers. The list is endless.

"Never forget, Hugh! This is humankind's legacy, and is mostly due to their ignorance of divine wisdom and weak discipline. By not using these two attributes, man allows me to create endless temptations to surround and infect their lives. Humankind does not yet realize that all creation in this universe is from his or her own power; until they do, this power will flow through the mind and be subject to mankind's conscious will, which is nothing more than desire!

"The same energy that existence was created from and still sustains all life is the same energy that gives you existence as humans, but it also has many other facets within its power. For as the universal mind power, it flows through all life in the amounts that each life form believes it to be. I am then within every mind that has ever existed and will ever exist. In reality, we are all one mind."

I consider what the old man is telling me and then ask, *"If man is the distributor for this power, then why do you create so much evil to infect humankind?"*

The old man laughs. *"I do not create evil, I only add form to evil energy as it flows from man's own thoughts. This much is true: man has created so much evil that it has become a part of that which I am, but as in all things, I am balanced with positive energies also. From your lust, I created the river beast; I choose the form, and you provided the energy that filled the matrix. From your innocence, I created Jotan; it was but a simple matter for you to create an attachment to the god child. However, both were only other manifestations of mind's power. Understand this as well as you can, Hugh; to most, I am either their God or their Devil.*

"Not everything I manifest has an evil nature. The Creator, namely you, decides this entirely. Soul has always possessed the power to create the required images and conditions for spiritual ascension. This power is given to humankind to use for Soul to climb the ladder to Heaven."

I send another question to the old man. "Then why, if there is a balance to all things, is my world filled with chaos and destruction?"

Abaddon stares deeply into me eyes for a moment, and then grinning wickedly, he replies. "Man created governments, laws, and religion with the initial intention of creating order; but by tempting his leaders with greed and a desire for power, riches, and control, humankind has over eons of time created a master who seeks only to extract the life forces from its citizens. For your leaders to stay in power, there must be chaos; this chaos trickles down into all humanity. As the conscious mind buries man in illusion and misery, Soul forgets its true purpose and destiny. Humankind does this primarily through visions of fear and their attachments; this serves my purpose, for even as humankind's own desires and fears create war, poverty, famine, and all the negative and positive aspects of your world, they blame it on me, either as their Devil, or even their God! Man thinks control is power, but their control is illusory, and really just another face of fear.

"This fear makes your leaders treasonous, treacherous, and mad for power. For their treachery, they receive wealth, luxuries, adoration, fame, and power and at my own bidding, they control endless worlds with this power. The very power your leaders use to create chaos is the same each man should use himself for his own personal enlightenment and growth. Man has a choice. He can distort this power and create a mangled, perverted version of the mind's power to be reflected in his reality, or choose Soul. Humankind has always had the choice to either live in the shadows or live in the light. Man needs only to take a small step toward the light to be there. If he chooses to pervert his energy, then he blocks the voice of the one Father who is calling each Soul back to it. Man blocks this voice by keeping his attention focused either on his outside desires or the gods of illusion that he creates within himself. He's so busy perverting the divine voice within, so absorbed are they, man simply won't listen to the calling. Instead, he continues to give the power away, and for what? Mostly just to gain a security blanket. For this blanket of illusion humankind hands their power over to an imagined God, religion, or government. They even give their power to their spouses or culture or society in general. But what's most important for my purposes is that he gives the power to his own ego, which I then use to subjugate him to my will or desire. It is this giving of Soul's power to the mind/ego, plus the attachment to man's outside world, that secures my existence for all eternity. In using the creative power of the imagination for his material desires, emotions and sensory feelings, man allows me to weave illusions from which very few ever escape."

I stare at the grotesque figure hunched over, with only his face exposed, and then I ask, "Why, if the leaders are so powerful and wealthy, do they exhibit so much anger and fear?"

"Human anger is created from the unknown; from fear come sadness and loss, which together create desire: mostly a desire to either want something, or to escape! Anger is an energy and it spreads and infects anyone that comes in contact *with it. It does not matter if the contact is through pictures, stories, music or a punch in the gut. These myriad of energy vibrations are constantly being projected into my power, which I am constantly sending back to the senders. The more anger they express, the more anger it is that comes back; this is the ever continuing cycle of the mind. So human existence continues with each life living within its limited sphere of consciousnesses, most believing they are the single most important being in existence.*

"Now we come to your next question of why I exist in the first place. I exist as the universal mind; the Creator uses the mind as a vehicle to distribute its power, which when stepped down into positive and negative energies, is not only for creation purposes but also to remind Soul of what it really is.

"From Soul's own choices, and partly from the misery caused by those choices, Soul learns and remembers. By remembering its divine purpose, Soul creates total freedom for itself, and thereby returns to its original source. This freedom is attained through a regimented trial of pain, pleasure, joy, discipline, success, failure, loss, and unconditional love. These are the fires that take an unaware Soul and temper it until it is molded into the Creator's own image. This freedom is part of the Creator's spiritual construct, which is wisdom, power, and freedom. These three aspects are instilled within Soul from its creation with the unconditional love of the divine Creator. What man does not realize is that the remembering or recognition of Soul is in reality Soul's divine rebirth.

"Some call this universal power unconditional love or spirit. In the true heavens, it is known as the Sound Current, the Word, Logos or the Voice of God. It has many names, but its most important aspect is that it is audible and can be heard, and therein lies the mystery and the hope of all life in the lower kingdoms.

"The Creator orchestrates the symphony of sounds that plummets its true offspring, Soul, into the fires of the universal mind. When Soul is ready, it will again pay attention to the Creator's divine baton and follow the music of the spheres back home. Soul's true home is not within the confines of the universal mind. No matter how sublime, the mind creates the manifold realities Soul resides in; all are like lewdness in the garden when compared with the father's true home. I exist solely for you to create either heaven or hell in the worlds within you. From your own creations, you build an attitude that determines your journey's end. It doesn't matter if it takes a thousand years or a billion years; in the Creator's eyes, you are already home."

I listen quietly taking in every word; my response rests on the certainty that Abaddon seems to relish in telling his side of existence. The Dark One continues. *"Soul is perfect in every way, for as a product of the Creator's essence, you can be nothing less. This statement includes all creation. Soul must, however, remember and accept its own perfection. Said even more simply, Soul must know itself!*

"I am the Warden, the Judge, the Punisher, the Savior, and the Redeemer, but most of all, I am the Gatekeeper. I cannot deny Soul when it begins to see through my illusions. However, I will continue to weave my prison bars of illusion and entrapment until the very last moment. Nevertheless, when Soul encounters the Sound Current or the voice of its true Father within itself, it is only a matter of experience and time before Soul is free of me."

I send a thought to the old man. *"So what you are saying is that you, the mind, are nothing more than the middle man, a subordinate between Soul and the Creator?"*

Abaddon goes silent for a moment, glaring insanely at me; how dare I question and demean him! From the deathly silence that surrounds us, he maniacally screams within my mind.

"I am the power, you fool! The power of the mind and of Creation itself! You dare to mock me?! You, the human worm trapped in your slug-like world; you who can never grow or see truth without me?!"

I smile within myself; I'm seeing a weakness, and the old man knows it.

Calming down, Abaddon becomes silent for a moment, then gaining control, he continues. His voice is no longer gravelly or wretched; instead, it is now soothing and beguiling. *"As I said, the Sound Current is literally the voice of the Father calling its offspring home on vibratory waves of power. The closer Soul comes to the center of creation, the more free it becomes. This journey home ultimately releases total freedom within Soul. Nothing can prevent Soul's escape from its prison of flesh once it listens to the calling. Your journey since you left your corporeal body on Earth has only been the final leg of a journey that started eons ago. I created the painful situations that eventually broke your lack of understanding. Nevertheless, even now I strive to stop you from achieving the one sole purpose of Soul."*

"Why?" I ask.

Abaddon smiles. *"Simply because when Soul reaches for the door to freedom, it becomes a liability to my own existence. In your achievement, you infect everything, including the Souls you interact with; and they in turn do the same to those they come in contact with.*

"As the mind, I have mastered the ability to spawn fears within man that are more terrifying and numerous than any real dangers could ever be. Because of this, man suffers more in his imagination than in his reality; this will continue as long as he does not know truth. Creation in the lower worlds allows humankind to encounter many defeats, but he must not ever be totally defeated; for this is what keeps life constant. For all the wins and losses in your life, and of all the Souls you meet in all your lifetimes, you are really the only one you will ever totally know.

"And now we come to the question of your life...You, Traveler, are the only true answer to the myriad situations in your life. You are the only solution. For in reality, you are a walking, breathing, thinking eternal Soul. Only one man in a million ever realizes this, and so it is to my own benefit to keep humankind deluded. However, at the same time it is to my own benefit to create the situations that eventually lead to humankind's freedom.

"Am I a contradiction? Maybe, but know this! I am forever partly truth and partly fiction. Each Soul must accept the cards life deals it. Once they are in hand, he or she alone must decide how to play those cards to win the game. You as Soul have played well, but now it is time to bet on what you hold. You began your journey with the wish to free your mother, but now there are other players in the game. As always, you yourself have given me the key to your final destruction, when your friend Kaylu was believed to have died from my attack down below. You see, young

seeker, it becomes quite easy to accept suffering or sacrifice yourself for others when you know you are an eternal Soul. This creates the illusion that you have attained the grace of a martyr over your fellow beings. However, this is only another subtle way of my keeping a man's ego alive without him recognizing it. The real test for a man comes when he feels hopelessness from the possible destruction of a loved one that he cannot save. I watched with glee your reaction to the pitiful condition of the little creature you call 'Kaylu,' and your desperate feelings of helplessness.

"Now you have a choice to make.

"You may walk away now with your mother. However, if you do, you assure Kaylu's death. The choice, as always, is yours. To save Kaylu, you must desert your mother! You cannot have them both!"

I stand silent. This can't be happening! I'm so close! The heaviness of me body only increases as I realize the hopelessness of my situation. How can I choose? Who has the right to make such a choice?

My mother is the reason for me journey, but I could not have made it without Kaylu. My love for both is boundless; to make a decision either way would tear me apart!

Whatever decision I make, I would carry lingering feelings of guilt and blame forever. I struggle to move, but the power of the Dark One combined with me own feelings of hopelessness hold me fast. Abaddon smiles a wickedly insane smile; his eyes flash a deepening madness, and then casually he projects his words again into me mind, *"To help in your choice, I will provide a few extra tidbits for thought."*

A window appears in me mind; peering through it, a scene unfolds within the vision. Me mom lies bound by what seems to be invisible restraints. She's alive! However, I can also see the deathly stillness that permeates her entire being. A great sadness wells up inside of me as I realize she is losing the battle with the negative forces surrounding her. Her limp form fills me with fear, anger, sadness, and a burning desire to help her. The vision fades; in its place, I now see the image of Kaylu lying injured and unconscious on the rocks. I watch anxiously as the image of his face begins to fade, but just before it is totally gone, it slowly, piece by piece, reconstructs itself; within seconds, I see and understand who Kaylu really is.

Instead of seeing Kaylu's face, I see the face of Melody! The image again begins to fade, and as it does, I hear and feel the evil insane laughter of madness coming from the old man.

"You see! You think you know your friend, but believe me, human! There are more things known in Heaven than ever in your world. For now you see and know that each human exists at several levels of consciousness, with each level representing just one of their own kingdoms. Even now you exist currently in your deepest kingdom; at least as far as the mind can take you. You might say this higher self is the Over-Soul—just as Kaylu is to your flesh and blood sister, and you are to your corporeal body of the little boy on Earth.

"All through your human existence, your higher self has guided, taught, warned, and constantly tried to communicate to you. The higher self is always struggling to remind you of your true purpose in life, but does man listen? Hardly! He's too busy listening to his own thoughts, his own excuses, or even his own stomach

noises; *Soul's true purpose is what I, the mind, must keep hidden from the masses! The purpose, of course, is to merge with the Creator as its individual offspring and become a co-worker with it. The spiritual application of this task is what lies hidden from man; each must find that on his own. Sometimes, a man meets his higher self in his dreams, or through contemplation, or even through an out-of-body experience. This higher self can and will teach the spiritual applications, if only the mind will listen. This higher self is the small voice within; it is the intuitive wisdom that is always whispering to your heart. It is the essence of simplicity and common sense. This higher part is your guardian angel, the true soulmate and even more, it is your true self! It is the one who I as mind keep you locked from knowing in my prison of fear!*

"*Until it finds the Sound Current, Soul exists in an incomplete existence to the conscious mind. This subconscious mind patiently waits for humankind to recognize itself as Soul. The mind hides this fact by whispering to the conscious mind that a Savior has come—or is returning, or is going to appear soon, or what have you—who will show him the way. They do not realize that the way is within themselves already, striving to be released. You are your own Savior, as designed by the Creator ITSELF. When you grow spiritually as a human in your conscious self, Soul begins to remember and contacts the conscious part of man on a subconscious level. This contact allows wisdom to be transmitted bit by bit to Soul's lower nature, which is humankind as you know it. This continues until humankind remembers its divine destiny.*

"*Soul's creative power sometimes spills over into your conscious human self, giving you bits and pieces of Soul's awareness. You take this awareness to enhance your daily life; it is an integral part of man's artistic and intuitive nature, even though man is barely aware of its existence. This cave I inhabit seems to you to be my domain. However, the jewels in this cave are symbols of all the minds throughout creation, each connected by the spiritual energy flowing from each Soul. Each is locked and held captive as if in solid stone. I call it the Universal Mind.*

"*Enough! You now know the truth. Decide! Which is it to be? Save your mother, or let her remain doomed under my eternal control? Or save your sister and friend, Kaylu, or let her die by your choice?*"

As I quietly listen to Abaddon, everything I hear seems linked to part of what I already know. As I stand gazing at him, a gentle voice, like a soft impression, manifests within me mind, "*Everything you have learned from the beginning of your journey has been for your benefit, even this!*" I let all my emotions disappear; all that can serve me now is to still the mind and operate from my heart.

Remaining silent, the Abaddon continues staring into me eyes. Under no circumstances am I going to allow twisted knots of fear intimidate me into making a rash or emotional choice. I'm beginning to realize this force that manifests as Abaddon, together with all of the other entities I've encountered, are all linked to me in some mystical way; a critical insight seems poised under the surface of my conscious understanding.

Listening carefully to the old man and remembering the words of Jotan, Morleck, Shakti, the wise man in the park, and others, I realize all of them exist for my benefit and survival. Abaddon just said that his power only exists because of me and the rest of humankind. If indeed this is true, then why would I be helpless to a power of my own making? Had not Jotan said that my mother is trapped in a prison of her own making? Is this dark world also of my own making? If it is, then am I not the lord and master of my own kingdom? Or must I choose to be the beggar again?

Letting myself fall into a sitting position, I close me eyes and stare into the eye of Soul. Abaddon remains silent for a moment, watching as I pull my attention from the outer world and project it within. The old man stretches his neck to peer closely at me; then with a cold viciousness, his screams of insane rage echo within me mind, "*Choose, boy! Before it is too late! The decision must be made!*" I ignore him and quietly begin to chant my name inwardly. The reaction of Abaddon is immediate. "*Stop! Stop now, you fool! Look at meeee! Make your choice now, or I will take them both!*" I sit still, listening inwardly to the HU. As I listen, I sense a powerful presence—a presence unlike anything I have ever known or encountered. A musical sound begins flowing through me as I place my attention on me inner senses. Melodious sounds form words echoing with a richness and depth that fill me with its simple message. "*Hugh, perceive creation as yourself; create the images you wish out of the love within.*"

I realize then the truth of what Abaddon had said. I must hold the cards dealt me, but I also realize that I do not have to play the game any longer; I could just stop playing!

Using my imagination, I begin creating the image of the old man in me inner vision. As the image begins to form, Abaddon screams again in rage, "*Do you know what you are doing? You neeeeed meeeee. I am the power! Only I create forms. You...you are merely human! Your mind is mine, and it always will be! Never will you escape my grip! Without me you are nothing!*"

A voice rich in tone and clarity again speaks within me, pushing out the ravings of the Dark One.

"*Know what it is that is before you. Face it...for what is hidden from you will be revealed only to you. Realize the kingdom is not some heaven in the sky; if it were, then the birds would be there before you. Nor is Heaven in the sea; if it were, the fish would be there before you. But the kingdom is inside you; and also outside of you. When you know yourself, then you will know Heaven, and you will know you are the child of the true Father. But if you know not yourself, then you dwell in poverty and you will become that poverty. By allowing yourself to be one, you will be full of light, but if you are divided, you will stay full of darkness.*"

I place a brilliant white light around my inner image of Abaddon, then I send this inner image a wave of energy that comes from me heart; the love makes the image of the old man shudder. Steadily, I continue to bestow unconditional love into the heart of the old man. Gentle but powerful words again take form as impressions within my mind.

"*I am here, my child, as I have been from the beginning; I am by your side with my hand on your shoulder.*" A feeling of great sympathy and compassion wells up inside of me. The feeling grows, expanding into a tremendous expression of gratitude and unconditional love. The inner voice floats throughout me filling me with a great light.

"*Know that you are Soul. Welcome, my beloved child; my love is enough for each and every individual Soul. It awaits each with joy and anticipation.*" No more thought, no more concern for how I feel; I am being touched by a universe of total incomprehensible love.

The mental image of the Dark One begins to shrivel and shrink bit by bit.

The inner voice again melts into me mind. "*When you make the two one, when you make the inside like the outside, and the outside like the inside, and the above like the below, when you become like a child, you will know the kingdom and be there.*"

The image of Abaddon becomes softer and kinder, vitalized with strength and youth. Tears form in me eyes as the deepest love continues to overwhelm all else. The inner image no longer belongs to the form of the Abaddon. In its place stands the image of a vibrant young boy—possibly ten years old, a boy with light brown hair and wearing a red shirt, jeans, and sneakers—and the image stands up and smiles.

At this moment I open me eyes.

Standing in front of me is my own human self-boy, smiling with a look of power, confidence, joy, and love. As the boy on the dais, I radiate light, and from this light I recognize an innocence I know so well.

The boy on the dais speaks within me heart and mind.

"*We are together again. You have freed yourself, and now you inherit the true kingdom that has always been ours, waiting only your recognition. As a child of the Father, you have duly prepared the kingdom within. By allowing the Father within to direct you as Soul, you have opened the lock to your universe. You have brought forth that which has always been within you, for what you have is what saved you, including the mind itself! You learned the secret of building your own kingdom.*

"*Know the Father welcomes you as the prodigal son returned, for only as a true child of the Creator can Soul inherit the kingdom within. By dreaming the image of the darkness into yourself, you have cleansed the last of the darkness that lived within you. You now know that your kingdom is not a place, nor is it a reality; the kingdom is not over there or up there, nor is it down there. It exists within as the total understanding of Soul. Since the mind is no longer the master, Soul is free!*"

No longer trapped with the heavy burden and weight of the mind, I feel light, energized beyond anything I've ever imagined. Advancing to the dais where my image stands, I reach out to unite with me inner self, but before I do, I ask, "Where is Mom?"

The young boy, who is none other than my child-self, steps off the dais and walks to the other side of the cave. As he does, the sound of stringed instruments floats in the ether above us. The music increases in tempo as we come closer to each other; at last my child-self laughs and steps forward. Amidst a great chorus, our two selves walk into one another, merging and becoming one.

I am new to myself; my hair stands up on the back of my neck as I look down at my body. I awaken to a new joy, openness, curiosity, and trust. An increased awareness, shattering in its simplicity, seems to explode within me, while a sense of wonderment and profound gratitude fills my heart and mind.

I step out from the center of the cave, and as I walk toward the rear, I notice a shadow on my left. I move closer and find a narrow opening in the wall. Suddenly, I see her!

Slipping through the wall's thin, craggy opening, I find my mother on the cavern floor, completely still as in death. Kneeling down beside her limp form, I reach out and take her in my arms. There is no sadness, no anger, no worry; I feel only unbridled joy that I am with her again. Lightly I kiss her forehead. Soul's love flows, enlivening her astral form and filling her heart. I watch amazed as she gradually revives; joy and love again overwhelm me.

"Mum! Oh, Mum! It's me, Hugh!"

Within seconds, she opens her eyes and stares up at the man she finds holding her in his arms. For a brief moment she stares, then taking a deep breath, she whispers, "Clark?" Me eyes glisten as I see her respond. That she called me Da's name only makes me smile more. She closes her eyes and mumbles Clark once or twice more; then she's quiet. Gently picking her up in me arms, I carry her back into the jeweled cave. We enter the mystically lit chamber, and as we do, a great sound erupts in the air around us.

A melodious blend of voices sings my name. The notes are high, as if sung by children. As I continue to the tunnel leading to the waterfall, the voices have grown into a loud chorus. As beautifully as angels, they all sing the holy sound of Hu in perfect harmony.

I remember Shakti saying that when a Soul wakes up and no longer is imprisoned within the dream of the lower worlds, the whole universe sings his freedom; so it is. Sunlight washes over us as I emerge from the cave; Mom is barely conscious, but she's alive.

CHAPTER 49 ~ TO LEAVE OR NOT TO LEAVE

Walking down the path toward my friends, one thought swims within me mind. Oddly enough, it is the one thing I hadn't thought about during this entire journey. Now that I have me mom, what do I do now?

Soon I approach where my comrades sit waiting. Morleck and Loren are kneeling over Kaylu, who is leaning against some blankets and coats. When I come into view, everyone looks up and sees that I am carrying my mom. Loren quickly rushes to my side to help me lay mother on a blanket. She looks at me with an incredulous look; she can't believe I actually succeeded in freeing me mom.

I move over to Kaylu, at the same time asking Morleck, "How is he doing?" Morleck nods, "He will survive."

With a sigh of relief, I move back to mom, and pour some water from me flask into a wooden cup. Holding her head up, I pour some of the liquid onto her lips, and soon she reaches out to hold the cup herself. Within moments, she begins to respond, becoming aware of all of us around her. Looking up at me, she has a confused look on her face, as if she didn't recognize me. "W-who are you? Where's Clark?"

I gently stroke her cheek. "Mom, look closely. It's me, Hugh; it's okay, it really is me."

She still has a perplexed and glazed look in her eyes. "Hugh? How can that be?" The only Hugh she knows is her ten-year-old son; but staring into this man's face, she recognizes his eyes and the gentle look she knows so well. "Hu-Hugh, is that really you? What has happened? How are you so changed?"

"Mom, it's a long, long story. I'll explain everything, but not right now; we have to leave this place. Can you stand?" With me help, Mom raises herself up. Just then, we hear a voice coming from behind us, calling out from the surrounding fog. Karla and Corwin are walking out of the last swirling tendrils of the thinning fog.

"Karla!" Loren shouts as she runs to her sister. Embracing her, Loren sobs, "Karla, you're safe! We thought we had lost you!" Davy then appears from behind Corwin. Everyone is back!

The journey back to the sea shore is uneventful, and doesn't take us nearly as long as the trip from the shore to the cave. Soon both boats are gliding back toward Soultraveler. The water is calm and the fog is dissipating.

Leaving faded gray skies behind us, Soultraveler floats in glimmering waters, waiting like a sanctuary for us weary travelers. I help me mum climb the ladder onto the magnificent ship and take her to my cabin. Leaving her in Loren and Karla's care, I go on deck to see the guards. Two empty shields are lying in the guards' quarters, reminders of the noble men who once used them. The loss of Elias is sorely felt, especially among the crystal guards. He is their second comrade to fall in our defense.

I'm neither tired nor hungry; all I want is to get Soultraveler away from this dismal area, and head out to open waters as soon as possible. I give the orders to the crew leaders to move out. The ship becomes abuzz with activity as the great sails are hauled up on the new masts that were stored below, riggings are tied and the helmsman turns the ship away from the black island. Ocean winds open the sails and Soultraveler moves swiftly across calm waters.

Standing at the rails, I watch the dark island fade into the distance as the ship moves out. The further the island disappears, the lighter the crew and I feel; a heavy weight is being lifted from not only our shoulders, but our minds as well. What I thought would be a bloody fight to the end turned out to be a battle with me own self. Abaddon was nothing more than a barrier instilled within me mind: another trap for Soul. With everyone warning me about Abaddon and its tremendous evil, I believed their stories and so created from me darkest part of mind what I just confronted. True, there is a universal negative force working against the freedom of Soul, but by me confronting my own dark self, I transformed my own negative energy to positive energy, which is how all existence functions. Positive forces, from the atom structure on up the ladder of creation, are constantly changing to negative and vice versa; man's attitude and imagination are the ultimate determining factors as to how this energy affects a person. In my case, my prior experiences with the Light and Sound prepared me for the encounter with the manifestation of what was left of me negative traits.

The sun's almost down. I sit on the bow of the ship on the silver throne, watching the ship cut through the water while contemplating the situation with me mother and myself.

"Hugh?" Mother stands at the end of the stairway leading up to the deck.

"Mother! Are you all right?"

"I'm fine, son; a little weak, but okay." Mum walks up the stairs toward me. I stand and take her hand to help her up the stairs.

"Mom, I can hardly believe you're here, here with me." Standing together on the great ship, Mum looks calm; the gown she's wearing is a light green with a white laced neckline. The girls had helped her bathe and fix her hair. Adding just a touch of makeup transformed her back into the woman that I had not seen in a very long while.

"Yes, I'm here, son, but I must admit I'm still somewhat overwhelmed by your transformation; surely, I haven't been gone for the many years that you have aged?"

"No, Mom, you haven't been gone that long. Actually, I don't know how long it's been; I lost track of time back when me journey began. What do you remember?" I motion her to take a seat.

Ann is quiet for a moment, then sitting on the silver throne, she replies with what seems to be great effort. "The last thing I remember is the accident, then darkness and being held in that horrible place. I thought I was doomed for eternity as life drained from me...but look at you; you've aged to the maturity of a young man, perhaps even thirty!"

I was silent for a moment, trying to think of an explanation for the events that led to this moment. The more I thought of everything that had happened, the more confusing me mind becomes just trying to find a beginning of me story. "Mom, inside I'm still ten. I may look and act older, but inside is the son you remember. I just don't know how to explain, or know even where to start to tell you what has happened."

Mom remains calm; she has a peaceful look about her that makes me feel comfortable and secure. I reach out and take her in my arms, embracing her as if I'm still the little boy she remembers. "It's so good to be with you again; you'll never know what it was like knowing you were trapped and going through so much pain!"

"No, son, from what I can see, we both haven't suffered the worse for our experiences. I, for one, feel like I've been given a new life. Something is gone inside—something that's tortured me throughout my life. I feel so different, so alive! But tell me. Do you know how to get back to Da' and Melody?"

I'm silent for a moment. How can I tell her I have no idea how to get back? Then looking into her eyes, I shake my head. "Mom, during this whole experience, most of the time I didn't know what was going to happen from one moment to the next, so I learned to trust in the Creator in ways so personal that to describe me relationship with spirit would only demean and undermine its true meaning, but I do know this! The Creator exists in both the bitter and the sweet; whenever answers are needed, somehow, some way they appear." I pull out the little book, <u>The Way of the Traveler</u>. "Consulting this is one of the ways that helped me throughout me journey; this is a gift I received from a Spiritual Traveler by the name of Jotan."

Mom abruptly turns her head, and looking deeply into me eyes, she says, "Jotan! Where have I heard that name before? It sounds so familiar; I just can't think of where or when I heard it." I hand the little book to her. She carefully opens it and glances through the pages. Loren appears from below and walks over and sits down next to me. Quite naturally, she puts her arm around me and snuggles close. Mom watches us with an odd expression on her face; she hasn't adjusted to the fact that I'm now more than just her little boy. "Mom, Loren has helped me in this journey in more ways than I can describe. We have become very close."

Ann raises her eyes to stare into Hugh's; she suddenly understands how close they really are. She looks into Hugh's eyes and says, "This is so much to take in; is there anything left of my little boy?"

Loren looks at me. She knows I'm from another world and that I'm now in a different body, but she is somewhat confused by what mom means by "little boy." I feel her questioning look, and think for a moment before speaking; not for the first time since I met Loren, I am tongue-tied and nervous. I stand up and walk behind the throne, and then putting me hands on Mom's shoulders, I open up. "Loren, back in me world, I am a very different person; the body I live in is young, quite young."

Loren's eyes widen. "What do you mean by 'quite young'?"

I look out over the sea and say, "Ten years old young..."

Loren's eyes widen even more; her mouth opens a little as if she's going to say something but nothing comes out. Then finally, she loudly whispers, "Ten! Ten years old! Ten years old?"

Mom calmly replies, "Yes, ten. That's the age of the boy I knew before this experience began."

I step from behind the throne. "Loren, listen. It doesn't matter; for me it's like another lifetime. It doesn't have to change our affection for one another."

Loren looks directly at me and says, "Affection! Hugh, whether you know it or not, I'm in love with you!" She didn't say anything more, she didn't have to. The confused look on her face reflected that her world just disappeared. One moment it was there, the next it's gone!

I take a few steps toward her. "I'm also in love with you; for me, it doesn't matter who I was before. What matters is that I'm with you now."

Ann looks closely at her son, and then exclaims, "Are you sure, Hugh? It seems there are so many barriers to stop you from being together."

I step closer toward Loren. "I'm sure, Mom. I think I was sure from the first time I met her back in the cave." Taking Loren's hand, I continue. "But I knew for sure when I saw you the first night at the inn singing with Karla."

Ann stands up beside us and says slowly and patiently, "This is all well and good, but have either of you thought of the future? Hugh, you and I need to somehow get back to our family; what happens to your love then? How will Loren feel about that?"

Loren is the first to speak. "She's right, you know. I agree; you can't live in both worlds at the same time."

I'm quiet for a moment. Reflecting on what she's saying, then I reply, "If I've learned one thing, it's that nothing is impossible. My young, boy self is lying in a hospital right now, yet here I am: moving, breathing and loving in a totally different reality. There might be a way, but I just haven't figured it out yet."

Loren steps into me arms; tears glisten her cobalt blue eyes. In her heart, she feels she is losing me, but she has known this ever since the first night at the inn. I remember her telling me one night that something within her has always told her that the very qualities she loves in me are the ones that would eventually separate us. I didn't understand then what she was trying to say; now I know, and that feeling is becoming a reality.

"Loren, you are and always will be a part of me. I won't let time and space be a deterrent to our being together." I take my mom's hand and Loren's in the other. "We can sit up here all night and not figure out what ultimately is going to happen, so let's just live in the moment and enjoy who we are right now. Mom, let's have dinner with my wonderful friends. Whatever happens, will happen; we'll cross that bridge when we come to it. Right now, let's get some dinner and discuss our plans with Morleck and the others."

Dandi and Kaylu are overjoyed to finally meet my mother. Both are thrilled to see that Mom has fully recovered; they can't give her enough attention, especially Kaylu. Mom's almost overwhelmed with the little Wuskie as he sits next to her, touching her hair and holding her hands as if he's finally met a long lost relative. Kaylu's like a little child, giggling and overly attentive to Mom's every need. I think it's amusing how he's being carried away by mom. I decide not to say anything about my experience with the Dark One, or when Kaylu's features had transformed into those of Melody: at least not at this time. Morleck is also enjoying Mom's company. Indeed, he seems to find Mom entrancing and fascinating as she seriously discusses not only her experiences with the Dark One in his cave, but then laughs and describes in great detail her home and about me as a little boy. She shares many of the things I did as a small child in me growing years—to my own discomfort. The crystal guards are somewhat reserved, but they, too, enjoy meeting her. They answer dozens of questions concerning their families and their lifestyles as far as being warriors, teachers and Travelers; Mother listens attentively to their stories, especially about their journey with me and our encounter with the Dark One.

Toward the latter part of the evening, Morleck draws me away from the festivities and leads me outside to the upper deck above my balcony outside me cabin. The moon is full and the water is still as glass. Soultraveler moves silently through the calm waters. The stars are out, and their unique brightness makes them shimmer and glisten as they reflect in the dark waters.

Morleck clears his throat and speaks. "Hugh, I have been thinking about your situation as far as you and your mother getting back to your earthly bodies. The more I have contemplated on it, the more questions I have about the real possibility of you both returning safely."

"What do you mean, 'returning safely'?"

"Well," he said nervously, "you need to understand the danger woven into your possible return."

I look at him with a slight fear rising in my chest. "Like what?"

"For one thing, you no longer are at the level of maturity of a ten-year-old boy; nor do you see your old world in the same perspective as when you left. You have a loving, intimate relationship with Loren. Your sense of time and space is drastically distorted compared to before you left. How are you going to function in the body of a ten-year-old boy after you have experienced so much and have even become a Traveler in your own right? Your mother's situation is not nearly as drastic as yours; she was mostly in an unconscious state as a captive of the Dark One. Even so, she has changed according to what she has shared with me. She is still bewildered by the adult you, versus the little boy she remembers, but she is becoming more accustomed to that change by the hour. I believe that physically both of you can successfully move back into your bodies, but for each of you, it is going to be a totally different experience mentally, emotionally, and spiritually. To be honest, I have never encountered anything like this, and I cannot advise you on what to expect. You may forget a large portion of this experience or maybe even all of it! And yet you may also retain all you have experienced and the skills and maturity you have gained. This would leave you feeling trapped by the physical limitations that your younger body and mind impose on you. Think about it, son! Can you really tell me you will be satisfied being a child again, knowing all you have gained and now understand?"

What he's saying is true; how can I go to school with me old friends? How can I be content living as a child with all the limitations it entails? Plus, I'm going to miss Loren and all that she taught me about love, life, and true feelings that centered deep within me heart. The old alchemist is bringing up some good points; maybe it would be better to send my mother home and let my physical body expire. I could continue my existence here, and have everything I could want.

"I don't know, Morleck; I don't know what to do. If I stay here, then what about my father? He has tried so hard to help me and Mom to get back, and he and Melody have been there for me when I needed them most. Do I just ignore them and concern myself with only my needs? Perhaps I have unfinished work with me family? Perhaps there's a plan the Creator wants me to be a part of? Morleck, the more I think of all the outside factors and variables, the more confusing the whole thing becomes."

Morleck puts his hand on my shoulder. "Perhaps we both are letting the mind get in the way again; the more we discuss and the more we think about the ramifications from whatever prospect, the more involved the mind becomes, and we both know what can happen then."

"You're right," I sigh. "I remember in the park before I met Jotan, the wise teacher there did something to me with his eyes; when I walked away, me mind couldn't deal with it. I couldn't contain the immense awareness released within me, but my heart could. I guess we could sit here all night trying to figure out what's right and what's wrong with both situations, but in the end, I think the heart needs to make the choice."

Morleck nods in agreement and says, "Then tell me son; what does the heart say?"

I'm quiet for a few moments. I am almost afraid of what needs to be said and done. Looking up at the stars, I then shut me eyes tightly, listening. My heart speaks to me. I say aloud, "I need to go home."

For the rest of the evening, Morleck and I read, study, and discuss The Way of the Traveler, trying to find techniques and spiritual applications that might allow me and Mum to re-enter our corporeal bodies. Just before the sun is about to rise, Mom joins us. Loren, Karla, Dandi, and Kaylu also come up to the balcony. I look at each of me friends.

In me heart, I am torn by the thought of leaving them, but I know it is the right thing to do. Morleck explains to my friends what we decided and why, and he also informs them we think we have found a way to go home.

Dandi's huge form moves alongside me. Taking me shoulders in his enormous hands, he pulls me close and says, "I will never, ever forget our time together, my young friend. In the journey you have shared with me, I have realized more of myself than I ever dreamed possible."

I embrace the gentle giant, and feel my heart warm with the love that passes between us. I finally reply, "I can't really say goodbye, because with what I have learned from you, I know now we are always together and will meet again."

Kaylu runs up next and hugs me, then using his projection technique, he pushes his thoughts to me mind. "*We have become a part of each other, but in my heart I know we have always been together. Thank you for the wonderful gifts you have given me; watching you grow has helped me to change in ways I don't even understand yet."* His words and feelings expand deep within my mind. *"I know I am losing you as my fellow traveler, but although I'm losing your presence, I have found something else. I always know that our friendship is for forever and I will see you in my dreams and contemplations."*

I don't want to let go of my little friend. His love carries his thoughts to a part of myself I have only experienced in the divine union of me true self.

As I step back, Karla rushes to embrace me, and I hold her tight; what an amazing girl, I think. I hold her at arm's length. "Karla, you truly are an amazing person. Take care of Davy, for he's quite the man and he loves you greatly. May the blessings be on both of you!"

Loren then steps in front of me. Her dark hair is spilling over her shoulders, and she's wearing a light green satin top and a darker green long skirt that is almost touching the deck. The sun is rising behind us, projecting light around her like a crown. Her amazing blue eyes are sparkling as tears glisten along the edges. She whispers in a half cry, "I do not know what to say or do…" I stare at this beautiful young woman who has taught me so much. Loren has been so unselfish and kind; even when I was afraid and did not know what to do, she was always there. I remember how playful and child-like she was when we were on the island sitting under the shade of the trees in the glen, listening so joyfully to my songs. Loren generously shared all she had with me, including Soultraveler. Loren has made me what I am now, standing before her as a man. She extends her hands, inviting me to take them in mine. As I touch her fingertips, I realize I may never see her again. Pain spears me heart and a tear slides from the corner of me eye as I step into her embrace for the final time. As we close our embrace, I whisper, "I can't say goodbye; me Soul will tear apart, for sure."

"I know, Hugh, but it must be so…But first, before you're gone, I want you to know what you have meant to me." Loren's voice cracks, and she pauses for a few seconds. Looking up into me eyes, she softly continues. "You have shown me a higher love than I could ever imagine in my life, but I realize that somehow I always knew this day would arrive. Oh, Hugh, thank you, thank you so much for sharing yourself with me. When my father died and Karla and I were left wandering in the caves alone, I thought life was over, but then I met you. My Soul filled with life again, and this is because of you. I have grown so much from what I once was because of your love and example. Your love has allowed me to be aware of what a wonderful experience it is to be a woman, and I love you."

I reach out and bring her into me embrace. How can I let go of someone who has become such a part of me? Me stomach feels light and me heart beats faster; warm flashes shoot through me like crashing waves. Breathing in her scent, me eyes close, and I try to burn her fragrance into me memory. Finally, tilting her head slightly, I lean down and kiss my first and greatest love. As our lips meet, our tears merge, and for a brief moment, we both wish our love could ascend to the throne of God.

I slowly step back and reach into my shirt for the packet of crumpled memory plants. I separate a few from the packet and hand them to Loren. "Keep these; when you want to see me, inhale their fragrance and I will travel from your memories into your heart."

Mom steps forward to my side. "I, too, wish to thank you all. I realize there's no way I can repay everything that you have done and given us, but I want each of you to know that my son and I will never forget your friendship and the wisdom and sacrifice you have given us."

Morleck quietly says, "It's time."

Morleck and Ann then turn and head down the stairway leading to the lower deck. Hugh hesitantly steps away from Loren and reluctantly follows them down the stairs.

Loren feels a sudden emptiness within her. Hugh is leaving, and there is nothing she can say or do to prevent it. How can she live her life, now or in the future? She has tasted the sweetness of true love, and once tasted, it always leaves a hunger for more. Karla silently embraces her sister, and then the entire group encircles and comforts her.

Hugh enters Morleck's cabin and joins Ann at the table. As Morleck busily works at a counter covered with tin canisters and bottles, he turns to Hugh and Ann and says, "Well, my friends, now we shall see what we shall see. According to The Way of the Traveler, it will take just a few moments for me to mix the required herbs. In the meantime, I need both of you to relax and focus on your home and your loved ones there."

"What is it you're mixing?" Ann asks.

"This is a very old tea mixture called Soma. It will relax you so that you can focus on what needs to be done."

Ann sniffs and stiffens at the tea's odor. "Are you sure that will bring us back home?"

Morleck pours a little water into a cup and replies, "According to what Hugh and I have read, it's definitely possible, but of course, I'm not one hundred percent sure." He continues to mix his herbs, talking as he does. "I would not even be attempting this if you both didn't have living bodies back in your reality. This is a very unusual case. We are attempting what is called 'Reverse transcendence.' Both of you have living bodies in your earthly reality, and have transcended to this more ethereal realm. Because you both retain your physical bodies, I know the silver cord is still connected to your consciousness, and this, my friends, is where you have to put your attention."

Ann has a confused look on her face. "What is a 'silver cord'?"

"Ah, that's a very good question," Morleck nods, "and believe me, as many times as I have asked that very same question, I have gotten as many different answers. I will try to make my explanation simple. The silver cord is a vibratory connecting stream of consciousness that each person has, sort of like rays of light coming from the sun, but in this case, the sun is Soul.

"For each person, the cord vibrates at the frequency corresponding with the person's metabolism. This frequency is unique and different for each life form.

When a person dies in the physical realm, his spiritual self leaves the physical body, which is made from the same elements as the world he lived in, and transforms into his astral body, which appears to be a mirror image or double of the person's physical form. This astral body is believed to be separable from the physical body during astral projection, or the out of body experience, as well as at death. Lucid dreamers also use the astral body when the person is aware that their experience is a dream; the astral body remains linked to the physical body by means of this silver cord. The astral body is composed of astral fabric, which is also the source of the entire astral dimension; it is like earth's physical matter, which consists of vibrating particles, but it functions at a much finer frequency. When we look at frequency and vibration from the perspective of the external creation, frequency is the cyclic pattern and vibration is the process when energy contracts and expands.

"This finer vibratory body moves by thought, and is controlled by the emotions. The Soul can be influenced by other spirits, and if the physical body is ready for death, Soul uses the silver cord to pull that person's consciousness to the next plane of existence; as it does, a body is being created for him based on the needs and traits of that individual Soul.

"When Soul has attained the higher awareness where he stops taking on bodies—whether from the physical, astral, causal or mental realities—then the silver cord is cut and discarded forever. But as long as a person is moving throughout the lower worlds, then the cord is of paramount value, because it is the very lifeline or the connecting rope of life for those inhabiting bodies ruled by matter, energy, space, and time.

"The unique aspect of this connecting cord is that its vibration and frequency are not the same in both the physical and higher planes; the closer the end of the cord is to its source, the stronger its vibration and faster its frequency. The cord functions on each plane according to that realm's vibration and speed in tune with the body that exists in each plane. As the cord extends closer into the next plane, the vibration either steps up or slows down, adjusting accordingly."

Still confused, Ann asks, "Why is it called a cord?"

"Most people who have had some type of experience with this divine aspect—whether by astral projection or near death experience—have described it as a silvery white cord that is attached to both their physical body and to their spiritual body. The image of a cord is the most popular way of describing the phenomenon."

I'm staring out the window, listening but not really paying much attention. I'm thinking about returning home and not seeing my dear friends ever again. Morleck pours some of the steaming drink into cups and hands them to us. "This tea is only to help you relax; it takes your own effort and intentions for you to make this reverse transcendence possible. As the drink begins to take a relaxing effect, try to move into an open and contemplative state. Think of your family, and the earthly reality that you came from, and place your attention on your physical body."

I am sitting in a comfortable chair next to me mum. When I reach out and take her hand, she smiles and we lock eyes: this will be the last time we know each other both as adults for a very long time, I think.

Morleck sits and softly says, "Begin."

Closing me eyes, I think of our home in Bristol. As I relax, me mind clears. Slowly, I try creating feelings and images of my old world; as I do; I begin to hear the dim sound of buzzing far off in the distance. I continue creating familiar images of home. I imagine Billy and me running through the woods with Cody at our side. I can almost hear the crackling of the autumn leaves; the buzzing sound becomes louder. As I continue thinking of home, I can actually feel the images without the need to physically see them with my normal vision; I am seeing by my inner eye. I listen to the closer buzzing sound by my inner ear. Sounds and familiar smells of the woods creep from my imagination into my inner senses. Peering intently through and into the eye of Soul, a soft round radiance appears within me vision. A diffused orange glow surrounds its edges and the illumination intensifies as it gradually moving toward the center. As I refocus my vision, I see new images fade in, then fade out from the center of the light. While watching the light and its images, I hear and feel the Sound Current moving through me. The current carries along me imagined images of home and the woods to the light. A low whistle like the sound of the wind when it blows through trees blends with my sight of the images. The center of light fades and collapses within itself, then it fades back again; gradually the images are beginning to have distinct features. At first, I can't make out what it is, but soon, bit by bit darker shadows within the image become clearer. I feel myself being absorbed into the characteristics of the image. Forgetting all else but what I am seeing and hearing, I feel myself slipping away. Sounds become louder, images become clearer; together, they overpower my senses. The great maple tree, in all its magnificent, crystal clear beauty, with all its colors and details, manifests itself within me vision. I feel myself being pulled closer as the tree looms before me.

Then there's a shift.

I'm looking up into the opening in the tree house floor. I feel my eyes momentarily rolling in me head, but then realize that it's not my eyes but the power of my attention focusing upwards. I reach for the rope hanging through the tree house opening, and as I touch it, I feel another shift. Now I'm entering the round opening into the tree house, yet at the same time I'm somehow moving through the top of me head: it's a weird, freaking feeling. As I'm moving through the hole in the floor into the room, I feel sluggish; heavy energy overwhelms me; and things seem to be moving in slow motion. Me thoughts seem delayed; I have to almost force me mind to think. No longer is me mind fluid, articulate, and alert. I can barely make out the Sound Current, and soon it completely fades. Everything within me vision darkens. I feel as if I'm trying to wake up, but it's so difficult! I no longer feel sounds or light. After a tremendously groggy moment, a spinning sensation engulfs me. A voice whispers from a dim light; getting louder by the second.

"Hugh! Wake up! It's me, Da'. Wake up, boy! Open your eyes."

The tree is gone; only an intensely bright, blurry light remains. I open me eyes. My vision is fuzzy and blurred...Da'?

My lips are dry, and my throat and tongue are so weak, so raw! I struggle to move my mouth to speak, but my voice is just a hoarse whisper, and I can only manage croaking out, "Da'!"

"Melody, hand me that pink water pitcher," a familiar voice says. I then feel the coldness of ice chips as they are gently placed into my mouth.

"Don't try to speak, son," the familiar voice continues, "you're just fine!" As the chips melt, coating my raw mouth and throat, I discover that I can move my jaws and glide my tongue again. "It's me, Da." My vision clears a little, but my eyes sting as bright glaring lights blast down on me from above. I try to adjust to the brightness. Me Da's image floats into focus.

Barely above a whisper, I croak in me now unfamiliar high-pitched voice, "Da'—I'm back! Where's Mom? Is Mom okay?"

Clark stares down at his son. The paleness of his skin and his shrunken form contrast deeply with the brilliant light in his eyes.

Melody stands behind Clark with her hand on his shoulder, her tearful face smiling.

Taking his son's hand, Clark whispers, "Mom's fine…You're fine…Everything's fine, lad; you're home."

Afterword

The Land of Hugh is a project that started a long time ago—actually back in the early seventies, when I was a young man in my early twenties. Up to that time, I was a man obsessed with fast cars, money, women, and any other pleasures the mind could dream up. I was not looking for answers to life, as I felt I knew all the answers that mattered anyway. I will admit, I did have those times when I would be alone in my private moments and the big question of "Why?" would melt into my mind. That "Why?" had many, many arms and legs that extended outward into every facet of my life. But I was not ready to understand this question, nor how it had been working in my life from the time I was born. Not ready to grasp the meaning of "Why?" into my life, I buried it deep down, covered by the excitement and pleasures of the mind and senses.

But the Creator—unknown to me at the time—has a plan for all of us, and the plan for me was about to explode within myself in ways I would never have foreseen.

In 1974, I was unexpectedly touched by something that I never believed existed. I was at a low moment in my life, and when this revelation found me, it changed by life forever. It was something that lasted for only a minute or two, but it changed me in ways that are still being defined every day of my life. I became a seeker, and in doing so, I entered a reality that was always within me, but always hidden. In this new reality, my life moved for the next forty years unknown to me toward this story. Without the influence of contemplations, dreams, out of body experiences, and unconditional love; "The Land of Hugh" would never have been born. All these things and more led me to my own knowingness.

Real spiritual experiences in our lives are very private, and if nurtured properly, they can someday bear fruit and allow the seeker to share his wisdom for those who are ready. The world has evolved since the early seventies, and more Souls than ever are ready to find their own truth within themselves. The actual story of The Land of Hugh has taken ten years to plan and come forth. The story is written to guide the reader through the maze of experiences one may have when opening their spiritual senses. The story is peppered with exercises and guidelines through dreams, contemplation techniques, meditation stories, and other experiences that Hugh goes through. All are woven together in a story that encourages the reader to turn each page with the expectation of discovery. None of the story's content is new; all has been said many times and in many ways. The way this story is told is meant to help the reader evolve as Hugh does, through the childlike attitude that Hugh experiences his journey. Hugh is the Soul within each of us that yearns to know truth, and if readers are ready, they will grow as the story unfolds, just as Hugh.

ABOUT THE AUTHOR

by

Cynthia Ann Humes

I met W. T. Lewis over a decade ago through quite ordinary circumstances, and I had no idea that he was a writer until one day he mentioned that he was looking for someone to assist him in editing a book. The problem, he told me, was that none of the possible editors he had encountered had any understanding of the philosophical ideas suffused through the novel. Those who had tried their hand on a few chapters, he explained, had actually introduced errors. They didn't comprehend that although the story begins as a boy's adventure story, it goes much deeper, delving into the spiritual realm, nature of the soul, and complex Asian and Western religious ideas. The story's intent was to simplify these metaphysical concepts and incorporate them into an exciting story about a young boy's spiritual awakening.

Mr. Lewis only knew me as an Information Technology professional, but in addition to being a Chief Technology Officer, I explained to him that I am also a professor of Asian religions and have edited and written a few of my own books. We agreed that I should read the first few chapters to see if I could possibly assist him. Since I am writing this introduction to him, the reader will have already anticipated that I liked the book so much that I agreed to help edit the work and assist him in its publication. I greatly enjoyed working with him in the process: we often discussed ideas such as mind, soul, the audible life stream, different levels of heaven, and even soul travel. We discussed how the characters in this story might experience these truths along the spiritual journey that Hugh takes in the story.

Mr. Lewis was born in the 1950s and came of age in the sixties. I have learned that within months of his birth, his mother died; as the youngest of nine siblings, and without a mother's love to guide him, he forged an independent and idiosyncratic path. Although his life seemed normal from the outside, his lively imagination and deep urge to learn and explore spirituality led him to read constantly and experiment with alternative spiritualities. To W.T. Lewis, reading (and sometimes re-reading) thousands of books that he loved provided an escape for his imagination, and planted the seeds for a spiritual revelation. The story of "The Land of Hugh" is the result of his life's journey through a spiritual maze that he was determined to simplify. His intent is for this book to help provide a vehicle for those who are searching to discover their own spiritual path. The big questions in life—such as "Why?", "What is our ultimate purpose?", and "Why we are here in the first place?"—haunted him throughout his young life. From the benefit of his direct experience with spirit and his intense reading, he has incorporated divine wisdom into a story that answers these and more questions about the human experience and its relationship with spirit. If he can help point the way through his actions and writing, and show what worked for him to those who are ready to experience something more than the mundane, traditional life, then he feels he will have accomplished something good for the Creator, this world, and himself.

—CAH

CPSIA information can be obtained
at www.ICGtesting.com
Printed in the USA
BVHW04*1108030518
515173BV00006B/60/P